GateKEEPERS

A Novel

by

Sheldon Robert Stone

&

Rudolf B. Schmerl

Domar Books, LLC
Beachwood

Sheldon Robert Stone is an award-winning architect
from Cleveland, Ohio. He is a Fellow of the
Society of American Registered Architects
and is the recipient of their
National Presidential Gold Medal.

Rudolf B. Schmerl is a retired faculty member of
the University of Michigan.

ISBN: 978-0-615-24184-5

contents

Prologue

In 1982, the Federal Trade Commission and the National Council of Architectural Registration Boards agreed to replace what had been the Boards' national licensure examination with a much more adequate and relevant test. Until then, most architects in the United States had submitted themselves to an examination whose shortcomings were more and more apparent, if not to the profession's gatekeepers, then to its practitioners. In California and Wisconsin, studies funded by their legislatures had determined that less than forty percent of the NCARB licensing examination was related to the tasks architects actually have to perform. The architectural licensing boards in both states had already proceeded to develop their own examinations, and discontent was becoming general.

But the examination also had its supporters. For one thing, it had the appearance of professionalism, as so many standardized examinations do. A number of its parts were prepared by external testing agencies in multiple choice format, regarded as "objective." Answer sheets, consisting of rows of circles either filled in or not by applicants, were coded to preserve confidentiality, sometimes also assured contractually between the examination boards and the testing services by prohibiting release of substantive information to the examinees about their performance. Supporters of the examination also argued that it served to protect the public's safety and welfare, assuring that only properly trained and truly qualified architects would be licensed to plan and design the nation's buildings, and to work with the construction firms that erected them. Evidence to the contrary was apparently less difficult to provide than likely to persuade those who required persuasion.

Most Americans are familiar with examinations serving to separate applicants for entrance to many of the professions, trades, and other occupations into two groups, those who pass and those who don't. They are familiar, too, with comparable examinations from their years in American schools and colleges, both private and public, almost all of which also use some sort of examination to justify admission to or exclusion from the next grade level, or a diploma, or a certificate or degree. And they are familiar, as well, with the arbitrariness of so many aspects of so many of these examinations: the selection and phrasing of the questions, the choice of the "right" answer from a group of often quite ambiguous responses, the amount of time permitted for their completion, the minimum score required for passing. Whether they are familiar with, or even want to think about, what Wizards of Oz sit behind the curtains, pulling the levers, ringing the bells, sounding the alarms, and why and how those Wizards make their decisions, is much less certain.

This story, based on one Ohio architect's experience with this system, is technically fiction. Many of the characters have been invented; a few are representations or syntheses of people the authors have known; and the story's key events will not be found in any archives. But the story also includes a few real persons and events, whether within the action or as part of the years in which the story is set. We trust that our readers will grant us the usual license to blend fact and fiction to the best of our abilities.

What is not fiction, however, is the architect's experience, nor his long struggle to see to it that no others in his profession would have to endure anything comparable. Neither is our conviction that, no matter how necessary it is to have measures of performance, those measures need to be transparent, reasonable, and always subject to improvement. Of course there is plenty of room for disagreement about desirable details, which will vary greatly from one profession to another, from one degree to another, and the like. And of course we can all proclaim that standards should always be as high as possible, that we want excellence in all things, that we must constantly be on guard to assure the best that we can be, whoever we are. It is quite another matter to examine why and how the system seems to operate as it does. Just as we hope that readers will recognize what we have invented and what we have not, we hope that they will see that we support what is now known as accountability, not only for institutions and individuals, but also for the *processes* used by institutions to assess the performance of the individuals they let in—or keep out.

SRS
RBS

Chapter I
Nathan, September, 1979

The room was pretentious, high-ceilinged, semi-paneled, somehow reminding Nathan that he was a visitor to power, the grandson of immigrants, one of the first in his family to go to college, one of the first to mingle with people in charge of things. People like these whose nameplates on the dais at the front of the room identified them, whether they were there or not, without any kind of indication of who they really were. Just a name: Mr. Schwartz. They were Congressmen, mostly from places of which Nathan had never heard, elected by people Nathan knew nothing about, fellow citizens with whom he had nothing in common, probably, except this system of the apportionment of power. Nathan had some recollections, mostly from the eighth grade, of how the system was supposed to work. Mrs. McMurtree had been quite clear in her presentations, and so had the textbook. The people chose their representatives in a republic. The representatives arranged themselves in groups like this Subcommittee to consider legislation about how people were to behave, how much they should pay for what, who should monitor their behavior, and what penalties would be exacted were there to be infractions. Something like that. Of course the President had to agree to the legislation the Representatives and Senators passed, and so did the courts, but much of what happened started here, with hearings like this, instigated by somebody on somebody's staff, whether officially or not. Mrs. McMurtree had not explained that part so clearly. But it hadn't mattered, because Nathan and his eighth-grade classmates had known even then that what she had explained was not how things worked but what they were supposed to believe, just like religious instructions. If you kept your mouth shut and just repeated what they told you, you wouldn't get into any trouble.

The Congressmen–there seemed to be only three or four, to Nathan's surprise, with an equal number of young staff members dripping solicitude and servility–were taking their chairs behind their name plates, muttering to the staff, shuffling papers, joking with each other *sotto voce*. A few people were sitting in what seemed to be the section for the audience. Nathan saw a man who looked vaguely familiar, but he couldn't place him, and the man looked away rather hurriedly. A young woman asked Nathan if he was there to give testimony. When he assented, she gave him a thick stack of paper and directed him to find a seat at a long table below the dais. He made his way toward one of the few remaining empty chairs, nodding to the men already sitting at the table. They did not respond. Perhaps, he thought, it was too solemn an occasion for good manners.

He looked at the top sheet of the stack the young woman had given him.

The Truth in Testing Act of 1979;
The Educational Testing Act of 1979
Hearings Before the Subcommittee on Elementary, Secondary, and Vocational Education of the Committee on Education and Labor – United States House of Representatives –Ninety-Sixth Congress – Subcommittee on Elementary, Secondary, and Vocational Education and Labor, Washington. D.C.
First Session On: **H.R. 3564** - *To require all educational admissions testing conducted through interstate commerce, and all occupational admissions testing (which affects commerce) to be conducted with sufficient notice of test subject matter and test results, and other purposes, and* **H.R. 4949** - *To require certain information to be provided to individuals who take standardized educational admissions tests, and for other purposes.*

Lawyer language, of course. How could whoever had drafted this be expected to talk about fairness and justice and transparency, especially of clear and reasonable criteria determining what score was needed to pass these damned things? No, "sufficient notice of test subject matter" and "certain information" were as close as Congress intended to get to specificity. The meaning was to be determined first by whatever agency might be told to enforce this legislation, if it ever got to that point, and second by the judge who surely would have to hear all the counterarguments presented by accrediting agencies and professional organizations and the rest of the enormous bureaucracy with vested interests in The Way Things Were. Nathan sighed.

His mind reverted to his awakening next to Cheryl in Jack Greenstein's apartment that morning, in the sleeping bag on the floor, while Jack's dad, Nathan's friend Sid, was still snoring on the sofa. It wasn't the most desirable arrangement, but hotel rooms weren't cheap in Washington. Sid had come to visit Jack. Cheryl had come, she had said, to be with Nathan and give him her support or at least a smile at the hearing. Well, she'd changed her mind. Sitting through a Congressional subcommittee's hearing on a beautiful, warm September morning when the stores were open in a big city she'd never visited before just lacked appeal to a twenty-two-year-old girl from Cleveland who knew how to dress herself to advantage. Nathan, staring at the papers in front of him, was uncomfortably aware of how his mind was drifting. Not for the first time, he wondered whether he and Cheryl had anything going besides physical attraction. She certainly hadn't seemed to pay attention when he had tried to explain how important this day was to him.

A man sitting on the dais cleared his throat and tapped the microphone in front of him. "Good morning," he said. The sign in front of him said that he was Mr. Erdmann. "Good morning," he said again, more loudly. "It's about 9:40, we're already a little late, so let's get this hearing underway. I was asked to begin this morning–the Chairman is on his way. I see Mr. Schwartz is here." A portly man was making his way to the dais, carrying an attaché case and breathing rather loudly. "We should begin because we have several witnesses waiting to give their testimony," Mr. Erdmann continued. "This is the fourth day of these hearings, and two more are scheduled on H.R. 3564 and H.R. 4949." He looked around him as if he expected a comment or a question, but no one said anything, and he cleared his throat again and went on.

"We have an interesting, indeed distinguished panel this morning. I think most of them are already at the witness table–if the others would take their places there--" Nathan was jostled in his chair as two more men brushed by it to take the remaining seats. "Thank you," Congressman Erdmann continued. "Even though some of our colleagues are not here yet--" he indicated the empty chairs on the dais on either side of him–"this will go into the record and we will establish the record this morning.

"The people on the panel this morning--" the Congressman, reading from his notes, was beginning to drone. Nathan did not recognize a single name from his copy of the materials, although he had heard of some of the organizations they represented. Various universities, of course, including some East Coast schools and a black college. Something called the National Association for Equal Opportunity in Higher Education. The NAACP. Probably the three black men sitting together, Nathan thought. Some sort of Center for something, represented by its Director of Research. Somebody from a testing outfit. A man representing the National Association of Occupational Licensing Reform. And Mr. Nathan Goldstein, from Cleveland, Ohio. He seemed to be the only witness without a Ph.D. or a fancy title. Mr. Schwartz took his seat in the middle of the dais.

"First I will call on Dr. Summers," said Congressman Erdmann, "and now I will relinquish the Chair to Representative Schwartz."

Dr. Summers reached for the microphone near him on the witness table and opened his mouth, but Representative Schwartz, no doubt far more experienced, was too quick for him with his own microphone. "Thank you, Representative Erdmann," he said, opening his attaché case and extracting papers and a yellow pad. "First let me apologize. It used to be that only death and taxes were certain. I can now add a third certainty, namely, that the Eastern shuttle from New York will be late, going or coming. Again, I apologize. Now, uh, Dr. uh, Dr. Summers." He beamed a smile at the wrong man.

"Good morning," Dr. Summers said, a little stiffly and more loudly than necessary, Nathan thought. "My name is Geoffrey C. Summers, Ph.D., and first of all I want to express to this august Committee my great appreciation for this opportunity to share my views about this crucially important topic that this Committee is examining. Let me begin by first describing, as briefly as I can, the rather extensive personal and professional background I bring to a discussion of this complicated topic and the proposed and highly significant legislation." Nathan's eyes grew heavy.

The cab ride to the Rayburn Building had been not merely interesting but fortuitous. It turned out that Nathan and the cab driver had an acquaintance in common. That had come out later in their conversation. First the driver, who had kept glancing at him in the rearview mirror, had rather casually asked him if he was from the Middle East. "You look like you might have Arabic ancestry?" he had questioned.

Nathan, suddenly aware that it was the driver who looked Middle Eastern, was immediately on guard. The driver, a dark, heavy-set man in his mid-forties, had a thick black moustache. "No," Nathan said, "at least not for many generations. My ancestors, the ones I know about, came from Germany and Russia."

"I know your name from my dispatcher," the driver said. "If you don't mind my asking, Goldstein is often a Jewish name, isn't it?"

What the hell is this, Nathan thought, looking at the driver's identification card on the dashboard. Davood DelAvar Bahman. An Arab himself, apparently. I don't have time for a discussion of Israel's right to exist, Nathan told himself, the hearings start at nine thirty. He didn't answer.

"Sorry if I'm getting too personal," the driver said. "I'm Iranian. You see my name–Davood Bahman. Davood is Farsi for David, like your King David."

Nathan didn't want to be rude. The man seemed friendly enough, and Iranian wasn't Arab anyway. "Your English is excellent," Nathan said, by way of making amends for his frosty silence a moment ago.

"I used to teach here, right here in Washington," the driver said, "at Howard's School of Architecture and Design. In the sixties and early seventies. I taught design." Nathan was amazed. "But in 1974," the driver continued before he could say anything, "I went back to Iran and taught architecture in Teheran." He pulled up at a red light. "A mistake, it turned out. My whole family was educated, you know, secular, and things began to become difficult. I came back here about a year ago, but as you see, I haven't found work as an architect and I haven't found a teaching position either." The light changed and he maneuvered the cab into a passing lane.

"Quite a coincidence!" Nathan said. "I'm an architect. In fact, that's why I'm here today, in a way."

"Really!" the driver said. "Where did you go to school?"

"At Ohio State University, in Columbus," Nathan told him.

"Ohio State!" the driver exclaimed. "I have a cousin who teaches architectural design at Ohio State! Habib Farzin! You know him?"

"I certainly do," Nathan said. "I took two courses from him. He's an excellent teacher. Well, this *is* a small world!"

"Habib and I grew up together, studied together, came here together," the driver said, "but he stayed here when I went back, and I think he's done well at Ohio State. He certainly likes it there, you know, the university, the town, his colleagues, his students."

"Well, his students like him, too," Nathan offered.

"He was telling me about one of them who got into trouble with the profession, he thinks," the driver continued. "He wasn't sure, but he thinks the student–who was working on some sort of research, an independent study as part of his master's degree in architecture–had his research stopped because it was going to step on a lot of toes, you know what I mean? It was just rumor, but Habib thought it might be true. You know anything about that? It happened some years ago. When were you there?"

Too small a world, Nathan thought. "No, I never heard anything like that," he said, ignoring the question. "How did your cousin happen to tell you about it now, do you remember?"

"We were talking about what's going on in Iran, and I was saying that I didn't think anything like that could ever happen here, you know, the thought police, everybody having to be very careful with the authorities, and he said he wasn't so sure, there had been the Kent State shootings, you remember, and of course the shootings at Jackson State in Mississippi which I knew about from my work at Howard University, and then he said that even closer to home, you know, at his school, there had been episodes–and then he told me about this student or the rumors. And some strange accidents."

"I see," Nathan said. "No, I don't think I ever heard about anything like that."

"Here we are," the driver said, pointing at the Rayburn Building. "Do you want the main entrance along Independence Avenue?"

"Yes, please," Nathan said. "What's the fare?"

"Eight twenty," the driver said. Nathan gave him a ten dollar bill and said, "Keep the change." "Thanks," the driver said. "I'll tell my cousin we met!" "Sure," Nathan said, "give him my regards!" He turned and looked at the building directly in front of him, and then at its surroundings. The cab pulled away.

The Rayburn House Office Building, named for the powerful Speaker from Texas, acknowledged as one of Lyndon Johnson's mentors, was constructed to help to accommodate the ever-increasing business of the United States House of Representatives. Politicians routinely campaign against big government, Nathan reflected, but the population keeps growing, problems keep multiplying, and the universities keep graduating people who need jobs. The Longworth and Cannon House Office Buildings are just to the east along Independence Avenue. The Capitol is visible to the north across the street. Nathan noted the Rayburn Building's white marble facade covering the exterior above the pink granite base, but his glance was caught by the two marble statues on pedestals on either side of the main entrance. One was the *Spirit of Justice*; the other was the *Majesty of Law*. Forget Mrs. McMurtree's eighth-grade civics class, Nathan thought, his heart lifting: this was what it was all about.

He walked up the series of exterior stairs to the building's main entrance doors, opened them, took a deep breath, and went in. Here we go, he told himself, an American citizen about to teach his elected representatives something about the reality they needed to align with the *Spirit* and the *Majesty*. He started to walk toward the gate barring him from the main lobby.

"May I help you, sir?" A uniformed guard behind him was motioning him back. Nathan was reminded of his conversation with the cab driver about what was happening in Iran. Uniformed guards at government buildings all across the world were supposed to prevent change. But he was here precisely to advocate change. One man's tempest in a teapot was another's revolution.

"Yes," he said. "I'm to go to Room 2175, to speak at a hearing at nine thirty--"

The guard, looking at papers on his desk, interrupted: "Subcommittee on Elementary, Secondary, and Vocational Education?"

"Yes," Nathan said, aware that all those polysyllables wouldn't have rolled so smoothly from his own tongue.

"Name?"

"Nathan Goldstein."

"Yes, you're on the list–may I see some identification?"

"I have the invitation letter," Nathan said, reaching for his breast pocket.

"No, let me see your driver's license," the guard said.

Nathan extracted his license from his wallet and gave it to the guard. The guard glanced first at the photograph and then at Nathan. Is he going to ask me whether I have Middle Eastern ancestry, Nathan thought, grinning to himself.

"OK," the guard said. "Through the gate, straight ahead to the elevators."

"Thank you very much, Dr. Summers!" Congressman Schwartz's voice, conveying genuine gratitude, probably that Dr. Summers had at last finished his presentation of his experience, reflections, views, opinions, and carefully considered suggestions, brought Nathan back to his immediate surroundings. "I think that we should defer questions until all witnesses have made their initial or formal presentations, in the interests of time, so if that's agreeable--" Mr. Schwartz glanced at the other Congressmen on either side of him, who nodded assent–"our next witness is Dr. Oldfield from the National Association for Color, uh, for Equal Opportunity–Dr. Oldfield?"

"Thank you very much, Congressman Swartz," Dr. Oldfield, a black man who looked very tall even sitting in his chair, boomed out in a deep, resonant voice, making everyone sit up. Nathan noticed the mispronunciation and wondered whether Dr. Oldfield would be subjected to hostile questions from the Congressman later. "We at the National Association for Equal Opportunity in Higher Education have long been concerned about the subject of this hearing today not only as educators dedicated to the advancement of *all* our students through equal opportunity for meaningful education but also as citizens aware that equity, true equity understood in relation to the widely differing historical, social, and economic circumstances experienced by generations of our citizens--" this was by no means the first time, Nathan thought, that Dr. Oldfield had introduced his subject in precisely this way. Maybe he should have rehearsed his own testimony a few more times himself. But Cheryl had chattered incessantly on the drive down from Cleveland, and Sid, the driver, had either expostulated on the incompetence of other drivers, whom he seemed to regard as rivals for the passing lane, or, during their lunch break at a roadside restaurant and once while Cheryl was napping in the back seat, had provided unsolicited fatherly advice. Nathan had tried to listen as politely as he could. Sid was about twenty years older than he was. They had met some six years ago when both were employed by the same architectural firm, Nathan as an intern and Sid as an architectural project manager, supervising construction jobs in the Cleveland area. They had stayed in touch after Nathan had resumed his studies at Ohio State in 1974. When Nathan, not long ago, had lost his job, spending too much time on his challenges to the profession, it was Sid who had kept him going with various small-scale assignments. So the unsolicited advice was a price Nathan had to pay. He remembered the lecture in the car.

"Nathan, I want to talk seriously to you while your girlfriend is snoozing back there," Sid had said when traffic was light. "Sure," Nathan had said, trying not to mind Sid's tone. "I know how important this testimony you're going to give at the hearing is to you," Sid continued, "and of course it's too late to try to talk you out of it, which I don't want to do anyway. But have you thought about how the outcome might affect your options to practice architecture, I mean, *really* thought about it?"

"Yes, I have," Nathan answered, trying to keep his impatience out of his voice. "I've thought about this very carefully for a long time, Sid, and it's something I feel I have to do, not just for myself, but as an architect committed to the integrity of his profession. I hope that doesn't sound pompous because I mean what I'm saying."

"Well, that's exactly what I was hoping you'd say, and no, you're not pompous, you're exactly right," Sid reassured him. "But what I worry about is whether you're aware of the risks involved and the consequences, the possible consequences, of what you're going to do at the hearing. You might be making a target of yourself, if you understand me."

"Sid," Nathan said, a little abruptly, "what makes you think I haven't already been one?"

Sid was astonished. "What do you mean?"

But Nathan had spoken more loudly than he had intended to, and Cheryl stirred in the back seat. "I'll explain later," Nathan muttered to Sid. Caught up in the conversation, Sid had slowed but was still in the passing lane, and a car behind him swerved, passing on the right. The driver gave them an angry look, and Nathan said, "Idiot. Be careful, Sid, or I won't get to enjoy giving my testimony to all those politicians."

Dr. Oldfield was clearly enjoying giving his testimony, however. He was concentrating, at the moment, on what he described as the inherent cultural bias in standardized examinations, and Nathan found himself listening with increasing discomfort. With friends like these, he thought, my case is going to be considerably weaker, just by association. Dr. Oldfield appeared to be saying that standardized tests, constructed by standardized test makers, that is, people who were of the dominant social group–white and upper middle class, was the implication--were intrinsically discriminatory. Such tests reflected the assumptions of the test makers about "core cultural knowledge." That core cultural knowledge was of course limited to what the dominant social group had accumulated in its climb toward dominance. It never included the survival strategies, the wisdom, the "street smarts" that the many other groups comprising American society had developed in their long and proud histories of accomplishment. Dr. Oldfield dared to say, he said, that he could easily construct a test of the mastery of such materials that not a single member of this distinguished Subcommittee would have a chance of passing. He elaborated this point at some length, with colorful examples of survival strategies, wisdom, and street smarts. Nathan squirmed with embarrassment. The Congressmen, he saw, remained completely impassive. The stack of paper to which Dr. Oldfield was referring as he spoke remained formidable. This was going to be a long morning, and Nathan was far down the list of witnesses.

The dominant social group. A memory from childhood floated into Nathan's vision, transporting him back to the old neighborhood in Cleveland, before his family's first move. He was four or five, not yet in kindergarten, and his family was living in what had since become the inner city, near East 105th Street and St. Clair Avenue. It had been a Jewish neighborhood, but most of the Jewish people had moved east, to Cleveland Heights, Shaker Heights, University Heights, depending on what they could afford. The Goldsteins, who were renters, might have been the only Jewish family still living on Nathan's street.

One day Nathan, who had never ventured very far from his house by himself, saw a number of white children playing on the front porch of a house about halfway down the block. On an impulse, he decided to walk down, introduce himself, and ask them their names. There was a stone path from the sidewalk leading to the front porch, and as Nathan took it toward the children, a boy approached him. Nathan smiled and said hello. The boy flung a handful of sand into Nathan's face and eyes. Nathan, shocked, stood there for a few seconds, then turned and started to walk home, crying. He had not seen his older brother on his bicycle across the street, watching the entire incident. His brother rode over and stopped him. "You go right back there," he said to Nathan, "and beat him up." Nathan turned around at once and walked back with clenched fists. When he reached the stone path, the children immediately ran into the house. At that moment, he thought, listening to Dr. Oldfield, he had joined the dominant social group. But his membership had been ephemeral.

The next witness, a Dr. Matthew B. Hayes, represented a national testing bureau that constructed, administered, retrieved, and scored hundreds of thousands, even millions–could that be right, Nathan wondered?–of standardized examinations every year. Most importantly, Dr. Hayes said, his bureau analyzed the results along various dimensions, demographically, geographically, and so on, as he would explain. With all due respect to the previous witness, Dr. Oldfield, Dr. Hayes said, although he would by no means claim that perfection had been achieved in the construction of these tests, the allegation that they were badly skewed by cultural bias toward one or another social group could *not* be supported by statistical evidence. Chairs scraped loudly both on the dais and at the witness table as Congressmen and witnesses turned to stare at Dr. Hayes. Nathan could almost feel the animosity emanating from Dr. Oldfield as Dr. Hayes continued. It was true, Dr. Hayes said, if certain variables were ignored, such as income level, micro- as well as macro-geographical locations, family size and structure, and parents' educational levels, that there appeared to be significant differences by race, especially on certain portions of the quantitative parts of the tests. But he wanted to stress, he said, that those variables should *not* be ignored if the tests were to be understood as they were intended to be understood, namely, as a kind of diagnostic measure of the test-taker's scholastic strengths *and* weaknesses. He had brought some charts and tables that would illustrate this important point, and with the Committee's indulgence, would now proceed to present them. Nathan relaxed once more, wishing he could smoke a cigarette. Everybody seemed to be taking as long as possible to say what he had to say.

Cheryl didn't do that, ever. Sometimes she was coy--when she'd told him that morning that she'd changed her mind about attending the hearing, she'd added, very seductively, that she'd make it up to him later with a surprise she was going to arrange–but she didn't go on and on, as Sid, for instance, sometimes did. Cheryl Weinglass got to the point. Within two weeks after they'd first met, she had moved into an apartment in his building. Within days most of her clothes were in Nathan's apartment. It wasn't just the seventies, it was Cheryl. She wasn't a Jewish American Princess, she was very independent, almost finished with her work toward her certificate as a physical therapist. She was self-confident, sure that if she persisted she'd get what she wanted, job, career, or man. On their second date, she'd told him that he turned her on, and she had meant it. But she enjoyed the way men looked at her, did what she could–a lot, Nathan thought!–to encourage them, and loved the attention. They had told each other that they were in love with one another, but that had not stopped Cheryl from flirting with other men, nor had Nathan ever felt remotely jealous when she did. They called it trusting one another. Nathan wondered about that from time to time.

He glanced at his watch. It was almost eleven thirty, and Dr. Hayes was showing no signs of slowing down. Nathan had agreed to meet Sid and Cheryl on the steps of the Capitol at a quarter past noon, if he could, so that they could have lunch together. If that didn't work out, he was to go back to the apartment after he had testified, and they would agree on where to go for dinner. Jack had said that he would be unavailable, but that he could recommend some excellent restaurants. Nathan tried to listen to what Dr. Hayes was saying, but it seemed to be more of what he had already said, in greater detail. Dr. Oldfield's frown now looked etched into his face. If any of the Congressmen had questions for Dr. Oldfield, Nathan thought, he would be sure to begin by saying something invidious about Dr. Hayes, or at least about his presentation. Maybe you didn't have to wait to be asked questions, Nathan reflected; maybe you could cut in somewhere at an opportune moment and say something like "If I may be permitted to comment on a related point--" even if the relationship remained imaginary.

Suddenly, when Dr. Hayes appeared to have concluded his explanation of a particularly complex chart and paused to make a transition to the next one, Congressman Schwartz interrupted, not with a question but an announcement. "It's now moving on toward the noon hour," Mr. Schwartz stated incontrovertibly, "and this may be as good a time for our lunch break, Dr. Hayes, as we're going to get. So with your permission I'm going to ask you to resume your very interesting presentation after we return, let us say at one fifteen, and now I'm going to entertain a motion to adjourn this hearing until that time."

"So moved," Mr. Contreras said. "Seconded," Mr. Whitburn said. "All in favor?" Mr. Schwartz asked. "Aye," all said. Chairs scraped as the Subcommittee rose more or less in unison, leaving Dr. Hayes standing at his flip charts. Nathan was delighted. He'd have time to run to the men's room and then meet Cheryl and Sid for lunch.

The men's room was a popular destination for witnesses, Congressmen, staff, and those few people who had comprised the audience–reporters, perhaps, Nathan thought. He did not see the man who had looked familiar. There was some deference on the part of the witnesses and staff to the Congressmen, but Dr. Oldfield, whose height was astonishing, took three strides and claimed a urinal ahead of a Congressman. Nathan wondered whether, if Dr. Hayes needed to relieve himself, a confrontation might occur over the wash basins. But Dr. Hayes did not appear–perhaps he had seen where Dr. Oldfield was going–and Nathan, waiting for his turn, heard Dr. Oldfield mutter something to the president of the black college standing behind him. "But Lloyd, of course he's going to defend the tests!" the president expostulated. "That's his game, not his sideline!"

Of course, Nathan thought. People were here to defend their interests, or to object to what they saw as inimical to them. Dr. Oldfield and Dr. Hayes would never agree about what constituted evidence of bias, discrimination, injustice. The Subcommittee already knew that. They knew what most of the witnesses would say. They knew that the biggest challenge confronting them today would be to stay awake while they were on the dais.

But they didn't know what he would say, even though he had submitted the requisite number of copies of his prepared testimony in advance. They wouldn't have read it, at least not carefully. They couldn't anticipate what kind of a scandal he was going to report. If Cheryl had a surprise for him, he had one for them. He finished up, washed his hands, and hurried out of the building to meet Sid and Cheryl.

*****

The hearing resumed some twenty minutes later than Congressman Schwartz had announced it would, largely because he did not return to the hearing room until then, and Mr. Erdmann had excused himself even before the morning session had been adjourned. Nathan looked around.

To his surprise, Dr. Oldfield had not returned, but the man who looked vaguely familiar was still in the audience. Nathan decided to use the time to review the testimony he would give when finally called upon. He would begin by stating that his testimony was presented in support of both bills the Subcommittee was considering but that, in the light of both his personal experiences with, and his research into, the architectural licensing process, what he had to say would be especially relevant to H.R. 3564, "The Truth in Testing Act." Then he would summarize his academic and professional background, but certainly not at the level of detail in which Dr. Summers had indulged himself. Then he would acknowledge the ugly fact that he'd taken and flunked the NCARB professional examination three times already. That would get their attention. He'd explain immediately that his testimony would relate not so much to *his* failures but to the *Board's* failure both to maintain his records adequately and to use the alternative legally available to them.

The dilemma, he thought, watching the Congressmen come in, some rather more flushed than their brief exposure to the September sun warranted, was how to hold their interest and yet provide a reasonably complete account of his struggles over the past several years. To judge from their performance this morning, they were very good at appearing to pay attention, even when they were probably doodling on their notepads or daydreaming about their girlfriends, as he had done. Well, he was not an actor. He had brought "exhibits," documents of various kinds, but he had no flip charts, no visuals, no models for their close inspection. This wasn't a charrette. He would have to slog through his story as best he could and hope they would confuse him with the rich scion of a major contributor to their political party, whichever it was.

Dr. Hayes finished his presentation at last, having bewildered most of his audience with statistical sophistication far beyond their grasp or interest. The next witness of the afternoon was the Director of the National Association of Occupational Licensing Reform, Samuel P. Jamison, Ph.D., as he announced. Nathan decided to listen carefully as soon as he heard Dr. Jamison's first sentences. Despite the pomposity of reminding the Subcommittee of his degree, his manner was pleasant and his voice sonorous. The Subcommittee, perhaps because they had been so bored by Hayes after he had attacked Oldfield's position, also seemed inclined to pay attention.

"Unlike common law or statutory law," Dr. Jamison began, "regulatory law has a much shorter history in our country, and continues to evolve. In regard to professional licensing, state regulatory agencies, acting as agencies of their respective state governments to protect the public's health, safety, and welfare, write and enforce rules to regulate and supervise our behavior. In a perfect world, these agencies would base their power on clearly defined, transparent rules. They would allow opportunities not just for *comments* by the public and the professions, but for some means of *participation* by both, participation in formulating and revising these rules as business and social environments, especially technological circumstances, keep changing. They would work to prevent malfeasance and nonfeasance. They would be able to justify their decisions and actions. If necessary, they would cooperate in review of those decisions by the courts. Unfortunately--" Dr. Jamison paused dramatically, taking a sip of water– "we do not live in a perfect world." Nathan sat up, ready, as he knew all of Jamison's listeners were, for a description of the imperfections in which they were mired.

"When the courts have ruled on the actions of these administrative agencies," Dr. Jamison continued, "they have almost always ruled on their side. To illustrate the effects of this combination of legislative, executive, and judicial power on the economy–that is to say, on creativity, on innovation, on curiosity and ambition, the very characteristics that make for progress in our competitive society--let me pose a hypothetical case. Let us say that a certain state, in which the automotive industry and its suppliers are major employers, taxpayers, and so on, has enacted statutes creating an agency to oversee the design of automobiles. Let us say, further, that the governor of that state, with his legislature's approval, has appointed executives from the major automobile companies and oil corporations to the agency's top administrative positions. And let us also say that most of these persons have every intention to return to their respective industries in some capacity when their terms of public service expire. Comparable situations are not unknown, I believe, in this city." Dr. Jamison took another sip of water. Nathan wondered about the wisdom of the last remark. But there was no doubt that he had the Congressmen's attention.

"Now I want to posit a young, upandcoming automotive engineer," Dr. Jamison said, "a brilliant young man who, while he was still a student at the state's university, had begun work on the design of a car whose engine would last half a million miles, whose transmission and exhaust system would last ten years, and whose miles per gallon would approach 100, all without a significant rise in the costs of production or important changes in the appearance of the vehicle." There were smiles and a few chuckles, but Dr. Jamison remained unperturbed. "As I said, this is a hypothetical case. In this scenario, then, the young man is successful in every respect: engine, transmission, and exhaust systems work exactly as intended, and the car does indeed achieve 100 mpg. The brilliant young man finishes college, is awarded his degree, and signs up to take the state examination which he must pass to obtain his license as an automotive designer, without which he cannot practice in this state either on his own or as an employee of one of the automotive companies. But his work in college has of course attracted a certain amount of notoriety. He has won prizes. His proud professors have written papers with him and presented them at well-publicized national conferences. He has published several articles on his own in highly reputable engineering journals. Is his profession waiting for him with open arms? Are the automotive companies ready to compete for his services with generous compensation packages and fringe benefits as soon as he has his license? Or is there another likelihood?" Again, Dr. Jamison reached for his water. Excellent timing, Nathan thought: he knows just when to heighten the suspense with these liquid pauses. I've got to remember that when I get on stage. I mean, when it's my turn.

"Gentlemen," Dr. Jamison said, sweeping the Subcommittee, which indeed included no women, with a glance from left to right–Nathan noticed, however, that a lady had taken a seat at the witness table–"we all know that another possibility is all too likely. The young man's revolutionary ideas would certainly be welcomed by consumers. The company that succeeded in obtaining his services would surely benefit substantially. Eventually, stimulated by his ideas, other engineers at other companies in the state would very likely enhance the designs of their own products and heighten the competition. If there were to be losers, they would most likely be foreign competitors, the very firms in Germany and Japan now competing more and more successfully with our own American companies. But in the short run, there is no question that all but one of the American companies, the one that hired the brilliant young engineer, would be at a serious disadvantage. And even that company would have to make massive new investments to take advantage of the young man's ideas. All the companies would be required to rebuild their engines, retool their cars, and change their strategic marketing plans. In the short run, costs would rise and stockholders would not be happy. And when stockholders are unhappy, it is unlikely that corporate executives will be comfortable, whether they are in temporary positions in industry or in temporary positions in government. I do not know the outcome of my hypothetical example, but I do know what happens in real life. Ideas have to be implemented in practice to see if they will work. If practice is limited to only approved practitioners, it is not difficult to avert the threat of innovation." Dr.

Jamison paused again, but this time he ignored his glass to fix the Subcommittee with a stare. Then he raised his finger, pointing not at the Congressmen but at the ceiling, as if an invisible but powerful Presence were there, listening. Nathan was delighted by the theatrics. This was a gesture that nobody could repeat without diminishing its effect.

Jamison had reached his peroration. "Gentlemen," he declared, "it is the position of the National Association of Occupational Licensing Reform that far too many governmental agencies entrusted with the machinery as well as the authority involved in the granting of licenses required to practice a host of professions and trades are unduly influenced by special interest groups whose short-term as well as long-term financial motivations do not serve the long-range interests of the American professional, the American worker, or the American public as a whole. The facts are unmistakable. State agencies are restricting entry to the professions and trades through the licensing procedures imposed on applicants for the licenses they must have, and they are doing so to prevent the competition and the innovations that they fear will endanger their own privileged positions. Thank you very much." Jamison sat back. For a moment, while the roomful of silence was a gauge of his impact, Nathan wanted to start clapping. The extent to which Jamison had anticipated his own remarks was almost uncanny. Nathan wished that he could be next, and almost raised his hand to volunteer, as if he were in school. But he wasn't and he didn't.

Instead, Congressman Schwartz introduced the only woman at the table, who had not been there in the morning. He noted that the Subcommittee had been happy to accede to her request, received last week, to present her testimony early in the afternoon, inasmuch as her difficulties in getting to Washington from Pocatello were almost as complex as the ones he had experienced in taking the shuttle from New York. The joke drew polite chuckles from the staff. Dr. Stephanie Sundhebel, he continued, was Director of the Office of Institutional Research and Long-Range Planning at—he stumbled over the name of a small college in Idaho, and Nathan saw Congressman Schwartz look questioningly first at a young staff assistant and then at Dr. Sundhebel. She smiled and shook her head either as if to confirm or to deny the name or the location, Nathan couldn't tell which. She was here this afternoon, the Congressman continued, to comment on the relationship between projected enrollments as these affected curriculum development, staffing, and investments in dormitories on the one hand, and, on the other, trends in applicants' achievement on standardized tests as these influenced the accreditation of post-secondary institutions like her own. The Congressman's fluency surprised Nathan until he saw him turn the page.

Dr. Sundhebel, a small, fluttery, bubbly, middle-aged woman much given to smiling and gesticulating, soon turned out to be the most challenging witness the Subcommittee had had to endure, and Nathan saw three members consult their watches before Dr. Sundhebel had finished reading the list of people at her college who had helped her prepare her testimony. He returned to reviewing his own, sure that he could find material he could either condense or leave out entirely. He could skip the few lines about NCARB's founding and so on, but he'd have to tell them that a certificate issued by NCARB entitled an architect to be admitted to practice in all fifty states and five of the territories. And he should also stress that although NCARB certification required all candidates to meet the "cut-off" scores, several states had modified those scores slightly, and in some states steps were being taken toward the elimination of the current examination. At this time, however–and he had to emphasize this point, he'd tell them--NCARB certification was necessary everywhere if an architect was to compete in the national architectural building market, where the big money was.

He had better not put it that way, he thought, although it would get attention. No, he'd say something about the nation's tradition of competition and incentive, as Jamison had done, and they would understand him perfectly.

He might refer to Jamison's earlier testimony, since it seemed to have been so well received, piggy-backing on what had already been asserted. For instance, he would present evidence that people had passed the NCARB exam who had no formal architectural education or training. How this assured protection of the public's safety, health, and general welfare, often alleged to be one of the examination's primary purposes, he would comment, obviously remained obscure. He would cite critics who had complained that the exam was a much better measure of test-taking skills than of architectural competence. He would tell the Subcommittee about the consultants to Wisconsin's architectural board, hired to investigate the abnormally high failure rate of Wisconsin's applicants. The consultants had found that the exam tested many skills architects did not need. California, he would inform them, had joined Wisconsin in these criticisms, and was also in the process of developing a replacement for the NCARB exam.

But there was much that, however relevant to him, he'd have to leave out of his testimony. He did not want to complain to Congress about his state's Legislature or official agencies: that would be certain to be self-defeating. Charnesky's death in that mysterious hit-and-run accident early last April had negated Spagnelli's instructions to Wheeler to have the Board of Examiners present at the next week's hearing, and when Nathan had tried to talk to Spagnelli, he'd turned away. Then, despite the evidence that Nathan and Peter Candor had produced about the NCARB exam's imprecision, unreliability, and arbitrariness, S.B. 15 had passed. After the bill had been signed into law by the Governor, Wheeler had sent Senator Madison a list of some four hundred names of Ohio architects who had been granted licenses under Section 4703.08 Part A of the Ohio Revised Code, well after 1931, the critical point that Charnesky and his Board had tried to keep hidden. But it was too late for the Senator to undo his colleagues' action: the vote had been twenty-nine to one. No, political defeats, for whatever reason, weren't something for public confession to Congressmen. Nor did he intend to mention that he hoped to involve the Federal Trade Commission or the Department of Justice in looking into the use of the examination as, in effect, a restraint on trade. He could use that phrase to describe the exam, he thought, without threatening appeals to agencies in the Executive Branch. He needed a comparison. He'd think of one.

And it wouldn't be wise, either, to say that he was going to take the exam again in December. They might just wish him good luck and ignore everything he'd said.

Dr. Sundhebel was in full stride, smiling, twisting in her chair with palpable excitement about faculty/student ratios and dormitory net square feet affected by variations in anticipated FTE enrollees–what were FTEs?–and Nathan saw that at least half of the Subcommittee's members had their heads down and were breathing very regularly. Well, his story would be a lot easier to follow, and much more dramatic. He would explain how the crucial term *"satisfactory"* in Section A--*"satisfactory evidence of knowledge of professional practice"*–evidence he had provided with extensive documentation, somehow became *"special,"* in the Board's denial of his application, stating that he had not provided "any evidence at the hearing which would show that he possessed any *special* qualifications for licensure...." This kind of semantic chicanery, he would say, in addition to the arbitrary, capricious, and selective use of the Ohio Revised Code that he had already demonstrated, illustrated the pressing need for Congressional action. To standardize the process across the nation, a conceptual framework was needed for the development of professional examinations of applicants for architectural licenses regardless of the location of their residences. Unlike physicians, whose practice was almost always confined to specific and limited geographical areas, architects, once licensed, could submit bids for projects anywhere they had obtained reciprocity. If competition between them was to be at all equitable, the manner in which they obtained their licenses clearly had to be fundamentally similar from one state to the next. State boards could retain their autonomy about required scores or mandatory sections, or even alternative examinations, if those were to be developed, but when it came to fundamental processes, individual applicants needed to know that they all had the same chance, whether they wanted to practice in Ohio or in Idaho or in New York. Congressman Schwartz might appreciate that last one.

He would emphasize his conviction that outsiders cannot and should not regulate a profession. Regulation should be left to the profession itself, like faculty governance or more generally academic freedom. Those ideas had been tested time and again, and proven meritorious. But the issue to be considered–this would be an opportunity to use one of Jamison's effective mannerisms, whether the glass of water or the stare– is whether the professions test and allow entry on a fair and equitable basis. For instance, the intern requirement, which varied over the incredible range of from two to thirteen years in various localities before an applicant was allowed to take the NCARB exam, simply produced a cheap source of labor, like so many agricultural workers who could not unionize for fear of deportation. Ah, that was the comparison he'd use. What appeared to be happening in architecture, he would say, was a pattern of restriction tantamount to *an unreasonable restraint of trade*. That would have to be emphatic.

He thought he had a very strong case, and he thought he had prepared it well. He hoped for questions and discussion, because then he could go into more detail, and refer more fully to the documents he had brought with him. But what he really wanted to tell them about, what had happened to him at Ohio State when he had worked on his master's thesis–how his research had been inexplicably stopped while he was in the middle of collecting his data, and how, nevertheless, he had been given his degree as if it had been a reward for his silence rather than recognition of his accomplishments–that he couldn't do. That wasn't a story that they could investigate. That was something that he would either have to live with and resent and wonder about for the rest of his life, or, just maybe, look into on his own.

How could he do that? Who would help him? Maybe Professor Rosenberg? Prescott, he knew, had suffered a fatal heart attack just after Charnesky had been killed, and, still angry and upset, Nathan hadn't gone to the funeral. But Rosenberg might know what had happened, and he had seemed both honest and fearless. He wasn't a particularly warm man, but still, he had been helpful, up to a point. Nathan reached for his pen to write himself a note, but suddenly Dr. Sundhebel was finished and Congressman Schwartz, once again overflowing with gratitude, was thanking her effusively. "Our next witness," the Congressman announced, "is Mr. Nathan Goldstein, architect, of Cleveland, Ohio."

Chapter II

Fleming, September, 1979

The bar was to the right of the restaurant, dark, quiet, well appointed with the usual furniture–leather armchairs, sturdy cocktail tables with wood veneers, large ashtrays, bowls of nuts and pretzels within easy reach, a thick rug of some kind underfoot, reproductions of paintings of eighteenth-century hunting parties on the walls, discreetly placed. Nothing obtrusive anywhere. Fleming, pleased, looked for the men he was to meet. All three were already there, drinking. He wasn't late, he thought–he was never late. They were early because they assumed he was picking up the tab. Maybe he would and maybe he wouldn't. He went to their table.

"Roger, there you are," one of them said. "Right on time!"

"Hello, Bill," Fleming said. Bill was William Meinrad, chief counsel of the American Institute of Architects, the AIA, of which Fleming was Executive Vice President. "Hello, Otto," he said to another man, shaking first Meinrad's hand, then the other man's. Otto was Otto Rune, also a lawyer, who worked for the National Council of Architectural Registration Boards, NCARB. "Ballard Warren," the third man said, rising and extending his hand. "Yes, of course," Fleming said. "I'm not sure whether we've met before, but it seems likely, doesn't it?"

"I think we have, once or twice," Warren said, "and of course we've talked on the phone a number of times."

"That we have," Fleming said. "I almost had your number in Cleveland memorized for a while!" They chuckled briefly and Warren, the president of the Cleveland chapter of the AIA, resumed his seat. The leather armchairs were too big to allow much intimacy around the cocktail table, but the three men showed no inclination to rearrange themselves elsewhere. Fleming saw a straight-backed chair at another table and went to get it. It was his meeting, he thought, but they didn't seem to be following his cues. He returned with the chair, annoyed that no waiter had come to help him with it, to hear Warren continue with something he had been telling Meinrad and Rune before he'd arrived.

"So this really tall black guy," Warren was saying, "gave him a look that would have frozen John D. Rockefeller, but the fellow just kept on with his statistical evidence and his charts and his tables, even though he must have known that those coons were upset as hell. I guess he had looked at the Committee and guessed correctly that he wasn't going to get any damnfool liberal nonsense about double standards from *them*, Democrats or not." Meinrad and Rune chuckled.

"Bring me up to speed," Fleming said quickly, looking at Warren. But a waiter approached and Fleming raised his hand, motioning to Warren to hold on while he ordered a drink. "A martini," he said to the waiter. "Very dry, please." The waiter nodded and turned. "Go ahead," Fleming said to Warren, feeling that he was taking control as he should.

"I was just telling Bill and Otto about some of the witnesses at the hearing before Goldstein spoke," Warren said. "I know you want to hear about Goldstein and his testimony and how the Committee reacted to his crap, and I haven't gotten to any of that. I was saving that until you got here, Roger."

"Good, thanks," Fleming said. "But first of all I want to know what the three of you think of the chances that these bills will ever see the light of day."

Rune, lighting a cigar, looked at Meinrad. "Slim and none," Meinrad said. "I wouldn't be surprised if they never get out of committee. But if they do, they're sure to die on the floor. And besides, I haven't heard a whisper about a companion bill in the Senate."

"That's the way I see it too," Rune said, blowing smoke away from his companions. "It's exactly the kind of thing every editorial writer in the country would denounce as federal intrusion into states' prerogatives, and of course they'd be exactly right. What would be next? National examinations for high school diplomas? Or drivers' licenses? Can you imagine how our friends in the trades would scream if somebody were to propose uniform federal examinations for masons and plumbers and electricians? Or mandatory continuing education, for Christ's sake?" They laughed. The waiter brought Fleming's martini and said, "Here you are, sir." Fleming let the waiter set the glass down in front of him without acknowledgment.

"National examinations for high school diplomas might not be a bad idea, in a way," he said to Rune, but including the others in his glance. "But what would that do to college sports? Football and basketball? I mean, how could the colleges recruit all those guys who can't read and wouldn't have diplomas?" They laughed again. Fleming took a sip of his drink and exhaled.

"You see how absurd the whole thing is, when you think about it," Warren said. "But I have to tell you, most of the witnesses they heard this morning, and this afternoon too, were on the other side. Not just the black guys, that was predictable, about discrimination and all that crap. Besides this one fellow with his statistics, I don't think anyone testified against either bill."

"Anyone there from any professional school?" Fleming asked.

"No," Warren said. "Just the usual liberal arts crowd. Unless you count education as a professional discipline–there was a lady who was some sort of administrator at a college out west somewhere who had a lot to say about teacher training and science education and that kind of thing. But her main purpose was, let's see, I'm not sure that she had a main purpose. She just had a lot of very confusing stuff to say. I think it had to do with how hard it is to predict fall enrollment and how changing the standardized examinations would make it even harder. But maybe not. I don't think anyone paid any attention to her anyway. But there was one man who did get attention–no, not Goldstein, although he seemed to cause something of a stir too–a man named Jamison from something called–" Warren pulled out a little notebook and flipped through it– "National Association of Occupational Licensing Reform. Ever hear of it?"

Meinrad and Rune shook their heads. "No, I haven't either," Fleming said. "Who are they? Where do they get their money?"

"Good questions," Warren said. "I don't know. I think he was put on the witness list late, you know, after the original list had been printed and distributed. Or maybe some strings were pulled to allow him to testify after the witness list had been compiled. I've heard that pulling strings is not altogether uncommon in this city."

The others laughed briefly and uneasily. Fleming wondered whether Warren was being a smartass, as if he were somehow morally superior to them. No, he just thought he was being clever. "What did this man– Jamison?–have to say?" he asked, re-establishing fellowship with his tone.

"Yes, Jamison. It wasn't so much what he said as how he said it that seemed to hold their attention. I don't mean that he paraded up and down, which a witness can't do anyway, and he certainly knew how to give a speech, but that wasn't it either. He gave them a hypothetical example, he called it, that they understood very well, of a really bright young engineer who had designed a new car that would last damn near forever and get great gas mileage without a huge increase in production costs. Then he said what a threat such a young fellow would be to all the companies that didn't hire him. Even the company that did manage to hire him would first of all have to make major investments in re-tooling all their plants all over the country, and what would the shareholders say to that, and how would that affect the compensation packages of the executives. You get the idea. So in this hypothetical example the bright young engineer would pose a major threat and the chances were that he'd be blackballed everywhere. The Committee understood that all too well. And this Jamison didn't neglect to point out what this sort of obstacle to innovation means nationally, you know, in the light of the foreign car companies who are beginning to get a greater share of the market every year."

"Damn," Meinrad said, speaking for the other two as well. "Where is this guy from?"

"I'm not sure," Warren said. "I suppose I could find out."

Fleming shook his head. "No, don't bother. I don't really see why we should worry too much about it. If any reporter does anything with it, it would be simple for the automotive companies to point to all their innovations and emphases on the public welfare since Nader exposed the Corvair as a death trap. They have excellent PR people, and they spend a fortune every month on fighting precisely this kind of argument. I don't buy that business about foreign competition. Made in Japan means that it's junk, as far as most of the American public is concerned. The Germans and Japanese may sell a lot of expensive sports cars, and a few expensive German luxury cars. And I'm sure that they still have the hippie market, you know, the tie-die flower-power holdouts left over from the Vietnam War years. But I can't see any serious trouble ahead for the Big Three, not for generations."

"Yeah, I think you're right, Roger," Rune said. "And it's something of a stretch, especially for congressmen who tend to think in terms of their constituents and voting blocks, to see the automotive industry's position as somehow symptomatic of other businesses, like construction and real estate development and the professions that go along with those."

"Symptomatic! Fancy stuff, Otto!" Meinrad teased his friend. Fleming felt that the conversation was beginning to drift. "Well, what about Goldstein, then?" he asked Warren. Meinrad and Rune sat straighter in their chairs.

Warren didn't answer right away. He was looking very appreciatively at a shapely girl in a well-filled cut-away blouse who had just entered the bar and was looking around, perhaps for someone she was to meet. Fleming, Meinrad, and Rune followed Warren's gaze and grunted in male agreement. She seemed to note their approval without looking at them directly, and sashayed to a table near them. Her high heels made her long legs seem even longer. The waiter came to her immediately.

"Yes, indeed," Fleming said. "Now, Ballard, you were saying about Goldstein?" The girl looked up for a moment, but the men had stopped staring at her and were speaking more softly.

Warren emptied his glass and set it down carefully. "Goldstein, yes," he said. "By the way, I think he saw me but I don't think he recognized me. We met once, maybe twice, in Columbus, but very briefly. On the other hand, he may have seen me at meetings when I didn't see him. I'm not sure. Anyway, he didn't testify until the afternoon, and then he had a lot to say. It all sounded very plausible except, of course, for the fact that he did flunk the NCARB exam three times and so far has not been successful in the courts. You know his case is before the Ohio Supreme Court now," he said to Meinrad and Rune. They nodded. "Roger told us," Rune said.

"What do you mean, 'very plausible'?" Fleming asked Warren. He finished his martini.

"Well, there was that language in the Ohio Revised Code that did give the Board the option to waive the examination if he met the criteria specified in that section. He was right about that. And he did meet the criteria, he was right about that too. He brought a lot of stuff with him, you know, letters, affidavits, documentation of all kinds he kept referring to. And that the Ohio Board's Secretary–I forget his name–Wheeler?-- said that he wasn't aware of that language, that sure didn't help our side. Damn fool. And there was another point Goldstein made, although he didn't press it as he might have, the fact that when he tried to see the questions and answers on the section of the exam that he flunked, you know, asked about it later on, he was told that all that had been thrown out and nobody had made any copies or anything like that. That wasn't kosher, if you pardon the pun."

"What wasn't kosher? What pun?" Meinrad asked.

Fleming laughed. "Ballard is alluding to Goldstein's ethnicity," he explained. Meinrad still looked puzzled. "Goldstein's a Jew," Fleming elucidated, "and kosher means that it's food they can eat without violating their religion. So if something is kosher, it's OK."

"He's a Jew? I didn't think of that either," Rune said. "That explains a lot."

"Right," Warren said, "I never met one I could trust, not one. They just don't play the game by the rules, if you know what I mean. Anyway, he went on and on about everything that had been done to him, you know how those people whine, and one of the Committee members did ask him some questions, you know, pretending to be sympathetic or outraged or whatever--"

"Which one?" Fleming interrupted.

"Which question?"

"No, which Congressman?"

"Schwartz, from New York, who was running the hearing."

"Oh, no wonder. Another Jew."

"Yes, that's right, of course he is. But nobody else asked him anything, and they didn't seem all that impressed by him, any more than by the other witnesses. Well, maybe a little."

"Anything in particular he said that seemed to impress them, did you notice?" Fleming asked.

"Yes, that California and Wisconsin were so unhappy with the NCARB exam that they're both working on new examinations for their applicants," Warren said. "And there was one other point he made that had them pricking their ears up, about the inconsistencies, from one state to the next, in the internship requirements for the kinds of experience the intern was to bring to the NCARB exam. This is *before* applicants can take the exam, you remember." The two lawyers looked surprised.

"He said that this was simply a way to cheapen the labor supply," Warren continued. "He even compared the interns to the Mexicans we allow in to pick vegetables and fruits. The Spics can't unionize because they're afraid of deportation. The interns can't protest because they'd be blackballed. That's not exactly how he put it, but the meaning was clear."

Warren's listeners shifted uncomfortably in their chairs. "You know how he described it?" Warren asked rhetorically, referring again to his notebook. "Like *an unreasonable restriction of trade*. That caused a stir, believe me."

"Well, that's bullshit," Meinrad said. "He's not a lawyer and doesn't know anything about it." Rune nodded quickly, but Fleming wasn't reassured. Nobody said anything for a moment, and then Meinrad and Rune glanced at their watches. The cocktail hour was running out. "One more thing," Fleming said to Warren, who was showing signs of following Meinrad's lead, "did Goldstein say anything, directly or indirectly, about his work at Ohio State?"

"Ohio State? Where he was a student?"

"Yes," Fleming said. "About the research he had started in some independent study project? Or about any of his advisors at the time, the professors, I mean?"

"No, he didn't," Warren said. "Why would he? That wouldn't have had anything to do with his flunking the NCARB exam three times or with his notion that the Board treated his appeals unfairly or any of that. Why do you ask?"

"Just curious," Fleming said. "I heard that he was something of a pain in the ass even back then, so I thought he might have trotted out all his old grudges."

"What grudges? He got his degree, didn't he?" Warren asked, turning to go with Meinrad and Rune.

"Roger, if we're done," Meinrad said. "Otto and I have to meet our wives–thanks for the drink--"

Bastards, Fleming thought. "You're very welcome, Bill, Otto," he said. "See you soon, I'm sure–Ballard, just one more thing," he said, putting his hand on Warren's shoulder.

Warren stopped while Meinrad and Rune waved and made their way out of the bar. Fleming watched them go past the restaurant and toward the hotel's lobby until they were out of view. "Ballard," he said, lowering his voice, "I'm certain that you understand how important it is that we keep all this to ourselves. You're sure Goldstein didn't recognize you in the audience?"

"Well, not a hundred percent, Roger, but I really don't think he did," Warren answered. "And I do understand that this is all confidential. I don't think we have anything to worry about as far as Goldstein's concerned, not now, not ever."

"Great," Fleming said. "You have to go?"

"Yes, my plane back to Cleveland–" Warren checked his watch. "Yes, I'd better get going right now. Let me split the drinks with you," he added, reaching for his wallet.

"Absolutely not," Fleming said, waving him off. "My pleasure. There's usually a cab on the corner right outside the hotel, so you shouldn't have any problem."

"Right," Warren said, offering his hand. "Next time, then."

"Next time," Fleming said, smiling and shaking Warren's hand. The smile disappeared as quickly as Warren turned and walked out. Didn't even thank me for the drink. Well, maybe he'll remember it if Goldstein's name ever comes up in his conversations in Cleveland. Fleming had learned, he thought to himself, that you had to pay for everything, especially for trust. The waiter approached with the tab. "Not yet," Fleming said, raising his voice and eyeing the shapely girl who had been watching his party break up. "Bring me another, and bring that lovely lady another of whatever she's having."

The girl looked up, hesitated, and then, brushing her thick, rather long hair back from her face, said, "Why thank you very much, kind sir." Fleming, pleased that he had gotten to first base, smiled, took the three steps to her table, extended his hand, and said, "Roger Fleming."

"Cheryl Weinglass," the girl said. She had a great smile, Fleming thought, probably extensive dental work some years ago. "So pleased to meet you," they said almost in unison, and burst out laughing. "Great minds are reported to think alike," Fleming said. "Are you waiting for someone? Am I intruding?"

"Well, yes, in a way–I mean, I am sort of waiting for someone, if he wakes up from his nap upstairs, but no, you're not intruding, Mr. Fleming, not at all."

"Roger," he corrected her, "and may I call you Cheryl?" She's at least three years younger than my daughter Ann, he thought. But that's not the point. Still, I'm not going to risk getting involved with some young stud fresh from his nap and eager to go again, either.

"Please do," Cheryl said. "Did your friends abandon you?" The waiter brought their drinks.

"No, we were finished, and one had to catch his plane back to Cleveland and the other two were worried about their wives," Fleming explained. "But I don't have any such encumbrances as those." Might as well push it as far as it would go. He took a big swallow of his martini.

But she ignored that hint and responded to the first part. "Cleveland!" she said. "That's where I'm from!"

"Really!" Fleming said, stiffening. Maybe there was more than one reason to be cautious.

"Oh, I meant to ask you," Cheryl said, "did I overhear you talking about someone named Goldstein?"

Jesus Christ, Fleming thought, don't tell me I've been trying to pick up Goldstein's girlfriend! "Goldstein?" he asked. "No, I don't think so. We were talking about looking into certain problems, professional problems that somehow have come to the attention of the Congress--" I'm talking too much, Fleming thought, must be this second martini– "and I may have told them to leave no stone unturned or something like that. They do some work for me from time to time," he added, thinking that it sounded lame even while he said it.

She gave him a peculiar look. She's not buying it, he thought. "Oh," she said. "I was just asking because that's my boyfriend's name, the one upstairs. He testified to Congress today, some Committee, I mean."

Confirmed. This was amazing. Fleming leaned back a little, just in case Goldstein should suddenly enter the bar, but he saw an opportunity. "Your boyfriend the one upstairs?" he smiled, now quite fatherly. "Are there other boyfriends not upstairs?"

Cheryl giggled. "Not really, no," she said. So she *was* a player, Fleming thought. "What did your boyfriend testify about? I'm just curious."

"Well, he's an intern architect, in Cleveland, you know, and he's had trouble getting his license to practice, although he did very well when he was in school–he went to Ohio State in Columbus--"

"Excellent school," Fleming said encouragingly.

"–yes, and then he didn't pass the exam for the license, you know, although he came close," Cheryl continued. She finished her drink. Fleming looked for the waiter. Might as well keep this little broad going, she might spill something interesting. And her teats weren't hard to look at either. But he positioned himself so that he could keep an eye on the entrance to the bar.

"Anyway," Cheryl continued, "he's going to take the exam again this fall and I'm sure he'll pass it, but this Committee is looking at examinations, you know, for getting into school or getting licenses, that kind of thing–I know about that because I'm finishing my studies to become a physical therapist--"

"Really! Very impressive!"

"–yes, and Nathan, that's my boyfriend, he felt that somehow the whole thing is unfair in one way or another, I can't really explain it the way he does. But that's why he testified today, to tell them about it."

"I see," Fleming said. "Very interesting." She didn't have any insights. But still, Goldstein's girlfriend! He shouldn't just let the chance slip by. "Tell me something, if you don't mind," he said, leaning toward her again, "you know you're an unusually attractive young woman, and I have a very good friend, as it happens, in Cleveland, a lawyer, very successful, unattached, recently had his heart broken–would you mind very much if I gave him your name and telephone number? I mean, you do go out once in a while with other people, don't you?"

Cheryl was clearly flustered and delighted at the same time. "Well, no–I mean, not exactly, not very often–what do you mean?"

Fleming took out his wallet. "I think I have his card with me," he said. "He's really very good-looking, tall, likes to dance, plays tennis, I think, drives a silver BMW, yes, here's his card: Richard Statton. Let me buy you another drink–what are you having?" He offered her the card and motioned to the waiter, who had reappeared.

"Oh, no, I'd better stop," Cheryl giggled. But she took the card and put it in her purse. "You're sure?" Fleming asked. "Another for you, then, sir?" the waiter asked. "Give us a moment," Fleming said to him, rather curtly. The waiter left. "You know, Cheryl, I can't ask Richard to call you if I don't have your number," he said, taking out his pen and offering it to her. "Well–ll–" she said, looking toward the bar's entrance. No one was there. "Oh, why not!" she said, taking the pen. "Do you have a piece of paper?" "Write it on the napkin," Fleming suggested. "Then, when I give it to Richard–he comes to Washington quite often on business–I can explain the romantic circumstances of our meeting."

"Oh, were they romantic?" Cheryl giggled again. Silly little broad, Fleming thought, she looks like she'd be great in bed but what else does Goldstein see in her, I wonder? "Absolutely," he said. "We've already established that great minds think alike!" She scribbled a number on the napkin and pushed it toward him. "Here's my number at work," she said, "and here's your pen." Time to go, he thought, I don't want to push my luck. He folded the napkin carefully, put it in his inside pocket, and took his pen. "You're sure you won't have another drink?" But he started to rise even as he asked the question. "No, I really better not," Cheryl said, looking at her watch. "Nathan will be down for dinner any time now."

"Cheryl, it's been great," Fleming said, "and I'm sure you'll hear from Richard very soon." That horny bastard thinks he's God's gift to women, and all I'll have to do is to tell him that this is one hot number, Fleming thought. He offered his hand and Cheryl took it. The waiter approached and Fleming, releasing Cheryl's hand, reached for his wallet again and gave the waiter too much money. "You need change?" the waiter asked insouciantly. The son of a bitch was getting even with him! "Hell yes," Fleming started to snarl when he saw Goldstein hesitate outside the entrance, not sure, apparently, whether to go into the restaurant or the bar. "No, keep it," he said hurriedly. "Bye, Cheryl!" He hurried toward the exit, leaving Cheryl with a surprised look on her face. He brushed past Goldstein at the door, trying to look the other way. "Mr. Fleming?" Goldstein asked. Fleming hurried on.

*****

Cheryl's surprise for Nathan had included a dinner reservation at the hotel's restaurant as well as a room for the night in the hotel itself. After Nathan had finished his testimony, they had met, as planned, at the Capitol again. Sid would pick them up in the lobby in the morning for the drive back to Cleveland, but the night was to be spent in all the delights that privacy could confer. "How on earth did you manage to save all that money?" Nathan had asked Cheryl, truly astonished. Cheryl was both pleased that her surprise had succeeded and annoyed by the question. "I can save money any time I want to!" she had declared. "I look for bargains, I'm careful about what I eat, and I'm careful with money, Mr. Big Shot, and you should know that!"

"All right, all right," Nathan had said, putting up his arm in mock self-defense. "I'm very grateful and absolutely delighted. It'll certainly be more comfortable than a sleeping bag on Jack Greenstein's living room floor."

"Not just more *comfortable*, Nathan," Cheryl said, licking her lips. That was just before Nathan had to return to the Rayburn Building to give his testimony. When he had joined her again at the Capitol, later that afternoon, they had gone straight to the room. Afterwards Nathan had fallen asleep, and Cheryl, deciding to take advantage of the cocktail hour, had left him a note and gone to the bar.

Cheryl Weinglass liked men. She had liked boys ever since the seventh grade, when they had begun to notice her, and she liked the effect that being popular with boys had on the girls she knew. By the time she was seventeen or eighteen, she had graduated from boys to men, even though she was still in high school, and she loved all the differences. That the four men sitting together, talking about Nathan Goldstein–she was *sure* that the handsome one with grey hair who looked distinguished and seemed to be in charge, had said something about Nathan–were all much older than she was did not trouble her in the least. Older men had more money, were more likely to buy you more than one drink, and weren't always so eager to cut to the chase. They were more likely to enjoy the repartee and the body language that went with it. They might not always be so great in the sack, but that wasn't all there was to the game, and when she was really horny, Nathan did very well. Or Bernie, about whom Nathan didn't know anything. She had been very careful.

She got up before Nathan, now heading toward her from the entrance, could see that there were two glasses on her table, met him halfway, took his arm, and started to speak before he could: "Well, Mr. Sleepy Head, it's about time! I'm starving! The restaurant is this way, come on--"

"Cheryl, hold on a second," Nathan interrupted, resisting her a little. "That was Roger Fleming at the door, just leaving as I came in looking for you! Were you sitting with him?"

"Who? What are you talking about, I've been waiting here for you, just had a couple of drinks by myself, that's all!"

"Really! All by your little lonesome?" He had meant to tease, but he sounded sarcastic and suspicious. Cheryl, an experienced in-fighter, leaped at the opening.

"Look, Nathan, don't start this shit with me," Cheryl said, "and don't question me as if you were the police and I am supposed to be some spy or something. We had a great afternoon, and now I'd like to have a great dinner, and don't start spoiling our plans for a great night, which is what you're going to do if you keep this up."

"Do you know who Roger Fleming is?" Nathan said, ignoring her threat. "I mean, do you even know who the hell he is? No, you don't," he continued, cutting her off. Her face was getting redder. "You don't know, you don't care, and I have to wonder what you just might have done just now, I really do."

Cheryl started to say something, then bit her lip. "Look, Nathan, either stop this right now and let's go to dinner, or forget the whole thing, give me the air fare and I'll go upstairs, get my things, and catch a cab to the airport. I mean it."

That stopped him. She's serious, he thought, and maybe I did go too far. But Roger Fleming! He had met Fleming at least twice, once in Cleveland and once at some meeting, and had corresponded with him when he was doing his independent study–in fact, he still had the letters they had exchanged–and the Executive Vice President of the AIA was just about the most valuable person to know in the whole country for someone just starting out in the profession. He knew *everybody*, not just every partner of the really important architectural firms, but bankers, lawyers, engineers, developers, real estate companies, and of course politicians. Politicians! Did Fleming know that he had testified to the Subcommittee today on the NCARB examination?

"Well, Nathan, what's it going to be?" Cheryl asked coldly.

Nathan sighed. "I'm sorry, I'm just still wound up from today. Let's go to dinner," he said, taking her arm. She relaxed a little and said, "All right then."

But it took some wine and some time to repair the damage their exchange had done to their earlier mood. Cheryl, aware of Richard Statton's card in her purse, felt guilty, defensive, and aggrieved all at the same time. Why shouldn't she enjoy what Nature had blessed her with, earning her the attentions of attractive men? She wasn't going to be young and beautiful forever, and now was the time to experiment, to investigate, to see just how she could combine what she had with what luck might contribute. But she hated getting caught in a lie and having to think of ways to justify herself. Nathan was just too possessive, and she couldn't put up with that. She wasn't one of those ridiculous girls who didn't mind being *owned*, practically, by whatever man they were sleeping with, not Cheryl Weinglass. If the new emphasis on feminism meant anything at all, it meant equal rights for women in exactly this way, and what was sauce for the goose was sauce for the gander. Or the other way around, however it went. She decided she'd start with a salad with oil and vinegar. And then the salmon, baked in that parmesan crust she liked.

Nathan, across the table, sipping his wine and studying the menu–the prices were outrageous-couldn't get past the thought of Roger Fleming finding out that he had testified against the NCARB examination to the Congressional Subcommittee considering legislation called "Truth in Testing." Would Fleming be open-minded and try to find out what Nathan had had to say? It would all be published in the *Congressional Record*, he thought. Or was Fleming likely to be displeased that Nathan had gone up against the establishment, no matter what he thought of the exam? Probably. Is this what Sid had meant about the possible consequences of his testimony?

"I'm ready," Cheryl said.

"What are you going to have?"

"I think I'd like the salmon," she said. "What about you?"

They were being careful with one another, he saw. At least she hadn't ordered the most expensive item on the menu. "The salmon sounds good," he said. If she was on her way to forgiveness, she'd tell him to order something else so that she could taste it. Did the fact that she'd made the reservation for the restaurant mean that this was her invitation too, not just the hotel room? Well, he couldn't ask her now.

"Order something else, Nathan, so that I can taste it," she said. "And don't forget, this is my invitation, part of the surprise. Order a steak." He was forgiven. She was really a sweet girl. He flashed her a grin and said, "No, honey, the room and what you have in mind are more than generous enough–the dinner's on me."

After dinner they returned to their room with a bottle of wine. Nathan knew that his credit card bill next month would be painful, but it had been a special day, and this was no time to call a halt to the celebration.

*****

Fleming hesitated outside the hotel, unsure about what he wanted to do and where he wanted to go. It was time for dinner but he wasn't

hungry, and he didn't like eating alone anyway. Both of his girlfriends–
he had long been divorced–were out of town. There wasn't anything
enticing in his refrigerator in his apartment. What was really on his mind
was the narrow escape he'd just had, avoiding Goldstein just by a step,
after flirting with his stupid girlfriend. He wouldn't have minded another
drink but he knew that he'd had his quota. He wasn't in his thirties any
longer, he told himself. He decided to go back to his office. Somebody
might be working late, although, with this nice weather, that wasn't
likely. Still, it was possible, and he could pretend that he had hoped for a
message from Congressman or Senator so-and-so, that was always
impressive. Or maybe some high official at HUD.

Besides, there was something he wanted to look up at the office,
whether or not anyone was there. Perhaps he shouldn't have mentioned
Goldstein's "grudges" at Ohio State in his brief exchange with Warren.
He didn't particularly trust Warren. He had gotten as far as he had, a
public relations man as the key official of a professional society,
complete with a very nice salary, an even nicer expense account, lots of
lucrative opportunities to make influential friends in high positions in
both corporate suites and in the government, because he didn't
particularly trust *anybody*. That he wasn't an architect himself had never
stood in his way at the AIA. The AIA Board wanted somebody who
understood politics, knew the major players, had an instinct for the
jugular, and when push came to shove didn't hesitate to protect their turf
however it had to be done. Any way at all. Fleming felt that he was *born*
knowing how to play that game. But sometimes, he thought, signaling a
cab, he might be *too* sure of himself, too certain that he was smarter and
quicker and more adroit than other people, and then, once in a while, he
might say something that he wished, later, he could take back. Too close
to the edge too often, he thought, giving the driver the address on New
York Avenue. Just literally a step ahead of Goldstein back there at the
bar, for instance. And with Warren: although it was reassuring to know
that Goldstein hadn't brought up that old business at Ohio State in his
testimony to the Subcommittee, he didn't want Warren to look into any
of that either. Not just Goldstein's ridiculous study, but what had
happened later. Jesus. He didn't even want to think about it himself.

He had been right about the weather. Nobody was working late at the
office. It was just as well, he thought. He walked past the reception area
and conference rooms and turned the corner to his own private office,
admiring, as always, his name plate and title to the side of the door. A lot
classier, he thought, not for the first time, than on the door itself. He
unlocked the door, walked to his desk to see what Louise, his secretary,

had put there after he'd left, and found various messages he could ignore and one he didn't want to. "Mrs. M. called and would like you to call her if you come back this evening. At her request, I'm also leaving a message on your machine at your home. She said you'd know where to call her." So Joyce was back early and her husband wasn't. Fleming was sure that Louise suspected that he was having an affair with a married woman. Her phrasing dripped disapproval. If she wasn't such an excellent secretary, and if she didn't know so damned much, he'd seriously consider reprimanding her. But that was always the problem with having to trust people's discretion, Louise's or Warren's or anybody's, you couldn't reprimand them as long as you had to trust them. He reached for the phone. No, he thought, first he'd check that file that had brought him back here in the first place. It was only about six thirty, plenty of time to reach Joyce, in more than one sense, he smiled to himself.

He unlocked his private four-drawer file cabinet with the key on his key chain–the only other key to the cabinet was in his jewelry box in his bedroom–and tried to remember how he had filed the material relating to Goldstein. It had been a long time, three or four years, since he'd had any occasion to look it up. It certainly wasn't under his name. He thought that he'd given it some kind of coded identification, something clever, so that just in case somebody was looking for a file labeled **Goldstein, Nathan,** he'd have to know something else about Goldstein. Of course. It was under **J,** as he had explained to Meinrad. He riffled the first few files–Jackson, Jacobson-- there's another one-- James, Jarrad, Jasperson, Jennings, Jewison–too far–there it was, just before Jewison. No label, he saw. Not necessary. He drew the file out. Some letters, that enormously long questionnaire Goldstein had developed for his study, some newspaper clippings, copies of articles about the NCARB examination. Two of the letters were from Goldstein to himself. He had answered the first, sidestepping neatly, but not the second. A copy of his letter was here. Then there were Goldstein's letters to Arthur Mercer, Warren's predecessor at the Cleveland AIA chapter. Mercer really deserved a lot of credit for stopping Goldstein, alerting Fleming as he had, even recommending to Goldstein that he contact Fleming directly. That had been brilliant.

He looked at Goldstein's letters. Yes, just as he'd thought–Goldstein had listed his advisors. Arnold Prescott and Harry Rosenberg–damn, still another one!–from the Architecture faculty. Maxwell Goodman, a marketing professor. Warren was very unlikely to know him. But he might have known Prescott and Rosenberg, especially Prescott, who had been so prominent in Ohio. As for Rosenberg–hadn't somebody told him that he'd just left Ohio State for Michigan, up in Ann Arbor, of all places? Yes: he'd replied that it wasn't as if a football coach had switched allegiances! No headlines in architecture professors switching schools! That had gotten a laugh. Practitioners and academics weren't always fond of each other.

Well, no, he wouldn't push this with Warren. There wasn't much chance that Warren would follow up Fleming's misstep, would even wonder about it. To hell with it. He replaced the file, sat down at his desk, reached for the phone, and dialed Joyce's number.

Chapter III
Nathan, November, 1979

The weather, that November day in 1979, was unpleasant in eastern Ohio, but the drive down to Columbus from Cleveland was mercifully uneventful. Interstate 71 South is flat and straight, mostly running through farm country. Nathan, still very familiar with the road from the dozens of times he had taken it during his seven years of undergraduate and graduate studies at Ohio State, found himself thinking about Cheryl and their leave-taking the previous evening. She had helped him load his car with his clothes, his books, and his little television set. Once again they had reassured one another that they loved each other, that they trusted each other, that they wouldn't even think about going out, as they called it, with anyone else. Once again he had doubts about all of it. There had been a girl years ago, whom he had first met when he was still in high school, who had somehow entranced him in ways that he couldn't describe, a girl about whom he still daydreamed, never erotically but not in any ethereal way either: Karen Sternberg. He had never felt quite the same way about anyone else. They had called each other and corresponded for a while after she had moved to California, a wonderful correspondence that had only gradually petered out as they'd gotten older, busier, involved with this person or that. But his feeling for her had persisted, somehow. After he had graduated from Ohio State and was traveling across the country from one architectural firm to another, interviewing for jobs, he had looked her up when he had come to the West Coast. He remembered that he had rented a car to drive from Los Angeles to the Bay area. The California coast had been breathtaking; nothing in his Ohio background had prepared him for such gorgeous scenery. But the trip had been completely unsuccessful, both professionally and personally. The interviews had all been an expensive waste of time, in some cases, even unpleasant, and he had found Karen only five months before she was to marry some nephrologist or endodontist or whatever he was. A plastic surgeon, he remembered.

What had drawn him to Karen? That was easy, he thought: she had made him feel that she was genuinely interested in him, in what he was saying, in how he saw things, in what he wanted to do and why he wanted to do it. She had a way of listening that indicated that he had, as the cliché had it, her undivided attention. Since she seemed to think that what he was saying was important or amusing or stimulating in some way, he felt that she thought that *he* was important or amusing or stimulating.

The only way that he knew that Cheryl found him stimulating was sexually. She wasn't merely responsive; she was just as likely to take the initiative as he was. He had known a fair number of girls who liked sex—this was the seventies, after all, and chastity was almost as quaint an idea for women as for men—but never a girl who liked sex as much as Cheryl did. And that's why, he realized, he didn't believe all those protestations of strict fidelity. Not only did he not believe that she wouldn't have anything to do with other men while he was in Columbus, preparing for the NCARB examination once again, he wasn't at all sure that she hadn't already been seeing someone else in Cleveland, at least sometimes. He remembered two occasions like holographs in his mind, still seeing her expression change, in one instance, from normal to shock to steely control. That time they had been in a restaurant, some months ago. They had been sitting at a table for two, Cheryl facing inwards, toward most of the other guests at their tables, while he, sitting across from Cheryl, had seen only the backs of the people who were leaving, walking toward the exit. Someone, a tall man, had obviously caught Cheryl's eye as he made his way past their table and Cheryl had recognized him immediately. She was normally an animated girl, whether talking or listening, but now, at least for a second, she froze and her face registered unmistakable shock. Then she recovered, almost visibly adjusting her features. "What is it?" he had asked, surprised and concerned. She didn't miss a step. "For a moment," she had said, "I thought that was Sean Connery coming by! He looked so much like James Bond, I couldn't believe it! Too *much*!" He had looked at the man's receding back, but the light was poor and he couldn't even tell what the man was wearing. And then he was gone, and Cheryl resumed their conversation. But he hadn't forgotten.

The other time, rather recently, had been quite different. He had gone downstairs to Cheryl's first-floor apartment with a pressure cooker she had wanted to try—she didn't have one and saw no reason to buy one when she could borrow his—and had come in just as she was hanging up the phone. He had hesitated. She had said, too quickly, "Wrong number," and then, very unusually, she had blushed. He was immediately positive that she was lying. "Here," he had said, "this is the pressure cooker, and here's the weight that you have to put on this little vent, I'd guess you'd call it, like a hat." "Ooooh," she'd said, giggling, "like a condom!" It was typical of her to say something like that when she was anxious to change the subject.

No, he didn't trust Cheryl, and the fact was that he didn't love her and she didn't love him. But there was no one else in *his* life, and at this point he wasn't interested in looking for anyone either. What he was interested in, what he was passionate about, was finally passing this damned NCARB exam, the reason he was returning to Columbus. Still, he'd call her tonight at nine, as they had agreed he would.

The 17th Avenue exit was coming up. It all looked very familiar. He turned right off the exit going west toward the campus, turned right again onto High Street, left on Lane Avenue, left on Tuttle Park Place, left onto Woodruff Avenue, and came to his dormitory, Neilwood Gables. "Hello, Columbus!" he said to himself, thinking of Philip Roth's *Goodbye, Columbus*. He had never read it but had always intended to, just to see what all the fuss was about in the Jewish community. "Makes fun of his own people!" An older cousin had denounced Roth with that phrase at a family gathering, he remembered, and then it had turned out that she hadn't read the book either. Well, maybe after the exam was behind him.

It took a while to complete the paper work with the Residence Director. His room was a stroke of luck: a single room with its own bathroom. Not that it didn't have the usual cell block feel, with beige vinyl floor tile and concrete block walls, painted a matching light beige. It was fine for a college student, but very spartan for a man almost thirty years old and accustomed to at least a little comfort. There was a single window, a single bed, a modest but sturdy five-drawer chest, a desk with a fluorescent lamp and a straight-backed chair, some shelves above the desk, and an armchair so old it had forgotten the better days it once must have seen. A pay phone was located down the hall. He unloaded his car, unpacked his bags, hung up his clothes, put his underwear and socks in the chest and his toiletries in the bathroom, and moved his car to the student parking lot, hanging the "Temporary Permit" tag he had just acquired on the rearview mirror. By the time he had finished, he found himself more in need of a nap than of dinner. His mother, Adele, had packed some sandwiches for him anyway, as always. The one person, he thought, he could always count on. *Always* in his corner, no matter what. He ought to call her tonight instead of Cheryl, or at least call her too. But first, a nap.

When he awoke, it was already nine, and, hungry, he remembered both the sandwiches and his call to his mother. Cheryl could wait a couple of minutes. He made sure that he had enough change for both calls. His mother was delighted that he'd called, that he was glad she'd packed the sandwiches–"I told you!"–and that he'd arrived safely. She urged him to get a good night's sleep and he promised that he would. Then he called Cheryl. To his surprise, her phone rang until her machine answered, and at the beep he said, "Hi, Cheryl, it's me. I'm fine, I'm checked in, got a parking permit for the car, and just unpacked. I'm pretty tired, I guess, and I'd like to turn in early–busy morning ahead of me–but if you're there, or get back in the next half hour, give me a call, and tell me you're OK." He checked the number on the pay phone and told her what it was. "Love you!" he said, feeling a twinge as he remembered his thoughts in the car, and hung up.

The sandwiches were very good, as he'd told Adele rather prematurely, but they made him thirsty, and he decided he'd go out for a beer–surely the Library on High Street was still in operation–after Cheryl had called back. He looked at his watch and decided to give her another fifteen minutes. He connected the television set to the wall outlet, placed it on the desk chair which he put next to the bed, pulled the aerial out, turned the set to what he remembered was the ABC channel in Columbus, and stretched out on the bed again. The armchair probably appreciated his choice. ABC was re-broadcasting its news program from earlier in the day. Sam Donaldson, the anchor, was saying, "Ted Koppel, our diplomatic correspondent, is standing by at the State Department with the latest on that. Ted?" Koppel came on, saying, "Thanks, Sam– State is doing what it can but for the moment, at least, that doesn't appear to be much. There has been no direct contact with the U.S. Embassy in Teheran. That building is under the total control of the demonstrators." Donaldson asked, "Ted, the Ayatollah's support for this action is ominous, is it not?" "Well, it may or it may not be ominous," Koppel answered, unhelpfully, Nathan thought. "The State Department is making a particular point to distinguish the Ayatollah Khomeini from the Iranian government. That's why it's being so restrained in its direct references to the government." Donaldson thanked him very much. Jesus, Nathan thought, and turned the set off.

Chickens coming home to roost, as Malcolm X had said in another context. The support the American government, Republicans or Democrats, he reflected, had given the Shah in Iran–ever since the overthrow, had it been in 1953?–of the elected socialist premier, an overthrow always associated with the CIA, had made the United States the target of hatred second only in virulence to that directed at the Shah himself. Muhammad Reza Shah Pahlevi, unquestionably a bloody tyrant, like so many others that the U.S. preferred to bloody Communist tyrants. We buy a lot of our oil from Iran, Nathan remembered, thinking of the drive down from Cleveland he had just completed. He recalled his conversation with the Iranian cab driver some weeks ago in Washington, the former architect, Professor Farzin's cousin. Were the driver's veiled hints at tyranny in Iran directed at the Shah, he wondered now, or at what the driver anticipated would occur with the Shah's inevitable overthrow? Or both?

He looked at his watch again. It was getting late, almost ten o'clock, and he wanted that beer. He had given her about twenty minutes extra. Time to storm his own Embassy. He got up, took his jacket, and went to the Library on High Street, one of his favorite places when he had been a graduate student on campus. It was *the* place for students living mostly within the northwest quadrant off campus. The beer was cold and the music was loud, and you usually ran into someone you knew. He went in, noting that not much had changed. Some things resist change very well, he thought. If it ain't broke, don't fix it. There was the same dark wood paneling, wood benches and tables adorned with a few more names and symbols since the last time he'd been here, and yes, probably the same foosball table, but updated pinball machines. The music was still loud, and the beer was flowing. Nathan found a stool at the bar. When the bartender came up, he asked for a Rolling Rock, in the bottle. Like old times, he thought: B.C. Before Cheryl.

He became aware that the fellow on the next stool was looking at him rather intently. He glanced at him without recognition, but at that moment the young man said, "You look familiar–are you in school here?" He seemed polite and genuinely curious.

"Not any more," Nathan said. "In fact, it's been a few years."

"When did you graduate?"

"In 1975," Nathan said, glad for the conversation.

"Well, not much has changed since then," the young man said. "I came in seventy-six, and this is my senior year. Some buildings have gone up, but nothing major. Man, you really look familiar. Do you live here in Columbus?"

"No, I'm from Cleveland," Nathan said. "Are you from around there?"

"No, my family lives in Dayton," the young man said. "Were you in a fraternity?"

"Yes, Alpha Epsilon Pi," Nathan said.

"Ah, I thought you might be," the young man said, beginning to grin. "Did you come to the AEPi open house here last year?"

"Yes, I did," Nathan said, grinning back. They exchanged the secret handshake. "Nathan Goldstein," Nathan said. "Norm Russell," the young man said. "May I buy you a drink?" Nathan asked. "Sure," Russell said. "I'll have another Bud." Nathan signaled the bartender. "I remember now," Russell said, "you were here, at the open house, with Jack Greenstein's dad, Mr. Greenstein, the architect, right?"

"Right again," Nathan said. "Sid Greenstein. So you know Jack?"

"Actually, not very well," Russell said. "He's a few years older than I am, like you, I think, but his dad, Mr. Greenstein, he was a big influence on me, a big help." The bartender brought the beers and Russell filled his glass. Nathan drained his Rolling Rock.

"How so?" he asked Russell.

"Well, I was in my third year of architecture school and had been trying to decide, for quite some time, actually, whether all that work, all those all-nighters were really worth it. I was having serious doubts. And my talk with Mr. Greenstein helped me to reach a decision. I decided to switch majors, to the Administrative Science program. I had to go to summer school, and I have to go again next summer, but at the end of next summer I'll have my B.S. in business. I feel it's the best decision I've made since I don't know when, and I give Mr. Greenstein a lot of the credit. He told me that I was among the few really lucky people in the world who had a chance to find what they wanted to do with their lives, what kind of work really turned them on, I mean. If architecture wasn't it, he said, then don't do it. He said that it wasn't just a matter of working harder. If I wasn't doing well, or as well as I had expected to, then that was a sign that I was trying to swim upstream against a current just too strong for me. Something like that."

That sounded like Sid. "You didn't do well in the architecture program?" Nathan asked.

"Honestly? No," Russell said. "I was an A- student in high school and never really had to work very hard, but in architecture I got mostly C's and had to work my ass off for B's. And there weren't very many of those. For me, used to doing well in school, you know, that was torture. And I know my family was very surprised and disappointed. And after all, they were paying the bills."

"But you're doing much better in the business school?"

"*Much* better. Mostly A's. Nothing below a B. And I really like the courses. The profs in architecture were pretty good, most of them, I guess, but I just couldn't seem to catch fire. You know what I mean?"

"I do," Nathan said. "As you can guess from my friendship with Sid, I'm an architect, and I love architecture, not just as art or for its fascinating history everywhere, but as an enterprise, you know, related to everything that people have done since they climbed down from the trees. But I do know what you mean. When it's all reduced to prerequisites and electives and required hoops to jump through, and to grade point averages and exam scores and God knows what else, that really tends to squeeze the love and the passion and the excitement right out of you." He reached for the second bottle and took a healthy swig.

"Yep, that's the way I felt," Russell said. "But not now. Hey, are you here just for the day?"

"No, I'll be here for a few weeks, in fact," Nathan said. "Why?"

"We're having a party–AEPi, I mean– this weekend, girls, beer, the whole thing, you know—how about coming by? Around nine?"

"Thanks, Norm, very much, but I can't," Nathan said. "I'm here to take the architects' registration exam next month, and I promised myself that I'm not going to do *anything* but cram. Just the sort of thing we were just talking about. To get to do what I want to do, I've still got to jump through some pretty convoluted hoops. No choice."

"Well," Russell said, "That's too bad, about your not being able to come to the party, I mean. I've heard that exam is a real bear–doesn't it last three or four days?"

"Yes, three days, but I've already passed the Ohio design section," Nathan said. "Now I need to sit for two days and take the NCARB exam."

"Well, I want to wish you the best of luck," Russell said, draining his glass. Fast drinker, this young guy, Nathan thought. "I've heard that only about a quarter or so of the people taking the test pass it," Russell said. "Is that true?"

"Yes, something like that, for people taking it for the first time," Nathan said. "I'd better get going, Norm," he said, finishing his bottle. "It's been a long day–I came in this afternoon, and need to get some sleep. Good luck in school this year!" He put the money for the beers on the bar.

"And good luck again to you, Nathan!" Russell said. He wasn't going anywhere yet, Nathan sensed. They shook hands. "Tell Mr. Greenstein I said hello!" Russell said. "I will!" Nathan promised and made his way out. Pay phones have no answering machines, he thought, and went straight to bed.

*****

After breakfast the next morning, and after checking the news–the hostages in Teheran had not been freed yet--Nathan, on an impulse, walked over to Brown Hall, the home of the School of Architecture. The building practically shouted memories at him. Even the examples of student projects adorning the walls, different as they were from the ones of his student days, were not really unfamiliar. Radical changes were occurring in medicine, often the result of almost magical developments in engineering, in both diagnosis and treatment, Nathan reflected, but the actual practice of medicine had simply become more of a bureaucracy, much more involved with insurance plans and statistical projections and demographic patterns. It was more and more of a complicated *business*, with stockholders and boards of directors and executives who might or might not have been physicians themselves. Certainly not practitioners any longer. He hadn't heard of any family physician driving up to his patients' houses, carrying his little black bag, in a long time. Most professions, including his own, seemed to be very good at resisting fundamental changes. The architect used to be practically both coach and quarterback in the planning, design, and building industries. Many planners and builders used to have architectural backgrounds. Now, like family physicians, they had been reduced to role players, and they had found ways to accommodate themselves to the system that had gradually evolved. Everything interlocked: education, accreditation, professional societies, examinations, registration and licenses, cooperation, contracts, money. Especially money. Of course there were exceptions. But perhaps they were so prominent *because* they were exceptions.

Nathan looked closely at a particular design of a high-rise office building, certain to be by one of the better students taking Professor "High-Rise" Charlie Baker's class. "High-Rise" Charlie, a very good teacher, Nathan remembered fondly, liked to show the work of his best students, and Nathan had been flattered that his own design had been selected for display when he had taken that class. This design was attractive and imaginative, and Nathan wondered where such a building might be constructed. He thought that it would require a rather large, well-landscaped area to establish its presence to maximum advantage. That meant, instead of an adjacent group of stores sharing a huge parking lot with the building's occupants and clients, it would need trees, plantings, walks, maybe even a fountain or some sort of park-like ambience sure to be denounced by the developer as wasteful.

The sound of approaching steps interrupted Nathan's musings and he turned to see the School's Assistant Dean, Frank Wilson, coming toward him, smiling, preparing to shake his hand. "Nathan Goldstein!" Wilson said. "How nice to see you again! I'd heard you were coming but I thought your appointment with Dean Toya was for next week?" They shook hands more warmly than Nathan had expected. He did not remember that Wilson had been so friendly at their last meeting, when he had told Nathan that he had to abandon his study.

"It is," Nathan said, "but I got in last night to start cramming, you know, and this morning I couldn't resist just a brief visit to the old battleground before I got started. And this will give me a chance to confirm my appointment with the Dean. How have you been?"

"Fine, fine," Wilson said. "Busy, you know, we're getting close to finals and it's always busy at this time in the quarter. Well, I'm sure Peggy will confirm your appointment with the Dean. Really nice to see you." He turned to go, but Nathan, suddenly yielding to his second impulse of the morning, touched his arm and said, "Professor Wilson, one question--"

"Yes?" Wilson asked.

"It's been a long time, I know, but this has been on my mind ever since it happened–do you remember my independent study project concerning the marketing of architectural services? I was working with Professor Prescott and Professor Rosenberg from our faculty and Professor Goodman from Administrative Science?"

"You heard that Prescott died suddenly, didn't you, and that Rosenberg left last term to go to Michigan? I don't know whether it was because of his wife's death a year or so earlier or not, although I'm sure Michigan has more money than we do," Wilson said by way of not answering Nathan's question.

"Yes, I did," Nathan said. He had known about Prescott, but not about Rosenberg. "Do you remember the project?"

"Yes, I do," Wilson said, looking uncomfortable, Nathan thought. "I remember it as very interesting and worthwhile, and I recall that I was the one who had to tell you that the study had to be shut down–but I don't remember why! I was just the messenger, Nathan, I do know that." He started to turn away again but Nathan wasn't finished.

"It was just after I had written to Roger Fleming at the AIA in Washington," Nathan persisted, "to ask them to participate in the research and he had written a kind of maybe in the future but not now answer. I wrote again to get the specifics or maybe even reconsideration, but I never got a reply. Do you know, can you tell me, if the AIA was unhappy for some reason with what I wanted to do? Did Fleming have anything to do with stopping the study?" He could see that, whether or not Fleming had been unhappy then, Wilson was now.

"I just don't remember, Nathan," Wilson answered. "I have a meeting with Professor Wilkes, and I've got to run now—stop in the next time you're in the building—nice to see you!" He waved and was gone. He knew something then and he knows something now, Nathan thought, and he simply doesn't want to tell me. But I just can't imagine that Fleming would have had anything to do with it. The Executive Vice President of the AIA, concerned about what one graduate student was doing way out there in Columbus? Not very likely! But why had Fleming ducked him in that bar in Washington in September?

He went to the Dean's office. The Dean was new—when Nathan had been a student in the School, Professor Webber had been the Dean, but Webber was retired now, replaced by a man recruited from the West Coast, a Nisei, if that was the right term, Ken'ichi Toya. But the Dean's secretary was still Peggy Pearsall, with whom he had always gotten along very well. She had treated him as a kind of distantly related nephew, and some of his fellow students had teased him about how much "older women" seemed to appreciate his curly black hair and hazel eyes. Ridiculous. Peggy must be in her fifties now. Besides, his hair was disappearing at breakneck speed, the curse that most of the men in his family had to endure for some unspecified crime, probably committed by an ancestor who had known Moses personally. He opened the door and walked in. There she was, bent over her IBM Selectric, fingers flying.

"Ahem," he said. She looked up and yelped with surprise and delight. "Nathan!" She got up and came around her desk to give him a hug. "Nathan Goldstein! You're a week early! How marvelous to see you! How are you?"

Maybe she *is* my aunt and nobody bothered to tell me, Nathan thought, grinning to himself as well as at her. "Fine, Peggy, I'm fine," he said. "And how are you?"

"Oh Nathan, about the same, just older, like everybody else," Peggy said. She had noticed his receding hairline. "There've been some changes here since you graduated, of course, and Dean Toya is very unlike Dean Webber, if you're curious about that. I'm sure you'll like him—I don't mean that you didn't get along with Dean Webber--" suddenly she looked confused and blushed. She knows something too, Nathan thought. Be careful, he told himself.

"Well, of course I heard about Professor Prescott's very untimely death—a heart attack, wasn't it?"

"Yes, that was a shock!" Peggy said. "He was on the phone with somebody, I heard, no warning at all, here one minute and gone the next, you just never know."

"And I understand that Professor Rosenberg left for Michigan?" Nathan asked.

"Yes, and that was pretty sudden too–nothing like poor Professor Prescott, of course, but still, he had spent most of his career here and until his wife died–did you know she was his second wife, by the way?– he had always seemed to be really at home here, the School, the University–he was a big Buckeye fan, you know–and the town too." Peggy knew everything about everybody, Nathan remembered, and he had always pretended to be very interested. Maybe that was why she liked him "Anyway, he did go to Michigan, and I don't think he's even visited here since then, although I heard he's coming next week. But you're here a week before your appointment with Dean Toya–you're not going to cancel it, are you?"

"No, no, on the contrary, I just stopped in to say hello to you and confirm my appointment for next week," Nathan said quickly, going on to explain, once again, how he'd wanted to visit before he got started with intensive studying for the NCARB exam. "Some pretty wonderful memories," he said to Peggy. "I'm so glad you feel that way," she said, lowering her voice a little, although the door to the Dean's private office was shut and no one else was in the room. "I thought you might be, well, maybe bitter."

"Why did you think that?" Nathan asked, lowering his voice as she had done.

"About the way your study was stopped," Peggy said, "especially after they had encouraged you so strongly and had even tried to get you some internal support, for an assistant and expenses."

"You remember all that?"

"I certainly do, Nathan," Peggy said. "It was so unusual. First all that show of support, then a couple of telephone calls and whispers, and then it all came to a halt. You remember, Nathan, that I helped with typing the questionnaire and setting up some of the meetings, so I felt involved too, you know. But what I wanted to tell you–well, there were a couple of things--" the phone rang and the door opened at the same time. A student came in rather hesitantly, looking at them with an unformed question on his face. "Excuse me, Nathan, just a minute," Peggy said, motioned the student to a chair, and picked up the phone. "School of Architecture, Dean's Office, may I help you?" Whoever it was had a complicated message or inquiry. Peggy picked up a pen and a note pad, said "Yes?" a couple of times, and then said "Just one moment, please," into the receiver and made a face to Nathan. "I'm sorry, Nathan, this is important, it's the Registrar's office and it's going to take a while." "Sure," Nathan said, still very quietly. "I'll be back soon, Peggy, we'll talk then--bye!" He smiled, waved, and left thinking about what she had started to tell him. A couple of telephone calls? Whispers? There *was* more to the story. It was good to have an ally, especially a secretary. They knew everything, and sometimes they kept records. He went back to his room and cracked the books.

At nine that evening, more than saturated with material that was beginning to seem as familiar and as uninspiring as his morning face in the mirror, he tried Cheryl's number from the pay phone in the hall. He let it ring ten times before he hung up to try again, thinking that he must have misdialed. After another ten rings, and sure, this time, that he had dialed correctly, he hung up to consider two alternative explanations. She was either out with somebody or she'd had an accident and was in the hospital. As soon as he had put his concerns into words, he was aware of another possibility: she was home, but he was calling at an inopportune time. What was not likely was that she was home and alone. Nor, for that matter, that she'd had an accident. Somebody would certainly have let him know. He decided to be optimistic and to attribute her absence to something relatively benign, perhaps involving one of her girlfriends. He'd call again in an hour. But enough of architecture for the moment– he'd catch up on the news.

Ted Koppel was not reassuring about the situation in Teheran, and the unanswered telephone in Cleveland, an hour later, did not assuage his mood either. He went to bed and slept badly. When he woke up the next morning, it was already eight thirty. Cheryl should be at work by now, he thought. He went to the bathroom, shaved, brushed his teeth, and got dressed, giving her a few extra minutes again. But she was normally very punctual and he was sure she'd be at her desk. He returned to the pay phone and called her at work. When she picked up her extension to say, "Cheryl Weinglass, may I help you?," he squelched all the clever openings he'd had in mind and said, simply, "Cheryl! It's Nathan!"

"Nathan! Oh, I miss you so much, Nathan!" Cheryl said, sounding more than normally cheerful, and yet somehow anxious as well. "I've missed you very much, too," Nathan said. "I've been trying to reach you at home, at nine as we agreed, last night and the night before, but I guess you weren't home? Is everything all right?"

"Yes, everything's fine, honey," Cheryl said. "Two nights ago? I was out with Kathy for a drink, maybe two–that was the day you left, and she invited me out to console me--and last night–well, yesterday was a really long day and I had a headache and went to sleep after dinner. I *thought* I heard the phone ring but I just couldn't seem to wake up, and I guess I thought I was dreaming–listen, Nathan, here comes my supervisor, we're not supposed to get personal calls, you know–call me tonight at nine, OK? Love you!" She hung up.

Sure, a headache, Nathan thought. Cheryl *never* got headaches. And she sounded almost glib. Since when did she go out drinking with that Kathy? Well, maybe she *was* blue when he'd left for Columbus, or at least it was sweet of her to say so. He'd just have to trust her, even if his suspicions weren't gone. Sounded like one of those corny country-and-western songs, he thought rather glumly, and decided to go to Charberts for breakfast. There were two Charberts, "clean" and "dirty," according to the students' tradition, if they were both still in business. He'd try "clean" Charberts first.

Charberts became part of his morning routine, as did, some days later, Ted Koppel's late-night broadcasts called "The Iran Crisis: America Held Hostage." The Carter administration's reasons for not taking immediate military action, endlessly discussed by commentators, critics, editorial writers, scholars, and the general public–especially its angrier members–seemed, well, reasonable, but there was no question, Nathan thought, that the seizure of the American Embassy was an act of war. He tried to concentrate on cramming for the examination, on telling himself that he had no choice when it came to trusting Cheryl, and that, as far as Iran was concerned, there was not only nothing he could do, there wasn't really anything to say. Nobody had asked him for his opinion. If anyone had, he would have said that he hoped that reason would prevail, even in Teheran. He called Cheryl regularly, they assured each other of their mutual love and fidelity, he suppressed his questions, and continued to study.

His appointment with Dean Toya was scheduled for the next Monday at ten. He made a point of arriving some fifteen minutes early, hoping that Peggy would finish what she had started to tell him the previous week. But if she didn't bring it up, he didn't see how he could. He couldn't say, "Remember last week when you were going to tell me why you'd been afraid that I'd have bad memories of my time at the School of Architecture, and I asked why you thought that?" Well, maybe he could find a smoother way. But when he arrived, there was another woman there as well, working with Peggy on some sort of schedule, and although Peggy welcomed him warmly, offering him coffee or tea and some left-over donuts, there was of course no way to return to last week's conversation. He accepted the tea, skipped the donuts, and sat down with *Architectural Record* in the waiting room to wait for the Dean. Peggy explained that Deans Toya and Wilson were in a conference

call with the AIA that had just begun. The implication was that Dean
Toya would probably be delayed. Nathan nodded.

The door to the Dean's private office opened at a quarter past the
hour, and a Japanese American came out with Wilson, just finishing a
sentence. Toya was of medium height, wore glasses, and looked much
younger than Nathan had expected. Early forties, Nathan thought, at the
most. And he's in very good shape. Wilson saw Nathan in the waiting
room and motioned him over to introduce him to the Dean. Toya's
handshake was firm and dry. Wilson and Nathan exchanged another
pleasantry or two, and then Wilson left and Toya ushered Nathan into his
office, closing the door. Nathan waited for a cue about where to sit–the
choice was at the Dean's desk, where the Dean would sit behind it and he
would sit in front of it, like an errant schoolboy, or in the much more
comfortable, cushioned chairs at a coffee table in the corner–and was
pleased that the Dean pointed toward the friendlier arrangement. The
evidence was that no one had sat there yet this morning.

"I'm very glad to meet you, Mr. Goldstein–or should I call you
Nathan?" the Dean asked. "Please do, Dean Toya," Nathan said.

"And you should call me Ken," the Dean smiled. Nathan was
surprised. He wasn't paying a social visit, and they certainly weren't on a
par professionally. "All right, thanks, Ken," he said. He reached into his
briefcase to pull out a legal pad on which he had written several
questions about the NCARB examination for the discussion he expected
would now take place, but before he could take his pen from his shirt
pocket, Toya held his hand up to stop him and said, "How's life going,
Nathan? I mean, personally?"

Nathan, now taken aback, said something innocuous–"fine, Ken, just
fine, I'm studying for the NCARB, you know, and--" only to be
interrupted again. "I know you're studying very hard, Nathan, and I'm
sure you'll do well, very well," Toya said, apparently dismissing the
subject. "I wanted to get to know you a little personally, if you don't
mind, because I've heard quite a bit about you. I understand that when
you were here you were one of our very best design students."

Nathan mumbled something.

"No, don't be modest," Toya said. "I heard about your hotel retreat
design for the Machu Picchu mountains in Peru. Professor Montague
was talking about it just the other day. You entered the Brussels Prize
competition with that design, didn't you? I don't remember, did you win
the Prize?"

"Yes, I entered the competition," Nathan said. Toya had touched on
a sore point, but he wasn't sure that he'd done it intentionally. What the

hell, he thought, tell him. "But no, I didn't win the prize. And frankly, Ken, I've wondered about it ever since. Another graduate student here, Brian Keating, asked me if he could send his entry along with mine, you know, in the same package, to save on the postage. You know how tight life can be for graduate students. So I said sure, and we did that, and guess what: his project was one of the international winners."

"Really!" Toya exclaimed. His surprise didn't seem feigned. "Did you get your originals back, or did you see the printed document with photographs of the winners' projects?"

"No, they didn't send anything back," Nathan said. "And I didn't know they issued anything showing the winners."

"Well, maybe they didn't do it that year," Toya said. "Those things can be expensive." There was an awkward pause. "So," Toya resumed, "tell me how your life is going."

This is very strange, Nathan thought. What's he after? He doesn't want to talk about the NCARB exam, which is the only reason I made this appointment, and –give it another shot, he told himself, you've got nothing to lose.

"As I said, Ken, life is OK for the moment. I'm working out of my apartment in Cleveland Heights, doing some design and drafting for an architect friend, and, as I was saying, studying for the NCARB–I really need to pass it this time and I have some questions I'd like to discuss with you." There, talking fast got it out, he thought. But again Toya smiled and said, "Oh, I'm sure you'll do fine, Nathan, I've got a strong hunch that you will, and my hunches are usually right. No, I meant life in general, not just work–there's more to life than work, as I'm sure you know. For instance, do you have a girlfriend?"

Damn, Nathan thought, where is this going? Why doesn't he want to talk about the exam? "Yes, sure, I've got a girlfriend," he said. "We've been going out for almost two years."

"Really!" Toya said. "That's a long time with one girl these days! You must be in love!" Nathan didn't know how to respond and said nothing. "I'm not sure how much you know about me," Toya continued, untroubled by the lack of connection, "so I'll tell you a few things about myself. I've been the Dean here, well, it'll be two years next spring, not quite as long as your romance. I lived in California all my life, and it wasn't easy to make the decision to come here, not just because of the climate. But I was an Assistant Dean, and I found I liked administration and if I may say so was good at it, and Ohio State provided this wonderful opportunity. I do miss California's climate and beauty, but I find the people very friendly here, for the most part, and I'm enjoying my work with the faculty." He crossed his legs, engrossed in his subject. Nathan hoped that he looked interested.

"I was born in this country," Toya continued, looking toward the window revealing the country of his birth, "but my parents were both born in Japan. They were both university professors, by the way. They taught at the University of Hawaii, the Manoa campus in Honolulu, before World War II, and then they moved to San Francisco. That's where I was born, in 1938. And not long after that, the Japanese bombed Pearl Harbor." Nathan repressed an impulse to look at his watch.

"It wasn't easy being Japanese in the United States at that time, not even in Hawaii, but especially not on the Mainland. You will have heard the story. We were put in an internment camp–I was not quite five years old, I think–for our own safety, they told us. My parents were naturalized citizens, and my sister and I were natives, of course, but none of that mattered, we were dirty Japs, you know, like your people in Europe."

Aha. So that's where he's been going all this time. Now we've bonded. What's next?

"How do you like your dorm room, is it comfortable?"

This is worse than driving in New York, Nathan thought, detours, construction, one-way streets, and sudden stops. "Yes, it's perfectly adequate," he said. "Very quiet, which is great for studying." Once more? No reaction from Toya. "I even have my own bathroom," he added, just to fill what had suddenly become a void. Toya looked at his watch. "Yes, we tried to find you something suitable," he said. "Nathan, I'm sorry, but I have a meeting at ten forty-five. I want to wish you the best of luck on your exam, I just have a hunch that you'll do very well. By the way, I don't know if you knew this about me, but I'm single. Maybe you know some attractive girl who might like to meet me? She could be white or Japanese or Jewish, I'm not prejudiced. Perhaps we could double date, especially if your girlfriend comes to visit you?" He got up. The meeting was over.

"Sure, Ken," Nathan managed to stammer, also rising. "I'll see if Cheryl knows a suitable person--" Toya extended his hand again and Nathan shook it. "Thanks very much for your time," he said almost automatically. "Of course," Toya said, "and let me hear from you if you think you could arrange something for me! So good to meet you, stop in again when you have time!" He found himself outside the private office. Several people rose expectantly and Toya began to welcome them. What a waste of time, Nathan thought. Maybe not. There was Peggy. But so was the other woman.

"Peggy, how are you?" he asked. "Very busy, I see?"

"Nathan, hello!" Peggy said. But she looked harassed.. "Yes, I'm afraid we're behind schedule with some things–before I forget, Nathan, Professor Farzin asked me to ask you to visit him in his design studio class this morning after your meeting with the Dean–it's in progress, but he thought he could break away for a few minutes to meet with you, if you have time. Oh, and Professor Rosenberg is in the building somewhere–I'm sure he'd love to see you, if you can find him! Ask Professor Farzin, he should know–do you have time?"

"I do, yes," Nathan said. "Thanks very much, Peggy! I hope you and I will get a chance to chat the next time I'm here!"

"Yes, I hope so," Peggy said "It's just that today–you understand."

"Sure," Nathan said. "Is Professor Farzin's class still in the design studio on the fourth floor?"

"That's right," Peggy said. "Not much changes here–oh, we do have a new drinking fountain in the hall, just outside the door, did you notice?"

"No, I didn't," Nathan laughed, "but I'll take advantage of it now!" He waved and walked out, stopping for a drink on the way to the design studio.

Professor Farzin, it turned out, had indeed talked to his cousin in Washington, DelAvar Bahman, and the cab driver had told him that Nathan had been his passenger. They chatted briefly about the smallness of the world, and how, especially now with the seizure of the Embassy in Teheran, what had seemed far away was in every American living room on television every night. "Ted Koppel is practically a member of my family!" Professor Farzin said. "I just wish he'd have some good news for a change!" Nathan nodded in rueful agreement.

"Nathan," Professor Farzin said, "the Dober report that was issued some months after your study was stopped, and that you copied for the architecture library, made a great deal of sense to me. Your study project was well ahead of its time-- that became clear to me when I read the report. Of course architecture and business have to link up if we're going to make real progress in all the many aspects of the industry! Absolutely! But what I want to stress is that the opposition you encountered was probably just the tip of the iceberg. There are all kinds of vested interests in keeping things as they are."

Nathan stared at Professor Farzin. "Opposition?" he asked. "I thought I was being encouraged! Both Professor Prescott and Professor Rosenberg, I'm really quite sure, were very encouraging! And although I don't know why the request for a grant wasn't ever submitted to the top administration, they did help with that proposal! What do you mean, 'opposition'?"

It was Farzin's turn to stare. "I don't want to accuse anyone of anything I can't prove," he said. "And you know, as a foreigner, particularly as an Iranian, I can't say that I feel completely secure myself. I'm sure you know what I mean." That's the second time in under half an hour, Nathan thought, that a Gentile has implied that I understand his feelings or experience because I'm a Jew. Maybe so. "Just let me say that I hope very much that you won't yield to any pressures, that you'll stick to your position, that you'll pass the exam. I'm sure you will. I'm certain you have a lot to offer the profession, Nathan, and I think that, in time, you'll be completely vindicated."

"Thanks very much for your faith in me, Professor," Nathan said, not entirely sure about what Farzin had just said. "I have every intention of doing my best. That's why I'm here again."

"I have to get back to my class," Farzin said. "Great to see you. By the way, Harry Rosenberg is visiting here today and tomorrow–I think he's with Jack Montague now–I'm sure he'd want to see you! Well, I have to go, Nathan--best of luck." They shook hands. Farzin returned to the studio. Nathan went to Montague's office to find him in deep conversation with Harry Rosenberg. They broke it off to welcome Nathan warmly, and Nathan found himself genuinely glad to see them both. After he had answered their questions about what he was doing and how well he felt he was prepared for the NCARB examination, he asked Rosenberg how he liked Michigan.

"Very well, actually," Rosenberg said. "Ann Arbor's much smaller than Columbus, of course, but it's a vibrant place, lots going on. I've joined a synagogue, and I'm very comfortable in the condominium I bought. I don't miss mowing the lawn or raking the leaves, I can assure you of that. The resident manager is quite a character, tells excellent stories about the many wives he seems to have had, but he takes very good care of the place with his people. And the neighbors, almost all of them owners, are mostly very nice. I've made a new friend, a professor of English, of all things, who lives in a unit not very far from mine, a bachelor, so we socialize a bit and he's been telling me about his department in his college–a different world from ours, Nathan!"

Nathan noted not only Rosenberg's use of his first name, which he hadn't done often in the past, but also the length of the answer, also unusual for the normally terse and still military man. Rosenberg must be excited to be visiting his old friends, he thought. "How so?" he asked.

"Well, Rubin–my neighbor's name is Walter Rubin–certainly knows what the world is like–he came to this country in the late thirties as a boy, a refugee from Germany, just with his mother, and I've gathered that their first years here weren't easy–but English professors aren't concerned with things like licenses and national examinations and professional standards that have to be met for the sake of the public. I'm not sure that they have much of a professional connection to anything outside the university. I think that's what I mean by saying that they live in a different world. Professional intellectuals rather than intellectual professionals, perhaps."

"And have you become a Michigan football fan?" Montague wanted to know.

"Absolutely not!" Rosenberg declared. "Once a Buckeye, always a Buckeye!" They laughed together. They chatted for a few more minutes and, after Montague and Rosenberg had wished him success on the examination, never mentioning what Nathan was sure they knew about his previous efforts, he left, thinking what a very strange morning it had been. Some weeks later he took the examination, eight hours each day, on two consecutive days. When he got back to his room and realized that he was done, he decided to leave Columbus immediately. It would take him no time at all to pack and check out of the room. He would be back in Cleveland and, he hoped, in bed with Cheryl well before eleven.

*****

Nathan considered pulling off Interstate 71 as he drove north through the cold December night to call Cheryl to tell her that he was on his way home, a day early. She'd get the message about what he had in mind. But there was something about his conversations with Professor Wilson, with Peggy, and with Professor Farzin that was nagging at him. It didn't have anything to do with Cheryl directly. Or maybe it did. He let his mind drift. There wasn't much traffic on the road, the car was running well, he was enjoying a cigarette, and he felt more relieved than he would have thought possible. It's over, he kept thinking, one way or another, it's over. I can relax. He turned the car radio on, but he didn't like the country-and-western nasal twangs that filled the speakers, and when he changed the station, it was somebody denouncing President Carter for not yet having invaded Iran, or not yet having dropped half a dozen nuclear bombs. He turned the radio off at once. Idiots were never in short supply.

Slowly the conversations with Wilson and Farzin and Peggy came back to him, and slowly they coalesced. All of them had, in effect, told him that somebody had stopped his independent study. Farzin had even hinted at the reason: he had been perceived as a threat. By whom, exactly? To whom? That wasn't clear. But that he had been a threat rather than a pioneer, as he had envisioned himself, that much was evident. He had been about to document the need for change, great change, in the practice of the profession. That had been seen as intolerable. And apparently he had missed a lot of cues.

That, he suddenly realized, was the connection to Cheryl. The cues. The missed calls. The absences. Those two episodes before he had even left Cleveland. Her too cheery tone too often. Her rather recently intensified social life with her girlfriends, because, she said, she missed him so much. No, he wouldn't call her from the road. He'd surprise her.

He parked his car in the garage behind the building. He noticed a silver BMW in Cheryl's parking space. She couldn't have gotten a new car, certainly nothing that expensive. He looked at his watch. It was only a little after ten. He had made good time, even stopping for coffee and a sandwich. The walk around the building to the entrance led him past Cheryl's first-floor apartment. A dim light was on in the bedroom and the ill-fitting shade permitted a glimpse of the interior. Overcome by conviction, Nathan yielded to impulse and positioned himself to squint at the light in the room. Not all Peeping Toms get caught, he thought, and if there was nothing to see, he'd hurry to the door.

But there was, and he didn't. Cheryl was getting fucked on the bed, from behind, by a naked man whose face he couldn't see. She was obviously enjoying it enormously. They finished and the man collapsed on top of her. Nathan stood frozen to his spot outside until a car's headlights swept down the street. Panicking, Nathan ran to the building's entrance. He hadn't endured all that agony in Columbus to get arrested as a *voyeur* in Cleveland. Then he stopped. Obviously he wasn't about to go to Cheryl's apartment. But what would be the point of going to his own apartment like this? He returned quietly to his car, deliberately not looking at Cheryl's window, and got his suitcases. The books, the television set, and the dirty laundry could wait until tomorrow.

But after he had carried his bags up the three flights of stairs, his anger boiled over. He called Cheryl. There was no answer. He waited a few minutes and called back, letting the phone ring and ring. There was no answer. He unpacked his bags, calling every few minutes, and finally, when he was on his third cigarette since his arrival, she answered. "Hello?" she asked. "Is someone there?" "It's me," Nathan said. His voice sounded hoarse even to him. "Nathan?" Cheryl asked. "Nathan, where are you? Did you finish your exam? Are you in Columbus?"

"No, I'm not in Columbus," Nathan said. "Never mind the exam. I'm right here in Cleveland. In fact, I'm upstairs in my apartment. In fact, I saw what you were doing an hour ago or whatever it was when I came in. Your friend had his BMW in your space and his cock in you, and you can't believe how much I never want to see you again, you no-good bitch." He hung up before she could and went to bed. Then he heard the sound of a car engine. He went to his window and saw the BMW pull out of the driveway and head down the street. His throat felt very dry. He went to the kitchen and poured himself a glass of water. In a water glass, he thought, not a Weinglass. To hell with it.

Cheryl moved out of her apartment by the end of the week. At the end of the following month, in January, 1980, Nathan received a letter from the Ohio State Board of Examiners of Architects. He had passed the examination.

Chapter IV
Rubin, April, 2005

The fence wasn't there.

He was strangely disappointed. Among the very few vivid memories he'd had of the place was the fence closing off the exercise area next to the Great Hall, a chain-link fence, no doubt not nearly as high as he remembered it–he had been eight–with barbed wire on top, angled inward. You could see New York's towers through the fence, and he remembered, or thought he remembered, staring across the dirty grey swirling water at those far-off towers, strange and not at all welcoming. What was the purpose of the fence? To prevent someone from plunging into the water and trying to swim to the city? He couldn't imagine such desperation. America. He wouldn't understand anything anybody said. Nobody would understand him.

He turned back to the Great Hall. They had eaten there, at long wooden tables, grouped by what the American officials considered the ethnicity which dictated dietary requirements or preferences. All the Asians, Chinese, Japanese, Koreans, whatever they were, had been seated together. He wondered, remembering the scene, how their normally different cuisines and ancient animosities might have affected their digestion. All the Jews had been grouped together as well, regardless of their origins. Institutions and their procedures could not, of course, take individual differences into account, regardless of the importance attributed to them by the individuals concerned. There had to be *some* workable principles of organizing things. So there they were, all Jews, sitting on hard wooden chairs, he thought. But maybe not. He was sitting between his mother and an awful apparition, a man with a dirty matted beard and earlocks and a skullcap, smacking his lips as he slurped his soup and munched his bread, with long dirty fingernails and earwax so thick that it looked ready to ooze down his neck. He looked at his mother. She had been watching him, anticipating his revulsion, and gave him the look he had expected. He was to say nothing, to keep his eyes on his bowl, to be polite. He did. But he knew that she understood and that she agreed with him.

He never forgot that man: ugly, dirty, smelly, repulsive, that was how the world saw Jews, all of them, no matter how clean-shaven, what they wore, how they ate, how carefully they cleaned themselves, hands, ears, noses, it didn't matter. His father's hands had always seemed to smell of soap, and their fingernails were always short and clean, but it didn't matter, the world saw his father's large brown eyes and curly dark hair and rather long nose and saw the same filthy Jew, *Jude, Judenschwein, Kauft Nicht bei Juden.* His father had tried to shield him from the signs, but he had seen them and the *Magen David* on the plate glass, yellow paint–or had it been white?–and the passersby, pretending not to notice.

But this was America. The flag fluttering up there showed white stars in a blue field on the left-hand corner, no hooked black cross. No drums. No shouting. *Wenn's Judenblut vom Messer spritzt.* Just a lot of very strange people, different colors, different eyes–narrow, some of them, in flat faces--and very different clothes. Different sounds: what strange languages they spoke. Not the German he knew, the little Hebrew he had learned, the few words of English he had practiced on the ship with his mother: *"I am sorry, I cannot speak English."* They didn't pay any attention to him, nobody spoke to him, he didn't have to say anything. It occurred to him that they were as scared as he was. Maybe more: maybe they didn't even know how to say *"I am sorry, I cannot speak English."* He felt better.

He turned the other way to look at the gigantic statue, green and silent, her arm held straight up, lifting her lamp. *Little lamp o' mine, Gonna let it shine....* Not only still there but new and improved, after the restoration resulting from the campaign led by that automobile executive. Lee Iacocca. Henry Ford II had fired him, he had heard, despite his great success with the Mustang. "But why?" Iacocca was supposed to have asked. "Because," Ford was reported to have said, "I don't like you." Very honest. In the university you almost never heard such honesty, certainly not in his university, where people were let go every year as not quite having lived up to expectations, not as productive as had been hoped, not getting along as well with colleagues as would have been desirable, not getting favorable student evaluations–as if anyone really analyzed those in relation to observed and documented performance of either instructor or students. "Because I don't like you." If a chairman or, ha! a dean, said anything like that, that simple, that direct, the ivy would peel off the walls. So Iacocca had gone to Chrysler and done a superb job, just as what'shisname, some years ago, who had been refused tenure at Michigan, had gotten a position at one of the top Eastern schools–Princeton? Brown?–and in no time at all had established himself as a first-rate scholar, not one of those babblers about French theory but a solid eighteenth-century scholar. Specialized in Johnson. His books had been very well received. Now he's big in the Modern Language Association too. What was his name? Something Armenian. He'd gone to Brown, he was quite sure, but the name wouldn't come.

He remembered not understanding why the statue was there when he had first seen her, what she was supposed to symbolize. *Freiheit.* What could that mean to a small boy? His mother must have tried to explain it to him, but he couldn't remember what she might have said. His wonderful, gentle, sweet, tough-as-nails mother. The enlarged photograph of that Russian Jewish woman with her two small children among the many displays inside had startled him, she looked so much like her. But the date was 1905, when his mother had been a child of seven, back in Berlin. What she had gone through! His early years, even with the fear, the beatings, the constant uprootings–as if roots could be grown in six months here, ten there, suitcases, suitcases–had been merely adventurous compared to what she had had to endure. Her father's death before she was old enough to know him. World War I and the ensuing chaos. The strain of her fierce mother who hated her enforced reliance on her two older brothers, themselves probably not flush with money. Then, earlier, there had been that awful second marriage, a crazy stepfather, only for about a year, but wiped from family stories, annals, references as if Winston had pushed him and everything associated with him down the memory hole in *1984.* Deleted before the age of computers, manually word processed out of existence. Never happened. Until he was well over thirty, when, one day, reviewing the family history once again, in his mother's little kitchen in Cleveland, he had told her that something he had wondered about for years–that probably wasn't true, more likely it had just occurred to him, but it made him sound so much more thoughtful about that history to claim that he had wondered about this for years–it was a way of pleasing her–was why her mother, young, attractive, very sociable, had never married again. "But she did," his mother had said. He was astounded. "What? She did? And you never told me? A secret all these years? Why, for God's sake?"

"It was terrible," she had said. The conversation, although it had been in her German and his English, came back to him as he stared at the statue. *Freiheit.* Bondage, by contrast, had so many different names. "The man turned out to be very sick. Nobody could have known. He seemed normal in every way until some months after their marriage.

Then –" she broke off. He waited, knowing she would never leave a story unfinished.

But there wasn't much more to tell. "He probably had syphilis," she had continued, "or that was what was conjectured. He had to be taken to an asylum, and he died there some years later. Your grandmother never spoke of him again and made it clear to everyone that he was not to be mentioned in her presence. She crossed him out, erased the whole business forever."

Somehow that finality precluded either further questions or any easy change of subject. He had probably been drying the dishes she had washed after their meal. She had a dishwasher but refused to use it for the few plates and bowls and utensils they had used. As for rinsing them to put in the machine until it was full, tomorrow or the next day, no, that wasn't an option either. How domestic details were intermingled with revelations of syphilitic stepfathers! And that had been more than forty years ago.

He glanced at his watch. The ferry wasn't due for about another half an hour. He went back inside. A museum–clean, well-lit, directional signs, exhibits–a most impressive collection of suitcases, trunks, bags, satchels, briefcases, boxes, sacks, everything imaginable. It reminded him of a similar display he had seen in the Israeli Museum of Art in Jerusalem, another, equally exotic collection of what people from all over had used to *schlepp* their precious few belongings to another strange land where they hoped they would be strangers no longer. A guard had barked at him "No pictures!" when he had taken out his camera, embarrassing him, the fascist bastard. This place, too, was a museum, even though here you could take pictures, no noises, no smells, certainly no odors emanating from the visitors. Well, good. There was enough here–the displays, the brochures, the staff, but especially the actual physical island in the water, the city over there, the statue, the gulls flying overhead or landing or walking in their graceless way to and from the garbage cans–to suggest both what had changed and what had not, and that was all that anyone could ask, of a museum, anyway. Or of memories.

Strange that he should think of Israel, despite the similar displays of baggage. Had they been arranged, he suddenly wondered, by the same curator? Or are there curators of immigration displays, trained in the types, origins, manufacture, materials, ethnicities, esthetics, significance, diversity–of course, diversity!–of baggage? A specialized graduate program, perhaps, within a broader field of study–museumology–complete with a chair or director, an executive committee, a staff, budget, fund-raising and grant-getting responsibilities, and inevitably a not entirely sympathetic dean to report to? If it hadn't been the same person, had they studied in the same program, perhaps under the same advisor? Imagine the possibilities! No, like Melville's Bartleby, he preferred not to. He was old and lonely and rambling, and what Israel had in common with America was only that they both were or had been refuges for refugees, and time and events had changed all that. Israel wanted to be a country like other countries, only with its own religion, for those who believed in it, or said they did, or were descended from people who believed in it, or said they did. Not good enough for this country, thank God. At least not good enough for enough good Americans who insisted on more, on *Freiheit* for everyone, damn it, everyone who could somehow manage to get this far, was not ascertainably defective in some way, and had fifty dollars. Or whatever it had been.

"Professor Rubin?"

He turned, startled. A middle-aged woman who seemed to be with some other people, standing a couple of steps behind her, looking on with apparent curiosity, was asking him if he was Professor Rubin. He had no idea who she was.

"I am," he said, acknowledging the fact but admitting nothing further.

"I thought it was you!" she said. Was she delighted because she had been right or because he was Professor Rubin? Or, more accurately, had been up to his retirement ten years ago? "I'm Sally Minglewood–I was Sally Triandos when I took your course, but I got married–actually, not to my husband Bill, he's there with our nephew and his wife, I'll introduce you–Bill, this is Professor Rubin, I told you about him at the university, and this is my nephew George, George Triandos and his wife Sophia, they live here in New York–Professor Rubin--"

"You're not married to your husband Bill?" Rubin said dryly. He had absolutely no recollection of this woman gushing all over him, and he had been enjoying his silent ruminations.

"What? Of course I'm married to Bill, what do you--"

"You said you had been Sally Triandos when you took my course–what course was that, by the way?–but then you got married but not to your husband Bill."

"Oh! No! Well, I see, but haha you know how it is, people make mistakes, especially when they're young–uh, you know, the course you teach in English literature, I think it was in my sophomore year. I don't remember what it was called–it was some years ago, haha. I guess you've had hundreds of students in it since then?"

"Thousands, more likely," Rubin said. "It must have been the survey course if you took it in your sophomore year, the last time and probably the first time students ever had to read anything written before they were born. When were you in my class?"

"Oh, it was quite a few years ago, of course–I don't remember exactly–but what are you doing here? Did you come through here into the country, or your family?"

"A grandmother," Rubin lied smoothly, ready to invent an entirely new life but more interested in breaking away. The woman's relatives were beginning to shift from one foot to another and their obligatory grins had long disappeared. "But here comes the ferry, I think," Rubin continued, thank you *deus ex machina.* He pretended to check his pockets for his ticket, knowing exactly where it was. "We're leaving too," continued Mrs. Minglewood, "we've been here for hours–my parents, George's grandparents, came through here and told us all about it, but I've never been here before and neither has George, even though he and his father, my brother, lived here all their lives--" there was no stopping her. Her husband took her arm to steer her toward the dock, but she kept right on.

There was only one way to escape once they had boarded the ferry. "Excuse me," he interrupted her description of her parents' confusion on their arrival, "but I need to find the restroom, so nice to see you again," and headed past husband Bill and nephew George in what he hoped would be the right direction, waving at them. They looked relieved. He obtained a similar feeling shortly. When he came out of the restroom, he hesitated, wondering which way was opposite of where they might have gone. Taking a chance, he went up the narrow stairs to the stern, clasping the railing, once again looking at The New Colossus.

The famous poem was remarkable, he thought, chiefly because its sentiments, now forever associated with the statue, had been so uncharacteristic of the opinions of so many of the time. Or, for that matter, of those of succeeding generations of many good Americans, right up to the present. There was an organization even now, something for a fair and sensible immigration policy, that occasionally published dry and plausible and horrifying projections of the impact of the hundreds of thousands of people who wanted to come to the States one way or another every year, anywhere at all, Idaho or Utah for God's sake, just to get out of Burundi or Nepal or Croatia or Zimbabwe or wherever people were starving or rotting or slaughtering each other, replacing one murderous thieving tyrant with a worse one every few years, desperate for any kind of work, shelter, something to eat, a chance for their babies. Of course the babies were the problem, the babies, so irresistible, that those poor bastards kept having, no matter what, drought, famine, genocide, tsunamis, earthquakes, the lemmings kept multiplying until there was nothing for it but to plunge into the ocean– swimming toward America?–and drown. He thought of what Gerald had said, when he had been so astonished by Gerald's contribution to that anti-immigration group–it was a very rare instance of disagreement between them–"For Christ's sake, Walter! Everybody can't live here!" The point was of course undeniable, but he must have looked abashed, for Gerald, glancing at him, had laughed: "What's the matter, Walter, now that you aren't tired, poor, wretched and yearning to be free any longer, you want to welcome all those millions that still are? You want me to tell them where your condo is, so that you can put up a few dozen AIDS victims from Uganda? Or maybe some desperate Palestinians from the West Bank?"

Gateway to freedom. That's what it said on the New York quarter, next to her tiny image. That's still how he thought of it, and yes, he felt guilt. Didn't all survivors? It wasn't just a matter of having made it here, a reasonably successful if not distinguished career, a nice place to live, good friends, a very comfortable pension–and he had never really minded not having his own family, not after what he had seen of those of too many of his friends'–no, it was the guilt of having survived, of being unable to explain to himself or to anyone else how his mother had gotten them out of Europe, out of that conflagration and destruction and mass murder, while close relatives, friends, classmates, teachers, old people, young people, children, everyone, had been swept away like so much trash. The Nazis had made Germany *Judenrein*, all right. The few Jews still there, survivors or returnees, and now, with the Russians, some few thousand real immigrants, were most unlikely to achieve anything remotely resembling the cultural contributions Jews had made to Eastern and Western Europe since their expulsion from Spain. And look at Spain for the last five hundred years. It wasn't just the defeat the English had inflicted on their armada in 1588, it was their own nationalism and religious fanaticism, culminating almost a century earlier in the expulsion of Moors and Jews both, that had reduced what had been centers of learning to picturesque tourist traps. Well, that was probably unfair–he had never been to Spain and couldn't speak Spanish–but it felt good to think it. Why should he be fair? It was enough that he felt guilty.

The ferry was approaching its dock. Should he try to get to the head of the line or hang back, hoping that the crowd would separate him from the Triandos woman and her tribe? He took a chance, pushed ahead as far as he could, and hurried off the ferry to the cab stand. It was going to be expensive to take a cab back to midtown, but he wanted to see the streets, relatively manageable on a Sunday afternoon, even if all New York cab drivers were insane and suicidal.

This one wasn't, he noticed. He glanced at the ID on the dash. Hashem Iskandar. He looked about thirty-five, large dark eyes, neat black mustache, no beard, hairy hand on the steering wheel. "Not too much traffic," Rubin offered.

"No, it's Sunday," Mr. Iskandar replied. The explanation was satisfactory but did not open other avenues.

"How long have you been driving a cab here?" Rubin tried again.

"Since I came," Mr. Iskandar said. "Three years now."

"You speak English very well," Rubin said. "You learned it at home, I assume?"

"Yes, in school," Mr. Iskandar said.

The man was a Palestinian, Rubin was sure, had recognized him as a Jew, and did not want to jeopardize his tip. But maybe there was more to it. Why be cynical about his motives? Why make these assumptions? Why couldn't he be generous and brotherly toward a fellow immigrant?

"Where was that?" he asked.

"Jerusalem," the driver said.

Now what? A Palestinian refugee, making him feel like a German. He couldn't say "Jerusalem the Golden!" or "Yes, I've been there, beautiful city," or, in fact, anything relevant. Well, maybe something friendly, upbeat, optimistic? "Are they gradually moving toward peace over there, do you think?"

The driver didn't respond right away. Stupid question, Rubin thought–he's undoubtedly thinking yes, when at last we cut all your goddamned throats, *wenn's Judenblut vom Messer spritzt* or the Arabic equivalent. But there was the matter of the tip. Stop it, he told himself.

"I hope so," Mr. Iskandar said. "I have many relatives there, and their life is very hard. Peace would be very good. But a just peace, a peace that makes life better for everyone."

Rubin was greatly relieved. Mr. Iskandar was not only a careful driver but also an astute diplomat. "What did you do in Jerusalem?" he asked. "Surely you didn't drive a cab?"

"No," Mr. Iskandar said. "I was a teacher."

"Ah!" Rubin couldn't help himself. "So was I! At least, until I retired about ten years ago."

Mr. Iskandar glanced at him in the rearview mirror, registering surprise. "Ten years ago?"

Definitely shrewd diplomacy. And it would work nicely–the tip would be generous, part guilt, part pleasure in the flattery. "Yes–after about thirty-five years, you begin to notice that the students are still the same age but they don't speak the same language any more that you do– and then it's time to move on. What did you teach?"

"I taught math and physics in a high school," Mr. Iskandar said. Rubin waited, but the driver didn't ask what or where he had taught. They were almost at the hotel anyway, on the other side of the street. "You can let me off at the corner, then you won't have to go around the block," Rubin said. "How much do I owe you?"

The light on the phone next to the bed in his room was blinking, an angry red rhythmic blink, not angry at him, he reasoned, angry at absence. The recording had been triggered by his absence. The robot had required only inaction to spring to life, quite the opposite of a biological dictate. The designer–or, of course, the many designers, organized into teams, reporting to different supervisors, arguing, backstabbing, ultimately taking credit where they could and blaming where they couldn't–obeyed much more traditional commands. Here was their product, another great technological advance, improving communications for all he knew across the globe, maybe somebody in Beijing with the wrong New York telephone number, blinking a red eye at him in this dreary room from which he could see only the dreary rooms in the great tower across the street, those whose blinds weren't drawn. He looked at the instructions on the telephone, adjusting his bifocals on his nose until finally he understood that he was to press 8. He picked up the receiver and followed instructions.

"Walter, I forgot when you said you'd be back from your sentimental excursion – give me a call when you get in, I'll be here. We're anxious to see you!" Typical. No name, no phone number, no time. He took out his address book and found Gerald's number.

"Hello?"

"Good thing I still know your voice," Rubin said.

"Walter! Walter, you old bastard, how the hell are you? Laura, it's Walter – finally, we've been waiting here for your call–look, we thought we'd take you out to dinner, what would you prefer, Italian? Chinese? Or a big juicy steak somewhere? How are you?"

"I'm fine, fine, just a little tired, Gerald," Rubin said. "First of all, I'd like to take a bath. Then maybe a short nap and then dinner–sure, anywhere you say, around here, that is–I don't want to go far--"

"Great, we'll pick you up, I know just the place on Fifty-second Street–when do you think you'll be ready? We might need reservations, it's Sunday--"

"Yes, that's been pointed out to me already today," Rubin said. "How about seven?"

"Seven it is! Unless we can't get in then. If it's not seven, I'll call back and leave a message if you're in the tub. Great! Laura says welcome to New York!" Rubin heard the phone click. Gerald was as quick and decisive as ever. People don't change, he thought; his mother had maintained that by the time a child is four or so, its personality is pretty much fixed. "But what about events?" he had asked her. "If circumstances change drastically, as ours did, or just one major unpredictable event occurs, a parent's death, say, then wouldn't the child's personality develop quite differently?"

She had considered the question carefully, as always. "I don't think so," she had said. As always, she had spoken in German, he in English. And as always, neither was troubled by the bilingualism. But with the exception of the occasionally untranslatable German word, or a particularly telling German phrase, he always remembered their conversations monolingually. "Changing circumstances or major tragedies do of course–natürlich--have effects on how the child develops," she had said, "but since different children react differently to very similar, even the same events, the differences must be expressions of who they are." If she had been an academic, she might have added "at their core," but thank God–Gerald would say "praise Jesus!"–there was nothing in the least pretentious about her.

No, Gerald had always been quick and decisive, and certainly his circumstances had changed drastically, and more than a few times. Laura was his third wife, and almost twenty years younger than Gerald. Now happily retired–Gerald was Rubin's age–he had been a college professor–they had met at the same university and become friends there– a school administrator, an official of a national educational organization, a private consultant (with his own company, a move that had left Rubin gasping with admiration), and, for a while, something with the federal government (about which Rubin had been quietly dubious).

Why were they–and had been for so long–such good friends? It was easy to list all the obvious differences between them, but what were their bonds? Not for the first time, Rubin pondered this question, adjusting the water's temperature to a pleasant warmth as he relaxed in the tub, regarding his small paunch, white chest hair, and thin limbs. Gerald Parker. An unusually big man–until the injury to his knee at the age of twenty-five, he had been a professional football player, a defensive tackle and by his own account, a very good one–he had, first of all, the easy self-confidence of so many big men, able to put anyone, male or female, child, geezer, crone, all but the chronically dyspeptic, instantly at ease with his charm, his smile, his amazing good looks. One look at Gerald and you immediately saw three things: his size, his color, and how handsome he was. Men (unless, of course, they were white bigots or black rivals) were almost always inclined to be friendly; women, many of them–only God knew how many there had been!–very friendly indeed. And then there was Gerald's personality, outgoing, warm, friendly, funny, a gifted storyteller, an excellent listener, and, if the conversation turned serious, both thoughtful and almost always well-informed. But there was more: Gerald was a sensitive man, attuned to nuances of all kinds, and could be surprisingly delicate whether he offered observations, suggestions, or criticism. Rubin got out of the tub and dried himself, luxuriating in the rubbing.

Gerald could also be direct and sarcastic, and Rubin had experienced both modes. But, on reflection, Rubin always concluded that he had deserved whatever Gerald's remark had been. Gerald had high standards for the people he cared about, and Rubin knew he was one of them. He had even been Gerald's best man, at his second wedding, to Madeleine, now some thirty years ago. The divorce, some five or six years later, had been a considerable disappointment to Rubin, almost a personal failure considering his role at their wedding, although he hadn't known Madeleine very well. At least they hadn't had any children. Just as well: not only did Gerald already have three from his first marriage, but Madeleine was white, which would have complicated matters. Justice was supposed to be color-blind, but damned few judges were.

Now there was Laura. A partner in a very successful New York law firm, which was why Gerald and Laura lived in New York. Rubin had always suspected that Gerald had fallen for Laura while he was married to Madeleine, and that was the reason for their divorce. But he hadn't asked, and for once Gerald's remarks, the few there had been, had been guarded, heightening Rubin's suspicions. Laura was gorgeous. Almost six feet tall, a glowing black complexion, a perfect figure–well, it had been perfect, but Laura was in her middle fifties now–and a striking, aquiline profile, suggesting perhaps some Cherokee or Iroquois ancestry. Gerald, who was considerably lighter than Laura–she called him, amplifying the description as the occasion might suggest, "that brown-skinned man"-- liked to tease her about her looks, proud as he was of them. "Some of us," he'd say, "obviously had some Caucasian in our kindling, but Laura, now, her great-granddaddy must have been the Last of the Mohicans, out for one more good time. So he went down to the quarters." Rubin grinned at the oft-repeated joke, which Laura always waved away like a pesky fly. Rubin was almost as enchanted by Laura as Gerald was. If only he had met someone like her, fifty or forty or even thirty years ago! Instead of Alice, instead of Norma, instead of Janet, instead of – never mind, he told himself, he wasn't going to get his nap thinking about *them*. He set the alarm for six thirty and fell asleep almost at once.

The reunion, in the lobby at a quarter past seven–CP time, as Gerald predictably told Rubin as he folded him into his big chest–was not quite as restrained as either man would have liked, but it had been almost four years since they had seen each other. They inspected each other for changes, and saw them. Gerald's were perhaps the more obvious: his hair had turned white and he had grown a short, well-trimmed beard, which made him look darker than Rubin remembered. Rubin's thinning hair was still gray rather than white, but he had shrunken an inch or so from his previous middling height, and his paunch was more pronounced. But their long, intimate, cherished friendship glowed in their faces.

Laura, too, had changed; her hair was gray now, and she had put on weight, but she was still very beautiful. She kissed Rubin warmly, once Gerald had released him, and apologized for being late. "That man's going to be late to his own funeral," she said in her low, husky, musical voice that instantly commanded the attention of every man within earshot, "and when he gets there, he'll *still* be on the phone."

"All right, let's go," Gerald said. "The reservation was for seven, and they aren't going to relax the rules for an old colored man."

But although the restaurant was crowded, their table was waiting for them. As they made their way toward it, following the *maître d'hôtel*, Rubin spotted a face–dark, Middle Eastern, mid-thirties, with a small mustache–he knew he recognized but couldn't place. The man was with three other men, of similar appearance but older. Rubin shrugged and held Laura's chair for her. "Always the gentleman," she smiled as she sat down. "You see, Gerald, Walter is still as quick as ever!"

"We'll see how quick he is when they bring the bill," Gerald said, grinning, and immediately added, "I'm joking, of course, Walter, this is our invitation and our pleasure. It's really great to see you."

"TIAA-CREF is wonderful," Rubin said, referring to his pension plan. "I'd be happy to contribute or, in fact, reverse the host-guest relationship."

"Out of the question," Gerald said. "Next subject?"

"Your children and grandchildren, of course," Rubin said. "We have to get those out of the way before we turn to what's wrong with the world and all the fools who never listened to us when we told them about it."

"Didn't we though!" Gerald agreed. "And you're right, I don't recall that they paid much attention to us. Maybe they were on to something. Anyway, the children are all fine, mostly, and the grandchildren–hey, we have another one, did I tell you? Bryan and Kimberly had another little girl, just three or four months ago--"

"*Six* months ago," Laura corrected.

Gerald fumbled in his wallet for pictures. Rubin relaxed, knowing that this would last at least through the salads. Gerald and Laura had five children altogether, three by Gerald's first marriage, one that Laura had brought to their marriage "from a previous relationship," and one they had had together, a lovely girl now in her early twenties, Rubin's favorite, Rita. She called him "Uncle Walter," and he loved her for it. She was completing pre-medical studies at Columbia. There were eight– no, now nine– grandchildren, and Rubin usually remembered the names of the older ones, but of the many blanks his memory drew these past few years, names seemed to be particularly prominent. He set about admiring the pictures and demonstrating that he knew whose images they were: "Charlie's gained some weight, hasn't he? Oh, but Keesha looks great here!"

The waiter cleared the salad plates and refilled their glasses of water. Out of the corner of his eye Rubin saw the four Middle Eastern men bend over their table, three listening intently to the other–not, Rubin noticed, the one who looked familiar. Laura was asking him something. "I'm sorry?" he asked, turning toward her.

"How are things with you?" she repeated. "How are you keeping busy?"

"Well, I wish I could tell you that I'm being very productive, but you always knew when I was lying," he said. "To tell you the truth, I'm not at all sure that I'm half as busy as I ought to be. I seem to have a lot of medical appointments, serving to help train the various interns and residents in one or another specialty at our Medical School, and then, inevitably, I run to the pharmacy to obtain the magic potions they've prescribed–run isn't quite the word, by the way, I should reserve that for what I have to do when Nature calls, as she does more and more frequently--"

"The light touch is all very well, Walter," Gerald interrupted, "but is something seriously wrong or are you just a typical old bachelor hypochondriac?"

"Oh, now, don't start consulting your calendars for my funeral just yet," Rubin said. "I do have high blood pressure and some unpleasantness with my kidneys, and I do indeed find myself unhappy with our nation's treatment of the frail and ill elderly, but on the other hand, my pension plan is truly wonderful, and Rita is in my will and let's change the subject."

"So, aside from your volunteer work for your Medical School, training the next generation of medical millionaires," Laura asked again, "how are you keeping busy?"

Rubin hesitated, unable to keep from glancing at the four Middle Easterners. One of them had taken a small notebook from his jacket's inside pocket and was jotting something down. The older man was still talking very intently. The man who looked familiar–where *had* he seen him?–was leaning back now, looking a little sceptical. "The main thing I've told myself that I'm doing," Rubin said, "is selecting and revising some old articles and trying to add a few new ones to a book I'm considering putting together, but--"

"About literature?" Gerald interrupted again. "Gerald, please!" Laura expostulated.

"No, not about literature," Rubin continued, "unless incidentally – about me, really. Autobiographical meanderings. Reminiscences, ruminations, reflections. What's it all about, Alfie, you know, half a century later."

"So that's why you visited Ellis Island today!"

"Yes. The old country, or as close as I plan to get to it."

"Are you going to give us a preview?"

"I wish I could," Rubin said. The four Middle Easterners seemed to be getting ready to go. The one who looked familiar was motioning to their waiter, and the older man was reaching for his wallet. "But you've read the ones I've published, for instance, the one about my work with historically black colleges, and the one about teaching American literature in the inner city–there, that's what I mean by incidental references to literature–and the one about my father's family, or what I could find out about them. It's to be a sort of dual perspective, personal and professional, of who I am and how I think I spent my time here."

The four Middle Easterners were getting up and Rubin and the man who seemed familiar locked eyes for a moment. Rubin saw a flash of recognition in the man's face. The other men moved and blocked his view.

"No social life?" Laura asked.

"What? Oh, you mean women? Single, divorced, widow predator types, looking for a poor old defenseless Jewish refugee--"

"Stop!" Laura said. "You're as bad as Gerald! Can I get a straight answer?"

Rubin realized that somehow he hadn't expected the Arab or Turk or Pakistani or whatever he was to be quite as tall as he was, and he was surprised that he had had any expectation at all. "Yes, of course," he said to Laura. "I do have a social life with some old friends from the University, and with neighbors in the condominium association, in particular, Harry Rosenberg–did you know him, Gerald?–he's retired from our College of Architecture?" Gerald shook his head. "No? No, that's right, he came from Ohio State well after your years at our School of Education. And once in a while, Laura, I do go out with a lady, to dinner or a movie or a concert or a lecture."

"The same lady?" Laura was not easily put off.

"Well, yes, the same lady. But don't read anything into that. We're both very comfortable with the way things are, and besides, she has children and grandchildren, and I'm certain that, however nice they've been to me, they wouldn't be nearly as pleasant if they thought that I had designs on her."

"So she has money?"

It was Gerald's turn. "Laura!" he said. "Stop badgering this old rascal, of course she has money! Why else would he be after her? At his age he isn't likely to present himself as a Lothario!"

"But that's how she sees me, I'm sure," Rubin said quickly, and they all laughed. The Middle Eastern men were moving out of the restaurant. The one who had recognized Rubin did not look back, but something about the back of his head clicked into place. It was Hashem Iskandar, dressed up and with friends. Arabs. Palestinians. No doubt plotting a terrorist strike.

"That man was my cab driver this afternoon," Rubin told Gerald and Laura. "I was wondering where I had seen him before--" the Parkers glanced in the direction Rubin indicated, but the men were gone–"but you know how it is, when you see somebody out of context, or whatever context you have mentally placed him in, you don't recognize him. Or if you do, it might be something of a shock."

"Exactly," Gerald said. "It happens to African Americans all the time. There was that story Carl Rowan used to tell about himself, after Lyndon Johnson, I think it was, appointed him head of the U.S. Information Agency and he got a nice big house in some posh Washington suburb and was out one Sunday morning mowing his lawn when a white lady pulled her Cadillac up at the curb and asked him how much he got paid for yard work. He said that he didn't actually get any money but that he did have the privilege of sleeping with the lady of the house. That woman took off like a bat out of hell."

They all chuckled. "The funny thing is," Rubin said, "that's the second time that's happened to me today. Only I was the one of context. I was thinking about things I was looking at on Ellis Island, you know, staring at the city and the statue across the water and remembering my mother when all of a sudden some woman asked me if I was Professor Rubin. Of course I wanted to say I was Gerald Parker, the famous football player--"

"Tell the story!" the famous football player commanded.

"–but I confessed instead that I was the famous Professor Rubin. She said she was Mrs. Manglewood or Singlestick or somebody, there with her husband and nephew and the nephew's wife and had been my student under another name a hundred years ago in my sophomore survey course. Sally – she had been Sally Triandos at the time--"

Rubin paused. Something had flitted across Gerald's face.

"Don't tell me you knew her?" he asked.

"I don't think so," Gerald said. "Certainly I never knew a Mrs. Manglestick or whatever you said, and I don't remember a *Sally* Triandos–could she have had a sister?"

"Oh, Lord, don't they all," Laura said.

"I have no idea," Rubin said.

There was a pause.

"Anyway," Rubin continued, "I managed to get to the men's restroom once we were on the ferry back to the Battery, and avoided her thereafter. The point was that, from her point of view, I was the one out of context. She had gone there with her husband, this Mingletwig, and her nephew and the nephew's wife because Ellis Island was where her parents had landed and she had hardly expected to run into her old English professor from thirty-five years ago. She asked me if I had come through there."

"Did you confess again?" Gerald asked.

"No, I lied and said it was my grandmother," Rubin said. "I don't know why I did that. I suppose to keep the conversation from getting out of hand, with one confession after another. Who knows where that would have gone? I'd probably be drinking *ouzo* at the nephew's house now, or shouting *Opa!* and clapping my hands to a bouzouki."

"Right," Gerald said. "Sounds just like you. And then you never would have returned my call, and we'd be worried sick about you wandering around in this big city preyed on by all kinds of people I won't even mention. Much better to invent a grandmother and be done with it."

They lingered over coffee, reluctant to call it an evening. Laura had appointments in the morning, so Gerald and Rubin agreed to meet for a late breakfast at Rubin's hotel. "There's something I want to talk to you about," Rubin said, "or actually to have you talk to me about, having to do with your time in Washington. When you were at the Department of Education."

"Yes?" Gerald asked.

"Let's save it until tomorrow morning," Rubin said, "but Harry Rosenberg, my friend from Architecture, has been telling me about an old case involving a man he knew at Ohio State that has stirred up a lot of questions in my mind–I'll tell you all about it tomorrow."

"Okay," Gerald said, signaling the waiter. "Tomorrow about nine."

"That means nine thirty," Laura said.

"I know," Rubin said ruefully, "but I'll be in the coffee shop at nine, trusting and abused as usual."

Chapter V

Rubin, April, 2005

"About what I mentioned last night," Rubin said, stirring a sugar substitute into his coffee and looking for the cream, "having to do with your time at the Department of Education--"

"You make it sound as if I had been *doing* time there!" Gerald laughed. "It wasn't like that. Here," he said, stretching a long arm to the next table and snaring a small pitcher of cream.

"Thanks," Rubin said. "I know you didn't *do* time in Washington or for what you did in Washington, although I suspect you should have– wasn't that during the Reagan administration? Or was Bush the First in office?"

"It wasn't quite three years, most of it during Reagan's second term," Gerald said. "I got out and went back to my company not long after Bush became president. And that lasted another seven years until I finally hung it all up, about the same time you retired from Michigan."

"OK, I've got the time frame now, I think," Rubin said. "I don't know whether what I want to ask you about still works in the same way as it did during your years there, but actually it's not what might have changed that I'm curious about, it's what hasn't."

"You're being awfully mysterious," Gerald said. "What exactly is the question?"

"What do you know about accreditation?"

"Accreditation of what?"

"Anything. Schools or school systems. Organizations that accredit them. Licensing organizations. Certifications. How is it decided that a medical school in the Galapagos, say, is not offering an up-to-the-stethoscope education? What difference does it make where a sawbones learned to dissect a cadaver if he can pass the state board examination in Wyoming or wherever he wants to practice? How did all this come to pass? Moses didn't descend Mount Sinai, as far as I know, bearing the Almighty's instructions about who is to design and administer the examinations intended to separate the rabbinical wheat from the illiterate chaff. Well, what *is* the process and how does it work and who's in charge? Are there vast differences between, say, certifying an electrician and attesting to the skillful and ethical practices of your neighborhood mortician?"

Gerald sat back, regarding Rubin contemplatively. "What is this all about, Walter?"

"I'm not sure yet," Rubin said. "Maybe nothing except my curiosity. Maybe a very belated recognition that, just because it's obvious that both performance and potential have to be evaluated periodically for organizations as well as individuals, our ways of doing so are as arbitrary and capricious as anything else we've devised, no matter how we dress them up as wise and honored traditions. Maybe it's a growing uneasiness on my part that my entire career has been spent in unconscious and unthinking participation in intrinsic corruption. Maybe--"

"Oh for Christ's sake not this guilt again Walter!" Gerald interrupted almost in one word.

Rubin held up his hand. "Maybe because I've been thinking about what could very well have been a murder in Columbus not quite thirty-five years ago, even though it's in the books as an accident. Closely followed by a heart attack suffered by one of Harry Rosenberg's colleagues."

"What?" Gerald said. "What murder? What are you talking about? Are you serious?"

"I'm serious, but I'm not sure of anything. So far all I have are some questions. They're not even my questions, not entirely. I told you last night, I've been talking to my friend Harry Rosenberg from Architecture, or I've been listening to him remember a case from the late seventies, I think it was, and the more I think about it, the more ramifications I see."

"What was the case?"

"There was a student, from Cleveland, as I recall, who was doing extremely well in Ohio State's School of Architecture, working on his master's degree with some sort of marketing study–I think he was doing a joint degree or maybe a dual degree with their Business School. This study involved architects in Columbus and the area. Something he was doing in the study, a survey of practicing architects, apparently caught the attention of the professional organization, whatever it is, that licenses architects in Ohio or the country–these are details I'm not clear about yet. Harry is quite a bit older than we are and tends to tell a story in his own way, and if he gets off the track, it's very hard to right the locomotive again. Anyway, somebody, apparently from this organization, leaned on the faculty to stop this fellow, I don't know on what grounds. But Harry tells me that stop him they did. But that's only the beginning."

Gerald signaled to the waitress while Rubin drained his coffee. "He'd like some coffee and I'd like some more tea, please," Gerald told her. "And could you bring another couple of slices of lemon?" Gerald gave her one of his patented smiles.

"Certainly, sir," the waitress said cheerfully, returning his smile. She was obviously delighted by him. "You old rascal," Rubin said enviously, "you may be in your dotage but you still got your mojo working."

"I wish," Gerald said. "But don't get off the subject. What murder?"

"As I say, I'm not sure it *was* a murder. Harry says that there was an inquiry and the death was ruled an accident, a hit-and-run automobile accident. But the coincidences stretch credulity. The man was the president of the state board of examiners of architects, the group that controlled the licensing examination. All that's changed now, but at the time, the association was pretty much part of a closed club, complete with political influence, and of course in an excellent position to influence business practices, to maintain ties with the construction industry, and so on. And the man who had a heart attack just a little later, while he was on the phone with another official of this same state board of examiners, and who was a colleague of Harry's at the university, was the president of the Ohio Architects Society." Rubin paused to look for the waitress. "I know this seems a long way from what I asked you about, but we'll get to it."

"Accreditation," Gerald said, indicating that he remembered the question.

"Yes. Now here's the first strange thing. The student, after having been praised by his advisor for his talents as a promising architect, was suddenly told to stop his work on his research, on the extent to which innovative business practices were communicated to and used by local architectural firms. He was told that he'd get partial credit for what he'd done, just to stop the surveys and interviews and data collection. The advisor, by the way, was the man who later had the heart attack. As far as Harry can remember, the student didn't get any real explanation. An application he and his professors had prepared for internal support from some source within the university was never submitted, even though it was ready to go. Anyway, he had no choice, so he did as he was told and then he took his licensing examination. He failed."

"Really! I thought you said that he'd been told that he was very promising!"

"Yes. Apparently he didn't fail by much, but he did fail. It's not that unusual, really, at least not in my experience–half the doctoral students in my department at Wisconsin, in the nineteen fifties, failed their preliminary exams the first time, as I did. And I have a friend, a Yale graduate, now on the Law faculty here at Columbia who failed his board exam in New York the first time. Said it was one of the best things that ever happened to him–what people now refer to as a wakeup call. Anyway, he failed, but he saw a way around it, in the Ohio law governing the licensure of architects at the time, to the effect that a combination of educational credentials, work experience, and recommendations from architects knowledgeable about the candidate's abilities could be substituted for a passing grade on the exam, if the licensure people went along with it. So he tried that. And here's the second interesting thing: he was turned down, even after a hearing complete with lawyers, held by the state board of examiners."

"Really," Gerald said again. "Thanks so much," he said to the waitress who appeared with the lemon slices, more coffee for Rubin, and another pot of tea for him. "You're very welcome, hon," she said, perkily, and bounced away. The two old men grinned at each other. "Almost like old times," Rubin said. "Or so I remember hearing."

"Never mind what you heard," Gerald said. "Is there a third interesting thing? I'm beginning to think of a question I want to ask, but finish the story."

"No, he wasn't black, but he was Jewish," Rubin said, "and that may or may not have something to do with it, I don't know. Harry thinks it does, but Harry, unlike me, is paranoid."

"Unlike you? Go ahead, what about the third interesting thing? There was another, wasn't there?"

"Not just one. The man tried the exam three more times, passing on his fourth try, by which time the faculty member I told you about, the professor who was also an official in the professional association, had had his fatal heart attack. I'm not sure how many years elapsed between the student's first failure and his ultimate success, but I do know that the advisor was in his grave when the man was admitted to architectural practice in Ohio."

"You said the other man's death was officially recorded as an accident?"

"Yes, the president of the state board of examiners. But the professor is supposed to have had that heart attack while talking on the phone to somebody at that board. Harry tells me that he'd had a bypass some years earlier, but that had been successful, and except for having to take his high blood pressure pills regularly, as I do--" Rubin was suddenly aware that he had forgotten to take them with him to New York–"he was reasonably healthy. He'd given up teaching, but he had maintained his private practice."

"What was strange about the other man's accident?"

"I don't know. I'm not sure that Harry does either. But the way Harry told me about it made me think that Harry wasn't satisfied with whatever was reported about it."

They sipped their beverages. "Before I tell you that I know almost nothing about accreditation," Gerald said, "and I don't, what happened to the man once he became a licensed architect?"

"Ah, yes, one more interesting thing. Eventually, Harry tells me, he became a successful practitioner but he didn't get over the experience. He felt that he had been humiliated, treated unfairly, singled out for at least temporary disgrace because he had been working on documenting the short-sighted, conservative marketing practices of the profession. And even before he passed the examination, he found a way to tell his story to a Congressional committee investigating the subject much more broadly."

"What subject? Accreditation? Licensing practices? I know Congress can and does stick its nose into lots of surprising things, but what motivated them to get into this one?"

"It was a subcommittee of the House Committee on Labor and Education or whatever its name was, chaired by Carl Perkins of Kentucky–"

"Perkins! Of course I remember him, his name is attached to all that vocational education money every year!"

"Well, it's nice to have your name attached to something like that, I'm sure. Anyway, the subcommittee was holding hearings on a couple of bills on testing, educational testing–this was in 1979, a little before the Iranian revolutionaries seized our embassy in Teheran. I think their excuse was that Carter had refused to surrender the Shah, who had come here seeking treatment for his cancer, to their judicial system. There has to be a god, don't you think? There are just too damned many ironies to explain away otherwise."

"Oh, I think there are a whole lot of gods," Gerald said. "And goddesses too, of course."

"Of course. Anyway, that's about it. So what do you know about accreditation?"

"Very little, as I told you," Gerald said. "I remember attending an accreditation meeting for an urban community college around 1970 or so, for what the North Central Association called 'Correspondent Status,' the first step toward full accreditation. It involved interviews of key administrators–maybe a couple of the trustees as well–and various faculty, staff, and student leaders. The interviews were conducted by the North Central representatives and some volunteer biggies, a president of an urban community college in another state, and so on. There were visits to some of the classes–as I recall, that was interesting, because that college had just started out renting space all over the city, or borrowing it from schools and churches–and of course the accreditation team, as it was called, looked at instructional materials and facilities and syllabi, and what I remember best is how relaxed everyone was about the money–there seemed to be very little of it. If I had been in their shoes, I would have been as nervous as a whore in church, pretending that the millage they didn't have yet was a sure thing next year and that their legislature was going to float them until then. But it was all calm, cool, and collected, and damn if they didn't eventually get their money, just as they had predicted."

"What was your role in this accreditation visit?" Rubin asked.

"I was there really as an observer," Gerald said. "But I was still on Michigan's faculty at the time, and a couple of the college's administrators thought that, if the question of cooperative agreements with established institutions of higher education came up–for instance, about universities recognizing certain community college courses as equivalent to theirs at the freshman level, say–I could offer some sort of reassurances. In fact, I couldn't, but they wanted me there anyway, probably to take up space."

"Yes, I can believe that," Rubin said. Gerald's coat size was still a 56. "I had no idea it was so complicated, that there were so many ramifications."

"There's no reason why you should have known–English professors don't have to concern themselves with this kind of three-dimensional bureaucratic maze until they stop explicating poetry and become administrators. And before you ask why they can't do both, it's because there's no poetry, absolutely none, in administration."

"Have you had any other experience with this process?"

"Well, in a sense, we all have had, as students–what are standardized examinations but accreditation? It doesn't end with the SAT or ACT that high school students take–those are just the beginning of the professionalization process, if you want to call it that. Doesn't a sufficiently high score, whatever that is, on a standardized exam mean that the examinee is to be accepted at the next level of whatever he or she is pursuing? I'm thinking of Rita, who just took the MCAT–the Medical

College Admissions Test—and if she gets a high enough score that will in effect say to the medical schools she's already applied to for admission that her undergraduate work has been accredited by her performance on the test. And you and I had to do something like that with the Graduate Record Examination, the GRE, and Laura had to do it not only with the LSAT to get into law school but then, when she finished that, she had to take the New York bar exam. We're all familiar with the system as individuals, just like this architect you told me about. Well, there are roughly comparable procedures for institutions and organizations, not uniformly so, and no doubt there are exceptions, but generally, yes, accreditation permeates everything. Think of a driver's license, a hunting license, a permit to own a gun or carry one, or even building a house—the structure has to pass inspection before it can be legally occupied."

"And then it can deteriorate and become home to drug dealers and their clientele," Rubin added.

"Yes, of course," Gerald said. "Nobody is claiming the system can detect senescence or that it's even foolproof on its surface. People cheat everywhere. Take continuing education courses, resulting in something called credits for whatever profession insists that it upholds high standards of contemporary practice by demanding that its members earn a certain number of such credits every three or five years or whatever it is. All kinds of professions, trades, occupations, make such demands. Dental hygiene. Real estate. Quality control chemists. You know what actually happens, maybe not always but in any number of instances?"

"What? The quality control chemists run off with the dental hygienists to clean up in some illicit real estate deals?"

"That too, probably, but what I have in mind is something much more mundane. The people needing the continuing education credits send in their names, identification, and fees—hear me now, *fees*—well ahead of the time the continuing education courses are offered. Not incidentally, it is quite common to offer such courses at resorts with golf courses, or near casinos, or other such attractions. The organization—this is the accrediting organization—sets up tables in the lobby of the hotel hosting the event, staffs the tables with people from the organization, whether permanent staff members or otherwise, equips those people with the registration information provided by the putative attendees, and—hear me again—the certificates of completion of the course. The putative attendees show up at the appointed hour, identify themselves to the staff members behind the tables, have the payment of their fees affirmed, receive their certificates and copies of the materials, if any, and *then* they have a choice: they can actually go into the adjacent auditorium and listen to the PowerPoint presentations, or they can take their certificates and head out to the pool or golf course or casino or, if it's not too early, to the bar to meet their friends, boys and girls letting the good times roll."

Rubin was fascinated. "I know about going to the bar instead of to the sessions at which all those papers are presented," he said. "I remember being told by a hotel elevator operator in Philadelphia, where we were having that year's meeting of the Modern Language Association, that English professors got the drunkest and tipped the least of any of the conventioneers the hotel ever hosted–but we don't have any continuing education courses, or at least no requirement. We can just pontificate about Pope or wax lyrical about Wordsworth or speculate about Shakespeare without ever having to prove to anybody that we have read the latest scholarship or still remember what we had to read as graduate students. At least, once we have tenure. After that, we devote ourselves to examining the young and finding them unworthy, whether they are undergraduates, or working on their dissertations, or trying to survive their probationary periods as junior members of the department."

"But that's very similar to what I'm talking about," Gerald said. "The difference isn't so much in the practice as in its presentation. Your tradition, the tradition of unlicensed pedagogy– interesting, isn't it, that teachers in the lower rungs of the educational establishment have to achieve some sort of certification before they are set loose upon our children, whereas you, at the top of the profession in universities and teacher training institutions, are in effect subjected only to the question of whether most of your influential colleagues like you well enough to grant you tenure–your tradition is that there is a general understanding of what competence, continuing competence consists of and is manifested by, an understanding pervasive throughout the profession, and not reducible to objective verification, for instance, through machine-scored examinations. The implication is--"

"Good Lord!" Rubin groaned. "What an idea!"

"Exactly my point," Gerald continued. He was clearly enjoying himself. The waitress came by again but he ignored her. "The implication is obvious. What you and people like you, other humanities professors, most social scientists, most people in the natural sciences, what you do is simply not important enough, as far as society is concerned, to bother you with periodic, relatively objective examinations of your continuing competence. But take professions that matter, medicine, law, engineering, dentistry, architecture, accounting, or the trades, plumbing, carpentry, electrical work, or serious social services, such as police and fire departments—hell yes, we insist that people who do work that matters to us demonstrate that they know what they're doing. Or at least have reasonably recent certificates."

"This is getting depressing," Rubin said. "Here we are, in our mid-seventies, and thus hardly able to claim that we still have a lot to offer, and according to your analysis, the fact that we haven't been asked to claim it since we took the GRE in our twenties proves that we never did. See, I told you I've been wondering about how I spent my life, and instead of reassuring me that it hasn't been a total waste—don't yell at me about guilt again, Gerald, people will stare—you prove to me, with all that objectivity you keep talking about, that it has."

Gerald laughed. "I'm not at all sure that I said that. But have it your way. I sure wouldn't want people to stare."

Rubin looked at his watch. "My plane isn't scheduled for departure until three, but you're supposed to be there about two hours early, so that they have time to see if any of your ancestors might have had suspicious DNA—do you have time for a walk? I'd like to get just a brief exposure to New York's stormy Monday blues."

"Sure," Gerald said. "Especially since it isn't stormy. Wasn't that the old T-Bone Walker tune? 'They call it Stormy Monday but Tuesday's just as bad'?"

"I think it was, and it usually is," Rubin said "I've got the bill. You paid for dinner last night."

"Don't mind if you do," Gerald said.

*****

LaGuardia was busy as always. Rubin took a book from the outside pocket of his carry-on and looked for an empty seat near the gate for his plane to Detroit. There was none. A large contingent of Middle Easterners, complete with more small children than seemed proportional to the number of their worried parents, was occupying the seating area. Arabs on their way to Dearborn, Rubin thought gloomily, using the children as a cover for their plans for martyrdom. He walked around the area, wheeling his carry-on, deliberately staring at the men to draw their attention to his plight: an old gentleman, book under arm, burdened with a suitcase, and no place to sit, damn it. Nobody noticed him. The men were either explaining the mysteries of American air travel to one another or to their wives, or spoiling the very small children who seemed to Rubin to be shrieking at intolerable noise levels, or engaged in last-minute remonstrances of some kind, perhaps about obscure passages in

the Qu'ran or the advantages of supporting Hamas over Fatah. This was
not a culture, Rubin thought grimly, that honored the elderly. Now if
they were truly Asiatic instead of merely *Middle* Eastern, and thus aware
of their obligations to their reputations, they would be leaping out of
their chairs to accommodate his obvious need, muttering pleasantries,
offering dates and figs, bringing coffee. They ignored him because they
recognized him as a Jew, that's what it had to be. He spied a vacant chair
and rushed toward it, reaching it barely ahead of a very pregnant lady,
complete with head scarf, suitcase, and a screaming three-year-old child
of indeterminate sex. He pulled up short, gesturing toward the chair:
"Please," he said to the pregnant lady. She threw him a glance he found
impossible to interpret and collapsed into the chair, hugging the
screaming child. Rubin resumed his peregrinations.

Not too many years ago, he thought, at Ellis Island, or the docks, or
at train and bus stations throughout the country, these people would have
been of different ethnicities, different colors, yelling in different
languages, but filled with similar anxieties, burdened by similar
obligations, trying to be buoyed by similar hopes. It was as if he were
visiting Ellis Island as a ghost from the nineteen thirties, refreshing not
his recollections but his understanding, looking forward because he was
able to look back. He could put aside his bitterness about the WASP
distaste for noisy swarthy foreigners, the explicit anti-Semitism of Henry
Adams, the virulent loathing of Irish "and dogs" not allowed in proper
Yankee establishments, and of course the fear and revulsion inspired by
Africans, East Indians, the "yellow peril," and, probably from the very
first, by the "salvages" encountered by the original European pirates and
murderers, carrying their guns and germs and steel wherever they went,
as Diamond's excellent book had it. If you examined the human record
carefully enough, what you had to admit was that superior numbers and
technology had allowed marauders to subject their victims to
unspeakable brutality everywhere and at all times, all the way up to
quota systems, admission standards, multiple-choice machine-scored
standardized tests, winks, nods, and gentlemen's agreements. Now here
were these people, in impossible circumstances at home, in very difficult
circumstances here, destined for very hard work, humiliation,
discrimination, outrages of various kinds for years to come, and that little
three-year-old screamer would go to the University of Michigan and
become a neurosurgeon. What a strange, wonderful country.

A familiar face, suddenly. It was the older man from the restaurant
last night, the one who had given the impromptu lecture to Hashem
Iskandar and his two companions. There he was in a chair, talking to a

lady and some other people gathered around them. He must be a tribal elder, Rubin thought, or perhaps even the patriarch–but was he sending his flock forth into the unknown, the wilds of the desert, complete with progeny and cell phones, to settle in the Promised Land of Dearborn and Wayne County, or was he in fact *leading* them there, a modern Palestinian Moses? If the latter, would he be permitted to set foot at Metropolitan Airport, or would he, after a glimpse of the desolation of Detroit from ten thousand feet, suffer a heart attack, unable to free himself from his seat belt despite the frantic ministrations of the stewardess–no, now the hostess–and thus ascend directly to Paradise, taking the short cut provided by Northwest Airlines? Rubin was aware that these multiculturally incorrect speculations, despite the amusement they afforded him, did not diminish the coincidences of the sequence of cab driver/restaurant/airport, Arabs following him, increasing in number, getting closer and closer to his home. Soon they would take over his condominium association in Ann Arbor, abolish the understanding that families with small children were to be kept to a minimum, and then turn their attention to the Jews.

A hostess approached the microphone and the crowd stirred. Men stood up and grasped carry-ons and briefcases, women clutched small children and gave commands to larger ones. Rubin fumbled for his boarding pass and, pulling his carry-on carefully between his fellow passengers, edged toward the gate, looking forward to his seat on the plane. Then it occurred to him that it would be sure to be next to two screaming children, or two overweight Arab ladies who would be afraid of touching his elbows. At least they wouldn't have live chickens in cages.

He was right about the chickens, but there were no children either, and he put his carry-on in the overhead compartment, nodded to the two Arab men in the window and middle seats, and sat down in the aisle seat, fastening his seat belt around him. He took his book–Sam Harris' *The End of Faith*–which he had just bought in a bookshop he and Gerald had visited, and opened it at random. "…we live in a country," Rubin read, "in which a person cannot get elected president if he openly doubts the existence of heaven and hell." Of course not, Rubin thought. Harris went on to point out that we don't ask our leaders to know anything in particular—unlike, say, hairstylists—as long as they affirm their "faith." Any believer would have a much better chance than any sceptic.

So Gerald was wrong, after all: surely political leadership was a profession that mattered, and it required no continuing education credits, no standardized examination, no machine-scored tests. Contrary to Lear, image is all. Well, a bulging campaign chest didn't hurt either.

But how was this different, except in scale and significance, from academic politics? Henry Kissinger was supposed to have said that the reason that academic politics were so vicious was that the stakes were so small, and that indeed would account for the intensity of the passions attached to the warfare characteristic of so many communities of scholars. But otherwise, the similarities were remarkable. What training was there for a departmental chairman, a dean, a vice-president? Of course there was something called "higher education"–he had known a professor of adult education who, annoyed by the pretentiousness of his colleagues in his local Institute of Higher Education, called it "the Institute of *Much* Higher Education"–but no distinguished academic leaders, no Robert Hutchins or Theodore Hesburgh or Roger Heyns, had ever emerged from such a burrow to lead his followers up the academic Alps. Fund-raising, yes, that ability was *sine qua non*. Or at least its appearance, at the interview stage. Boards of trustees or their hired headhunters were as subject to being conned in this respect as in any other, although you wouldn't think that ascertaining the facts about a given candidate's proven fund-raising track record, as it was always called–the image was amusing, all those middle-aged men in track suits, martinis in hand, huffing and puffing after a potential donor–would be difficult to do. There would be records, deposit slips, letters accompanying major gifts if for no other purpose but to reaffirm, once again, the conditions of the gift: " ... for a young lady of Caucasian descent and Episcopalian heritage, to be known after our late mother as the Katherine O'Brien Vanderbilt Hilton Jones Scholarship, for the purpose of subsidizing the annual costs of up to but not more than 50% of an undergraduate year at a suitable institution of higher education in the United Kingdom ...." Or a building–an auditorium or a gymnasium, or an addition to an art museum, or an executive wing for the Business School's summer institutes for executive seminars for executives. Rubin chuckled to himself and then, realizing that the man next to him, reading a newspaper in Arabic, had glanced at him and the book in his hand, pretended to be merely clearing his throat. The humor in *The End of Faith* might be difficult to explain under the circumstances.

He put the book in his lap so that the title didn't show and closed his eyes. Air travel, particularly short flights fully subscribed, was best tolerated, he had found, with a cat nap in the middle. The younger children had quieted down and the older ones seemed to be occupied with whispering either to each other or their parents. He could hear only part of a conversation, apparently coming from the row behind him, some in Arabic, some not. What was not in Arabic had to do with money. Somehow, Rubin found this reassuring and nodded off.

*****

The weather, when Rubin emerged into it from the airport, was miserable: cold, gloomy, threatening rain or worse, the kind of weather a bachelor, in particular, might be expected to loathe because there would be no light or warmth or cheer when he finally got home. But Rubin was not that kind of bachelor. He liked to be in charge of his things: not just what they were but also how they were arranged. He liked order, especially if it was the order he had selected to suit his taste. He did not mind other people's relatives, pets, piles, litter, or disarray, but he was always aware that his tolerance was directly related to his ability to escape them all. And he enjoyed his car, waiting for him in the parking structure, questioning neither his time in New York nor the pleasantness of the journey. It was an expensive, powerful Chrysler, complete with almost all the gadgets he could have added, less than a year old. Its motor was quiet, its windows closed off the noise of the road–there wasn't much except for the trucks that Rubin passed effortlessly–and his favorite FM station's music reverberated from the car's six speakers. It was a local college station that specialized in jazz and although, for Rubin's taste, there was far too much modern jazz by musicians he had never heard of, occasionally there would be something by Ellington or Basie or small groups, Brubeck or Peterson or Mulligan or the MJQ, and then he would be transported back fifty years to what seemed to him, then, the Rubin with potentially wonderful futures: magical events no one could predict, chance meetings, unexpected opportunities, someone's recognition of his abilities, his eagerness, the difference he could make, the women he could fall in love with, the books he could write, the speeches with which he would enthrall innumerable audiences. It was all there, in Joe Williams' goin' to Chicago, movin' on down the line; in Johnny Hodges' inexpressibly sweet alto, painting a blues so indigo nobody had had them without that exact mood; in Brubeck's dialogues with Paul Desmond, or in Peterson's amazing right hand, or in Mulligan's deeply authoritative statements of how things really were, or in the Modern Jazz Quartet's unending discoveries of gorgeous lyrical complexities. He had been in his mid-twenties and although absolutely nothing else had been clear, those things had been. Racing west on I-94 in the gathering dark, occasionally weaving around a slower truck or car, glancing in the rearview mirror for blinking red and blue lights, Rubin was not the retired professor identified on the license he would have to proffer were those lights to materialize into a matter-of-fact state trooper, but a graduate student of uncertain but brilliant future.

All was as he had left it in his condominium, with the exception of his telephone recording machine, blinking as the hotel telephone had blinked at him in New York. "Just a minute," he told it, aware of fulfilling the stereotype of the single person living alone, resorting to conversation with inanimate objects as well as with himself. First, there were clothes and bathroom items to be put away, ablutions to be performed, mail to glance at–almost always bills, request for contributions, and catalogues for more products than any thirty civilizations could have imagined. Then there was the question of something to drink, tea, for instance, on a chilly night. He decided that tea would be welcome and set about making it. Then, when the water was in the kettle, the Earl Grey next to the cup he had selected, and the spoon on the counter, he pushed the button. There were three requests for donations to worthy causes to which Rubin had sent small amounts of money some months ago, a teenager's giggle, a hang-up, and then suddenly an old man's voice.

"Walter," the voice croaked–he recognized it instantly as Harry Rosenberg's, and something was obviously wrong–"Walter–oh shit I forgot you were going out of town–see if you can reach–never mind..." A dial tone droned and then a machine said "If you'd like to make a call, please hang up and ..." That was all.

Rubin looked at his watch. It was not even six o'clock, and he dialed Harry's number, thinking that if, as he expected, he got no answer, he could try to reach Harry's neighbor, the old lady, or perhaps the condominium manager, Wayne, or even 911. The kettle whistled. No one answered Harry's phone. Rubin couldn't remember whether Harry had an answering machine. He poured his tea and found the condominium association's directory. The office would be closed, but maybe he would recognize Harry's neighbor's name–certainly the address–if he saw it. Yes, here it was: Genevieve Mullins. He had met her several times, but they had only exchanged pleasantries about the weather or the tulips or whatever flowers were in bloom. A small wrinkled woman who seemed suspicious of him and perhaps of Harry as well, even though they had been neighbors for twenty-five years. He dialed the number.

"Hello?"

"Mrs. Mullins?" he asked, aware that he couldn't remember whether she was or ever had been a Mrs. "This is Walter Rubin, Harry Rosenberg's friend–we've met several times--"

"Who?"

"Rubin, Walter Rubin," he repeated. "Harry Rosenberg's friend. I'm calling because I'm concerned about Harry–he left a strange message on my telephone recording machine, and--"

"What? Can you speak up? What about Harry?"

"That's what I'm calling you to find out, Mrs. Mullins," Rubin said more loudly but still politely.

Suddenly the old lady seemed to connect. "Harry's in the hospital," she said. "He had a stroke or something, but he managed to call Emergency and they came and took him away, it was late Saturday night, woke me up of course which is how I found out. I think his son is with him, at least that's what I was told when I called earlier today, called the Hospital."

"Good Lord," Rubin said. "Do you know where he is in the Hospital? What unit, I mean? Which hospital, by the way?"

"The University Hospital," Mrs. Mullins said. "No, I don't know where he is, you have to call the Information Desk. That's all I know."

"Thank you very much, Mrs. Mullins, I'll call right away," Rubin said, but she had already hung up. He checked the number for the University Hospital's Information Desk and dialed, somehow convinced that he was too late. Harry was about eighty-four, he thought, and had long had high blood pressure. So did Rubin, among other "conditions," as he had learned to call them. The thought of his own mortality was not new, but Harry's rasping voice and incomplete request somehow sharpened the realization. A young woman's voice, pleasant, almost solicitous, asked him how she might help. "I'm calling to find out about Professor Rosenberg, Harry Rosenberg," he said. "I've just learned he had a stroke, I think, on Saturday night and was taken to the University's Emergency Service?" He was reminded, as he repeated what Mrs. Mullins had told him, of his conversation with Sally Triandos on Ellis Island: everything had to be repeated, re-established as the context changed. While he was asked to wait a moment, he thought of Gerald's story about Carl Rowan and the white woman who had asked how much he charged for lawn care. He anticipated the question he was about to be asked and decided to lie as he had to Sally Triandos.

"Are you a relative?" the young woman asked him.

"Yes, I'm a cousin, we're very close," he said. "Do you need my name and address or anything? I'm also retired from the University," he continued hurriedly, "on the faculty, actually–how is Harry, I mean Professor Rosenberg?"

"I'm afraid he's in the Critical Care Unit," the young woman said. "I have no other information at this time except that there is someone related to him in the Family Waiting Room. Only one person, and two are permitted."

"Thank you very much," Rubin said. "I really appreciate the information. You've been very helpful." He had long since learned that there was no such thing as excessive courtesy to the staff once you had claimed special privileges as a faculty member.

"You're very welcome," said the young woman. He thought she might add that she hoped for the best, but that would have been excessive on her part, apparently.

He finished his tea, unsure of what to do. He had met Harry's son several times–a bald man, rather stout, with blue eyes, he remembered, didn't look like Harry at all–and had no particular impression of him. He was in some sort of business. No, he had been in some sort of business but had gotten out of it because–he couldn't remember. Sometimes Harry's stories seemed very involved. What was his name? Alvin? Albert? No.

Well, he supposed he had no choice: he was Harry's friend as well as neighbor, and he couldn't very well tell Harry, if he recovered, that he thought he was going to die, it was a cold night, he had just unpacked, and besides his son, Alvin or Albert or whatever his name was, was already there. He could at least try to find out what Alvin or Albert knew. There wasn't much chance that whatever medical *factotum* was on duty would tell him anything, even if he tried the fellow faculty member routine. *Nobody* not on the Medical School's faculty was a fellow faculty member, except maybe a really important Vice President, or the President himself, of course, or a Regent. But there were gradations of fellowship within the Medical faculty as well. The gorilla of the School was the Internal Medicine department. Other units could be important, but they were lesser breeds, no question about it. Patients referred from one specialist to another, as Rubin had been, eventually got glimpses into the dynamics as well as of the School's hierarchy. He remembered a neurosurgeon studying his chart and noting the specialists his primary care physician had already referred him to: "Well, she's trying the shotgun approach to your problems, isn't she?" He changed his clothes, made sure that the recording machine was on and the stove off, left a light on in the living room, and drove to the Hospital.

Alvin or Albert was not hard to spot in the Family Waiting Room. He was the only person sitting by himself, reading a magazine. Several small groups of people were gathered elsewhere in the room. If there really was a rule limiting the number of visitors to two per patient, it obviously wasn't enforced, at least not at this hour. He walked up to Albert or Alvin and said, "Mr. Rosenberg?" The man, startled, looked up, surprised, no doubt, to be addressed by a man in an overcoat instead of a white lab coat complete with ID tag and other indicators of officialdom. His eyes were disconcertingly large and blue. "I'm Walter Rubin," Rubin said quickly, "your father's friend and neighbor—we've met before—I just came back from out of town and found a message from your father on my recorder."

"What message?"

Not very courteous, but the man is under stress, of course, Rubin thought. "It was incomplete but it was clear that something was wrong, just from the sound of his voice," he explained. "So I called Mrs. Mullins and she told me that Harry had had a stroke, she thought, but that you were here, so I thought I'd come right away."

"Yes, yes, I understand, I remember you, you're another retired professor and you live in the same condominium complex as my father."

Damn, Rubin thought, stress or not, this man was downright rude. "That's right, I do, Alvin," he said.

"Marvin," the younger Rosenberg corrected.

"Marvin, of course, sorry. What have they told you about your father, if I may ask?"

"I don't think he's going to make it," Marvin said without any particular emotion. "They haven't exactly said that, just about 'very serious' and 'monitoring very closely' and all that crap, but I can tell, it's not going to be long either. He's almost eighty-four, I think."

"So he did have a stroke?"

"They think so. I don't know. What difference does it make, whatever it was? They reached me in Minneapolis yesterday, and I barely had time to call my sister in Tampa and cancel my appointments in Minnesota and catch a plane to Detroit, which I hate, by the way, and now the old bastard's gonna die and leave me with a thousand details. Sarah probably won't come until the funeral, provided she can get a new outfit, if she can tear herself away from her goddamned cats for God's sake." Marvin stared angrily at Rubin as if Rubin had started to defend Sarah or her cats. Sarah was apparently the sister in Tampa. Maybe not.

"Sarah is your sister?"

"No, of course not. Sarah is my wife. My sister lives in Tampa, I told you. Minna. Jesus, I thought you said you were a friend of my father's, didn't he tell you anything?"

Rubin was beginning to be very sorry that he had come. "Is your sister going to join you, then?"

"Join me? What do you mean, join me?"

"Is she coming here to be with you and see your father?"

"Look, you've got the wrong idea about all this," Marvin said. "I don't exactly know why I should have to explain it all to you if you're such a good friend of my father's, but let me ask you something first: are you going to help me with all this? I don't know this goddamned town, I don't know who to call, I don't even know a rabbi for Christ's sake. I've never even buried anybody before. When my mother died my father took care of everything with her family, I was barely involved. So are you going to help out?"

Rubin saw no way out. This wasn't Sally Triandos asking him if he had come through Ellis Island himself. "Of course," he said. "Anything I can do. But shouldn't we wait first of all--"

"Mr. Rosenberg?" It was a young, tall, trim doctor in a white lab coat, glowing with health and solicitude. William Simpson, M.D., said the heavy black print next to his photograph on his badge. There was more, something about his affiliation with a Hospital department. Rubin had a vision of a possible visitors' badge: Walter Rubin, Ph.D., Friend and Neighbor. No photograph.

"Yes?" Marvin almost barked.

The doctor glanced at Rubin. "You're also a family member?"

"No, he's not," Marvin said, and Rubin found himself smiling awkwardly and retreating a few steps. Dr. Simpson took Marvin into a little room Rubin had not noticed earlier at the far end of the Family Waiting Room. This was his chance to escape. He hadn't even taken his overcoat off. He felt his car keys in his pocket. It was obviously all over for poor Harry, and the son was nobody Rubin wanted anything to do with. Three steps and he would be out of sight, down the hall, back to the parking structure, let this jackass Marvin struggle with Minna or Sarah or the cats about the details of Harry's funeral, why the *hell* had he said he'd help? Maybe Marvin hadn't heard him?

Rubin took off his coat and sank into a chair, waiting for Dr. Simpson to finish telling Marvin how Harry had died.

Chapter VI
Rubin, April, 2005

The local paper carried the announcement of Harry Rosenberg's death in its regular column of recent departures–for reasons Rubin once knew but couldn't remember, the paper had long since stopped publishing announcements of births, marriages, and divorces in what had been a widely read and highly informative feature–but the obituary that appeared a few days later was perfunctory, probably released by the Dean's office. The Dean was probably a young man or, these days, woman who hadn't known Harry. Perhaps she had met him at one of those obligatory Christmas or, these days, holiday season's parties. It wouldn't have mattered: she must have given the task of writing the obituary to one of her assistants, read it over hurriedly, muttered "Very nice," and sent it on to the paper. There was no picture.

> Professor Emeritus Harry A. Rosenberg of the University of Michigan's Alfred A. Taubman College of Architecture and Urban Planning passed away last Monday at the University Hospital. He was 84. He came to the University from Ohio State University in 1979 and retired ten years later. He is survived by two children, Marvin of Minneapolis, Minnesota, and Minna of Tampa, Florida. Cremation has taken place. Contributions in Professor Rosenberg's memory may be made to the American Heart Association.

Damn, Rubin thought, there was a lot more to say about poor old Harry than that. He had served in the Army in World War II and had been in combat–Rubin thought it had been with the Greek underground. He had gone to architecture school on the G.I. Bill, somewhere in New York, Rubin remembered. He had been married twice, the first time to the mother of that awful Marvin and the Minna who had not, after all, come up to Ann Arbor, and that had ended in divorce. Then he had married again. Harry had been very happy with his second wife, Susan, a

Gentile, until her death of some sort of cancer almost thirty years ago in Columbus, well before Rubin and Harry had met. Harry had not only taught at both Ohio State and Michigan, he had been in private practice before that. As a professor, Harry had published a fair number of articles in architectural and real estate journals, and had served on various faculty committees (work that, to Rubin's considerable astonishment, Harry took very seriously and of which he was surprisingly proud), particularly on committees delving into ethical matters: proper relationships between faculty and sponsors, questions of conflict of interest, relationships between faculty and students. It was that last one that made Rubin grimace. He had had more than one affair with graduate students, including his own, and although he was sure that those had been poorly kept secrets, he still didn't believe that consensual sexual relations between people who were legal adults, whether they were supervisor and secretary, other people's spouses, teacher, student, regent, janitor, coach, cheerleader, athlete, straight, gay, citizen, alien, tall, short, or of different colors were even remotely the institution's business. Harry had vigorously disagreed. They had not quite quarreled about it, but it was as close to a quarrel as they ever came. "Come on, Harry," he had said testily. "I'm not talking about taking advantage either of underage adolescents or of emotionally volatile or vulnerable people, and yes, I know there are sexual predators of both sexes and all persuasions–straight, gay, and switch hitters. I'm talking about mature people who are sexually attracted to each other and who don't happen to share the official view that any sex outside the connubial bed is necessarily immoral, unethical, damnable, and institutionally corrosive. Do sponsoring agencies inquire about the applicant's marital fidelity? Do tenure committees? How is this nonsense different from the loyalty oaths of the fifties, for Christ's sake?"

"There is absolutely *no* relationship between those issues," Harry had snarled. "Loyalty oaths did not involve power relationships between individuals but conformity with the prevailing political ethos. They were ridiculous because no communist would have hesitated to sign them. The people who were offended by having their patriotism questioned were very often people who had already demonstrated their loyalty to this country."

"That's all very well," Rubin had answered, "but the question here is what business it is of the University if I decide to see whether Alice Horowitz is just teasing me or if she really would go to bed with me."

"Who is Alice Horowitz?"

"Who *was* Alice Horowitz? Peter Horowitz's wife and a graduate student in the Department and a damned good lay, as I was by no means the only one to find out. They eventually got divorced, several men after I was out of the picture, and he moved on to some school out west–I don't know what happened to her."

"Rubin," Harry had fumed, "sometimes you really disgust me." And he had gotten up–the argument had taken place in Rubin's living room–and stalked out. It had been a while before they saw each other again.

And now Harry was dead and here was his totally inadequate obituary. Rubin liked reading obituaries. Occasionally they were painfully fundamentalist, stating that George or whoever had gone to join the Lord in the room that Jesus had prepared for him–Heaven as a kind of Holiday Inn, with the Son of God as the manager, angels no doubt running vacuum cleaners and changing the sheets–and sometimes they were saccharine, suggesting, instead of grief calling for public acknowledgment, pride in the association with the wonderful person who had graced this Earth with his or her presence, as if the mourners' social status had been elevated accordingly. Rubin's all-time favorite obituary, which he had clipped and filed in a folder labeled "Miscellaneous," was one of a former colleague, running two full newspaper columns, amounting to a hymn not to God but to the man's virtues, talents, versatility, charm, brilliance, tact, grace, wit, on and on, composed and revised several times by its subject in the weeks preceding his death. It reminded Rubin of the old joke about the retirement dinner for the *shul's* venerable rabbi at which half a dozen speakers did homage to the old man's scholarship, wisdom, insight, strength, leadership, and so on, and when the last speaker was praising the rabbi's generosity of spirit, the rabbi, unable to contain himself any longer, jumped up and shouted angrily: "And what about my humility?" Rubin's delight in that story never diminished, no matter how often he told it.

But there was another obituary, also written by its subject, that Rubin truly admired, of a genuinely cheerful and generous man, an Episcopalian priest as certain of his prospects as he was joyful about them: "Well, at last!" his announcement of his death began. Rubin had not known the man and was immediately sorry he had not. There had been a spirit, he was convinced, whose joy in life as preparation for the joy to come would surely have cheered his parishioners everywhere, as these last words must also have done. Talk about arriving at the Pearly Gates with a smile! That sweet chariot must have been a gasser, as Louis Armstrong might have said, Rubin chuckled to himself.

Well, what about poor Harry? There had been no funeral, no service. Cremation, forbidden by Orthodox Judaism, was certainly not what

Harry would have wanted, but it had apparently not occurred to him to mention that in his will. No one sat *shivah*, no one recited the *kaddish*. Marvin, whose relationship with his father was apparently as poor as that with his other relatives, had insisted on simplicity, speed, and (a word Rubin had never really understood) "closure." The closure included inspection of Harry's condominium for items Marvin thought he or his sister might want, and, to Rubin, the quite astonishing revelation that Harry had willed a two-drawer metal file cabinet and its contents to his "good friend and neighbor Walter Rubin." The file cabinet was to be delivered when the realtor to whom Marvin had entrusted the sale of the condominium prepared it for inspection by potential purchasers. Marvin had told him nothing further.

He decided that he would not write a letter to the paper about Harry, at least not until he had had a chance to see what the file cabinet contained. He expected World War II memorabilia, perhaps some old photographs, maybe a diary, or even a manuscript of some sort. There was enough time to write a letter, if he decided that he should. Marvin would not approve, but Marvin would probably never see it, and to hell with Marvin anyway. Poor Harry. His children must have taken after their mother, of whom Harry had never spoken to Rubin. There was time.

The telephone's ring roused him from contemplating the letter he would not yet write. It was Evelyn. "I saw the paper this morning," she said, "to find your friend's obituary. Why didn't you tell me, Walter?"

He had told her, on the phone a day or two ago, about his trip to New York, his visit to Ellis Island, his reunion with the Parkers, even about the book he had bought and not yet finished reading, but not about what he had found waiting for him upon his return. The reason was simply that Evelyn, who was a year older than he was, took news of anyone's death very badly, whether she had known the person or not. She had met Harry several times and seemed to like him well enough, so Rubin had anticipated exactly the display of emotion now apparently in store for him, to be compounded by accusations of insensitivity. But of course he couldn't tell her that.

"I guess I wanted to absorb it myself first and then tell you about what happened at the Hospital and what happened later," he said, marveling, as he often did, at his ability to improvise. Too bad he had never had a chance to study music. "It was pretty grim, with Harry's awful son Marvin. I'm sorry, Evelyn, that I didn't tell you, but I think I was in something of a state of shock about it myself, maybe without fully realizing it. I'll tell you all about it, of course."

He could sense that she was adjusting her attitude from aggrieved to sympathetic. "His awful son Marvin?" she finally managed to ask.

"Yes," he said. "It was obvious that there was no filial emotion *there*. He was very put out at having to come in from Minnesota, at Harry's impending death, which seemed to be an awful imposition, at his sister in Florida, at his wife and her cats, and I think at me for having been his father's friend or not having taken care of everything for him, or maybe just because he needed to be angry at somebody. He was not easy to deal with, believe me."

"I'm sure he was terribly upset," Evelyn said.

"I'd like to think so, but I don't, not in the way you mean," Rubin said. "Anyway, what about dinner tonight? Do you have plans or shall we go out? I could pick you up around six thirty, how would that be?"

It worked. "That would be delightful," she said, clearly pleased by the turn the conversation had taken. "But let's not go to one of those awfully expensive places, this should just be a nice dinner, nothing fancy, all right?"

"You pick it," he said, pleased with himself. "See you at six thirty." The doorbell rang. He hung up and went to the door. It was a large man with Harry's bequest.

*****

The two-drawer metal file cabinet did indeed contain World War II memorabilia: some old photographs of Harry in uniform, by himself and with other American soldiers and men who, Rubin guessed, were Greek fighters, against a background of mountains and, in one instance, a burnt-out railroad car off its tracks; some medals that Rubin, a civilian all his life, could not identify; a packet of letters tied with a frayed string; and, to Rubin's surprise, a German pistol and a box of cartridges. He knew nothing about firearms, but the pistol, when he examined it, appeared to be in excellent condition. It was wrapped in some sort of oiled brown paper, cracked and crumbly in places, but the pistol was shiny and seemed perfectly functional. Rubin figured out how to make certain that it wasn't loaded–it wasn't–and re-wrapped it carefully. The cartridges were sure to be much too old to use. He caught himself, surprised again: why and for what did he want to use them? Was he planning to learn how to shoot at his age, or perhaps try to supplement his pension at the expense of a local bank? Anyway, there was a lot more in the file cabinet, and he replaced the pistol, the cartridges, the medals, the letters, and the photographs.

There was a file of Harry's reprints, articles, mostly, but also letters to editors of journals and newspapers and "in-house" publications issued by both universities for which Harry had worked. Rubin decided to examine them in due course, as he put it to himself. First he would conduct a general survey of the contents, aware that what he was really doing was assessing what *he* was going to leave if he could think of someone to leave it to when he had his stroke or heart attack or whatever it would be. How did Harry come to pick him as his legatee? And why these items? The reprints would have been more appropriately donated, Rubin thought, to the Architecture library, or still more appropriately to the trash bin, considering their age. The World War II memorabilia could have gone to a historical library, whether the University's or some other collection, with or without the pistol. What had made Harry think that Rubin would be interested in any of this, let alone want it? It wasn't as if Rubin didn't have plenty of stuff of his own, postcards, manuscripts, reprints, trinkets, paraphernalia, leftovers from his mother's possessions, gifts, souvenirs, and far too many books that he had no idea what to do with. He had a will, instructing Gerald (who, he had decided years ago, would not only survive him but would, however reluctantly, consent to dispose of his remains) to whom to offer the accumulations ("yes, to the Salvation Army and whatever waste disposal firm Ann Arbor has a contract with!" Gerald had shouted when Rubin had revealed how their friendship would end), but he really didn't care what happened to his "things," not now and certainly not later. He had not kept his deathbed promises to his mother about distributing certain of her treasures to certain of her friends, and for once he felt no guilt about it. The time to give something to somebody other than an institution was when both were alive and clear in the head. If you had children, they could get the money, if there was any, to help them get on with their lives—which was pretty much Marvin's attitude, he realized. And if you didn't, then leave the money and anything else of value to a good cause, a university or library or museum or hospital. Keep it simple. A friend of his, the lawyer in New York, was a specialist in inheritances, estates, and taxes, and knew exactly what a probate court was—Rubin was always uneasy about legal terms and thought that a probate court should examine the deceased's probity, not the final nastiness of a rich man's revenge upon his survivors—and Rubin's impression was that much of that kind of law had to do with figuring out how to keep dead people's money out of the pockets of the people they had liked least, former spouses, present children, greedy relatives, and governments of all kinds. Politicians made a great virtue of opposing what they called "the death tax" on behalf not of the people about to die but of those hoping to inherit. Those people not only voted but might also contribute to election campaigns.

There were some leather-bound notebooks which Rubin left for later, some family files apparently going back to the nineteenth century–Harry's parents had come from Russia as small children, fleeing the 1905 pogroms–and materials from the years Harry had been in private practice, drawings, maps, correspondence. Strange that he would have kept this stuff. On the other hand, who knew why anyone kept anything? His mother had kept some porcelain figurines that she had inherited from two aunts who had died before Rubin was born, and his mother had wrapped them carefully and brought them to the United States, along with some furniture and china and *Shabbat* candlesticks precious to her, and eventually she had her own apartment and displayed what she had saved from Europe to her admiring visitors, other refugee ladies who came for *Kaffee und Kuchen* and reminiscences. What the hell. She had polished the candlesticks and furniture lovingly and regularly, and Rubin had never questioned her affection for them or what they represented. Harry was entitled to similar respect.

There were separate files for his work at Ohio State and Michigan, and Rubin was about to reach for the Michigan files, thinking he might spot some familiar names, when he noticed that one of the Ohio State files was relatively fat and subdivided by colored folders. It had a label: **Nathan Goldstein**. Wasn't that the student Harry had told him about, whose story he had just related to Gerald in New York? He got up. It was time for a cup of coffee, and the file could be examined more leisurely at the kitchen table.

It was an accordion file, holding perhaps eight colored folders, subdivisions of various kinds: "Goldstein's Project: Questionnaire, Responses, Data Analysis"; "Committee Meetings;" "Correspondence, Notes on Phone Conversations;" "AIA Materials;" "Goldstein's Congressional Testimony;" "Clippings, Misc."; and a thin folder labeled "Prescott." It held a newspaper clipping–an Arnold Prescott, a former professor of architecture and president of the Architects Society of Ohio, had died suddenly–a lengthy obituary–that's ironic, Rubin thought–a copy of the death certificate–why in God's name did Harry have *that*?– and a printed program of the memorial service held at the departed's church. There were also some hand-written papers, notes of some kind, in a folder without a designation. What was an AIA? He looked at the contents and saw the stationery: American Institute of Architects. Aha, Rubin thought, this one will amount to something, not like pronouncements from the MLA or the Four C's, the Modern Language

Association and the Conference on College Composition and Communication. This one will have the unmistakable smell of serious money. No silly pretenses, as in the academy, of upholding the inviolable standards of pure scholarship. Where to begin? At the beginning. He would rearrange the files chronologically. To understand anything, how, for example, a man like him had to remove tufts of coarse simian hair from the tops and insides of his ears almost every day, it was helpful to remember that he was descended from creatures who probably gave no more thought to their appearance than did that Jew on Ellis Island who had disgusted him at the dining table. Evolution was not a steady uphill climb toward some ethereal condition, while flights of angels sang the traveler to his rest, but an uneven, haphazard, often accidental mix of progression and regression, emergence and disappearance, now very gradual, now astonishingly fast, with far too many variables at work to permit prediction of eventual destination. Aside from the macromolecular trail, all there was, concretely, were the fragments, the blurred traces, the debris of the more recent part of the journey. He remembered a couplet from a poem he had never published: *How hard it is to shape from shards More than a form the past retards.* So the first question was how Harry had met Goldstein, and what he thought of him. He set to work, arranging the dated materials with the earliest on top and putting aside undated papers–there didn't seem to be many–for later examination, for "content analysis," he thought, smiling dryly at his inability to escape academic language.

> Interesting meeting today with a student from Cleveland, a Jewish boy–I can't remember the last Jewish student we had and already I'm nervous about this one–who did his undergraduate work here. Don't think he took any courses from me, I would have remembered him. Tall, good-looking boy, nice manners, excellent record, but something about him seemed immature to me, maybe too trusting or even naive. He hasn't been in the Army.

That was Harry. His Army service had been of great importance to him, although he had never told Rubin much about it. The file had refreshed Rubin's recollections. Harry had been trained as a demolitions expert and, with some other American and British volunteers, had parachuted behind the lines in Greece after the Germans had bailed the Italians out and occupied the country. Harry and his unit had fought with the Greek underground, blowing up German troop trains and killing the bastards however he could. Harry wouldn't have put it that way. Harry was an American, not a refugee. Harry hadn't personally known any of his aunts, uncles, and cousins murdered by the Nazis, and Harry's father had not disappeared during *Kristallnacht.* Rubin had never figured out what, exactly, the Germans represented to Harry. Well, Harry was as dead as the Germans he'd killed, and eventually what mattered was who was left alive.

Like this Nathan Goldstein. Tall and good-looking? Maybe, but Harry had been short–five six if he stood very straight, which he always did–and although stocky and muscular, not good-looking. A craggy face, a big nose, eyes set too close together. Still, there had been something about Harry: he somehow seemed authoritative, sure of himself and his subject, whatever it was. Rubin thought that he probably had been an effective teacher, well-organized, comprehensive, responsive to well-considered questions, fair, punctual. In a word, Rubin grinned to himself, military.

The next item was just a list of names: "Goldstein's Committee, Contacts, etc." The only name that meant anything to Rubin was Prescott, about whose death Harry had a separate file. He had died suddenly. Was Harry suspicious about the manner of Prescott's death? It suddenly occurred to Rubin that perhaps Harry thought that Goldstein had had something to do with it. Goldstein had not finished his project, Rubin remembered, and his committee or someone on his committee had stopped him. Whatever the reason, Goldstein must have been not just disappointed but furious. The study was no doubt the most important thing Goldstein had ever undertaken, and it was probably intended as the spring board for what was to have been a brilliant and lucrative career. What had happened to Goldstein instead? He had failed the licensing examination several times. He had lost an appeal to the State Board. He had eventually gotten his license and gone into private practice, emerging from obscurity for a brief moment to tell his story, such as it was, to a Congressional subcommittee at a sparsely attended hearing which had had no known effect. And then he had faded, like most people, into whatever unremarkable course his life had taken, listening to no accolades but his own.

Like Rubin. Like Harry. Like most people. But maybe he had done something that neither Rubin nor Harry nor most people had ever done, not even Harry blowing up German troop trains in Greece: maybe Goldstein had gotten even for personal reasons. Was that what Harry had suspected? Did he have proof? Was he afraid? Why had he kept this pistol and these cartridges all these years? No, that was silly: the pistol was most likely a trophy, a scalp wrested from a fallen enemy, a remembrance of Harry's heroic youth, having nothing to do with events taking place half a world away more than a quarter of a century later.

Rubin glanced at his watch. It was later than he'd thought, almost six o'clock, and he was to pick Evelyn up at six thirty. He had to bathe, shave, and pick something to wear–Evelyn always commented on his clothes, especially if he wore a tie she had given him. He didn't feel like wearing a tie tonight. Maybe a turtle neck, slacks, a sports jacket, as if he were fifty-five instead of seventy-five. He sighed, arranged the papers in several piles on the far end of the kitchen table–where Harry used to sit, he realized, when he came for tea or coffee--and headed for his bathroom.

*****

"Oh, I like that tie!" Evelyn exclaimed when she opened her door to his ring. She lived across town in a well-maintained neat house in a well-maintained neat neighborhood. It was not a really expensive neighborhood–there were no McMansions nor any of the solid houses from the nineteen twenties within a mile or two from campus, whose value had rocketed to unbelievable amounts in the last two or three decades–but they were nice, rather predictable houses with flowers and bushes in front and small yards behind, somehow projecting middle-class respectability. The people who lived in them paid their bills on time and had adequate health insurance, even now. Evelyn's husband had been a professor in the School of Business Administration and had known something about investments. Her house had been paid off many years ago. She drove a nice car. She was generous to her children and grandchildren. Her husband had left her in a comfortable position, comfortable enough so that she could visit a daughter in Hawaii and another in Florida at least once each winter. Rubin had hinted that he would be receptive to an invitation to join her in Hawaii but so far she had just seemed to regard his enthusiasm for her photographs and picture postcards as the normal reaction to gorgeous scenery anywhere. At least she hadn't invited him to visit her at her daughter's in Florida. Rubin had been to Florida and despised it.

"Of course you do," he said, smiling, and leaning forward to kiss her cheek. "That's why you gave it to me."

She smiled. "Yes, that's true," she said. "Come in. Do you want something to drink before we go? A glass of wine? White or red?"

"No, thanks," Rubin said. "I'm rather hungry, although I don't know why–it's not as if I had missed any meals recently. Did you decide where we're going?"

"Let's go to that Middle Eastern place on the east side," Evelyn said. "I'm in the mood for some sort of shawarma and rice. Is that all right? Would you rather go somewhere else?"

"No, that's fine," Rubin said. "What's that place called–Scheherezade's or something equally literary?"

"No, that's what it used to be called, but it was sold recently and renamed Jericho's Wall, I think. I don't know if it's been remodeled or if they have a new chef or different menu, but they do have a new sign and when I drove by the other day on my way to Ypsilanti they seemed to have refinished the parking lot."

"Jericho's Wall! Let's hope that Joshua isn't playing the trumpet tonight!"

Evelyn looked puzzled. Literary allusions were not her strong point. "They don't have a band there, Walter," she said.

"Just as well," Rubin grinned. "It would be too much ethnicity for me." He helped her on with her coat and escorted her to the Chrysler, opening the door for her. A nice, elderly, old-fashioned couple, he thought, as she settled into the curved leather seat. He knew she liked his car. Hers was several years older, and although perfectly adequate, not nearly as luxurious. She was careful with her money. On the way to the restaurant he told her about Harry's stroke, Marvin at the hospital, and subsequent developments, but he did not mention the two-drawer metal file cabinet.

Jericho's Wall hadn't been totally transformed from Scheherezade's, but the walls had been painted with new murals and Rubin recognized the Dome of the Rock, the Al-Aqsa Mosque, and a market scene in East Jerusalem. Another mural depicted a dusty street, sunlight almost bouncing off the walls of the buildings. Three or four men were lounging or crouching in the shade of a wall that ran off the picture. Jericho's Wall? Resistance fighters? Hamas? The previous owners had been Lebanese; the new owners obviously were not. Rubin felt a twinge of uneasiness, and then he felt annoyed with himself. He was never uneasy, he reminded himself, when they went to a German restaurant. In fact, then he liked to show off his remaining German to whatever waiter or waitress seemed to be German. They usually weren't, but he got to say *Sauerbraten und Rotkohl*, rolling the *R* so that Evelyn would roll her eyes. Why be uneasy here? Nothing but absurd guilt, as Gerald would have been quick to assert. He helped Evelyn off with her coat, hung it up with his own on a coat rack near the door, and followed Evelyn to the table she selected. The restaurant, he noticed, was half-empty. They would be conspicuous. The place was well-lit and clean, reminding him of Hemingway's story. A waiter approached: young, swarthy, lean, handsome, mustachioed.

"Good evening," the waiter said with just a faint accent. "Welcome to Jericho's Wall. Have we had the pleasure of serving you on a previous occasion?" Rubin groaned inwardly but Evelyn was delighted. "We used to come here once in a while when it was Scheherezade's," she said, "but this is our first visit since it's changed ownership. You've made a lot of changes, haven't you?"

"Yes, quite a few," the waiter said. "Especially on the menu, as you will see. May I bring you something to drink? Coffee or tea? Water? A soft drink, perhaps? We don't have a liquor license yet." He put two menus on the table and looked inquiringly at them.

"Perhaps later," Evelyn said. "Water will be just fine for now. Walter?"

"Yes, a glass of water, thank you," Rubin said. He had spotted the man behind the cash register and had recognized him. He was the older man he had seen first in the restaurant the Parkers had taken him to in Manhattan, with three other Arabs, and then the next day at LaGuardia. One of the other three men had been his cab driver from Ellis Island. To his surprise, Rubin remembered his name: Hashem Iskandar. Impulsively, he turned to the waiter, but the young man had gone to bring them their glasses of water and some pita and hummus.

"Walter?" Evelyn asked. "Is something wrong? You look as if you had just thought of something?"

"I've seen that man before," Rubin said. "The man behind the counter, at the cash register. I saw him in New York. Twice, in fact. Odd, he must have been on his way here."

Evelyn turned to look at the man behind the counter, then glanced inquiringly at Rubin. "It's just a coincidence, I'm sure," she said. "Where did you see him?"

Rubin explained, mentioning Hashem Iskandar, but not going into detail about their conversation or his internal conflicts. He had learned early in their relationship that Evelyn was not curious about what it meant to be either a Jewish refugee or a secular Jew with rather pronounced prejudices against all forms of religion or, for that matter, a Jew of any kind. That was all right with him: he knew a lot of Gentiles, mostly white but not all, who felt exactly the same way. Once you knew where the boundaries where, what walls not to try to breach, as it were, you could have completely satisfactory relationships with people whose beliefs or practices struck you, in themselves, as totally irrational. Evelyn occasionally went to church, some sort of Presbyterian congregation in a building that could only be described as very substantial. Laura Parker went to an AME church with her mother whenever she visited the old lady in Nashville. Rubin understood that rather more readily than Evelyn's pleasure in maintaining her membership in the First or Twenty-third or whatever it was Presbyterian. Some denominations–Unitarian or Amish or Mormon or Quaker –seemed to him to have either too much theology or not nearly enough, like Chassidism or the Jewish Cultural Society. He had avoided discussions of religion with Harry because he knew that Harry would have been irritated both by his ignorance of tradition, ritual, and Jewish learning, and by his inability to suppress his scepticism. Aside from fellow atheists or agnostics, Rubin was actually most comfortable with Roman Catholics, whether they were fallen, nominal, or devout. The first usually retained affection for their parents' beliefs because that is how they remembered their parents. The second were much like himself, always ready to declare an identity in the name of a religion, regardless of the facts of the case. And the third were secure in their fortress of faith Rubin wouldn't ever question, not even with the help of Sam Harris. Evelyn's Presbyterianism wasn't a serious disability, and besides, her Christmas and Easter celebrations inevitably involved her cooking, of which Rubin was very fond.

Evelyn ordered a shawarma plate with lamb, and Rubin, true to his declaration of hunger, ordered a combination plate: shish kabob, shish tawook, shish kafta, and grape leaves stuffed with ground lamb. The food was delicious. The waiter stopped at their table several times to inquire about their satisfaction and bask in their compliments. They decided to skip dessert but to have tea with lemon, and that too was very good. Rubin felt relaxed and confident. When the waiter stopped at their table again to ask if they wanted more tea and to place the bill discreetly at Rubin's elbow, he asked him if the man at the cash register was the owner.

"Yes, he is, he is my uncle," the waiter replied. "Would you like to meet him?"

"I would indeed," Rubin said. "Not that I don't trust you to convey our delight, it's just that I'd like to tell him personally."

"Certainly, sir," the waiter said, smiling and turning away.

"Here," Rubin said, stopping him and returning the check with his credit card and a ten dollar bill, aware that it was a generous tip.

"Thank you very much," the waiter said. "One moment and I will ask my uncle to come over." He went to the man at the cash register.

Rubin found Evelyn looking at his with some surprise. "Do you mind?" he asked her. "No, not at all," she said. "It was very good. But I've never known you to do anything like this."

Rubin shrugged. "Just an impulse," he said. The waiter came back followed by the older man, who was smiling broadly. "This is my uncle, Mr. Alhumaidi, the owner of Jericho's Wall," the waiter said. He put Rubin's credit card, bill, and receipt on the table. Rubin pocketed the card and receipt and signed the bill. Mr. Alhumaidi stuck his hand out, murmuring "You enjoyed your meal?" "It was excellent," Rubin said, shaking his hand. "I'm Walter Rubin, this is Mrs. Broadhurst, and we both enjoyed our meals very much. We'll tell our friends, you can be sure." Mr. Alhumaidi smiled at Evelyn and said, "So glad you found everything satisfactory. You like Middle Eastern food?"

"Oh, yes," Evelyn said. "Almost all of it–Arab, Turkish, Persian, we love it." Rubin winced at the combination. Evelyn's ecumenical approach to cuisine might have unpleasant political overtones in this setting. But Mr. Alhumaidi exhibited no discomfort. "Good, good," he said, and, as Rubin and Evelyn rose, held Evelyn's chair for her. "Thank you," Evelyn said. As they made their way to the coat rack, Rubin turned back to Mr. Alhumaidi. "By the way," he said, smiling, "how's Hashem Iskandar?"

He saw at once that he had made a serious mistake. Mr. Alhumaidi's face turned darker and his black eyes glittered at Rubin for a long moment. "You know Iskandar?" he growled. His voice was suddenly different. His friendly demeanor had disappeared. Rubin couldn't understand what he had done.

"I saw you with him in a Manhattan restaurant not long ago," he managed to say. "I had met him earlier that day–but he didn't see me in the restaurant," he finished lamely. Mr. Alhumaidi didn't answer but kept glaring at Rubin. "Well, thanks again for a great meal," Rubin said, taking Evelyn's arm and turning toward the door, "good night!" "Good night!" Evelyn added, stepping out quickly with Rubin and leaving Mr. Alhumaidi quivering with hostility behind them. She's noticed, Rubin thought–but it was too obvious to be missed. Is she going to comment?

"What happened there, Walter?" she said when he had started the Chrysler and eased it toward the exit of the parking lot. "He was so charming and then suddenly when you asked him about that cab driver, he got so cold–maybe they are enemies, you know, different tribes or religions or whatever it is with Arabs–well, we can't go there again!"

"I have no idea," Rubin said, pulling too quickly into traffic. The driver he had cut off blew his horn at him angrily. Goddamnit, Rubin thought, that's two men who've wanted to hit me in about two minutes. I'm too old for this. I've been too old for this for many years. At least Evelyn didn't say anything.

"Be careful, Walter," Evelyn said.

He tensed his jaw. "Sorry," he said. "I don't know what was eating Alhumaidi or whatever his name is–as far as I could tell in New York, there wasn't anything between him and the others, no argument or anything like that. He was doing all the talking. But not only was I too far away to hear anything, I wouldn't have understood it anyway."

"No, of course not. But we can't go there again. That's too bad, it really was delicious."

"Well, I have to admit that I would feel pretty awkward going back," Rubin acknowledged. "We'll just have to write it off as another impenetrable mystery we'll never solve, like so many others puzzling us in these our golden years." Even as he tried to put a light spin on whatever had happened, he realized that he didn't think it was funny and that he still had Harry's possible suspicions of Nathan Goldstein on his mind. He regretted his words at once.

"Another mystery? What do you mean?"

He hesitated. He certainly wasn't going to tell her about Harry Rosenberg and Nathan Goldstein when he hadn't yet had a chance to look into whatever had occurred in Columbus all those years ago, if anything had. "Oh, you know," he said. "Don't you feel sometimes, when you look back at things you've seen or things that happened, that what you once thought you understood you're no longer so sure about, or what you didn't really understand at the time hasn't become any clearer in the intervening years? You've probably come to accept some things without understanding them very well, as I have. Those kinds of mysteries."

"Yes," Evelyn said thoughtfully. "I've had to accept a number of things I really don't understand, about Lizzie in particular, but some other people too." Lizzie was her younger daughter, the one in Florida. Rubin had met her when she and her two children had visited Evelyn in the summer, and Lizzie was, as she liked to put it, very much her own person. She certainly wasn't her husband's: they had divorced years ago.

"Who else?" Rubin asked. He knew that Evelyn wanted to expand the view that he had suggested.

Evelyn didn't answer right away. That usually meant that she was thinking about William, her late husband. He was right.

"There were some things about William," Evelyn said slowly, "things I never understood, you know personal things, Walter, I don't want to go into details--"

"Sex, you mean," Rubin said.

"Well, yes, mostly, but there was more to it, I think–you know, I never was quite sure, but I think it had to do with the way William was brought up by his mother–did I ever tell you that William never knew his father?"

"Yes, you did."

"He never knew his father. I don't know what that would mean to a boy growing up at that time, you know, in the twenties and then the Depression. It couldn't have been easy, of course. At least William didn't have any siblings. But that meant that he was all his mother had. That couldn't have been healthy."

"Oh, I don't know," Rubin said. "That's pretty much how I grew up in this country, just a few years later."

"Yes, you told me," Evelyn said, "but you had known your father in Germany, before all that awfulness, so that's really quite different. I mean, you remember your father. William never knew his father."

"Yes, I remember my father," Rubin said.

"Well then. Anyway, I thought for some years, and maybe I was right, that William's– umm– peculiarities isn't quite the right word–had to do with the way his mother brought him up, but I was never really too sure. Maybe not. So it will stay a mystery. Now Lizzie, that's another story entirely."

The lights in Rubin's rearview mirror seemed unusually bright. He adjusted it. "How do you mean?" he asked.

"Oh, she was always independent," Evelyn said. "I used to think that William tended to spoil her, especially in comparison with the way he was with Helen, you know, Lizzie was the little one, but I don't think it was William so much as it was Lizzie. She could always be awfully determined to have her own way, to do things her way, when she wanted to do them and not a moment before. Her teachers used to tell us that too. I don't know where she got that from. Helen was hardly ever any trouble at all, and William and I were reasonable, I think, certainly we tried to be, but Lizzie just had to do things her way or not at all. I think that was a large part of the trouble with her marriage, she just couldn't understand that having her way meant that she was bossing Jim around, at least that's how he saw it until finally he couldn't stand it any longer and left."

Rubin had heard much of this before, but Evelyn hadn't finished. He knew the next turn her mind would take just as he turned the Chrysler into her street. The car behind him, he noticed, turned as well.

"What I'm worried about," Evelyn continued, "is how she's bringing up those children. She thinks that they should be independent and make their own decisions and that's how they'll learn to take responsibility for their own lives, but what she doesn't see is that they're likely to make some terrible mistakes at their age and with all these modern social pressures, and then it will be too late."

Rubin pulled into Evelyn's driveway. The car behind him drove slowly further down the street. He couldn't make out what it was. He got out of the car, came around it, and opened Evelyn's door. "Thank you, kind sir," she said. "Are you coming in?" He had left the engine running and was surprised by the question. "I'm really rather tired," he said, "but I'd love to have a rain check, even though it's not raining."

"All right," she said. She seemed vaguely disappointed. She could talk about her daughters and her grandchildren for hours on end. He walked her to the door. "Good night, then, Evelyn," he said. "I'll call you very soon." She offered him her cheek and he kissed it. "Good night, Walter," she said. "The meal was great even if his behavior was strange!" "Yes, it was," Rubin said. "Good night!"

He got back into his car and drove down the street in the same direction he had come. There was the car that had followed him, across the street, pointed in the opposite direction. The driver must have anticipated that Rubin would turn the Chrysler around in the street outside of Evelyn's house so that he could follow it. Rubin sped up, turned a corner, drove quickly to the end of the block, doused the lights, turned another corner, and waited. He saw a car rush by on the street he had just left. He waited a few more minutes. No cars came in either direction. Hew drove home, circling his condominium's area before pulling through the parking lot to his garage. No one was in sight. He remembered Harry's German pistol and wondered how he was going to obtain ammunition for it.

Chapter VII
Nathan, July, 1974

In July, 1974, two weeks after Nathan had turned 25, and had finished his MBA at Case Western Reserve University in Cleveland, he took a vacation from his job with a small architectural firm in Cleveland Heights, and, with his girlfriend, Nora Sheppard, went to a KOA campground some twenty-five miles west of Toronto. Nora was in her second year at the Cleveland Institute of Art. They had met when Nora walked up to Nathan, who was playing Frisbee with a friend on the lawn adjacent to his Overlook Road apartment building in Cleveland Heights, and introduced herself. Nathan was very glad she did: Nora was stunning.

The KOA campground was almost full. People had come in campers pulled by or perched on pickup trucks, or in recreational vehicles, or with tents, and there were even a few only with sleeping bags. Nathan and Nora had his old tent and two sleeping bags, serving as mattress and blanket, and had taken full advantage of the tent's privacy during the night. They had planned to rise at dawn, with a whole day's sightseeing ahead of them. In particular, Nora, whose major was sculpture, wanted to visit the Henry Moore Sculpture Centre at the Art Gallery of Ontario, as well as the Royal Ontario Museum whose East Asian Galleries are famous for their collections of Chinese art and archeological artifacts. Nathan's top priority was the Ontario Science Center. But when they woke to the sounds of the world outside their tent, birds, voices, a motorcycle engine, bits of conversation from their neighbors in a camper hitched to a pickup truck, their desires were reignited, and they made love even while the odor of the bacon sizzling on their neighbors' charcoal grille drifted over them. When they finished and fell apart, breathing heavily, they realized that the family preparing its breakfast was separated from them only by the tent and a few feet of grass. They glanced at each other with mutual amusement and embarrassment, wondering how noisy they had been. "Never mind," Nora whispered, "they're too busy with their own appetites to have been disturbed by ours." "I hope you're right," Nathan whispered back, "Because now I've got to go out there, say hello, and start our own breakfast." "Fine," Nora said, still whispering, "you take care of the diplomacy and I'll take a shower." They grinned at the division of labor, put on enough clothing to go outside, and set about their tasks.

The night at the KOA camp was to be the first of two, for Nora had never been in Toronto before, and Nathan's previous visits to the city had been too brief to satisfy his curiosity. Toronto was much bigger and varied than Cleveland, with a wonderful variety of peoples from all over the world, and yet it combined a unity, a civility, and an energy in ways that Nathan had not experienced in his own country. New York, for instance, was certainly energetic, but nobody would characterize it as civil. On the other hand, Southern or Southwestern cities known for hospitality and friendliness were not famous for their energy. As for unity, what seemed most apparent about cities in the States, North or South, was their racial divide. Nathan had been trained as an architect to observe not only where people lived but how they managed to do so, in physical terms, and that training had been both refined in some ways and broadened in others by his study of organizational principles and successful business practices. But this was a vacation with Nora, and he would try hard not to lecture her about alternatives in urban development. As soon as he thought of the phrase, he realized it sounded like a seminar, and chuckled to himself. But if he had already spent too much time in school, why had he made up his mind to go back for more? He broke the eggs into the frying pan and concentrated on having breakfast ready by the time Nora reappeared from her shower, fresh, lovely, and ravenous.

Toronto fascinated them both, and much of their conversation that evening had to do with what they had seen and what they still wanted to see. That led to other places they wanted to visit, first in North America, and then, as their imaginations soared, anywhere, regardless of distance, cost, or obligations.

"OK, seriously, now, Nathan," Nora said. "Have you decided what you're going to do this year?"

Nathan had been talking about the Seven Wonders of the World, and suddenly he was brought back to Cleveland Heights. He sighed. "Well, I had been thinking that I'd continue to work in Cleveland," he said. "But I think I've changed my mind. I've been looking into architectural licensing. It turns out that a number of states are beginning to consider requiring a professional architectural degree as a prerequisite even to take their licensing exams, and this might also affect reciprocity. My

B.S. in Architecture, which represents a four-year program, isn't considered a professional degree."

Nora looked concerned. "So what do you think you're going to do? What is a professional degree?"

"A five-year Bachelor's and a six-year Master's. I've got an appointment with an assistant dean at the School of Architecture in Columbus next week. Depending on what he tells me, and how it goes, you know, generally, I'm seriously considering continuing my education there for my Master's in architecture. But I want to find out what graduate business credits they might accept at OSU from Case Western to help meet the elective requirements. I've already got quite a bit of work and money invested in those credits."

Nora was silent. Nathan had known that his answer, as gently as he had tried to phrase it, would lead to an inevitable question. She asked it.

"What about us? I was hoping that we could continue to see each other."

"Yes, that's what I'd like too, Nora," Nathan said. "I really care about you. I have family in Cleveland, your family lives close to Columbus, they're not that far from each other anyway, and my Mustang runs well, as you saw. Since we'd both be in school, we'd both be busy with our work, but we'd probably have breaks at more or less the same time, certainly for Thanksgiving and Christmas. So our vacations should be just about the same. We'd go to the Greek islands or the Great Wall or the Pyramids, as we were just saying," he smiled, trying to lighten her mood.

"I really don't want you to leave Cleveland," Nora said, "but I do understand. I could visit you at Ohio State, right?"

"Of course!" Nathan said quickly. "I would want you to visit. I'd show you around–and I'd show you off–for instance, Brown Hall, where the School of Architecture is located–"

"Oh, I'd like to see Brown Hall," Nora interrupted, "but I want to see the fun things too. You know, the student hangouts, the bars. Your apartment."

"My apartment?"

"Yes, your apartment," Nora said, smiling. Then she leaned over and kissed him.

That Friday, July 12, major American newspapers printed excerpts from the enormous report issued by the House of Representatives' Judiciary Committee about the abuses of power committed by the Nixon administration, then in its second term. Deception and corruption had apparently become the *modus operandi* at the highest levels of government. Impeachment of the President of the United States was moving more and more rapidly from possibility to probability. Nathan, whose interest in national politics was at best mild, and who was not, in any case, a supporter of Richard Nixon, enjoyed his blissful weekend.

*****

A few days later Nathan parked his car in The Ohio State University garage near 15th Avenue and High Street and proceeded toward Brown Hall for his one o'clock meeting with Professor Frank Wilson, the assistant dean he had mentioned to Nora. He had known Wilson when he had been an undergraduate at the School of Architecture, but not well, and had no particular impression of him. But he was glad that he was seeing Wilson rather than the dean, Charles Webber, a brusque, rather unpleasant man. Webber didn't seem to like students much, and he apparently was also regarded as intimidating by his office staff, Peggy Pearsall and some other ladies. Now Peggy, there was someone he liked and who liked him. He opened the door to the Dean's office and there she was.

"Nathan Goldstein!" she cried out warmly. "It's been a long time! How *are* you?" She came toward him to give him a hug. He was pleased: she didn't give hugs out freely.

"Fine, Peggy, I'm great, happy to be here," he answered. "How are you? How are things?" He glanced to the left, at the door to the Dean's private office.

"I'm fine too, Nathan," Peggy said. "Nothing much has changed, he still keeps us hopping around, especially at budget time. You're here for your appointment with Dean Wilson?"

"Yes, I am," Nathan said. "I want to explore the possibility of graduate work, Peggy! You'd have to put up with me for quite a while again!"

"Oh, I think we could manage that," Peggy said. "Coffee? Tea? I hope you had lunch?"

He hadn't, but found it easier to tell her that he had, rather than munch a donut. He accepted a cup of tea. She wanted to know what he had been doing and he told her about his job in Cleveland. At exactly one o'clock the door to the right, to the assistant dean's office, opened and Wilson came out. "Mr. Goldstein?" he asked. "Yes," Nathan said quickly, breaking off in mid-sentence to Peggy and nodding to her–he knew she understood. She seemed a little flustered, anyway, probably because Wilson had opened his door before she could announce Nathan's arrival. The sixties and early seventies had changed many things on many college campuses in the country, but deans were still deans, staff were still staff, and the status of ex-students remained indeterminate until they made their wants known.

Nathan found, however, that Wilson had done his homework, having read his letter carefully and studied his transcripts. "There's no problem," Wilson told him. "You received both your undergraduate degrees from Ohio State, in architecture and business administration, your grades toward your MBA at Case Western are excellent, and your application to enroll in our Master's program in September is certain to be approved by the admissions committee."

Nathan was delighted. "I do have a question," he said, "about how many credits I might be able to transfer from the MBA program to meet the requirements for the elective credits for the Master's of Architecture here."

"Forty quarter hours," Wilson replied. "I've already looked into that. You'd need only fifty quarter hours more. So you've already earned almost half of your total required credits."

Nathan flushed with pleasure. "Great, that's great, more than I expected!" he said. "I can tell you right now that I'll definitely enroll. Thanks very much! But I do still have a couple of questions."

"Yes, go ahead," Wilson said.

"Well, of those fifty quarter hours, how many would be for core course work?"

"Thirty-five," Wilson said. "That would leave fifteen quarter hours. You could elect those in courses directly related to the architectural curriculum, which is what I'd suggest."

Nathan hesitated. He had come to what was for him the key question, even though he had already and emphatically told Wilson that he would enroll. He hoped to avoid specifics at this point–they'd be premature and might prejudice developments.

"Professor Wilson," he said, "as you can see from my transcripts, my undergraduate business major was marketing. In my graduate work in business, I focused on organizational behavior. For those fifteen quarter hours we're talking about, would the School of Architecture be open to my designing an independent study project, combining architecture, marketing, and organizational behavior? I know I'd have to come up with some sort of research design, of course, and formulate the objectives very clearly, but I just want to raise the question in general terms at this point."

Wilson considered the question. "You don't have anything specific in mind yet?" he asked.

"No," Nathan said. "Do you think the School would be open to something like that, or is that too much of a departure from tradition?"

"No, I don't think so at all," Wilson said. "We've engaged in collaborative work with other units several times, and it's not unusual elsewhere. John Wade, the dean at Milwaukee, has been pushing sociology and economics as part of his undergraduate curriculum, and Leon Pastalan at Michigan is a professor of architecture despite his not being an architect. He's a sociologist, as I remember. His specialty is actually gerontology, and his interest is in designing space and spatial arrangements that will accommodate the elderly and their needs. He's made quite a reputation for himself, deservedly so. So I don't think that what you might develop along the lines of business practices or however it goes would be at all radical here. But your faculty advisor, who hasn't been assigned yet, would of course have to approve and be closely involved."

"Of course," Nathan agreed.

Wilson was seized by an idea. "I know who'd be interested in this!" he exclaimed. "Prescott! Do you know Arnold Prescott?" Nathan shook his head. "He's an Adjunct Professor and doesn't teach full time," Wilson continued, "and has his own practice here in town–but what really convinces me that he'd be the ideal man for you to work under is that he's also the President of the Architects Society of Ohio. *Lots* of contacts everywhere, throughout Ohio, of course, but also in Washington, at the AIA. The only trouble is that he's very busy, as you'd expect. But I know he'd be interested in this–what do you think about having *two* advisors?"

"Two?" Nathan was surprised. Sounds like double trouble, he thought.

"Yes, I don't know that Arnold would agree to take you on in a big project by himself–architecture is more and more a collaborative enterprise, as I'm sure you'll agree, with your business background. But he's definitely the one you should work with. I have it!" Wilson was clearly in a creative mood, ideas lighting up like fireworks. "Harry Rosenberg! You know him, of course."

Why 'of course,' Nathan wondered. "I know his name, and I think I know him by sight," he said, "but I haven't actually taken any classes from him." Wilson seemed astonished. "I think he was on sabbatical when I had planned to take one of his courses," Nathan explained.

"Well, I'll talk to both Arnold and Harry on your behalf," Wilson said. "I think it will work out. They get along, so don't worry about getting caught in the middle, as sometimes happens." Nathan thought it best to look blank. "But there should be somebody from the business program," Wilson added. "Is there someone over there you'd like me to ask to serve on this committee, which is what it's getting to be? Or still better, that you could ask?"

"Yes, Professor Goodman, Maxwell Goodman, in the College of Administrative Science. I think we had a very good relationship. I'd be happy to ask him–he always seemed to like my work, and he's regarded as one of the top marketing professors in the country. His book is used almost everywhere. Well, on a great many campuses, anyway." Nathan was delighted by the conversation. Everything seemed to be falling into place. "I'd be glad to ask him," he repeated.

"Good, do that then, and I'll talk to Arnold and Harry, as I said," Wilson said. "That will work out well, I think. I've heard of Goodman but I haven't met him, so it's just as well that you talk to him. Now I'd like to ask a few questions too."

"Of course," Nathan said.

"Are you currently employed in Cleveland?"

"Yes, I am, and have been for some time," Nathan said. He named the three firms he'd worked for in the last two years.

"Good, so you have practical experience. Have you told your current employer that you're planning to return to school this fall?"

"No, I wanted to meet with you first," Nathan said.

"Yes, that makes sense, but now I want you to inform your employer of your decision as soon as you can. It's very important that we maintain good relations with practitioners throughout the state."

"I understand," Nathan said. "I'll tell them when I go back to work on Wednesday."

"Good, that'll be fine," Wilson said. "Now what about housing? Do you want our Housing Bureau to help you find something suitable?"

"No, that's not necessary," Nathan said. "I've lived alone in the past couple of years and prefer that to roommates or a dormitory, and I know the area quite well, I think. I was planning to look for a small apartment after our meeting."

Wilson smiled. "So you were pretty sure that things would work out?"

"Well, I certainly hoped so," Nathan said.

"All right, then, I think that's it. You should have the letter confirming your admission and the details we've discussed within a few days–the Admissions Committee can handle this with me on the phone– and I'll call them this afternoon or in the morning. Please send your acceptance letter back to me just as quickly as you can. Oh, by the way, here's a stroke of luck: we have an office available that you could use for your independent study project, so include a request for office space in that connection in your acceptance letter. That way I'll be able to justify, even though it'll be *post facto*, assigning the space to a graduate student, which is very unusual. I think only two graduate students have had their own offices in the past, at least since I've been in this position."

"After the fact?" Nathan didn't understand.

"That's the way things work, everywhere. The university is no exception. First the agreement, then the paperwork. What matters is what the record shows, and that will be the date of your request. That's another reason for you to get that acceptance letter back to me ASAP. I'm certain that somebody, probably a retired professor, is going to ask me for that office for this year, so if I can tell him that I've already assigned it to someone for a research project, that will save me a hassle I just don't need."

"I see," Nathan said, grateful for the explanation and even more for the office space. "Thanks very much again! I'll be certain to request space for the project in my letter, then, and I'll get it to you by return mail, you can be sure."

"Good, I think we've settled everything then, Nathan," Wilson said. Nathan was pleased that he had progressed from Mr. Goldstein to his first name. He rose, shook Wilson's proffered hand, thanked him again, and left, telling Peggy how well things had gone. "Better than perfect!" he told her. In the afternoon he found a wonderful loft-style apartment in the west quadrant off campus at a price he could afford. The two-story unfurnished apartment had an open-ceiling living room and a kitchen with space for a dining table and chairs on the first floor, and a bedroom and bathroom on the second. The bedroom was open to and overlooked the living room, separated by the stairs and a guard rail. Better than perfect, he said to himself. He liked the phrase almost as much as his new circumstances.

The next week, on July 24, the Supreme Court of the United States, with an 8-0 vote, ruled that the President had to furnish sixty-four tapes to the Special Prosecutor, now Leon Jaworski, investigating what had become known as the Watergate burglary. The tapes had been secretly recorded in the Oval Office two years previously. Nathan saw the headline in the paper, but only glanced at the article below it.

*****

Two months later, Nathan settled into his new apartment, found a few additional items of furniture he thought he needed–a spare bureau for his bedroom so that overnight guests could be comfortably accommodated, for instance–and made separate appointments to meet with Professors Prescott, Rosenberg, and Goodman. Classes would not start until the following week but most professors were already in their offices, making preparations, organizing files, duplicating handouts, putting on their armor, as Nathan remembered overhearing one saying when he had arrived early one September in one of his undergraduate years. It wasn't clear whether the professors were the besieged Trojans warding off the invading Greeks, or, instead, the Greeks themselves, assaulting the students' ignorance by force or by stratagem. But Nathan liked the image either way. Hector at the xerox copier, Achilles preparing overheads. The first days of September brought the usual, almost tangible excitement on campus everywhere, in the buildings, on the lawns, people greeting each other again after the long summer, eager to start despite their protestations to the contrary. The days were still very warm but the nights were cooler, and talk of the coming football season was almost obligatory, even among people whose interest in the game, the team, the tradition, was at best perfunctory. Football was a much more pleasant subject than what had happened three weeks earlier in the nation's capital, where Gerald Ford had just become President. But Nathan avoided both topics as best as he could.

His first appointment was with Maxwell Goodman on the third floor of Hagerty Hall, a four-story tan brick-and-stone building in which Nathan had taken most of his undergraduate business courses. Most faculty offices were off the same corridors that students took to the classrooms. The arrangement did not facilitate conversations in the faculty offices once classes began, and Nathan was glad that Goodman had agreed to see him before the quarter started.

He was exactly on time and knocked on the door, hearing, as he had expected, a shout of "Come in!" He followed instructions. Goodman, a big balding man, dressed as usual in a blue oxford-cloth button-down-collar shirt with a tastefully matching tie–Nathan had never seen him wear anything else–rose from behind his desk to shake Nathan's hand. They exchanged quite genuine pleasantries, and Nathan was flattered to hear that he had been one of the better students in Goodman's two marketing courses that he had taken.

"You said something on the phone, Nathan, about hoping I could serve on a committee of advisors you want to put together for an independent study project?"

"That's right," Nathan said. "Professor Wilson, the assistant dean in the School of Architecture with whom I talked before deciding to come back for my master's in architecture, recommended that the College of Administrative Science should be very substantively involved in the study I have in mind, and--"

"Well, what *do* you have in mind, Nathan? I remember the independent study you did with Professor Foster and me, on modular housing, during your last quarter with us. Your work was very good. Did you know that Professor Foster expanded your study, and has become very active as a consultant in the modular housing industry?"

"No, I didn't know that," Nathan said, taken aback.

"Well, of course, you did only the preliminary work, but I think you did explore the topic very interestingly, and Foster has done extremely well, picking up your ball and running with it, for a seasonal metaphor."

Nathan didn't appreciate either the revelation or the metaphor, but repressed his thought to answer Goodman's question. "Well, I'm glad to hear that the study was useful," he said by way of transition, "and I suppose that in a general way it's part of what led me to the study I'd like to do now, with your approval and guidance, and of the other two faculty members in the School of Architecture."

"Two?"

Nathan explained the scheme that Wilson had developed, and which, he had learned on the phone, Wilson had already proposed to both Prescott and Rosenberg.

"I see," Goodman said. "That's a reasonable division of labor for us, but I hope it won't prove too complicated for you, getting all of us to agree and so on. But what exactly is your study to be about?"

"I'd like to apply what I've learned about marketing and organizational behavior to real-world architectural practice, especially after what I've seen in the working world in the last two years. My hypothesis, if I can call it that, is that architects aren't very good at marketing their services and adapting to their clients' needs as those evolve. I'd like to do some research on the marketing methods they use and are familiar with, probably through a survey accompanied by selective interviews, in relation to their involvements in the markets in which they're active. To my knowledge, no such survey has ever been conducted or at least reported. It should yield quite a mass of data. I'd have to have some help both with the design of the questionnaire and with the statistical analyses of the data to meet the usual requirements of reliability and validity, but I don't see why there would be any special problems with either of those. Those aspects of the work are handled quite routinely in survey research."

"Yes, in polls, for instance, of voting behavior or intentions, or in studies of consumer behavior–but what about sampling?" Goodman asked.

"Well, I don't have a ready answer to that yet," Nathan admitted. "At first I thought of asking just the architectural firms in the Columbus area to participate, mostly so that I could follow up the survey with interviews at firms responding with especially interesting data. Then I thought, no, that might be too parochial, I should include firms in some other big Ohio cities as well, Cleveland, Cincinnati, Akron, Toledo. Then I thought why not the whole state, but I rejected that as too ambitious and threatening to take much too long, without any clear benefits in either validity or reliability. So I'm open to suggestions."

Goodman smiled. "Perfectly reasonable," he said. "That's something the committee will have to work out at the beginning of the study, of course. But I share your optimism, I don't see any insuperable difficulties there."

"Then you'll serve on the committee?" Nathan asked.

Goodman smiled again. Nathan's enthusiasm was obvious. "Yes, I will," he said. "In fact, I look forward to it. I think you've got a great idea, I already know that you do first-rate work, and although I don't know your two architecture professors, I'm always open to widening my circle of acquaintances. That's on the assumption that they'll agree also, of course."

"Dean Wilson has already talked to them and told me that they're both open to the idea," Nathan said. He was excited and delighted. "And I have appointments with both of them later today. On the basis of my conversation with Dean Wilson in July, I really think they'll agree. I certainly hope so!" he added fervently.

"All right, then, Nathan, let me know as soon as you can, and as I said, I look forward to this joint enterprise!" Goodman extended his hand. Nathan shook it, said thanks, promised to call as soon as he had news, left Hagerty Hall, and walked to the oval to relax before his luncheon meeting with Arnold Prescott. So far, so great, he thought. Better than perfect. If Prescott agrees to be one of my advisors, I'll have a very well-known marketing professor and a very well-connected professor and practitioner of architecture on my committee, and if the study produces some really useful results, as I think it will, I'll be in an excellent position when it comes to considering job offers. He indulged himself thinking of the letters of recommendation Prescott and Goodman would write on his behalf to some of the best and biggest architectural firms in the country. He had heard of professors who, upon being asked for letters of recommendation by their students, had told them to draft something for their signatures, a way of asserting both their importance and their virtue: too busy for such mundane tasks but also too kind to refuse. Goodman would never insult him like that, he was sure. Prescott was already demonstrating his interest and kindness by inviting him to lunch at the Kon Tiki, a well-known Polynesian restaurant on Olentangy River Road, about a twenty-minute drive from campus. As for Rosenberg, well, he'd have to wait and see. Now it was time to go to lunch.

Nathan arrived about five minutes early, but Prescott was already waiting for him in the lobby, looking for a young man in a blue shirt and tan khaki pants, as Nathan had described himself. "Nathan Goldstein?" he asked him. Prescott was about Nathan's height, quite trim, bald but with a neatly cropped fringe of grey hair. He was in his late fifties or early sixties. He was very well dressed, wearing a tie and well-fitting sport jacket. His demeanor was pleasant, but something about him, something indefinable, put Nathan on guard. Nathan confirmed his identity and Prescott said, "I've got a table reserved and I've been told it's ready. I eat here quite often. Let's go in, then." As they made their way to their table, Nathan noticed that the place was rather fancy and the guests looked affluent. His slacks and open-collar shirt were too informal, he felt. Prescott hadn't warned him to wear a tie. They sat down and Nathan saw, as he picked up his menu, that Prescott didn't. "The prime rib here is excellent," Prescott said. "I'm going to have that, and I think you'd enjoy it too."

"Yes, I love prime rib, but I don't have it very often," Nathan said.

"I know how students have to eat," Prescott said. "But you're my guest, remember, so order it if you like." Why not, Nathan thought, it'll be a long time before I eat this well again. And when Prescott suggested that they both have a drink first, he accepted that too, ordering a scotch on the rocks while Prescott told the waiter he'd have his usual. The waiter knew what that was–a vodka martini, extra dry with two olives. Nathan was duly impressed, as Prescott had obviously intended.

After Nathan had answered Prescott's preliminary questions about where he lived and whether he had a car–he'd had to sell his Mustang but had acquired a used Chevy–Prescott asked him about his family. "What do your parents do? Do you have any brothers or sisters?" The waiter's arrival with their drinks gave Nathan a moment to wonder why Prescott wanted to take this route to the subject of his independent study. Prescott seemed bluff and hearty, what with prime rib and a drink before lunch, but what did Nathan's family have to do with anything? The waiter asked whether they'd decided on what they'd like, they gave him their orders, the waiter said "Excellent choice"–he had probably been trained to say that, Nathan thought, not quite the way Pavlov trained his dogs–and Prescott waited for Nathan's answer, quite expectantly. But before Nathan could say anything, Prescott said, "Wait! First, a toast–to your success at Ohio State!" Nathan, smiling gratefully, said "Thanks, I certainly hope so" for the second time that day, and clinked glasses with Prescott. They each took a sip and Prescott said, "Now, tell me about your family. I'm interested in getting to know you as a person."

Well, at least this part won't take long, Nathan thought. "Not much to tell you," he said. "I have one older brother. He works for one of the Cleveland-based Fortune 500 companies. My dad died about four years ago, in 1970. We moved to Beachwood, just outside of Cleveland, when I was about ten or eleven. Now my Mom has an apartment in Mayfield Heights. She works part-time, but is thinking about working full-time. That's about it, Professor."

"What kind of work did your father do?" Prescott asked.

"He was a driver-salesman for a local bread company," Nathan said. The waiter came back with a basket of bread and their salads. Prescott began to eat, but when Nathan followed his example, he asked him to describe his plans. Nathan, chewing and swallowing, managed to say, "Plans?"

Prescott, smearing a pat of butter on his bread, said, rather sternly, Nathan thought, "Yes, plans. Professor Wilson asked me to meet with you to discuss my acting as one of your advisors on the independent study you have in mind. He said that Professor Rosenberg–have you met with him yet?"

"No, not yet, but I have an appointment with him," Nathan said.

"–that Rosenberg would consider joining us. I'm an Adjunct, you see, only part-time, and have a practice here in Columbus and other professional obligations. Perhaps Wilson told you."

"Yes, you're the president of the Ohio Society of Architects," Nathan said.

"The Architects Society of Ohio," Prescott corrected him. It seemed to matter. Damn, Nathan thought, this isn't going as well as I'd hoped. "Yes, sorry, that's what I meant," he said.

"Yes. It's quite unusual for a student to have two advisors, but as I understand from Professor Wilson, you want *three*, someone in the Administration Sciences School?"

I will *not*, Nathan said to himself, correct his nomenclature just because he corrected mine. "Yes," he said, "Professor Maxwell Goodman, who has already agreed, this morning, in fact. Professor Goodman's expertise is in marketing." Prescott looked blank. "He's quite famous in his field," Nathan added. "His book has been adopted in business schools throughout the country, and I've done quite well in coursework I've taken from him. In fact--" I'm talking too much about Goodman, he thought--"a study I did in one of his classes concerning modular housing was, in a way, part of what led to my idea for the independent study I hope you and Professor Rosenberg will help me with." All this tiptoeing and careful balancing! What is this, a ballet?

"Go on," Prescott said, resuming mastication. I'm sure they serve great food here, Nathan thought, but will I get to eat it? Maybe luncheon meetings weren't such a great idea. But he put his salad fork down and explained, as he had to Maxwell Goodman, what he had in mind. Prescott listened carefully. Nathan finished just as the waiter brought the main course. Nathan began to carve up his prime rib, waiting for Prescott's reaction.

It was slow in coming. First Prescott watched disapprovingly as Nathan relinquished most of his salad to the waiter, who had to clear the table. The salad had been sacrificed to the explanation. Nathan finished his drink and waited for Prescott either to respond or to begin eating. Meetings in faculty offices were much less complicated, he said to himself. It took him almost no time to change his mind.

"I'm very impressed, Nathan," Prescott began. "I don't mind telling you that what you've described sounds not only very well thought out but really important. I would very much enjoy acting as one of your advisors. Definitely yes. And so, I'm happy to tell you–this will be a little surprise for you–will Professor Rosenberg. Of course you must keep your appointment with him this afternoon and tell him all this in detail again, but he called me this morning and asked me to make the decision for both of us. He trusts my judgment, you see."

Nathan was indeed pleasantly surprised but couldn't resist a question: "So when you asked me just now if I'd met with Professor Rosenberg yet, you knew I hadn't?"

"That's right," Prescott said, smiling broadly and spearing a stalk of asparagus. He seemed to think he had played a joke on Nathan. "That's right, I knew you hadn't. Just wanted to heighten the suspense." He chuckled, obviously pleased with himself. He cut his meat. "Go ahead, eat," he said. "It's very good."

Nathan did as he was told, and agreed. "I see why Professor Rosenberg trusts your judgment," he said, pointing to his prime rib, thinking that the flattery was not only genuine but appropriate, and would serve to keep the conversation on track. The second assumption was wrong.

"Now are there things you'd like to know about me?" Prescott asked.

"I—well—what would you like to tell me?" Nathan replied. It was the best he could do, but it was good enough.

"Well, first of all, you should know that I was divorced from my first wife, for reasons that don't concern you, about six years ago, and remarried last year, so I'm a sort of a newlywed. But I'm also a father of one son, a couple of years older than you are, Nathan, with whom I haven't spoken in almost two years, even though he lives here in Columbus."

Nathan, amazed by these unsolicited confidences, tried to look as sympathetic as he could while chewing his beef.

"My son has always had a hard time accepting advice, and has made decisions without considering consequences more often than I care to tell you," Prescott continued. This is a very strange man, Nathan thought. His sense of privacy is as weird as his sense of humor. But he *is* the president of the Architects Society and a practitioner and in position to help me enormously, he reminded himself, listening attentively as Prescott went on. "He doesn't get along with my new wife or her children, who are also adults," Prescott was saying. "And after he walked out of the house a year ago last Christmas Eve after a lot of shouting and yelling, I don't think it would be possible for my wife just to welcome him back."

Nathan swallowed. "I'm sorry to hear that," he said. "I hope things will work out in time."

"Yes, I hope so," Prescott said rather abruptly. "Nathan, I'd like to meet weekly with you, here, for lunch—let's make it every Wednesday, subject to adjustment as necessary, if I have to go out of town or meet with a client--so that I can stay involved in your research and monitor your progress. Wilson said that you're planning on fifteen credits for this research, is that right?"

"Yes, fifteen," Nathan said. The prodigal son had apparently left the conversation as suddenly as he had left his father's house.

"So your research would be completed in three quarters?"

"Yes," Nathan said.

"All right. Please have a preliminary outline, but as detailed as you can make it, completed by next Wednesday for distribution to me and Rosenberg and Goodman. Now, do you participate in any sports?"

"Yes," Nathan said, less and less astonished by the way Prescott's mind leaped from one subject to another without any apparent connection. "I play some golf and enjoy biking."

"Do you fish or play tennis?"

"I've fished a few times, and I do have a tennis racket, but I haven't used it since high school."

"Maybe you can brush up on your tennis," Prescott said. "I belong to a Christian group and we spend one week during the spring at a men's camp just north of Columbus. If you're interested and things go well this year, perhaps you'd consider attending as my guest."

"That's very kind of you, perhaps we can work that out," Nathan said, smiling and nodding just enough to hide his thought–what the hell is this now?–without feigning enthusiasm. Prescott misinterpreted his answer anyway.

"Good, good," Prescott said. "The camp is on a lake stocked with largemouth bass and blue gill every year. Do you have fishing gear? Never mind, I have some extra rods and reels you can borrow. By the way, I hope you aren't, umm, let's say excessively modest. We all get back to Nature at camp, and we swim in the lake in the nude." He watched Nathan carefully.

"Then I'll be easy to find," Nathan said.

"What do you mean?"

"I've never been outside in the nude," Nathan said, "so I'll have the whitest ass there."

Prescott burst into a surprisingly loud laugh. People turned around to stare. And, Nathan thought, I'll probably have the only circumcised penis. A Christian camp, just what I always wanted.

"Good, you have a good sense of humor," Prescott said when he recovered. "Now, I reviewed your course schedule and saw that you are taking Montague's graduate course in Design, my course in Professional Practice, and your independent study. So you're not enrolled in Rosenberg's courses?"

"No, "Nathan said, once again shifting gears. "Perhaps next quarter, depending on what he's going to offer, but now I want to concentrate on getting off to the best start possible."

"Yes, of course. Rosenberg and I aren't friends socially, but we're on a very collegial basis, I think I can say that, and I can tell you that he's tough but fair. Saw a lot of action in the war–World War II–but won't talk much about it. Have you taken any work with him in the past?"

"No, I haven't," Nathan said.

"Ummmm. Well, as I say, Harry is fair. He will judge your work fairly. And he will be helpful to you. But don't expect any extra consideration. You won't get it."

Nathan had no idea what Prescott meant, and thought it best not to ask.

Prescott looked at his watch just as the waiter came back to ask if they'd like to see the dessert tray. "No, thank you, just the check please," Prescott said. Then, realizing that Nathan hadn't yet declined dessert, he explained: "I have a business meeting in town, and have to leave–next Wednesday, then, here, at noon, with your outline, as we discussed." The waiter gave him the check and, without looking at it, Prescott gave him a credit card and rose. "Thank you very much for everything, Professor," Nathan said, wiping his hand on his napkin and then offering it to Prescott. "Excellent lunch, thanks for agreeing to work with me, and I'll have the outline with me next Wednesday."

"Yes, yes," Prescott said, taking Nathan's hand for a moment and looking for the waiter to return. Suddenly he was in a rush. The waiter came back, Prescott signed the bill, pocketed his credit card, waved to Nathan, and made his way out. Nathan followed at a distance. Less than perfect, he thought as he hurried to his car. His appointment with Professor Rosenberg was at two o'clock, and it was already one thirty. Prescott's description of Rosenberg suggested that he'd be wise to be early.

He succeeded. The door to Rosenberg's office was open, allowing the breeze to flow through from the window, and Nathan, seeing a short man bent over his desk, writing, knocked gently on the wooden frame. Rosenberg looked up, saw Nathan, looked at his watch, shrugged, and motioned Nathan to enter. "I'm a few minutes early, Professor," Nathan said. "Nathan Goldstein."

"Yes, fine, have a seat," Rosenberg said. There was just a hint of New York in his voice. He pushed whatever he had been writing in–it looked like a diary, Nathan thought–to one side and took a folder out of his inbox. Nathan sat down in the chair Rosenberg had pointed to, in front of his desk. All these non-verbal cues, Nathan thought, indicative of the very different personalities he'd have to orchestrate somehow. This man is clearly anxious to be seen as in charge here. Maybe if he were taller, he'd ask me to sit in a more comfortable chair.

"All right," Rosenberg began. "Tell me first of all if Professor Prescott has agreed to work with you on this project you have in mind."

"Yes, he has," Nathan said immediately. "Just now, at lunch."

"Good, then I'll participate as well," Rosenberg said. "Did he tell you that I had asked him to make a decision on my behalf as well as his?"

"Yes, he did, eventually," Nathan said.

"Eventually?"

Nathan explained. Rosenberg was not amused. Nathan remembered that Prescott had acknowledged that they weren't friends "socially," whatever that meant, just good colleagues. He waited, watching Rosenberg make a note on a piece of paper in the folder.

"All right, what's the project?"

Nathan went over his idea once again, mentioning his work with Maxwell Goodman. Since Goodman did not know Rosenberg or Prescott, Nathan had assumed that Rosenberg had not heard of Goodman, as Prescott had not. But Rosenberg was familiar not only with Goodman's name but also with his book. Further, Nathan saw, unlike Goodman and Prescott, Rosenberg took notes. When Nathan finished, he looked at Nathan for what seemed a long moment.

"Where are you from?" he asked.

"Cleveland," Nathan said. "Cleveland Heights, most recently."

"Have you been in the service?" Rosenberg asked.

Nathan was startled. Everybody has different personal questions, he thought. "No, I haven't," he said. Rosenberg did not seem perturbed.

He stood up, and Nathan saw that he was indeed quite short, but muscular, as his short-sleeve shirt showed. He had dark eyes and a big nose. He spoke evenly, clearly, enunciating his words precisely but without any exaggeration. The New York accent was just discernible. The question was whether the meeting was over already.

"Did Professor Prescott give you an assignment?"

"Yes, I'm to have a detailed outline ready by next Wednesday at noon," Nathan said, "with copies for you and Professor Goodman."

"What will the outline include?"

"The key hypothesis, some examples of the survey questions, some indication of the statistical methods to be used in the analyses of the data, some indication of the expected utility of the study."

"What about the size and nature of the sample? Are you talking about a random sample?"

"Frankly, that's the key question I need help with at this time," Nathan said. "I've already mentioned this to Professor Goodman, but it didn't come up in my conversation with Professor Prescott."

"I see," Rosenberg said, bending down over his desk to write another note. "We're going to have to settle that very soon, at a meeting of all four of us. Not at a restaurant," he added. Nathan nodded in agreement.

"All right," Rosenberg said. "Your idea has merit, but its

implementation remains an open question, obviously. Did Professor Prescott say that he'll send the outline to Professor Goodman and to me after he's gone over it with you?"

"No, that's still up in the air, I think, "Nathan said. "I had assumed that it would be my responsibility, but now I'm not sure."

"I think it *should* be your responsibility," Rosenberg said. "After you and Professor Prescott have worked on it, tell him that you'll take that responsibility. He's a busy man. Good to meet you. I think that it will be an interesting project, depending on everyone's cooperation." He was clearly ending the meeting, but Nathan was confused. "But you've all agreed," he said.

"No, I mean the cooperation of the firms you're going to ask to participate in the survey," Rosenberg explained. "And whoever else might be involved."

Nathan didn't understand that either but decided not to ask. "Thanks very much, Professor Rosenberg," he said, rising. He saw Rosenberg put the paper in the file and reach for what looked like the diary he had been writing in. "I'll bring you the revised outline, then, as soon as Professor Prescott has approved it."

"Good, do that," Rosenberg said. "Goodbye." He did not offer Nathan his hand.

"Goodbye," Nathan said, and left. Less than perfect, he thought again. But he was on his way, nevertheless.

*****

The next weeks went by quickly. Nathan's weekly lunches with Arnold Prescott at the Kon Tiki included his progress reports, and Prescott was always encouraging and helpful. He had even introduced Nathan to some important people they'd run into in the restaurant. One was a Paul Charnesky, President of the State Board of Examiners of Architects, who actually sat down at their table in the Kon Tiki and listened to Prescott's description of Nathan's project with much interest. On another occasion, also in the restaurant, Prescott saw two architects he knew from Cleveland, an Arthur Mercer and a Ballard Warren, and called them over. They also told Nathan that he was doing very important work after Prescott had introduced Nathan and asked him to tell them about it. Thinking of his future, Nathan asked for and got the business cards of both Cleveland architects. A meeting with all three of his advisors settled the issue of sampling: he would have a number of categories of firms, by size and volume of business, in the state's major cities, and invite the firms that matched those criteria to participate in the study, but he would restrict requests for interviews to selected firms in the Columbus area, simply for practical reasons. While he was working on preliminary versions of the questionnaire, he also drafted a letter of invitation to participate in the research, to be sent to the firms that fit his categories in the cities they had agreed on. He had thought that Prescott might help him to solicit some key firms through his personal contacts, but it was agreed instead that simply listing his committee members and their various titles in the letter of invitation would be both more effective and more diplomatic. To his delight, Peggy Pearsall volunteered to do some typing for him as her time permitted, and his desk in his office was soon covered with manuscripts, notes, and brochures from architectural firms around the state. Better than perfect, he was saying to himself again.

He was particularly pleased with his design class and its instructor, Jack Montague. The professor had liked Nathan's work from the beginning–Nathan was designing a hotel retreat located in Machu Picchu in Peru–and frequently called the other students' attention to Nathan's progress. One November afternoon Montague came to Nathan's drafting table in the studio and motioned to him to step away, out of earshot of the others. "Nathan," Montague said, "I've discussed your design with some other people, and brought them in to look at it when you weren't here, so that your head wouldn't get too big from the compliments, and the consensus is that you should enter it in the Brussels Prize competition, the Prize for Architecture."

Nathan had *thought* his work was good, but he was nevertheless surprised and very pleased. "Really!" was all he could manage at the moment.

"Yes, really," Montague said. He combined a very direct manner with a warmth and friendliness that Nathan found charming. "Some people here had the impression that you were a kind of businessman's architect, but it's clear that you've blossomed into an excellent building designer. You must have noticed that I've used your work as a kind of exemplar for the other students. Take the next step and enter the competition. If you need some funds for the entry fee and the shipping costs, I might be able to find some support for you, but time is short, and you need to make up your mind almost immediately."

"The School is already being very generous, with office space and some secretarial services for my independent study project, and I do have the money for the expenses involved," Nathan said. "And I'll certainly enter the competition, with this encouragement! I'm flattered and delighted!"

"Excellent," Montague said. "You'll need to prepare a color rendering of your hotel. You've taken great advantage of the hillside approach, and a perspective looking from the Machu Picchu ruins could be very dramatic. Have you given any thought to the perspective drawing?"

"Yes," Nathan said. "I've been looking through a number of books with photographs of the ruins, and there was one I remember that does show a view from the ruins. I've already been in contact with Academy Blue on Fifth Avenue–they can burn an enlarged photo into an erasable sepia print. I think I could erase a part of the sepia drawing, sketch in the building, and then color the entire drawing."

"Could you do this and include it with the final project due next Wednesday?"

"Yes," Nathan said without hesitation, thinking now I've got to. He had already started on some drawings. He devoted the entire weekend to the project, working through the nights, sleeping a few hours during the days, skimping on meals, even neglecting to shave or answer his telephone. The prospect of earning some form of recognition in the Brussels Prize Competition was intensely motivating. To get the benefit of Montague's criticisms and suggestions, and to have time to revise and complete the work for mailing by Wednesday, he wanted to have everything done for Montague's critique by Monday morning's class. He arrived in the studio bleary-eyed and tired, but he was ready. He arranged his presentation boards on top of his drafting table and waited for Montague to come over. Montague was talking with another graduate student, Brian Keating, a tall, thin fellow with a pony tail and, for Nathan's taste, exaggerated mannerisms. Nathan thought that Keating was going on too long about too little, but then he realized that he was irritable not only because he hoped but wasn't sure that Montague would be pleased but also because of lack of sleep. Control your excitement, he told himself. Montague finally finished with Keating and walked over to Nathan's drafting table.

"Good morning, Nathan," he said in his usual warm way. "Let's see what you were able to complete over the weekend!"

"I completed four thirty-inch by forty-two inch presentation boards," Nathan said. "Drawing One," he continued, showing his work as he described it, "includes a Site Plan and Floor Plans. Drawing Two shows additional Floor Plans and the Front Elevation. Drawing Three includes a Side Elevation, Sections, and an Interior Lobby Perspective. And Drawing Four includes a Detailed Exterior Perspective, another Interior

Lobby Perspective, and the color rendering perspective we discussed, looking from the Machu Picchu ruins across the mountain toward the proposed hotel." Montague studied Nathan's drawings for some time. Nathan grew a little nervous. Finally Montague turned to him, smiling. "Excellent work, just as I expected," he said. "You must have burned the midnight oil over the weekend! Have you completed the Brussels Prize registration documents?"

"Yes, I have," Nathan said, delighted by Montague's praise. He saw Keating looking at them, and inferred that Keating had heard Montague's comment and question. "And I've found a crate that will hold my drawings. Actually, it's a little larger than what I need, but I'll add filler paper to secure the packaging. It will work quite well, I'm sure."

"Very good," Montague said. "I think your chances for some sort of recognition are excellent with this quality of work, and just your entry in the competition, by itself, does the School credit. Nathan, I've also been hearing good things about your independent study project from Harry Rosenberg, and it sounds very interesting, quite relevant to my own practice. Would you stop by my office after winter break to tell me about it when we both aren't quite so busy?"

"I'd be glad to, Professor," Nathan said enthusiastically. He wasn't at all tired, he decided. So Harry Rosenberg had told Montague nice things about his independent study? That was more, so far, than what he'd done for Nathan. Well, in a way, this was better. Rosenberg was reserved but he meant what he said, when he finally said it.

That afternoon, as Nathan was wrapping his presentation boards for shipping in the crate he had procured, he was approached by Brian Keating, with whom he had previously exchanged only short greetings. "Hi, Goldstein, do you have a moment?" Keating asked.

Nathan hesitated. He wanted to finish what he was doing. "What's up?" he replied, non-committally.

"I'd like to ask a favor," Keating said, "in connection with the Brussels Prize competition?"

Is he asking me or telling me, Nathan thought. "Yes?"

"I mean, it's sort of a loan, the favor, I mean, something I'd pay back next quarter--" Keating seemed to need encouragement to finish his own sentences. "Yes?" Nathan said again.

"Well, what it is, I'm entering the Brussels Prize competition too--" Keating nodded at Nathan's crate--"or want to, but I don't have enough bread for both the fee and the shipping."

What, he wants me to lend him the money? We barely know each other! Nathan remembered that Montague had offered to try to find him "support" for these costs. Apparently Montague hadn't succeeded on behalf of Keating. Or hadn't offered to try. "Yes?" Nathan said for the third time.

"Well, what it is, of course I've heard, I mean I know that you're entering your Machu Picchu design in the competition–good luck, by the way–and I see you're packing it up now, and I was wondering, if there's room in your crate there–it looks like there is–for my drawings too, would you mind including my drawings with yours, and we could split the shipping costs? I mean, I would pay you back next quarter, you know?"

Nathan hesitated. So the favor Keating wanted wasn't just the advance of the money–which was what it would be–but also the use of the crate and shipping materials. He probably hadn't found anything as suitable as what Nathan had. Considering that they really didn't know each other, this was some *chutzpa*. "I need to get this out this afternoon," he said, hoping that Keating wouldn't be able to meet his implicit deadline..

"Oh, my drawings are mounted and ready for shipment, and I'm sure they'll fit," Keating said, inspecting the crate. "You could still use some of this filler, in fact, y'know?"

Oh what the hell, Nathan thought, just help the guy out. "Sure," he said. "Bring them over and we'll include them."

"Great, thanks a lot, Goldstein," Keating said. "I like your name, y'know? Anybody named Goldstein, I figure has got to be mellow, y'know?" He laughed a high-pitched laugh. Nathan smiled uneasily and watched him hurry off. Something indefinable about Keating bothered him, but he dismissed the feeling. When Keating returned with the drawings, they packed the crate very carefully. "You want me to take this to the Post Office?" Keating asked. "You look tired, man, you probably should hit the sack."

"No, I'm OK," Nathan said. "I'll take care of it. I'll get an extra receipt for you," he added, implying that he'd be the one to go alone. And, he thought, to keep whatever change the Post Office would make.

Keating looked disappointed. "Yeah, OK then," he said. "Thanks again. Sure, get an extra receipt. I'll have the money for you next quarter, fifty-fifty, right?"

"That's right," Nathan said.

*****

The winter quarter began in January, and the weather and Nathan's mood were both foul as he drove to the Kon Tiki for his weekly lunch with Prescott. He and Nora had broken up over the holidays, and although Nathan had seen it coming for some time, and had made no particular effort to maintain their relationship, he had not taken her accusations lightly. She had said, although at much greater length, that he was more involved with his work than with her, and that she wanted to be more important to someone than that, and that she missed her old boyfriend, and that, in fact, she had already been seeing him again. She hadn't quite called Nathan insensitive and self-centered, but that's what it all came to, and he didn't see himself in that light, and didn't want anyone else to, either. "Architecture isn't a hobby for me," he had said, raising his voice. A mistake. "And you mean that's all sculpture is for me, a hobby?" she had yelled. It was indeed what he had meant, but he hadn't meant to hurt her. It was too late. She was gone within minutes. He was sure her old boyfriend would be a great comfort to her. Now he was a few minutes late for his lunch with Prescott, who was always punctual.

Prescott was waiting for him in the lobby. "Busy morning?" he asked, his right eyebrow raised, always a sign of his displeasure. Nathan explained that Professor Spencer had given a guest lecture in design studio, on solar energy, partly in connection with the U. S. Department of Energy's call for proposals for a national Solar Energy Research Institute. There had been a lot of questions and they had gone beyond the scheduled time. Professor Prescott snorted dismissively. "Solar energy!" he said, leading the way to their customary table. "The technology isn't here for that yet, certainly not on any cost-effective basis. And especially not in Cleveland, where you get so few days of sunshine in the winter." Nathan hadn't suggested anything to the contrary, but he agreed quickly, sensing that Prescott hadn't forgiven him for making him wait.

They began to talk about Nathan's questionnaire. Nathan had a pilot ready for testing, with follow-up interviews with three or four firms in the Columbus area. Four firms had already agreed to participate in such interviews and Nathan was ready to schedule the appointments as soon as his committee approved the pilot. He had a copy with him. Prescott reviewed it quickly while they waited for their meals. "Good, Nathan," Prescott said, sipping his vodka martini. He seemed mollified. "You'll take this to Rosenberg and Goodman?" "This afternoon," Nathan said. "I'm anxious to push ahead."

"Yes. But first tell me your basis for this group of questions here–the kinds of services the firms offer different kinds of clients, and the range of fees they charge. I see that you have them distinguish the ways in which they sell their services, and that you're also asking them to specify the geographic distribution of their markets."

So he hasn't really approved it yet, Nathan thought. I just can't get used to his style. He leads me in one direction, then reverses field.

"Well, the conceptual framework of marketing," he said, aware that he was giving Prescott a summary of Goodman's introductory lectures, "includes four areas, called the four P's of marketing: product, price, promotion, and place. I'm sure the taxonomy is basically a mnemonic device, but it does help. First, product, the kinds of services that companies offer. Obviously, there's a huge variety. Second, price, not just how much, but the ways they charge for the services they offer, for instance, a flat fee, or a percentage of the construction costs, whether the initial bid or the actual expenditures, and so on. Promotion has to do with how they sell their services: personal contacts, sometimes through boards and club memberships, professional and civic associations, of course, or brochures and other print materials, different categories of advertising, in other words. And then place, their channels of distribution. The questions about place are a bit more difficult to phrase clearly and get focused for service businesses like architecture. It's much easier for product-oriented companies. A soap, for instance, can be sold at drug stores, grocery stores, convenience stores. I think that architectural firms vary more, in this respect, by geographical markets–you know, local, regional, national, that sort of thing. It isn't as clean as I'd like, but this is still the pilot, and my hope is that, with the interviews and what I'll learn from them, I 'll be able to refine this set of questions for the final version of the questionnaire."

The waiter brought their food, but for once Prescott hesitated. "Something occurs to me," he said. Nathan waited. "A few years ago," Prescott continued, "the Department of Justice conducted an investigation of the American Society of Civil Engineers, specifically, of that Society's prohibition of competitive bidding. The AIA also had an ethical ban on competitive bidding. Legal action against the engineers was almost certain. I don't know if the AIA actually got together with the civil engineers, but they were certainly watching, and both groups dropped their bans on competitive bidding at about the same time. Did you know about that?" He tucked his napkin below his chin and picked up his knife and fork.

"No, I didn't," Nathan said. "I take it that the Department's concern was price-fixing, collusion of some sort." Prescott nodded.

"Do you think that removal of the ban, or to put it positively, the encouragement of competition among the firms, might somehow affect participation? Or the responses I would get?"

"I didn't see anything the AIA would find objectionable in your questions," Prescott said, "and I think I know their concerns very well. I just wanted you to know that this was an issue not long ago. As far as I know, the AIA is comfortable without the explicit ban. Tell me how you plan to use the data you're going to collect." Prescott attacked his meal. Nathan was once again forced to postpone his

"I'm assuming that we're going to get a wide range of responses," he said. "The respondents aren't going to have similar educations in business and marketing. I don't know what to expect when it comes to specifics, but on the basis just of my experience with the Cleveland firms I've worked for, I'm pretty sure about that in general terms. So I think the data are going to show a whole range of problems that different firms have in maintaining and expanding their businesses. If that's right, and if I can sort those problems into different categories, then I'll be able to make suggestions and recommendations to the respondents that I believe they will want to consider. And that's the appeal I'm using, too–tangible benefits for participation. For the time it takes to complete the questionnaire and participate in the interview, they get a consultation on how to improve their marketing strategies and materials. The ones I'm not going to interview will get a written summary of the results, so they'll have something tangible too." He began to eat.

"What I like about your approach," Prescott said, "is that I'm one of the architects you're describing, an architect with no formal training in business, only practical experience. And the world has moved on since I began my practice, that's certain." Satisfied, Prescott changed the subject once again. That afternoon Rosenberg approved the pilot questionnaire. Goodman had had to go out of town, but had left a note saying to go ahead if Prescott and Rosenberg approved. Nathan sent the questionnaire out the following day and scheduled his first interviews. He was making good progress, he felt.

Three weeks later Nathan gave Prescott a verbal progress report. The preliminary questionnaires had been returned, the interviews had been held, the data looked extremely promising, and distribution of the responses into predetermined and some additional categories had not been difficult. Nathan was almost ready to produce the final version of the questionnaire and mail them to the full sample of firms that had agreed to participate. His excitement was heightened not only by Prescott's praise but also by a way, suggested by Professor Goodman upon his return, of overcoming an important technical difficulty the pilot work had uncovered. The difficulty was that much of the information to be elicited by the questionnaire was confidential, inhibiting the firms' willingness to answer all his questions. He had been implicitly asking for their trust in his discretion, promising to keep their individual responses confidential and to publish the data only in aggregate form. "That's probably not good enough," Goodman had said. "This sort of thing is now subject to approval by an IRB–an Institutional Review Board–set up in response to the federal requirements governing research on human subjects. We have a number of IRB's throughout the University, not just in the health fields. We have one in our College, and you could probably get them to review the questionnaire if Architecture hasn't set up its own IRB yet. Serious business, after the Nuremberg trials and in this country, the revelations about the syphilis study at Tuskegee."

"Human subjects?" Nathan hadn't heard anything about it from either Prescott or Rosenberg. Another unexpected hurdle. Goodman caught Nathan's disappointed tone.

"Yes, even architects are considered human," he teased Nathan. "These are federal guidelines I'm talking about, Nathan, with the full force of law. Everybody has to comply. There have simply been far too many abuses committed in the name of research, not just biomedical and psychological, but across the board, and confidentiality and anonymity are key concerns. The research has to be designed not just to obtain answers to the questions the researcher has posed but also to do so in ways compatible with normal standards of confidentiality, privacy, and so on. The subject doesn't have to answer questions he doesn't want to answer. He doesn't have to give reasons. He can withdraw at any time, without penalty. He gets a copy of the voluntary consent form the investigator has to provide. Things like that. There's quite a bit more, as you can imagine, in the biomedical fields and engineering fields."

"Voluntary consent form?"

"Well, in your covering letter or in an introductory paragraph at the beginning of the final version of the questionnaire, you can explain to the reader, whoever is going to respond, that the response itself will be considered his voluntary agreement to participate, because that's true. But that's what I'm saying isn't enough. You'll know who submitted what information when the responses arrive. There's no need for you to know that, and that's the problem. I know you're going to provide the return envelopes and postage and ask them to be sure not to include any identifying information. But some people won't pay attention, and they might send the responses back in company envelopes, or include a letter on company stationery, and that would mean that you should eliminate their response. Ah, I think I see a way to avoid that."

"How?"

"Have someone else code both the questionnaire and the return envelope. Have him keep that code separate from all the other materials, so you won't know it or see it.   When the responses arrive, your accomplice–that's not the word, but I can't think of it just now–can check off the company's name on the distribution list, destroy the return envelope after he's made sure that no identifying information remains, and when you've got all the responses you think you're going to get, he can destroy the code, leaving you only with the list of firms that participated without being able to say who sent you what."

"I see," Nathan said, grateful for the suggestion. "Is this going to take a lot of time? Should I try to get a friend to do this or should I hire somebody?"

"No, don't get a friend," Goodman said. "That wouldn't look right. Yes, for appearances' sake alone, you should hire someone. It'll just be a few hours at whatever the going rate is now. Are you running short?"

"I've been very careful," Nathan said. "Now I'll be even more careful. Can you suggest someone I should try to hire?"

Goodman shook his head. "No, sorry," he said. "Why not ask Prescott or Rosenberg? They probably know some architectural student who'd be interested and could use a few extra dollars."   Nathan reported this conversation to Prescott at their lunch, ending with Goodman's suggestion that an architectural student could be the confederate. "Do you know anyone you could recommend?" he asked Prescott.

"Do you know Brian Keating?" Prescott asked. "He's a good fellow, very nice, really, and I think he'd be interested. What are you planning to offer?"

"Yes, I know him," Nathan said. Keating hadn't yet paid him the money he owed him, and he'd been reluctant to ask him for it. It wasn't that much, but he wanted it back, and this could be a good way of reminding him. "I don't know the hourly rate for graduate students," he continued, "but it shouldn't be hard to find out. Should I ask Professor Rosenberg about Keating?"

"Is that necessary? Well, just to keep Rosenberg's nose from getting out of joint, haha, maybe you'd better," Prescott said, pleased with his joke. Nathan didn't think much of it, and kept a straight face. "Well, now, Goodman's been very helpful with this," Prescott continued, "and now let me try to be as well. Especially if you're going to incur additional costs for Keating or whoever you get to help you. Nathan, I want you to look into opportunities to get some financial support for your work, a grant of some kind. Considering how far along you are, I don't think that there's time to submit something to an external sponsor, wait for the review, and then, probably, negotiate the amounts and categories of expenditure. A much faster way to get consideration for a small grant, and that's what we're talking about, is to see what internal sources are available, you know, little pots of money that the central administration has in less than well publicized locations."

"Not the Dean?" Nathan asked.

"No, definitely not the Dean," Prescott said. "Not that he doesn't have discretionary funds, he certainly does. But I'm sure that he's not about to support anything involving me as an Adjunct, or Rosenberg, or you–as a graduate student, I mean. No, there are some sources in central administration, I'm sure, and I'd like you to look into them. I'd sign on as Principal Investigator or whatever it's called, and Rosenberg and Goodman would be listed, but the salary and wages would be for you and Keating, if you work that out, and there'd be money for mailing and supplies and secretarial services. No indirect costs, of course, covered in an internal grant."

Nathan was surprised and pleased. Prescott seemed to know a lot more about these business practices than he'd let on. And the idea was as welcome as the prospect of having to pay an assistant out of his own pocket was unpleasant. "Where should I look first?" he asked.

"I think there are some University publications, updated every year," Prescott said. "Start at the Library–the Reference Desk. Those are wonderful people. What they don't know they make a point of finding out. Extremely helpful." They concluded their lunch shortly thereafter. Nathan's mood was once again upbeat and eager. The weather hadn't improved, but he didn't notice.

*****

The application Nathan was to prepare for signature by his committee and, it turned out, the School of Architecture–Assistant Dean Wilson would do that, Prescott decided–had to be discussed by all concerned, and Nathan brought a draft to a meeting in Wilson's office. On the way in–he was the first to arrive–he exchanged pleasantries, as usual, with Peggy Pearsall, who seemed well informed about his progress. Apparently Wilson had said something to her about it. The committee arrived a few minutes later, and Nathan found himself introducing Goodman to Wilson. The application was to be submitted with Prescott as Principal Investigator to the Office of the Vice President for Research, who had, Wilson explained and Goodman confirmed, "seed money" for work that could be expected to lead to proposals to external sponsors for much larger amounts of money. Those proposals could indeed include requests for reimbursements of indirect costs, and those reimbursements, when they came, kept the seed money pots well seeded. Nathan was fascinated by these revelations of the internal mechanisms of the Ivory Tower, not the sort of thing graduate students normally heard about. So what students usually assumed about all the differences between the Ivory Tower and the "real world," as they always called it, apparently didn't hold up under close inspection.

There was a problem. The application form asked for supplementary materials "such as survey instruments, IRB approvals, letters of support and/or endorsement, etc.," to be included as appendices. Nathan's questionnaire was ready, and Goodman had helped to obtain his college's Institutional Review Board's approval of the proposed use of human subjects. But he had, as yet, no letters of support. "I've contacted Mr. Warren in Cleveland, the new president of the AIA chapter there," Nathan told them. "I met Mr. Warren some months ago at the Kon Tiki when he happened to be there with Mr. Mercer, who was president of the chapter at the time, and Professor Prescott was kind enough to introduce me. They expressed interest in this study, and gave me their cards, so I thought Mr. Warren might send a letter of the sort needed here. I talked to him on the phone a couple of days ago, and he just called me back this morning."

"Yes, good," Prescott said. "Good move. Ballard Warren's ambitious and enterprising. You know him, Harry?"

"I do," Rosenberg said. Once again, very non-committal, Nathan thought. Prescott didn't seem to notice. "How did your call go with Ballard, then, Nathan, this morning, I mean?" he asked. "He said that he'd called Mr. Roger Fleming in Washington about it," Nathan said.

Goodman didn't react but the three architects seemed startled. "That's the Executive Vice President of the AIA, the national," Wilson explained to Goodman. "Oh, that's very promising!" Goodman exclaimed. "Would they be a possible sponsor of a larger study, later?" But before anyone could reply, he continued: "No, hold that thought, what about the letter of endorsement? That would serve our purpose very nicely here, a letter from the national organization."

"Well, are you going to get support from Fleming, Nathan?" Prescott asked.

"I'm not sure, to be honest," Nathan said. "Frankly, I thought Mr. Warren was being rather cautious on the phone, I don't know why. When

I asked him if I could count on a letter from him, representing the Cleveland chapter, he said he wanted to give Mr. Fleming some time to think about it and then he'd discuss it with him. He said that AIA had been thinking of doing some such survey themselves, so I suggested the possibility of some cooperation, for instance, a survey conducted jointly. He did ask me for a copy of the final version of the questionnaire, and I got the impression that a lot depended on that. So I've already sent it to him. The questionnaire isn't confidential the way the answers will be, and I have to agree that they need to see what I'm asking them to endorse."

"Don't you think that we have enough here to go forward, with or without the AIA's endorsement?" Rosenberg asked the others. "We have the questionnaire, the list of firms to be invited to participate, the human subjects business, three full professors–I think we should go ahead and submit the application."

"We have a few days yet, Harry," Wilson said. "There's no reason not to wait to see if Fleming or Warren or both will send a letter. I think such a letter could be very helpful, and Nathan deserves every chance. Let's hold off until the last minute." Nathan thought that Goodman might ask his question again about the AIA as a possible sponsor of a larger study, but Goodman didn't say anything. Wilson looked at Prescott and Goodman. They nodded in agreement with him. "So if I get the letter," Nathan asked, "I should rush right over to make sure that it's included, right?"

"If indeed it's an endorsement," Wilson said. "And for the time being, let's assume that it will be." They agreed on that note and ended the meeting.

But Fleming's letter, which Nathan received a full five days after it was dated, was not an endorsement.

Dear Mr. Goldstein:

I do appreciate your sending a copy of the questionnaire, via Mr. Ballard Warren, that you intend to use in your Marketing/Architecture project. It is certainly most comprehensive and well thought out. I can see why it is going to be necessary to have interviews with the firms rather than leaving it to them to fill out by themselves. Certainly you are including questions that are of considerable interest to AIA, but you go considerably beyond what we have contemplated in our survey for architectural firms.

One of the difficulties of our working out some joint relationship is the present status of our survey of firms. We have at the present held up making such a survey until we have a better fix on economic conditions. It will be quite expensive and we want to be sure that our income will be adequate to undertake such a survey.

Consequently, any discussion between us as to how we may work jointly could result only in the delay of your project. Naturally we will be most interested in the results of your survey. I am asking the Department of Professional Practice to review your questionnaire although I must say it appears to me to be most comprehensive.

Sincerely,

Roger Fleming, Hon. AIA, Executive Vice President, American Institute of Architects

cc: Mr. Ballard Warren
Mr. William Meinrad

*****

Peggy Pearsall was no snoop. Neither was she exempt from normal curiosity about and reactions to the people she worked for. In her mind the people she worked for fell into very distinct categories. There was, first of all, the Dean, Charles Webber, her immediate boss, whom she didn't like much and of whom she was afraid. The Assistant Dean, Frank Wilson, was pleasant enough, certainly polite as Webber was not, but he seemed afraid of the Dean too, and Peggy was careful not to let him know how she felt. Then there were the professors. She didn't actually work for them as she did for Webber and Wilson, but she was almost always glad to help them if she could, and she was very friendly with almost all of them. But aside from two special friends on the staff, also secretaries, the people she liked best were the students. "We're here for them," she liked to tell other secretaries. "It's very simple. If there were no students, there'd be no university, and we'd all be out of a job!" But she never said such things in front of Dean Webber.

And of the students she liked best, Nathan Goldstein was among her three or four favorites. She liked his good looks, his ability to make just the right amount of small talk, his apparently genuine interest in her and her family—he often asked about her children—but most of all she liked his manners. He was well brought up, anyone could see that, she told her friends. Probably the influence of his mother, whom Nathan had mentioned more than once to Peggy. When she had volunteered to help Nathan with typing his questionnaire and letters, in such time as she had, she felt not charitable but important, as if she were somehow a fellow researcher in his study. She was very pleased to help him, she had said, and she meant it.

The Dean didn't like having to call Peggy on the phone when he needed her ("as if I were the secretary, and she was the boss!" he had growled at Wilson), and she hated the buzzer he had installed, so much so that for once she had asked him to remove it. They had compromised on a speaker arrangement. He flipped a switch under his desktop, the light went on at a small speaker next to her typewriter, she pressed a button if she was there to let him know that she was waiting for his instructions, and he'd tell her what he wanted. Once or twice he forgot to turn the switch off after they'd finished, and she had to press her button to let him know that she could still hear him.

That happened again a day or two before Nathan received Fleming's letter. Peggy had answered the phone: "School of Architecture, Dean's Office, may I help you?" to hear a woman say, "Mr. Roger Fleming from the Washington office of the AIA, for Dean Charles Webber, please." "One moment, please," Peggy said, and buzzed the Dean, whose office door was closed, as always. "Yes?" Webber said gruffly. "Mr. Fleming from Washington for you, Dean," Peggy said. "Oh," Webber said in a quite different tone, and then, apparently without realizing it, flipped the switch while picking up his phone. Peggy had hung up but immediately realized that she could hear every word he said. She was about to press the buzzer to alert him when she heard him say, "Nathan Goldstein? His study is what?" Peggy's hand froze in midair. No one else was in the room. It was clear from Webber's tone that something was seriously wrong. She lowered her hand, ashamed but overcome more by concern than curiosity.

Webber didn't say anything for a while and Peggy breathed very quietly. Just as her shame was beginning to get the better of her, Webber said, "No, Roger, I understand that very well. You don't need to spell that out for me. Of course I remember the Justice Department investigation. Your point is well taken." Then he listened again. But what did this have to do with Nathan? "So what do you want me to do about Goldstein?" Webber asked. Peggy held her breath. "Yes, of course we can stop his damned study," Webber said. "But isn't that the absolute extreme? Are you so sure that Goldstein is jeopardizing–" he broke off to listen again. The only way Peggy could listen to them both would be to pick up the outside line, very gingerly, and that she wouldn't risk, not even for Nathan. Just a moment longer, she said to herself.

"So you're lobbying to implement selection of architects based on qualifications, for government projects? I think I know what you mean by qualifications. Who are you talking to, on the Hill, I mean?" Another pause. "Good, those boys can be very helpful," Webber said. There was another pause. She couldn't press the button to alert Webber to his speaker. It was too late for that, she told herself. "Now hold on, Roger, I think I know what you're getting at, that's not at all comparable to lobbying for the profession's interests," Webber said, getting louder. Another pause. "Yes, we're up for renewed accreditation next year, you know that, the national team is being put together now. I know some of the people on the accreditation team who've already agreed to serve, Larson and Morgan–who?" Another pause, but only a brief one. "No, I don't know them," he said. "And you'd talk to them about what?" Webber's voice was getting fainter but she had no trouble hearing him. "You'd tell them that?" Another pause. "I see," Webber said. "That's a pretty persuasive way to put it, Roger. All right, we'll shut the damned study down. I'll get Wilson to do it, and to come up with some sort of explanation. Prescott will be upset, and so will Rosenberg, but I'll handle that. For the greater good, that sort of thing. All right, Roger." Another pause. "Yes, Roger, I'll let you know. Give me a few days. Certainly by next week." Another pause. "All right, Roger." Peggy, sensing that the conversation was almost over, decided at that instant that she had to go to the ladies' room.

She came back to see that the light was still on. The Dean's door was still closed, but two voices were now audible over the speaker. The other voice was Frank Wilson's. The Dean must have called him in without going through Peggy, which was very unusual. "We don't have any choice, Frank," Webber was saying. "Fleming represents the Board of Directors very well, and if I pick a major fight with Fleming by going to them, I'll lose. I'm not in this business to lose. I don't intend to jeopardize accreditation. I may not like that son of a bitch Fleming, but that's not the point. Now you encouraged Goldstein--" "But Charlie!" Wilson yelped–"and you damn well are going to stop this study. That's what you're going to do. How, that's up to you, Frank. But if Prescott and Rosenberg give you any shit, and they will, tell them the truth, this is bigger than they are and if they have anything to say about it, they can say it to me. I've handled tougher customers than those two, a weirdo and a little kike." Peggy rushed back to the ladies' room, shocked. When she returned, the light was off and Webber was waiting for her. "You weren't in the office?" he asked, a bit more pleasantly than usual.

"I went to the ladies' room and I'm afraid I stayed a while, something I ate this morning, I think," Peggy said. "Was there something you wanted?" Webber gave her a long searching look. "No, nothing," he said. "Hope you're all right," he said, going back to his office and closing the door. It was the nicest thing he'd ever said to her, she thought.

*****

The next morning Peggy appeared in Nathan's design studio to tell him that Professor Wilson wanted to see him in his office right away. "About what?" Nathan asked, unpleasantly surprised. He was working on a passive solar design problem that he found absorbing. Then he noticed Peggy's expression. "Is something wrong?" he asked her. "Nathan, please, just go to his office as soon as possible," she said. "I have to tell him that you're on your way."

Very mysterious, Nathan thought. Does this have something to do with Fleming's letter? We could still submit the application to the Vice President's office, as Harry Rosenberg had wanted to do. "I'll be there in a few minutes, tell him, please, Peggy," he said. "And thanks for the personal delivery of Dean Wilson's message! I'm treated like royalty around here!" Peggy gave him a strange look and left. Nathan worked for a few more minutes, stopped, and wondered whether perhaps it had something to do with Brian Keating. For some reason he wouldn't explain, Harry Rosenberg had made it clear that he was not to hire Keating, grant or no grant. "Not suitable for this project," Harry had declared. "Find someone else." Maybe Prescott had leaked something to Keating before that, that he would get a few hours' worth of work, and now Keating was furious, perhaps had complained. And he still hadn't paid Nathan the money he owed him. He went to Wilson's office, noticing that Peggy was not at her desk in the reception area. The door to Wilson's office was open, and Wilson waved him in.

"You wanted to see me, Professor, urgently?"

"Yes, Nathan, I'm afraid I have mixed news for you," Wilson said. "I'll get right to it. The School of Architecture has decided that the direction of your marketing research is not exactly on target, let's say, with the architecture program. The work you've completed up to this point, in the School's view, is outstanding, and we've all learned a lot from it, and we can give you five credit hours–with an A grade–for what you've already done. But instead of continuing, we want you to work with Professor Rosenberg for the other ten credit hours you need, during the spring and summer quarters. Professor Rosenberg--"

Nathan, too shocked not to interrupt, did so. "The School? 'We'? Who is the School, who is 'we'? You encouraged me from the very first, my committee, all of them, has been very encouraging and helpful–I don't understand what you're telling me!"

Wilson's face changed. "Your committee doesn't set policy for the graduate program," he said coldly. "The Dean and the Executive Committee do that. I'm telling you that what you've done is very good, has earned you five credits, and now you have an opportunity to work directly with Professor Rosenberg. I strongly recommend that you take it."

"What about our application for a grant from the Vice President's office?" Nathan asked, still in shock and disbelief.

"It hasn't been submitted," Wilson said. "You knew that it required the Dean's signature, and under the circumstances, it didn't get that far."

"Under the circumstances?"

"I've just explained them to you, Nathan," Wilson said. "Twice, I think. See if you can get an appointment with Professor Rosenberg." The meeting was over. Somehow Nathan staggered out of Wilson's office. Peggy still hadn't returned to her desk. On the way out of the building Nathan saw a new notice on the School's main bulletin board.

The School of Architecture is proud to announce that Brian Keating, a first-year graduate architecture student, has been awarded 14th place in the International Brussels Prize competition. Congratulations, Brian!!!

There was no mention of Nathan Goldstein.

Chapter VIII
Rubin, May, 2005

It was much less complicated than Rubin had expected. "Can I help you?" asked the fat man behind the counter, rather gruffly. He clearly had recognized Rubin as a civilian in all pejorative senses. "Yes, I think so," Rubin said. "I've come into possession of a pistol, a Luger P-08—"

"Yeah? How? Were you in the war? World War II? The Big One?"

"No," Rubin said, "I was too young, but – "

"But that was from World War II, right? German officers' weapon. Great pistol, wonderful balance. Those people really understand guns."

"I'm sure they do," Rubin said, "certainly better than I do. What I – "

"How'd you get it? Antique store? Gun sale? Y'got a permit?"

Rubin was getting annoyed. The man had himself confused with a detective on a television cops-and-robbers program. Next he would morph into a prosecuting attorney. "Yes, I have a permit," he said. He had just obtained one, as well as a safety inspection certificate. "What I want to know is whether you have any ammunition it would take in case I'd like to use it for target practice."

"Well, it's hardly a target pistol," the fat man said, confirmed in his contempt for the elderly fellow who knew nothing about guns. "But I suppose you could use it for that. Sure. Any nine millimeter rounds-- here–" he reached for a box of cartridges and put it on the counter. "You know how to load it?"

Rubin flushed. "Refresh my memory," he said, pushing the box of cartridges back to the fat man, aware that he wasn't fooling him.

"Right," the fat man said. He unlocked the display case under the counter and selected a pistol from the many revolvers and automatics. "This isn't a Luger, it's a Walther, but close enough," he said. He took the clip out of the handle. "Individual rounds are loaded into this clip," he explained. "The clip is inserted into the bottom of the grip," he continued, suiting the action to his words, "and the shells are fed into the chamber each time the trigger is pulled. You put the rounds into the clip first, of course. The first round must be racked, it's called, from the clip to the chamber manually." He showed Rubin the slide release. "This latch acts as the safety release." That seemed to be all he wanted to say.

"OK, I think I've got it," Rubin said. "How much is a box of cartridges?'

"Eight fifty plus tax," the man said. Rubin gave him a ten. The man rang up the sale, made change, and put the box into a paper bag. "Y'mind telling me how you got the Luger?" he asked Rubin again, this time more politely. "From a friend," Rubin said mysteriously, lowering his voice. "He used to run around with Norm Mailer and Irv Shaw and Jimmy Jones and those guys. Not Herm Wouk, though."

"Who?" the man asked, baffled. "Thanks," Rubin said, put the box of cartridges in his shopping cart, and walked away. You should be ashamed of yourself, he thought.

The store, some twenty miles south of Ann Arbor, was part of a national chain specializing in hunting and fishing gear and outdoor supplies of every imaginable kind. It was crowded with people of all descriptions, families of three generations, including mothers and grandmothers, small groups of men of varying ages, men by themselves, a group of four or five women unaccompanied by either men or children, and, to Rubin's surprise, an Amish family at the display of fishing poles. Stuffed game birds waddled or nested under the glass counters. Dozens of animal heads, most of them with horns or antlers, were mounted high on every wall. Several very large taxidermic exhibits attracted admiration from every demographic segment of the customers and visitors milling through the store, especially from the children and, Rubin noticed, the Amish family. One exhibit was a huge display of stuffed animals in various poses on a simulated mountain—wolves and polar bears facing off over the carcass of a musk ox, brown bears, otters, buffalo, mountain sheep, foxes, weasels, coyote, deer being eyed by a cougar, elk, antelope, a bobcat stalking a snowshoe hare, raccoons, on and on. Another was of African game animals, lions killing a buffalo, an elephant charging at the visitors, a rhinoceros about to spear a male lion somehow leaping vertically into the air, one paw extended to ward off the huge beast, doomed, Rubin was sure, to be hoisted on the rhino's petard. Elsewhere a great moose was crossing a shallow pond populated by large live fish, swimming between the moose's hooves and simulated rocks. Bemused, Rubin wandered around the displays, thinking that the work was of "museum quality," aware as he thought of the phrase of his reference points: the University's Museum of Natural History and the great museum in Manhattan, forever associated in his mind with his first year in the United States. Then he discovered a long darkened hall of aquaria with various kinds of live fish and an occasional turtle. Again, the quality of the displays was comparable to those of some of the best zoos Rubin had visited. A serendipitous occasion, he thought to himself: he had gone to find cartridges he could use in the Luger, without yet having puzzled out why, and had found a semi-private zoo of living and dead creatures intrinsically fascinating, and with no entrance charge. He decided to take his time, look at the clothes and boots and equipment just out of curiosity–he had never gone camping and had no interest in it, but some of those jackets looked both warm and comfortable–and perhaps try the lunch menu in the restaurant upstairs. He had seen a sign to the effect that today's specials were elk, venison, and buffalo. He would have the elk: he felt adventurous.

*****

His FM station in the Chrysler was playing a National Public Radio program whose "host" was a woman who probably really didn't know any more than she seemed to. Rubin knew that she was highly regarded for her interviewing skills by local radio interviewers. This seemed to mean that they wished that they too had nationally syndicated programs, perhaps even hers. Somebody had had to replace Johnny Carson, after all. No, that was different: Carson was supposed to have been a comedian, or at least a comic. Adjectives had a way of becoming nouns in show business, as did verbs. Fun, however, was no longer a noun, as in "that's so fun!"

This woman wasn't fun. She was annoying and predictable. She was interviewing the Executive Director of the Fulfill a Fantasy Foundation, established, Rubin learned, to help children between the ages of three and eighteen, afflicted with a terminal illness or disease or injury of various kinds–

"HIV? Heroin addiction? Abortion-induced trauma?" Rubin snarled at the Executive Director.

"Uh, leukemia, that sort of thing?" the Interviewer Woman asked helpfully.

"Oh, yes, leukemia, multiple sclerosis, many, many diseases," the Executive Director continued. "We consider all nominations on an individual basis–"

"*Nominations?*" Rubin yelled.

" – from anywhere in the contiguous United States–"

"What's the matter with Alaska, Hawaii, Puerto Rico?" Rubin yelled.

"–of children in such a terminal state but still able, you know, to travel in some sort of way and who have expressed a desire, you know, or have a fantasy that they want to fulfill before, you know, and we try to see to it that they–"

"Uh, what kind of fantasy–" the Interviewer Woman tried to interrupt.

The Executive Director wasn't an Executive for nothing: "– that they have an opportunity, now we can't pay the expenses of their families or companions, you understand, but *their* expenses, those we cover, you know, transportation, hotel, meals, tickets–"

"But not if they're terminating in Alaska, Hawaii, or Puerto Rico?" Rubin shouted.

"What kind of fantasies?" the Interviewer Woman insisted. "What are the most commonly expressed fantasies, what do they most often want?"

"Explain what you mean! Don't be so terminally obscure!" Rubin shouted.

"Oh, most often of all? What do they most often say their most cherished fantasy is?"

"Yes!" Rubin shouted and the Interviewer Woman affirmed.

"It would have to be Disneyland," the Executive Director said. "Definitely Disneyland, oh, by far. But a clear second is shopping sprees, you know, at the mall, and that's true for both boys and girls of all ages, after Disneyland, definitely the mall, that's what the children want."

"Jesus Leaping Christ," Rubin muttered. It was an oath of his own invention and he was very fond of it. What had he expected? The Vatican? The Western Wall? Mecca? A trip on the space shuttle? An African safari? Buckingham Palace?

"Really!" said the Interviewer Woman. "But you know, that's not really surprising, is it? I mean, of course, they're American children, ill or not, isn't that right, so what would we expect? Isn't that wonderful, in a way?"

"Um, yes, I suppose so," the Executive Director said. "Of course they're American children from the contiguous United States, although we've never, you know, actually checked whether they're, you know, *citizens*. I mean, I'm not sure we could actually, you know, *do* that–"

Rubin groaned and turned the radio off. He was reminded of an essay he had read years ago by a professor of anthropology at Michigan–what was his name?-- a fantasy itself, actually, about what a team of archaeologists and anthropologists found ten thousand years from now in a dig in some location in what had been, in the remote twentieth century, a place called Southern California: the fragments of a statue. When put back together, it turned out to have been of a giant rat with a vacuous grin and white gloves. Clearly it had been a god worshiped by the primitive inhabitants of the region at that long ago time. The Rat Worshipers, the anthropologists decided to call them. Not much else had been discovered about them. *How hard it is to shape from shards More than a form the past retards,* he thought again.

What if that store, or its ruins, somehow survived into, say, the twelfth or thirteenth millennium? Complete not only with most of its stock but also its displays intact? After global warming, global freezing, as the carbon dioxide layer in the atmosphere, thick with the ashes of studies by the fossil fuel industry to the effect that human activities had no measurable effect on the environment, blocked the sun's rays from reaching much of the planet's surface. The glacier then covering the Midwest might somehow just prevent disturbance of what had been the Michigan peninsula by man, beast, or bacteria. Say that somehow a giant air bubble had been trapped by the ice, covering that store and its parking lot. Gradually the ice melted, and then, one wonderful day in 12,005, the bubble was released, flinging huge shards of ice in all directions and uncovering the remains of the store Rubin had just visited. Paleozoologists, archaeologists, anthropologists, professors specializing in all sorts of disciplines would hurry to the scene, collect mounds of data, and proceed to publish completely erroneous articles in scholarly journals about the fauna and flora of the North America of ten thousand years ago, getting promotions and tenure and honors for discoveries impossible to match south of the glacier's reach. No doubt the scholarly journals of that time would get a cartful of letters minimizing the importance of the discoveries from aggrieved professors excluded from the dig. Some things could be counted on to last, such as the behavior of distinguished faculty.

All very well, Rubin thought, driving well below the speed limit, but it was time to try to understand why he had bought a box of fresh cartridges for the Luger. And don't tell me, he thought, smiling indulgently, because the ones that Harry had left were certain to be too old to be used.

It wasn't just because someone had followed him the night he'd taken Evelyn home from Jericho's Wall. It wasn't just because Mr. Alhumaidi had been so visibly upset when he had inquired about Hashem Iskandar. There was something else at work in the back of his mind. It had to do with something a long, long time ago. There was a feeling of–how to say it?–a *surfeit* of threats of violence, too many threats, too much violence. Suddenly he remembered the display of suitcases in the Great Hall on Ellis Island. Too many suitcases. And those lions killing the buffalo in that display he had just seen. Too many lions. It was time to react, like the rhinoceros: the Luger, once loaded, would be his great sharp horn.

But what lion did he seek to impale?

Too many suitcases. He had a recurring dream, one that he understood all too well but could nevertheless not release from his mind, of himself at an indeterminate age, hurrying through a terminal of some kind–train, plane, or bus–to catch whatever it was, suitcase in hand, through a crowd of travelers themselves equipped with luggage of all kinds, when suddenly his suitcase opened, spilling his clothes, his toiletries, his possessions onto the floor, forcing passersby to step around him as he tried, frantically, to stuff everything back into his suitcase. In his haste, he tried to force shirts and socks and underwear into the suitcase without paying attention to the latches, and the suitcase jammed and wouldn't close, and he had to start over, knowing the bus or train or plane would leave without him. Nobody offered to help. People just stepped around him, muttering imprecations, complaining about his clumsiness. Somewhere in the terminal policemen or security guards, or huge men in brown shirts with those insignia that terrified him, had noticed the disturbance he had created and were coming to investigate. He always woke up at that point, sweating, his heart pounding. He had had that dream for years, that one and the one about the train that he and his mother had waited for, it seemed for hours, trying to be inconspicuous in the station, worried that, with the few people at that hour of the morning, they were all too visible. The train was late, dallying somewhere, indifferent to their anxiety, and it was getting lighter with every passing minute, showing their Jewish faces more and more distinctly. His mother's fright was almost palpable, and he was terrified. He always woke up before the train came, even though it had actually come, if not on schedule, at least in time on that cold morning so long ago.

Enough, he thought, enough. *Dayenu.* It had been, all things considered, a long life in this country, a good life, once they had gotten settled in Cleveland, even though there had been times that he had heard his mother cry at night when she thought he was asleep. It had taken years to get settled. First they had lived in New York, with a friend of his father's, a fellow veteran of the first world war, when his father had still been a German. His friend had gotten out relatively early, about 1935, before the gates started closing everywhere. Gottesmann. Herr Gottesmann was married and had three children, all older than Rubin, and too busy acclimating themselves to English and New York and the schools they attended to pay much attention to him. A small scared boy that they had been told to be nice to, even to protect, because somehow he had lost his father back in Germany. But there were conflicts, Rubin remembered, about the space they took up, sleeping in the living room, about the bathroom they had to share with the five Gottesmanns, conflicts if not overt,   then expressing themselves in tensions Rubin saw in his mother's pale, drawn face and nervous manner. She had had no difficulty getting a job through one of the Jewish relief agencies. She was an accomplished typist, could take shorthand, and her schoolgirl English, although far from perfect, was sufficient to allow her to call herself bilingual. But her pay was very low, and what she could afford to contribute to the expenses of the Gottesmann household was not always sufficient to satisfy Mrs. Gottesmann, especially once, he remembered, when she had diverted grocery money to buy her son his first pair of long pants.

It hadn't been easy for the Gottesmanns either, Rubin was sure. He remembered them with difficulty. Although his mother had always stayed in touch with them, exchanging High Holy Day greetings and occasional short letters throughout the year, he and the Gottesmann children had never corresponded or kept track of each other. After the senior Gottesmanns had both died, his mother would occasionally remind Rubin how grateful he should be to them for having helped them *"wieder anzufangen,"* to begin again, and he would nod or grunt in agreement. But what he remembered was the tension.

The Gottesmanns' little apartment was on 142nd Street, at what was then the edge of Harlem. The children in the school Rubin had to attend were mostly Irish, Italian, and black. As a newcomer in strange clothes who couldn't speak English, and especially as a rather small boy who didn't know the signals, Rubin was vulnerable in the schoolyard, on the streets, and even in the overcrowded classes, where the teachers couldn't possibly see or hear everything. He had to learn to fight. He had had some experience in Germany, and equipped himself with a small screwdriver that Mr. Gottesman never saw again. He carried it so that the blade protruded just slightly between the forefinger and middle finger on his right hand. Fortunately for him, his next encounter was with the largest boy in the class, who had often been in trouble, a black boy who, sitting behind him, wiped his muddy shoes on Rubin's jacket draped over the back of his chair. Rubin spun around in his seat and stabbed the boy below the knee. The boy screamed, the teacher–again luckily for Rubin, a man–sprang down the aisle, ignored Rubin, grabbed the black boy, and hustled him out of the room. The other boys stared at Rubin, the whites with admiration, the two other black boys, both only about Rubin's size, with uncertainty. "Man," one of them said, looking at the white boys for confirmation, "you crazy. He gonna wait for you after school and *kill* your ass."

"He better not even try," said a big Italian boy threateningly to the black boy. The other white boys muttered agreement. Rubin glowed. He had made a friend. Later, in the schoolyard, where the other white boys wanted to see the knife they were sure he carried, Rubin learned that in this country it was the black children who were the dirty Jews. The lesson was confirmed by the school's Jewish principal, who expelled the large black boy that afternoon.

Eventually, after about a year, Mrs. Rubin got a promotion and they were able to leave the Gottesmanns' apartment for a tiny place of their own, still within walking distance of the school Rubin attended. He was very glad about that. He hated being the new kid. But it was not to last for more than a few months. Mrs. Rubin's employer, a German Jewish department store–the owner's grandfather had begun in the traditional way, selling *shmattes* to other immigrants–decided to close. The war in Europe was spreading, and it would not be long, it was clear, before the United States would be involved in more than LendLease. New opportunities beckoned to those with cash to invest. The question of what, if anything, to do with the employees–Rubin, listening to his mother reminisce about it years later, always imagined a very short meeting at which the owner announced the decisions he had made and, wet with sweat and red with embarrassment, hurried out–was settled, in Mrs. Rubin's case, by referring her to one of the owner's *mispoche,* or rather, to the woman's husband, a Polish Jew who had a much bigger store in New Orleans. She was to write directly to him: he expected to hear from her, she was assured.

Somehow it worked out. Mr. Dembowitz agreed that he needed someone who could take shorthand, could type, had experience. She would be his Executive Secretary's assistant. He was sorry that he couldn't offer to pay her moving expenses–the other employees would be sure to find out, and he had never done anything like that for them--but maybe the relief agencies would help, and her pay would be quite a bit higher than what she was getting from "the German." Besides, New Orleans was cheaper than that awful New York, and the *shvartzes* weren't nearly as dangerous. All this on the phone in Mr. Gottesmann's apartment–the Rubins didn't have a phone--Mrs. Rubin's first long-distance call in America, one eye glued to the clock, the other on her list of questions. Rubin remembered it well, including his confusion about what he should feel. He had been sitting at the kitchen table next to her, transfixed, hating the idea of another move, another new school, but aware how desperately she wanted this job, how devoid of choices they were. Mr. Dembowitz and Mrs. Rubin came to an agreement and Rubin, looking at his mother's glowing face, knew how he should feel.

For a day or two, however, what seemed to be another insuperable barrier blocked their way south: the relief agency had no money to pay for their move. "Not in the budget," the caseworker told Mrs. Rubin, who was almost in tears. There was no alternative: she had to go back to Mr. Gottesmann, promising him that it would only be a loan. She would pay it back with interest, just like to the bank. Rubin, driving his expensive Chrysler back to Ann Arbor, recalled the scene with almost the same hot sense of humiliation he had felt sixty-five years earlier, when he had witnessed it. The truth–although Mr. Gottesmann had not confessed it that afternoon–was that he didn't have that much money to lend her, regardless of interest rates. Two Greyhound bus tickets weren't the problem: it was the expense of moving the Rubins' few things, the hotel bill while Mrs. Rubin looked for an apartment they could afford, the month's rent in advance she would have to come up with, the meals, the local bus fares. But he knew someone who knew someone. Give him a day, two days at the most, he would come up with something, it would work out.

It did. The someone who was known to the someone Mr. Gottesmann knew had a connection to another relief agency–sometimes people in the position of the Rubins were astounded to discover the rivalries between American Jewish agencies about who was to get the credit for the frayed lifelines they could throw the refugees struggling to stay afloat–and the New Orleans chapter agreed to finance their trip and first weeks in the city. Mr. Dembowitz, it turned out later, had made a call or two as well. There was to be a *quid pro quo,* clear from the enclosures in the letter Mrs. Rubin received from the New Orleans agency: a list of synagogues and temples as well as of Jewish organizations seeking volunteers to help them with their work. Mrs. Rubin sighed and signed up for secretarial work for three evenings a week with an organization somehow involved in assisting refugee scholars, musicians, authors, museum curators, and the like, to find "suitable positions" in the southern United States. Maybe, she said, they could furnish a typewriter so that she could do some of the work at home. And she explained to her son that, if he really didn't want to become *bar mitzvah,* which would necessitate Hebrew classes and attendance at a synagogue, he would at least have to go to Sunday School at the Reform temple. Rubin protested–even that seemed unreasonable to him–but Mrs. Rubin's sense of obligation would brook no bargaining.

What lion, he thought again as he pulled into his condominium's garage, the door rising in magical response to his thumb on the opener he kept in the car, did he want to impale? He might resemble a rhino in certain respects, he thought, what with his rather large nose and leathery skin, but it would be an old rhino, not one inclined to combat, certainly not with a lion. Still, there had been too many lions, however long ago, and if he personally had gotten away with nothing worse than some scratches or maybe a bite, he hadn't forgotten them. Sometimes he thought of Harry, blowing up German troop trains, and felt a strange envy. Sometimes he thought of the enormous void, never filled, left by his father's disappearance. November 10, 1938. Berlin. The acrid smell of smoke. The noises. His mother's mounting panic when it grew later and later and his father still had not come home. Although she had sent Rubin to bed, he heard her on the phone, calling everyone who might have seen him, who might know something, who might, just might, tell her that he was hiding, he would be home in the morning. Rubin put his packages on his kitchen table–he had bought a jacket as well as the cartridges–took off his coat, noted the unblinking telephone recorder, took in his mail, went to the bathroom, and put the kettle on the stove to make himself a pot of tea.

As he sipped his tea at his kitchen table, his glance fell on the pills he took every morning, one to prevent kidney stones and several others to prevent heart attacks and strokes, all in brown plastic bottles with caps he could unscrew. No children ever visited. The bottles seemed relatively full, although he had not had his prescriptions refilled in some time. He thought of the array as his pharmaceutical life support system. Had he remembered to take the pills this morning? Maybe not, but he didn't have to take them every day, he was sure. They were getting more expensive, too, he thought, and his co-pay had also recently gone up for visits to his doctors' offices. What the hell do people without health insurance *do* in this country, he asked the little brown bottles silently. They offered no clue.

Harry Rosenberg had taken pills too, but different ones. It didn't matter. Presumably the ones he had taken had extended his life for an indeterminate time, but ultimately it didn't matter, as Marvin would have been certain to declare. Gone. A few lines in the paper four or five weeks ago, his belongings distributed or thrown out, his condo for sale or maybe already sold, his ashes in the atmosphere, contributing to global warming, gone. He *should* write that letter to the paper. Why hadn't he done so already? Because Harry wouldn't have wanted him to? Actually, that probably wasn't true. Harry wasn't adverse to praise or recognition. He finished his tea, rinsed the cup, put it in the dishwasher, and went to his computer, aware of his incessant reliance on one machine after another, all of them mysterious, like his pills.

To the Editor:

Professor Harry Rosenberg's death not long ago deserved more than the perfunctory announcement it received in your paper a day or two later. I cannot speak knowledgably about his work as an architect, as a teacher or as a scholar in his discipline, or as a colleague at the University. Those who can, should. I knew him first as a neighbor and then as a friend in the condominium complex where we both lived. Harry was a proud man, proud of and loyal to his family, his friends, his institution, his country, and his religion. He was a combat veteran of World War II, proud of his service in the United States Army in a cause he never questioned. He was conservative in his views, a bit old-fashioned in his dress, courteous, thoughtful, a gentleman in the best sense of the word. He expressed himself forcefully but carefully; his reliability and sense of responsibility were unmatched; he took serious things seriously, and first among those was his fellowship with other human beings. We are all diminished by his passing.

Rubin read over what he had written without much conviction that he had said what he had wanted to say. A cliché or two, he noticed. The rather obvious echo of Donne's famous poem in his last sentence was certain to be mocked by the seventeenth century people–there were still two or three–now remaining in the Department of English Language and Literature. He could imagine how some of the younger people, "the posts," as he called them--the post-Marxists and deconstructionists "working in theory," the feminists and post-modernists, the whole tribe of babblers--would snicker at his praise of someone he described as "conservative." "Old Rubin is praising himself," they would laugh, "that's how those bourgeois liberals wind up." What he really wanted to say about Harry was that he had been clear about things that had become very murky, confused, debatable, or, in modern parlance, "nuanced."

Harry's world had been simpler, and so had his values, and there had been great advantages to the kind of clarity those values conferred. It wasn't a question of being right or wrong, it was a question of knowing what one had to do. Harry, right or wrong, thought he knew what he had to do and went out and did it, and Rubin felt envious and lonely. To hell with it. He signed the letter–*Walter S. Rubin, Professor Emeritus of English Literature*–and sent it off via e-mail. Let the jackals howl, he thought, grinning. He couldn't remember whether there had been any stuffed ones in the African diorama in the outfitters' store he had just visited.

He didn't think much about his years as a professor of English literature any more, although he had loved literature and teaching both. He remembered some colleagues with warmth and affection, but those had died or moved away. South, usually: Michigan winters and arthritis were not a happy combination. Some others he recalled with amusement, occasionally with regret, especially if he had respected them and they had left for other universities. There had been two or three with whom he had quarreled or had pretty much ignored as inconsequential, intellectually in general and politically within the Department. One of them was still teaching and sometimes he ran into him and his wife at the Farmer's Market or at a rather fancy grocery store they both favored, and they would chat for a moment, aware of their dislike for each other. But on the whole, Rubin spent little time reflecting about his professional life, certainly not in proportion to his ruminations about his early years.

He had let the Parkers think that his main activity now was writing and re-writing articles for a kind of memoir about what he had tried to do in all those years. But although he had notes and outlines and knew pretty well which of his old articles he might revise for inclusion in the book he had described to Gerald and Laura, he hadn't written anything new. All he really had was a working title. *A Transplant in the Halls of Ivy: Reflections of a Refugee College Professor.* He wasn't at all committed to what followed the colon. "The babblers," the critics and theorists influenced by Derrida, Butler, Habermas, and "their ilk," the "victims of that French disease" (another of his favorite self-coined descriptions of the most fashionable persuasion dominating literary criticism and "alleged" scholarship of the past several decades) were quite enchanted by titles with colons in their middles, as they were by cutesy parenthetical ambiguities that would, they hoped, suggest their nuanced sensitivities, their exquisite awareness of metatext and irony. That was in itself a solid reason never to use a colon in a title. But the phrase–*Reflections of a Refugee College Professor*–seemed clumsy, ambiguous, strangely evasive as well. What kind of refugee? What kind of professor? What college? Why should anyone care? Still, the rather botanical first part of the title pleased him. Michigan liked to call itself "the Harvard of the Midwest," which might suggest only a waxen imitation of ivy, but still, ivy, and he certainly was a genuine transplant.

He didn't miss the Department, he didn't miss academic politics, he didn't miss teaching–how many times had he had to confront the students' brave new world with its so many goodly creatures and to give Prospero's response?–and he didn't miss thinking about literature. He still enjoyed it as much as ever, and once in a while was delighted by a new book or a new writer, but he no longer had to *think* about it, to prepare lectures or mediate class discussions or listen to presentations at scholarly conferences or God forbid serve as a member of a panel discussion. That was all to the good. What did he miss, then? He missed his parents, particularly, of course, his mother. He missed his really close friends, especially the Parkers. He missed Harry. Suddenly he realized that he missed never having had Harry's opportunity to shoot back. Not that he was sorry he hadn't served during the Korean war, when he had applied for and received one student deferment after another. He had never been mad at any Koreans, he used to say. He wasn't even sure where the place was. But Germans, the people who had murdered his father, simply and solely because he was a Jew, alone, unprotected, trying to get home to his wife and son late that evening in 1938, that was different. And those nameless, faceless, howling Germans who had done that so long ago had never paid for it. Whatever had happened to them, whether they had frozen to death at Stalingrad or been burned in the conflagrations at Dresden or Hamburg, or been shot by Russians or hung by partisans, they had not paid for murdering Solomon Rubin, 42, *Kaufman*, of Osnabrücker Strasse. He wasn't envious of Harry after all. Harry was only doing his duty, not avenging Solomon Rubin or anyone else.

So that was why he had bought the cartridges for the Luger. He wanted revenge. At least he knew it wasn't justice he wanted. Justice had to do with fairness, with making sure that the rules applied to everyone in the same way, that people who had been prevented from learning how to read and write weren't required to prove their acquaintance with the classics before they were allowed to vote. You could abolish slavery, but no justice could atone for it. No, justice was something to be arranged, to be negotiated, to work out in a court or at the Hague or at Camp David, a compromise affirming that time had passed, and that the future had to be different from the past. That wasn't for him. A piece of his mind had frozen forever on that November night in 1938, and he wanted revenge on people who must have died years ago. Or at least on *ersatz* Germans, if he could find any.

How stupid. How degrading. The lion was an anonymous group of young German thugs beating and kicking his father to death in some miserable alley, and then celebrating their victory for *das Vaterland* in a smoky tavern, drunken Nazis singing their bloody songs. Some mangy lion. After all these years! And was that the connection, then, to Hashem Iskandar and Mr. Alhumaidi? *Ersatz* Germans?

The saunter down Memory Lane had turned into a journey of discovery, apparently. And this new continent that his Columbus self had found had been there all the time, just like the Caribbean islands that the *Nina*, the *Pinta*, and the *Santa Maria* had finally come across. But he didn't like what he saw through his spyglass. A crazy old Jewish professor who demonized Arab immigrants to the United States because Nazis had murdered his father in Berlin more than sixty years ago. A nutty old Jew who had seen too many celluloid avenging angels gun the villains down, the dirty dogs. Interesting mixed metaphor, he thought– unable to keep his academic self from supplanting the Columbus persona–angels, white wings fluttering from their shoulder blades, halos askew, snarling like Jimmy Cagney, blasting dirty dog villains with their Colt .45's.

Columbus wasn't just an off-course discoverer, though, it was also a city, the home of Michigan's alleged rival if you took the football business seriously. It was where Harry Rosenberg had discovered something that Rubin had not yet identified, something that might have contributed to Harry's decision to leave Ohio State and come to Ann Arbor. Quite a decision, actually, for a man approaching the end of his career in academia. Of course his wife–the second wife--was dead by that time, so whatever ties they had had to Columbus through her relationships and activities would presumably have been attenuated. But still, he had colleagues, friends, students, knew his way around, probably went to football games. Rubin had been to Michigan's stadium only for graduation ceremonies in which, once in a while, he had had to participate, but Harry had liked football, the campus, the town. His house in Columbus had been near the bluffs overlooking the Olentangy River, a house, he had told Rubin with obvious pride, he had remodeled quite extensively. He had even shown Rubin before-and-after Polaroid pictures of the remodeled kitchen. On the other hand, maybe his wife's death had been another reason he had decided to leave Columbus, especially his house. No doubt he had remodeled it for her. Well, he'd never know about that now. But the Nathan Goldstein file, which he hadn't examined in detail yet, might still yield some clues.

Rubin sighed, selected a Louis Armstrong CD with "I Gotta Right to Sing the Blues" on it, the 1931 version with the gorgeous trumpet solo after Louis had finished the vocal, pushed the button, and felt himself transported, as he almost always was, by the warmest voice he had ever heard. He had heard Armstrong play in person many times, and once had even talked to him for what must have been at least fifteen seconds, and treasured the memory. He adored Armstrong, aware that his own cautious streak of cynicism was quite at odds with Armstrong's joyous affirmation of life with all its pain and longing. Rubin had fallen seriously and permanently in love with jazz in New Orleans in the early 1940's, when his mother and he had lived in what would now be called an integrated neighborhood, with black neighbors on one side and a black cemetery around the corner and the all-white school he attended three blocks down the street. Years later, in Ohio, he learned a key difference between the South and the North from a black perspective. "In the South," a black friend had explained to him, "they don't care how close you get as long as you don't get too high. In the North, they don't care how high you get as long as you don't get too close." The insight was worth volumes of sociology and history both. The children in that Louisiana elementary school had not thought less of him because he lived next door to two black ladies, mother and daughter, to whom, on his mother's instructions, he always wished a polite good morning or good evening. But his refusal to say "nigger" (he said it once in front of his mother, as an experiment, and she almost slapped him: he never forgot that), his discomfort when they used the word, his incredulity when they tried to teach him what white children in the South had been brought up to regard as self-evident about black people, all that earned him their scorn, even contempt. His mother had a similar problem at Mr. Dembowitz's store, where her supervisor, in response to Mrs. Rubin's observation that she saw little difference between the way black people were treated in New Orleans and what she had experienced as a Jew in Nazi Germany, cried out, "How can you make yourself so low to compare yourself with *them*?"

Later Rubin came to understand why New Orleans Jews shared their white Gentile neighbors' prejudices against black people so thoroughly: because they were so anxious to continue to be perceived, first of all, as white. That was clear enough. But how they could identify themselves with the white police, for instance, with their uniforms and guns and clubs, brutalizing black people of all ages, that was completely inexplicable. His Sunday school lessons at the Reform temple were almost exclusively devoted to Jewish history, from which theological implications could be inferred but were rarely made explicit. The periods of Jewish slavery were discussed vividly, especially, of course, in relation to holidays and festivals–Passover for the liberation from bondage in Egypt, where Moses, Rubin was impressed to learn, had killed an overseer–later he would think of the overseer, always shown whipping a slave in the texts they used in class, as Simon Legree–and Purim, for release from the Persian Haman who was, the children were told, that period's Hitler. Well, then! Couldn't they see that the New Orleans police were the storm troopers, that the "Colored" signs on drinking fountains and restrooms, the movable wooden slats in the holes on the backs of the bus seats, slats marking the diminishing area into which black people had to crowd as more and more whites got on, were nothing but local versions of *Juden sind hier nicht erwünscht?* Without even that ironic gentility of phrase? But black people in New Orleans were not sitting by the rivers of Babylon, *yearning* for Jerusalem. They might sing songs about crossing the Jordan, which Rubin later learned meant the Ohio, or about finding freedom with the Lord or in their graves. But that was different. They weren't yearning for Africa. On those special Sunday mornings on which his mother sent him to a little grocery store "the other way" with thirty cents for ice cream for them both, Rubin would stop first outside a black Baptist church to listen to the singing and then, after he'd bought a pint of vanilla from the quiet black lady in the store, go around the corner where he could listen outside a black bar to the Albert Ammons or Pete Johnson or Big Joe Turner records already playing on the juke box. Once he was so mesmerized by the music that the ice cream started to melt and he had to run all the way home, thinking of an excuse to tell his mother. No, they weren't displaced Africans. They were black Americans, serving in the Army, fighting the Germans and the Japanese; or local garbage men donating their time to help the all-white Boy Scout troops with scrap metal collection drives for the war; or working in the kitchens of some of the white families whose sons he visited after school. They were Americans, which is what he wanted to become. When, years later, he read about Marcus Garvey, he thought it revealing that the immigrant from Jamaica had been most successful with his Back to Africa movement in Harlem, not in the South where, at his time, most black people lived.

They weren't even all black. The ladies who lived next door were light brown. The daughter had blue eyes. There was a black whorehouse–Rubin learned what that was from some boys in his class whose older brothers, apparently, bragged about their visits there–not far from the bar where his ice cream had started to melt. Once he had seen a police car stop there and a big blond cop, buttoning his shirt, come out, grinning, and get into the car, saying something to the officer behind the wheel. He pressed himself against the wall of the bar building, frightened, and they didn't see him. When he was in his early twenties, in a nightclub somewhere, he heard Odetta sing *"Cap'n holler Hurry! Gonna take my time,"* and that scene came back to him. White psychopathology about race, when he thought about it as an adult, *was* so shot through with unexamined hypocrisy that it amounted to a form of mass schizophrenia, not unlike what had gripped the Germans in their decade-long hysteria.

First it had been jazz that had drawn him to American black people, and then he realized that his sense of identification with black Americans came from his identification of the New Orleans police with uniformed Nazis. But there was something else, something even more positive than Armstrong and Basie and Ellington. He was still a teenager in Ohio when he first wondered why he was often more comfortable with black acquaintances than with white friends, often even with Jewish friends. It was because they expected less of him precisely because he was white. If he didn't understand a reference, an expression, a cue, a signal, well, that was no surprise, he was white. He was often tested by black acquaintances, especially when he was the only white boy in a group and one or two of the black boys weren't at ease with his presence, but somehow his responses passed muster, and they relaxed. White boys, however--especially, he thought, Jews–expected him to know things or agree to things that he didn't know or didn't agree with, and since he was their color or even their ethnicity, they would give him no slack as an outsider. He remembered an argument he'd had in high school in Ohio with a brilliant Jewish boy, orthodox, refined, gentle, modest about his abilities–he was by far the best student in all his classes, and Rubin respected him greatly--when the boy had maintained that Jews *were* better than other people, any other people. Rubin had been shocked. At once the argument turned on what it meant to be God's elect. "Where was your goddamned God when the Nazis murdered my father?" Rubin had shouted angrily. "Chosen for what?" And he had said other things, profane, obscene, so blasphemous that the boy had never spoken to him again.

Once he had seen genuine hatred in a black boy's eyes, hatred as pure as what he had seen in the blue eyes of the German boys who had caught him one afternoon on the way home from his all-Jewish school in Berlin. Then he had been seven, but he always remembered. In New Orleans he was about twelve, coming home with two friends of the same age from a public swimming pool white people could use, when a large black boy, perhaps sixteen or seventeen, very dark, very muscular, came riding up to them on a milk-delivery bicycle. The bicycle had a normally sized rear wheel but a very small front wheel, over which a large wire box had been bolted to hold quart and half-gallon glass bottles of milk that the delivery boy had to take to white ladies' houses, and to hold the empties they returned. He had obviously completed his deliveries and rode up to them with an empty glass bottle in his hand, sputtering at them: "You – you – you – !" He couldn't get more than that out, but was swinging his bottle at their heads. Clearly something had just happened to him, probably at the last house he'd delivered milk to, and he was beside himself with fury. Rubin, closest to him, managed to squeak "We didn't do anything to you!" while the other two boys shrank away, terrified, and the black boy, eyes still glittering, rode off. The other two boys, now ashamed and denying their fear, vented exactly as Rubin had known they would, about sending them all back to Africa. He was quiet, debating whether to tell his mother that evening. He decided that he would not, knowing how she would once again remind him of what the two of them had escaped in Germany.

He sighed again. Louis had finished declaring his right to sing the blues a long time ago. It was getting dark. The elk sandwich had been very satisfactory, and he wasn't hungry in the least. Maybe, he thought, he'd have a snack later, although that probably wasn't a good idea. His doctor had cautioned him about the importance of regular habits, eating at the same times, mild but regular exercise every day, taking his pills without fail–damn it, his pills. He probably *had* forgotten to take them today. Now he'd have to wait until morning. But doctors, primary care or terminal care or all the ones in between, enjoyed their authority far too much to be obeyed so obeisantly. They spoke a medicalized Greek. They pretended to remember his name, as if he didn't know that they had just looked it up on the chart the nurse had given them on their way into the examining room. They didn't bother pretending to remember anything about his various ailments or the drugs–the "medications"–they were currently trying on him, curious about what his reactions might be. They glanced at the thickening file of charts or, in recent years, at the computer screen always angled away from him, to reacquaint themselves with his "conditions." Their average age seemed to be about seventeen or at best twenty-nine. At least, unlike the technicians who took his blood pressure or the occasional nurse, they didn't call him "Walter." He was "Mr. Rubin." His Ph.D., acquired almost half a century earlier, earned him nothing when he sat in front of them on the examining table, coughing on command.

He considered looking at the Nathan Goldstein file again, trying to trace whatever had gone wrong for Goldstein through Harry's diagnoses and prognostications. It would have been uncharacteristic of Harry to have become suspicious of Goldstein, whatever reasons he might have had, without following up. He remembered how Harry had gotten involved in the condominium association, first as an architect with strong opinions about the extent of esthetic eccentricity that was to be tolerated, and then as a citizen, concerned about repairs to the external features, roofs and gutters, walks and lights, about the equity of the periodic assessment fees, the use of "common areas," problems with the maintenance crew or management company, and especially the use of the "club house." Harry had been a good neighbor, no question about it, but he had also been something of a busybody. There was nothing he could do about people's rights to have pets–that had been decided at the very beginning, long before Harry had bought his two-bedroom unit–but he did not hesitate to let everyone know that no cat had better come near his bird feeder, and that no dogwalker would be safe from his wrath without the appropriate equipment. Rubin agreed with Harry about the dogs–who, after all, wanted to slide around the parking lot?–but he didn't know of anyone who neglected to take the pooper scoopers and plastic bags on their daily rounds with Fido. As for the cats, they were much too fat to be a serious threat to Harry's beloved cardinals and blue jays. Hawks, now, those were another matter, but Harry never mentioned hawks as a threat to songbirds. Harry's unit on the edge of the condominium association's property faced a little woodsy oasis across the line, and occasionally a crow or hawk landed on a bough of one of the few remaining large trees, eyeing Harry's bird feeder. But intra-avian predation was apparently acceptable to Harry, as feline assaults were not. Everyone has his prejudices, Rubin thought.

He took the Nathan Goldstein papers, now arranged chronologically, from the drawer and began to go through them once again. They seemed to tell a straightforward story of Harry's meetings and correspondence with Goldstein. In particular, there was quite a lot about Goldstein's development of his questionnaire, comments and suggestions about the items to be included, and notes about the confidentiality with which the responses had to be treated. Apparently someone had suggested   a coding system that would permit follow-up with architectural firms that had not yet responded to Goldstein's request for participation, or had not yet returned the completed questionnaire in the self-addressed stamped return envelope that Goldstein would provide. The code would assign three-digit numbers, in no particular order or pattern, to all the firms asked to participate. The numbers would be printed on Goldstein's original solicitation, on the questionnaire, and on the return envelope. As the responses came in, the code would permit identification of the respondent, whose number would then be blacked out on the list of participants, preserving their anonymity and thus guaranteeing the confidentiality of their answers. After an appropriate interval, the remaining firms would receive the follow-up request, repeating Goldstein's promise to share aggregated results as well as his suggestion that all participants, by learning how to improve their marketing and other business practices, stood to gain highly tangible benefits from the research. The code would, in fact, make a second such follow-up, some time later, very easy. When no more responses arrived, the code would be destroyed and data analysis would begin.

But there was a condition. Goldstein himself could not know the code without violating the very confidentiality he was to promise the participants. He would have to have an assistant to assign the code, to keep track of the responses as they came in, without, of course, opening the envelopes, and to do the follow-ups when Goldstein decided it was time. The assistant would have to be paid, probably by the hour, but not much time would be required. Goldstein planned on a "universe" of no more than a hundred or so architectural firms in Ohio's metropolitan areas, hoping for a response rate of perhaps fifty percent.

Professor Prescott had apparently suggested that one of Goldstein's fellow graduate students in architecture, a Brian Keating, might be the assistant. Goldstein, amenable to the idea, had written to Harry, saying that he knew Keating from Professor Montague's design class, and asking what Harry thought. To Rubin's surprise, Harry had printed a big **NO** in the margin of Goldstein's note, and then seemed to have thought better of it: *"Discuss with Goldstein in person, but carefully."* On the bottom of Goldstein's note, Harry had written two initials: *"P.D."* What did *that* mean? Nobody with those initials had surfaced anywhere in the file. How am I supposed to tell the players without a program, Rubin wondered. A cryptographer, he told Harry, I'm not.

Why was he puzzling about all this, anyway? It was Harry's mystery, not his, and now it would never be solved to Harry's satisfaction. Was it a way to avoid beginning serious work on that book of essays? That seemed likely, but there was something else. It had more to do with Harry than with him. It had to do with Harry's naiveté, with his implicit but nevertheless almost palpable faith in "the system," whether that meant academia or business or even the nation as a whole. Rubin, the cosmopolitan who didn't fit in anywhere, the eternal refugee, the permanent outsider, had never shared that faith, not even at Ellis Island. He remembered any number of times that he had bitten his tongue rather than respond to Harry's declarations of belief in people's fundamental decency, in the integrity of most institutions as well as individuals ("despite a few bad apples," Harry would always concede, finding reassurance and confirmation in the cliché), in the solid philosophical bases of what he took to be the nation's essential principles. He hadn't read much history. Harry was a damned good American. For all Rubin knew, he voted Republican. The thought made Rubin laugh.

So if Harry had come across something really ugly at Ohio State, involving colleagues and students, the institution, maybe even the profession, he would have had a very hard time reconciling whatever he believed had happened with his more general view of the worlds he lived in. And, knowing Harry, Rubin was sure that he would have done something about it. And because Rubin wished that he could have shared Harry's faith, wanted to believe what Harry had believed, especially now that he was old and questioning what he had accomplished in his life, he wanted to know what had shaken Harry so badly that he had left Columbus, kept these files, and entrusted them to his "good friend and neighbor, Walter Rubin." It seemed worth the effort.

But not just now. He would take another look in the morning.

Chapter IX

Nathan, 1975

The winter quarter ended shortly after Nathan had been summoned to Frank Wilson's office to learn that his study had been aborted on the Dean's orders. He called his mother, Adele, in Cleveland. She was, as he had known she would be, delighted to hear that he wanted to visit her for a few days. She was also, as he had also known she would be, immediately concerned.

"Is something wrong? Are you all right?"

"Well--" Adele could always tell when something was troubling him, and there was no way he could reassure her convincingly. "I've been better, Mom," he said. "I'm OK, don't worry, but work is very complicated at the moment, and I'm tired and I need a break."

"What do you mean, complicated?"

"I've been told to change directions in the work I'm doing with a couple of my professors, and I didn't expect that," Nathan said. At least he wouldn't have to go into details at this point. But it wasn't enough. "And then I didn't win anything in the Brussels Prize competition I told you about and I'd hoped for at least an honorable mention, after all the encouragement I got. So that was kind of disappointing."

"Of course it is!" Adele said indignantly. "Those things are probably fixed, Nathan, you know, with all kinds of things going on they never want you to find out. I'm sure your entry would have won a prize otherwise. What time will you be here, in time for dinner? Any special requests?"

"Yes, I should be there in time for dinner," Nathan said, "but don't go to any extra trouble, I love all your cooking, you know that. Well, maybe you can surprise me with one of those desserts, but you pick it. Love you, Mom. See you Thursday, then."

"And I love you, Nathan," Adele said. "You take care of yourself and I'll have one of your favorite desserts ready for you on Thursday. Bye!" They hung up and Nathan felt a little better already. He took his coat to go to the Library Bar on High Street. He had already picked up the materials Professor Rosenberg had left for him in his office, but he'd take them to Cleveland, he decided, and review them there. Intellectually and emotionally, they were no substitute for the marketing study he had wanted to do so passionately. They weren't uninteresting, dealing, once again, with modular housing, but they had nothing to do with fundamental visions of architects and their roles in society, with the profession and its potential contribution to the nation. He knew that sounded very high-falutin'. He knew that he was a twenty-five-year-old graduate student from a working class family at a state university, not a New England Brahmin at Harvard, connected by birth, marriage, and especially money to generations of people who took their power for granted. What of it? How old had Einstein been when he published his world-changing papers on mass and energy, on gravity and electromagnetism? How old had Newton been when his professor at Cambridge had stepped aside for his brilliant student? How old was Darwin on the *Beagle*? How old had Jefferson, Hamilton, and Madison been when they decided that their ideas, not those of the British aristocracy, were the ones to guide the development of what would be a unique nation in all of man's history? Vainglorious comparisons, of course. But the time to try to see how far you could push your ideas was when you were young and energetic, when you had little to lose and much to gain.

But that was the problem, Nathan reflected, as he turned his collar up against the wind on his way to the Library. He did have something to lose. Just because you didn't have much didn't mean that you could afford to lose it. What he didn't want to lose was his chance to become an architect, a licensed, registered architect, either with his own practice or as a member of a firm working throughout the country on one exciting project after another. That was what he had been working for all these years in school, working very hard, resulting in very good grades, marvelous contacts, excellent prospects. He wasn't going to throw all that away in one uncontrolled outburst of rage and fury, not in Wilson's office, not anywhere. Precisely because he wasn't a New England Brahmin, he had to play their game by their rules. God *damn* them. He opened the door to the Library. A couple of beers, a few games of pinball, and the familiar faces of his friends would help immeasurably.

*****

The traffic on Highway 71 North was heavier than Nathan had

expected for a Thursday afternoon, and Nathan arrived in Cleveland a little later than he'd thought. His mother, he knew, would be getting anxious. She always hoped that he'd be early. She lived on the fifth floor of a fifteen-story apartment building in Mayfield Heights, one of Cleveland's eastern suburbs. The building was one of three in a high-rise complex. The landscaping was sparse, the lobby was now just a bit shabby and smelled too strongly of the janitor's cleaning supplies, and occasionally the elevator took its time coming either to Adele's floor or to the ground. But that was usually a sign that a tenant with a disability, perhaps one of the old people with a walker, had been struggling to get on or off, and Nathan's mother was invariably patient about such things. Her parents had come "from the old country" with next to nothing but their character and determination to work hard. Adele felt that they had done well and that she had upheld the tradition. Nathan agreed with her. That tradition was a very large part of his own motivation.

He parked his car near the building's entrance in the area designated for guests and went inside the main door to the panel of buttons numbered by apartments, just outside the heavy security door. Security was critically important. The crime rate in the central city had been increasing as unemployment of the unskilled and unschooled had enhanced the attractions of the drug trade. In some respects Cleveland was much like other American cities: desperate and hopeless people in the center, surrounded first by a ring of frightened fellow citizens fiercely clinging to their respectability, and then, further out and all three sides–south, west, and especially east, with Lake Erie lapping at the area's northern shore–by the large, even ostentatious homes and spacious green lawns of the wealthy. Adele's building was in a respectable area, prizing its safety. Police cars cruised the neighborhood quite regularly. Nathan pushed the buzzer for Adele's apartment and smiled at the almost instantaneous response, letting him through the security door. Of course she probably thought "Finally!" even as she pushed the button. He went into the lobby but paused there a moment to look around. The two-story lobby was decorated handsomely but not pretentiously. A contemporary brushed steel chandelier hung from the ceiling. The chairs, upholstered with some sort of tan fabric, looked comfortable. The potted plants, real or not, were a nice splash of untamed green. By contrast, the few pictures on the walls, mostly still lifes and landscapes, were muted and unobtrusive. Everything was clean. Still, there was just that faint smell of Lysol. He pushed the "UP" button next to the elevator shaft. When he got off the elevator at the fifth floor, he saw his mother peeking through her partially open door.

Adele, who stood just over five feet, had silver hair, a trim figure, sparkling dark eyes, and was still a beautiful woman. "Nathan!" she called, loud enough to make him put his finger to his lips as he hurried down the corridor past the neighbors' apartments to her smile and hug. He was twenty-five, almost six feet, with graying hair and a receding hairline, but he knew that he was her youngest child and nothing could change that. The contrast with the security system of the building seemed almost palpable. True security, he thought as he kissed her cheek, was knowing that you could always count on someone, no questions asked.

Adele's apartment was a comfortable one-bedroom, one-bath unit with a long balcony, accessed from the living room and affording a wonderful view of an adjacent wooded area. The apartment's foyer opened into a dining room with a small kitchen adjacent to the right, and a step-down living room beyond. The walls were all painted off-white. There were some pictures on the walls and a few plants near the windows. The beige carpeting went well with Adele's furnishings, most of which were familiar to Nathan from the home he'd grown up in. Photographs of family members displayed around the apartment always caught Nathan's eye, although he knew their every detail, even, of the photographs of himself, when they were taken. Some of the photos were of Nathan's parents, together; some of them were with the two boys, Nathan and his older brother Aaron; and one was of his father by himself. He always inspected those pictures lovingly. The photographs inside the china cabinet in the dining room of Aaron and himself at their respective *bar mitzvahs* (each holding a *siddur*, wearing a dark suit, a handmade *tallit* embroidered with silver Hebrew lettering around the collar, blue horizontal striping, and white macrame fringes, and, on their heads, white *kippahs*, also embroidered with silver) did not hold his attention. He lingered, but only for a moment, at the photographs of their high school and college graduations, and of Aaron and his family. He was reminded of Professor Prescott's request to tell him something about his family, and of his very brief answer. It was as good an answer, he felt, as a question like that deserved. Better. As if all that struggle, all those hopes, all that love, all that pain could be encapsulated in a few words over a drink. Even these photographs could only evoke memories, not describe them. He went to the bathroom to wash up. Dinner was waiting, of course.

Adele had made roasted chicken and potatoes and vegetables, and motioned Nathan to the table while she brought the food from the kitchen. He let her put his portions on his plate, knowing how she loved to do that, stopping her finally with "Enough already, Mom!" Also tradition, he thought. So was her question just a minute or so later: "So, Nathan–are you dating any nice Jewish girls?"

"Mom, don't start, please–I'm not dating much at all this year, I'm concentrating on my work."

Adele was undeterred. "One of my friends here knows a very sweet girl, from what she tells me is a wonderful family. I could get her number and you could call her this weekend."

"Mom, please!"

"I know you have to finish college and get yourself established, but it wouldn't hurt to find a nice Jewish girl, you're twenty-five and nothing is more important than family." Adele was adept at marshaling incontrovertible facts into formidable array.

"This is delicious," Nathan said pointedly. Adele shrugged. "Tell me how your marketing research project is going," she said.

The briefest way, this time, would be the best way. "Mom," he said, "they decided–the Dean himself, I think–that they didn't want the research to go forward." She was astounded. "Pardon me? What? What did you say? Why in heaven's name not?"

"I'm not sure," Nathan said truthfully. "I don't really understand what they told me. I think various people, including my advisor, Professor Prescott, tried to give me some hints from time to time. Again, I don't really know that. But it's possible that somehow what I was trying to do was a threat to somebody. I don't really see how getting information that promises to improve the practices of the profession could be threatening, but that's the feeling I got."

"Does this put your graduation at risk? If they felt you were doing something wrong?"

"No, Mom, they gave me an A for the work I had completed, and now I'm to work with another advisor, Professor Rosenberg, on research he's doing on modular housing--"

"Rosenberg?"

"Yes, he is, Mom," Nathan confirmed. Some questions were best understood implicitly. "Seems nice enough, very straightforward. Not the warmest man I ever met. I think he was some sort of hero in World War II, although I don't know any details. Anyway, I might have to go an extra quarter in the fall, but not more than that, and no, my degree is not in jeopardy."

Adele fell silent for a moment, digesting what he had said.

"Is Stan coming over?" Nathan asked her. Stan Goldberg was her "Significant Other." He was a social worker, having attended Western Reserve University, before it merged with Case, on the GI Bill after

World War II. He was a widower, about Adele's age. His children, long grown, lived in Chicago and Indianapolis, Adele had told Nathan, who had wanted to know everything about the man seeing his mother. Nathan had quickly come to like Stan very much, partly because it was obvious how he felt about Adele, partly because he was glad that his mother had someone special in her life. "Yes, after dinner," Adele said. "He wanted to take us out, but I wanted to have a chance to have a quiet meal with you, just the two of us, so we could talk, just like this. I knew something was bothering you."

"You always do," Nathan said, "and you always did. We must be related."

She smiled and waved him off. "So this is not a major setback?" she asked.

"It won't have been once I have my degree and my license," Nathan said. "If I take the long view, eventually this won't have been a major setback, no. Right now I'm still confused and angry, and mostly disappointed, I think. I just don't understand it. But let's not dwell on it, Mom, I don't really have anything else to tell you about it."

"All right," she said. She saw that he was almost finished with his chicken, as she was. "How about some dessert now? I made a raisin cake, and you could have some tea with it."

"Let's wait until Stan gets here," Nathan said. "Isn't he a fan of your cooking and baking, just as I am?"

"Yes, he's very flattering," Adele said, pleased by the suggestion. "Let me clear the dishes and you relax in the living room." When she finished in the kitchen, she joined him in the living room and they talked about Aaron and his family, especially how the children were progressing. Nathan promised to call Aaron over the weekend.

Stan arrived about an hour later with bagels and blintzes from the Jewish bakery he and Adele both favored. "For your breakfast tomorrow," he explained. "Nathan, how are you? So good to see you again!" They shook hands warmly. "Adele, you look wonderful," Stan continued, giving her a kiss on the cheek before he even took off his coat. "How are things?" Nathan saw his mother glow and he liked Stan even more. At Adele's instructions, they took their places at the dining table and proceeded to do justice to her raisin cake.

Stan had just bought a new car, a Honda Civic, for its excellent gas mileage. He worked in Akron and drove at least seventy miles a day. "You remember how gas prices jumped after the *Yom Kippur* war, when the Arabs imposed the oil embargo and Nixon called for voluntary gas rationing and told us to turn down our thermostats?" Stan reminded them. "And the price of a barrel of crude rose from, what was it, about three dollars to five dollars? I remember some gas stations were charging a buck and a quarter a gallon!"

"Yes, I remember that, it wasn't even two years ago," Nathan said. "And our regular station, Ernie's, allowed only ten gallons per customer and was closed on Sundays."

"Nathan, do you remember I called you and said you shouldn't turn back your clock, you know, daylight savings time wasn't over?" Adele asked. "During the oil embargo? I remember I overheard some people in a restaurant talking about it and blaming the Jews for the whole thing."

"So what else is new?" Stan asked. "That's our function. Never mind that the Egyptians invaded when Golda was asleep at the switch. Of course they blamed the Jews."

Adele didn't like the turn the conversation had taken, even though she had provided it. "That wasn't a normal time," she said. "Nathan, please don't ever feel that being Jewish is a major issue in this country, the way it was for your grandparents in Germany and Russia. It's better here for the Jews than anywhere else, better than it's ever been."

"I hope you're right, Mom," Nathan said. "But the recession is having a big effect on construction and therefore on the architectural profession. It's not like medicine or law. Not only is the job market very tight in architecture, there aren't many Jewish architects and fewer Jewish architectural firms, even around the country as a whole."

"You're saying your chances of finding a good job with a good firm are slimmer because you're Jewish?" Stan asked.

"Well, I don't think they're improved because of that!" Nathan grinned. "As you said, so what else is new? But I'm planning to look everywhere, East Coast, West Coast, South, Midwest, everywhere, once I'm finished with my studies and have my degree."

"I hope you find something close to Cleveland," Adele said. "I want what's best for him, of course, but why shouldn't what's best for him be in this area?" she asked Stan.

"Of course!" Stan agreed immediately.

"Let's see what happens," Nathan said. "I haven't even begun to look yet. First things first!"

*****

Michael Kaplan had been Nathan's best friend since they had been classmates in junior high school. They had been roommates in their undergraduate years at Ohio State. Nathan could talk to him as to no one else. They had arranged to meet at Michael's apartment in Ohio City, just across the Cuyahoga River from downtown Cleveland, the following evening. On the agenda were pizza, beer, a Cavaliers' game on television, but mostly conversation. That was understood, as always. They discussed the Cavaliers, they reminisced about their adventures when they had hitchhiked from California to Cleveland five years earlier–on one occasion they had been threatened by four skinheads whom they had scared off with karate tactics–and they recalled athletic feats when they had been in high school. Nathan had been a wrestler and Michael had been captain of the football team.

Michael, now a social worker in a group home, was about to change his life. He was engaged to a girl from Columbia, South America, whom he was to marry in the fall. They were seriously considering moving to Tucson, which they had recently visited and where there were job opportunities for both. Nathan asked the obvious questions. "Isn't Tucson unbearably hot in the summer? What about your folks here, what are they going to say about your living so far away?" "Have you heard of air conditioning?" Michael asked in turn. "And long distance calls? And airplanes that fly in all directions? And when it comes to weather, what makes you think my parents wouldn't appreciate having somewhere to stay in Arizona when Cleveland is freezing over in January?" Nathan had to concede all points. The conversation turned to his studies in Columbus.

It didn't take Nathan long to tell Michael what had happened to his independent study project. "They shut you down without warning?" Michael asked. "What did you fuck up?"

"Nothing," Nathan said. "I don't think it was anything I did. I think it was what I was trying to do."

"That doesn't make any sense," Michael said.

"I know," Nathan said, "and that's what's bothering me."

"No explanation at all?" Michael asked.

"The best I could get out of my major professor," Nathan said, "the one who takes me out to lunch almost weekly, was that the time wasn't right for my study. He was very flustered by my questions. What I think or maybe suspect is that somehow somebody complained to the Dean, somebody in the AIA, maybe right here in the Cleveland chapter. But I can't prove that. And why somebody would complain, somebody seeing the project as a threat, I don't understand that. But what I really don't understand is why a complaint, if that's what happened, would result in such drastic action. Michael, I got a lot of encouragement when I started, from everybody. The assistant dean, the same guy who told me that the

Dean had decided to stop the survey, had been very helpful at the beginning, even got me my own little office. The committee–three professors, not just one advisor, which was already unusual–was very supportive throughout." Nathan got up, can of beer in hand, to pace up and down in Michael's small living room. Michael watched him appraisingly.

"I did learn a lot from the whole experience," Nathan continued. "About questionnaire design, how to phrase a question so that the response can be coded easily for statistical analysis, how to code the questionnaires themselves so as to preserve their anonymity–did you know about the regulations governing the use of human subjects, even in survey research?" Michael shook his head. "Well, I do now," Nathan said. "And of course I know the names and addresses of one hell of a lot of architectural firms in Ohio, and I even visited some for the preliminary interviews I did as part of the pilot they had me do. So it hasn't been a total loss, not by any means. But it's been a loss, no question about that either, and I just can't understand what happened."

"So where are you now?" Michael asked.

Nathan stopped pacing, sat down, and explained what he was to do with Professor Rosenberg. "It may take me an extra quarter," he said, "but I'll have my degree by the end of the year, and then I hope new doors will open."

"This will be your fourth degree, right?" Michael asked.

"Yes, the master's in architecture will be my fourth. Why?"

"I wouldn't have predicted that you'd be in school this long," Michael said. "I remember when we were roommates how you used to build architectural models in our apartment, all those all-nighters for your design courses. I thought you wanted to get out of school and into practice just as fast as you could. You know what I think? I think you changed soon after your father died. Right?"

Nathan nodded. "Yes, his death had a very powerful effect on me. He was still so young, really, and he had worked so hard, he was cheated, I felt, terribly cheated out of what he deserved. I think that somehow subconsciously, you know, without really thinking about it–young guys don't do that–I had expected him to grow old slowly and eventually retire with my Mom to a little comfortable house in the suburbs somewhere, a house that maybe my brother and I would help them buy, and to enjoy his old age and his grandchildren and his garden, you get the picture. Norman Rockwell stuff way back in my mind somewhere, as I say, without really being conscious of it. This is the first time I've thought about that at all. You must be more stimulating than I ever gave you credit for."

"About time you found out, then," Michael teased back. "But what about the change, you know, after your father died?"

Nathan thought for a moment, searching for a place to begin. "I always respected my Dad," he said. "He worked hard every day. He worked for the same company for over twenty years. He used to get up at four a.m. on work days and wouldn't get home before four thirty or five in the afternoon. He always took care of the outside of the house, you know, shoveling the snow, cutting the grass, painting it when the time came for that. He wasn't big on chores inside, but I remember that he did wash the floors down once in a while. You know he didn't make a super living jumping up and down on a bread truck every day. We lived in the poorer section of Beachwood, and the Jewish community there is pretty well off, on the whole. I was very aware of that."

"So it was about the money for you, at that time?"

"Maybe at the beginning," Nathan said, "you know, when I first started thinking about college. Funny, when you talk about something you begin to understand your own feelings more clearly. No wonder psychology is so popular. Imagine getting paid to listen to somebody figure out what the hell happened in his life."

"How much?"

"How much what?"

"How much are you going to pay me? I'm sitting here listening!"

"Hey, you invited me, remember? Lured me here with pizza and beer? This is the price you have to pay!" They laughed with affection for each other.

"Go on," Michael said.

"All right. This is going to sound sort of pompous. After my Dad died, I realized that what I wanted to do wasn't just to make a lot of money. I wanted to make a difference, the way he had done in my life–in my family's life. I'm not stupid, I know how important money is, but after a certain minimum, it's not enough. You're a social worker, you know about this. Real satisfaction comes from making a difference in people's lives, from building something solid, something lasting, from helping to change things for the better for a lot of people, not just yourself. Don't you feel that way?"

"Yes, you know I do," Michael said. "And I wouldn't call that pompous, I'd call that idealistic."

"And what I wanted to do–what I still want to do–is to combine business principles with architectural practice in ways that help everybody, the profession, its clients, and the community as a whole. The study I had started was to be the foundation for all that. That was the change, Michael. That's what I came to after my Dad died and I realized that life is short and if you're going to do something worthwhile, you had better get started. Does that make sense to you?" "Very much so," Michael said. Then he asked, "How old was your father when he died?"

"Only fifty-four," Nathan said. "He had had a heart attack earlier, when he was forty-seven. A warning. But he had to go back to work, of course."

They sat silently for a while. Then Nathan said, "I want to tell you something about my Dad, but please don't repeat it to anyone." Michael gave him a look. "I know you won't, Michael, I just want to emphasize this. My Dad had the Kinsman route at the time the neighborhood was changing. It wasn't as safe for a white man as it had been a few years before that, before the race riots, you remember. The year before my Dad died, he was robbed by a black man while he was delivering bread to the stores on Kinsman. The guy put a gun in my Dad's mouth, took all his money, and told him that honkies weren't welcome in the neighborhood any more. When my Dad told his supervisors what had happened, they moved him to the west side and put a black driver on the Kinsman route."

"There are still a few white businesses down there that have a good relationship with the black community," Michael said.

"Well, not the bread company," Nathan said. "Anyway, they changed his route, and I think he was more upset about that than about being robbed. He had many good customers on the Kinsman route, black as well as white, and an entirely new route on which he didn't know anyone was pretty stressful. Very stressful. I think I told you that my Dad had his last heart attack while working in his truck. He was found inside his truck on the 130th Street exit ramp off 71 South. I never got the whole story on that. I don't know who found him, I don't know how long after the heart attack, I don't know how he got to the hospital or when. What I remember is standing next to his hospital bed, talking to him. His doctors told me later that he never heard a word I said, that he was in a coma with extensive brain damage because of the loss of blood flow during his attack, but I always felt that he heard me. I think he did, Michael." Nathan paused. Michael waited.

"Anyway," Nathan continued, "on this new west side route, Dad had one customer who always gave him a hard time, really nasty, whenever Dad delivered bread and pastries and so on. I don't recall that Dad ever complained about any other customer, ever, anywhere. But this guy got to him. He was an Arab. One time when my Dad was leaving his store, he overheard him call my Dad a dirty Jew. He said it loud enough for my Dad to hear. It was as if he was daring Dad to complain or start some kind of trouble. Well, Dad felt that at his age it would be hard to find a new job, especially after he'd just been transferred from the Kinsman route because he was white. In other words, he wasn't at all sure that his company would back him up. He had tried to find a new job after his first heart attack, when he was forty-seven, but eventually he went back to work for the same bread company. But that guy was a thorn in his side, I know that. And I know that he really missed his old route on Kinsman."

"And you think that work became so unpleasant for your father, with the Arab and the new route, that this somehow caused his heart attack?"

"I think it was probably a contributing factor," Nathan said. "I don't know, of course. I wonder about it. I didn't want to look into it because who knows what that would produce, and I was concerned about the effects on my Mom and my brother and his family. You start lifting the cover off something, you don't know what you're going to find."

"Like your situation at the University," Michael said.

Nathan was startled. He hadn't thought of the comparison. "Well, in a way, yes, I suppose so," he said. "You don't know. Sometimes it's better not to know, for instance, if you can't do anything about it. I can't do anything about the way my father died. I can't help wondering about it, that's all."

"And about how your study was stopped, or why?"

"My feeling is that I should buckle down, do this new work on modular housing, get my degree, pass the NCARB exam, and start my career, that's what I think I should do," Nathan said. "You know, be like you. Only my Mom wants me to find a nice Jewish girl and stay in this area, not like you," he added mischievously.

"What a surprise!" Michael said. Their mood lightened. They finished the pizza and had another beer. Michael promised to let Nathan know about his wedding plans as soon as his fiancée told him what they were. Nathan laughed and promised to come to whatever remote location she picked, provided it was in the United States. Then he drove home. It was midnight and he knew that Adele would be worried.

She was still up, waiting for him, but he reassured her easily, telling her how great it had been to see Michael and how they had enjoyed the Cavaliers' game and their pizza and beer. He didn't mention either the conversation about his father or that Michael was thinking of moving to Tucson once he was married. As much as Adele had always liked Michael, she would have been more enthusiastic if Nathan's best friend were providing a suitable example by marrying a nice Jewish girl. As for

Tucson, she had already expressed her hopes the previous evening, ostensibly to Stan but clearly directed at Nathan, that he'd find a good job close to home. So instead he chastised her gently for not having waited for him to pull out the sofa bed in the living room, and she asked him if he would like a brownie and a glass of milk for dessert, to which he assented. Adele said, "I'm going to sleep. If you want, watch the television for a while."

But neither was ready for sleep, and Nathan heard Adele's bedroom television set, very faintly. She was watching an old movie. He could hear Humphrey Bogart's distinctive rasp. He turned on the set in the living room to find the same movie, also keeping the volume low, and got under the covers of the sofa bed. On the end table next to him was a large framed photograph of Nathan and his father, Martin, taken just after his high school graduation ceremony. The light from the television set was bouncing off the photograph, illuminating different areas as the television picture changed. Nathan stared at the photograph, first at himself in a dark suit, and then at his father, wearing a grey suit, on his left side and shaking his right hand. He remembered how firm the grip had been, and how his father's pride shone in his eyes. Martin had not graduated from high school. He had had to go to work.

It was getting very late. Nathan grabbed the remote and shut off the television. The moonlight entering the room combined with the parking lot lighting reflected from the pavement, but Nathan closed his eyes and fell asleep almost at once.

He was standing on a polished stainless steel plate with raised patterning. There were no walls or ceiling. He was surrounded by an impenetrable darkness on all sides, prevented from falling into it only by the polished stainless steel floor below his feet. Suddenly the steel's color changed to a semi-gloss painted black finish, and light from a source he could not see made the floor's raised diamond patterning more evident. Then the flat steel plate began first to flex and then to warp. Nathan's footing slipped as the plate changed form. Now he was sitting beside his father. The steel plate below his feet was wrapping itself over a portion of the engine protruding into the cab of his father's bread truck. His father, next to him in his brown vinyl driver's seat, was folding a small sheet of paper, but not before Nathan had recognized it as a handwritten list of two and three letters Nathan knew to be initials, with adjacent three-digit numbers. Marty unzipped his chocolate brown uniform jacket to slip the folded sheet into his shirt pocket.

Two- and three-story red brick buildings with stores along their first floors, glass windows gleaming dully, lined both sides of the street behind parked cars. The sky was turning grey and snow was blowing. Marty carefully backed the truck into a parking space in front of a small grocery store. He had not noticed Nathan next to him, and Nathan realized that he was invisible. Once, when he had been six or seven, his father had taken him to work and Nathan had helped him deliver bread that day. He wanted to ask Marty if he remembered that, but he could not say anything. Marty slid the driver's side door open, eased himself out, and went to the rear doors to open them. Turning in his seat, Nathan saw his father take a large flat tray and load it with pastries and loaves of bread packaged in plastic. He somehow flowed out of the truck to follow his father into the store, where Marty stacked the fresh bread and pastries neatly onto shelves and removed several loaves about to go stale. Then he walked over to the checkout counter where the owner was waiting for him. Nathan saw the grocer pay Marty for the bread and pastries. Then he seemed to be asking him some questions. Nathan couldn't hear what was being said, but he saw Marty take the paper out of his shirt pocket and write something on it. The grocer gave Marty another three dollars. Marty put the paper back in his pocket, took the stale bread, said something to the grocer, who smiled and waved goodbye, and went back to the rear of the truck to put the stale bread on a "Return" shelf. Nathan flowed behind him, still invisible.

Suddenly a young black man appeared behind Marty, demanding change. Marty, startled, said he didn't have any. "You not hearing me, man, I said give me your money!" Marty started toward the driver's side of the truck. The black man pulled a gun out of his pocket, stuck it against Marty's back, and ordered him into the service alley next to the store Marty had just left. "Give me your money!" Marty pulled some dollars out of his pocket and handed them over. "Your numbers money!" the man snarled, stuffing Marty's dollars into his own pocket with one hand and putting his gun into Marty's mouth with the other. "Listen up motherfucker, I'm a blow your fucking head off in three seconds you don't give me the money, what's it gonna be?" Marty unzipped his jacket, reached inside to a zipped pocket, and pulled out a thick wad of bills. The black man grabbed it and said, "Now get the fuck outta here, honky, this ain't your neighborhood no more, you got that?" Nathan flung himself on the man to get his gun, but neither the man nor Marty saw him. The man was gone as suddenly as he had appeared. Marty walked back to his truck just as a black Cadillac sedan with heavily tinted windows pulled up in front of him. A young white man in a grey felt hat and a black leather coat got out of the driver's seat and called him over. They shook hands. The man pushed Marty hard against the rear passenger door and ordered him into the car. Nathan suddenly found himself in the back seat of the Cadillac listening to his father explain what had just happened in the alley to an older white man neatly dressed in a grey sharkskin suit with a big diamond ring on the little finger of his right hand. "He put a gun to my head," his father explained. "I had to give him all the money!"

"How much we talking about?" the man in the sharkskin suit asked.

"About two hundred," Marty said.

"You still got the slips?"

"Sure," Marty said.

"Hand them over," the man in the sharkskin suit said. Marty gave him his list.

"You can't work for me here no more, Marty," the man said, pocketing the paper. "We're in a turf war here on Kinsman, and I need someone younger, a tough guy, someone scary. You can sell your bread here but you can't run numbers for me here no more."

"I've worked for you for over ten years!" Marty protested. "I've been one hundred per cent loyal and honest! I always--"

"I know that, Marty," the man interrupted. "So don't worry about the two C's, all right? You did right by me, I know that, so I do right by you. But you can't work for me here. You're a family man. You got, umm, you got responsibilities."

Suddenly Nathan found himself on the corner of the street he had grown up on, walking toward his home. His father was walking next to him. "Nathan," his father was saying, "sometimes you need to go with the flow. Sometimes, yes, you have to fight. You'll know when. But sometimes you need to go with the flow." "But what about when you were robbed at work?" Nathan asked, never questioning that his father could hear him now as well as see him. "I had a family," Marty said, "a wife, two sons who needed me--look, my life was almost over. Yours is just beginning." The street began to change. One-car attached garages expanded into two. White painted wooden homes became red and blue, or turned into brick. Nathan felt lost. His father had gone. "Dad, Dad," Nathan yelled, "where are you, Dad?"

"Nathan, are you all right?" It was Adele. "You're shouting in your sleep! Were you having a nightmare?" Nathan was immediately wide awake and sat up. "I'm so sorry, Mom, I'm fine," he said. "Sorry I woke you, just a dream, please go back to bed. Too much pizza, I guess, but I'm fine now, really."

"I could make you a warm glass of milk."

"No, please, thanks, Mom, please go back to bed, really." She said all right and went back to her room. Nathan pondered his dream, knowing that it was a strange continuation of his conversation with Michael. But what in the hell was that all about, "sometimes you need to go with the flow and sometimes you have to fight"? The milk suddenly sounded good, although it didn't need to be warm. He went to Adele's small galley-type kitchen and poured himself a glass. Then he returned to the sofa and slept soundly.

The next day he returned to Columbus. His mother had packed the left-over chicken for him, along with some soup, canned foods, cereal, cookies, and pastries. He had protested a bit, but took everything. It made her happy.

*****

Nathan got back to Columbus by four the next afternoon. He had had time, driving down, to think about his conversation with Michael and the dream it seemed to have produced. The dream reinforced his feeling that whatever had happened in Brown Hall, whatever mysterious opposition his projected survey had suddenly stirred up, he had to finish his studies and get his degree. Unlike his father's Kinsman route, his neighborhood had changed overnight. The people in charge now were nobody he knew, nobody he recognized. Apparently they had changed the rules of the game, or maybe the game itself, and he was somehow out of date. But he still had the option offered to him, to assist Professor Rosenberg with his work on modular housing. A few more months at worst. Then the professional degree. Then the job interviews and the NCARB. And then his career would begin at last. He knew he could do the work. What was required now was calm and perseverance. After he had unpacked his bag and put the food away as Adele had told him, he laid out the drawings and materials Rosenberg had given him. He hadn't gotten to them in Cleveland as he'd planned. The clock, he told himself, was ticking.

He made the most of both spring and summer quarters, attending class, completing his projects, doing well on the exams. The fall quarter of 1975 was to be his last. He needed only to finish his work in Rosenberg's modular housing studio. His relationship with Rosenberg had become friendlier, but Nathan's favorite professor was Arnold Prescott, quirky though the man was. They continued to have lunch at the Kon Tiki every other week or so. On such an occasion, on the first day of October, Prescott surprised Nathan with a revelation and a proposition.

"Nathan," Prescott said, stirring his extra dry vodka martini with the little plastic sword still skewed through the two olives, "I've been having some health problems for a while, specifically, angina."

"I'm sorry to hear that, Professor," Nathan said.

"I think we've known each other long enough and well enough now, Nathan," Prescott said, "for you to use my first name." He made it sound more like an instruction than an invitation. "All right, Professor Arnold–I mean, Arnold," Nathan said. Prescott smiled, but Nathan could see that something was wrong with his eyes. "Have you seen your doctor recently?" Nathan asked.

"Yes," Prescott said. "I'm scheduled for surgery next week, and that's what I want to talk to you about. I'm going to be out of commission for a while, and I'd like you to take over my Professional Practice course. I know you just took the course yourself this last year, but you did very well in it, and you've had some practical experience."

"But the students are graduate students, like me," Nathan said.

"They respect you," Prescott said. "I'm sure that won't be a problem. In fact, if you'll agree, there won't be any problem. I've talked to Frank Wilson and he's agreeable. There'll be a small stipend for you, proportional to the time period, of course. And Nathan, you're my first choice. If you don't want to do it, I'm not sure I have a second at this point."

"Well, of course I'm flattered, honored, even," Nathan said, "and a stipend wouldn't be necessary, but I have to ask, how much time do you think will be required?"

"You'll need to grade the midterm papers, teach the remaining weeks–as you know, the class meets twice a week–and grade the finals. That exam is all ready, you don't need to prepare a new one. You do have to submit the final grades to the Registrar by the due date, which is one week after your graduation. You're just working with Harry now, isn't that right?" Nathan nodded. "Well, I think you can do it. It will take some hours each week, but I've talked to Frank Wilson and he's agreed that you'll be paid. So contact him today or tomorrow and he'll make the necessary arrangements."

Frank Wilson again. Another favor from Frank Wilson? The last one didn't work out so well. On the other hand, go with the flow. "All right, Arnold," Nathan said. "I'm really very flattered, and as I said, payment isn't necessary."

"Yes, of course it is," Prescott said sharply. "Never undervalue your professional work, Nathan, whatever it is. If you want to do something *pro bono*, do so on behalf of a client who is truly needy, not Ohio State University. Make a donation as a wealthy alumnus, not as a graduate student watching his bills. Now, have you given any more thought to attending our Christian camp next summer, as my guest?"

His health may be poor but his style is the same as always, Nathan thought. This is not the time to disappoint him. "Yes, I'd love to attend, thank you very much," he said. "I plan to be working by then, though–you said it's for an entire week?"

"Five days," Prescott corrected. "You might find the job you're looking for right here in Columbus. Then it shouldn't be hard to work the camp into your schedule. I might need some help in my own practice by then, you know. Who knows, possibly some day you could become my partner!"

"Thanks very much again," Nathan said, "even for just raising the possibility!"

"Let's see what happens," Prescott said more reflectively. "My partner and I separated two years ago, and I've been working as a solo practitioner since then. The economy is slow now, especially for new buildings. I don't really know what my needs will be in a few months. But let's keep it on the table. Are you looking at any particular cities, where you'd like to locate?"

"Yes," Nathan said. "Cleveland, of course, and Chicago and Atlanta, and San Francisco and Los Angeles–and now Columbus!"

The next day's meeting with Wilson produced the necessary details without incident, although Nathan was on edge and Wilson seemed nervous. Peggy, too, had welcomed him, he thought, with something of a question in her face, even though she knew why he had come. Drop it, he said to himself. Go with the flow. I'll graduate in just a few weeks more.

The class went well. The students had no problem accepting him as Prescott's substitute, and after the jitters of the first few minutes, Nathan found that he enjoyed teaching. Prescott had been right–the work did not take an exorbitant amount of time. And the work for Rosenberg began to be very interesting, much more so than he'd anticipated. In the meantime, through periodic telephone calls to Mrs. Prescott, Nathan learned that Arnold's surgery had been successful, but that his recovery was taking longer than the doctor had expected. Nathan had sent a card and a potted plant to the hospital and was pleased to hear that both had survived the hospital. The plant, Mrs. Prescott told him–Betty, she said to call her–was now in their family room.

A week or so before Nathan's graduation, Prescott called him at his apartment to ask whether he was still planning to attend the men's camp the following summer. It was scheduled for the second week of August, and Prescott had a brochure ready to mail to him, providing instructions and directions. "Yes, I am, Arnold," Nathan said, somewhat to his own surprise. But the man had been good to him, was recovering from major surgery, and Nathan sensed that his acceptance would please Prescott greatly. He was right. Then Prescott asked about the Professional Practice course. Nathan told him that everything was on track. He planned to move out of his apartment the day of his graduation, taking his belongings to Cleveland, where he would stay at his mother's place until December 5. That day he'd return to Columbus, pick up his students' final papers, and then grade them in Cleveland during the next week. He'd come back on the eleventh to turn in the final grades to the Registrar the following day, when they were due.

"Do you have a place to stay on the eleventh?" Prescott asked.

"I'll probably stay at the Ohio Stater on High Street," Nathan said. "The price is right and it's right across the street from campus."

"Betty has been busy taking care of me, and there are some complications to that, with the bathroom and so on," Prescott said. "Otherwise I'd invite you to stay with us. The next time you're in Columbus, we'd be delighted if you'd stay here, Nathan."

"Thanks very much once again," Nathan said. "Of course I understand. We all want you to get completely well just as fast as you can, Arnold."

"Yes, well, come to my house at least for lunch on the twelfth, after you've turned in the grades," Prescott said.

"Great, I'll do that," Nathan said. "About noon?"

"Tell you what," Prescott said, "Betty may want to adjust that–why don't you confirm your hotel reservation a couple of days before you come in and then I'll leave a message for you there–where did you say you'll stay?"

"The Ohio Stater on High Street," Nathan said.

"Right, I'll make a note right now–one second–OK. I'll leave a message for you there about the time to come here for lunch on the twelfth."

"Fine," Nathan said. "How are you progressing generally?"

"Well, maybe a bit more slowly than we'd all hoped, but I've taken a few short walks in the shopping mall and my wind is getting better. I still have some pain from the surgery, but it's not major. The doctor said I could probably go back to work, at least a few hours a week, in about a month. And I've gotten all sorts of get-well cards and good wishes that have cheered me up, Nathan, former students–Brian Keating sent a wonderful card, rather sentimental, I must say, and candy that I can't eat, and would you believe it, I got a card from the Dean himself, Webber, I mean, and Wilson too, oh, and from people in the profession around town and around the state too, Ballard Warren, Arthur Mercer, even a card from Roger Fleming in Washington. I forgot to tell you, Nathan, he called me while I was still in the hospital, and even asked about you–I guess you had corresponded with him."

"Yes, you remember," Nathan said, thinking suddenly that Prescott didn't remember. "The AIA was considering doing its own survey about the time I wanted to launch mine, and I had written to him after talking to Warren about doing the work jointly."

Prescott was silent for a long moment. "Nathan, I'm rather tired," he said. "Good luck finishing up and congratulations on your graduation next week. I'll leave that message for you. Good-bye." Nathan heard the phone click.

*****

The phone rang next to Prescott's bed a few minutes later. He let it ring, still thinking that he should never have mentioned Fleming to Nathan, still remembering the scene in Webber's office when the Dean had refused to explain to him and Rosenberg just why the AIA wanted Nathan's study stopped. Rosenberg, furious at the way Webber had insulted both of them with his assertion of decanal authority, had stalked out. The phone kept ringing and finally he picked it up.

"Hello?"

"Arnold?"

"Yes, this is Arnold Prescott, who's calling?"

"It's Roger Fleming, Arnold, from Washington at the AIA, how are you doing?"

"Roger, how nice of you to call," Prescott said. The room seemed very warm. "I'm doing a lot better, I think, still have a ways to go, I'm afraid."

"Yes, well, try to be patient, Arnold, I'm sure it's tough, but patience and peace and quiet will help you greatly, I'm sure. Arnold, I won't keep you long, but tell me, are you still heading the state chapter of the AIA or did you relinquish that under the circumstances?"

"No, Roger, I'm still serving as the president, that's very important to me personally as well as professionally," Prescott said. "I'm looking forward to resuming my duties at least in a limited capacity next month, when I'll also return to work for a few hours a week. My board has been very understanding and supportive."

"Good, I'm very glad to hear that, Arnold," Fleming said. "Can you tell me anything about what's going on in Ohio on the qualifications-based selection issue, selection of architects?"

Prescott was surprised. So Fleming's ostensible solicitude was a cover for whatever was really on his mind. "We're not directly involved as a professional association," he said. "Except for such testimony as may be requested by the Legislature or various boards. But as you can understand, I haven't been involved with any of that since even before my operation. I can give you the names of the people—there haven't been more than a handful—who have either testified or been asked to appear, I'm not sure which at this point."

"No, that's all right, thanks," Fleming said. "Is anyone working on our behalf with the Legislature?"

"Oh, of course, as always," Prescott said. "The key people are anxious to have their interests represented adequately, that's always the case. Your paper on techniques that the national AIA thinks would be most effective is quite useful, by the way, although we've modified it somewhat to our particular circumstances, as you can imagine. Ohio has its particular character, just as other states do."

"Yes, of course, I expected that," Fleming said. "We're hearing that from Texas and South Carolina and Vermont too, so that's no surprise. But we think the program is working quite well and that qualifications-based selection will be the basis for architectural practice in the future, pretty much throughout the country. Uh, Arnold, just by the way, any news about your student, Goldberg or Goldstein, what was his name?"

The room was definitely too warm. He'd have to ask Betty to turn the heat down after the phone call. "Goldstein, Nathan Goldstein?"

"Yes, that's the fellow. He was going to do that survey and had written to us about it here."

"Yes, I remember," Prescott said. "What about him?"

"His name came up at the last board meeting, I don't recall quite in what connection, just that a couple of the directors were talking about people's hidden agendas and ulterior motives, you know, the hidden politics of what we all have to put up with. Goldstein's survey came up as an example."

"He's doing well," Prescott said, ignoring whatever Fleming was implying. "In fact, we hired him to take over my graduate course here when I went into the hospital, doing a fine job with that, and he's scheduled to graduate next month. I just talked to him a few minutes ago, and he's going to come by for lunch after he turns the grades in for my course next month."

"Oh? When is that? Not when he graduates?"

"No, that's earlier," Prescott said, more and more puzzled.

"Graduation is at the end of November, and then he's going home, Cleveland, and he's taking the final reports with him to read them there, but he has to come back to turn his grades in on the eleventh, and he's coming for lunch the next day. Roger, what's this about?"

"Well, to tell you the truth, Arnold," Fleming said, "I'm not so sure that we did right by him, and I was a little bothered by the doubts the fellows raised about his motives for that survey last spring. I'd like to keep track of him in case I hear of a suitable opportunity for him somewhere–you know, I do hear of some good jobs opening up in various parts of the country–and frankly, I'm impressed by your favorable judgment of him. So I'd just like to know what's going on with him just in case I can steer him to some opportunity, you see."

"Yes, I see!" Prescott said, very pleased. The room seemed quite comfortable. "That's very good of you, Roger!"

"So he won't be staying with you, then, when he comes next month?"

"No, he's going to get a room at the –just a minute--" Prescott consulted his note–"the Ohio Stater, right by campus. Do you mind if I tell him of your interest, Roger?"

"I'd very much rather you didn't do that, Arnold," Fleming said at once. "I can't make any promises, you realize that, and I certainly wouldn't want to disappoint him again, absolutely not. So let's just keep this between us at this point, Arnold. I'm really glad you're on the road to recovery and I wish you the best of everything, always."

"Thanks, Roger," Prescott said. "I won't say anything to Nathan, then. Good to hear from you!"

"Goodbye, Arnold," Fleming said. Prescott heard him hang up. Betty came in. "What a strange conversation that was!" Prescott said. "Who was it?" she asked, taking the receiver from his hand and hanging up. "Roger Fleming from the national AIA," he said. "He wants to help Nathan Goldstein find a good job after he graduates, but he doesn't want me to mention anything to Nathan." "Oh, that's so nice of him," Betty said. "How are you feeling, dear?" She straightened his blanket and moved to fluff his pillow. "I'm a little tired," Prescott said, smiling, "but not so tired that I couldn't use a kiss!"

*****

The Ohio Stater's chief attractions for parents and friends of Ohio State students were its location and especially its rates. It was much cheaper than the new high-rise Holiday Inn on Lane Avenue just west of the campus. But it had not aged gracefully. The white paint was peeling off the brick exterior walls. The interior finishes in the common areas were worn. The furniture in Nathan's room, on the first floor, was replicated dark wood plastic laminated finish. The double bed was positioned flush against the rear outside wall backing up to what the students called "Pearl Alley," officially North Pearl Street, which they used as a short cut to avoid traffic on High Street. The main purpose of the alley, which ran north and south behind the commercial buildings along High Street, was to let delivery trucks bring goods to the loading docks and garbage trucks haul the leavings away. The alley, lined with dumpsters, smaller trash receptacles, and litter all along its length, was the view that greeted Nathan when he slid back the heavy patterned drapes covering the window. The room was stuffy. The noisy through-wall heating and air-conditioning unit didn't circulate the air to Nathan's satisfaction, and although it was cold outside he wanted to open the window for a few minutes. He noticed that the latch was broken and that the window couldn't be locked. He slid the aluminum-framed glass panel open with some difficulty–the frame stuck first by the sill and then by the header–but he managed to wiggle it open and slid it back and forth to loosen some of the accumulated debris. The air felt good. He decided to go for a walk around campus and to leave the window open a crack. Then he went back to the television set, turned it on just loud enough so that it could be heard in the hall and out in the alley, and left for campus. He had already picked up the note at the desk, confirming his lunch at Prescott's house the next day, when he had registered.

His return to campus seemed anti-climactic after his graduation. Adele had been so proud that she had twice asked strangers to photograph the two of them, Nathan in his cap and gown, Adele in one of her best winter outfits, beaming. They had talked at length on the drive down and back, about what he had accomplished, what he hoped to accomplish, how proud she was of him, how proud the whole family was–and then, of course, about how she hoped he'd find the prescribed girl and the perfect job right in Cleveland. He reminded her that he had already scheduled some interviews on the West Coast as well as in Atlanta and Chicago, and intended to try to set up some more in those areas. She tried to change the subject, but he could tell that her mind was still on what she wanted for him and for herself. "Maybe," he said, "after I pass the NCARB exam, with some more practical experience, I'll have a better chance with a Cleveland firm. And you know I've already sent out quite a few inquiries there anyway."

"When will you take the exam?" she asked.

"Next December, in about a year," he said.

"That's not so long," she conceded. "By that time something will have opened up in Cleveland. Something good."

"From your mouth to God's ear!" Nathan said, grinning at the old expression. She was pleased.

He got back from his stroll around campus and his dinner at the McDonald's on High Street–Adele would not have been pleased by his choice of restaurants, he knew–in time to call the Prescott's. He reached Betty, who told him that Arnold was resting but that they both were looking forward to his visit tomorrow. "So am I," Nathan said. "Just in case Arnold needs to call me tonight about something–anything at all, I'm in Room 144 at the Ohio Stater. You have the number?" "Yes, of the hotel," Betty said. "I'll tell him." They said goodbye. Nathan checked the folders with the students' final reports and the grade sheets to be delivered to the Registrar in the morning, put them in his attaché case on top of the plastic laminated dresser, and tried the television set. Only local channels were available, and reception was poor. He had brought some magazines and read for a while, but by midnight he decided that it was time to turn in. He remembered that he'd left the window open and closed the sliding glass window, but he couldn't lock it. He left the light on in the bathroom and left the door slightly ajar for just enough light to make out the shapes of the furniture. He was asleep within a few minutes.

He woke up with a start. His bed had moved. He opened his eyes and, in the dim light from the bathroom, saw a man in a ski mask squeezing his way through the window, bracing himself with one foot on the edge of the bed. The man stood at the foot of his bed for a moment, looking at him, and Nathan could see that he was tall, thin, and, from the openings in his mask around his eyes and mouth, black, and that he was about to attack. In an instant Nathan was up on top of his bed in a karate stance. The man took a step backwards, and then grabbed the attaché case that contained the student papers and grades Nathan was to submit the next morning. As the man glanced at the window he had just come through, Nathan hit him solidly on the side of his neck. The intruder swung at Nathan, hitting him, but Nathan caught the next blow with his left arm and counter punched again and again, twisting his fist with each blow, hitting him in the ribs and kidneys, putting his full shoulder weight into each blow, all the while yelling, "Get the fuck out of my room! Get the fuck out of my room!" The intruder dropped Nathan's attaché case and stumbled toward the window, gasping, putting his head through the opening and struggling to raise his knees to the sill. Nathan hit him three more times as the man fell out onto the pavement below. He pulled himself up and ran down Pearl Alley. Nathan closed the window, sprang to the phone, and called the front desk.

The night manager, as he called himself, turned out to be a kid in his late teens, nervous, flustered, even embarrassed–but not, Nathan noticed, shocked or even surprised–asking how the intruder had gotten in, where he was now, whether he should call the police, what Nathan wanted him to do. That's it, Nathan thought, getting dressed and packing his things. "Look," he said, "your window is broken and it's obviously been broken a long time. That's how he got in and how he got out. You can't see him now because I threw his ass out and he ran away. Call the police if you like, they can always file another report, which is all they're going to do. I don't care what you do, just move over and let me use that phone." The kid backed away and Nathan called the Holiday Inn on Lane Avenue. Yes, they had a room, but it was very late–Nathan, looking at his watch, saw that it was about three a.m.–was he associated with the University? Yes, Nathan said, he was with the School of Architecture and he had to turn in his grades in the morning, and would be there within a few minutes. "We'll expect you shortly, then," the lady said. Nathan hung up, grabbed his bag, and brushed past the night manager, saying, "Thanks for all your help." He left him standing befuddled in the room and shut the door behind him.

It took him a while to fall asleep at the Holiday Inn. The struggle with the intruder at the Ohio Stater probably hadn't lasted two minutes, but the excitement hadn't worn off. He had given a good account of himself, Nathan thought, but maybe he should have tried to subdue the bastard and held him for the cops somehow–they could have questioned him. Maybe this wasn't just happenstance that the guy had picked his room with the broken window lock. Maybe there was more to it. But after he had lit his second cigarette–he had lucked out and gotten a room in which he could smoke–he began to relax. Let's not get paranoid, he told himself. You did good. That was a time to fight and you did. He stubbed out his cigarette and fell asleep.

Five hours later, after a light breakfast, he checked out, wincing a little at the full night's bill for forty-five dollars, and drove to Brown Hall. Peggy was delighted to see him, as always, and congratulated him on his recent graduation. Nathan realized that he had missed an opportunity to bring Adele to the office to meet Peggy, but then he thought no, Webber and Wilson might have been there too, so it was just as well. He gave Peggy the students' final reports, and she also took the grade sheets, explaining that she had to go to the Registrar's office that morning in any case. Wilson was at a meeting somewhere, and the door to Webber's office was closed as usual. Peggy didn't mention him and Nathan didn't ask. They chatted briefly about Nathan's impending job search, and the classes she was taking in education, and he promised to stay in touch. She gave him a hug and wished him every success.

It was still too early to go to Prescott's house and Nathan took another walk, this time around the Oval, in the heart of the campus. It was cold but not bitter, and he sat down on one of the many benches, admiring the various buildings surrounding the Oval. Almost all his memories of his undergraduate and graduate days here were very pleasant, some extremely so, bringing smiles no matter how often he reviewed them. Still, there were the two major disappointments of the past year, the study he hadn't been allowed to carry out and the mysterious fate of his entry in the Brussels Prize competition. Those wounds hadn't healed. At least the scar tissue was still fresh.

The mystery of last night's intruder pressed on his mind. That the hotel hadn't fixed the lock on the window, even though the room was on the first floor and backing into an alley, all right, that wasn't so surprising, given the general state of disrepair the place was in and the kind of night manager they employed. But why didn't the night manager seem surprised? Did they have break-ins on the first floor every night? Were all the window locks broken on all the rooms along that corridor? If not, had the man tried every window until he found one he could enter? Was he just a thief or robber, or did he want something else? He hadn't been armed, apparently. Was the guy just supposed to scare him? Why? Well, he'd gotten more than he'd bargained for, Nathan thought with satisfaction. A time to fight, he thought again. He got up to drive to his lunch at Prescott's house.

Nathan arrived exactly on time and Betty, who had seen him park in their driveway, opened the door for him as he walked up. "It's so good to see you again, Nathan," she said. They had met several times before and Nathan liked her. She was an attractive lady in her early fifties with a bright smile and a pleasant demeanor. "And you too, Betty," he said. "How's Arnold?"

"It's not one of his better days, I'm afraid," she said. "He's waiting for you in the living room. Please excuse him, he's still in his robe, he just wasn't up to getting dressed this morning."

"No problem," Nathan said, suddenly aware of his jeans. "I'm pretty informal myself, as you can see." "You're fine," she said. "Arnold, Nathan is here!" Nathan, standing in the foyer, could see Prescott on the sofa in the living room. "Yes, come in, come in, Nathan," Prescott said.

His voice wasn't very strong. "Come in, sit down here, so we can chat."
Nathan went in and carefully shook Prescott's proffered hand. The grip
was weak. Prescott was wearing navy blue pajamas with satin piping and
a navy blue cloth bathrobe. His feet were up, resting on a white-cased
bedroom pillow on a dining room chair Betty had put next to the sofa for
that purpose. Nathan, who had never been in Prescott's house previously,
noted that the furniture, both in the living room and what he could see of
the dining room, was in the "Prairie" style inspired by Frank Lloyd
Wright's designs, including the trademark diamond overlays on cabinet
doors and end tables, and wood slats on the sides and backs of the sofa
and chairs, allowing the leather and fabric upholstery to show through. A
fire was burning in the rough-cut stone fireplace, and Barbra Streisand's
voice came out of the stereo, very softly.

"Sorry, can't squeeze your hand yet," Prescott said, smiling feebly.
"I'm a little tired today."

"It's very good to see you, Arnold," Nathan said, hoping he'd struck
the right tone. "Thanks so much for having me over for lunch today."

"Lunch will be ready in about half an hour," Betty said. She had
followed Nathan into the living room. "Can I fix you a drink, Nathan?"

"I don't suppose you'd let me have a vodka martini?" Prescott asked
before Nathan could reply. "You know I can't," she said. "You're still on
medication and will be from now on, remember? What about a glass of
wine?"

"All right," Prescott said, looking sorrowfully at Nathan. "A glass of
the merlot, then."

"That would be fine for me too," Nathan said quickly.

"Good," Betty said. "Be back in a moment."

Prescott looked at his brown leather slippers encasing his feet on the
chair. "I've been trying to get Betty to buy an ottoman," he told Nathan,
"but she maintains that it wouldn't fit with the way she's arranged the
living room. I think it would fit just fine, but as you either know already
or will find out eventually, women think that they were born in charge of
interior decorating. I had most of this furniture before we were married,
and I stood firm on keeping these pieces–told her it was an architect
thing. So she's redecorated the rest of the house and I've learned to
appreciate country-style furniture. Well, sort of." Betty came back with a
tray bearing two glasses of wine, offering one to Nathan first. Nathan
took it, waited for Prescott to take his, lifted his glass, and said, "To your
complete recovery, as soon as possible!"

"I'll drink to that, thanks!" Prescott said. "So would I, but I'm still
busy in the kitchen!" Betty said and left the room.

"What influenced you to get the Frank Lloyd Wright Prairie Style pieces?" Nathan asked, returning to Prescott's subject. "I think it's very attractive and fits very well in your home."

"I always admired Wright," Prescott said. "I never met him, but I admired him, not just as an architect but as a man. Did you know that the AIA shunned Wright? They saw his building designs as much too far outside the mainstream. They were opposed to the direction he took. But he wouldn't compromise his ideas or his ideals, his vision, you could call it. And now just about everyone agrees that his innovations have stood the test of time. Still, I have to admit that he's more revered by the historians and the general public than by the members of the profession. But he's kind of a hero of mine."

"If you'd been president of the Architects Society of Ohio in Wright's day," Nathan asked, "would you have been one of the people who shunned him even though you admired his work?" Prescott seemed startled by the question and didn't answer immediately. "Well, as president of the Society," he said, rather slowly, still thinking, "I suppose I'd have to follow the members' wishes. I might not agree with them, of course. But I told you, I didn't know Wright personally. If I had, that probably would have made the decision more difficult."

"Suppose you had, I'm just curious about this, suppose you'd known him personally, and knew him to be honorable, and you thought that his work and ideas ought to be more influential," Nathan asked, "would you still go along with what the membership wanted?"

Prescott was silent so long that Nathan grew uncomfortable and sorry he had pressed the question. Just as he was about to change the subject, Prescott said, "Yes, I guess so, but I wouldn't feel good about it. I think I'd know that I lacked the courage to follow my personal convictions, and I'd wonder whether I was submitting to majority rule not because it was right but because it was in power. Now let me ask you: what would you have done in this position?"

"I would have supported Wright," Nathan said, but not defiantly.

"You're showing your youth," Prescott said. "Young people think they can change the world. Then they get older and find it hasn't changed much at all, they've only gotten older. The changes that people like to point to when they talk about revolutionary new this and revolutionary new that usually aren't changes in behavior."

"Innovation, though, in ideas, in technology, in the ways we work, whether together or alone, does seem to me to be at the core of our nation," Nathan said. "Maybe I'm naive. Or as you say, just young."

"How was your stay at the Ohio Stater last night?" Prescott asked.

He'd had enough of the conversation about Wright, Nathan saw. "Very exciting," he said. "Too exciting. I had a big scare."

"What do you mean?"

"A man broke into my room, came through the window–it had a broken lock, the maintenance in that place is very poor–and tried to attack me. I fought him off and threw him out, the same way he had come."

Prescott stared at Nathan uncomprehendingly. "Are you serious?"

"Absolutely," Nathan said. "The night manager, he called himself, was of no use–can you imagine, he didn't even seem surprised?–and I checked out in the middle of the night and went over to the Holiday Inn. I know it's hard to believe, Arnold, but that's exactly what happened at three o'clock this morning."

Prescott stared at him, almost too long, Nathan thought. Then, without any change of expression, he asked, "What about your job prospects, Nathan, anything lined up yet?" It was Nathan's turn to stare. After all this time, I'm still not used to his herky-jerky style. It's unbelievable.

"Not yet," he said. "I've got some appointments in various cities, with more to come, I think, but so far nothing really promising."

"If you're still available next spring," Prescott said, "I might need some help in my office. I'll have to see. But I want you to keep in touch, no matter what."

"Of course," Nathan said. Betty came back. "Gentlemen," she said, "lunch is served at last!"

Chapter X
Rubin, May, 2005

Rubin's mood, the next morning, was considerably more cheerful. He made himself a pot of coffee before he took his bath–showers, he had always maintained, were for boys in physical education classes–shaved carefully, brushed his teeth for rather a long time, pleased, as usual, by how sturdy they seemed, and deliberated whether he should get dressed or enjoy breakfast in his underwear, slippers, and robe. It was a cozy white terry cloth robe with a collar, a breast pocket, and a matching belt he could knot over his stomach. He succumbed to its embrace. Then he pushed his two whole wheat slices of bread down in the toaster, poured his coffee, mixed in the requisite cream and sugar substitute, and congratulated himself for remembering his pills. Three varieties for high blood pressure; one for acid reflux; one for kidney stones; the child's aspirin to unclog the arteries; and one for–what was it? General aches and pains? Stupidity? To counteract the side effects of all the other pills? Or to accord some measure of equity to all the drug companies competing for his life?

He had recently read an article in one of the many magazines to which he subscribed about the relationships between physicians and drug salesmen, or more formally, representatives of the pharmaceutical companies. Apparently it was common practice for reps to visit private clinics, medical partnerships, solo practices, and even, to Rubin's surprise, practitioners at medical schools, laden not just with free samples of their products and the associated brochures and propaganda, but also with small gifts for the office staff: a potted plant for the reception area, for instance, or pizza for lunch, or coffee mugs, key rings, pens and note pads, bearing their companies' logos. Outright bribes. Rubin recalled how publishers' representatives, years ago, occasionally brought free books to professors of English, called "examination copies" under the pretense that they would be returned if the professor decided not to "adopt" the book as a required text for one of his classes. But that particular fringe benefit had pretty well dried up over the years as book prices had soared, competition had intensified, and reading, as the major activity of most forms of higher education, had withered. Pill popping, however, prescription or over the counter, was more popular than ever, not just for recreational purposes among the young and their imitators, not just for identifiable diseases and visible decay, but also for the New You that so many of his fellow citizens hoped to become: slimmer in the waist, hairier on the head, more pleasant, energetic, relaxed, in control. New ailments, new psychoses, new sources of stress, dysfunction, and maladjustments, announced, it seemed, weekly, were always and miraculously accompanied by a new pill or a new regimen or a new curative now available through prescription provided you were not pregnant, had no history of renal failure, and had had no liposuction in the past eighteen months. The money flowed in like the mighty Mississippi.

To judge from his daily quota of unsolicited e-mail from what might be the homebound contingent of pharmaceutical representatives, Rubin thought that sexual dysfunction, attributable, in particular, to male organs of microscopic size, appeared to be the most common and therefore most profitable problem afflicting American men: profitable, that is, for the companies flooding the nation's computers with excited announcements of the remedies they had ready. They had certainly put their chips on that number. He wondered whether the reason he could afford all these pills for high blood pressure every day–or at least on those days he remembered to swallow them–was because thousands of his neighbors were swallowing "enhancement" pills. If so, he was all for it. Their problems with their tiny pricks kept his hypertension under control. Things balanced out. Maybe there *was* a god, chuckling somewhere.

Where did all these corporate wizards of potency come from, these autocrats of alchemy, these Parkes and Davises, Warners and Lamberts, Mercks, Glaxos, Lillys, Upjohns, Pfizers, Pfezzers, Pfees, Pfis, Pfos and Pfums? Were their origins back in the nineteenth century's snake oil salesmen in their covered wagons, setting up shop in the next town square, hawking their self-distilled whisky as cures for stomach ailments, hair loss, melancholia, foot fungus, and respiratory difficulties? A rapid-patter *spiel,* a cheerful demeanor, a hearty laugh, and--for two dollars--good health and a warm glow in a little brown bottle? The artists among them had prospered, relegating their less talented colleagues to other professions or at best to village drug stores, relying more on vanilla ice cream than on Mrs. Naborly's QuickFix Regurgitant to make a living. No snake oil salesman could have continued indefinitely with just a single covered wagon. Three or four generations later, a campus of research buildings surrounding corporate headquarters, a staff of thousands, an advertising budget in the multimillions, fame on every television channel, actors and actresses of all ages vying for the infinitely dramatic roles of crone and geezer, yuppie and spouse, snotty kid and bleary parent, unable to breathe, walk, eat, sleep, eliminate, have sex, tolerate spring, commit introspection, or achieve wisdom without (the sky clears, the music becomes louder and cheerier, the faces look ever so much happier) The New Pill, not yet banned by the Food and Drug Administration.   Rubin, still munching his toast, was entranced by his vision. But, he decided, that last bit, the Food and Drug Administration, one of Teddy Roosevelt's contributions to the Republic, was a sour note, ominous, even. Think of thalidomide. Vioxx. Anthrax. No, that was a disease, not a drug. Hard to tell the bugs from the bugkillers without a program.

The phrase reminded him of the Nathan Goldstein saga. Who was P.D.? Why had Harry objected so strongly to what'shisname, Brian somebody, as Goldstein's assistant? Especially after Prescott had recommended him? Come to think of it, what was the relationship between Harry and Prescott, other than that both were members of Goldstein's committee? They had been colleagues, but had they been friends? Was the fact that Harry had kept the clippings about Prescott's death, along with the obituary and the program of the memorial service, indicative of some bond between them? Something stirred in the back of his mind. He had read the newspaper account of Prescott's heart attack, the obituary, and the program of the memorial service, and he had just seen something that tied in with them. He got up, got dressed, and went to his "study"–it was also the smaller bedroom, but Rubin had had to offer it to overnight guests only very rarely –where he had found a place for Harry's file cabinet. He took the "Prescott" folder out of the **Nathan Goldstein** accordion file, and once again read the account of Prescott's demise, the obituary, and the program of the memorial service.

He found what he was looking for in the program, the name he had run across in Harry Rosenberg's notes on Goldstein's questionnaire. Brian Keating. Remarks by colleagues and former students. No children had spoken, no relatives. Keating had been Prescott's student, which was no doubt the reason Prescott had recommended him to assist Goldstein with the code for the questionnaire. Keating wasn't identified in any other way, but Prescott's colleagues were all identified by title–Professor Harry Rosenberg, Professor Jack Montague, Dean Emeritus Charles Webber. A Ballard Warren was listed as President of the Cleveland chapter of the American Institute of Architects. Rubin remembered that

Prescott had been an official of the Ohio chapter of the AIA. Keating was one of only two people listed without a professional affiliation. The other was a Sean O'Bannion. Probably another former student. Well, if they had their own companies, or were working for other architectural firms, a program of a memorial service for a former professor probably wasn't the place to advertise. Now if they had gotten jobs with pharmaceutical companies, that might be a different story. What with dramatized advertisements for laxatives, aphrodisiacs, breath fresheners, toilet paper, vaginal rinses, denture fasteners, penis stiffeners, and for all he knew navel lint softeners on television every twenty minutes in every American home, who was to say that an eye-catching arrangement of pills alleged to prevent arrythmia, on display at a small table placed ever so delicately just next to the open casket, would be considered in bad taste?

So Harry had offered some remarks about Prescott at the memorial service as well. He checked the file of Harry's reprints. Yes, there was a manila folder behind it, marked *"Miscellaneous, Unpublished."* It did not take him long to find what he was looking for.

Arnold Prescott

Arnold Prescott was a leader of the profession of architecture. He was an indefatigable advocate of the highest professional standards, moral as well as esthetic. He was a vigilant guardian of the profession's interests. He was a tireless campaigner for the recognition of its importance, not merely in the local community but in the larger society. His colleagues, recognizing his commitment, his dedication, and his great abilities, asked him to assume the leadership of our State's chapter of the American Institute of Architects many years ago, and he did so willingly, graciously, and I believe successfully in all respects throughout his long and distinguished period of service.

As my colleague at Ohio State University's School of Architecture, Arnold impressed me in particular for his close, occasionally warm relationships with many of his students: for many, he was more than their teacher, even their mentor, he was their friend. You will hear from two of them in a moment, and they will, I am sure, tell you more about that. My own observations included another instance, however, in which a graduate student of much promise somehow failed to complete work of great interest to both Arnold and myself. But Arnold found a way not only to hide his disappointment but also to salvage the student, helping him to find a new direction and seeing him through completion of his degree. What might have been a tragic turn of events for the young man turned out to have been nothing worse than a detour. It was Arnold who deserved much of the credit for that, and I am sure that many, many other students, colleagues, and friends could share similar anecdotes illustrating his care and concern.

We will all miss Arnold Prescott, a fine architect, a fine leader, a fine teacher, and a fine man.

What a strange elegy, Rubin thought, what a mix of cliché, banality, and grudging respect! And the reference to what clearly had to be Goldstein? What had possessed Harry to allude to that story, not the happiest he could have told? There *was* something wrong between Harry and Prescott. At least from Harry's point of view.

The telephone rang. For a moment Rubin debated whether to let the machine answer it, but he decided that it was too early in the morning for solicitors. Evelyn was out of town. Perhaps it was someone he might want to talk to. If not, he could claim, if it was a stranger, that Professor Rubin was in Paris, and if it was not, that he had something on the stove and would call back. Or perhaps something more imaginative, something improvised for just this occasion. "Hello?" he said cautiously.

It was Gerald. "Walter, glad you're in–I–umm--how are you first of all?"

Something was wrong. Gerald never began hesitatingly unless he needed a moment to find how or where he wanted to start with whatever he had on his mind.

"I'm fine, Gerald, even better now that I'm talking to you," Rubin said, aware that his concern was in his voice. "What's up?"

"Well, what's up. Quite a bit. Laura is in Nashville–her mother's very sick, in the hospital, in fact, and probably won't pull through. This at a time when she's supposed to be in court on some damned merger or hostile takeover or whatever it is, I never can understand high finance and the legal tangles these pirates get themselves into. I don't suppose there's ever a good time for a parent to die as far as their children are concerned, though."

This did not sound like Gerald at all. "Go on," Rubin said.

"Yes, there's more," Gerald continued. "I was thinking–look, do you have any plans? Are you going anywhere? Is your calendar all booked with women and important scholarly stuff and lectures you have to give or attend or whatever you retired Michigan professors do?"

Now that sounded more like Gerald. "Yes, of course, I'm terribly busy, especially with women," Rubin said. "But they'll all wait patiently, I'm sure. What have you got in mind?"

"I was thinking of flying out to see you," Gerald said. "I could call Laura in Nashville to let her know, and come out this afternoon or evening, if you're sure it's not an imposition and I'm not forcing you to disappoint a vast throng of your admirers, both of them."

Yes, Gerald was definitely recovering. "I'd be absolutely delighted, Gerald," Rubin said. "Make your arrangements and call me back to let me know when to pick you up. Stay as long as you like. Whatever it is, I can listen for hours. But tell me that it's not something between you and Laura."

"No, no, no, don't worry about that, Laura doesn't even know about it yet, which may or may not be part of the problem–it's Rita. Look, I'll tell you–"

"Rita!" Rubin felt a stab of pain. Rita was his darling, almost as if she had been his own daughter.

"Walter, I don't want to go into the whole thing over the phone. I'll call you back within thirty minutes. I'll stay overnight, but I'll probably go home tomorrow or at least the next day. I'll call back in a few." Gerald hung up. Rubin did too, very slowly, staring at the phone. What could it be? Had she gotten herself knocked up? Gotten married? To some imbecile? That wouldn't be his Rita, as bright and ambitious and charming a girl as any in the Western Hemisphere, she wouldn't let herself fall for some clown, some snake oil salesman, with nothing but a flashy smile and a line of jive–but who could explain what so many women saw in the men they wound up with? Vain, egotistical, the type who, when they were on the prowl, checked their reflection in every store window, worried about their hair, who alluded to clothes and whisky and cars by brand names or in-group designations–years ago, "deuce and a quarter" for a Buick 225--and they still had charming, attractive women hanging on their every stupid word. They probably weren't the ones who bought the pharmaceutical enhancers he had associated with the affordable price of his hypertension pills. Could Rita have fallen for somebody like that? And Gerald had killed him?

Well, he had better clean up, put Harry's folders back in the file cabinet, check the hide-a-bed, change the sheets, put out the towels in the guest bathroom, see what groceries he might need–they'd go out to dinner, of course, and he would not let Gerald pay–and try to curb his impatience. What could it be? Rita had always been so sensible, so quick to see the humor in things, so funny, so delightful. Never mind curbing his impatience, he'd ask Gerald when he called back. No, he wouldn't; he wasn't going to be the Jewish mother. Gerald wanted to tell whatever it was his way, and it was his story.

*****

Rubin's first inquiry was about Laura's mother in a Nashville hospital, but Gerald had no news. He was to call Laura later that evening at her mother's house, where she was staying with other relatives. They went to Rubin's Chrysler.

"Nice car," Gerald said, carefully easing himself into the front passenger seat. Rubin had neglected to adjust it, and Gerald's first move was to search for the lever. "Brand new?" He found the lever, pushed the seat back as far as it would go, and tilted it back. There were some disadvantages to his height and bulk

"Sorry, I should have thought of that," Rubin said. "Evelyn isn't quite your size. It's not quite a year old. Not Evelyn, the car."

"Yes, I followed the explanation," Gerald said, now struggling to adjust the seatbelt around himself. "She must be one tiny lady."

"Oh, I don't know," Rubin said. "Big enough for me. All set?"

"Let 'er rip," Gerald said. "This is a new parking structure, isn't it? To go with the new terminal? Of course I haven't been out this way in some years, so what's new to me might be old hat to you."

"That's right," Rubin said, checking his shirt pocket for the parking stub. He had already paid the fee at one of the automated Pay Parking Ticket Here machines inside the terminal. It had blessed the stub with an imprimatur and returned it to him for deposit in the automated Exit Here machine, which would raise the barrier as soon as it had eaten the stub. Rubin always wondered what employment the people who had been replaced by the machines had found to support what, he was sure, were their large and desperate families. Whatever it was, it couldn't possibly provide health insurance. "It's part of the new McNamara terminal, brought to you exclusively by Northwest Airlines on its way into Chapter 11, and of course assorted taxpayers, all of whom believe that they live in a free-enterprise system. So, I'm not sure, maybe it was finished four or five years ago. When was the last time you were here, by the way?"

"Longer ago than that, I think," Gerald said. "I think we stopped on our way to Chicago for that family reunion. Yes, Rita was about ten or eleven, so it was at least ten years ago. I had that damned Buick, I remember that. This is a Chrysler, isn't it?"

Rubin let the power window down again, pleased, as always, with the luxury, and inserted the parking stub in the waiting slot. "Yes, a Chrysler 300," he said. The barrier rose and he shifted into drive, carefully pausing at the opening to the road leading back to the highway. Good place for an accident. "Ten years. Just about the time I retired. You too, I think."

"That's right," Gerald said, "ten years ago. Right now it seems more like twenty years ago. My God, Walter, we're both seventy-five. How are you feeling, incidentally? What you said in New York was rather troubling, you know, about running around to too many doctors and swallowing pills by the dozens."

"How am I feeling?" Rubin repeated. "As you said, seventy-five. Very nice for a summer day, but not so great for a worried uncle anxious to hear how his favorite niece has upset her father so much that the man flew six hundred miles west to tell me all about it." He waited. Gerald didn't answer right away.

"I'm confused, Walter," he said, finally. "Confused and somehow angry, not at Rita but—well, I'm not sure what I'm angry about. It's not who, anyway. And it all has to do with being black in America, still, after all this time, well off as I am and rather successful and certainly aware of how much and how fast things that I never thought I'd see change *have* changed after all. But man, what baggage we have all brought with us, all of us, black, white, whoever."

Rubin, waiting for Gerald to continue, turned off I-75 to the westbound lanes of I-94. Gerald, a huge presence next to him, was very far away.

"Rita blew the interview," Gerald said suddenly. "It was so unlike her. She had done reasonably well on the MCAT, it turned out, perhaps not brilliantly, but completely adequately, and she was called in for an interview. She hadn't expected that an interview would be necessary—no, that's not the word—involved, maybe, so perhaps she was a bit on the muscle when she went in. I'm guessing about that, though. The interviewer wasn't a faculty member but one of these professional Negroes from the Minority Recruitment Office or Support the Colored Children Program or whatever they call themselves now, and in no time at all Rita was all fangs and claws. And when she's like that, she's just like Laura. I hadn't expected—"

"Hold on, Gerald," Rubin interrupted. "This was at Columbia? The medical school? Her first choice, as I remember?"

"Yes, all of the above–I don't remember whether I told you but she took the MCAT about the time you were in New York, and got the results some time after that, of course, and that's when she was contacted to come in for this interview. Anyway–"

"Do you know her score?" Rubin couldn't help himself, but as soon as he asked he regretted that he had. Rita had done adequately, Gerald had said.

"Yes, she got a 31 out of a possible 45. Not great, but the minimum for admission to a fair number of medical schools–including yours, I looked it up–is around 24 or 25. I think it's scored something like the ACT, not the SAT. Of course the whole thing is about to change–the SAT already has–I'm not sure about the ACT. You must have heard that there have been problems up and down the line, as is to be expected with these machine-scored, computerized examinations administered to the masses all over the country under all kinds of circumstances. Anyway, the guy really pissed her off, assuming, first of all, that she'd need financial aid and a mentor and an orientation–you know, he might have had the right name but the wrong file–but he didn't seem to realize that, having done her B.S. at Columbia, she knew the university very well, and in fact had participated in some programs for premed students, and wasn't interested in how supportive and encouraging his Multicultural Diversity Minority Program or whatever it's called wanted to be of everyone the less white the better."

"He said something like that?" Rubin asked, incredulous.

"Well, no, he wasn't that dumb or blatant–I'm giving you Rita's version, which may have included some imaginative editorials. But in no time they were shouting at each other about affirmative action."

"Oh Christ," Rubin groaned.

"Exactly," Gerald said. "Rita isn't Ward Connerly, but she certainly has all kinds of reservations about affirmative action–no, she despises it, at least as a policy. She says it's just another way of not seeing black Americans, no, black people. Lump them all together and they disappear, she says. In our case, we're not disadvantaged, she had an excellent education, she wasn't brainwashed to think she's white, she's been active in one or another community program for years, and she doesn't need to hear any lectures on what it means to be black, not from Cornel West, not from Amiri Baraka, and certainly not from some jive brother whose main function is to color up the dean's Christmas party."

"Say what?" Rubin said. They both grinned.

"Well, I'm not in a mood to be charitable," Gerald continued. "Now here's the thing. I don't really disagree with Rita about affirmative action. It's insulting as hell. I don't remember asking for special consideration when I played ball or when I got my degrees or when I worked for the government or had my own company. It never occurred to me that I was disadvantaged because I was black or because my parents hadn't gone to white schools in Alabama or because their grandparents had been slaves or because some white overseer raped my great-grandmother. Or whatever happened. Nobody gave me anything I didn't earn, and I understand Rita's anger. But there's another side to it. In fact, there's more than one other side to it."

Rubin waited.

"Look, you know what?" Gerald said. "I'm hungry. Is there a place where we could get something to eat on the way to your condo? It's almost seven o'clock."

They were approaching the exit to Ypsilanti and Rubin had an idea. "How about some Middle Eastern food?" he asked Gerald. "Rice and lamb and chicken shawarma? Pita and hummus?"

"What's shawarma?"

"It just means shredded, I think. I know a place between Ypsilanti and Ann Arbor. Very good food, although the owner doesn't like me."

"Sounds very interesting," Gerald said. "Let's try it and you can tell me–no, let me guess why the owner doesn't like you. You climbed on a table and declared that God meant the Israelites to have the whole Arabian peninsula, from the Red Sea to the Euphrates, all the way south to the Indian Ocean, especially the oil."

"Yes, something like that," Rubin said, taking the exit. "The trouble was, the table was shaky and I fell into the soup. Made quite a mess."

"What was it, really?" Gerald asked.

"I'm not sure," Rubin said, "but it started the night you and Laura took me out to dinner, in New York, after I had visited Ellis Island. I took a cab back to the hotel–"

"Oh yes, it's coming back to me," Gerald said. "The cab driver was in the restaurant with some other people and you recognized each other."

"Yes," Rubin said, "and one of those other people turned out to be the owner of the restaurant we're going to now. Not long after I came back from New York I took Evelyn out to dinner, and she had noticed this place along Washtenaw Avenue–it used to be something else, also Middle Eastern, and she was curious. So we went and I recognized the owner from the New York restaurant–come to think of it, I had also seen him the next day at LaGuardia, he was on the same plane going back to Detroit–and I remembered the name of the cab driver, and asked this man about him. He--"

"You remembered the name of the cab driver?"

"Yes, and not only that, I still do. Hashem Iskandar. Isn't that amazing?"

"Astounding," Gerald said. "I thought you had particular trouble remembering names?"

"Normally I do, but for some reason I can't explain, I remember Mr. Iskandar's name from his license, and I remember this man's name as well, Mr. Alhumaidi. How do you explain that?"

"I don't," Gerald said. "But I've never been able to explain anything about you anyway. Damned immigrant who couldn't speak a word of English when he stumbled off the boat, winds up as a professor of English for Christ's sake. Is this the place? Jericho's Wall?"

"This is it," Rubin said, carefully easing the car into a parking space he selected with Gerald's size in mind. "Jericho's Wall. When Evelyn told me of the new name for the place–I guess they remodeled it as well–I joked that I hoped they wouldn't have a trumpet player, but she didn't catch the allusion. Oh, well, you don't have to know the story to appreciate the food."

They got out of the car. "So what's the punch line?" Gerald asked.

"There isn't one," Rubin said. "We came here, I recognized Mr. Alhumaidi from the New York restaurant and LaGuardia, and after a very good meal I asked the waiter to ask Mr. Alhumaidi to stop at our table so that I could compliment him personally. So of course he did and of course I did and Evelyn did and we were beaming at each other like brothers in Christ when I asked him how Hashem Iskandar was. Was *that* ever a turd in the punch bowl!"

"How did he react?" Gerald asked.

"Like a thunderclap. His face changed, he demanded to know how I knew Iskandar, I thought he was going to hit me. I said something about how I had seen him in the restaurant with Iskandar, who had been my cab driver, grabbed Evelyn, and got the hell out. Maybe Iskandar owes him money or refused to marry his daughter or is backing another faction of some Kill All the Jews group in the old country. I thought you might ask him."

"Oh, just what I flew out here to do," Gerald said. "Are we going to order takeout or shall we eat inside at a table?"

"By all means, inside at a table," Rubin said, holding the door for Gerald. He saw Mr. Alhumaidi behind the counter, the handsome young waiter, and some other people, and saw, as well, that all eyes were on Gerald, as always. The waiter rushed up, smiling.

"Welcome to Jericho's Wall," he said. "Your first visit, I think?" He hardly seemed aware of Rubin.

"Yes, thank you, but I've heard so much about you from my friend here," Gerald said, including Rubin in the conversation just as Mr. Alhumaidi, also smiling, joined them. The two Arabs glanced at Rubin, smiled and nodded, and clearly did not remember him. Business had been good, Rubin surmised.

"The table by the window?" Mr. Alhumaidi asked Gerald, saying something in Arabic almost simultaneously to the young waiter, who immediately disappeared.

"Yes, fine," Gerald said. "OK, Walter?"

"Fine," Rubin said, watching the dynamics unfold and pretty sure that he knew what Gerald was about to do. Seventy-five, white-haired, not quite as straight as he used to stand, but still very much in charge. They sat down at the table. The waiter materialized, bringing water, menus, napkins, and utensils, and, this time without any perceptible signal from Mr. Alhumaidi, evaporated again. "You are from out of town, I think?" Mr. Alhumaidi asked. "But you know Middle Eastern foods?"

"How is your chicken shawarma?" Gerald asked by way of answer. As smooth as ever, Rubin thought. A few minutes ago he had never heard the term. Now you'd guess that he had just written an article for the New York *Times*' food section on the intricacies of shawarma, chicken, beef, or lamb.

"Ah, we think it's very good," Mr. Alhumaidi said. "Would you like to taste it?" They were obviously becoming fast friends.

"Yes, indeed!" Gerald was enthusiastic. Mr. Alhumaidi excused himself and went to bring a sample. "I think I know what you're doing," Rubin muttered. "First," Gerald said, "as Hippocrates instructed us to do, praise the man's chicken shawarma." Rubin nodded in agreement. Mr. Alhumaidi returned with a generous sample of various meats. Gerald tried them all, praised them all, and selected the chicken, as did Rubin. The waiter brought pita, hummus, and fattoush. They began to eat. After about fifteen minutes, Mr. Alhumaidi inquired whether everything was satisfactory.

"Excellent," Gerald said. "Of course my friend here had told me how much he had enjoyed his meal here. But he was not the first one to tell me about your restaurant: I heard about it first in New York, from a cab driver."

"Really!" Mr. Alhumaidi said. "In New York! A cab driver! We are famous in New York? Who was he, if I may ask?"

"Ah," Gerald said. "Names are not always easy to remember. Hasan Something? No. Al-andar? No. Alkandar, perhaps?" He looked inquiringly at Mr. Alhumaidi. Rubin chewed vigorously.

It worked. "Hashem Iskandar?" Mr. Alhumaidi asked, simply ascertaining the possibility.

Gerald took a drink of water. "Perhaps so," he said. "That could be it. I do know that, after I had said that I was going to Detroit–he took me to the airport–he recommended this restaurant very warmly. Apparently he knows you?"

"He should," Mr. Alhumaidi said. "He is my nephew, my sister's son. And now he is part-owner of Jericho's Wall: he has just invested some money. At first he did not want to do so, but when he heard how good business is, he changed his mind. We are going to expand out in back as soon as we get the building permit."

"He did not tell me that he was an owner!" Gerald said.

"If he had, you might not have believed his recommendation," Mr. Alhumaidi said.

"Well, now *I* shall recommend Jericho's Wall, and as far as I know, we are not related," Gerald said. Mr. Alhumaidi laughed. "Maybe not, but we don't have to be relatives if you also wish to invest in the restaurant," he said. "There are still opportunities!"

Gerald smiled. "I think you are already very successful, if this meal is any indication," he said, "but I appreciate the offer. I assume that I do not have to make an immediate decision?"

"No, no," Mr. Alhumaidi reassured him. "Come back tomorrow, try the lamb, and let me know then how much you would like to invest!" They all chuckled. Mr. Alhumaidi returned to his place behind the counter. When, a few minutes later, Rubin paid the bill and once again left a generous tip for the waiter, Mr. Alhumaidi thanked them both and reminded Gerald that he was expected the following evening. Gerald did not quite promise to come.

"Well, you solved that mystery," Rubin said, easing the Chrysler into traffic, careful, this time, not to cut off anyone else. "Well done!"

"You mean the mystery about why he yelled at you the last time you were here?" Gerald asked.

"Yes," Rubin said. "I must have asked about Iskandar just after he had refused to invest any money in his uncle's place, and Alhumaidi was furious at him and anyone who said he knew him, like me, an unsuspecting passenger in his nephew's cab. All perfectly logical, or at least consistent with what we know of human nature. Just as is the fact that neither he nor the waiter remembered me–remember what we were saying in New York about the importance of context? I was with you, not with Evelyn, so I was out of context and not memorable. Which brings us back to Rita."

"How does that bring us back to Rita?"

"Since the Iskandar/Alhumaidi mystery is solved–I remember telling Evelyn that it would be permanently inscrutable, like so many other things, and we would just have to live with it–I'm sure that's not the only thing I've been wrong about in my long life but at the moment I can't recall any other examples–anyway, since you've solved the mystery of the angry Arab restaurant owner, it's time to return to the angry daughter, victim of an affirmative action conspiracy at Columbia. You were telling me that although you basically agree with Rita about how degrading affirmative action is, there's more to it."

"I see. From previously angry Arab to presently angry daughter. Walter, your mind is like a steel trap. A steel trap designed by Rube Goldberg. But that's very much in context, isn't it?"

"How do you mean?"

"Well, you picked this restaurant to see if the change of context, substituting me for Evelyn, would change the man's behavior, and you think it did, erasing your memory from his cortex, when for all you know he remembered you perfectly well, decided not to pursue your rude inquiry about his now reformed nephew who has apparently recognized his familial obligations, and instead set about recruiting yet another investor, obviously flush with money. Thank you for dinner, by the way–it really was very good."

Rubin was amused. "All right, your alternative explanation is plausible, I'll give you that," he said. "Now will you get back to Rita?"

"Let's get settled in your place with some wine or whatever you have, and yes, that's what I want to talk about," Gerald said. "Or vent, maybe. But the first thing I have to do is to call Laura. She should be at her mother's place by this time–even if she could stay at the hospital, there isn't anything she could do and she'll be more comfortable at the house."

"Did anyone else from the family come into town?" Rubin asked.

"Her brother was to fly in from Los Angeles some time today, and there are Laura's cousins in Nashville, and some other people. I'm sure there are people with her." Gerald was quiet, then resumed, as if he had heard Rubin ask what he was thinking. "You know, I never got along very well with Laura's people, and although we never discussed it openly, I know she knows it and is troubled by it. She was quick to tell me that I didn't have to fly down there with her, that she would call me if and when the time came."

Rubin didn't think it was necessary to acknowledge how astutely Gerald had guessed what he had wondered about. "What was between you and Laura's relatives?" he asked.

"Probably a number of things–I'm sure they all thought I was too old for her, for one, and then the fact that I had three children already by my first wife, and that I had been married twice before–actually, I was still married to Madeleine when I met Laura. And then, although I don't remember that anything was ever said openly, that Madeleine was white, I'm sure that was a topic of conversation among some of Laura's family. Having committed treason once, who could tell when I might betray racial solidarity once again?"

"You're not serious?" Rubin asked. "You really think they asked themselves that about you?"

"Walter, as close as you are to being a soul brother, at least in your heart, there are subtleties within subtleties to this business of being black in white America that simply can't be put into textbooks. Isn't there anything comparable in Jewish families? A new husband whose previous wife was a *shiksa*, what would the family say?"

"Welcome back, Prodigal Son!" Rubin said. "Or what's the matter, she called you a dirty Jew? But I don't really know. I know of Jews who divorced Jewish wives to marry Gentiles, in fact I've known a couple of them personally, but I can't recall having heard of a Jewish man who divorced his Gentile wife to marry a Jewish woman."

"Interesting," Gerald said. "Sounds like a topic for Oprah or one of those television shows like hers: *Men Who Marry Down: Why Jews Won't Do It and the Brothers Will*." They both chortled at the thought. Rubin pulled up at his garage and worked the magical door opener. "Open Sesame!" Gerald said. "Very nice! There *are* other places to live besides New York!" They got out of the car, retrieved Gerald's carry-all from the trunk, and went in.

"Let me show you your room, complete with private bath," Rubin said. "There's a phone on the desk, and you can make your call there."

"Thanks," Gerald said, following Rubin, "I have my cell phone in my bag."

"No, use my phone," Rubin said. "I just heard that the phone companies charge double for long-distance calls on cell phones, both the caller and the receiver of the call."

"Really!" Gerald said. "In that case, I *will* use your phone, thanks."

But about ten minutes passed before Gerald reappeared. He looked distressed. Rubin started to ask about Laura's mother, but Gerald shook his head: "No, Mrs. Mayberry's still resisting the Lord's call," he said. "In fact, she seems to be a little stronger, although she's not conscious yet. But Laura's talked to Rita, and is *not* happy."

"White or red?" Rubin asked, pointing to the bottles on the sideboard. He had the glasses ready.

"What's that red?" Gerald asked.

"It's a merlot," Rubin said. "But I've got some others here if you'd—"

"No, the merlot is fine," Gerald said. "Make it a full glass, I think I need it."

Rubin poured the merlot for Gerald and another glass for himself.

"Thanks," Gerald said, taking the glass, sighing, and sinking into the largest armchair in the room, at Rubin's gesture. "Man. *Not* happy. They're really very much alike, mother and daughter. Apparently their conversation wasn't at all like mine with Rita."

"Yes, I wanted to hear about that," Rubin said.

"Well, as I said, I don't have any use for affirmative action either, at a personal level. A quota to you always meant a ceiling, so you fought against quotas because they kept you out. Only so many undesirables at a time. But a quota to us means a floor, at least so many to prove not that we were qualified but that Whitey was making amends for centuries of murder, rape, and slavery by letting us take sociology sitting next to Miss America. How could Whitey be guilty of anything when he had such an obvious commitment to Diversity? Wrote learned books and articles about how Diversity was so educational for white boys and girls? Your own university, making the case for Diversity to the United States Supreme Court, what was that case not long ago?"

"There were two cases on the use of racial and ethnic preferences in admission to the University's programs," Rubin said. "We lost the one on undergraduate admissions, *Gratz v. Bollinger*. Bollinger was the Michigan president who went to Columbia, by the way. But we won the one involving racial preferences for law school admission, *Grutter v. Bollinger*. Incidentally, I think the Supreme Court got it exactly assbackwards. But save that thought for later."

"You followed the cases so closely that you remember their names?"

"Gerald, you know that I've been involved with one or another aspect of this issue all my life, not just here at Michigan," Rubin said. "Sure I followed them. Even after I retired. The Supreme Court decisions didn't come down until the summer of 2003."

Gerald took a healthy swig from his glass. "Good stuff," he said appreciatively. "What do you mean, the Supreme Court got it assbackwards? Now you're a Constitutional scholar and a legal expert and Court critic as well as the world's foremost authority on–what was it? Something having to do with Chaucer?"

"No, of course not," Rubin said. "Never mind all that, continue with what you were saying. Have some more wine."

"Don't mind if I do," Gerald said. "What was I saying? Oh, about my conversation with Rita. Well, I guess I was supportive. The arguments to be made for some sort of affirmative action, as far as I can see, don't have anything to do with Rita. They either have to do with kids whose backgrounds are quite different even though their abilities may be similar, or they have to do with institutional responses to the miserable K-12 education that far too many black youngsters have been condemned to, post-secondary institutions, I mean. So I was supportive. I did suggest to Rita that if Columbia is still her first choice, and I don't see why it shouldn't be, she might have some fence repairing to do. That didn't go over very well either. So I said that she shouldn't judge Columbia's medical school by one condescending jackass in the Minority Recruitment Office. Turns out that she felt he was coming on to her at first and took her response badly, which is how they wound up in a state of war."

"So it wasn't just that she was insulted as being perceived as a twofer? Female and black, double credit for the scorekeepers and report writers?"

"I'm familiar with the term," Gerald said. "Yes, she was insulted, of course, and properly so, but the man was apparently obnoxious personally on top of all that. If she has any more to do with him she'll probably start telling him about his mother, so I told her just to think about it, sleep on it, take a couple of days, talk to her friends, not make any rash decisions. I think she'll be all right. She's not foolish. Unless Laura stoked the fire again, damn it."

"Why, what did Laura say to Rita?" Rubin rose, refilled Gerald's glass, refilled his own, and took another bottle out of the cabinet.

"Hey, that's fine, thanks," Gerald said. "This will be my last glass. Laura seems to have told Rita to keep her eye on the ball, or words to that effect. Laura wants Rita to go to Columbia even more than Rita wants to go to Columbia. For one thing, Laura wants Rita close enough to home to keep reasonably informed about what's going on. For another, there's a young man who seems to be very fond of Rita and--"

"Really!" Rubin couldn't help himself.

"Yes, and Laura is very impressed by him, more than I think Rita is, at least at this point. And for a third, there's another young man of whom Laura is not at all fond, and he's in Atlanta, Rita's second choice. Emory University."

"And Rita likes this other young man rather more than Laura wishes she would?"

"So I am led to think."

"Jesus," Rubin said. "And I'm only the uncle, so to speak. I don't envy parents. Too complicated for me."

They sipped their wine in silence for a moment. Then Gerald said, "You were going to tell me why you think the Supreme Court got those decisions assbackwards."

"All right," Rubin said. "But how will this help you vent about being black in white America?"

"Oh, something will come up, I'm sure," Gerald said. "Go ahead."

"Well, I have two arguments to make, one each corresponding to exactly what you said–the kids who aren't like Rita, and the responses of colleges and universities to the pressures to open the gates to all Americans. The first has to do with what you always hear, that no one should be judged on the basis of his race, color, and so on. Of course no one should. But the implication is that the way not to do that is to pretend that history has had no consequences. And the way to pretend *that* is to ignore history as much as possible."

"Walter, get to the Supreme Court!"

"Well, how is educational achievement assessed at the point of entry, the Ellis Island, to the land of opportunity, college? What, really, are the measures of all that merit we are told whites possess to such a statistically significant greater degree than their black classmates? There are two measures. One is grade point average, GPA. As if public high schools were any more alike than private schools! As if we could measure what it means to earn good grades in a ghetto school where good grades are regarded by the cool set as racial betrayal! As if good grades in a rural high school of a hundred and fifty kids suggested something similar to good grades at the Bronx High School of Science! And the other measure is a standardized test, whether the SAT or the ACT, whose value as a predictor rather than as a limited evaluation of past performance is, at best, statistical, not individual. In fact, that's one of the great ironies in this whole debate. The opponents of affirmative action, these new conservative organizations with their wonderfully libertarian-sounding names–the Center for Individual Rights and the Center for Equal Opportunity, for instance–argue for decisions to be made on the basis of test results whose predictive value, if any, has nothing to do with either individuals or opportunity!"

"How do you mean, 'if any'?" Gerald asked. "Don't the SAT and ACT scores correlate pretty well with GPAs achieved in college?"

"I'm told three things about that," Rubin said. "One is that, yes, they do correlate fairly well with later academic performance, but only for undergraduate liberal arts courses. The second is that psychometricians don't agree with each other, any more than do other people. Just look at the arguments about the IQ tests. There's never been much consensus about what, exactly, they measure, if anything. And the third, of course, is that much more research is needed. In the meantime, we have these damnable standardized tests and the kids' high school GPAs, as if they were as holy and indisputable as batting averages and football rankings. Something to count, so that's the end of the discussion."

Gerald looked thoughtful. "The thing I liked about sports," he said, "is that the outcome was usually clear. There was a winner and a loser. Oh, of course I can remember some very questionable calls by a referee, especially if I was accused of a late hit on a quarterback, but generally, the better team won. Rankings are of course nonsense, whether of football teams or universities. Comparing batting averages over different time periods is also ridiculous, comparing things that can't be compared, although you do get the notion that Ted Williams and Cool Papa Bell could both hit the hell out of a baseball. But you're saying that our national fixation on sports shouldn't be carried over into scholastic measures to make predictions about who will succeed and who won't? How do gamblers make any money, then?"

"Oh, come on!" Rubin snorted. "How much insight is required to bet on a white kid whose family members are college graduates, whose annual family income is, say, around a hundred thousand or more a year, who has been raised to do well academically with all kinds of supplementary activities and programs from nursery school on, as opposed to a black kid whose parents are divorced and didn't finish high school, who grew up in a neighborhood whose residents were more familiar with cops and rats than with public libraries, with violence in the streets than with picnics in the park, with--"

"All right, all right, I get the picture," Gerald interrupted. "So the bet on the white kid is on the total package, not just the standardized test score or the GPA."

"You know it," Rubin said. "The score is the result of any number of things never acknowledged in the discussion. That's a huge difference between analyses of success in sports and success in school. In sports, coaches, training, facilities, everything is taken into account. Look at the usual carping about the New York Yankees: Steinbrenner buys the best players. Well, a wealthy white school district doesn't just buy the advantages offered its students in the school buildings, computers, libraries, and well-trained teachers, it's also populated by residents with computers and libraries and god knows what else *at home*, acquired before the kids toddle off to kindergarten. The schools take credit for the education and the enrichment, as it's called, that the parents provide. Isn't that obvious? But it's not acknowledged."

Gerald sipped his wine. "What's the second argument?"

"What?"

"You said you had two arguments," Gerald reminded him. "You've just pointed out–at some length, I might add--that the issue of merit, as defined operationally in American education, turns on some pretty dubious kinds of evaluations of past performance interpreted as predictors of future achievement. OK, since we're talking abstractly, or at least in general terms, I'll sign on to most of what you said. So I think I see your point about undergraduate admissions, although I'm not fully convinced, frankly. You haven't said anything about poor white kids with academic potential. But are you also going to tell me something relevant to what Rita did? Or might do?"

"I don't know if I can tie my ideas about affirmative action to Rita's situation," Rubin said. "I don't know if I even want to try. I think you gave her good advice–she should cool down, sleep on it, talk to her friends. But I do understand Laura's concerns, and instead of getting mad at Columbia for insulting her, perhaps Rita should forget about this fellow in Minority Recruitment and just register for her classes. Who knows how long he'll be there, anyway? Don't these types usually move on to some big job in Washington?"

Gerald roared.

"No, no, for Christ's sake, Gerald, I didn't mean you! Really! Although, come to think of it, you never did tell me--"

"Never mind all that, get on with your second argument! At this rate we'll be talking until you have to take me back to the airport!"

"The second argument is much simpler. Colleges and universities practicing affirmative action because they recognize the glaring inequities in what's available to the masses of black youngsters in high school are essentially committing themselves to remedial education, no matter how that term might grate on certain sensibilities. The remedies are usually a combination of financial aid, tutoring, social support, role models, and in some instances, transitional programs designed to help eighteen-year-old kids who've never been away from home before, let alone in a majority-white environment, to make some very complicated adjustments. But it's not enough to make these efforts, not enough to have sensitivity training sessions for white faculty and staff, not enough to have a Center for African-American Studies with distinguished black faculty members, not enough to try recruit more black students, faculty, and staff, not enough to have some black asses sit in high administrative positions–"

"Walter!" Gerald made rapid circular motions with his free hand.

"All right. In my view, the essence of the matter is the degree the university offers, whether it's a bachelor of arts or of science or of business administration or whatever it is. That degree has to mean that its recipient, regardless of race or color, can now perform at least at the same minimum level as any other recipient. If he came in as a freshman needing remedial work in English or math, or help with realistic self-appraisal or study habits and self-discipline–my impression is that a lot of black kids come to Michigan and similar schools without any idea of the competition they're going to face, and aren't helped to face it by their tutors and counselors--there's only one way to check whether those universities have actually provided the remediation they've promised."

"You mean the same standardized tests you've just been attacking?"

"But they're not the same, or shouldn't be the same, not to the test-takers, not after four or more years of undergraduate work, not if the universities haven't just been passing them along. Affirmative action, as I understand it, means leveling the playing field. It doesn't mean using different standards of performance in the game itself."

"So the national discrepancies, by race, on the Graduate Record Exam, the MCAT that Rita took, the LSAT that Laura took years ago to get into law school, and the rest of them, those discrepancies indicate what?"

Rubin drained his glass. "I'm going to have another," he said. "Are you sure you wouldn't like some more--"

"No, I'd like an answer to my question," Gerald said. "What do those national discrepancies indicate to you?"

"That the same old scam is going on, of course," Rubin said, pouring himself more wine. He was becoming more and more animated, knowing that very soon he would be very sleepy. "Black kids don't matter all that much. Give them their degrees. Let's not have any problems about the grading system. Maybe they'll do all right eventually. Pass them on. Keep a lid on things. If they can't get into Michigan's professional schools, there are other law schools or medical schools or graduate programs that will probably take them. I don't know why that point isn't relevant to the white kids who claim that they've been denied admission unfairly. I'll ask the Center for Equal Opportunity."

"And your solution?"

"Why do I have to have a solution? The issue was why I think the Supreme Court got it assbackwards. Because I think that admission to undergraduate programs, certainly for freshmen or recent high school graduates, should indeed take their race and personal circumstances into account, whereas admission to professional and graduate programs should not. By that time, if the universities are doing the job they claim to be doing, there shouldn't be any discrepancies by race in the performance on those tests."

"What's this about personal circumstances?"

"Well, take Rita. I guess this *is* relevant to Rita. Here she is from New York, a graduate of an excellent private school, grew up in midtown Manhattan, doesn't know much about the ghetto except what she learned from participating in community action programs, has highly educated and relatively wealthy parents, has traveled in the Caribbean and South America, speaks a fair amount of Spanish–no, I don't blame her a bit for being insulted if all that Columbia sees is her color. Of course she's right, and so are you. But what if she were from up around 125th Street, didn't have a father, just a sick mother and younger siblings, had to work part-time to help support the family, and had nevertheless managed to get a B+ average in her Harlem high school? Had kept her nose clean? Had a teacher who saw what she could do and wrote her a really stirring letter of recommendation? And so on. Why the hell *not* offer her the financial aid without which she couldn't hope to go to any college, why *not* have various tutorial and other supportive programs available for her, why *not* try to make it possible for her to learn what the college has to teach?"

"I think you're contradicting yourself now," Gerald said. "On the one hand, you're arguing that individual differences among students need to be considered in admission to college, differences that include their personal circumstances, the schools they went to, and so on. On the other hand, these differences are to be subsumed according to race or color. I haven't heard you argue on behalf of affirmative action for poor white kids."

"I think the history is a bit different, Gerald," Rubin said, annoyed. "And I haven't singled out race or color as the distinguishing marker, as if all black or brown people had identical educational histories. I'm talking about the great numbers of African American kids, not foreign students from Africa who may have stopped off on their way here for a couple of years at Oxford or Cambridge. Do you want me to run through all that again?"

"No, hell no," Gerald said quickly.

"Look," Rubin said, ignoring Gerald's reaction, "the history really matters. White immigrants to this country, as far as I know, generally overcame the disadvantages they faced within one or at the most two generations. They lost their accents, learned machine politics, formed unions, and Anglicized their names. Some of them had their noses bobbed as well. Their ethnic neighborhoods did not function as prisons, and they began to leave them fairly soon anyway, again, within a couple of generations. With some exceptions, Jews, for instance, they were not redlined as blacks were, just about everywhere, regardless of the size of the down payments they offered. White immigrants earned enough money, eventually, to save some of it, and began to move up the ladder, not in all fields and not everywhere, but generally, with enough success for some of them to become really wealthy. No, they weren't welcome at Harvard or Yale or Princeton, but they did pretty damn well for themselves at CCNY and Brooklyn and other urban colleges. And eventually they did get into Harvard, Yale, and Princeton, and even joined the faculties and became administrators. A few of their 'firsts'"– Rubin held up the index and middle fingers of both hands to signal the quotation marks–"are still notable to their descendants, Cardozo and Brandeis as the first Jewish Supreme Court justices, for instance, but white ethnic 'firsts' have pretty well disappeared from public view and public memory. Not so of Hispanics and Asians, and certainly not of blacks, and women now have their own special categories anyway. So no, I don't think I'm contradicting myself at all. Context is everything." He got up, tried to take a bow, and instead reached for the new bottle.

"Lord, this Jewish boy can *talk*!" Gerald said, regarding him with a wide grin. "But can he drink?"

Rubin put the bottle down. "Good question," he acknowledged. "The answer is, probably not. Let's go to bed. What's the plan for tomorrow?"

Gerald got up and stretched, yawning. He was immense. "Laura is going to call me here before ten. On your phone, by the way. Then we'll see. If her mother is stronger, I'll stay another day or so, if that's all right."

"Of course," Rubin said. He was suddenly very tired. "I'll get the lights, go on up."

"You know, Walter," Gerald said, "I had expected to say something like thanks for listening, but I'm not sure that you didn't do most of the talking as well as the drinking."

"And I'm not finished!" Rubin said, motioning his friend up the stairs. "Good night!"

Chapter XI
Nathan, January, 1976

On a Sunday afternoon in early January, 1976, Nathan took a cab to Cleveland's Hopkins Airport, paid the driver, checked his ticket, and, taking his suitcase and carry-all, made his way into the terminal. The wind wasn't nearly as biting at the airport as it almost always was near the lake, but Nathan was glad to get indoors. He went to the Continental ticket counter to check his bag and get his seat on his flight to Atlanta.

"Do you have a seat preference?" the attendant asked him.

"On the aisle, near an exit," Nathan said.

She checked her list and said, "Yes, we have one available—are you aware of your added responsibility as the occupant of this seat to assist the flight attendant in case of an emergency?"

"Glad to help, but I hope I won't have to," Nathan said. She was not amused. She wrote the seat number and gate number on his ticket's outside flap, explaining what they were as she did so, and put his suitcase on the conveyer. "Thanks very much," Nathan said, but she was already motioning the next passenger in line to come forward. Not a job I'd want, Nathan thought as he looked for his gate. People don't want to hear that what they choose to buy might entail added responsibilities.

He had almost half an hour before departure, plenty of time to call Sherry Barnett in Georgia. He had met Sherry in his one semester at Washington University in St. Louis, where he'd started work on his MBA before he'd transferred to Case Western. Sherry, some years older than Nathan, had been a high school math teacher before deciding to return to school for an MBA. She had helped him one evening with matrix algebra. They had stayed in touch over the intervening three years, and now Sherry, who had gotten a job with the Atlanta Braves, was to be his host during his job search in Atlanta. He dialed her number from a pay phone across from his gate. They had agreed that he'd call to let her know if the flight was on schedule and to discuss plans for a meal. When he arrived in Atlanta, he was to rent a car and, following the directions she had already given him, drive to her apartment in

Dunwoody, drop his bags, and then, perhaps, take Sherry out to dinner.

But she'd made a beef stew, and the two bottles of merlot he had in his carry-on bag would go nicely with that. It would be a quiet evening at her place.

The security arrangements of the red brick three-story walk-up building in which Sherry lived were similar to those of Adele's building in Mayfield Heights. Nathan entered the lobby, found the number for Sherry's apartment on the panel, pressed the button, and entered the building when she pressed hers upstairs. He walked up the stairs to her apartment and pressed another button. Sherry opened the door. She was wearing a long grey Atlanta Braves' tee shirt over a pair of red gym shorts and was barefoot. She was tall, rather thin, with long, wavy, reddish-brown hair. She gave Nathan a hug and kiss on the cheek with more enthusiasm than he'd expected. But when he looked for a place to put his suitcase and carry-all, she told him to put them next to the sofa. "I want to be upfront, Nathan," she said. "I'd be more comfortable if you slept on the hide-a-bed. I'm glad to be able to put you up while you're here, but I don't want any complications."

"Of course," Nathan said, but she wasn't finished with her explanation. "I just broke up with my boyfriend last weekend," she said, "and I'm sure he'll be calling. In fact, there's a chance that he'll come by. I don't want him getting any wrong ideas and making a scene."

"I completely understand," Nathan said. "Sorry to hear that it didn't work out. I've had that experience once or twice myself, and it's always painful."

"It was my idea, frankly," Sherry said. "It's Cliff who's having a hard time accepting it. I don't think he *has* accepted it, so that's another reason to be careful." She motioned him to sit down. "Can I get you anything, first of all? Dinner's ready, in the crock pot, but we don't have to eat right away."

"Let's start on the merlot," Nathan said, opening his carry-all and giving her the two bottles. He sat down while she took them and found an opener and two glasses. "Another reason?" Nathan asked, sitting down on the sofa. She understood but hesitated. "Well, I know him from work," she said. "The Braves. He's a ball player. If anything were to become public, you know, some sort of public scene, that would be very awkward for me." She poured the wine for both of them, gave him his glass, and sat down in an armchair opposite the sofa. "To your success tomorrow!" she said, raising her glass. He reached across, clinked glasses, and said, not "From your mouth to God's ear!" as he would have liked to, but "Thanks, I'll certainly drink to that!" They both took a sip.

For a moment he thought that Cliff the ball player had been thrown out of the conversation, but Sherry was just beginning.

"*Extremely* awkward," she continued. "Originally, I thought my job would be in marketing, but it's turned more into public relations. I help arrange events, work with the media, try to put on a good face for upper management. So I'm a pretty visible member of the organization. I met Cliff last summer when the Braves drafted him in the second round, out of Oklahoma State. So last summer was his first with the Braves' minor league clubs. He and his agent were in negotiations here in our Atlanta office, and that's where I met him. I couldn't keep my eyes off him." She paused for another sip. Nathan knew he was in for the whole story.

"I guess the whole thing is my fault–I pursued him, frankly," she continued. "My boss found out, and strongly suggested that my involvement with a player, even one still in the minors, wasn't good for any of us–him, the Braves, or me. Especially when he was a good deal younger than I am."

"Oh?" Nathan couldn't help himself.

"Almost seven years younger," Sherry said. "A man would brag about that sort of thing, but a woman isn't supposed to even admit it."

"Right, it's an unfair double standard," Nathan said.

"And stupid and totally unrealistic. Anyway, his career is really beginning to take off, and here I am, making emotional problems for him. He just can't accept that I'm the one who initiated breaking up. He always did that with his previous girlfriends, or so he says. So he's calling me several times a day, and I keep worrying that he's going to make some sort of scene and it'll get into the papers–you know how sports journalists are, no different from the entertainment reporters hot after all the gossip and scandals about singers and actors–and then my job is going to be on the line."

Maybe you should have thought about that earlier, Nathan thought. "Oh, this will blow over soon, Sherry," he tried to reassure her. "He'll find someone new, and so will you. You're much too attractive to be alone for very long, you must know that."

"I don't know about that, but I always had the feeling that Cliff had a couple of girlfriends elsewhere, you know, on the road, like musicians," Sherry said. "I don't really know, but I heard something about it. Anyway, let's eat. I know you have a big day tomorrow and want to get to sleep early."

Nathan woke up the next morning to the sound of the shower. On an impulse, he knocked on the bathroom door. She heard the knock, turned the water off, and yelled, "I'll be out in a minute!"

"Don't hurry," Nathan called, amused by the implication, although there was no other facility in Sherry's apartment. "Just wanted to know if you'd like me to make breakfast?"

"You'd be a dear if you made coffee," Sherry shouted through the door. "The coffee maker is right next to the sink, and the water, filter, and ground coffee are already in it, so just turn it on. There's some raisin bran in the cupboard to the right of the sink, and milk and juice are in the fridge."

"Do you want cream or sugar in your coffee?" Nathan asked.

"No, just black, that's fine," Sherry called back.

The coffee maker was very quick and he knocked on the bathroom door a few minutes later, holding a cup of coffee on a saucer in his other hand. She was audibly drying her hair with her hair drier, and he knocked harder. "Yes, out in a minute," she called. "I have your coffee!" he replied. She opened the door wrapped only in a blue towel, holding the drier and reaching for the cup, saying "Thanks, Nathan," when her towel dropped to the floor, the coffee cup almost suspended between their hands. "Shit," she cried, taking the cup carefully from his hand, "close the door!" He did, but not quite as quickly as he might have, and called out, "Did you spill that? Should I bring you another cup?" "No!" she shrieked, but he heard her giggle as he turned back to the kitchen.

A few minutes later she emerged from her bedroom, fully dressed, made up, and with the empty cup, ready to go to her office. Nathan confirmed that he had the directions she had given him for his first appointment at ten, and she told him that traffic had been steadily getting heavier in the Atlanta area and that he should give himself plenty of time. They agreed that he'd take her out for dinner that evening. Neither mentioned the bathroom door, but it stayed on Nathan's mind.

Nathan took Sherry's advice and arrived in downtown Atlanta at a quarter to ten. He parked his car in a structure in the Fairlie-Poplar district, only two blocks from Hastings & Hastings Associates, where his first interview was scheduled. A good omen, he told himself. He had time for a cigarette before he entered the building, a mid-rise brick and decorative stone structure. The Hastings & Hastings office was on the fifth floor, visible from the elevator lobby, distinguished by its large glass openings, cut aluminum logo, and name prominently displayed on a cherry-stained wood panel above the glass entrance doors. He went in and approached the receptionist, identifying himself and stating that he was there for his meeting with Mr. Thomas at ten. The receptionist, checking on Mr. Thomas's readiness, learned that he was in a meeting and needed another fifteen minutes. Nathan declined the offer of a cup of coffee and, following instructions, sat down in the lobby in a Marcel Breuer chair to leaf through a couple of architectural magazines. No one else was there but the receptionist. Twenty-five minutes later a man entered the lobby, asking if he was Mr. Goldstein. Nathan stood up, nodding.

"Sorry about the delay, we have an important project underway in Florida, I'm John Thomas, please have a seat, both our conference rooms are in use right now," Mr. Thomas said hurriedly. "I only have a few minutes so let's get right to it–tell me more about your background."

Nathan unzipped his black leather portfolio case, pulled out a copy of his resume, and gave it to Mr. Thomas. "I think I sent you one with my letter," he said, knowing that indeed he had, "but I thought another copy might be useful."

"Yes, thanks, I'll just take a quick look to refresh my memory," Thomas said. "I've been so busy this morning, I didn't get a chance to review the copy you sent." Right, Nathan thought, watching the man's eyes scan the lines. "Work experience, yes," Thomas said, flipping to the second page, "education, uh huh, yes, good, community activities?"

"Yes, I included those," Nathan said. "The volunteer work with Head Start while I was in high school was of course a long time ago, but I enjoyed it and learned a lot, I think, and then the work with minority-owned businesses while I was getting my MBA seemed relevant."

"Yes, of course," Thomas said. "Commendable, very commendable. Uh, have you decided on a direction in the profession?"

"I'm most interested in the business aspects of the practice," Nathan said.

"Could you be more specific?"

"Yes, marketing activities and also on the front end of projects, when programming information is gathered from clients."

"I see," Thomas said. "Those business activities are typically handled by our partners or others with extensive experience in the profession. I can understand, with your degrees in business, why that direction attracts you, but you'd need to work under people with more experience."

"I'd expect that, of course," Nathan said.

"Do you have some examples of your drawings?" Thomas asked, looking at the portfolio.

"Certainly," Nathan said, turning the open portfolio around on his knees to face Thomas. This would be a lot easier if we were sitting at a table, as I'd expected we would, he thought. "This photograph is of a still life drawing I did as an undergraduate, in ink and charcoal."

"Nice," Thomas said, flipping through the pages.

"This drawing," Nathan said, trying to get the man to pay attention, "is an addition to the downtown library in Columbus, Ohio."

"Yes, good use of the masonry arches here, along the outside covered arcade," Thomas said, turning the pages. "You seem to be a good draftsman." He came to design drawings for a proposed hotel retreat in Machu Picchu in Peru. "Is this an apartment building or a hotel?" Nathan explained. "That's an interesting design solution," Thomas said. "I like the way you've leaned the building against the mountain side." "I tried to synthesize the building with its natural surroundings," Nathan said. There was a brief pause. Thomas had not looked at all the drawings, but he was obviously finished with them.

"I, uh, I have to tell you that actually we're not hiring people at this time," Thomas said. "The economy has slowed down, and we've been feeling the impact. In fact, we've had to let several of the junior people go just in the past two months. But even if we could offer you something now, for your first two years or so, it would be in the drafting department."

"What would that involve?" Nathan asked. "Would there be opportunities for advancement into the business aspects of your practice?"

Thomas seemed surprised that Nathan wanted to pursue the possibility. "Well, in your first year, if we had an opening, and as I say at this time we don't actually have one, you'd be working on details–stair details, wall sections, that sort of thing."

"Do you follow the various levels of intern architect experience recommended by NCARB?" Nathan asked.

Thomas chuckled. "Unfortunately, no, but I'm not sure that any of the large architectural offices can really afford to follow those recommendations," he said. "We're looking for production from our intern architects, and it would be too costly to train them in all aspects of the practice. Smaller firms can do that better. You listed three architectural firms in your resume as former employers–so your experience was pretty broad, am I right?"

"Yes, for the most part," Nathan answered. "Two of them were very small, one to four-man offices, and they really attempted to provide a broad range of experience, from preliminary design through construction documents. The other one was of medium size. They had me focus on drafting details of the kind you described."

"Umm," Thomas said. "Well, there are similarities and differences everywhere, of course." He wasn't looking at his watch but Nathan sensed that the interview was about over. "I'd certainly be willing to work my way up from the bottom," he said, "but as I said, I'd appreciate opportunities for advancement in which my business background would be a factor."

"Yes, if things got to that stage, that would no doubt be taken into consideration," Thomas said. "So you're open to moving to Atlanta?"

"Oh, very much so," Nathan said. "I already have a couple of friends here."

"Good, good," Thomas said, rising. "I'll be in touch with you in a few days if we're interested. Enjoy your stay here."

"Thanks very much for your time," Nathan said. "I hope to hear from you."

"Goodbye," Thomas said, shaking hands with Nathan firmly but quickly. He was gone. Nathan took the elevator down and looked at his watch. His first interview, scheduled for an hour, hadn't even lasted thirty minutes. He had two hours before his next appointment. It was at Benton Associates, within easy walking distance. Benton's offices were in a historic eleven-story English-American brick-and-limestone triangular building between Peachtree, Broad, and Poplar Streets. The building, constructed in 1897, was Atlanta's oldest "skyscraper." Nathan had seen it before, but decided to use his time to inspect it again and perhaps some other buildings in the downtown area. His interview with John Thomas had been disappointing, but he liked the feel of the city.

Interior renovations were in progress, Nathan saw in the lobby. A sign, headed "Please Excuse Our Dust," announced that the property had recently been acquired by the Hamilton Bank and Trust Company. Sales and acquisitions in a city's downtown suggested brisk business, Nathan thought, and he wondered about Thomas's claim that the economy's slowdown was producing a discernible impact locally. He saw the building's directory next to the elevator bank. Benton Associates were on the top floor. He looked forward to the view. But he still had plenty of time and decided to take a look at the Hyatt Regency hotel, on the corner of Peachtree and Harris, famous for its twenty-two-story atrium that he had last seen on his visit in 1972. The atrium had influenced his design for the hotel in Machu Picchu. Mr. Thomas seemed not to have noticed.

The cylindrical glass-enclosed elevators at the Hyatt Regency ran on an exposed track and cable system, providing a wonderful panoramic view of the open atrium. Nathan enjoyed it thoroughly on the way up to the Polaris restaurant, which rotated on a cylindrical base on top of the hotel like a slowly spinning flying saucer. The hostess led him to a table by a window, he studied the menu and gave the waiter his order, and gazed out, admiring the downtown skyline. He saw several new high-rise buildings under construction. He could see cranes lifting materials and workers installing steel framing and outside finishes. No doubt about it, Nathan thought, Atlanta was booming. This city would be a much better place than Cleveland to begin his career. He felt optimistic.

The decor at Benton Associates was more traditional than that at Hastings & Hastings. A number of renderings and photographs on the walls in the reception area showed work the firm had done for some of its clients–J. P. Morgan, Sears, Goldman Sachs, Dupont, Union Pacific. Very Fortune 500, Nathan thought. "May I help you?" the receptionist at the desk behind him asked. "Yes, sorry, admiring your projects here," Nathan said and introduced himself. "I'm here for my one o'clock meeting with Mr. Reston."

"I'm sorry, Mr. Goldstein, but Mr. Reston phoned about fifteen minutes ago to say that he'd be unable to meet with you today," the receptionist said smoothly. "His morning meeting with a client became extended into a lunch invitation, and he has another meeting at two and won't be back today."

"Oh, I see," Nathan said, disappointed. But she wasn't finished.

"And he asked me to tell you that he'll be out of the office tomorrow and Wednesday. He asked that you leave your resume and that I give you a company brochure."

"Oh," Nathan said. He had already mailed a copy of his resume to Mr. Reston, but drew another out of his briefcase. But she wasn't finished.

"Here you are," she said, handing him the brochure and taking his resume without looking at it. "Mr. Reston will call you in Cleveland, perhaps next week, to see if another time might be arranged for your interview."

"I won't be there," Nathan said. She looked at him as if he had farted. "I mean, I'm traveling to various cities during the next couple of weeks," Nathan explained more gently, "so please tell Mr. Reston that I'll call him next week from wherever I am, for that purpose."

"I see," she said, still a little miffed. His response obviously hadn't been part of her script. "Do you have a business card with your address and phone number?"

"I don't but that information is at the very top of my resume," Nathan said. "Thank you," he said, turning to go.

"And thank you, Mr. Goldstein," the receptionist said, smooth as ice once again.

And once again he had more time than he needed to get to his next interview, this time at Paterson Architects in downtown Atlanta's Centennial Hill district. He walked to Georgia State University's campus, thinking that the exercise would keep him from brooding and the collegial environment would restore his optimism. But his three o'clock interview at Paterson was similar to his interview at Benton: his conversation was limited to the receptionist, who explained that no one was able to meet with him that afternoon. The main difference was that he did not get a company brochure in trade for the extra copy of his resume.

He came to a pay phone on his way to the parking structure where he had left his rental car, and decided to call Sherry to see if she wanted to meet him downtown for an early dinner. He thought he could walk around the area until then, as he had been doing. But she wanted to go home instead and in fact was ready to leave. Cliff had called three times, although she had spoken to him only the first time, and she had told him that Nathan was staying at her apartment while he was looking for a job in Atlanta.

"You what?"

"I know, I shouldn't have," she said. "It just sort of slipped out. I guess you were on my mind."

"How did he react?"

"Oh, he got all jealous, you know, accused me of sleeping with you—I told him we were just friends and that you were sleeping on the sofa and that since he and I are no longer dating, it was none of his business—but that only got him madder. So I told the receptionist here to tell him that I was in a meeting. But I think I better get home before he shows up—who knows what he might do."

Just what I need, Nathan thought. "OK," he said, "I'll come there too. You'll probably get there before I do, so I'll press the buzzer and you ask who it is before you let me in." She agreed and told him that she thought she'd be home in about forty-five minutes, well before he could get there.

When he got to her building, she let him in as arranged, and when he came upstairs told him to pour himself a drink while she took another shower. "Pour one for me too," she called as she headed for the bathroom. "OK," he said, picked up the bottle of scotch, and noted that Sherry had remembered his favorite brand, Dewar's. "Strange Days" by The Doors finished playing on the turntable while he put a few ice cubes into the two glasses that Sherry had left on the counter, and James Taylor's "Sweet Baby James" dropped down next. Just then the apartment door buzzer sounded. With Sherry still in the shower, Nathan started toward the intercom but stopped himself, remembering what she had told him. I really don't need this, he thought. He knocked on the bathroom door again, remembering the morning. "Sherry, someone's buzzing you from the lobby downstairs," he called. "Don't answer!" she yelled immediately. "I'll be right out!" She emerged a second or so later in a very short cream-white silk robe, put her finger over her lips as she ran past Nathan to the intercom, and said "Yes?"

"It's me, Cliff," a voice answered. "I need to talk to you, Sherry, now!"

"Cliff, I told you it's over so just go away!" Sherry said. She sounded determined but nervous. I *really* don't need this, Nathan repeated to himself, unsure about what, if anything, to do.

"Sherry, I left one of my mitts in your apartment and I want it, I need it now," the voice insisted. "I'll go after I get it." Yes, sure, Nathan thought. There would be a fight, they'd wreck the apartment, the police would come, there'd be a story in the paper, Sherry would lose her job, he would never be able to show his face in Atlanta again–the whole sequence of undesirable events flashing instantly in front of him was as clear as James Taylor's song still playing on the turntable.

"Hold on," Sherry said uncertainly. "I just got out of the shower–just a minute." She released the intercom button and ran to Nathan, pulling him toward the bedroom. "I do have his glove here, I have to return it," she whispered even though Cliff was still downstairs. "Just hide in the bedroom, please, please, no heroics, I don't want any trouble!" She must have had the same vision I just had, Nathan thought. "Please, Nathan, just hide in the bedroom! Hurry!"

"In the bedroom?"

"If he starts searching around the apartment, just hide under the bed, hurry, Nathan!"

The headline would read "Promising Brave Minor Leaguer Finds Aspiring Architect Under Ex-Girlfriend's Bed in Dunwoody, Apartment Trashed."

"Can't I just wait outside?"

"No, he can see my apartment door at the top of the stairs from the glass entry door, Nathan, *please!*"

"All right," Nathan said and went to the bedroom while Sherry ran to the closet for Cliff's glove. Then she pressed the intercom again. "Are you still there, Cliff?"

"Damn right I'm still here!" She pressed the buzzer and within seconds Nathan heard loud knocking on Sherry's apartment door. She unlocked the door but left the door chain attached.

"If I let you in, Cliff, do you absolutely promise to leave the instant I give you the glove?"

"Yes, damn it!" She undid the chain and opened the door. "Here," Nathan heard her say. "Now go."

Nathan heard the man push his way in. "I gotta talk to you, Sherry," he mumbled. Then there were the sounds of a tussle. "Come on, baby--"

"Don't! Let me go! You promised!"

"He's here now, isn't he?" Cliff snarled. Nathan tensed behind the bedroom door. If he bursts in, I'll jump him, to hell with hiding under the bed–but the door opens out and if he just opens it carefully and comes in slowly, where should I be?

"No, he's out on his job interviews, I told you, now go, get out, you promised!"

"You're fucking him, aren't you?"

"I told you no and it's none of your damn business!"

"I bet he's here now!" Nathan heard something that sounded like a shove and a step toward the bedroom. "You never trusted me," Sherry yelled, "but it was you who was sleeping around, and don't think I didn't know it!"

"What? What? You're a lying, cheating bitch, I never--"

"No? What about that girl in Clearwater?"

"What girl in Clearwater? You don't know what you're talking about!"

"Don't play innocent! One of the other girls in the office has a friend on the team, and she tried to warn me before I got hurt–so stop lying and just get out!"

"Who? Who on the team?" Cliff's tone was suddenly defensive.

"Never mind! You didn't keep it a secret! Now get out, I'm telling you!"

There was a moment of silence. Nathan wished he could peek out to see the scene, but it was over. There were some heavy steps, the door opened, and then slammed loudly. Cliff had taken his glove and left. Nathan opened the bedroom door to see Sherry, tying her robe more securely around herself–so there *had* been a tussle, Nathan thought–at the living room window to watch Cliff drive away. "Nathan?" she called as she closed the vertical blinds. He stepped into the living room to find her on one of the two bar stools at the counter opening to the kitchen. "I really need this drink now," she said, motioning to him to join her. He did. They clinked glasses and drank and looked at each other. "Whew," she said. "Give me a hug, Nathan." He did. The next album, "Aqualung" by Jethro Tull, dropped on the turntable. Sherry continued to hold him tightly. They kissed. He reached inside her robe and she began to unbutton his shirt and stroke his chest. They went to the sofa. All the song tracks on "Aqualung" played, followed by "Led Zeppelin II."

Later they decided to eat in again. After dinner they went to Sherry's bedroom.

*****

Nathan had scheduled two interviews for the next morning, Tuesday, both in Decatur, but they netted him only two more company brochures in exchange for additional copies of his resume. He wondered, after learning that his appointment at the second firm had been cancelled some days earlier when a client had requested a meeting at the same time, whether receptionists everywhere were trained to make smooth, even fluent apologies to unwanted applicants whenever a client's schedule took priority. Which was, of course, always. Form follows function, Nathan reminded himself.

His flight from Atlanta via Phoenix to Los Angeles was uneventful. He had appointments with architectural firms in downtown Los Angeles, Beverly Hills, Sherman Oaks, and Pasadena over two days, Wednesday and Thursday. Not a single interview materialized. Every person who had agreed to meet him had, he learned, conflicting obligations. The apologetic and ever-so-courteous receptionists began to blur in his mind. On Friday morning Nathan paid his motel bill, filled his rental car's gas tank, and began his trip to San Francisco. The four-hundred-mile drive, he thought, would refresh him, giving him a chance to reflect, to reassert his optimism, and, he knew from previous experience, to invigorate his spirit with the sheer natural beauty of the scenery. State Route 1, Highway 1, the Pacific Coast Highway, the Cabrillo Highway, the Shoreline Highway, California 1–it was all more or less the same road, and gorgeous.

He had rented a bright red 1976 Mustang II with a black vinyl interior and an automatic transmission in memory of his first new car, a jade green, three-on-the-floor, 1969 fastback Mustang with a 302-cid V-8 engine. The new Mustang handled well, but it didn't have his 69's power. This Mustang was shorter and lighter and got better gas mileage, but it didn't give him the same feeling of empowerment. Of course better gas mileage was a good thing, but still! He smiled to himself, wondering whether this nostalgia for the 1969 Mustang was the first sign of aging. Then he felt the top of his head and decided that, no, he'd been familiar with certain such signs for some time now. That's all right, he thought, I haven't had any complaints yet.

He stopped for lunch at the Nepenthe Restaurant along the ocean side of Highway 1 in Big Sur, the ninety-mile stretch from San Simeon to Carmel between the Pacific and the Santa Lucia Mountains. He chose a table on the terrace and drank in the view, turning his head to absorb the windswept cypress trees, the rugged canyons, the steep sea cliffs, the pristine coastline. Everything made sense. He had been in California twice before, in 1969 and again the following year. That trip had been cut short by Marty's sudden death. This view was like a dream, a dream he wanted to commit to memory. It was balm for his spirit.

He had tried to express something of this mixture of thought and feeling on the essay examination required of all M.Arch. students at Ohio State University. He had argued that the development of architecture, like that of art, music, and poetry, reflected man's evolving understanding of nature. The principles of harmony, also known as ecological balance to environmental scientists, were fundamental to natural communities of plants and animals within their particular climatic and geological settings. Particular harmonies differed, of course, as in music, as in meter and rhyme schemes, as in paintings, but harmonies there had to be, and good, certainly great architecture was nothing if not harmonious, with itself and with its surroundings. Of course harmonies could be and were frequently destroyed: volcanic eruptions and earthquakes, hurricanes, forest fires, drought, the introduction of alien species in the natural world, and in man's, pestilence, war, starvation, and death. Something about the Four Horsemen of the Apocalypse, Nathan recalled vaguely. He hadn't read much of the Bible, certainly not the New Testament. The Book of Revelations, he remembered from conversations with religious Christian friends. John, the last survivor of Christ's Apostles, in his late eighties, had dictated his visions or whatever they were in that cave on Patmos to a fifteen-year-old frightened boy, Stephen, who was later anointed into sainthood himself by the early Christian Church. The visions were of the doom to come, and mankind's sole hope for its avoidance. California's original inhabitants never got that message, Nathan reflected. But they probably knew a lot about harmony. The waiter brought the ground steak sandwich, tossed green salad, and large coke he had ordered.

He was in no hurry, he realized. He had no interviews until Monday. He ate his lunch quite leisurely, left money on the table for the bill and the tip, and walked to his Mustang. Nathan drove a couple of miles north up Highway 1 and noticed a sign: Pfeiffer Beach. Nathan parked his car and walked down to the ocean. He found a large, inviting rock on the hillside and sat down. The rock was warm. He stared at the waves lapping on the shore below him with a steady, almost rhythmic beat. Harmony everywhere. He lit a cigarette to enhance his contentment even more. Suddenly a Golden Retriever wearing a cowboy red bandana around her neck rushed by, turned either at the smoke or the glimpse of Nathan, and barked joyfully. Someone was coming. But the dog was so happy, the lunch had been so good, and the view was so magnificent that Nathan, to his own surprise, didn't mind at all.

"Molly! Wait up, sweetie!" A female voice, followed by its owner, a tall, slim, red-haired woman in blue jeans and a sweat shirt holding a short thick branch in her hand as she ran to the dog. Molly started toward her and then, as the woman raised her arm and flung the stick toward the water, dashed after it. A wave beat her to it, and retreated with the stick, but the dog, undeterred, leaped in, grabbed it, turned, and ran full speed to Nathan. "Molly, come here!" the woman yelled. Molly rested her wet chin on Nathan's knee. "I'm so sorry," the woman said, approaching them, "she's gotten your pants all wet!" Nathan laughed and said, "That's OK–I think she wants to play." The dog dropped the branch at Nathan's feet and put both her front paws on his lap. He stroked her head and scratched behind her ears, and said to the woman, "Hello–my name's Nathan."

The woman seemed to have been waiting for the introduction. "Hello, Nathan," she said. "My name's Gwen. Do you by chance have an extra cigarette?"

"Sure," Nathan said, and gave her one and a light with his Zippo. She took a deep drag, thanked him, and sat down next to Nathan. The dog, perhaps annoyed by the smoke, wandered off. Gwen took another drag on her cigarette and asked Nathan whether he lived in the area.

"No, I'm from Cleveland, Ohio," Nathan said, not sure whether identifying the state as well as the city was necessary.

"Isn't that the city with the mayor who set his hair on fire?"

"Yes," Nathan said, "but at least not on the same day that the river caught fire."

Gwen laughed. Maybe she hadn't heard about the river, just the mayor. "Are you here on vacation?"

"No, I'm looking for a job," Nathan said. "What about you? Where are you from?"

"I'm from Louisville, Kentucky?" Gwen asked him. Nathan was familiar with the more and more common interrogative intonation intended both to convey information and simultaneously to imply the hope that it would be understood by the listener. Nevertheless, it grated on his ears. "My girlfriend and me came out here last week on vacation," Gwen continued, "but I haven't seen her since Tuesday when she hooked up with some surfer we met in Santa Barbara the day before, y'know? So I've been staying with my sister in Lucia. Molly's her dog," she added, looking around. The dog was nowhere in sight but Gwen didn't seem perturbed. "She's not really my girlfriend," she continued, letting Nathan leap back over both dog and sister. "We just work for the same company in Louisville. I'll never go on vacation with her again. She wants to move out here and she told me she really likes this guy, so who knows?"

Nathan, declining to speculate about the non-girlfriend's chances, asked, "What kind of work do you do in Louisville?"

"I work in Accounts Receivable for General Electric? My friend works in Payroll. We met about a year ago. We had some fun here the first few days but damn, I'm really mad at her now. My sister works during the day, and I don't like being alone all day, just dogsitting, y'know? Hey, what kind of work are you looking for?"

"I'm hoping to find a job working for an architectural firm," Nathan said. "An architect," he amended.

"An architect," Gwen said, dropping her cigarette and grinding it out with the sole of her sandal. "Cool."

"Well, I'm not licensed yet, but I hope to take the exam next December," Nathan explained without knowing why.

"Don't you have to go to college for that?"

"Yes, now almost everybody does," Nathan said. "In fact, there's talk that eventually you'll have to have a degree to take the exam to become a registered architect. That's not true everywhere now. In some states you can take the exam without a degree if you have thirteen years' experience working under a registered architect, but that's expected to change soon." Too much detail for Accounts Receivable, he thought.

"Thirteen years' experience! Wow! That's a lot! So, do you have a degree?"

"Yes, I received my Master's last November," Nathan said.

"Wow, your Master's! And you still have to take a test?"

"That's the way it works," Nathan said.

"Jeez, doesn't really seem fair," Gwen said. "Have you got any jobs lined up yet out here?"

"Not yet. I dropped off my resume at some firms in Los Angeles, and I'm scheduled for some interviews around San Francisco, but so far I haven't gotten any offers."

"Well, good luck, Nathan," Gwen said. "I'm sure you'll find

something, with a Master's and all. Hey, do you have a girlfriend back home?"

"No, I don't," Nathan said. "How about you, do you have a boyfriend?"

"No, I just got divorced about two months ago," Gwen said. "Some guy I met in high school. I got pregnant, we got married, and it just didn't work out. All he did was drink and get laid off from whatever lousy job he could find. Finally I said enough. This was supposed to be a celebration vacation, y'know? My girlfriend was such a shit to just leave me alone here!"

"Is your kid here with you?" Nathan asked.

"No, my Mom is watching her–she's the one who came up with the idea that I should get away for a couple of weeks. My ex really tried to make things difficult at the end. He doesn't have any money to pay me child support payments, and my lawyer got the judge to give me full custody because of his drinking problem." She paused, apparently bored by what she was saying. "Hey, if you're free for the next couple of days we could hang out," she continued much more cheerfully. "My sister's cool, I'm sure she'd let you stay with us. Or am I being too forward? Is it the California air?"

"No, no," Nathan said chivalrously. "I'd love to take you up on that. The problem is that I'm supposed to meet some friends in San Francisco, and I still have a long drive ahead."

"Uh huh. Too forward. My Mom always told me that the man should make the first move–she said that's the reason I got pregnant, that I didn't wait for him to make the first move. Hey, I better get going–I told my sister I'd clean her house today while she was at work. Molly!" The dog appeared suddenly, tail wagging, bounding up to Gwen.

"Hey, do you have a pen?" Gwen asked Nathan.

"Yes, I do," Nathan said and gave her the pen he carried in his jacket.

"Any paper?"

"Let me see," Nathan said. He found someone's business card from one of his visits to a Los Angeles architectural firm and gave it to her.

"You're Juan Gonzalez, AIA? I thought you said your name is Nathan?"

"No," Nathan laughed, "that's a man who was supposed to interview me for a job in Beverly Hills, but he was in a meeting."

"Well, Juan or Nathan, here's my work phone number in Louisville, so if you're ever in the area, you know, give me a call."

"I will," Nathan said. "Who knows what might happen?"

Gwen got up, gave Nathan his pen and the card and a kiss on his cheek, and said, "Really great to meet you, Nathan—you're right, who knows what might happen?"

"And I hope you have a great time while you're here, Gwen," he said.

"Hey, I was trying to, but you have to meet your friends in San Francisco!" She laughed. "Let's go, Molly!" They were gone. Nathan waited a minute or two and went back to his car. He wanted to get to San Mateo for dinner and a motel room. He had no friends in San Francisco. But there was a call he'd promised himself he'd make when he got to San Mateo.

*****

He found a small motel not far off the U.S. 101 exit ramp at San Mateo, a white stucco two-story building with an orange clay tile roof. The doors to the sleeping rooms on the first floor were all accessible from the exterior. Steel stairs, located strategically, went up to a balcony serving as an exterior corridor on the second floor. The building was entirely surrounded by a sun-baked asphalt parking lot, featuring a few planters with low, rather desiccated shrubs. He parked near the entrance and went in.

No rooms were available on the second floor, where Nathan, remembering the break-in at the Ohio Stater the previous month, had wanted one, but the man at the desk promised that several second-floor guests would be leaving in the morning. "How many nights are you staying?" he asked. "Four," Nathan said. The clerk offered him a choice of rooms on the first floor, one that faced traffic or one in the back which, he pointed out, would be quieter. But Nathan, still thinking of the Ohio Stater, chose the one that faced traffic and, presumably, lights from the parking lot. Once bitten, twice shy, he said to himself. He paid the man cash, showed his driver's license as requested, and asked whether the motel had a laundry service. The man directed him to a laundromat a few blocks down the street. Nathan took his bags to his room and unpacked them, making sure that he hung up his two suits for the interviews as neatly as he could. Then he made his call to 411, Operator Assistance.

Karen Sternberg had lived in Cleveland until 1962, when she and her family had moved to San Francisco, but Nathan had not met her until the following year, when she had come back to Cleveland to visit friends. They were both fourteen. For Nathan, it was love at first sight. He saw her only a few times more that summer, but they wrote to each other–not often, he admitted to himself, remembering, but often enough so that, when he and Michael, on their travels around the country in the summer of 1969, got to California, he met her again. She was attending college and living in San Mateo. They spent part of an evening together, and they had kissed and hugged, and he still tingled at the recollection.

"Number please," the operator said.

"Karen Sternberg in San Mateo," Nathan said.

A pause. "There's a K. Sternberg in San Mateo but no Karen."

"What's the number please?" Nathan asked. The operator gave him the number and he wrote it down on the first page of the new white legal pad on which he hoped to take notes during his interviews. "Thank you," he said. "'You're welcome," the operator said, "and thank you for using Pacific Bell." Nathan stared at the number. His heart was pounding. His palms were moist. This is ridiculous, he thought. Either it's Karen or it's not. If it is, either she's still free or she's not. If it's not Karen, I'll learn that very quickly and then I can decide how else I might find her. If it is Karen, I'll know almost as quickly whether she's still free or not. If she is, she will probably want to see me. If she isn't, well, I probably won't want to see her. He put his pad and pen down and turned on the television. He surfed the channels for about thirty minutes without paying much attention to either pictures or voices. Finally he turned it off, calm at last, and dialed the number on the pad. A woman answered during the third ring.

"Hello?"

"Is Karen Sternberg there, please?" Nathan asked.

"No, she's out this evening, who's calling?"

"This is Nathan Goldstein, an old friend of Karen's--"

"Nathan Goldstein from Cleveland?"

"Yes!" Nathan said, very pleased.

"This is Nancy–Karen and I share a house together. She's talked about you over the years, wondering whatever happened to you."

"Well, I just finished my Master's degree in architecture and I'm looking for work in the San Francisco area," Nathan said. And I'm very single and totally unattached, he wanted to add.

"Are you in San Francisco now?"

"No, I'm at the Blue Sky Motel right off U.S. 101."

"You're only about five minutes away!" Nancy said excitedly. "I know Karen would love to talk to you. Call her tomorrow after maybe two o'clock–I'll tell her you called and that you'll call back."

"Thanks very much, Nancy, I certainly will," Nathan said. "And please give her my best regards."

"I will!" Nancy said. They said goodbye and hung up. Nathan's heart was pounding again. So she had wondered about him over the years? Had told her roommate about him? Excellent. On the other, she wasn't there–probably out on a date.   Well, of course she was, he told himself, annoyed–a beautiful, smart, funny, and sexy girl like that, did he think she'd be home on a Friday night? He suddenly felt the need to move, grabbed his key, and left the room to walk to the parking lot. The cigarette he lit there as he sat down on a retaining wall around one of the low shrub areas did not have its usual calming effect. He walked down to the street. The few street lights did not encourage exploration. He returned to his room and went to bed. It had been a long day and, despite his excitement, he slept soundly.

In the morning, after he'd showered, shaved, and brushed his teeth, he took his duffel bag full of his soiled clothes and walked to the laundromat two blocks away. He exchanged two one-dollar bills for eight quarters with the coin changer, bought a package of laundry detergent for fifty cents, and threw all his clothes, regardless of color, into a single washing machine. Flouting the first commandment of Laundry Protocol made him feel defiant and adventurous. He added the detergent and inserted three quarters into the coin receptacle next to the machine's front loading door. The glass window in the door allowed him a view of the action. He looked around. The only other people in the laundromat were a young Hispanic woman with a baby in her lap, reading a magazine, and, some seats away, an elderly man in worker's clothing, with thick white hair, a large white mustache, and a dark, very wrinkled face, showing years of labor in the sun. You could see that he had been very handsome. He was sitting in a folding chair staring into a front-loading-door dryer through its glass window, watching the clothes within tumble over and over. He seemed hypnotized, watching the dryer's action without moving, without even taking his eyes from the sight. He's seeing something else in there, Nathan thought. All by himself. Not even a morning paper to read. He's looking at his life, Nathan decided, spinning in there, round and round, and when he takes it out, it will be warm and dry but a little more worn than it was. All that hard work for all those years and that's what he has, a seat in a laundromat watching his old clothes spin dry. But he's kept his dignity. If I were to try to talk to him, he would be suspicious at first, some young gringo condescending to him, but then, seeing that I was just being friendly and cheerful, he'd warm up and talk a little, perhaps not much, but a few pleasantries. Would he tell me what he sees in that dryer?

Could he tell me what I might glimpse in mine? Nathan hesitated, not sure that he really wanted to try to strike up a conversation.

Suddenly the baby began to cry. Its mother immediately stood up, holding the baby and rocking it gently side to side, softly rubbing its back and humming a song of some sort. The baby stopped crying and rested its head against its mother's shoulder. She sat down again in front of her active dryers and picked up her magazine. The dryer in front of the handsome elderly man stopped spinning and he picked up a white plastic basket on the other side of his chair, opened the dryer, and put the rumpled clothes into his basket. Then, erect, looking neither right nor left, he walked out. Nathan watched him through the window, feeling that now he was the clothes in his dryer, looking out. The elderly man went to an old red Ford station wagon parked directly in front of the laundromat. The car's paint was oxidized from too much time in the sun. Some dents and scratches were visible on its fenders and one of its doors. The man put his basket on the passenger seat, walked around the car, and started the engine. Some black smoke left the exhaust. He pulled the car away from the curb and drove away. Nathan found himself wishing him goodbye and good luck.

A few minutes later Nathan's washing machine completed its cycle. He pulled the wet clothes out, stuffed them into the dryer the elderly man had used, set the machine to "Sturdy Cotton," and inserted the required two quarters. Somehow using the same machine the man had used gave him a sense of kinship. But he wouldn't stare at his clothes: he was hungry and wanted breakfast. He had seen a small diner a few doors away. He hardly noticed what he ate, still absorbed by the old man in his old Ford.

When he returned to the motel with his clean dry laundry, he checked at the counter and found that a room on the second floor had indeed become available. He made the switch and immediately felt secure physically. But as soon as he placed the pad with Karen's number next to the telephone, in anticipation of the call he was to make after two o'clock, he realized that he had almost four hours of anxiety ahead. There was only one way to deaden that, to throttle his wishful thinking, to black out the images flooding his mind. He turned the television set on and watched Saturday morning cartoons, as mindless and predictable as always, quieting millions of children of all ages all across the continent. When they had finally Looney Tuned Out, he found a spaghetti western, good guys galloping after bad guys across dry prairies and into towering canyons, guns blazing, demonstrating amazing marksmanship from horses running at full speed–and then, laconic drawls, quiet acknowledgments of inviolable principles and loyalty to the death, hard-eyed, square-jawed men who might drink too much sometimes, would certainly kill each other, but would never cheat at cards. Nathan remembered scores of movies he had seen as a youngster. Nothing had changed, and somehow that was reassuring. But now it was two o'clock. He dialed the number.

"Hello?"

"Hello–is this Karen?"

"Yes–is this Nathan?"

"Yes, it's Nathan," he said, tension oozing away. "How are you, Karen?"

"I'm fine, Nathan, wonderful to hear from you–Nancy told me you called yesterday–you're in town?"

"Yes, until Tuesday evening," Nathan said

"And you've completed your master's degree? And you're looking for a job in this area?"

"Yes–I see Nancy told you everything!"

"Well, congratulations, Nathan! I remember your telling me about wanting to be an architect the last time we saw each other–when was that, Nathan?"

"In 1969," Nathan said, with a pang of regret: didn't she remember?

"And you have some interviews scheduled here?"

"Well, no, not officially–I spoke to several firms on the phone and they said to stop by when I'm in the area, so I'm hoping that one or two will take the time to meet with me Monday or Tuesday. I think they might be interested in what I have to offer not only as an architect but also as someone trained in business administration–I have a master's in that too, so that should help."

"You've been busy since we saw each other last!" Karen said. "Or since we've been in touch–it's been three or four years!"

"Yes," Nathan said. "I'm sorry, I haven't asked how you are or what you've been doing."

"I didn't give you a chance!" Karen laughed. "Well, a lot has happened. I graduated from the University of Arizona with a degree in business, moved in here with my best friend, Nancy, and Nathan, I'm engaged to a wonderful man."

Nathan swallowed hard and said, "Congratulations, Karen, that's wonderful. Tell me about him."

"We started dating two years ago when he was in his residency. He finished that up last year, and he just joined a very well known plastic surgery practice in San Francisco. Our wedding is planned for June."

Nathan dug his fingernails into his palm and said, "Congratulations again, Karen, I'm very happy for you."

"Thank you, Nathan," Karen said.

"Do you think you might have some time during the next couple of days to have lunch or possibly meet for a drink?"

"I'd love to, Nathan," she said, "but Bruce and I are driving down to Ventura this weekend to spend some time with his family, and we won't be back until Tuesday evening. I'm sorry, Nathan, but I hope you understand."

"Of course," Nathan said. "I was just calling to say hi. I've thought about you often and I'm sorry we lost touch."

"That happens in college," Karen said. "You appear to have focused on your education, and that's great. Remember, I finished three years ago, and things happen after you enter the real world. I certainly wish you all the best. Look, if you do get a job in this area, please give us a call. I'm sure Bruce would love to have you over."

"Thank you," Nathan said. "Maybe I'll take you up on that, if things work out here."

"I hope so," Karen said. "Good luck, Nathan!"

"And best of luck to you, Karen!" Nathan said. They said goodbye almost simultaneously and hung up. Sure, Bruce would love to have me over, Nathan thought. She didn't even tell me his last name. How am I supposed to find her number, tell the operator that I'm looking for Karen the wife of Bruce the famous plastic surgeon?

So that was that. Gone forever. The door permanently slammed shut. Do not knock on this door. Do not press buzzer. Go away. Bruce would *not* love to have you over. The last thing Bruce and his family in Ventura would want is some architect Karen knew as a schoolboy in Cleveland, for God's sake, calling up to ask if he could come over. Come over and play. No, it was the game that was over, and it was time to recognize that it had been a fantasy all along.

Maybe it was all for the best, Nathan thought. Karen had somehow been a romantic ideal,   provoking emotions and setting a standard that no other girl he'd ever met had rivaled. It was time to see the women he met not as imperfect Karens but as whoever they really were.

Still, for the moment, there was no denying the dull ache somewhere inside. Nathan spent the remainder of the weekend watching television, leaving his room only for meals and short walks. On Monday morning he began his visits to the five architectural firms in San Mateo and San Francisco, which, he hoped, would have someone interview him. No one was available. He dropped off his resume at each, took the company brochures, and, on the next day, returned his rental car at the San Francisco airport and boarded a flight for Chicago.

*****

Nathan had scheduled two interviews, one for Wednesday and one for Thursday, but had phoned three other firms in downtown Chicago only to be told that they weren't hiring. He decided, nevertheless, to visit each one to leave his resume and to see if someone might discuss future job possibilities with him.

His Wednesday morning meeting was at Worthmore, Jennings, and Stevenson Architects in the hundred-story John Hancock Building on Michigan Avenue. The building had been highly acclaimed, justifiably so, Nathan thought. He admired the powerful X-braced exterior walls providing structural support and helping to withstand the very high winds blowing off Lake Michigan. But the building did not fit in well with its surroundings. The nearby structures were not only much smaller but also less massive. Nor were the strong winds in the plaza and the loud noises from the street dampened effectively.

He took the elevator up to the thirty-ninth floor, recalling that he had read that the Hancock elevators were among the fastest in North America, traveling at 1,800 feet per minute or twenty miles per hour. From the ground, they reached the observatory on the ninety-fourth floor in thirty-nine seconds. He had not read any reports about what people did with all the time they saved.

Nathan entered the Worthmore, Jennings and Stevenson lobby and waited for the middle-aged woman who, despite her absorption in her typing, appeared to be the receptionist, to notice him. He did not dare to lean on the counter, custom-designed maple with inlaid burled walnut, serving as an effective barrier between the receptionist and visitors. Suddenly she stopped typing, pushed her glasses up her nose, looked at him and asked if she could help him.

"Yes," Nathan said, pleasantly surprised by her courteous manner, "my name is Nathan Goldstein and I have an interview scheduled with Mr. Jennings at eleven."

"Yes, Mr. Goldstein, he's expecting you. He's still interviewing another young man, but that's running well beyond what he had scheduled–the applicants from Harvard always seem to get special attention–so I'll let him know you're here right on time for your appointment. Please have a seat." She gestured toward a seating arrangement a good twelve feet away.

"Thank you," Nathan said, and followed instructions. Harvard. Was that a way to let him know that people from Ohio State shouldn't have such high hopes as Worthmore, Jennings and Stevenson? Especially Ohio State people named Goldstein?

He picked up an architectural magazine whose cover page showed a photograph of a high-rise office building, designed by the firm, that had won an award. He looked around and saw that the lobby's walls displayed numerous such awards from the city, state, and national American Institute of Architects for such office buildings, as well as for government and industrial projects, hospitals, and various interiors, not only around the United States but also internationally. Worthmore, Jennings and Stevenson was among the largest architectural firms in the country. No wonder Harvard graduates applied for jobs here.

The receptionist's phone rang and she answered, speaking softly and nodding. When she hung up, she said, "Mr. Goldstein, Mr. Jennings is free now and will be out in a moment." "Thank you," Nathan said again, thinking that Harvard must have left by another door. Pretty classy: you don't want Harvard bumping into Yale, for God's sake. A slim young man, not more than ten years older than Nathan, entered the lobby from an interior door, approached him, and said, "Mr. Goldstein?" "Yes," Nathan said, rising, "Mr. Jennings?" "Please call me Steve," Jennings said, shaking Nathan's hand. "We can meet in one of our conference rooms–this way, please." "Thank you, Steve," Nathan said. "And please call me Nathan." How had a man no older than thirty-five gotten to be a partner in such a large, internationally prestigious firm? Great talent? Superb connections? Both? Architects, unlike artists, musicians, or poets, Nathan thought, remembering his musings on the shore of the Pacific after his meal at the Nepenthe Restaurant, usually didn't achieve significant professional success until they were in their late forties or early fifties.

They passed a very large conference room that appeared to have seating for at least thirty people. Nathan, looking through a glass wall running its entire length, saw a very long stained cherry conference table, the most up-to-date leather chairs on either side, and an array of audio-visual equipment and display boards. The next room, even larger, but with glass windows instead of a glass wall along the corridor, was a drafting room. Nathan caught a glimpse of perhaps fifty young men and women hunched over drafting tables, moving parallel rules and triangles up and down the boards as they drew lines.

Jennings stopped at a closed door, said "Here we are!" to Nathan, and opened the door to a much smaller room to find six young men sitting around three white rectangular tables, moved together, leaning over and discussing several drawings. They were as surprised as Jennings was. "Something you need, Steve?" one of them asked. "Yes, I have this room reserved from eleven to noon," Jennings said. "We reserved it for the whole morning," the man said. "Another snafu, sorry, but we have no other room available." "What are you working on?" Jennings asked. "Getting ready for the noon meeting with the contractor on the New York midtown project," the man said. Jennings looked nonplussed. "OK," he said, and turned to Nathan. "Let's just meet in my office." "Sure," Nathan said. *Good thing they're only scheduling meetings here, not trains.*

Jennings, leading Nathan down another corridor, looked at his watch. "I'm sorry, I won't be able to give you the full hour," he said to Nathan. "My next meeting starts in forty minutes and I can't be late for that one. Here's my office," he said, opening the door to a room considerably larger than the one they had just left. The furniture included a small conference table, a large desk, chairs, a credenza, and a book case, all in matching contemporary cherry wood design. Nathan noticed a number of photographs on the wall of Jennings with various notables. He recognized Mayor Daley and Senator Percy. All the people in all the photographs were white men.

Jennings sat down at the conference table and motioned to Nathan to join him. "We have more room here to spread things out," he said. "Why don't you begin by telling me about yourself?"

Nathan hesitated–should he pull out another copy of his resume?–but said, instead, "Well, I've been traveling around the country looking for a position that offers experience in the business aspects of the profession. You may have seen on my resume that, in addition to my degrees in architecture--"

"Yes," Jennings interrupted, "you have degrees in business as well, I saw that on your resume. Very impressive. As I recall, your MBA is from Case Western." Nathan nodded. "I've taken a few business courses at Northwestern" Jennings continued, "but those have all been prerequisites in accounting and finance. My Dad–the Jennings in Worthmore, Jennings and Stevenson–wants me to enroll in Northwestern's evening MBA program, but I've been too busy here. By the way, he's the one who suggested that I meet with you."

"I see," Nathan said, thinking that he'd just gotten the answer to the question he'd posed to himself about Steve.

"Do you feel that your business training has been beneficial, or let me put it this way, what ideas could you share with us?"

"I think I could assist with gathering information for building programming, as well as with marketing services," Nathan said.

"Marketing is something I'm involved with myself," Jennings said. "Now, I mean. My first eight years here involved some design, drafting, and field work. Would you be willing to start in our drafting department–learn the business?"

"Yes, I would," Nathan said, "but I'd appreciate knowing that I'd be considered for business development positions in the future."

"That might be possible," Jennings said, "but we're pretty much old school when it comes to marketing."

"Old school?"

"We don't advertise our services," Jennings explained. "We feel that degrades the profession. We develop new work through personal contacts." Also known as the good ole boy network, Nathan thought, hoping his expression did not betray his reaction. "We've developed our network of business contacts over the years in the corporate, governmental, and institutional markets," Jennings continued. "Part of my job is to maintain and strengthen those relationships. You know, lunch or dinner, or maybe golf at the country club." He looked at his watch again.

"Part of my work for my master's in architecture at Ohio State," Nathan said, "was a study of how architectural firms in Ohio, mostly in the Columbus area, market their services. I found–"

"Was the AIA involved in your study?" Jennings interrupted.

"No, not directly, but we did have some contact both with the state chapter and the national office."

"Interesting," Jennings said. "My Dad sits on a national AIA task force concerning marketing. I'll ask him if he's familiar with your study. This was just last year?"

Oh shit, Nathan thought. "Yes, last year, but the study got only as far as the development of the questionnaire. I did learn quite a bit during the process," he added, aware that the vagueness was not helpful. Jennings looked at him a second too long. Is he going to ask me what happened?

"So, in your opinion," Jennings asked, "what are the business courses most applicable to the architectural profession?"

"Well, I think they're all important, from accounting to organizational behavior," Nathan said, relieved to get away from the subject of his study. "They provide a perspective--"

"I'm not familiar with courses in organizational behavior," Jennings interrupted again. "What are those?"

"I suppose it's a specialty within social psychology," Nathan said. "It deals with improving communication, for instance, with job performance and evaluation criteria, with job satisfaction, with management techniques. Abraham Maslow, Douglas McGregor, Frederick Hertzberg are big names in the field. Some aspects could be applied to improve programming in design work."

"Interesting," Jennings said again. "I see that you brought your portfolio–would you show me some examples of your work, please?"

Nathan unzipped his portfolio and presented examples of work he had done both in college and at his positions with firms in Cleveland. After some minutes during which Jennings alternated praise with exclamations of "Interesting!" he said, "I wasn't aware that Ohio State had such a diverse architectural program."

Diverse? What the hell does *that* mean, Nathan thought. "Just curious," he said, "may I ask where you went to architectural school?"

"Harvard," Jennings said promptly. "Most of our interns attended the top schools in the country."

"May I ask, too," Nathan continued, "what are your starting salaries for interns? Approximately?"

"They vary, based on education and experience," Jennings said smoothly, "but the average is about twelve thousand. A number of recent graduates have offered to work without compensation just to get the experience of working here. Excuse me," he said, "but I have to cut this a bit short. I have a luncheon meeting. Please call me next week so that we can discuss our mutual interests a little further."

"Thank you, Steve," Nathan said. "I certainly will."

"Let me walk you back to the lobby," Jennings said, rising. "It's a bit complicated, the maze here, I mean." Nathan followed, thinking that he didn't get to verify his hypothesis of a private exit.

He found a restaurant for lunch and spent most of the afternoon in visits to several downtown Chicago architectural firms, dropping off his resume and stating his availability for an immediate interview. Without exception, he was told that someone would be in touch with him should the firm have any interest in his services. It was a formula familiar to everyone, courteous, safe, robotic. Nathan, tired from travel, time zone changes, and frustration, went to bed early.

His meeting the next morning, at ten, was scheduled with the president of Grundstein & Sons International, one of the largest engineering and architectural firms in the United States owned by a Jewish family, the first such firm Nathan would visit since beginning his trip. Grundstein's headquarters were on West Fulton Street east of North Jefferson Street in a five-story red brick building which looked historic but exhibited signs of recent and extensive renovation. The brick had been cleaned and repointed. The exterior windows, glass, and doors had been replaced with materials that probably had been chosen to match the original design details. The entrance was through a large, attractive detailed brick arch. Business was apparently good. Nathan walked up the stone stairs leading to the main glass double doors and entered the building. The lobby's interior architecture seemed to synthesize the building's past with various contemporary details, including the lighting, furnishings and colorful artwork on the walls. The directory showed that Grundstein & Sons International was on the top floor. The elevator moved there slowly, almost gently. It certainly wasn't in competition with the Hancock racer. When the door slid open, Nathan saw that the elevator shaft was set back about fifteen feet from the lobby. The passengers would not spill out over their predecessors waiting in the reception area.

The design was similar to that of the main lobby on the first floor, combining original architectural details with contemporary light fixtures, furniture, and art on the walls. As did their competitors, Grundstein & Sons displayed renderings and photographs of buildings the firm had designed on the walls, as well as awards they had won. Nathan, after a brief inspection of the lobby, announced his presence to the receptionist and stated that he was there for his meeting with Mr. Atwater at ten. She asked him to have a seat while she called Mr. Atwater's secretary. Nathan sat down. The routine just did not vary. Mr. Atwater would ask him to call him by his first name. Nathan would say thank you and ask to be called Nathan. They would establish his educational credentials, work experience, and interest in marketing and other business aspects. Mr. Atwater would hem and haw and say that was his bailiwick, and ask Nathan what he would say to starting in the drafting department. And so on. And then, this afternoon, Nathan would fly home to Cleveland, having wasted a great deal of money and time without anything to show for it, not even a date with Karen, let alone a job offer.

"Mr. Goldstein? I'm Sharon, Mr. Atwater's secretary. Mr. Atwater will see you now." A friendly, middle-aged woman in a dark blue suit and a white blouse. Nathan followed her into a corridor, passing a room marked "Conference" and a series of open doors to offices with or without people in them, until they came to a secretarial area just outside a corner office, also with an open door. "Mr. Atwater, Mr. Goldstein is here," Sharon said to the inside. "Please show him in!" a man's voice said.

Atwater's office was large, with a high ceiling, with a commanding view of the lake looking east down West Fulton Street. Atwater, a slim middle-aged man about Nathan's height, rose to shake his hand. "Good to meet you, Mr. Atwater," Nathan said. "And good to meet you, Nathan–please call me Larry," Atwater replied, motioning Nathan to a chair and resuming his seat behind his desk. A departure from the conference table, Nathan thought, but first names first, and that's par for the course. To his amusement, the cliché seemed particularly appropriate in this office: on the long credenza behind Atwater's desk, between photographs of what Nathan assumed were Atwater's family members, were several golf trophies. There were also rolled up drawings, and on one side wall, between several book cases, were some contemporary paintings. They looked like originals.

"Let me begin by telling you that we've reviewed your resume in some detail since we spoke on the phone," Atwater said. "In fact, we've contacted two of your references and the feedback was excellent." Nathan sat up. This was not at all what he had expected to hear. This was exciting.

"First, I know you're from Cleveland–have you been to Chicago before?" Atwater asked.

"Yes, a number of times," Nathan said. "I have two good friends who live here, both former college classmates."

"Good, good–so you'd be open to moving to Chicago>"

"Absolutely," Nathan said. "It's a great city."

Atwater smiled. "What do you think the best fit for you would be, professionally?"

"Well, as you know from my resume, my education has combined work in business with work in architecture, and I'm hoping to find an opportunity on the business side of things, if not right away, then within a reasonable amount of time."

"Yes, I had thought as much," Atwater said. "I should tell you that I've discussed your background and credentials with Mr. Grundstein–the Chairman of our Board–he remains very active in the firm. I'll be direct, Nathan: we're interested in making you an offer. But first I want to get to know you."

Finally! Is the iron warming up or already hot? "That's exciting, Larry," Nathan said. "Does that interest include having me work on the business side of the company?"

"Yes, but not right away. We would want you to develop a solid understanding of how we do business. But in two or three years, assuming that everything worked out to our mutual satisfaction, there might very well be an opportunity for you under our vice president for business development. My question now has to do with what it would take to have you consider an offer. I suspect you've gotten several really attractive offers in the last few weeks as you've visited architectural firms around the country, and I need to know how to compete with those."

This was much too refreshing for clever answers. Honesty is the best policy. "No, no firm offers of any kind, to tell you the truth," Nathan said. "I won't say that my interviews have gone badly, but neither have they resulted in anything except don't call us, we'll call you. Well, a couple of people said to call them next week, but what you just said has been by far the most encouraging thing I've heard."

Atwater looked intently at him for a long moment. "I'm surprised, frankly," he said. "As I said, your credentials are excellent, and your references just about said that we couldn't find a better candidate. I wonder what's at work here. On the other hand, you just got your master's a month or so ago, and it takes time to make a decision. Let's take a tour of the office."

They got up and Atwater took Nathan through all the departments. Everyone was friendly. Nathan felt more and more at home. This is the place, he said to himself. He liked Grundstein, he liked Chicago, and he particularly liked Atwater. When they were finished, Atwater, shaking Nathan's hand, said, "If this all works out as I hope it will, Nathan, you just might take my job here some day. Maybe I could be your mentor for your first several years. "He smiled warmly. "But I don't expect to retire before some time during the nineties!"

"Thanks very much," Nathan said, also smiling. "We still have a lot to discuss, but I'm certainly very favorably impressed. Should I expect a formal letter from you? Or should I call you next week to discuss the missing details?"

"Yes, please feel free to call me," Atwater said. "These things take some time internally to clear with all the people who don't really want or need to make personnel decisions, but would get their noses badly out of joint if they weren't consulted. So yes, I may have some preliminary news for you next week—I'll talk to Mr. Grundstein again—so call me next week, by all means."

Nathan, not quite ecstatic but close to it, took a cab back to his motel, picked up his bags, checked out, and proceeded to Midway Airport. He had more than an hour before his flight's departure. He checked his bags through and found a pay phone. He was too excited not to call someone really important to him. His mother picked up the phone after two rings.

"Hello?"

"Mom, it's Nathan–I'm in Chicago, at the airport, and my flight lands in Cleveland at five thirty. Can you pick me up?"

"Of course I can! I haven't heard from you in two weeks! How did your interviews go? How are you feeling?"

"I'm just fine, Mom," Nathan said, laughing. "My last interview, here in Chicago, went very well. I'll tell you all about it. Don't come into the terminal, Mom, just wait in the car at arrivals at the last gate number– I'll need to pick up my bags and that always takes a while, so I'll meet you there about a quarter after six, OK?"

"In Chicago? Don't you also have a couple of interviews scheduled here in Cleveland?"

"Yes, I do, Mom, next week–I have to go now–I'll see you in a couple of hours!"

"Have a safe flight!" Adele said. "I can't wait to see you! Love you!"

"And I love you, Mom," Nathan said. "Bye!"

Chapter XII

Rubin, May, 2005

Rubin awoke to the ringing of the telephone next to his bed and reached for it, groggily. But he was too late. Gerald had picked up the phone in the study, and Rubin, hearing Laura's voice, hung up. He could hear Gerald talking softly in the next room, and wondered about the long pauses. Perhaps Mrs. Mayberry had taken a turn for the worse after all. Strange phrase, "taken a turn," as if she were out for a walk, apparently in a bad neighborhood. He got up and made his way, rather unsteadily, to his bathroom. That was enough of a walk for the moment.

By the time he had bathed, shaved, gotten dressed, and gone downstairs to the kitchen, Gerald was already there, dressed, humming, looking for cups and saucers, acquainting himself with Rubin's coffee maker, searching the refrigerator. "Good morning," Gerald said. "How is the Black Panther this morning? Ready to resume snarling, fulminating, lecturing? Another glass of wine, perhaps? Or is the mouth a little fuzzy, the tail dragging on the floor, the eloquence in need of lubrication?"

Rubin gave Gerald a long look, conveying, he hoped, bile and malice. "I can see why people don't like you," he said. "You have no milk of human kindness in your circulatory system. You hum at ungodly hours, and quite badly. You have no sense of rhythm. You have neglected to put the cream on the table. You have probably spilled something in the refrigerator, since you are blocking my view of it. Your pathetic attempts at humor are, well, pathetic. How is Laura's mother? How is Laura?"

"Mrs. Mayberry is making a miraculous recovery, praise Jesus," Gerald said, "which, in fact, is what she is doing. She's still in the hospital, but Laura says she's much stronger, and the doctors are saying that it looks as if she'll be able to go home in a few days. Laura is going to stay there until her mother is settled in and the nurses' visit routine has been established. She's already called her office in New York, and they're telling her to stay in Nashville as long as she thinks necessary."

"Great!" Rubin said. "What are *your* plans, then?"

"Well, since I don't have to go to Nashville, and since I don't have anything pressing at home, I thought I'd stay at least until tomorrow and hear the rest of whatever it is you have to tell me about being young and black in America. I want the truth right from the horse's mouth, so to speak. Or whatever end you represent after your performance last night."

"Performance!" Rubin growled. "What do you mean, performance? I explained any number of things you had never considered previously and overwhelmed you with perspicacity and logic. That was no performance, that was insightful analysis, and should have convinced you that *I should* be on the Supreme Court in Thurgood Marshall's seat instead of Uncle Clarence."

"Oh, I won't argue *that*," Gerald said. "But before you pick up where you left off, let's have some breakfast. The shawarma has worn off, and I need sustenance."

"Yes, I need more than coffee too," Rubin assented. "Sit down and let me take over. I have far more experience than you in the kitchen, I'm sure, especially with breakfasts. Sit down—you're much too big to work around."

"Don't mind if I do," Gerald said. "But can I have some bacon with my eggs? Or ham? A slice of ham would be good. Eggs over easy. And toast, please, whole wheat. Do you have any strawberry jam? Or raspberry? And I'd like a tall glass of orange juice. Skip the home fries, I'll have more toast. I suppose grits would be too much to expect. And a glass of water with ice, please–"

"Jesus Leaping Christ!" Rubin burst out. "I may have more experience *making* breakfast, but I can't match yours *eating* it! No, I don't have any damned grits, but I can handle the rest of it, now sit down and watch the coffee perk and don't start humming again."

The two old friends grinned at each other. "I'm glad about Mrs. Mayberry," Rubin said. "For Laura's sake."

"I know," Gerald said.

Rubin set to work. Gerald began to hum again but broke off when Rubin, looking straight at him, put his finger over his lips. There was a small television set in the kitchen and Gerald turned it on, searching for a news channel while Rubin broke the eggs over the frying pan. He found a "headlines" station and poured coffee for both while watching a reporter in Baghdad describe the latest suicide bombing in which dozens of people had been killed and injured in a mosque. It wasn't yet clear, the reporter said, who was responsible: so far, no group had claimed credit.

"Claimed credit!" Gerald and Rubin echoed simultaneously, incredulous and disgusted. They looked at each other. Gerald, in silent agreement, turned the set off. Rubin took four slices from a loaf of whole wheat bread and put them in the toaster.

"I once had a student," Rubin said, continuing his preparations, "a very nice and bright young man, from some small town around here somewhere–you know, an affluent, predominantly white suburb–who was apparently fascinated by various of my perspectives, which I never took the trouble to hide, and set about converting me to all the self-evident truths he had absorbed in his large Irish Catholic Republican family. He was an unusually attractive kid, funny, quick, not the least intimidated by a mere professor or anyone else. We stayed in touch after he finished his baccalaureate--he went on to get a master's degree here in whatever he was studying, industrial psychology or something like that, whatever that is–and we would have lunch once in a while and exchange opinions. I'm afraid that I confirmed all his fears: I was a liberal, I had doubts about the perfection of unregulated free enterprise, I could not reconcile the idea of a loving omnipotent deity with the facts of human history, and so on. Nevertheless--" the toast popped up and Rubin apportioned the slices–"nevertheless, he invited me to his wedding a couple of years later, and I went and met his dozens of brothers, sisters, uncles, aunts, and hundreds of cousins. But I was most impressed by his mother, a beautiful charming lady, truly gracious to her son's Jewish atheistic socialist professor who, she said, was such a frequent subject of her son's conversation." Rubin paused to distribute the eggs and ham and put a pitcher of orange juice on the table. Gerald, helping himself, said, "I know that you're going to make a connection of some kind to something here, but the suspense is excruciating."

"Yes, that's intentional," Rubin said, spearing a piece of ham for himself. "Somehow or other the lady answered my thank-you note, in which I also expressed my high opinion of her son and best wishes for the future, and, in a very pleasant way–really–asked me whether her son's impression, that I did not believe in God, was accurate. As I said, she had been most hospitable and charming, and I was disconcerted by the question. But I didn't think I could ignore it either. So I replied at probably too great length--"

"Why am I not surprised?" Gerald said.

"–suggesting that religion of almost any kind, certainly all the so-called major religions, had been the source of enormous bloodshed and violence and misery throughout human history, whether these religions worshipped one god or many gods or were dedicated to secular deities like dictators or ideas of nation or race or dialectical materialism."

"Aha," Gerald said. "The connection is emerging."

"Yes," Rubin said. "I wrote and revised my letter very carefully, not in expectation of being persuasive but in hopes of not giving any offense, because I really liked the boy and the mother–well, I had been flattered to be invited to the boy's wedding and I was really very well treated."

"I get the picture," Gerald said.

"To my dismay, Mrs. Sullivan–yes, I do remember the name–answered at length herself, dismissing what I had said about human history–naturally I had supplied a fair number of examples, not omitting the Crusades or the Inquisition or the usual methods of converting the heathen–as irrelevant. She didn't *quite* say that you can't judge the Creator by his creation, but that's what it seemed to come down to. Since that makes no sense to me, I didn't answer. And I haven't heard from my former student since then, either. But I can't hear about these murders in a mosque now without thinking about Mrs. Sullivan and whether she sees the connection to, say, the Troubles in the country of her ancestors."

"No, of course she doesn't," Gerald said, pouring himself more coffee. "Good eggs, by the way. And for a Jewish boy, you know what kind of ham to buy. Put another couple of slices of toast in, please."

Rubin obliged. "Why do you say of course she doesn't?"

"Because her idea of God and her understanding of her church have nothing to do with human behavior as it is, only as she thinks it ought to be. I know a lot of people who feel similarly. And it *is* a matter of feeling, Walter, not ratiocination or command of historical evidence or ability to make anthropological comparisons. My mother-in-law, as devout a colored lady as you'll find anywhere, feels very close to Jesus–especially now, I'd guess–and is quite certain that she'll meet up with all her friends and relatives, even the ones she quarreled with, in Heaven. I think she imagines Heaven as a kind of perpetual church service, with lots of singing and stirring sermons and praise the Lords and Amens. And everybody dressed in his or her Sunday best, and the children well behaved, with their faces shining and their hair combed, no unruly nappy heads anywhere. Now this lady has been married even more often than I have and from what I hear she wasn't exactly a nun in between times, and when she was young she knew all about letting the good times roll. Maybe she came to Jesus a little late in the game, but what of it? The Lord is merciful. He understands. His hand moves in mysterious ways His wonders to perform. And every one of her husbands is going to be up there in Heaven with her, even Mr. Williams, Laura's father, as crooked a card sharp as ever hid an ace up his sleeve, last seen somewhere in Memphis under inauspicious circumstances. Police custody, in fact. If Mrs. Mayberry has doubts about anyone's salvation, it's mine, not George Williams'."

Rubin was fascinated. "Why would she have doubts about your chances?"

"Oh, because I was married to a white woman once, and because I don't go to church regularly, and because my people were from Alabama, which is even further south than Tennessee and almost as bad as Mississippi, and because I didn't go to Fisk, and because I'm a couple of shades lighter than she is. All very good reasons why Jesus would hesitate about letting me through those Pearly Gates. My point is only that religion isn't rational to begin with, so no, your student's charming mother isn't going to wonder about Irish Catholics and Protestants murdering each other over the centuries, any more than your rabbi is going to apologize for all those Philistines Samson slew with the jawbone of an ass."

"You know my rabbi?"

"Man, everybody knows your rabbi. One of those aggressive loudmouths, always stirring up trouble with the *goyim*."

"That's him," Rubin said. "But the code word is *abrasive*, not aggressive. Jews aren't aggressive–that's a Gentile virtue associated with sports and investments, you know, bold risk-taking, John Wayne courage in the face of overwhelming odds. We're *abrasive*, which means ill-mannered, loud, not fit for the Ivy League or restricted neighborhoods."

"I see," Gerald said. "Sounds familiar, for some reason. I don't know whether Mrs. Mayberry ever gave any thought to your people and their standing with Jesus–probably not–but if she did, I don't think she'd be optimistic on your behalf."

Rubin drained his coffee. "More toast? Coffee? Anything?"

"No, thanks, that was very good, but I've had plenty," Gerald said. "But as long as we're on the subject of your future, tell me what you're going to do when you can't make breakfast for yourself, let alone for a visitor from out of state."

Rubin looked at Gerald and saw that he was serious. He abandoned his impulse to give a jocular answer. "I appreciate your concern," he said, smiling at his own formality, "but I don't really know what to say. I take all these pills--" he realized suddenly that he hadn't taken any this morning, and reached for the little brown bottles–"and they will keep me going for an indefinite period, and then I suppose somebody from the condominium association will find me either incapacitated or dead. I haven't made any arrangements for assisted living or long-term care or any of those warehouse storage plans that haven't quite made it into Medicaid yet. But I don't intend to outlive Social Security or to exhaust my medical insurance."

"No? What will you do?"

Rubin hesitated. "I don't know if I will actually have the guts to do what I think I should, if I can," he said. "A stroke or a heart attack, if it doesn't kill me, could very well prevent any action on my part unlike, say, cancer. But if I can, then I think I should make my own arrangements for my departure, rather than serving to train more medical students in the appropriate facial expressions and mannerisms to accompany their pronouncements to the about-to-be bereaved. Sorry, I don't mean to be frivolous, Gerald, but this subject always makes me angry."

"Angry?"

Rubin poured himself some orange juice and began to extract his pills from their containers. Gerald watched, expressionless. "One moment," Rubin said, starting to swallow the pills in no particular order. When he finished, he gave Gerald another long look, this time ending it with a shrug, and resumed. "Yes, angry, partly at society in general, but specifically at the medical profession. They welcome us into this world, at least those of us who are born into reasonably affluent families in this country. They give us expensive advice about how to live and what to eat and so on, and what *not* to do as well, of course. They assure us that we have the best health care system in the history of the world, certainly better than that of any socialist country like Canada. They see to it that they and their dedication to our welfare are portrayed in movies and on television by handsome actors and gorgeous actresses capable of performing weekly miracles with technical expertise Nobel Prize winners would envy. But when it comes to ushering us out of this world and into the grave, they knuckle under to churches and pastors and fearmongers, and let us suffer in pain and panic, to say nothing of what our families have to endure, with, at best, morphine for us and condolences for our relatives."

"But Walter," Gerald asked, "what would you have them do?"

"Take concerted public action, as they do on behalf of the victims of AIDS or tuberculosis or dozens of other such diseases. The disease I'm talking about here isn't death but our denial of it. Of course I'm sure that there are hundreds, maybe thousands of physicians who do what they can quietly, on an individual basis, but I'm talking about the profession. Look at the enormous waste of energy, emotional capital, and of course money represented by the Protracted Death Denial Industry. You don't have to admire Jack Kevorkian to realize that our interests in mitigating human suffering get almost no legal, social, or political expression when it comes to the most universal and democratic fact about our existence, that it will end. Oregon passes a most carefully restricted assisted suicide act and the Attorney General sees high crimes, never mind misdemeanors. A woman braindead for over a dozen years, existing only as an assortment of tissues kept pulsating through some complicated engineering, becomes a political football for people who want to run for president. Right-to-Lifers who are convinced that abortion is murder and that aborted fetuses suffered terribly pay no attention to the torture that adults very often have to endure while dying, while their relatives watch for days, weeks, even months on end. I can't imagine that this would be the situation if the medical profession, witnessing all this, were to break its silence. How is their silence so different from what greeted the ovens at Auschwitz? Or the genocide in Darfur? You choose the comparison."

Gerald was silent for a moment. Then he repeated his question: "So what will you do?"

"I've got a pistol," Rubin said. The silence lay between them like a heavy blanket.

"'I do believe you think what now you speak,'" Gerald started, and Rubin concluded with the Player King's next line, "'But what we do determine oft we break.'"

Gerald nodded. "I saw my mother die, Walter, and she fought for every breath with all her strength, which, poor thing, wasn't very much. And didn't you tell me years ago that that's pretty much how it was with your mother?"

"I said that I don't know whether I'll be able to do it," Rubin said. "But I certainly don't want to wind up in some nursing home stinking of formaldehyde, sitting in my own shit in a goddamned wheelchair while some big underpaid undertrained aide slaps me around for making a mess again."

"Some big *black* underpaid undertrained aide," Gerald amended Rubin's vision. "Some woman about my size but a lot meaner."

"I suppose so," Rubin said glumly. "How did we get on this cheerful subject, anyway?"

"I don't remember," Gerald said. "I'm getting to be as forgetful as you are, and I can't understand that–I'm at least two months younger. Anyway, about your mother, about whom you've told me quite a bit– there was one thing you didn't tell me that I'm curious about, and that was how or why she managed to get the two of you out of New Orleans to Cleveland."

"A lot more easily than she managed to get the two of us out of Berlin," Rubin said. "I never did understand how she did that. But as far as getting to Cleveland, I do know. That was in 1945, just about the time the war ended, the war with Japan, I mean. She had a friend–you know, Gerald, I've told you how indefatigable she was about staying in touch with people, writing letters almost every evening–she had a friend, a woman she had been in school with before World War I, believe it or not, when they were both little girls–who had married a Jew–she was a Gentile–and had gotten out of Germany in the very early thirties. I think they went to England first. I'm not sure what they did for a living, but they had no children, so there was a whole set of complications they didn't have to worry about. Eventually they came to the United States and settled in Cleveland. I can't remember what the husband did there, but his wife, Gertrude, got a good job with a publisher. Well, that was the connection. Gertrude kept her eyes open, ears to the ground, all that, and she heard about an opening that she persuaded my mother to apply for. It was with another division of the company, but still in Cleveland. My mother got the job, loved it, and of course she was delighted to be reunited with Gertrude. She really was a very nice woman–I knew her quite well. And that's how we came to Cleveland, where I finished high school."

"A couple of years later, right?"

"Yes. And then, some years after that, things got a lot easier, financially, I mean. I must have told you about it? Forty acres and a mule?"

"What? No, I don't remember you passing for black at the Freedman's Bureau. What's this? Do you even know what a mule looks like?"

"Sure I do," Rubin said. "They come in all shapes and sizes but mostly they're from Columbia, they're pregnant or they look pregnant, and they're about fourteen. Custom agents with trained dogs arrest them at the airports in Miami and Dallas in our never-ending war on drugs, all praise to law enforcement agencies everywhere."

It was Gerald's turn to give Rubin a long look. "Not that kind of mule, Walter," he said. "What are you talking about?"

"Reparation payments," Rubin said. "What the Germans–the post-Nazi Germans–called *Wiedergutmachung Zahlungen*. The literal translation might be 'Payments to make things well again.' Gertrude and her husband had found a lawyer in Germany and had applied for these payments under the program the German government established for survivors of the Nazi period. The survivors had to prove that they had been deprived of their relatives' lives and/or their own or their relatives' liberty or property, or in some cases other tangible assets such as employment, and there were lots of forms, and it all took quite a bit of time. That's why it was very helpful to have a lawyer on the scene. Of course the program was very controversial in Germany, where almost no one had ever been a Nazi and certainly had not been in any way responsible for what was alleged to have happened to the Jews. Gertrude's husband, I remember now, had actually been employed by the German government, the Weimar Republic, I mean, and was of course dismissed soon after the Nazis took over in 1933. So his case had to do with the loss of his job and pension. My mother's case, as the widow of the murdered Solomon Rubin, and as the person then solely responsible for the care of her young son, was obviously quite different. But among the really crazy things about the Germans was that, at least until the very end, they kept amazingly complete records, even of their own crimes. Like Richard Nixon and those tapes that he must have regretted to his dying breath. The lawyer that Gertrude recommended to us was very good, and eventually not only did my mother get a substantial amount–a monthly payment for the rest of her life–but I got some money too, in my own name. That made a huge difference. It's how I paid my tuition, room, and board in graduate school at Wisconsin, along with the scholarship money. And of course my mother's savings, over the years, amounted to quite a bit. I'm in surprisingly good shape, financially." He got up and began to clear the dishes from the table.

"Let me help you with that," Gerald said, rising.

"No, it's easier if you just sit there," Rubin said. "This kitchen is small and you really aren't."

Gerald resumed his seat. "Reparation payments," he said slowly.

"I might still be able to find the name of the lawyer," Rubin grinned, "but I doubt that he could do much for you now. That was fifty years ago. And I suspect that what you have in mind for reparation payments took place even longer ago."

"Not only that," Gerald said, "but you're going to tell me that, like so many others of your complexion, you weren't even here when my people were kidnapped, brought over in chains, forced to pick cotton, brutalized, lynched, all the things you explained to me last night. You're going to say that your forebears were grubbing in the garbage of some Russian *stetl,* barely keeping body and soul together, completely unaware of what was going on here. You never heard of Judah P.

Benjamin, right?"

"And you never heard of the Spingarn brothers or Julius Rosenwald
or Jack Greenberg? Or Malcolm X or Louis Farrakhan, on the other side
of the divide? Actually, I'm in favor of reparation payments, as I tried to
explain last night. That's what affirmative action is, it seems to me, or as
close to reparation payments as it's politically possible to get. There are
some other such things, federal support of historically black colleges in
the Higher Education Act, for instance, or nationally funded research on
sickle cell anemia, or on other health and social issues especially relevant
to black Americans. All of them are reparation payments. Three cheers
for all of them, as far as I'm concerned." Rubin put the dishes in the
dishwasher, shook the soap crystals into the container, closed the door,
and started the machine, thinking of his garage door opener. And if the
mechanized gates didn't work you called a repairman, another form of
reparation. The analogy seemed worth trying on Gerald. "Quite
amazing," Rubin said, gesturing to the dishwasher. "We make these
machines, dishwashers, garage door openers, elevators, to clean our
dishes or let us in or out or up or down, and when they break down, we
call somebody to come fix them. And we make our societies to clean
something, or let some of us in or up, or keep some of us out or down,
and when they don't work, we call somebody to come fix them.
Napoleon or Kwame Nkrumah or Jesus. Or we take the kids to
Disneyland."

"Disneyland? Too poetic, Walter, I don't follow that."

"Fantasy works very nicely to keep most of us dreaming of better
days in better places, with more suitable roles to play. Heaven for Mrs.
Mayberry, no doubt catching the pastor's eye as her contralto rings out
from the choir." Gerald chuckled. Rubin, encouraged, warmed to his
theme. "Marx had something to say about that, you remember. And look
at the popularity of all these books and films about lords of the ring,
hobbits, miracles on 34th Street, Harry Potter, spaceships, Jurassic parks,
Da Vinci codes, angels, demons, Santa Claus, teen-age werewolves,
exorcisms, magic, and all the rest. How is that different from lotteries
and Las Vegas, astrology, fortune telling, belief in an afterlife,
Hollywood romances, airport paperbacks, gossip magazines?"

"Or sports," Gerald added. "Fame and fortune, adoring women, fast
cars, jewelry, notoriety, television appearances, magazine covers–these
days, that dream must be responsible for more junkies and alcoholics
and abused wives and neglected children and misery in the ghetto than
the Ku Klux Klan. For every Muhammad Ali or Michael Jordan or
Walter Payton, there must be ten thousand kids who haven't bothered to

learn to read because they're out bouncing basketballs or doing the Ali shuffle or practicing broken field running in parking lots."

"Exactly," Rubin said.

"But if you can't be rich, what's wrong with dreaming about it? Isn't that universal?"

"Probably," Rubin said. "But dreaming about it rather than working for it will keep you from becoming richer, contrary to all the crap graduating seniors are told at their commencement ceremonies. And believe me, I've attended too many of those. Usually it's some kid from the graduating class encouraging his or her classmates never to abandon their dreams. That speaker is wildly applauded, especially if his clichés are brief. Adult speakers, trying to caution the graduates about the hard work and compromises that lie in wait, like so many thugs in an alley, don't have a chance. For another thing, wanting to be rich is just another way of saying that you want more, not just more of what you've got but more than others have. That's a guarantee not just for disappointment but for divisiveness. All your relatives will try to manipulate you and accuse you of favoring someone else. And for still another, with only few exceptions, most of what people have to do to get really rich is pretty awful, if not downright criminal. Buying cheap and selling high. As if, once you've got your pile, you'll get a chance to do something really important. All you're going to get is a fancy funeral, and you'll be too dead to enjoy it,"

"Man!" Gerald said. "You *had* a good breakfast! All this doom and gloom! Let's go for a walk–I need to stretch my legs, and you can show me around your condominium complex. Any colored people live here?"

Rubin nodded. "Yes, Dr. Parker, we practice diversity here. We have African American residents, Asian American residents, Christians, Jews, Muslims, Hindus, Buddhists, non-believers, other faiths, non-faiths, Democrats, Republicans, dog owners, cat owners, pet haters, bird feeders, aquaria tenders, indoor orchid growers, widows, widowers, divorced people, married people, retired professors with or without spouses of various genders–at least four, I think–the only creatures in short supply here, thank God, are small children. They're not exactly prohibited, you understand, and on weekends some grandparents among us tolerate their presence, but I can't tell you that this is a child-friendly environment."

"Well, you have to draw the line somewhere, I understand that," Gerald said. "Ready?"

Rubin went to get a cardigan. Gerald took a light jacket. When they left, to Gerald's surprise, Rubin locked the door.

*****

It was a good morning for the two old men, the best that Rubin, at any rate, had had since he had returned from New York to find Harry Rosenberg's last message waiting for him on his telephone answering machine. After their walk around the condominium complex, which Gerald, to Rubin's quiet satisfaction, admired enthusiastically, they drove to the University's campus and then around the town. Gerald was astounded by the changes that had taken place since he had last visited Ann Arbor. "It's not just the growth," he told Rubin. "I knew that, of course, but it's the feel of the place that's so different. New York changes all the time, too, but somehow its neighborhoods feel different only gradually. Here it's as if everything is straining in all different directions at once, up and out and inwards too, even down in some instances, with your underground Law Library and below-level parking. I realize that the school, to expand at all, has to grow into the town, but now it's begun to do that on the fringes as well as in the center, and somehow that seems diseased. University office buildings and medical clinics out by shopping malls and interstates. Like a cancer metastasizing."

"The University as a cancer?" Rubin laughed. "There are a lot of local people–landlords, shop owners, construction workers–who wouldn't see it that way."

"And a lot who would, I bet," Gerald said. "Especially old people like us. We like things to be stable. We're always telling young people to put things back where they belong, and we don't mean just tools or books or kitchen utensils. We like borders, and we want them to stay where they were when we first saw those colored maps, the green and pink and purple countries in our geography books–do kids still study geography, do you know?–unless, of course, they were in Africa and the colors were those of the English or French or Portuguese. This debate about immigration, you know, amnesty and citizenship or fences and border patrols, all that--"

"Oh, that know-nothing fascist *Amerika Über Alles* organization you belong to?"

"–the low wages California growers pay their illegally imported Mexican help versus the high prices we'd have to pay for our cucumbers if real Americans picked them–that's by no means the whole story. You start to round it out when you add the question of English as a national language, and how the national anthem would sound if you were to try to sing it in Mandarin, but at the very core of things is how comfortable we are with change. And the answer is, not very, or maybe not at all. Whatever happened to the old neighborhood? It's gone to hell, is what happened, even if it's all cleaned up, gentrified, trees growing in Brooklyn--"

"Really! In Bed-Stuy, too?"

"–wherever, things just ain't what they used to be, as the song says. So we tell kids how baseball was absolutely ruined by the designated hitter rule, which I believe is true, by the way, and how there was no parking problem when people took streetcars and buses in addition to the subway, and how, even though times were damned hard in the Depression, at least we didn't live in Red states or Blue states but in the United States, under the spreading apple tree."

"I don't think you got that one quite right."

"No? Don't sit under the apple tree with anyone else but me?'

"Yes, but not the spreading apple tree. That was a chestnut."

"You were a professor much too long, Walter, but you can stop now. My point is that immigration is seen as a threat all right, but it doesn't just threaten to lower wages and to raise taxes, it threatens whiteness. We're going to be a much darker country than we have been, with all that implies, and white folks don't like what they see ahead of them."

"No, I don't suppose they do," Rubin agreed. "But I'm not sure that white folks are quite as monolithic as they appear to non-whites. People who *aren't* white in this country are somebody in whatever group they say they belong to, but nobody except some Aryan Nation idiot would simply say he's white. White is negative, it just means not being somebody who isn't white. It doesn't say who you are. There's no white language, white music, white art, white religion, nothing substantive of any kind in whiteness. You have to be *something*, Swedish, for instance, or Croat or Serb, or at least Lower Slobbovian. White people have been killing each other with unrestrained enthusiasm all the years they have refused to be white together, whether as Englishmen and Frenchmen or Catholics and Protestants, just as black people have been gleefully killing each other in Africa and brown people in India and so on. And from what I've heard, Puerto Ricans and Cubans and Mexicans are quite sure that their differences are important, no matter how often they have to say that they're Hispanic or are called Latino."

"True but irrelevant," Gerald declared. "Just the other day I heard some news commentator claim that Mexico has its own 'guest worker' program. I don't know whether there's anything to that, but let's say that there is. Mexico wouldn't be threatened, not in language, not in religion, and very likely not in color. I think that Guatemalans would blend right in. But not in Iowa they wouldn't."

"Is there an anti-immigration organization in Mexico, do you think?" Rubin asked.

"Well, if there isn't, maybe they'd be open to the idea," Gerald said. "Want to go down and see what we could organize? How's your Spanish?"

"Non-existent," Rubin admitted. "Send me a postcard."

They were silent for a while, driving west along the Huron River until they came to a sign indicating a public park a thousand feet ahead. "Want to stop for a while by the river?" Rubin asked.

"Sure," Gerald said. "We aren't going to get mugged, are we?"

"You never know," Rubin said. "But it's not even noon. I don't think muggers get up this early. And anyway, this is Ann Arbor, not the Bronx." He turned into the drive. There was a guardhouse in the middle, where the drive was divided into entrance and exit lanes, with barriers. But the barriers were up and no one was inside the guard house to collect the entrance fee. A sign read "Park closes at 10 p.m." Rubin said, "The state's perennial budget crisis has permitted us unrestricted access." Gerald nodded. Rubin drove a longer distance than he remembered to the parking lot, where there was only one other car, a rather rusty older Chevrolet, Rubin noticed. He parked the Chrysler away from it, near a path. Gerald got out and Rubin, first checking something in the console, followed, locking the car. They could see the river perhaps a hundred yards away, beyond a shelter and some picnic tables with attached benches. A building with a sign and arrows, obviously containing public restrooms, stood a short distance away on the other side of the parking lot. No one was in sight. The park was very clean and well maintained, like Jericho's Wall, Rubin thought. "Shall we sit at a table or go down the trail?" he asked Gerald.

"Let's sit down and look at the water," Gerald said. "This is very nice. I don't remember it, but it must have been here when I taught at the School of Education."

"Yes, it was," Rubin said, motioning Gerald to lead the way. The path to the river was rather narrow. "It was here when I came to Ann Arbor, a couple of years before you did. We met on some committee shortly after you came, as I recall. But we didn't go out on picnics or anything equally frivolous–we just met and argued and interviewed some people and wrote a report to whatever vice president had appointed us." They reached a picnic table. "How's this?" Rubin asked.

"No, let's sit closer to the water," Gerald said, pointing to another table. "Do you remember who the vice president was? What was the report about?"

Rubin hesitated. "I don't remember the vice president's name," he said. "That would be too much to expect after all this time. But the report had to do with ways to recruit more minority faculty, staff, and especially students. Back in those days, you remember, you were a minority, and you probably even referred to yourself as a minority, which you won't do once your projected demographic revolution is complete."

"That depends on the circumstances," Gerald corrected him. "We've learned a lot from you white boys. Whatever the numbers are, if I can derive some advantage from calling myself a minority, or an underrepresented minority, or a historically and traditionally oppressed minority, then that's me, absolutely. On the other hand--"

"Yes, yes, sit down. The river's high here, isn't it? And fast. Nice spot. What's that down there? Ducks?"

"Yes, I think so," Gerald said. "It *is* nice. Peaceful. Very relaxing." They sat quietly for a while, on the same side of the table looking toward the river, watching the water swirl by. The weather was balmy. Birds flew into the trees above their heads, apparently to inspect them. Rubin surmised that they were hoping that lunch would be served. Suddenly they heard a sharp sound, a twig snapping under a foot, or something being opened. They spun around in their seats and found themselves looking across the table at a semi-circle of four or five leering long-haired young men in t-shirts and jeans, some with grotesque tattoos on their arms. Several had knives. One was armed with a club. They were within a few feet of the table between them.

"Goddamn!" said the one closest to them. "The big one's a nigger."

"That don't mean he don't have money or a watch or something," another one grunted. Rubin put his right hand in his pocket.

"That's right, get your wallet, old fart," said the first one. He appeared to be the leader. There was something wrong with his eyes, pale blue and protruding. "And your car keys, too, motherfucker. That your car, the Chrysler, or the nigger's?"

Rubin felt Gerald tense. He put his left hand on Gerald's arm to restrain him for a moment, and almost in a fluid motion, got up, drawing Harry's Luger out of his right pocket, racking the first round into the chamber as he had been shown in the sporting goods store. The click was audible to everyone. "Freeze," he said, aware that he sounded like a television cop. "Drop those knives and that club, very carefully." The men were astounded. Rubin slowly pointed the Luger at the man with the strange eyes. "Now. *Do it now.*" The man dropped his knife, open-mouthed, his strange eyes getting wider. "Don't–don't–"

Rubin swung his arm to point the gun at the others. "I've got plenty of bullets for all of you," he said. They began to drop their knives. The one with the club seemed reluctant to let it go. Rubin took aim and he dropped it. "Don't move, not one of you," Rubin said. "Gerald, you got your cell phone? Call 911."

Gerald, getting up, fumbled in his pocket. Rubin kept looking at the men and pointing the gun at them, now at this one, now at that one. "Walter," Gerald whispered, "I left it in my bag at your place."

"What do you want to do?" Rubin muttered back.

Gerald hesitated. "Make them take their shoes off and wade across the river, single file," he whispered. "All except this marble-eyed son of a bitch."

"What are you going to do? You're seventy-five, for God's sake!"

"Yes," Gerald whispered, "but you've got the gun." He was back in charge, Rubin realized.

"All right," Rubin said loudly to the five men. "Take your shoes off. Very slowly and carefully." They hesitated. "I really would like to shoot each one of you bastards," Rubin said quietly, hoping that his manner conveyed conviction. They decided to believe him and stepped out of their shoes, all gym shoes of one kind or another. "Now line up–not you, Ugly," he said to the leader, "line up one at a time at the water and start wading across, you first," he said to the one who had held the club, "as I tell you to go. Go to the other side and stay there. Not you," he said to the leader again, who was beginning to look very worried, shifting from one foot to the other. He had no socks, Rubin noticed.

"I–I can't swim," said the one who had held the club.

"It's shallow here," Rubin said, "and if it isn't, then learn fast. *Now go!*" He pointed the Luger at the man's chest. The man started to pick his way across the river. There seemed to be a lot of sharp stones. "Now you!" Rubin barked at the next man.

"Wait!" Gerald said suddenly. "Get the keys to their car!"

"OK, which one of you has the keys?" Rubin growled at them. "You?" he snarled at the man with the strange eyes, raising the Luger toward the man's forehead.

"No, no! Davis, give him the goddamn keys for God's sake!"

One of the other men reached in his pocket and withdrew a set of keys. "Throw them over here, *very carefully*," Rubin said. The man did so. Gerald bent down and picked them up. "All right, they're GM keys," he told Walter. "Let's get this show on the road."

But as the fourth man entered the water, under Rubin's unwavering gun, and Gerald approached the now visibly frightened man with the strange eyes, there was a yell from the first man, now in about the middle of the river, as he stepped into a hole and disappeared. The man behind him stopped. "Keep moving or I'll shoot you!" Rubin yelled. They turned to look at him and as he took aim and watched them scurry toward the opposite bank, he heard two thuds behind him, almost simultaneously. Gerald had smashed the leader in the face and the man had collapsed on the ground, bleeding and unconscious. Gerald gathered the shoes and knives and went some fifty feet up the river to a spot where the bushes shielded him from view. The first man surfaced down river, holding his head. Gerald came back, empty-handed.

"Must have hit a rock," Rubin said, gesturing toward the man in the middle of the river. "Let's get going," Gerald said. "I threw their keys into the river too." They stepped around the prostrate body on the ground and hurried to the Chrysler. Rubin pressed the automatic opener on his key and they got in. "Did you kill that son of a bitch?" Rubin asked, starting the engine. "I don't think so," Gerald said, rubbing the knuckles of his right hand, "but I suppose I rearranged his face. Jesus, Walter, I haven't hit anybody in about twenty-five years."

"Only twenty-five years? Gerald, you were fifty even then! What was the occasion?"

Gerald hesitated. Rubin realized that, although they weren't ready to talk about what had just happened, Gerald's quarter-century-old memory wasn't pleasant either. Drive carefully now, Rubin told himself, heading east back toward town. No need to hurry.

"Some drunk got fresh with Laura at a party, pulling at her or her clothes," Gerald said quietly. "She told him to stop. Then I saw what he was doing and I stopped him."

"He didn't know she was with you?"

"I don't know, but he found out. The trouble was, I broke his jaw, and he sued me. Extensive dental work, humiliation, psychological damage, and punitive damages. It would have been quite a bit of money."

"Would have been?"

"I had a very good lawyer," Gerald said, smiling.

"Laura?"

"Sure. It was the sort of thing you keep in the family," Gerald said. It was Rubin's turn to smile.

Chapter XIII
Nathan, 1976-1977

"How did your interviews go?" Adele asked as she pulled her Chevy Impala away from the curb, Nathan in the passenger seat, his bags in the trunk. Their initial greeting and embrace had been warm but brief in the cold January wind.

"There may be an offer from a company in Atlanta, and perhaps another two from companies in Chicago," Nathan said. "In fact, I'm pretty sure that I'm going to get an offer from one in Chicago, which is going to be very attractive, I think. Grundstein and Sons International."

"Grundstein?"

"Yes, it is, Mom," Nathan said, responding to the question implicit in her tone. "They have several offices in the United States and some in Europe and Israel, but if I get an offer and take it, I'd start in the Chicago office."

"But you have some interviews here in Cleveland too, you told me."

"Yes, including one at Becker, with Sam Becker himself."

"Yes, where you worked before. But you didn't like Mr. Becker, I remember, Nathan."

"No, not much, and there were some other people there who weren't a lot of fun to work with either, but I think I could get Becker to listen to my ideas about marketing architectural services, and I've already done my time in his drafting department. So that might be a better position, if he's open to some new ideas. And as much as I liked the man in Chicago, and the whole setup there, there's a problem there I'm not at all sure I want to tackle at this point."

"What's the problem?"

"I'd have to take still another exam to get my Illinois license. Here, in Ohio, I'd have just the national professional exam, which I'd have to take in Illinois too, of course, but in addition, Illinois requires a proficiency exam for the license. And you know, after all my years in school and four degrees, I've had more than my fill of exams, hoops, hurdles, barriers of all kinds. The fewer of those, the better."

"But you've always done well, Nathan," Adele said. "You always got very good grades."

"I don't like the odds, Mom. About three applicants out of four fail the exam the first time around. I'm tired of having to prove myself over and over. I want to get started with my career. One of the reasons I went back to get my master's degree in architecture was to avoid the equivalency exam and to increase my chances of simple reciprocity across the country after I pass the professional licensing exam. The equivalency exam is on the subjects I've already passed on the college level. It was designed to screen out the applicants who don't have degrees in architecture."

Adele didn't answer right away. Then, glancing at Nathan, she asked, "So you think you could work for Becker?"

"Yes, to get started. I wouldn't expect to spend the rest of my life there, but it would be a beginning. But Mom, I haven't even had the interview."

That evening, despite Adele's concerns that Nathan was tired from his long trip and should get to bed early, he went to see Michael Kaplan and found himself explaining, once again, the dilemma he anticipated he'd have if he got offers from both Grundstein and Becker. Michael was much more explicitly puzzled than Adele had been.

"You liked the guy at Grundstein, and you don't like Becker? How is that a dilemma?"

"It's not that simple," Nathan said. "Assuming that I get reasonably comparable offers from both, there's still the equivalency exam in Illinois, and I don't want to cram for another exam I have only a twenty-five percent chance of passing the first time. I want to get to work. I can't even be sure that I'd pass the exam the second time I'd take it, if I don't pass it the first time."

"There isn't any way to improve your odds?"

"The best way is to sidestep the exam altogether, which I could do by staying in Ohio. If I were a doctor and faced a similar discrepancy, you know, two exams in Illinois and only one in Ohio, and had competing offers to join the staff of a hospital in Chicago or another in Cleveland, and the chances of passing the extra exam in Illinois were only one out of four, wouldn't you tell me to take the position in Cleveland?"

"As you said, it's not that simple," Michael said. "But let's wait and see what kinds of offers you get, if you get them. When is your interview at Becker's?"

"Tomorrow afternoon," Nathan said, glad to change the subject.

The next day, after an unsuccessful interview at the Houston Company–why, Nathan wondered, did so many companies agree to meet with him only to tell him that they weren't hiring but would keep his papers "on file"? Was there something about his appearance that they wanted to see for themselves?–Nathan stopped for lunch at a diner he hadn't visited in over a year, Our Gang Restaurant on Chagrin Boulevard in Beachwood. The restaurant served lunch to the Beachwood business types on weekdays and catered to Beachwood residents on evenings and weekends. It was the kind of place where people ran into friends and acquaintances. Nathan got a seat at the counter, glanced at the menu, gave the waitress his order, and felt a tap on his shoulder. He turned to find a man he'd met in the MBA program at Case Western, Elliott Ross. Later he'd done a marketing study for Ross for which he'd never been paid. After the initial pleasantries, which included bringing Ross up to date on his interviews–the next one, in an hour, was to be at Becker and Associates–he decided to ask about it.

"Just curious, Elliott," he said. "Did that study I prepared for you about the apartment complex along with the two comparable properties ever lead to anything?"

"No," Ross said. "Your report was very good, but the investment group I was with at the time decided to pass. There were reasons to be cautious."

"Does that mean I won't get paid?" Nathan asked.

"Sorry, Nathan," Ross said. "The way we work is that if a project doesn't go forward, nobody gets paid. And you know we never discussed your fee."

"Well, if we had," Nathan said, pursuing his point, "how much is that kind of report typically worth?"

"If the project goes forward, I'd say, typically, about twenty-five hundred. Hey, I have to get back to a meeting. Good luck with your interviews. Let's have lunch–call me this week!"

"I will," Nathan said. "Do you have a card?"

Ross gave him his business card and waved goodbye. Nathan finished his lunch, left a tip, paid his bill, and drove to his appointment at Samuel Becker and Associates about a mile down Chagrin Boulevard near Green Road. It was all very familiar, like Ohio State's campus, but Nathan couldn't decide whether the familiarity was comforting or somehow smothering. He remembered Grundstein's offices in Chicago and his growing sense of belonging there while Mr. Atwater had taken him on a tour of the departments. He didn't have that sense here.

Becker's offices were on the second floor of a four-story pre-cast concrete building, one of three in a complex that led to many other office and commercial buildings along the boulevard's business corridor. The buildings had windows on all four sides, affording views of a well-landscaped setting. Nathan had worked there for almost a year while getting his MBA at Case Western. He entered the firm's lobby and there was the receptionist/secretary, Betsy, at her IBM Selectric. She looked up as he came in and said, "Nathan, how are you? Are you finally done with school?" as if he had been on an extended vacation which, had she been asked, she wouldn't have authorized.

"Yes, I am," Nathan said pleasantly. "Got my master's in November. And how are you, Betsy? You're looking well!" Nathan's relationship with Betsy had always been delicate. She often felt that people took advantage of her good nature, a side of her character, Nathan thought, that she kept well hidden. He was determined to try for a better footing.

"Thanks, I'm fine, except that they're driving me crazy as usual," Betsy said almost in one breath. "We've been really busy and Roger's been giving me specs to type up almost every day. We could really use some help. Are you coming back to work here again?"

"I'm not sure," Nathan said. He wanted to add that it wouldn't be to type any specs, but instead said, "I'm to meet with Mr. Becker about that very question. I'm a couple of minutes early, I think."

"Yes, you are, but let's see if he's ready for you," Betsy said, very much in charge. "Have a seat there while I check with Linda." Linda was Becker's executive secretary. Nathan sat down in the chair to which Betsy had pointed. Betsy called Linda and told her than Nathan had come in early. At least she didn't say *too* early, Nathan thought.

Becker was ready and Nathan went to his large corner office with two walls of continuous windows. Becker was sitting at his drafting table. He got up and said "C'mon in, Nathan, let's sit on the sofa," and took Nathan's extended hand in a very firm grip.

"Sam, good to see you again," Nathan said, recovering his hand. Becker was a big man and proud of it. "Sit down, sit down," he said. But instead of sitting on the sofa, Becker took a side chair and Nathan followed suit. Becker opened a box on the coffee table between them, took out a cigar, and pulled a gold cigar cutter and matching butane lighter out of his pocket. He took rather longer than necessary to snip off the cigar's end, hold the lighter to the cigar, and draw on it several times to ensure that it was lit, watching Nathan watch him. "Would you care for one?" he asked Nathan as an afterthought. "They're Cuban. Steve brought them back from Canada last month." "No, thanks," Nathan said, "but if you don't mind, I'll have a cigarette." He pulled out his pack of

Marlboros and his Zippo. "Sure, sure," Becker said. He waited a moment, took another puff on his cigar, shifted his weight in his chair, and as Nathan inhaled, asked, in a rather different tone, "So, you finished your master's at Ohio State?" The preliminaries were over.

"Yes, last November," Nathan said again.

"Congratulations," Becker said. "And you've been looking for employment?"

"Yes, around the country. I just came back last week," Nathan said.

"I did the same thing about twenty years ago," Becker said "But then I realized that all my connections were right here in Cleveland, so I decided to stay here. This business is seventy-five percent connections. Maybe eighty."

"Yes, they're enormously important, of course," Nathan said.

"Right. Eighty percent. Maybe more. Have you gotten any offers from these companies around the country?"

"A couple of interviews went well, especially one in Chicago, but nothing's definite yet," Nathan said.

"When do you plan to take your licensing exam?"

"This coming December," Nathan said.

"I read recently that Illinois requires all their licensing applicants to take the equivalency exam in addition to the professional exam," Becker said. "Most states only require the professional exam, for people like you, with a five- or six-year professional degree, like your master's. It might be easier for you to get licensed in Ohio." He squinted at Nathan through his cigar smoke.

"Yes, you're right, Sam," Nathan said. "I'm aware of that, and that could be a factor. Didn't you have some legal issues with the exam when you took it?"

"Yeah," Becker said. "When I took it, the Board–the State Board of Examiners of Architects, sounds medieval–had just decided to require an internship year after you graduated before you were even allowed to take the exam. I thought to hell with that, changing the rules in the middle of the stream, that's crap, so I hired a lawyer. They folded and I took the exam right after I graduated. But never mind that, let's cut to the chase. We feel we know you, you having worked here before, and we think you could fit in well here, and we're certainly busy. What's it going to take to bring you back?"

Nathan sat up and put his cigarette out to hide his excitement. "Frankly, I didn't expect things to move so quickly," he said. "You must have something in mind?"

"Yes, we do," Becker said. "Let's go for a little walk," he said, rising and motioning Nathan to accompany him.

Nathan followed Becker to a vacant office. "As you might remember," Becker said, "Charlie Carlton and I have the only two private offices here in our headquarters." Carlton was Becker's vice-president. Nathan remembered him as a sycophant, always agreeing with Becker about everything. He must have agreed that Becker should offer Nathan a position, no matter what he really thought. "This is the only other private office, right next to Charlie's, and it's vacant, as you see." Becker put his meaty hand on Nathan's shoulder. "It could be yours."

Nathan looked around. It was about twelve by twelve, with a view of the Deville Apartments across the boulevard. There was a simulated dark wood plastic laminated desk of the standard size, two chairs, and a credenza. On the desk were an ash tray, a daily appointments calendar, a pad of yellow lined paper, a telephone, and a plastic pen holder with pencils and ballpoint pens in it. "Sit behind the desk," Becker said. "Try it out, see how it feels."

Nathan sat down in the chair behind the desk and Becker sat down in the other chair. "How's it feel?" Becker asked, stage manager and director.

"Fine," Nathan said, "just fine. What kind of a job do you have in mind for me?"

Becker pulled the ash tray closer to him and deposited the cigar's ash, which had grown dangerously long. He puffed on the cigar and once again looked at Nathan appraisingly. All this drama, Nathan thought– Becker must have seen an old Edgar G. Robinson movie last night. "You have a degree in marketing," Becker stated as fact, not as question. "I want you to consider a position with us as our Director of Marketing. That's the job I have in mind for you."

"Director of Marketing," Nathan repeated. "Would you want me to focus on the Ohio market opportunities?"

"No," Becker said. "Nationwide. We opened our office in Miami because of our retail and multi-family projects there. That's the model. I'm licensed in thirty states and it's not difficult to get reciprocity today. The question is where, what would be the best places to expand. We've completed several housing projects for Emerald City Enterprises, and that's where I want to start expanding. When can you start?"

Careful now, Nathan told himself. This sounds great but there's still Grundstein, extra exam or not. "To be honest," he said, "working on the business side of things is exactly what I'm looking for. This certainly sounds like a great opportunity, Sam. But I'd like to discuss this with my family, as you can imagine. Could I have until Friday to get back to you?"

"Friday, yes, that'll be all right," Becker said. "By the way, the starting salary is $14,000."

"Would you be willing to go to $15,000?" Nathan heard himself asking.

"Not to start, no, but after you've proven yourself–let's say in about six months–I'd be willing to raise you to $15,000."

"That sounds fair," Nathan said, thinking actually it sounded more like poker.

"OK, then," Becker said, getting up. "Give me a call by Friday. If you decide to join us, I want you to start no later than the middle of next week. I have to get on the phone now, Nathan."

"Sure," Nathan said, rising and sacrificing his hand again. "I'll call you by Friday." He drove back to his mother's apartment in Mayfield Heights tasting the title in his mouth. Director of Marketing. No proficiency exam. $14,000 to start. My own private office. Becker is a straight shooter. A raise after only half a year. I'm Director of Marketing at Becker and Associates. Just the professional licensing exam, the NCARB, unavoidable anywhere. He imagined his business cards. The office would pay for them. Maybe there was a standard format, logo and everything, and only the individual names, titles, and private extension numbers would vary. Director of Marketing. He parked the car, rang the buzzer, got on the elevator, and floated up to the fifth floor. His mother was peeking out of her apartment's door down the hall.

"Well? How did it go?"

"Becker gave me an offer," Nathan said, grinning.

"Do you think you'll take it?"

"The position is Director of Marketing. I'd get my own office. The starting salary is $14,000."

"Did you take it?" Adele was smiling at Nathan, at the news, at the world.

"Not yet, Mom. I still want to talk to Grundstein in Chicago. I owe them that, and maybe to myself too." Adele had to agree. She fixed Nathan a brownie and a glass of milk. Chicago, in the Central Time Zone, was an hour behind Cleveland.

Mr. Atwater got to the point, when Nathan called him, almost as quickly as Becker had, once Nathan told him that he'd gotten an offer from a Cleveland company. "I want to firm up our offer to you, Nathan," he said. "I know you want to get to work as soon as you can. The cost of living is a little higher in Chicago than in Cleveland, so your starting salary with us would be $18,000, which would include full health care costs. You'd also get a $25,000 life insurance policy and two weeks' paid vacation. Your performance would be reviewed after your first six months. After your first two years with us, your vacation would increase to three weeks per year. When can you start?"

"That's a wonderful offer," Nathan said. "I'd like to have a couple of days, say until the end of the week, to make my decision, if that's OK."

"Is there anything I might say to make you more comfortable about moving to Chicago?" Atwater asked.

"Well, there is one issue that concerns me," Nathan admitted. "It's the licensing exam. I've heard that Illinois is one of the few states in the country that require all license applicants to take the proficiency exam as well as the professional exam."

"That's true," Atwater said. "At this point you have to take both. There's some movement to change that, to require the proficiency only of those applicants without professional degrees, and your master's qualifies as a professional degree. But as matters stand at the moment, you do have to take both."

"I plan to take the professional exam in December," Nathan said. "That requires two years' experience with a master's, and I just about have that now."

"We could help you with both exams," Atwater said. "Some of our young architects recently took both, and we make it a practice to help our staff to get their licenses. You could take the proficiency in June and still take the professional exam in December. And we have some contacts on the State's architects' licensing board that might be useful in your preparations."

"That's very generous of you," Nathan said. "I really appreciate that, and everything else about your offer. Very generous. I just need a couple of days–you understand, this is a crucially important decision I have to make now."

"I do understand, of course," Atwater said. "Call me Friday morning, then, if possible."

"Yes, I will, you can be sure," Nathan said. They said goodbye and hung up. Adele, who had been listening to every word Nathan had said, asked, "Is their offer better than Becker's?" "In some ways, yes, and in others, no," Nathan answered. "Grundstein is offering $4,000 more per year to start, but Becker is offering me the position of Director of Marketing. With my own private office."

"Which offer do you think provides the better opportunity in the long term?" Adele asked.

Nathan was taken aback. His mother, as usual, had asked a question he hadn't considered, and it was, as usual, the right question. "Grundstein, hands down," he said. They looked at each other. "Is there someone you could discuss this with?" Adele asked. "I don't mean Michael, I mean someone in the profession?"

"Good idea," Nathan said. "I could talk to Sid. Sid Greenstein. He used to work for Becker, and knows him quite well, in fact."

"Yes, you should do that, Nathan," Adele said, pleased. "You always respected his opinion, and he likes you."

Nathan looked at his watch. "I'll call him tonight, Mom," he said. "Or tomorrow if he's not in. Now I think I'll start calling all the other companies who said I should call them when I got back to Cleveland."

"Another brownie?" Adele asked.

"You want me to ask people if they want to hire me with my mouth full of brownie?" Nathan asked. She waved him off.

Every one of the other architectural firms Nathan had visited gave him one of two answers to his inquiry: either they weren't hiring "at this point in time," or they would keep his application materials on file for future opportunities. Nathan did not ask about the file's shape, but he had no difficulty imagining it.

He reached Sid Greenstein after dinner the next evening. "I need your advice, Sid," Nathan said. He could almost hear the older man adjust his face as well as his posture, ready to dispense wisdom and anecdotes.. He described the two offers he'd gotten, including Atwater's promise of help with preparation for the exams in Illinois, the promise of a raise after six months at Becker's, the much higher salary at Grundstein, the much higher position at Becker's, the benefits at Grundstein, the private office at Becker's. Sid listened carefully. He didn't say anything for what seemed like a very long moment when Nathan finished.

"Sid?" Nathan asked.

"Yes, I'm here, I'm thinking," Sid said.

"And what are you thinking?"

"I'm thinking that I don't want to prejudice you, Nathan," Sid said. "You know I don't like Becker personally. He's successful, I know that, but he's crude, he's hot-tempered, his ego is so big it belongs in a freak show, he likes to play the big *macher* in the community, and when it comes to putting his money where his mouth is, sometimes he does and sometimes he doesn't. On the other hand, he and I are about the same age, and maybe I'm jealous. I don't know. I guess I think you're more flexible than I am, Nathan, you might not mind Becker's style nearly as much as I do, so maybe you should ignore all that. But there's something else that's bothering me."

"What's that?" Nathan asked.

"You said that the man at Grundstein offered to have some of his younger people help to prepare you for the exam, but the way you told me that, Nathan, makes me think that's not enough for you. I thought it was really nice of him. What do you want him to do?"

"I don't think I want him to do anything, Sid," Nathan said. "I don't want to take the damn exam, that's all. It's about stuff I've already demonstrated that I know and can do. I have a master's degree, and I don't see why I have to keep proving myself over and over. OK, I have to take the professional exam everywhere, I know that, so I'll do that. But why should I take another stupid exam in Illinois when, once I pass the professional exam in Ohio, I'll probably get reciprocity anyway?"

Again there was a pause. But before Nathan could ask what Sid was thinking about now, he told him. "I know you have a master's degree, Nathan," Sid said. "You don't have to remind people. The question isn't what you have but what you don't."

"I don't have a license, you mean?"

"No, I mean you don't seem to have the confidence you need to take the proficiency exam, Nathan, and that's what I don't understand. Does this have to do with what they did to you in that study you didn't get to finish at Ohio State?"

"No, of course not, that's not related at all," Nathan said impatiently. "I told you, Sid, I just don't want to take the exam. It's not that I don't think I can pass it–on the contrary, I think I already have, and so does the State of Ohio. That's why I don't have to take it in Ohio. What happened to me in Columbus, with the survey I wanted to do, has nothing to do with this."

"No?" Obviously Sid wasn't convinced.

"Look, I can't explain what happened there, that's true," Nathan said, more quietly. "I don't understand why the study was stopped, or who, or how, and maybe it was a lot less peculiar than I thought, and maybe it wasn't, but I really don't see what it could possibly have to do with choosing between Grundstein's offer and Becker's."

"It has to do with your sense of risk, or maybe your sense of control, your understanding and acceptance of a world in which you can't have guarantees," Sid said. "Maybe the effect of whatever happened to you down in Columbus was to make you more cautious about what you see as risky, or maybe--" Sid suddenly broke off. Then, before Nathan could say anything, he continued. "Look, Nathan," Sid said, "I can't tell you what to do, I don't know what you should do. I know that if it were me, extra exam or no extra exam, I'd accept Grundstein's offer faster than a Jew would leave Russia, if only he could, but that's me, and as I told you, I don't like Sam Becker. What I think is that just maybe I have more faith in you than you have in yourself, at least right now. So I think you'll do just fine, whatever your decision is. And what I *know* is that I certainly hope so, Nathan, because you've worked hard, and you're one of the good guys, and I think you'll be a really fine architect one of these days."

Nathan was touched. "Well, thanks very much, Sid," he said. "I mean it, I really appreciate that. And I didn't mean to put you on the spot, not at all. I know it's my decision and I'm the one that will have to live with the consequences, whatever they turn out to be. Thanks so much, Sid. You're a good friend."

After he hung up, he saw Adele waiting expectantly. He smiled. "I still don't know, Mom," he said. "Sid said that he doesn't like Becker, but that's him, not me, and he said that if he had the choice, he'd choose Grundstein faster than a Jew would run out of Russia, but that's him, not me, and he's worried that somehow I lost my self-confidence because Ohio State stopped my independent study there last spring, but that's him, not me."

"Who said that's him, not me, him–he–or you?"

They laughed. "We both did!" Nathan said. They laughed again. "I'll think about it all day tomorrow," Nathan promised. "I have to. I have to let them know on Friday morning."

The next morning, after breakfast, Nathan went to the Cleveland Museum of Art, wandering around its magnificent Asian art collection, hoping that the serenity of the landscapes would somehow calm his mind and clarify his choices. Whether it was the landscapes or the beautifully classic building or the Museum's grounds, lovely even in January, it worked. Cleveland was home. Ohio had already said that his degrees and experience were tantamount to the required proficiency. It would be Becker. He went home and told Adele. She was overjoyed.

*****

In the next several days Nathan found an apartment in the Case Western neighborhood, a good used car, and a mix of new furniture from the May Company and used furniture from a sale at a students' housing unit. He got settled quickly, painting the apartment, scrubbing and waxing the floor, and arranging the furniture to his satisfaction. As agreed with Becker, he went to work on the following Wednesday.

"Good morning, Betsy," he said cheerfully as he entered. "Hi Nathan, good to have you back, Mr. Becker left a few folders for you on your desk," she said in her usual staccato style. "He wants you to become familiar with some of our current projects and clients, he's going to be at the Miami office until Monday, when he'll be back here, and wants a– let's see–" she consulted a note–"a preliminary strategic business plan for discussion when he gets back. If you have any questions, you're to talk to Linda, she has the instructions, and discuss ideas with Mr. Carlton, the coffee machine is in the copy room, you remember, and the cups are in the cupboard above the machine."

Nathan managed a "Thanks!" but Betsy had already returned to her Selectric, and he went to his office. There were, indeed, a few folders on his desk, in two piles, for a single stack would have been precarious. He sighed and got started. By the late afternoon, he had voluminous notes and many questions, none of which he could ask Linda or wanted to discuss with Carlton. Instead, he spent the next day at Case Western's Sears Library, researching various retirement housing associations and pension funds, as well as developers and architects involved with retirement housing projects around the country. By Friday afternoon he had drafted a preliminary strategic marketing plan, with which he approached Betsy.

"Betsy, could you type this up for my meeting with Sam when he gets back on Monday?"

"Can't you see I'm busy typing these specifications? You can't just drop something on my desk in mid-afternoon and expect it back the same day! OK, you don't remember our procedures, and you're in luck, this isn't due until Tuesday–but this is an exception! Don't do this to me again!"

"Sorry," Nathan said. You catch more flies with honey, he reminded himself. "I really appreciate your help, Betsy, thanks a lot. I have to review this with Sam when he gets back on Monday. So thanks for helping me out." Don't overdo it, he thought, she's nasty, not an idiot.

"OK," she grumbled. "Just don't do this again."

She gave him the typed copy about two hours later. "Thanks so much, Betsy," Nathan said, perhaps too heartily. But by that time she had been abused by someone else. "Richard Little gave me two letters to type that he insists have to go out today," she said bitterly. "I don't get a chance to catch my breath, I swear!"

"Dick hasn't changed?" Nathan asked politely.

"Not Dick," Betsy said, "he hasn't changed since he was in diapers!" She laughed, delighted with her joke. She used it often.

She's difficult but a very good typist, Nathan thought, which was probably why Sam had kept her on. There were no mistakes. He took the report and went to the copy room to make three copies: the original and a copy would go to Sam, he'd have a copy, and he'd make one for Carlton, just in case. He lifted the machine's cover and placed the sheets under the glass one at a time. At the fourth page a flashing red light indicated that the machine was out of paper. He inspected the cabinets and found new packages of paper. He took one and figured out how to open the machine's front panel and insert the new stack. Just as he was closing the panel door, Dick Little entered the copy room, pipe between his teeth, exhaling smoke.

"Hi, Dick, how's it going?" Nathan asked.

"Who said you could put paper in the copy machine?" Little demanded by way of answer.

Nathan was amazed by the question. "The machine just ran out of paper," he said. "I'm in the process of preparing a report for Sam."

"I don't care who you're preparing a report for," Little snarled. "Maintenance of the copy machine is my responsibility and I don't want you fucking up the machine, it's too important to the drafting department, got it?"

"Hey Dick!" Nathan said, growing warm. "All I did was put some paper in the machine to make copies! Don't get so excited!"

"Don't you have ears? I'm telling you not to touch the machine except to make copies. If the machine needs paper, come to my desk in the drafting room, and ask me. And don't tell me how excited to get. Got it?"

This is my third day and second confrontation and the boss isn't even here yet, Nathan reminded himself. "OK, Dick, sure, next time I'll ask you," he said. Little turned without saying another word and left. Nathan finished making his copies, still shaking his head over the absurdity of Little's assertion of importance. The world was hierarchical, not collegial, in any setting, in any environment. Deans in colleges, bosses at work, seniors lording it over juniors, every wolf an alpha when the alpha's out of sight. Newcomer, greenhorn, rube, beware. He was reminded of the television program "All In The Family": among the standing jokes was Archie Bunker's predictable annoyance whenever the Meathead, his son-in-law, was in "his" chair. Now *there* was a subject not addressed in any standardized examination he'd heard of: space and its use as expressions of the identity and status of its temporary occupant, from copy machine to Kinsman Road to the Promised Land to sarcophagus and Egyptian pyramid.

The meeting to discuss Nathan's preliminary strategic marketing plan was held in Becker's office the following Monday. Although Becker had not told Nathan that Charlie Carlton would attend, he was there, and Nathan was glad that he'd made the extra copy for him. The fact did not elicit comment. Nathan sat on the sofa, waiting while they skimmed the report, sitting in the side chairs on either end of the coffee table. Carlton was just a couple of seconds behind Becker's rapid pace.

"What do you think?" Becker asked Carlton, even before he had finished.

"Ummm," Carlton said, turning the page. "Looks pretty comprehensive, Sam. Why don't we give Nathan a chance to make a few calls and see what kinds of responses he gets?"

"Let's discuss strategy for a few minutes," Becker said. "Tell us your thoughts, Nathan."

"The report is based on the four P's of marketing," Nathan said, reminded of his explanation to Professor Prescott of the essence of the matter. "Product, Price, Promotion, and Place. Other marketing variables include an analysis of the competition, governmental regulations, and overall business conditions. The report's organization reflects all those."

"That's too abstract for me," Becker said. "Be more specific."

"OK. First about the four P's. Our product is the services we offer, program review, preliminary design, design development, construction documents, construction monitoring, and post-construction services. Our building design services include multi-family residential, shopping center, hotels, light industrial, and office buildings. And of course the particular area you assigned to me to begin with, Sam, retirement housing. Pricing is a little more difficult to analyze. As an AIA-associated company, I assume we've complied with but perhaps are moving away from the fee schedules previously mandated by the AIA?"

"We never really kept to those," Becker said. "They're a good guide for government-type work, but our clients are primarily developers and they've always demanded that their architects be price-competitive. They typically get a few architect bids to make sure we're in line. I'll handle the pricing when we have something definite to bid on. What were the other two P's?"

"Promotion and Place," Nathan said. "Promotion has to do with how we promote our services–personal selling, advertising, brochures, articles about the firm and our work in magazines and so on."

"Have you seen our brochure?" Becker asked.

"Yes, Betsy gave me a few copies last week," Nathan said. "It's really well done."

Becker grunted, his usual acknowledgment of a compliment. "You know that we insert pages of various projects so that we can target our clients' needs?"

"No, I didn't know that," Nathan said.

"Before you send out any brochures, bring them to me and I'll see what should be inserted, depending on what you're working on," Becker said. "What's the last P?"

"Place," Nathan answered. "Place includes the channel of distribution. For instance, General Motors sells its cars through a network of dealers around the United States, Canada, and other locations around the world. We have our Cleveland and Miami offices."

"I told you we're looking at retirement housing opportunities around the country," Becker said, an edge to his voice.

"Yes, I know," Nathan said. "Our nationwide goal to penetrate several retirement housing markets requires us, first of all, to have architectural licenses in the states we intend to do business in."

"I'm certified by the National Council of Architectural Registration Boards," Becker said, "and they assist us when we need reciprocity. That shouldn't be a problem for us. I already told you that we're licensed to practice in thirty states around the country."

"Yes, I remember," Nathan said.

"OK," Becker said, rising. Carlton got up as well. "Get started on this, Nathan, and let me know how it's going on by, umm, Thursday. I have to make some calls."

Nathan was surprised by the meeting's brevity and the abruptness of its close. "Don't you want to discuss competition, government regulations, the business environment?" he asked, not yet getting to his feet.

"Not right now," Becker said. "Charlie, you want to take Nathan to your office and hear about all that?"

"Ummm, I've got to make some calls myself, Sam," Carlton said.

"OK, Nathan," Becker said. "Get to work. Charlie, a couple of things before you go." Nathan got up, took his copy of his report, and started to leave. He had not yet closed the door to Becker's office when he heard Becker ask Carlton, "What the hell was he talking about with all those P's and Q's?"

"I have no idea," Carlton said, "but I don't think there were any Q's."

Nathan sighed and went back to his own office. He also had some calls to make.

The first one was to the American Association of Homes for the

Aging. He reached the director, a Mr. Jenkins, explained who he was and what Becker and Associates did and were interested in doing, and asked if the Association's membership list was available.

"Yes, to our members," Jenkins said. "Would you be interested in joining AAHA?"

"Very much so," Nathan said, "but I will need Mr. Becker's authorization."

"We have three kinds of member classifications," Jenkins said. "Provider, Business, and Associate. Since you are a vendor, you'd be in the Business category."

"What are the yearly dues?" Nathan asked.

"How many employees does your company have?"

"Not counting clerical and other support staff, we have thirty professionals in our two offices."

"Your annual dues would be three hundred dollars," Jenkins said.

"Thanks very much," Nathan said. "Please give me until this afternoon to obtain authorization, and I'll phone in the information."

"Do you have a facsimile machine in your office?" Jenkins asked. Nathan assented.

"Good, if you'll give me the number, I'll fax you the membership application. It's only two pages, so it should take only about twelve to fourteen minutes to send."

"That'll be fine," Nathan said, and gave Jenkins the number.

They hung up and Nathan went immediately to Becker's office, thinking that Becker should understand this without any P's and Q's. He heard no voices and knocked on the door. "Yes?" Becker called out. Nathan went in and explained the benefits of joining the Association.

"How much?" Becker asked.

"Three hundred a year," Nathan said. Becker picked up his half-smoked unlit cigar, pulled his gold butane lighter out of his shirt pocket, put the cigar in his mouth, and lit it carefully, almost crossing his eyes in the effort to avoid lighting anything but the cigar. Nathan waited. Becker drew several quick puffs, held the cigar with his right hand, put his lighter back in his shirt pocket with his left, and stared out the window for about a minute, puffing on the cigar. He turned to Nathan.

"OK," he said. "Tell 'em we'll join. See if they'll send you a copy of their membership list today—you said they had a fax machine. Go make more calls and let me know how things are going tomorrow."

Nathan returned to his office. The AAHA membership application arrived in the tray of his fax machine. He called Mr. Jenkins back to tell him that they would join as a business member and asked for a copy of the membership list. Jenkins agreed to send it. The nine pages took almost an hour to come through. Nathan began to call the members, one after another, filtering the vendors out from the retirement home operators, owners, and developers. Those were the members who might provide Becker with business opportunities. At the end of the day he gave Betsy eight legal pad pages of client contacts and asked her to transfer the data to four by six cards, one for each client, listing company name, contact person, address, phone number and a summary of the client's current and anticipated needs for architectural services. She agreed reluctantly, but since she was caught up with her other work, could think of no reason why Nathan couldn't have the cards "some time tomorrow."

Nathan went back to his office. All in all, he thought, a good day.

*****

The winter ended and spring and summer passed more quickly than Nathan could believe. A surprising candidate, the Governor of Georgia, a nuclear engineer and peanut farmer, emerged from the crowd of Democrats eager to challenge President Ford in the November election. Nathan paid little attention. His job and its complexities, including his relationships with Becker and his colleagues, occupied his mind fully. But he never had to remind himself of the NCARB examination he was to take in December. In addition to an all-day eight-hour examination requiring the applicant to prepare, by hand, a graphic building design solution, to include a site plan, floor plans, sections, and elevations, there would be a two-day, sixteen-hour examination in four distinct areas: environmental analysis, building programming, design and technology, and construction. The questions would be long and detailed, but the four or five possible answers for each, from which he was to choose the single most appropriate, would be exceedingly brief, allowing no explanations or qualifications. Machine-scored tests were relatively easy to administer, to score, to keep anonymous through a confidential coding scheme, to distribute and retrieve, and best of all, as far as the examiners were concerned, to hide behind. Their impersonality helped to diffuse confrontations between aggrieved test takers and the official purveyors of bad news. The news usually came in a formal letter that few disappointed recipients thought worth challenging. Not that the tests were beyond criticism: on the contrary, they were often described, both in the professional literature and on private grapevines, as irrelevant, ambiguous, outdated, culturally biased, deliberately tricky and confusing, and–if the aggrieved and disappointed test taker, sputtering with rage, could think of nothing more cutting–idiotic. Nathan had spent far too many years at all levels of American public education not to be thoroughly familiar with the vagaries of machine-scored tests. The kindest thing he had ever heard them called was arbitrary and capricious. It was his familiarity with machine-scored tests, he told himself, that made him take the NCARB examination so seriously.

Ohio's State Board of Examiners of Architects usually provided preliminary information about the type of building that would be the subject of the "design" examination, and Nathan was not anxious about it. Design was one of his strengths, he felt. Multiple choice or multiple guess was another matter. He ordered the Architectural License Seminars study materials and practice exams in September, giving himself three months to get ready.

The four volumes, one for each area to be covered by the examination, arrived on a Friday, and Nathan spent the entire weekend acquainting himself with the materials. On Monday morning, well before dawn, Nathan awoke with a start, realizing what it was that he had not been aware that he had been trying to remember. About a year and a half earlier, shortly after his independent study project had been abruptly and mysteriously aborted by the School of Architecture, he had obtained a copy of a report submitted to the American Institute of Architects by a well-known architectural firm, Dober, Paddock, Upton and Associates, Inc. The report–*A Preliminary Report to the American Institute of Architects Task Force on Design/Build*–was directly related to his study. He had heard of it from Prescott or Rosenberg or perhaps both. He had called the Washington headquarters of the AIA, reached a secretary who must just have had a fight with her boyfriend, and was at his most charming and persuasive, suggesting that his colleagues on the faculty, Professor Prescott in particular, the president of the Ohio Society of Architects, had assured him that the AIA would want him to receive the copy as quickly as possible, in the light of his own very closely related research. Her hesitation implied that his request was far from routine. He asked her name so that, when he was next in Washington, he could come by and thank her personally, perhaps over lunch or a cocktail. Her name, it turned out, was Daphne, and since he was on the faculty at Ohio State, she was sure that it would be all right, and she'd mail him the copy that afternoon and her extension number was–he hadn't written it down, he remembered that.

He found the report in his box of materials from his master's program at Ohio State. He had noted the date he'd received it: May 6,

1975. The report itself had been presented to the AIA Task Force more than a year earlier, on March 11, 1974, almost exactly a year before he and his committee had prepared that application for an internal grant that Dean Wilson had first encouraged him to draft and then had told him had not even been submitted. What, in the Dober report, had seemed so relevant to him when he had read it in 1975? He glanced at the first section, "The General Problem," and saw what he had underlined.

Next to an underlined and yellow highlighted, passage, he had written: "find out why the profession of architecture is losing market share in a growing construction market." It's the profession's reputation for not understanding the business aspects of the building industry from building programming through construction, he thought.

He continued to read. *"There is considerable evidence to suggest that clients who once turned to architects are now turning to others, and claim in general terms that architects do not understand the clients' problems and furthermore are unequipped to deal with them."* That's what's happening today, he thought.   Instead of retaining architects, clients turned to package dealers who provided comprehensive real estate construction services -- management of the architect from programming through design, and then management of the building construction process -- more accountability and better management control of the process. I understand why the AIA secretary had been more than a bit reluctant to release the study. And why the AIA never made the report public. A resistance to change and their desire to keep the profession's lack of business acumen an internal matter.

"Neither the architectural schools," he read, *"nor the registration examination, nor licensing requirements typically require the architect to have an understanding of systems analysis, project management, social and behavioral theory, financial management and analysis, or business organization theory."* These are all part of the design and construction process -- I studied each and every one of those topics to earn my BSBA and MBA. But, according to Dober, none of them is expected to appear within the NCARB exam. How am I supposed to change my thinking? I earned my architectural and business degrees concurrently -- I see things differently from a broader perspective.   After mankind learned to cook with fire, do they expect me to eat raw meat? Maybe not, but the exam would likely be undercooked. Nathan sighed.

The report emphasized that if architects were to continue to play a leadership role in the increasingly integrated and complex construction industry, their education must provide a thorough understanding of the management skills, needs, expectations, and processes included and expected within the building development and construction industry. I've already done that, thought Nathan.

The Dober report, he realized, had changed nothing. The materials he had just begun to study contained nothing of this perspective. That would be crucially important to remember when he took the NCARB examination. But it was greatly comforting to recall that he was not alone in his conviction that the profession had to change, to evolve, to synthesize traditional emphases with new disciplines, new techniques, new ways of understanding a changing world.

What was not at all comforting, about an hour later, was to find that his car had been stolen from the parking lot in front of his building. After reporting the theft to the police, Nathan took a cab to the office. Becker was already there.

"Good morning, Sam," Nathan said. "Do you have a minute?"

"C'mon in," Becker said. "How are the marketing calls going?"

Nathan took a side chair facing Becker's desk. "Good," he said. "I think Applebrook Homes in Cincinnati wants to meet with me next Monday. I have to call their V. P. of Development today to confirm that."

"Great," Becker said. "I want Charlie to come with us to attend the first few marketing calls."

Nathan noted the "us." "Of course," he said. "I appreciate that. But what I want to talk to you about is taking a couple of weeks off to study for the NCARB exam. It's scheduled for the second week of December."

"You get only two weeks' paid vacation, remember," Becker said.

"Yes, I know," Nathan said.

"When would you start your vacation and when would you be back?"

"I need to take off from November 23 until December 14."

"That's three full weeks," Becker said. "So one week without pay."

"Yes," Nathan said. "Two weeks to study and one week to take the exam."

Becker hesitated. Contrary to Nathan's expectation, he did not reach for a cigar. Not that tough a decision, apparently. "OK," Becker said. "One week without pay. Give Linda a note so she can mark it on my schedule. Everything else going OK?"

"Actually, no, not today," Nathan said. "My car was stolen this morning. I went out to the parking lot at six thirty and it was gone. I already reported it to the police."

Becker was genuinely sympathetic. Street crime in Cleveland, its likely perpetrators, and its probable causes were all subjects on which he had many opinions, all picturesque, all expressed with great conviction. Nathan was quickly sorry that he'd mentioned it. But Becker had not forgotten what to him was the main message. "Well, the cops might recover the car, or more likely it'll be replaced by your insurance company," he assured Nathan. "Get one of those steering wheel locks for your next car, you need it in that neighborhood. Have to work on a design now, Nathan. Try to schedule the meeting with Applebrook for about two in the afternoon–we usually use a charter service to fly to Cincinnati. Let me know later today what you've set up. Don't forget, I want Charlie to come with us."

"Right, I'll let you know as soon as I've got it confirmed," Nathan said. But his first calls were to his insurance company and his car dealer to arrange the lease of a car.

He worked out a mutually convenient time for his meeting with John Weston at Applebrook Homes in Cincinnati--next Monday at two–and told him that both the president, Mr. Becker, and the vice-president, Mr. Carlton, would attend as well. His tone was intended to convey the importance of the potential relationship Becker and Associates hoped to enjoy with Applebrook Homes. Weston, in turn, reminded him that Applebrook was looking at properties in Charleston, West Virginia, as well as in Columbus. Nathan assured Weston that Becker and Associates was fully licensed in West Virginia as well as in Ohio. Becker was in conference, so he told Linda about the scheduled meeting and gave her the note about his vacation plans–already approved, he wrote, by Sam in that morning's conversation. That's going to be some vacation, he thought. But if he passed, his next vacation would be the real thing. Maybe Paris. Or Rome and Athens. Or Jerusalem. Nothing in Ohio, certainly.

*****

Nathan arrived early to work again on the following Monday, driving his leased car that the insurance company had agreed to pay for. Linda was already there, typing some materials that Becker wanted included in the proposal to Applebrook Homes. "Good morning!" Nathan said enthusiastically. He was looking forward to the day. "Everything all set?"

"Yes," Linda said. "Your flight's scheduled to depart at ten thirty at Burke Lakefront Airport. I need about another fifteen minutes on the proposal. Sam asked that you make the copies for three brochures, you know, punch the holes and assemble everything along with the other materials, so let me get this finished as quickly as I can."

"So we need to leave here by nine thirty to make our flight," Nathan said, "and it will take me twenty minutes to copy everything and assemble three brochures–we're cutting it a little close!"

"Yes, and Sam wants to take one more look at this when he comes in–he should be here by nine. It's always this way with Sam–everybody runs around just before we leave for meetings. I'll bring this to your office after he's approved it."

"OK, thanks," Nathan said. "Good luck to all of us!" But it was ten minutes after nine when Linda brought him the inserts for the brochures.

"We're cutting it close!" Nathan said again, taking the inserts. "I know," Linda said. "Sam was on the phone and just gave me the OK." Nathan went directly to the copy room to assemble the three brochures. He found the matching blank pages used for copying inserts, but, remembering the scene with Dick Little, ran to Little's cubicle. Little was reviewing drawings. "Hi, Dick, I'm in a rush to prepare some brochures for a meeting in Cincinnati this afternoon, and I have to--"

"Can't you see I'm in the middle of something here?" Little snarled.

"Sorry to interrupt, but Sam, Charlie, and I have a plane to catch!"

Little gave him a long look and apparently decided that Nathan just might be telling the truth. "I'll be there in a couple of minutes," he growled. Nathan went back to the copy room to wait for him. When Little arrived, almost ten minutes later, to ask what he needed, Nathan said, "I'm really behind schedule–please put these blank pages in the copy machine so that I can complete the brochure."

Without a word, Little snatched the pages from Nathan's hand and yanked the copy machine's door open to insert the pages. Just then Becker burst in. "What the fuck are you doing in *here*?" he yelled at Nathan. "We have a flight to catch at ten thirty!" Little stood aside. "I'm putting the brochures together," Nathan started to explain when Becker threw his half-smoked, mostly chewed unlit cigar directly at him. Nathan raised his arm and blocked the wet cigar, but immediately saw the stain on his suit jacket's sleeve next to the three buttons. "Hurry up, goddamnit!" Becker yelled and stormed out. Little, now just outside the door, was smirking. Nathan rushed to punch the holes in the new pages for brochures and said angrily, "I *told* you I was in a hurry!" "We all have problems," Little answered and walked off.

Nathan finished binding the brochures with the new inserts and hurried to Becker's office, but heard his name called from the lobby. Becker and Carlton, wearing their overcoats and carrying their briefcases, were motioning him to hurry up. "Be right there!" he yelled and ran to get his top coat and briefcase. "They just took the elevator to the garage," Betsy called as he rushed by her desk. "Sam said he'd pick you up at the garage entrance door!" The elevator didn't respond immediately to Nathan's push of the button, and he ran down the three flights to the garage, opening the door just as Becker pulled up in his cream-colored Lincoln Continental. Carlton, rolling down the power window, told Nathan to get in the back and Nathan jumped in, the car still moving forward under Becker's impatient foot. The Lincoln's tires squealed as Becker turned hard around the corner toward the underground exit, flinging Nathan against the side door, and then, when Becker slammed on the brake just in time for the overhead door to clear the car's roof, Nathan was thrown against the back of the front seat. This was his punishment, he knew, for the delay, and he kept his mouth shut tightly as Becker maneuvered the Lincoln into the left lane to turn west onto Chagrin Boulevard just as the traffic light turned yellow. By the time Becker, tailgating the car ahead of him, went through the intersection, the light had turned red. Becker sped into the passing lane. He had not gotten far before a police cruiser, lights flashing and siren wailing, pulled him over.

"Shit!" Becker said. "We'll miss our plane!"

"It's a charter flight," Carlton said quietly, to Nathan's delight. "They'll wait if we're a few minutes late." Becker was not used to dissent, implicit or otherwise, from his right-hand man, but he was busy fumbling in his wallet as the policeman, leaving his lights flashing on the roof of his cruiser, approached on the street side of the car.

"Here it is," Becker said, pulling out his membership card in the Fraternal Order of Police "Will that help?" Carlton asked. "We'll see," Becker said. "I gave a lot of money to the Mayor's campaign the last time around, and he introduced me to some of the Beachwood cops." There was a tap on the window. Becker pressed the power window button. The officer was already holding his ticket pad in his hand.

"Sir, you just went through that red light back there and now you appeared to be speeding, so I'm going to have ask you for your driver's license," the policeman said. Becker looked at the man's name on the brass bar pinned next to his badge. "Sorry, Officer Holden," Becker said, in as pleasant a way as Nathan had ever heard from him. "I didn't realize I was speeding, and I thought the light was yellow when we made that left turn." He offered him his driver's license and, Nathan saw, the membership card. The policeman inspected both. Nathan couldn't see whether there was a bill between the license and the membership card. "You're Mr. Becker," the policeman said. "Yes, I am," Becker said.

"Haven't we met?" "Yes, at City Hall, last year," the policeman said. "Right, right!" Becker exclaimed, too heartily, Nathan thought; Becker didn't remember the cop from Adam. "How're things going, Officer Holden?" "Real good, Mr. Becker," the policeman said. "I made sergeant last year, and my oldest boy is graduating from high school end of this term." "Excellent!" Becker said, still in hearty mode. "Very glad to hear it!" The policeman returned the license and the membership card. "So do us both a favor, Mr. Becker, and ease up on the gas pedal, OK?" "Thanks, I will," Becker said. "Really, I didn't know I was speeding." "Well, I didn't actually clock you on the radar, and maybe my view of the traffic light was, umm, obstructed," the policeman said. "Have a good day!" He walked back to his cruiser. "Thanks, I'll be careful!" Becker called, put his license and membership card back in his wallet, rolled up the window, and grinned at Carlton. He started the engine and drove down Chagrin Boulevard.

"You got out of another one, Sam," Carlton said.

"Doesn't hurt to know the right people," Becker said. "I keep telling you, life, business, everything is connections. Who you know and who knows you. Ninety per cent of the story."

Carlton turned toward the back seat. "How you doing back there, Nathan?"

Nathan was trying to rub the wet cigar stain off his suit jacket's sleeve. "Fine, Charlie," he said.

"It always seems to get crazy when we have a plane to catch," Carlton said. Was he apologizing for Becker and his driving? "You'll get used to it."

"Sure hope so," Nathan said, smiling to cover what he was feeling.

Becker turned right onto Warrensville Center Road and left onto South Woodland. Nathan saw the needle move across fifty on the speedometer as they passed a sign showing the speed limit as thirty-five. Carlton glanced at his watch and said, "Sam, we should be there by about ten twenty, and our flight isn't scheduled for departure until ten thirty, right?"

"Right," Becker said, ignoring the implication once again. "North Coast Aviation."

"Burke Lakefront Airport?" Nathan asked. He wasn't going to act the guilty schoolboy, silent and ashamed in the corner. Becker didn't answer.

"Yes," Carlton said.

"Are we going on a Lear Jet?" Nathan asked, pressing his point.

"No," Carlton said, "maybe next time, if we get this job. The last time we flew to Cincy with North Coast we were on a twin engine Cessna 310. It's a six-seat plane, including the two for the pilots."

"The last time I flew on a small plane," Nathan said, "it was with Sid Greenstein."

"The same Sid Greenstein who used to work for us?" Carlton asked.

"Yes," Nathan said. "It was a single engine Cessna. He had just gotten his license and asked me to tag along when he did touch and goes."

"Did you enjoy the flight?" Carlton asked, maintaining the conversation against Becker's studied silence.

"It was OK," Nathan said. "I recall dropping my stomach somewhere over the Richmond Heights Airport."

Carlton laughed. "So what's Sid doing now?" he asked.

"The last I heard," Nathan said, "he was working as a pilot for North Coast Aviation."

Becker swerved to the right. "*Really*?" Carlton asked, a bit loudly.

Nathan laughed. "Just kidding," he said. "Sid's working as a field architect for Franklin and Franklin Architects."

"Very funny," Carlton said. "I was just about to suggest that we drive to Cincinnati."

Nathan laughed again. "I'm sure Sid would get us there safely."

"Maybe so," Carlton said, turning back to the front, picking up one of the brochures Nathan had assembled.

The flight to Cincinnati was uneventful except that Becker suddenly started to speak to Nathan again, as if nothing had happened. They had buckled themselves in, the plane had taken off, and Becker turned to Nathan and said, "Tell me about Applebrook Homes."

All right, Nathan thought, don't apologize. Bosses don't do that. They don't have to. "They've been in business for about ten years now," he said. "They're affiliated with the Episcopal Church, and they manage about twenty communities in four states–Ohio, Kentucky, West Virginia, and Pennsylvania. Those range from twelve-unit zero lot-line homes to mid-sized apartment buildings for assisted living. John Weston, whom we're meeting with this afternoon, told me that they're presently serving more than twenty-five hundred elderly and disabled residents."

"And they're planning new communities?" Becker interrupted.

"Yes, their five-year business plan calls for adding about two hundred residents per year," Nathan said, glad for the opportunity to show he had done his homework. "Weston said that their two upcoming projects were in Columbus and Charleston, West Virginia. He didn't specify all the other locations they have in mind. I think he wants to keep most of the information confidential until our meeting, when he hoped we'd develop a working relationship."

"Good job," Becker said. Finally, Nathan thought

The cab ride to downtown Cincinnati took only about twenty minutes, leaving them time for a fast-food lunch before their two o'clock meeting with Weston. They arrived for their meeting a few minutes early, introduced themselves to the receptionist, and were shown to the conference room. Nathan found himself holding the door for Carlton and Becker. Becker immediately went to the back of the room and sat down at the head of the conference table, which had seating for eight. Nathan followed Carlton, who sat down at Becker's immediate right and motioned Nathan to sit next to him on the same side. Weston would have to sit across from them, at Becker's left. It all seemed very calculated.

When Weston came in a moment later, Nathan rose and introduced himself, Becker, and Carlton. Weston shook hands with all three and thanked Becker and Carlton for coming down with Nathan. "I understand," Weston said, "that Nathan has told you about our plans to construct housing for two hundred new units per year for elderly and disabled residents. We're seeing a growing demand for elderly and assisted living."

"Yes," Becker said, "Nathan told me. Some of our other clients are also very optimistic about opportunities for growth." He went on at some length about his company's experience in the general area of housing for a special segment of the population. Nathan tried twice to add something to Becker's description of their services, especially how they could be adapted to Applebrook's specific design and housing program needs, but each time Becker cut him off. Carlton and Nathan took notes. Weston discussed Applebrook's interests in the Columbus and Charleston locations, asked for proposals for both projects, and ended the meeting very pleasantly, indicating that he looked forward toward the development of a mutually rewarding relationship.

The conversation in the cab back to the airport consisted mostly of Becker's lecture to Carlton concerning the strategies to be employed in the two proposals they were to write. Eventually Becker turned to Nathan and said, "Good job in arranging this meeting."

"Thanks," Nathan said. "I appreciate your coming today so that, in the future, I might be able to handle some initial meetings on my own."

Becker frowned. "That might take some time. I hope you realize that if I hadn't come today, we probably wouldn't have been asked to prepare these two proposals he asked us for."

Nathan was too amazed to nod assent. He had worked out most of what had been discussed at the meeting with Weston before they had left Cleveland.

*****

A few days later, Nathan parked his newly acquired 1976 Oldsmobile Cutlass in front of the main office of the International Brotherhood of Teamsters off Chester Road next to Cleveland State University. The Cutlass had been partly paid for by the insurance on his Chevrolet Monte Carlo, which the police had found stripped of most of its usable parts. Still sitting in his car, Nathan took one of his business cards from his wallet–Nathan Goldstein, MBA, Director of Marketing, Becker & Associates–and a small blue box from his suit jacket's inside pocket. He opened the box, took out a gold pin engraved

**Safe Driving – 16 Years
Continental Baking Company**

and unscrewed the safety clip on the back. He pierced his business card, inserted the award pin post, and screwed the safety clip on. Then he put the card into his shirt pocket and entered the building. He found himself in front of a speaker and a button, which he pushed to announce his presence. The receptionist, using the intercom, asked him to identify himself.

"I'm Nathan Goldstein, with Samuel Becker and Associates," he said.

"Do you have an appointment?"

"No," Nathan said, "I just want to leave my business card for Mr. Presser."

The receptionist could see Nathan through the inner glass door. She pressed the buzzer to let him in. He walked up to her, smiling, said "Thanks," and handed her the business card. She could see the gold award pin fastened to it.

"Oh, one of our award pins," she said. "Do you want to leave this card here for Mr. Presser?"

"Do you think if you took it in to him, he might take a couple of minutes to meet me?" Nathan asked, giving her his warmest smile.

"I don't know," she said, smiling back. "This is a little out of the ordinary. He's a very busy man. Give me a moment and I'll see what I can do."

Nathan sat down in the waiting area and picked up a magazine featuring an article about the International Brotherhood of Teamsters. He turned to it and found that it was about pending legislation affecting the Teamsters, in Ohio and across the nation. He hadn't gotten very far when the receptionist returned to tell him that Mr. Presser would see him now. He got up, making sure that his shirt was tucked in and his tie was straight, and followed her to a corner office. The receptionist motioned to him to stop in the corridor, knocked lightly on the door, and opened it halfway.

"Mr. Goldstein is here," she said into the office. "Should he come in?"

"One second," said a husky male voice. "Al, tell Tony not to worry." He was on the phone. "Al, everything will be OK. Don't worry about it. It's already taken care of. Goodbye, Al, say hello to the missus." The sound of a hangup came into the corridor. "Angela, tell Goldstein to come in!" The receptionist motioned to Nathan and he went in.

Presser, sitting behind a very large mahogany finished desk, was wearing a white spread collar shirt with the top button undone. His black and grey patterned tie was pulled down, allowing his thick neck to bulge over the collar. His hair, mostly black, was parted on the left, providing enough hair for a comb-over. He extended his hand to Nathan over the desk.

"Always good to see a family member of the Brotherhood, but you appear too young to have been driving safely for sixteen years. Whose pin is this?"

Nathan, shaking Presser's hand, said, "That's my father's pin."

"Who's your father?"

"Martin Goldstein."

"Goldstein, Goldstein," Presser said, looking at the card under the lamp on his desk. "Hmm, Continental Baking Company. Was your father the man who worked for Wonder Bread and had the Kinsman route?"

"Yes," Nathan said, surprised. "How did you know that?"

"It's my job to know our members," Presser said. "I was sorry to hear that your dad passed away a few years ago. It was on the west side, after they moved him from the Kinsman route."

"I'm very surprised that you know so much about him," Nathan said.

"Let's just say that we had some mutual friends," Presser said. "Your dad was a hard-working and honest man. I recall that Wonder Bread wanted to move him up to supervisor, but he wanted to keep the Kinsman route." Presser smiled. ""I heard that it was a very profitable route–used to be a lot of Jewish-owned stores in that area. I won't go into details, but there were others who wanted to move your dad up. He always said that he was happy with what he had and that his family came first. Yes, he was a good man."

"Thank you, thank you very much, Mr. Presser," Nathan said, moved.

"What can I do for you today?" Presser asked.

"I'm an architect now," Nathan began, "well, an intern architect. I plan to take my exam in December--"

"Excellent," Presser interrupted. "Always glad to hear when our members' families do well. Where'd you go to college?"

"Ohio State, for my master's in architecture, and Case Western for my MBA," Nathan said.

"The apple doesn't fall far from the tree," Presser said, smiling. "Your dad was a very smart man. I see you work for Becker," he continued, looking at the card. "He's a good guy, but he's got a big ego, you may know that already." He looked at Nathan who thought it best to remain expressionless. "I suggest you put your time in there and move on after you get established, you know, make your own connections. How can I help you today?" he asked again.

"Mr. Becker hired me to expand his retirement housing business," Nathan said, "and I thought that maybe the Teamsters' pension fund might be investing in something like that."

Presser looked at him shrewdly. "I was just talking about some better investments with one of our directors last week," he said. "I just might have much more influence in the Central States Pension Fund very soon. When did you say you plan to take your exam?"

"In December," Nathan said.

"Give me a call in early January," Presser said. "I may have some opportunities for you by then."

Nathan rose to shake Presser's hand, but Presser wasn't finished and he sat back down. "I've heard some things about the architects' intern program," Presser said. "Heard it was a sham to provide cheap labor for the big architectural firms. You know anything about that? Did you ever think about getting some union representation?"

"I'm trying to stay low key now," Nathan said, "but you're right about the intern program. There are no consistent training programs in place, and the interns get paid very little."

"You know there are times when you have to go with the flow, and times when you have to fight."

Nathan was startled. "Yes, I know–and I remember a dream I had not long ago in which someone told me that too, in those very words."

"Dreams are good," Presser said. "Follow your dreams. They will keep you young. You'll do well some day. Call me in January. Oh, one more thing–do you have an extra business card?"

"Sure," Nathan said, handing him one. Presser took it and gave the other one back to Nathan. "Thought you'd want to keep that," he said, pointing to the award pin. "Yes, thanks, that's very valuable to me," Nathan said, shook Presser's hand, and left, smiling to himself. This was one visit he wouldn't report to Becker. Not just yet. Connections were very important, of course, but so was timing.

*****

The next several weeks included Jimmy Carter's defeat of Gerald Ford, attributed by the pundits more to Ford's pardon of his predecessor and his own lackluster campaign than to the Georgian's appeal to the voters. For the time being, at any rate, the Watergate scandal and its revelations of widespread corruption at the White House and at Justice had been put behind the national curtain on the past. Bitterness about the defeat in Vietnam continued to fester, not only among those convinced that a noble cause had been betrayed by draft dodgers and radicals but also among those persuaded that the entire effort, beginning with the Kennedys, had sacrificed lives, morality, and truth to notions of national interest dating back to the Neanderthals. Nathan had remembered to vote but had not otherwise exercised the privileges of citizenship. His examinations were scheduled to be given at Taylor Hall on the Kent State University campus on December 7 (environmental analysis and programming), 8 (design, technology, and construction), and 9 (a written/graphic examination on a branch bank, additional program requirements to be provided at the examination). The first two would be multiple choice. He had begun to read the study materials for the third time, using a blue highlighter over his previous yellow marks as if to imprint the essentials into the very core of his memory. He went to the Sears Library at Case Western Reserve University to read architectural and building magazines, looking for articles on branch bank design and construction. He visited newer branch banks in the area, inspecting their physical features, taking notes, and always careful to introduce himself, presenting identification and assuring the manager that he was there to prepare himself for his architectural licensing examination, not to case the joint for Willie Sutton. By Friday, December 4, he felt so prepared that he was about to burst. Instead, he went out to a restaurant, a movie, and a neighborhood bar. He was ready.

Taylor Hall housed Kent State University's College of Architecture and Environmental Design. Nathan arrived in plenty of time to find Jim Wheeler, Executive Secretary of the State Board of Examiners of Architects of Ohio, already in the examination room. Wheeler was there as the senior proctor. Nathan had been introduced to Wheeler by Prescott at the Kon Tiki, and Wheeler had been there on other occasions when he'd had his weekly lunch with Prescott. But they had only exchanged pleasantries, and Nathan had no particular impression of the man.

"Good morning, Mr. Wheeler!" Nathan said. "Guess I'm in the right place!"

"Hello, Nathan," Wheeler said. "Yes, I expected you here this morning, you're on the list."

"Isn't the exam also being offered in Columbus today?" Nathan asked.

"Yes, why do you ask?"

"Just curious why they sent you all the way up here today," Nathan explained. The question had seemed to bother Wheeler.

"Yes, well, umm, one of the other proctors called on Friday and said he couldn't come, illness in the family, so I came to Kent in his place. There are lots of open seats, as you see--" Wheeler gestured around the large room–"so find a seat to your liking."

"Thanks, good to see you again," Nathan said. Something had rung false about Wheeler's explanation, but it didn't matter. He looked around. Only a few people had arrived before him. Drafting tables and wooden stools were neatly arranged in straight columns and rows across the room. He selected a place and took his Number 2 pencils, erasers, sharpener, dictionary, and a can of Coca-Cola out of his briefcase and arranged them to his satisfaction. More people entered the room. By five minutes to eight, the room was almost full of young men and a few women whispering to each other, and Wheeler went to the front of the room. He tapped a pointer on the blackboard for attention and the low hum stopped immediately.

"We should be getting started in about five minutes," Wheeler announced. "I am now going to distribute the test booklets and answer sheets. Do not, repeat, *not* break the seal on the booklet until I tell you to." He walked up the center aisle, counting out the booklets and answer sheets in accordance with the number of people in the row, and giving them to the people on his immediate left and right. By the time he was finished it was eight o'clock and he was back in the front of the room.

"Use your Number 2 pencils to break the seals on your test booklets *now*," he said, reading from a card. "Note that your booklet has an assigned number on its cover. Enter that number, along with your name and address, on your answer sheet in the indicated spaces. As noted on the cover of the booklet, this morning's multiple-choice NCARB exam is on environmental analysis. Answer all questions to the best of your ability, that is, if you're not sure about the correct answer, make your best guess. Make absolutely certain that your answer's number corresponds to the number of the test question. We will be checking the test booklet number against the answer sheet number, so remember that you *must* turn your test booklet in at the end of the examination with your answer sheet tucked in the booklet.

"You are allowed to eat snacks at your table. The rest rooms are just outside the entrance doors. If you have any questions during the examination, raise your hand and either I or one of the other proctors will assist you as best we can within the testing guidelines. The examination will end precisely at noon. The two clocks on either side of the room are exactly correct, and we will write the time remaining in thirty-minute intervals on the chalk board in the front of the room. You may begin now. Good luck," he added as an afterthought.

Nathan opened his test booklet, wrote his name, address, and number on the answer sheet, and inspected the test. As he had known, the test consisted of a series of paragraphs describing a situation or problem or "case," each followed by one or more questions, which in turn were each followed by four or five answers, (A) through (D) or (E), of which he was to choose the correct one. Some of the questions were very clear, with obvious answers. Many were not. He set to work. All around him he heard sighs of exasperation, people shifting on their stools, and, once, a muttered curse. He kept his head down, pleased, however, that he was not alone in his mounting irritation.

If the morning's portion of the NCARB exam had been an exercise in confusion, frustration with poorly worded questions, ambiguous and inadequate answers, testing the limits of self-control rather than knowledge and judgment of the practice and techniques of architecture, the afternoon's examination, on building programming, was worse. Nathan read one question and its possible answers three times.

A real estate manager who has been designated as the Owner's Representative according to the AIA B141 Owner-Architect agreement provides the architect with a building program for a new four-story corporate headquarters to be located in Columbus, Ohio. The real estate manager informs the architect that the building must be completed and ready for occupancy within 18 months. What would be the next step for the architect?

(A) Immediately begin the Schematic Design Phase.
(B) Verify the minimum square footage allowances for each office space.
(C) Present alternative finish materials to the client.
(D) Meet with his consulting engineering team, including civil, mechanical, electrical, and structural.

The AIA B141 Owner-Architect agreement was a topic included in the graduate level course he had taught for Professor Prescott. The architect's responsibilities included review of the owner's program, determination of the requirements, and subsequent agreement with the owner about them.

Highly relevant to such agreements, Nathan had taught his students, were Maslow's hierarchy of needs, McGregor's motivation models, and Hertzberg's theories of organizational behavior. Nothing in the question indicated the strong probability that the program provided by the owner's representative to the architect would be incomplete, and that what the architect most likely would have to do would be to solicit additional information. The architect should consider the building program preliminary. Then the architect would have to find out, as best he could from the owner's representative, how the program was developed. Ideally, the architect would then survey all relevant people in the owner's organization or firm to increase the program's scope and to verify that the information thus elicited was complete. Such information had to include predicted needs for specified periods of time to ensure that the completed building would meet the owner's long- as well as short-term organizational requirements. The lack of such forecasting, Nathan thought, was often the primary reason why so many owners of new company headquarters found that their buildings did not meet their expectations.

He looked at the clocks Wheeler had called to their attention and realized that he was spending far too much time on this one question. What choices could he eliminate?   (B) and (C) were clearly inappropriate. His choice, in the real world, would be (D), call in the consulting engineers, but that was in the B141 Design Development Phase, not in the Schematic Design Phase. That included a review but not verification of the owner's program. None of the phases in the B141, Nathan thought, even discussed verification of the owner's program; the

B141 considered only review and evaluation of the information on which to base the design. That left (A), immediately begin the schematic design phase. That must be what they're looking for, Nathan thought, and filled in the circle below (A) with his Number 2 pencil.

The next morning's examination, on Design and Technology, was no better. Among the very first questions, knotting Nathan's stomach, was this.

During the Contract Document Phase for a new high school, the architect learns from an article in the local newspaper that a new highway extension was recently approved and funded by the state legislature. The highway extension is to run alongside the community planning the new high school, and includes a new entrance and exit ramp near the community's central business district. The newspaper article predicts significant business and residential growth for the community.

The architect is bound by the AIA B141 Owner-Architect Agreement. Taking the newspaper's predicted residential growth into consideration, the architect projects the proportionate increase in student population, and, after review of the site and plans for the building, concludes that the site is not large enough for the projected increase. The next day the architect phones the school board's designated representative, authorized under the AIA B141 Owner-Architect Agreement to act on the board's behalf. The representative instructs the architect to disregard the newspaper article and proceed with the Construction Documents to ensure the building's start and completion in accordance with the previously agreed-upon schedule. What should the architect do?

(A) Follow the board's designated representative's instructions to complete the Construction Documents in a timely manner.
(B) Stop the project and call the Mayor.
(C) Complete several schematic drawings to further illustrate that the high school, as planned, will not accommodate the future student population, and try again to persuade the representative to stop the

Construction Documents and consider alternative sites.

(D) Complete several schematic drawings to further illustrate that the high school, as planned, will not accommodate the future student population, and call the president of the school board to schedule a meeting.

Nathan was reminded of television programs like "Let's Make a Deal" and "The Price is Right." But there was no laugh track here, and this wasn't entertaining. His first thought was that any architect with integrity would have to bring the projected impact of the highway extension to the designated representative's attention immediately. Then he thought about the architect's legal responsibilities to follow the AIA B141 Owner-Architect Agreement and respect the instructions to complete the Construction Documents in a timely manner. School boards are elected on their own almost everywhere, eliminating the idea of calling the Mayor. But choices (C) and (D) were not inappropriate; the architect might be wise to illustrate the impact of the projected population growth schematically. But if the designated representative continued to tell the architect to finish the Construction Documents, insofar as (C) and (D) could be considered violations of B141, then (A) would be the only choice left. Besides, the B141 considered only review and evaluation of the program information provided by the Owner, in this instance, the school board, not verification. Could the school board have made its plans without knowing what the legislature was about to do with the highway extension? Nathan was reminded of the series of questions allowing only affirmative answers: Is the Pope Catholic? Is a frog's ass watertight? Obviously the B141 exhibited concern only for the architect's potential liability, not his responsibility to verify the realism of the Owner's program. Otherwise the issue of the highway would have been raised and resolved during the Schematic Design Phase.

He glanced at the clocks and was dismayed to find that he had taken almost eight minutes to struggle with this one question. Decide, damn it! he told himself. All right, then (C): his education in business as well as in architecture, his acquaintance with theories of organizational behavior, his practical experience, and his sense of integrity combined best in that answer, at least of this choice of four. If this had been "The Price is Right," would the prize be behind Door Number (C)?

*****

By the third week after the examination, Nathan was rushing home every evening to check his mail, to look for the letter informing him that he had passed and was now licensed to practice architecture in the sovereign State of Ohio. Soon after New Year's, he phoned Jackie Presser's office, and was told that Presser was traveling but wanted to talk to Nathan when he returned in the first week of February. Now he had two things to anticipate. But the first was resolved some weeks later with a letter from the State Board of Examiners of Architects in Columbus. He let it lie unopened on the sofa next to him while he watched the sun sink in the west. This will either be one of the best days of my life or one of the worst, Nathan thought, and reached for the letter.

January 18, 1977

Mr. Nathan Goldstein
2570 Overlook Road
Cleveland Heights, Ohio 44106

Dear Mr. Goldstein:

We are sorry to inform you that you have failed the design portion of the NCARB Professional Examination. Your scores are as follows:

Environmental Analysis	82
Building Programming	84
Design and Technology	73
Construction	78

A minimum score of 75 is required for each section. Please be advised that all four sections of the NCARB Professional Examination must be passed simultaneously in one sitting. Therefore, you are required to retest in all four sections again. You are eligible to take the test again in December, 1977.

In addition, your score on the Ohio written and graphic test was a 73. Therefore you need to take this test again as well.

Very truly yours,

James P. Wheeler
Executive Secretary

It was one of the worst.

Chapter XIV

Rubin, May, 2005

The drive back to Rubin's condo was quiet, after Gerald's explanation of the last time he had belted somebody in the mouth. It was well past lunch time, but Rubin wasn't at all hungry after all the excitement at the park, and he couldn't imagine that Gerald was either. They had had a good breakfast. He pulled the Chrysler into the garage and they went into the condo. Gerald went straight into the downstairs bathroom to wash his hand.

"Do you have any iodine or disinfectant, Walter?" he called. "I cut my knuckles on that little punk's teeth."

"Yes, of course," Rubin said. "Is it a bad cut?"

"No, I just don't want to get his AIDS bugs into my blood stream–that would be hard to explain to Laura," Gerald said. "She goes to Nashville to tend her sick mother and I run off to Ann Arbor, whoring around with Good Time Walter, getting into fights and--"

"Here's the iodine," Rubin said. "I'll do it." Gerald dried his hand and Rubin swabbed the injured knuckles. Rubin reached for the band aids in the medicine cabinet but Gerald shook his head. "Do you want anything? To eat or drink, I mean?" Rubin asked.

"I wouldn't mind a tall glass of water with plenty of ice," Gerald said. "But nothing to eat, thanks. Let's sit down and talk about what happened. I'm bursting with curiosity."

"Harry Rosenberg left me a file cabinet with all kinds of papers, personal things, and World War II memorabilia in it," Rubin said, anticipating the obvious question and getting Gerald his glass of water. "And the gun as well as some ammunition was in one of the drawers. But before you begin to interrogate me about it, shouldn't we call the police? Or the sheriff?"

"For what?"

"To have them send a car out there and arrest them."

"Man, we're the ones likely to be arrested. Assault with a deadly weapon. And don't tell me you've got a permit for that thing–Harry didn't will you one, did he?"

"I've got a permit to own it," Rubin said defensively. "But I don't have a permit to carry a concealed weapon, no. Here." Gerald took a long drink and they sat down at the kitchen table. "Then don't call the police," Gerald said. "I want to go home to New York, where I've never been mugged in my long life. I want to get out of this criminal-infested college town with crazy knife-wielding peckerwoods trying to rob a poor old defenseless colored man sitting quietly at a picnic table by a meandering stream. You said there wouldn't be any muggers. I'll never trust you again."

"Gerald," Rubin said, "stop that and listen. You knocked that man cold and the other one may have a concussion. We could call the sheriff without identifying ourselves, just tell them we heard a disturbance out there as we were driving up or something like that, and we think they should send a car out, and then hang up."

"You're concerned about their welfare? You want to send them flowers and a box of candy?"

"No, I want those bastards arrested and jailed. I think they were high. They were probably in the restroom when we drove in, doing crack or cocaine or whatever they were high on, and I'll bet they all have long records, and I really think we should call."

"What if they trace the call? Walter, I'm not kidding, we're not guiltless in this. This wasn't just self-defense. There are grounds to arrest us, you because of the gun, me because I hit that creep. I probably did some damage. I'm serious. I really mean it, don't do this."

Rubin looked thoughtful. "They can't trace the call quickly. Suppose I put on an accent, call the sheriff, tell them just enough to stimulate their interest, and hang up without identifying myself."

"But why, for Christ's sake?"

"If we had been in a car accident, caused by the other driver, some drunk, and had gotten away without a scratch ourselves, but left him lying in the street, injured, would you tell me not to report it?"

"That's not what happened and you know it. So it isn't that you want their asses hauled off to jail, you want to assuage your guilty conscience for carrying a gun illegally, for waving it under their noses—Walter, tell me the truth, if they had hesitated much longer about dropping their knives, if they'd tried to call your bluff, if that's what it was, would you have shot them? You had that thing cocked and your finger was on the trigger!"

Rubin was silent.

"Damn!" Gerald said. "You *were* going to shoot!"

"I think so," Rubin said. "Now we'll never know."

"Why? We could have given them our wallets, your car keys–the insurance would cover theft, surely--"

"To hell with that," Rubin said. "Why did you hit that bastard?"

Gerald hesitated. "I did, didn't I," he said. "A good reason not to call the sheriff, as I said. But that's not the same as pointing a loaded gun at them. I guess you were pretty convincing. I couldn't believe that you would–I mean, how long have we known each other? And known each other *well*? But at the same time I couldn't believe it, I thought you *would*, just as they did!"

"All right, I won't call the sheriff," Rubin said. "You didn't answer my question."

"You didn't answer mine."

"I'm not sure I can," Rubin said. "There was something about that old car in the parking lot. It seemed so out of place. Maybe I just sensed danger the way an animal might sense a predator, without seeing it or even smelling it, and yet I didn't want to tell you–what would I have said, I sense danger? Here at this peaceful picnic site? I'm going to take Harry's pistol with us?–and I didn't want not to go to the river, either. So I took the gun from the console as we got out of the car and slipped it in my pocket. I put it back in the console before we came into the house, by the way."

"OK, but that's not all I meant," Gerald said. "Why do you have it? Are you worried about some former student, still angry about the C you gave him? Or some former colleague whose book you tore to shreds in your review in some widely read literary journal, circulation of at least fifty-four?"

"Yes, exactly," Rubin said. "Some of these college professors are so overly sensitive, you just can't tell what they might do if a senior scholar and critic like me tells them that their little books are much too long. Senior scholars have a duty, you know, to guard the gates, to maintain standards, to prevent the frauds and sleazebags and wannabes from infiltrating the ranks of The Profession. You must know all about that, you were a professor."

The two old men tried to smile at each other. It didn't work. Gerald waited. Rubin sighed. "All right, I'll try," he said. "I don't know what you'll think of this, but here's my explanation. Believe it or not, it has to do with my visit to Ellis Island. That trip brought back a flood–no, a trunkful of memories. About my mother. About our early years in this country. What we were just talking about last night. And about Berlin. About my father. How he disappeared. How he was beaten to death. I don't know how my mother found that out, but she did, and somehow, over the years, although of course I never learned the details, I learned enough to know that he was attacked and beaten to death by Nazi thugs on *Kristallnacht*, November 10, 1938. And somehow that stayed deep within me, eating at me all these years, not just a sense of deprivation, Gerald, some feeling that there was unfinished business, terribly important unfinished business. World War II hadn't finished it. The establishment of a place to go for the survivors, who weren't wanted anywhere, certainly not where they had come from and not where they went either–that hadn't finished it. My father, who had fought for that goddamned country for four years, beaten to death for his race in an alley in the city of his birth, of his father's birth, his grandfather's birth. Contrary to what they all had so fervently believed, they were never Germans. My father, a man who had loved me, who had loved my mother, who hadn't been able to get us out in time–I know he tried, my mother told me. He failed, at least for himself. Maybe that's what gave my mother the courage, her desperation after she lost him. I know she and I got out illegally, somehow boarding a train in Berlin without having our papers checked at the station. She managed that, I don't know how, as I don't know how she had managed to get friends first to store and then to ship her things to the States once she had an address to give them. All these crucially important details of what I suppose could be a college course somewhere, 'Variations of the Refugee Experience.' I've told you some of this story." Rubin got up a little shakily and got his own glass of water. Gerald waited.

"Then Harry's present to me–did I tell you that Harry was some kind of war hero, blowing up German troop trains behind the lines in Greece in World War II? He must have taken the Luger off some German he'd killed, I don't know. There was some ammunition for the gun in the file cabinet, as I said, but I got rid of that, and went to a sporting goods store a few miles down the highway and bought a new box, partly to have the man show me how to load the gun and so on. He didn't have a Luger but he had a gun a lot like it, and the lesson wasn't that difficult. And there was something else about that store, taxidermic displays, Gerald, intended for hunters, I'm sure, although I have no idea what emotions they're intended to provoke in hunters–I suppose a great lust for expensive weapons, now that I think about it–anyway, the displays were amazing, extremely well done, and there were several of African game animals, a whole gang of lions like those thugs attacking some miserable buffalo, I remember that. But the one that I found riveting was of a huge rhinoceros about to spear a male lion, which had somehow been wired or whatever it's called to hang vertically in the air, as if he were leaping up, trying to block the rhino's enormous horn with one paw–but you knew that the horn would be in that lion's midsection in the next second, and that the rhino would stomp that cat into the ground, leaving damn little for the hyenas and jackals and vultures. I hadn't seen that display, of course, when I decided to keep the gun. When I decided to get new ammunition for it. When I decided to have the man show me how to load the gun and rack the first round, he called it, into the chamber. But somehow that display explained what I had done, a visual metaphor for my subconscious, if you like. The Luger was my horn. I was preparing myself to fight back. Some nights after I had come back from Ellis Island, I took Evelyn to Jericho's Wall and after the unpleasantness with Mr. Alhumaidi I told you about, I pulled out of his parking lot too quickly, and cut somebody off. He blew his horn and then I think he followed me all the way back to Evelyn's house and was waiting for me down the block. Well, I had had enough, more than enough, of violence and beatings. I can't handle any physical confrontations at my age, and was never much good at them anyway. So no more running from the lions. The next Nazi bastard was going to have to look at the wrong end of Harry's Luger." Rubin stopped. He was breathing rather heavily.

"You all right?" Gerald asked quietly.

Rubin took a sip of water and nodded.

"So these thugs were Nazis?" Gerald asked.

"You heard what that bastard called you," Rubin said. "Why did you lay him out?"

"Yes, that might have been part of it," Gerald said. "But I don't have any complicated autobiographical or psychoanalytic explanation for hitting the guy. I just don't like being threatened like that, maybe because I haven't had that experience very often. Not since I was about twelve. And I was about six feet two then. Maybe bigger."

Rubin looked at Gerald appraisingly. "Jesus," he said. "I don't know if I was much over five feet by my twelfth birthday. Wasn't it Nietzsche who said that anatomy is destiny?"

"I don't know," Gerald said. "German philosophy never held my attention. So the reason you started carrying a gun without a permit, and the probability that you would have shot those men at the river an hour or so ago, both have to do with what happened in Germany in the nineteen thirties? That's what you were going to explain to the sheriff? And not long ago the sovereign State of Michigan entrusted the education of its young people to you through its agents the Regents of the University?"

"Not entirely rational, is it," Rubin said.

"No, Walter, it isn't. Not entirely, not at all. I can't tell you that what I did was rational either, and I'm not proud of it, I suppose–although I'm not ashamed of it either, the creep had it coming–but my reaction was instinctive anger in the context of the situation."

"And mine?" Rubin asked.

"You want revenge, Walter, revenge for your father, for the camps, for mass murder, for what you and particularly your mother had to endure, for the thousand betrayals and humiliations and moments of terror you and your mother went through–and all the time you know, Walter, you have to know, that there is no such thing as meaningful revenge, there is only retaliation. Only another act of bloodshed, another Hatfield shooting a McCoy or McCoy ambushing a Hatfield. So-called capital punishment, even when the right guy gets the needle, does not deter the next murderer. So-called justice for the relatives of the criminal's victims brings no one back to life. If it brings smiles to anyone's face, that's just another sick son of a bitch smiling. Suppose you had shot that marble-eyed mugger right between his buggy blue eyes–how could that possibly make up for what the Germans did to your parents? To everybody? What the hell does revenge ever accomplish?"

Rubin sat silently.

Gerald got up. "I'm sorry, Walter, I don't mean to pile it on like that," he said. "But I think you should get rid of that gun, and I think you should be honest with yourself–you're much too smart not to know that life isn't fair, as Kennedy said. You can't have revenge for what happened, any more than I can. All you can do, if you want to, and if you get the chance, is to try to help somebody who needs help, or try to fix something that needs fixing, at least to some extent."

"I know you're right," Rubin said. "My mother would have said exactly that, about helping people. The funny thing is, I remember thinking very similar things about revenge and justice, how the one is impossible for the very reasons you just gave, and how the other always requires some kind of compromise, some give and take. I thought about that in the car on the way back from the sporting goods store, after I had bought the ammunition. I even thought about Mr. Alhumaidi at Jericho's Wall, and why I was amusing myself imagining that Arab immigrants were after me, having recognized me as a Jew. I know you're right. I've been indulging myself in my own fantasies, just like Mrs. Mayberry."

Gerald started. "I'd better call Laura," he said.

"Of course," Rubin said. "Call her from the phone in your room."

"OK," Gerald said and went up the stairs. Rubin got up, opened the refrigerator, and inspected the contents. Nothing appealed to him. He decided that he'd suggest dinner out again, perhaps at an Italian restaurant this time. He went into the living room and saw last night's newspaper. He'd brought it in when he'd gone out to meet Gerald at the airport, but hadn't read it. He looked at the headlines: bombings in Iraq, Republican denunciations of Democratic critics of the war and the administration, the lack of health insurance for the poor, the cost to the automotive companies of health benefits for their unionized retirees, the loss of both manufacturing and white-collar jobs in the state, the booming economies of India and China. And there, on the editorial page, among the letters to the editor about the eternal truth of God's word, the absurdity of the theory of evolution, the inalienable right to bear arms as guaranteed by the Second Amendment, the precocious talents of the children in Mrs. Hessendorf's sixth-grade musical production at St. Aloysius' Elementary School, was his letter about Harry Rosenberg. He read it carefully--the Ann Arbor *News* was remarkably indifferent to spelling, hyphenation, grammar, and proofreading, not just in its sports columns--and was pleased to find it free of error.

Gerald came down the stairs, smiling. "Mrs. Mayberry is going home this weekend, they think," he announced, "and Laura is going to stay until she's settled at her house. Her brother has to go back to California, but someone else can take over by the middle of next week. She's talked to Rita, and Rita's apparently using her head again. So things are looking up."

"You didn't say anything about what happened just now, I hope?"

"No, hell no, Walter," Gerald said. "And I don't plan to. So the question is do I ask you to take me to the airport now, before the police find the body at the riverbank, and read about your arrest here in the *Times* at my favorite coffee shop in Upper Manhattan, or do I repay your hospitality and marvelously arranged entertainment by taking you out to dinner tonight and catching a flight back in the morning."

"The body at the riverbank," Rubin repeated. "Did you hit him that hard, do you think?"

"Hell, I don't know," Gerald said. "For all I know, he was high on heroin, had one or more incurable diseases, a weak heart, congested lungs--I didn't just pat him on the cheek, I know that. I don't think he'll pull a knife on anyone again soon, I'm pretty sure of that."

"No," Rubin agreed. They looked at each other. "Gerald, you're more than welcome to stay as long as you want, you know," Rubin said.

"I have only one clean pair of drawers and pair of socks left," Gerald said.

"I have a washing machine and a dryer," Rubin said, "and there are excellent men's clothing stores in Ann Arbor, full of New York merchandise. And if your credit card is over the limit, mine isn't. What did you tell Laura, about when you'd be back in New York?"

"I told her I'd call her back, either today or tomorrow," Gerald said.

"Tell you what," Rubin said. "Since I lied to you about the lack of muggers in our local parks, and since we both like Italian food, let me take you to a really good Italian restaurant here in town tonight, and tomorrow morning to a men's store that caters to football and basketball players and is sure to have at least a few things in your size. Call Laura tonight and tell her you'll meet her at the airport when she comes back from Nashville next week. In the meantime, stay here and let's have some more adventures."

Gerald laughed. "That didn't end the way I thought it would! What kind of adventures? Bar fights? Visits to massage parlors? Confrontations with the local gendarmes, pretending we're fraternity pledges?"

"No, no, I can't handle any of those," Rubin said "I was thinking of a good dinner at Anthony's and then maybe some jazz at the Firefly, or maybe there's a good movie or even a play somewhere, there's a very good theater in Chelsea–although I suppose with your sophisticated New York tastes, you wouldn't be interested in anything that didn't cost an arm and a leg?"

"Well, the dinner seems like a good idea, anyway," Gerald said. "But as for entertainment, I think I'd prefer old-fashioned conversation. Walter, we're not going to get many more chances like this. We ought to make the most of it."

Rubin was touched. "Why, you sentimental old man," he said. "All right. In the meantime, read my latest publication." He gave Gerald the newspaper, folded to the editorial page. It took Gerald a moment to find Rubin's letter. He read it quickly, then again, more slowly.

"Shall I venture a guess about what you liked about Harry Rosenberg? Or perhaps what impressed you about him?"

"Sure," Rubin said.

"The clarity of his convictions," Gerald said.

Rubin grinned. "Especially, you mean, in contrast with the murkiness of mine?"

"If that's the way you want to put it," Gerald said.

"Yes, I suppose so, on both counts," Rubin said. "For a while I thought I was a little jealous of Harry about that clarity, never having enjoyed any of my own, about that and what he did in Greece, when he was very young--"

"His military service?" Gerald asked.

"Yes, with the Greek underground–I don't mean that I think of it as romantic or as the stuff of a Hollywood war movie, but as a chance to fight back. Then it occurred to me that that's probably not how Harry saw it. I do know that he had relatives in Russia or wherever it was that his parents were from who didn't get out, because he mentioned that to me, but he didn't know them, and he seemed to know very little about them, for that matter. He never told me much about his parents. Working-class people, came to this country when they were small children, that sort of thing."

"Did he have any brothers or sisters?" Gerald asked.

"He had a younger brother, I know that, because he talked to me about him once, in a very strange conversation that really had more to do with his second wife, who died in Columbus some time before he left Ohio State to come to Michigan, and who was the great love of his life. I don't remember exactly how he, the brother, came up in the conversation. Harry was probably telling me about relatives, his wife's and then his–he had two children by his first wife, by the way, and I've met the son, a crude, unpleasant man–so I suppose that's how his brother came up. I don't recall that he had any other siblings."

"Why do you say it was a strange conversation?"

Rubin thought for a moment. "It was some time ago," he said. "I remember it was a winter evening, cold and blustery, two winters ago, I think. Harry was here for a late-night snack, wine and cheese or whatever it was, and I had been talking about my mother, and asked him about his family. It developed that although he had loved his kid brother very much, at least when they had been small boys, that proved to be a source of great pain to him after puberty, because the brother turned out to be a homosexual and Harry couldn't stand it. There seems to have been a silent or unspoken conspiracy between the two brothers that their parents were never to find out. You understand, this was in the late nineteen thirties. As far as Harry knew–I remember that he repeated that several times, emphatically, so it must have been very important to him–they succeeded–the parents never knew, never suspected. At least that's what Harry chose to believe."

"What happened to the brother?"

"As I remember, he joined the Navy and was killed in action, and Harry, although he grieved for his brother, also thought that perhaps it was for the best–I don't really know whether he meant best for their parents, best for himself, or best for his brother. I didn't ask him to explain what he meant. I listened and tried to look sympathetic."

"Did you succeed, do you think? Weren't you genuinely sympathetic?"

"I don't know if I succeeded, Gerald, but no, I wasn't genuinely sympathetic. Obviously I don't understand homosexuality, but I've known a number of homosexuals–there were four or five in my department alone, and there are other units at the University where they aren't at all rare, or however you want to put it–and they're no more alike than anybody else, that's clear to me. How could Harry's love for his brother be overcome by shame? Or revulsion? Or both? Now his first marriage, that seems to have been the kind of mistake that a young man, totally in thrall to sex and the rapture of having found a girl who'll let him, is certain to make and certain to regret, if marriage is the girl's ultimate requirement and social expectation, and when Harry couldn't stand whatever her name was any more, and was making enough money to pay the alimony and child support the judge set, he acknowledged his youthful error and started his life anew. Or at least that part of it. But I've never had a brother, or a sister either, so maybe Harry's reaction isn't all that inexplicable to someone else. What about it, Gerald? You have brothers and sisters–older and younger both, as I remember?"

Gerald hesitated. "Not any more," he said. "At least no older brother or sister. They both died within the last three, no, four years."

"You never told me!" Rubin said, remonstratively.

"No, I didn't," Gerald said, with no inflection. "John, my older brother, died in Atlanta, after a long illness–emphysema that developed into pneumonia–did you ever meet him?"

"I don't think so," Rubin said. "But you've told me quite a bit about him, how he was almost your younger father, not just a role model and great influence."

"Except for his damned smoking," Gerald said. "Not that he ever encouraged me to take it up. I tried it one time, thought it was awful, and couldn't understand how he had become so addicted to it. But it didn't kill him until he was almost eighty. Isn't that strange? Nat King Cole was still in his forties, I think, and John lasted about thirty years longer with the same damned habit."

"Were you with him when he died?"

"No. That's bothered me ever since. I can't remember what I was doing or why I thought I had time to get to Atlanta to see him, and I wonder, more often than I like, whether he was aware that he was dying and wanted me to show up. We were very close. There are some things that are hard to forgive yourself for."

Rubin was surprised. Gerald was remorseful about very little, but it was clear that he meant what he had just said. But he didn't seem to want to say any more about it.

"That's true," Rubin said. "I wonder whether Harry had similar thoughts, later on, about his mixed emotions concerning his brother."

"Anything about that in that file cabinet he left you?" Gerald asked.

"You know, I never finished looking at all the contents," Rubin said. "I got so involved in tracking down what he had about Goldstein–you know something? I didn't finish that either!"

"Goldstein?"

"His former student, Nathan Goldstein, from Cleveland," Rubin reminded him. "I told you about him over breakfast in New York."

"The fellow you think Harry suspected of having killed somebody?"

"Yes," Rubin said. "He was important enough to Harry for Harry to have referred to him in the brief speech he gave at his colleague's funeral, Arnold Prescott--"

"Hold on a minute," Gerald interrupted. "I can't tell the players without a program."

Rubin nodded. "Of course," he said. "Sorry. But I'm not at all sure that Harry described all the *dramatis personae* in what he left me, nor that his characterizations were complete or even accurate as far as they went–after all, he was an actor himself in this Ohio tragedy, not an impartial observer and certainly not the omnipotent playwright. All right, let's see what I can remember. I'll begin with the King and his court, that is, the Dean and the Assistant Dean and the key professors, introducing minor players as they appear on the stage, lords and ladies, office staff as servants, students as rude mechanics and apprentices, and of course foreign dignitaries and remote, possibly hostile princes and potentates and their emissaries--"

"Walter!" Gerald interrupted. "Please! I enjoy Shakespeare in the Park or on PBS, but no more seminars, and no, I won't take a test at the end of the hour!"

"You won't let me have any fun at all, Gerald," Rubin said. "First you analyze my heroism at the river as misplaced ahistoricity and psychological scar tissue, and now, just as the old pedagogical juices are beginning to bubble in my Shakespearean cauldron, you tell me to put a lid on it."

Gerald gave Rubin a long look. Rubin sighed and told him who Prescott was, and Goodman and Wilson and Webber and Peggy and Brian Keating–"Brian Keating!" Rubin suddenly cried. "I think I can guess why Harry told Goldstein that no, Keating shouldn't be his assistant in his study!"

"What are you talking about?" Gerald asked.

Rubin explained what he had learned about the role Prescott had proposed for Keating in Goldstein's research project, neither of which had come to fruition.

"And why do you think Harry vetoed that idea?"

"Because it occurs to me that Keating might have been a homosexual, or that Harry thought he was," Rubin said.

"That would have been enough, just a suspicion like that, to make Harry blackball Keating, so to speak?"

"I think so, given Harry's shame about his younger brother," Rubin said. "Walls within walls, with armed guards everywhere, keeping the undesirables out. Caste systems, color lines, sexual conformity or at least the appearance of it, political correctness, standardized examinations, family connections, legacy admissions--Jesus, Gerald, everywhere you look there are barriers to participation in the human enterprise, subtle, overt, behind the scenes, out in the open–all in the name of somebody's standards of what's acceptable. Grades, jobs, marriages, birth, family, alma mater, country club, sexual behavior. Maybe that's what fascinates me about Harry, now that I'm getting to know him better in death than I knew him in life. A first-generation American, son of working-class emigres, familiar with a sexual deviant, as he must have thought of him, from his own family, becomes a fierce warrior in a cause he seems to have regarded as a matter of duty, not principle. Or duty *was* the principle. Then, dissatisfied for whatever reason with practicing his profession, he decides to teach it, emphasizing high personal as well as professional standards. I'll show you his eulogy of Prescott that he gave at Prescott's memorial services. And why does he refuse to allow a graduate student in his department to work in a colleague's research project? If I'm right, because he thinks the student is gay. What a mess of contradictions!"

"So your interest in Goldstein is really interest in Harry?"

"Maybe so," Rubin said. "I never heard of Goldstein, or anything like what happened to him at Ohio State, until Harry started telling me about him. And I thought it was strange that Harry was still so involved so many years later with whatever happened in Columbus. Unless, of course, Goldstein did kill that official or was somehow responsible for Prescott's heart attack and Harry blamed himself for not having stopped Goldstein before it was too late. But I don't know, at least not yet, whether Harry really thought that. I have the feeling that something or somebody else was involved, and that Harry had a notion of what was going on, and maybe the reason he willed me all these files was that he hoped I'd find out and–this is going to sound ridiculous–clear his name."

"Clear whose name?" Gerald asked. "Goldstein's?"

"No, no, his own–Harry's," Rubin said.

"I guess I don't understand," Gerald said. "Clear his name of what charge?"

"Inaction," Rubin said. "In the court of his own conscience."

"Aha!" Gerald said. "One of those!"

"Yes," Rubin said. "Like you, a moment ago."

Gerald stared at Rubin. "You mean, my regrets about not having been at John's deathbed," he said. "I see. I think I'm beginning to like your friend Harry more and more. I don't understand his problem with his brother, any more than you do, but I can imagine how he might have worried about Goldstein, and how that would eat at him."

"Let me show you a copy of his remarks at the service for Prescott," Rubin said. "He referred to Goldstein, strangely enough, although not by name."

"Sure," Gerald said. Rubin got up to get the file, but paused on his way. "You know what's really strange?" he said. "Harry's dead. Did he think his conscience would survive him?"

"Well, if Mrs. Mayberry hadn't decided to stick around a while longer," Gerald said, "maybe she'd be explaining all this to Harry about now. Get the copy of Harry's remarks at the memorial service."

Rubin came back with the copy and handed it to Gerald, who read it quickly. "I'm not sure that I see what you're talking about," Gerald said. "The reference to Goldstein is really quite vague, and doesn't suggest any suspicions–on the contrary, 'a graduate student of much promise,' 'nothing more than a detour'–those aren't expressions that make my ears prick up."

"No, but what about 'work of great interest to both Arnold and myself' and the fact that of all the things he might have said to illustrate Prescott's virtues, he chose Prescott's support of Goldstein? It seems to me that it's the very vagueness that's strange. Why not identify this 'work of great interest' to an audience made up largely, I'd guess, of architects? And if you want to pick a student whose professional life was saved by Prescott, why choose one who didn't complete his project? Don't you sense some sort of code here, intended for whoever in the audience had been on the other side of whatever the dispute was, in effect saying that Prescott was on Goldstein's side and maybe he was right and you were all despicable?"

"Are you sure you aren't reading more into this than there really is?" Gerald asked. "You may have been influenced by what Harry told you here, years later, an old man's growing obsession with some mistake he became convinced he made, and now you interpret what he said at Prescott's funeral in that light, not as simply meaning what he said."

"A mistake he thought he made?"

"Well, when do you think Harry began to suspect that Goldstein was somehow implicated in that official's murder and Prescott's death?"

"Ah, the old questions from the Watergate investigation!" Rubin said, smiling. "What did the President know and when did he know it? You're right, I should have begun there with Harry's suspicions, if that's what they were, and if they were put to rest by whatever he learned subsequently. Gerald, I simply don't know. Not only that, I don't know how to find out. I'll go through the remaining papers in the file cabinet soon, and if I can't put Harry's nagging conscience at ease then, he'll just have to toss and turn for eternity, worrying about it. Are we over our episode at the river, or is there any more to say about it?"

"Not by me," Gerald said. "But if you see anything in the paper about it tomorrow or the next day, tell me. I'll be curious to see how two old guys like us get blown up into a large gang of armed blacks from Detroit who robbed and beat these innocent white students who were simply conducting biochemical experiments while investigating the ecology of the local public parks."

Rubin grinned. "Is that the story you want me to phone in to the paper?"

"No," Gerald said, "that's the story the paper will print without any help from us."

*****

Gerald left three days later. His prediction of the story the paper would print turned out to be reasonably accurate but incomplete. The men, arrested by sheriff's deputies alerted to their presence by church ladies who had gone to the site for a picnic but had fled at the sight of muddy, barefoot, tattooed men, still dripping water and propping up one of their fellows whose face looked seriously damaged, had indeed claimed to be the innocent victims of a vicious attack by armed robbers, all huge, all black. The deputies, however, told the reporter that they had found drugs and drug paraphernalia in the suspects' vehicle, that all the suspects had police records, and that their descriptions of their assailants were completely inconsistent and unverifiable. Two suspects were taken to the infirmary, one with a concussion, the other, who had lost four teeth, with a broken jaw. The other three were jailed on charges of possession of illicit substances. Rubin and Gerald were delighted, and Gerald did not hesitate to point out how right he had been to dissuade Rubin from calling the police. Rubin granted the point, but made another. "This version of events, Gerald," he said, "apparently will live as history. The only people who know what happened are those five bastards and the two of us, and none of us has any interest in getting the truth out. Imagine some doctoral student at the University, writing his dissertation in sociology, say, basing his analyses of crime and race relations at the nexus of local picnic sites on reports such as these, furnished by tired deputies to weary reporters. Not only is this fable now history, gospel, as it were, it will become part of the fodder consumed by policy makers, officials, high government muckety mucks. For all you know, somebody like Ronald Reagan or his speech writers will use this fantasy in an election campaign. I can't wait to see what the spin will be. The NRA is certain to see the possibilities. Make sure *you* pack a six-shooter with your six-pack! Pull a pistol from *your* cooler!"

Gerald laughed. "The function of history is to provide slogans, Walter," he said. "Now they're called sound bites, but it's the same thing, whether it's a call to war or a journalist's jazzy headline for some local atrocity. Remember the *Maine*! If it doesn't fit you must acquit! And gave her mother forty whacks! Let down your bucket where you are! Now there's a really interesting distortion–you can't imagine the number of young blacks who, without ever having read a word by either DuBois or Washington, are convinced that Booker T. was an accommodationist Uncle Tom and DuBois was the model for Malcolm X. Never mind that Washington was telling Mister Charlie that the brothers could speak English and were used to hard work and that there was no need to import a lot of honkies to work in the coal mines or the steel mills, or that DuBois had about as much use for blackleg preachers, whether they pounded the Bible or the Qu'ran, as he did for the untalented ninety percent, what matters is whether what you choose to believe makes you feel good."

"Are we back to religion?" Rubin asked.

"No, thanks," Gerald said. "I'll leave all that to Mrs. Mayberry, praise the Lord. What time do we have to leave to get me to the church on time? I mean, the airport? You know they're going to search me, just in case I'm a Black Muslim disguised as an elderly Baptist, so I should probably be there an hour or so before departure."

Rubin, reviewing the conversation on the way back from Metropolitan Airport, smiled again. Gerald had been right, of course. What matters is whether what you choose to believe makes you feel good. Or, if something makes you feel good, whether you are then inclined to believe it. That would explain a lot of marriages in their early stages. Very early. On the other hand, Gerald and Laura had been very happy, as far as he could tell, for many years now, and he knew other people who seemed to have become very comfortable with one another over the years, old feet in old shoes, taking on each other's shapes. He felt lonely, and decided to call Evelyn when he got back.

Evelyn was glad to hear from him, but she was unavailable for socializing in the immediate future: a daughter and grandchildren were taking all her time and energy. She said she'd call him when they were safely on their way home. Rubin was left with the book he didn't seem to want to write, or with puttering around his condominium, or with completing his inspection of the contents of Harry Rosenberg's two-drawer metal file cabinet. The book was not a contender and the puttering took almost no time. That left the cabinet.

Besides the packet of old letters from which he had not yet removed the string that held them together, there were three leatherbound old-fashioned notebooks and several manila folders, one of which held both original and copies of articles clipped from assorted newspapers and magazines. The headline of a copy of what was obviously a very old front page of a paper he'd never heard of, the New York *American*, caught his eye. The subtitles were equally intriguing:

**HARRY THAW KILLS STANFORD WHITE
ON ROOF GARDEN
SHOOTS ARCHITECT
IN BACK AS HE SITS
TALKING TO WOMAN**
Slayer, Captured, Gives Police False
Name, but Is Immediately
Recognized.

A TRAGIC OPENING NIGHT

Singing Girls Pluckily Keep Up the Music as Shots
Ring Out–Prisoner Refuses to Say a
Word in His Cell.

"Harry Thaw," the article began, "multi-millionaire, social exquisite, and noted clubman, last night murdered Stanford White, the famous architect, on the roof of Madison Square Garden. He shot him twice in the back and, as the victim whirled around in agony, another bullet sped into his stomach, and White dropped lifeless, at a table where he had been laughing and fingering a glass in company with a woman."

Rubin had a vague memory of what he had read about this particular crime of the century. White, a very famous architect indeed–hadn't he helped to design Madison Square Garden, ironically the scene of his bloody demise?–had, years earlier, seduced a sixteen-year-old girl who had later become a well-known actress and the wife of the very rich Thaw. He even remembered her name, and knew why: Evelyn Nesbit. But she had apparently continued her relationship with the architect. Thaw had found out about it and had put a stop to it as described in the article. A familiar story, except for the social prominence of the people involved, which was all that made it news. The question was why Harry had made and kept a copy of this front page.

Rubin read on, enjoying the reporter's melodramatic style, thinking that he should play a version of "Frankie and Johnny" or at least "I'll be Glad When You're Dead, You Rascal You" on his CD player for suitable accompaniment. "There are two versions of the dramatic shooting," he read. "One is that Thaw saw the architect with Mrs. Thaw, and, approaching the couple, said:

"'You've stolen my wife, you' ----

"Excitement Blurs the Facts

"The other version is that the society man entered with his weapon and waited for White to appear, killing him without saying a word. There was such tremendous excitement that the real story of that moment of revenge may never be known." Then why had the article begun by claiming that Thaw had first shot White in the back–twice–and then, when "the victim whirled around in agony," once in the stomach? Suppose the Ann Arbor *News* reporter had been similarly indecisive or lazy or eager to compose an entry for the annual Best Washtenaw County Crime Story Award: would the paper then have printed all five versions of what hadn't happened at the river as furnished, respectively, by all five thugs? How was the public ever to know the truth about anything if reporters didn't do their jobs?

The thought provoked others. Did the public ever know the truth about anything anyway? The full truth, if there was such a thing? Did the public care? Did it matter, in the long run? Who now, a hundred years later, really gave a damn about Stanford White, famous architect, infamous profligate, widely known for adultery as well as architecture? And about Thaw, or Mrs. Thaw–Evelyn Nesbit–or for that matter, that whole social scene of the very early twentieth century? What else was going on then? The copy of the old front page was not fully legible, but the headlines of the articles were all readable. Another murder–"Girl Slain in Rowboat by Her Suitor," complete with a picture of Miss Katherine Stryker, "Keyport girl whose body, with that of her sweetheart, was found in Raritau Bay yesterday," read the caption– the headlines continued: "Battled with the Frenzied Youth and Screamed in Vain for Help – His Suicide Followed–Fellow Townsmen Draw Mantle of Charity Over Case, Calling it 'Accident'"–what else? "Five Ice Trust Heads Sent to Jail for Year – For First Time in History of the Nation Monopoly Chiefs are Thus Punished –Action Taken in Toledo – Conspiracy and Extortionate Prices the Charges Which Brought Convictions" – well, there had been a lot more times of that kind of thing in the history of the nation since then, but probably not nearly enough convictions, Rubin thought–and about halfway down the page, in much smaller type, an article circled in red, presumably by Harry: "Jews Flee in Terror of More Massacres–Black Hundreds Spread the Propaganda of Slaughter in Many Towns." The dateline for the four sentences that comprised the article was St. Petersburg, June 23. "The agitation affecting the Jews is still manifested in a deluge of appeals to members of the Duma for protection against possible attacks." The next several lines were blurred, but Rubin could decipher that the Black Hundreds–then the Russian equivalent of white lynch mobs in the United States, Rubin thought–were spreading the rumor that Jews had brutally killed–he couldn't read who or what the Jews were rumored to have killed. June 23? Passover was long past, Rubin thought. The old blood libel was that the Jews killed a Christian child to mix his blood in what they consumed for Passover, as reported memorably in *The Canterbury Tales*. Well, the Russians weren't much concerned with calendrical niceties. If it was time to lynch Jews once again, for Christ's sake, the date didn't matter. June 23, November 10, the important thing was–he could read the last sentence: "The dispatch added that the town was greatly agitated and that the Jews were fleeing from threatened danger."

Harry's parents. They had come to the States about that time, small children, as he had been a small boy when he had arrived in 1939. Harry's parents. That was why the article was circled in red. Harry had probably gone on the web to look up whatever there was about Stanford White, found this page about the famous murder, and there, serendipitously, elsewhere on the page, was a report about events much more closely related to Harry than anything that had affected the history of American architecture. What was it the feminists liked to say? "The personal is political"? Well, yes, but vice versa, resoundingly.

And these other stories–poor Miss Stryker, the rascally ice trust heads found guilty in Toledo–they too reverberated down the years, closely echoed in one crime after another, crimes of passion, crimes of greed, year after year. O.J. Simpson, found innocent in criminal court by a jury of his peers (Gerald had said invidious things about those peers) but mysteriously guilty in civil court. Enron. Milken. Boesky. He couldn't remember all the millionaires who, in the last twenty years, had screwed their stockholders, investors, employees, pensioners, and of course the public, that wonderful abstraction that mattered only in politicians' speeches and civics textbooks. Why would anyone remember Teapot Dome? Rockefeller? Carnegie? Toledo ice trust heads? Although that last one was so picturesque, so readily translatable into marvelous cartoons, it really deserved some longevity.

Ecclesiastes came to mind, and Rubin got out his Bible to find the passage. "The thing that hath been," he read, "it is that which shall be; and that which is done is that which shall be done; and there is no new thing under the sun. Is there any thing whereof it may be said, See, this is new? It hath been already of old time, which was before us. There is no remembrance of former things; neither shall there be any remembrance of things that are to come with those that shall come after." That seemed definitive. In a way, its resignation was almost comforting, blunting hope and therefore the possibility of disappointment.

But this had not, apparently, been Harry's perspective. What he had said indirectly about Goldstein at Prescott's memorial service was that, with Prescott's help, Goldstein had persevered and had succeeded. Disappointment had been averted or overcome. Things had worked out, at least for Goldstein. Like Harry's parents, he had escaped and made good. Or at least survived. For a moment Rubin wondered just what *had* happened to Goldstein. No doubt he had gone into his father-in-law's business and lived happily ever after with a fat wife and too many spoiled children. Or maybe not.

Rubin replaced the copy of the old newspaper page in the manila folder and took out the three leatherbound notebooks. Each had a little strap with a snap button holding the book shut. He opened one and looked at the title page. *"Personal Diary: 1941-50."* The capitals, *P* and *D*, were large and elaborate, as were the numbers. Nine years: Harry had gone to the war and then to college on the GI bill. There would be something about whatever her name had been. Maybe something about his brother. He leafed through the notebook quickly. Harry hadn't crossed much out–he had let the thoughts fly. Rubin noticed different inks, corresponding to the sometimes surprisingly long chronological gaps in Harry's narrative. Almost nothing for 1947 and 1948. He put the notebook down and picked up another, again turning to the title page: "*Personal Diary, 1950-75.*" A quarter of a century, covering almost three times the length of time reported in the first diary, but the same number of pages. He looked at the spines of both books but saw no evidence that any pages had been torn out. Nor were there any missing pages in the third book: on the contrary, to his surprise Rubin saw that Harry had not come close to filling it. The title page read "*Personal Diary: 1975–,*" with a blank after the dash. He found the last entry in about the middle of the book. He read it several times, checking the date. Then he looked at the date of Prescott's memorial service on the copy of the remarks he had shown Gerald.

So that's what Harry had suspected. It wasn't Goldstein at all. What, if anything, had Harry done about it? There were still some folders Rubin hadn't inspected carefully. And there was that packet of old letters, tied with a string.

Chapter XV
Nathan, 1977-1978

The weekend was torture. The letter squatted toad-like on the sofa where Nathan had left it, emanating an evil miasma throughout the apartment, the kitchen, the bathroom, the bed. Sleep was impossible. At 3:00 a.m. Nathan awoke for the third time from the same nightmare, sitting in a classroom with many other people, filling in circles on an answer sheet with a Number 2 pencil without having the question booklet. Then he found the booklet but the answer sheet had disappeared. He raised his hand for help and a man came to his desk and said, "We changed the test, didn't you hear the instructions? And you were to bring a Number 4 pencil, not a Number 2!" The man took Nathan's Number 2 pencil and broke it, laughing, and suddenly everyone else in the room was laughing and pointing at him. "He brought a Number 2 pencil!" a long-haired girl cried, laughing loudly. She looked familiar but he couldn't think of her name and then he woke up.

He did not answer his phone all weekend. He remained in his apartment, eating very little, trying to stay still, occasionally staring at the television set but barely aware of whatever program was on. He had never experienced such torpor. But Monday came and he knew he had to rouse himself. He made his way to the bathroom, glanced in the mirror, and shuddered. His eyes were bloodshot. He had three days' growth of beard on his face. He looked either as if he had been running from the police or as if he ought to. He got into the shower and stayed so long that he suddenly worried that the other tenants wouldn't have enough hot water. He got out and shaved very slowly and carefully with a new cartridge. The after-shave lotion helped to revive him. He got dressed, considered but rejected the thought of breakfast, started toward the door, and saw the letter where he had last left it, now on the coffee table. He took it, sat down on the sofa, and read it again.

It was a couple of minutes after eight o'clock, and he was already well behind schedule, but he pulled his phone to the coffee table and, looking at the number on the letter, dialed it. State bureaucrats were supposed to be at work by eight in the morning. Not that they would be—they'd come in late, gossiping, make their office coffee, discuss their weekends, all the while letting the phones ring, probably mocking all the unsuccessful applicants calling to see whether there hadn't been some terrible, gut-wrenching mistake. He imagined a scene something like his dream, everyone in the office giggling and pointing at the ringing telephones. "There's another flunkee, slobbering and crying into his phone! How pathetic!" A woman answered.

"State Board of Examiners of Architects, Lorraine speaking, may I help you?"

"Uh--" he looked again at the hateful letter and saw the name—"uh, is Mr. Wheeler in?"

"Yes, he is," Lorraine said cheerfully. "May I tell him who's calling?"

"This is Nathan Goldstein," Nathan mumbled. "In Cleveland," he added, not sure why.

"Thank you, Mr. Goldstein," Lorraine said, as if he'd paid her a compliment. "One moment, please, Mr. Wheeler will be right with you." Apparently the sun was shining brightly in Columbus. It wasn't in Cleveland.

"Yes, Nathan, this is Jim Wheeler, how can I help you?"

"Yes," Nathan said, as if Wheeler had already offered to help. "I'm calling about your letter dated January 25 that I received on Friday, about the architect's exam."

"Yes?"

"I–I never expected this," Nathan said.

"Yes, all applicants hope to pass, I know, but the fact is that most need to take the exam more than once before they succeed," Wheeler said. He was very smooth.

"Yes," Nathan said, getting flustered. What did he want? He remembered. ""Does the Board have any materials that would better explain the test? Or the results? For instance, the distribution of the scores?"

"The only thing I'm allowed to show you are the answer sheets," Wheeler said.

"You mean the computer-scored answer sheets, the ones where I filled in those little circles?"

"Yes," Wheeler said. His tone was beginning to change.

"I don't see how I'd learn anything from those," Nathan said. "How about the test questions and answers, together?"

"Oh no," Wheeler said. "We're not allowed—our contract prohibits that. Those materials are confidential. Just the answer sheets."

"Confidential? What do you mean?"

"We have a contract with the testing service we use that prohibits release of that information, because it's their property, you see, and so we are obligated to treat it confidentially, and all we can let you see, as I said, are your answer sheets. Even then that's under restricted access."

Damned double talk, Nathan thought. "How restricted?"

"Well, I could schedule a meeting, here in my office. You'd have to inspect your answer sheets here, but you couldn't make copies or take notes or anything, that's what restricted means in this instance." Wheeler's tone was definitely no longer friendly.

Nathan squeezed the phone as hard as he could and controlled himself. "When?" he asked.

"When?"

"When would be a good time to meet?"

"This week I'm free on Thursday morning until noon," Wheeler said slowly, "and after two in the afternoon on Friday, but then just for a limited time."

Right, Nathan thought, get an early start on your weekend. "OK," he said, "I'll be at your office at two on Friday. I'll be coming in from Cleveland."

"All right," Wheeler said. "I'll pencil you in. Please try to be on time."

"Yes," Nathan said. "Thank you," he added, not sure whether Wheeler was still on the phone, and hung up. He looked at his watch. It was 8:15. I'm going to be late for work, Nathan thought, jumped up, grabbed his briefcase, and ran out, just remembering to lock the door. He backed his car out of the leased space behind the building and drove off rather faster than usual, tailgating the car ahead of him to make the right turn onto Green Road before the light turned red. C'mon, c'mon, Nathan yelled at the car ahead of him as the light changed to yellow and then, as he turned, to red. Fifty yards down Green Road he saw flashing lights in his rear view mirror. Nathan pulled his car to the curb and continued to look in the mirror. A Beachwood police officer got out of his squad car behind him, adjusted his hat, and walked toward him. Nathan lowered the window before he could tap on it. "Driver's license, please," the officer said in a neutral tone. Nathan pulled his wallet out, took the license from it to give to the officer, and noticed his name plate over his breast pocket. It was Officer Holden, the same cop who'd let Sam Becker go without a ticket back in September, now examining his license. "I was parked in front of the Ground Floor Restaurant," the cop said, matter-of-factly, "and saw you drive through the red light."

""Officer Holden," Nathan said, smiling and ignoring what he'd just been told, "we met back in September, when I was in the back seat of Sam Becker's car."

The cop looked at Nathan again. "I know Sam Becker," he said, "but I don't recall ever meeting you. Is this Cleveland Heights address current?"

"Yes," Nathan said. "I thought the light was yellow when I completed most of my turn."

"I saw you under the light," the cop said, "and it was red. I'm going to give you a traffic violation but if you so desire you can contest it in the Beachwood Mayor's Court." Yeah, right, Nathan thought, I'll get this dismissed when pigs fly. The cop finished writing the ticket and gave it to Nathan. "Have a nice day," he said without smiling and returned to his squad car. Sure, Nathan thought. He waited for the cop to pull away and then drove carefully to the entrance drive to the underground garage just down the road and parked his car in his designated space.

When the elevator let him off on the second floor, Nathan went to the seven-foot-high wooden door to Samuel Becker & Associates, thinking, as he turned the knob, I hope Betsy doesn't ask any questions about the exam. She didn't, nor did she greet him, but Nathan saw her glance at her watch as he mumbled "G'morning," and passed her desk. It was almost 9:30 and he was an hour late. But nobody was in the hall and he swallowed his half-formed explanation, going directly into his office.

The day dragged itself around like a dog with a broken leg. Nathan tried to concentrate on his work but started nervously every time he heard a step outside his door. What would he say if Becker or Carlton or one of the others came in to ask about the exam? Two other interns in the office had taken it. He had seen them at Taylor Hall at Kent State University. But no one came in. Finally it was time to go home. He left quietly and drove carefully back to his apartment. The letter lay where he had left it. He fixed himself a TV dinner, watched television, went to bed early, and had another restless night.

Although Nathan arrived on time on the next day, it was otherwise very similar until late in the afternoon. Dick Little, accompanying his arrival with a cursory knock on the door, walked into Nathan's office. "Goldstein, we're getting together after work at the Ground Floor bar to celebrate Matt's passing the registration exam–just to let you know." Nathan fought to control his face. "Thanks, Dick," he said as pleasantly as he could, although the announcement wasn't quite an invitation, "but I have a date right after work tonight."

Little stared at Nathan just a moment too long. "Suit yourself," he said. He turned to go out, but looked back at Nathan. "How'd *you* do?"

Nathan could feel the blood rush to his face. "I passed all the parts except design," he said. "Missed it by two points."

Little gave a snort, impossible to interpret. "Better luck next time," he said, and left. He's going to tell everyone right now, Nathan thought. That's it.

The next morning Charlie Carlton came to Nathan's office. "You know," Carlton said, after the preliminaries, "most of the guys here had to take that exam two or three times. I had to take it three times myself. Sam is one of the very few who passed it the first time."

"I guess you heard I didn't pass," Nathan said. His heart was pounding.

"Yes, Dick told me yesterday at the celebration for Matt at the Ground Floor. Look, I'm sorry you didn't pass, but as I say, most of us go through this with that exam. It's not a problem. I spoke to Sam, and he said it's no big deal, just focus on your work. You're doing well here."

"Thanks," Nathan said. "I'm concentrating on work while I'm here at the office, but it does seem to be on my mind when I get home."

"Sure," Carlton said. "It'll pass in a couple of weeks. I've been through it."

"By the way," Nathan said, "I'm driving down to Columbus on Friday to look at the exams."

"Really!" Carlton said. "Are you sure that's a good idea?"

"Well, no, not sure," Nathan admitted, "but anything they can tell me will help me understand what I got wrong, and that way I think it'll be helpful next time."

Carlton's expression showed his doubts, but he shrugged and said, "Good luck." Then he left.

*****

On Friday morning, before leaving for his meeting with Wheeler in Columbus, Nathan phoned Jackie Presser's office. Angela told him that Presser was traveling, but wanted to meet with Nathan as soon as possible. They set up an appointment for the next Monday, and Angela said, "You know, I probably shouldn't tell you, but Mr. Presser was really impressed with you, not just because your dad was a teamster but because of the way you used that to meet him and talk to him."

"Thanks," Nathan said. "That's good to know. I'll be sure to keep that our secret."

"Good," Angela said. "My head is full of secrets, one more won't bother me." Nathan wondered whether she was referring, however obliquely, to some of the things he'd heard about her boss. He didn't pursue it. You didn't ask questions about Jackie Presser if you wanted to do business with him.

Nathan was a few minutes early to his appointment with Wheeler, and browsed through a copy of the NCARB newsletter in the reception area. An article presented the development of the new, computerized NCARB exam as a major step forward in the effective evaluation of applicants. The standardized exam would, the article declared, prove especially advantageous to state licensing boards concerned about uniform evaluations of applicants, whether the issue was reciprocity or the mobility of architects as part of the general tendency on the part of American professionals to change their residences several times during their working lives. What about advantages for the applicants, Nathan wondered.

"Mr. Goldstein?" It was Wheeler. He's called me Nathan in the past, Nathan thought, so this is already a signal that we're no longer friends. As if we ever had been. "Yes, Jim," Nathan said deliberately. "Good to see you again." Nathan, getting up, offered his hand and noticed that Wheeler shook it briefly and reluctantly. "We'll talk in my office," Wheeler said, re-establishing dominance as he motioned Nathan down the hall, leading the way to his office.

Wheeler indicated the chair Nathan was to sit in and sat down behind his desk. A file rested on top. Before Nathan could say anything, Wheeler cleared his throat and took two sheets out of the file. Nathan saw that they were the computerized answer sheets on which he had darkened the little circles with his Number 2 pencil, in one column after another. "These are your answer sheets," Wheeler said needlessly, pointing to Nathan's name printed in pencil on top. Nathan saw how many of his original answers he had erased to select another circle to fill in. The sight brought back the whole experience of the examination, and for a moment he hung out of time in a maelstrom of panic, disgust, anger, and frustration. He tried to remain impassive. "And the test booklets with the questions, and the multiple choice answers?" he asked.

"As I explained on the telephone," Wheeler said stiffly, "we're not allowed under our contract to show those before or after the examination."

"But what can I learn from these sheets by themselves?" Nathan asked.

"They are all I am permitted to show you," Wheeler said. "I explained all this on the phone, you'll remember."

"I was hoping to learn something today that would help me do better next time," Nathan said, as evenly as he could. "It seems to me that people who don't pass the examination the first time they take it at least ought to benefit from the experience, learning something that the practice exams don't convey, what the people who write the questions have in mind as the best answers and so on."

"I'm not sure I understand what you mean," Wheeler said. "The practice materials are intended for exactly that purpose, and applicants are expected to use them quite intensively as they prepare themselves for the most important professional examination they'll ever take."

Pompous ass, Nathan thought. "I used them intensively, believe me," he said. "But when I did I could figure out, pretty much, anyway, why the testing people regarded one rather than another answer as the best one, because I had both the questions and the multiple choice answers to study, whereas here all I've got are these little circles and numbers, and obviously you can't expect me to remember what questions or answers these refer to."

"Whether you do or not," Wheeler said, "these are all I'm allowed to show you, as I think I've said several times now."

They sat and stared at each other for a moment.

"So I have to take the entire professional NCARB exam over again, all four parts?" Nathan asked.

"That's right," Wheeler said.

"I passed three parts and I have to take those over again too?"

"That's right," Wheeler said.

"And the test is offered only once a year, in December?"

"That's right," Wheeler said. "But you can take the Ohio graphic design problem again in June."

"The graphic test where the design solution is in my hands, not the multiple choice NCARB exam, is that right?"

"That's right," Wheeler said. "This has all been communicated to you previously."

"Well, I'd appreciate some additional information," Nathan said. "How often does the State Board of Examiners meet?"

"Once a month," Wheeler said. "Why do you ask?"

"Because what you've been allowed to tell me is of no use to me," Nathan said, "and maybe the Board could give me some insights."

"Are you sure you want to do that?" Wheeler asked. "I can't

remember a single instance of any applicant, whether passed or failed, who's requested a meeting with the Board since I began working here."

"Do I have a right to meet with them?"

"Yes, the Board would hear your grievance, if that's the direction you want to go in," Wheeler said.

"I'm not sure that I've got a grievance, but yes, I'd appreciate an opportunity to meet with them," Nathan said. As long as I can continue to be polite, he thought, I've got a chance of getting heard.

"Their next meeting is scheduled for February 15," Wheeler said, checking his desk calendar. "That's a Tuesday. Ten o'clock. There's usually a fifteen-minute break after the first forty-five minutes, and although they won't like it, and some of them will probably leave the room, I can schedule you for those fifteen minutes at ten forty-five. But not more than fifteen minutes. Are you sure you want to do this?"

"I think it's important to learn something from this experience," Nathan said again.

Wheeler stood up. The meeting was apparently over. "OK, see you on the fifteenth," he said. Nathan rose and extended his hand. Again Wheeler shook it reluctantly. "Thank you," Nathan said and started toward the door. Then he turned and said, "How about my recommendation letters? Are they available for inspection?"

Wheeler looked at Nathan's folder. "Yes," he said, "but they won't help you pass the exam. Their purpose is to help us determine your eligibility to sit for the exam, that's all."

"But I'm allowed to see them?" Nathan asked again.

"Yes," Wheeler said. He pulled them from the file and placed them on his desk in front of the chair in which Nathan had been sitting. "Thank you," Nathan said, sat down again, and started to read the letters. There were three, one from Prescott and two from previous employers, all on the preprinted forms supplied by the State Board of Examiners. Respondents had to check little boxes arranged in columns from "Excellent" to "Not Applicable" in relation to statements about the applicant's abilities and character. Each respondent had marked the box under "Excellent" in each category. There was space for "Additional Comments (Optional)" and Prescott had used it to write that Nathan was considered one of the top students to have graduated from Ohio State University's School of Architecture, and that several professors believed that he had the potential to demonstrate brilliance in the architectural profession. Nathan finished reading the letters, pushed them back toward his file on Wheeler's desk, said "Thank you" again, and left. Wheeler hadn't answered.

*****

On Monday morning Nathan phoned the office and told Betsy that he had a meeting with Jackie Presser but would be at work before two. The meeting went very well. Presser, reading at his desk when Nathan knocked on his door, smiled and said, "Nathan, good to see you, come in, have a seat!" Nathan thanked him and shook his hand before sitting down.

"I've been so damn busy lately," Presser said, "but I did want to follow up on our conversation about the work you want to do related to our Central States Pension Fund."

"You have a great memory!" Nathan said, genuinely impressed.

"Part of the job requirement," Presser said. "I have to remember who said what to whom, and what I can repeat and what I can't, and who to and especially who not to, you get me?" He smiled, but it was a glinty smile. "OK, the Central States Pension Fund. We have some projects coming up here in Ohio and also in Indiana. You said that Becker has experience in retirement housing projects."

"Yes, we have significant experience with retirement housing," Nathan said, "including high rise, mid rise, and lower density type developments." He reached into his briefcase, pulled out a brochure he had put together over the weekend about housing retirement projects, handed it to Presser, and waited. Presser inspected it carefully. "Yes, this is the kind of work we're looking for," he said. "I'm familiar with a couple of the projects Becker completed for Emerald City Enterprises, and--" his phone rang. "Mr. Presser," Angela's voice came over the intercom, "Tony Scardello is on the phone--can you take his call?"

"Tell him I'll be with him in a minute," Presser said. "OK, Nathan, this looks good," he said. "I like what I see. But you're getting this chance because your dad was a teamster, I want you to understand that."

Nathan stood up. "Thank you very much, Mr. Presser," he said. "I do understand that. You won't be sorry-- we won't disappoint you."

"I'm sure you won't, Nathan," Presser said, rising and shaking Nathan's hand with one hand while reaching for the phone with the other, "I'm sure you won't--or else."

Nathan was startled, as Presser, grinning now, had apparently intended. "I love saying that," he added, turning to the phone. "We'll work very hard for you," Nathan assured him as he made his way out. Was that supposed to be funny, Nathan wondered--he didn't sound as if he was kidding.

Later that afternoon Linda appeared in Nathan's office to tell him that Becker wanted to hear about his meeting with Presser. Jesus, Nathan thought, he could have buzzed me or even come the few steps himself instead of sending his executive secretary to fetch me. But he's the boss and never misses an opportunity to demonstrate it. He took his notes and some extra copies of the brochure he had given to Presser, and followed Linda to Becker's office.

"Nathan, yes, come in," Becker said when Nathan hesitated at his door. "Close the door. I wanted to talk to you about following up with Jackie Presser."

"Great," Nathan said. "I was just finishing my notes from our meeting this morning when Linda came to get me."

"Good timing," Becker said. "So you met this morning?"

"Yes," Nathan said. Hadn't Betsy relayed his message? "He wants us involved in some work for the Central States Pension Fund, retirement housing projects pending in Ohio and Indiana."

"Did you tell him about the projects we completed recently for Emerald City Enterprises?" Becker interrupted.

"I did," Nathan said, and handed Becker a copy of the brochure. "I had prepared this over the weekend and gave him a copy—he seemed impressed."

Becker leafed through it carefully. "This is very good," he said slowly, looking at Nathan. "Did you do this by yourself?"

"I went over the materials with Charlie about a week ago," Nathan said, "and put it together on Saturday, after I'd been told on Friday before I went to Columbus that Presser wanted to meet this morning. Otherwise I would have brought it to you first for review and approval." Tell him what he wants to hear, Nathan thought.

"Ummmm," Becker said. "Well, as long as Charlie had input, OK. It looks really good. You say Presser was impressed?"

"He seemed to be—yes, I think so, because he said he liked it and was going to give us a chance." Never mind the real reason, Nathan thought.

"You got his phone number there?" Becker asked, pointing at Nathan's notes.

"Yes," Nathan said, consulting his notes. He took a piece of paper from the pad, scribbled the number on it, and gave it to Becker. "Thanks," Becker said. "I'll call him tomorrow. You met with him twice, right?"

"Yes, twice," Nathan said. "The first one really to set the second one up, and then this morning to make the sale."

"Good job," Becker said, nodding and almost smiling. No time like the present, Nathan thought. "Sam," he said, "when I began working here you said you'd consider raising my salary to $15,000 after my six-month review. I've gotten indications from you, as just now, that my work is more than satisfactory, so I'd appreciate taking some time to discuss my salary."

"Yes, I recall discussing that with you," Becker said, no longer on the verge of a smile. "But I'm going to have to ask you to be patient. You've been doing good work, and we've been extremely busy this year, but the fact is that our clients have been slow, some of them very slow, in paying. We're close to having a cash-flow problem. Let's talk about this again this summer. But Nathan, yes, you did a great job with Presser." He turned in his chair, indicating the end of the conversation.

Nathan got up, controlling himself. "Yes, thanks, the meetings with Mr. Presser went very well," he said and left Becker's office. If I'd passed the NCARB, he thought, I would have gotten the raise today. He probably thinks I don't have anywhere to go. But my question is whether this is where I want to stay.

*****

Nathan was a few minutes early for his meeting with the State Board of Examiners of Architects in Columbus. To his surprise, Wheeler was at the receptionist's desk, looking through some papers. "Good morning," Nathan said, as pleasantly as he could. Wheeler looked up, expressionless. "The Board is on their break just now," he said. "They should reconvene in just a few minutes."

"Yes, I'm a little early," Nathan said, waiting to be asked to sit down. Wheeler said nothing but returned to his papers. Nathan sat down. Some copies of recent magazines were on the coffee table, including two about current events–Jimmy Carter's inauguration, the reaction of foreign governments, problems in the Middle East–but Nathan was in no mood to think about any of that. Wheeler got up, took the papers, and left. Nathan waited. Suddenly Wheeler was back.

"The Board will see you now," he said, motioning Nathan to follow him. Nathan did, entering a large conference room, where a group of well-dressed middle-aged and older men, all white, were sitting at a long table covered with papers, ash trays, coffee cups, packets of sugar, creamers, glasses, and pitchers of water. The man at the head of the table, who looked familiar, was passing documents to them from two large stacks at his right and left, alternating stacks and direction. Wheeler took the chair next to his, pointing Nathan to the vacant chair at the foot of the table. "All right," said the man, continuing to pass out the documents, as Nathan was about to sit down, "are you Mr. Goldstein?"

"Yes, I am," Nathan said, hesitating.

"You don't need to sit down," the man said. "We have just a couple of minutes to listen–as you see, we're very busy."

Nathan felt himself flushing with anger. Control yourself, he thought. "May I ask with whom I'm speaking?" Everyone stopped and stared at him, one man in mid-gesture of passing the documents to his neighbor. "I'm Mr. Charnesky," the man said. "I'm the president of the State Board of Examiners of Architects. Jim Wheeler has advised us that you have some sort of grievance about the NCARB examination you didn't pass last December. Is that correct?"

Charnesky, of course, Paul Charnesky. Prescott had introduced Nathan to him at the Kon Tiki, and Prescott had told him about Nathan's study in considerable detail. "Partly correct," Nathan said. "I didn't pass, that's right, but I don't know that I have a grievance. I have questions, and I'd like to learn something about the exam that will be of use to me the next time--"

"Didn't Mr. Wheeler show you your answer sheets?" Charnesky interrupted.

"Yes, but--"

"Didn't Mr. Wheeler advise you that the Board is under contract and we aren't allowed to show you the NCARB exam booklets or the answers?"

"Yes, but I'd like the opportunity to see more than the computerized answer sheets," Nathan said, raising his voice to prevent another interruption. "I don't know which questions I got right and which I got wrong."

"All applicants are limited to the same information," Charnesky said coldly. "No exceptions. The rules apply to everyone."

"Mr. Goldstein," said another man, sitting several chairs to Charnesky's right, "Mr. Wheeler told us that you're currently employed by Becker Architects in Cleveland in – in a marketing position? Is that correct?"

"Yes," Nathan said, "that's right, but--"

"Well, Mr. Goldstein," the man continued blandly, cutting Nathan off, "for what you're doing in the profession, you don't even need a license!" His lip curled. The men on either side of him nodded and smiled.

Nathan's neck felt very warm. "I've also worked under the supervision of licensed architects, doing design and construction documents and field observations," he said, "and my future plans are to utilize all my business education and skills for the improvement of the profession."

"No doubt very commendable, your plans and all that," Charnesky said, "but that's not what this Board is concerned with. You've received all of the information on the NCARB exam that any applicant is entitled to and would get, and that's it, you get no special favors, I don't care who you are or who you work for. If you're still confused about what you're to do to pass the exam, if you're going to take it again, talk to Mr. Wheeler here, who can advise you what criteria you have to meet to sit for the examination."

"Does that mean--"

"Mr. Charnesky has just told you that your time here is up, Mr. Goldstein," the same man who had spoken earlier interrupted, shuffling the papers in front of him. "We have a very full schedule. Goodbye."

"Thank you for taking the time to hear my concerns today," Nathan said, careful to keep his voice level. No one looked at him. Nathan walked out, followed by Wheeler. "I guess I'll be talking to you about the next NCARB exam," Nathan said. "Yes, do," Wheeler said. He seemed to want to say something else: I tried to tell you that you were wasting your time? You should have listened to me, it would have saved you the trip down here? Charnesky doesn't like pushy Jews? But he just held the door open for Nathan and said goodbye, as had the man who had told him that he didn't need a license to do what he was doing.

*****

March arrived two weeks later with every intention of verifying at least the first part of the old saying. The winds blew in from the lake with what seemed to be personal hostility. But when Linda, Becker's executive secretary, congratulated Nathan on his work with the Teamsters' Central State Pension Fund, telling him that she was typing two proposals for retirement housing projects in Ohio and Indiana, Nathan felt the warmth of success. "Really!" he said. "When did all this happen?"

"Sam followed up with Jackie Presser after your last meeting at the Teamsters' headquarters," Linda said.

"You think Sam might see me for a few minutes?" Nathan asked.

"I'm sure he will," Linda said, "although Charlie's with him. I think the door's open."

Nathan walked the few steps to Becker's office, hearing Becker and

Carlton laughing about something. He appeared at the open door and Becker, still grinning, waved him in. "C'mon in, Nathan," Becker called, "we're just talking about Jackie Presser and how tight a ship he runs. His people don't get toilet paper unless he approves the brand. But it's still two-ply for the guys behind the wheel, four-ply for the union brass." It seemed to be the same joke he had just made, but he grinned at Carlton and they both chuckled.

"Yes, Linda was just telling me about the proposals she's typing up for the Teamsters," Nathan said. "Great news. I'm glad I was able to develop this for the company."

Becker's smile disappeared as if Nathan had wiped it off with a Brillo pad. "*You*?" he said. "What makes you think *you* developed our connection with the Teamsters?"

Nathan's mouth fell open. "What makes me—what are you—are you joking?"

"No, I'm not joking," Becker said, bristling visibly. "I've known Presser for years, when you were still in knee pants. You think you introduced me to him?"

"You know that I met with Presser twice, talked to him several times on the phone, and prepared that brochure he liked so much," Nathan said angrily.

"Yeah, the brochure that Charlie here had to review and revise from your rough drafts– listen, don't take that tone with me, Nathan. You've got a lot to learn and the first thing is to lose that *chutzpah*, you understand me? It was my calls to Presser that got us this work, I was the one that closed this deal." Nathan glanced at Carlton, who was sitting silently in his chair, his face blank. He obviously wasn't going to say anything. Becker glared at Nathan, just daring him to continue the argument. Nathan fought for self-control.

"Sam," he said, more quietly, "I know I brought in the Central States Pension Fund opportunities. If you don't want to give me credit for it, that's your decision." He turned and walked out, not closing the door. "He's pissed off I didn't agree to that raise, that's all," he heard Becker tell Carlton. Nathan stopped in the hall and started to turn back, but caught himself. The son of a bitch.

In his office, behind the closed door and at his desk, still shaking with anger, Nathan got out a business card he had kept tucked in his wallet and dialed the number. No raise in sight, that was clear, no credit for the new work. Life was dumping on him. Flunked the exam, no raise, "you don't even need a license to do what you're doing...." Condescending bastards, Charnesky and that other guy, both of them, just like Becker. "Shaker Square Neighborhood Association, may I help you?" said a woman's voice.

"Yes, please," Nathan said. "This is Nathan Goldstein. Is Chuck Schneider in?"

"Hold on, please," the woman said. A moment later a man asked, "Nathan?"

"Yes, hello, Chuck," Nathan said. "Do you have a moment to talk, or is this a bad time?"

"Yes, I've got a minute or two, what's up?"

"You remember when we ran into each other last month and chatted, and you said to give you a call if I ever considered making a move from Becker?"

"Ah," Schneider said. "You're, uh, considering?"

"I certainly am," Nathan said.

"Excellent timing as far as I'm concerned," Schneider said. "I was about to put an ad in the *Plain Dealer*. I need help with design, and as I remember you're interested in that."

"Yes, I am," Nathan said.

"Can you meet me tomorrow for lunch? Say twelve thirty?"

"Any place you say," Nathan said.

"Great," Schneider said. "Meet me at the Rapid Stop restaurant along the rapid line in Shaker Square, OK?"

"See you there," Nathan said. He felt better.

The meeting went very well. Schneider, who had been Nathan's employer while he was taking courses toward his M.B.A. at Case Western University in the summer of 1974, was now working for the Shaker Square Neighborhood Association on renovations at the Shaker Square retail center. The money came from a "Community Development Block Grant" from the federal government, but through the City of Cleveland. Schneider was rather vague about who, exactly, was involved, or how it all came together, and Nathan sensed that there were questions better left unasked. Schneider reported to an Executive Director named Eugene Wentworth, but was free to hire an assistant.

After lunch Schneider took Nathan to his office at Shaker Square. The Shaker Square retail center, Schneider told Nathan, had opened in 1929, developed by Otis and Mantis Van Sweringen, the brothers who had developed Shaker Heights. It was designed as the second shopping center and the first planned community in the nation, and included one of the largest concentrations of multi-family housing in Cleveland. Schneider, with obvious pride, said that the Shaker Square retail center and surrounding apartment complexes were expected to be listed in the

National Register of Historic Places.

The Shaker Square Neighborhood Association had been established to help to revitalize the retail center. The center had lost many previous customers to more recently developed enclosed shopping malls. A number of locally owned retail tenants in Shaker Square were struggling, vacancies were increasing, and as a consequence of the loss of rental income, much of the necessary regular maintenance had been deferred. "Our job," Schneider told Nathan, "is to come up with plans to improve the buildings and the site, including landscaping and sidewalks. And we've got to be sensitive to all the criteria used by the National Register."

Not only would Nathan not have his own room at Schneider's office, his drafting table would be just a few feet from the secretary's desk, and the secretary, Olga somebody, a fat, frowzy woman, and Nathan took an instantaneous and mutually recognized dislike to one another as soon as Schneider introduced them. No privacy here, Nathan realized. And this woman is going to be much more part of my life than Betsy has been at Becker's. But the sooner I escape from Becker, the better.

"What do you think?" Schneider asked.

"Great," Nathan said, watching Olga compress her lips. "Do you have a few minutes to discuss some details outside?" Olga's body language was unmistakable. "Sure," Schneider said. "Let's go around the Square. I'll be back in under thirty minutes," he told Olga. She grunted neutrally and bent over her typewriter.

"OK," Schneider said when they got outside, "the details. Are you interested?"

"Absolutely," Nathan said. "I know I enjoy working for you, and I really like this project, it's very appealing to me for a lot of reasons. And I want to be completely honest, Chuck: I've got to get out from under Sam Becker, for my own mental health."

"Uh-huh," Schneider said, suggesting that no explanation was necessary. "Would you be able to start in two weeks?"

"Yes, but we need to talk about salary and benefits."

"What's your current salary?" Schneider asked. "And what are your benefits?"

"I'm at fourteen thousand now, but I'm due for a thousand dollar raise, and I have health care coverage," Nathan said.

"OK," Schneider said. "I can offer you fifteen to start and I'll include health care. What do you think?"

"I'll tell Becker I'm leaving in two weeks, is what I think," Nathan said, grinning.

"Great," Schneider said. "Call me at the office later in the week and we'll set up lunch again and you can fill out the paperwork then. I'm delighted, Nathan."

"So am I," Nathan said. They shook hands and parted. Nathan's departure from Becker and Associates was not as pleasant but almost as expeditious.

*****

Nathan began his new job at the Shaker Square Neighborhood Association toward the end of March. In June he took the Ohio graphics design examination for the second time, and failed it again, once again very narrowly. Although Nathan's answers were drawn and written in Nathan's own hand, he decided not to chance a repetition of his painful experience with the State Board of Examiners, but simply to take the graphic exam again in December when he would take the NCARB tests for the second time. In November he repeated the previous year's routine: he took time off from work, closeted himself in his apartment with the four study books for the four NCARB tests and went to the Case Western Reserve University Sears Library to find and study additional articles, this time for the Ohio graphics design examination on interpretive nature center design and construction. He supplemented his reading with visits to the Cleveland Metroparks, taking careful notes about what he saw. On December 11 he drove to the Kent State University campus and registered at the Kent Motor Inn near the campus. Once again the examinations were scheduled to be given in Taylor Hall. And once again, when Nathan got there on Monday morning well before eight o'clock, he found Wheeler there to proctor the exam.

"Good morning, Jim," Nathan said, as pleasantly as he could, "here we go again!"

"Hello, Nathan," Wheeler answered. "Yes, here we go again. Good luck today!"

Nathan noticed the use of his first name and the good wishes. Maybe his previous impression of the man had been unfair. Maybe Wheeler had been so stiff and nasty in his office because he'd seen Nathan's inquiry as somehow a challenge to his authority, despite Nathan's efforts to be clear about his purpose. Who could tell? He smiled at Wheeler and selected a drafting table near the door, arranging his Number 2 pencils, eraser, sharpener, dictionary, and cans of Coca-Cola, one of which he opened as he sat down. Other intern architects were coming in and the

room soon seemed full. At eight o'clock Wheeler cleared his throat and
gave the examinees their instructions. They were identical with the ones
Nathan had heard the previous year.

The questions, too, for all their apparent neutrality of tone, conveyed
the familiar hostility of a schoolyard bully: "Hey kid! C'mere! C'mere, I
said!" Nathan looked around the room and saw many of his colleagues
shifting uncomfortably in their seats, erasing answers, scratching their
heads. How the *hell* were they supposed to answer? Stupid choices,
stupid circles to fill in, what exactly was being measured? Certainly not
his knowledge of what an architect has to do in the actual practice of his
profession. And it got no better over the course of the examinations. On
the last day, Nathan found himself staring at a question on the
examination on construction as if it were in a foreign language:

> During the early Construction Phase of a new office
> building project, the architect observes uncovered steel
> rebar reinforcement stored onsite. Upon closer inspection
> the architect observes that the rebar is coated with surface
> rust. The architect advises the contractor of his concern
> about the surface rust during the weekly progress meeting.
> The contractor's response is that the rebar is scheduled for
> placement in previously excavated foundation trenches on
> the next day and that the concrete pour is scheduled for
> one day after that. The architect questions the contractor
> on the cost of cleaning the rebar by hand wire brushing.
> The contractor answers that the cost will be approximately
> $2,000 and that the foundation pour would be delayed by
> at least two days, and that other delays are likely in the
> other trades as a result of such an action. What should the
> architect do?
>
> (A) Instruct the contractor to wire-brush clean all of
> the steel reinforcement prior to placement.
> (B) Accept steel reinforcement with surface rust.
> (C) Instruct the contractor to excavate the trenches
> one foot deeper.
> (D) Instruct the contractor to excavate the trenches
> one foot wider.

Nathan's first thought was that any architect worth his salt would call
his structural engineer for advice, since he knew that most architects do

not perform their own structural design. But the information provided in the question was incomplete. He glanced at the clock on the wall and realized that once again he was spending too much time on a single question. Eliminate the least sensible answers, he told himself: neither widening nor deepening the foundation would address the issue. Accept the rebar with surface rust? Or wire brush the rebar and accept the increased costs and delays? He remembered a conversation he'd had some time ago with Sid Greenstein on this very topic. Ironically, it had to do with a project that Greenstein was handling for Becker while he was working for that bastard. The rebar, Greenstein had told Nathan, had been delivered to the site about two weeks before the foundation trenches were to be excavated. Seeing the rust, Sid called the structural engineer, who came to the site, took a wire brush from his briefcase, and cleaned a few sample areas on some of the rebars in not much more than fifteen minutes. Then he made some measurements. "He told me," Nathan remembered Sid saying, "that the minimum dimensions, including the height of the deformations, met all of the specification requirements. Prestressing was not a condition. So I accepted the rebar with the surface rust, but I insisted that it be free of mud and other non-metallic coatings."

OK, Nathan thought. There's no mention here of prestressing requirements, minimum dimensions, height of deformations, or weight. But wire brushing all of the rebar is going to add to the cost and delay progress significantly. Nothing in the information provided seemed to justify that course of action. He filled in the circle below (B) on the answer sheet.

*****

He returned to work the following week, determined to be optimistic despite the queasiness he felt whenever he thought of the letter that would arrive from Columbus before the end of January. The queasiness proved to be justified. Wheeler's letter informed him that, although this time he had passed the Ohio written and graphic examination, he had again failed one of the four NCARB tests. But this time the letter produced anger, not self-pity. And the anger suddenly brought an insight he had never previously considered. First he called Wheeler to make an appointment to see his file. Wheeler's surprise was almost palpable. "I showed you what was available last year," he told Nathan. "Nothing has changed–I still can't let you see the NCARB test booklets or answers."

"Nevertheless," Nathan said, "I'd like to see whatever you *can* show me in my file."

They agreed on a date and time in February. Almost as soon as Nathan heard Wheeler hang up, he dialed the office number of a friend who was a lawyer, Frank Leighburg, whom he had met during his years at Case Western Reserve University. After the requisite pleasantries, Nathan told him what was on his mind. "Something's wrong," Nathan said. "Considering how close I've come to passing without quite making it, twice, now, I'm beginning to think that something's wrong. It's all very well to tell me that nobody can see the questions and answers after the fact, and that they can't make an exception for me–I understand that–but how could I have done so well in my coursework, and worked in private practice as well all these years, and still not be able to pass these stupid exams?"

Leighburg was silent for a moment. "Do you have a theory?" he asked.

"I'm beginning to think I do," Nathan said, "although it's more a feeling than a theory. Theories are supposed to be based on facts, and I don't have any facts. But I sure as hell have a feeling. Two feelings, really."

"And they are?" Leighburg prompted.

"One is related to the number of Jewish architects in Ohio, or for that matter, around the country," Nathan said, knowing Leighburg's ears would prick up immediately. Leighburg's parents had survived a Nazi concentration camp in Poland. "When I met the State Board of Examiners of Architects in Columbus to ask about the exams I flunked the first time, I was dismissed as if I'd violated some code merely by raising the issue. I remember the president of the Board telling me that they weren't going to make an exception for me no matter who I was or who I worked for. There was an edge to that remark, you know, I was asking for something I wasn't entitled to, as if I had tried to pull strings."

"You're a pushy Jew," Leighburg said.

"Exactly. The second thing, and this just occurred to me, is that I might just be being blackballed. When I was in the master's degree program at Ohio State, I had started work on a research study that at first was encouraged by everybody–I had a very supportive committee, three professors, and the assistant dean was very helpful at first too–and all of a sudden, without any satisfactory explanation, they stopped the study. I must have pissed somebody off, and I think it was people in Ohio, maybe even here in Cleveland. As I said, Frank, this is a feeling, I don't have any hard evidence."

"What was the study?" Leighburg asked.

"It was to be a survey of small architectural firms in the Columbus area, having to do with their knowledge and use of marketing in competition with big firms."

"A survey?"

"Yes, you know, questionnaire, coded responses, statistical analyses, availability of results in generalized form, nothing unusual in social science terms, but apparently revolutionary in the architectural profession. As I say, I was stopped cold and it didn't happen."

"And you don't know why? Who stopped you?"

"The school. I was told by the assistant dean, the same man who had been so helpful, that I was to stop and do something else. I wanted the degree, Frank, so I did as I was told. I had a lot invested at that point, believe me."

"Yes, I understand," Leighburg said. "Anything else?"

"I have another meeting scheduled with the Executive Secretary of the State Board of Examiners," Nathan said. "Late in February. I just can't believe that they'd give me the same bullshit twice."

Leighburg didn't comment. "OK," he said, "call me back after you've met with him. But in the meantime, go to the main library and start looking at whatever might be relevant to your situation in the Ohio Revised Code. They have a complete copy. It's just possible–no, I think it's probable–that you'll find something we can use."

"Will do," Nathan said. "Thanks very much, Frank."

*****

Nathan's meeting with Wheeler began with the reaffirmation, on Wheeler's part, of the impossibility of showing Nathan his test booklet and answers. "OK," Nathan said. "How about the Ohio graphic/written design problems, the two failures from December of 76 and June of 77, and the one I passed last December?"

"I'm sorry," Wheeler said, his voice shaking audibly, "those aren't available to you either."

"But those aren't national exams, those are Ohio exams!" Nathan expostulated. "Are you telling me that you're under contract with another testing agency that prevents you from showing me exams I've passed as well as failed?" He was almost shouting. Wheeler was visibly nervous.

"No, I'm not precluded by contract from showing you the Ohio design exams," he said. "But I can't show them to you because–I'm sorry to have to tell you this–we've discovered that they've been destroyed."

"*What?*" Nathan shouted. He heard the secretary scrape her chair on the floor in the outer office, probably turning in alarm toward Wheeler's door.

"I don't have an explanation," Wheeler fumbled, "perhaps they were mistakenly left near a pile of material that was to be discarded–perhaps one of our temporary clerks–we get some not so well trained people--"

"I don't think you believe that any more than I do," Nathan said. "This is outrageous, and it's a violation of the Ohio Revised Code. I want to make another appointment to appear before the State Board. I'll tell you when after I talk to my lawyer. I'm not going to let this slide." He got up. This time there was no question of a handshake. Nathan stalked out, leaving the door open, and brushed by the visibly frightened secretary. He threw her an angry glance and she wilted into Wheeler's office.

He called Leighburg the next day. "OK, Frank," he said. "I had the meeting with the Executive Secretary–a Jim Wheeler–and I've looked into the Ohio Revised Code, and I've got some news for you."

"Go ahead," Leighburg said.

"First of all, Wheeler told me that all three of my Ohio graphic/written design exams, the two I failed and the one I passed last December, had been destroyed. He tried to blame some anonymous clerk, but that's transparent crap. Not only did the bastard lie, but those exams should have been available for my review under Ohio law. I did what you told me, Frank, and went to the library. Very instructive."

"Do you have a section number?" Leighburg asked.

"Yes, I certainly do," Nathan said. "It's Section 4743.02 of the Ohio Revised Code. I've got it right in front of me–I copied it out–shall I read it to you?"

"Please do," Leighburg said.

Nathan read the section slowly:

> The examination papers of each applicant examined by boards, commissions, or agencies created under or by virtue of Chapters 4701. to 4741. and 4757. of the Revised Code shall be open for inspection by the applicant or his attorney for at least ninety days subsequent to the announcement of the applicant's grade; provided, papers not graded by members of examining boards or their employees and which by terms of a contract with any testing company the papers are not available for inspection; but it shall be the applicant's right to have any such paper regraded manually, upon written request of either himself or his attorney made to the board within ninety days after announcement of the grade.

"I've already talked to Wheeler today, to tell him about the requirements of the Code," Nathan continued. "You know what he said?"

"What?" Leighburg asked.

"He said that he wasn't aware of those provisions! I think he's a liar! I think he threw all three of my Ohio exams out himself before our meeting, and I'd really like to know who told him to do it!"

"Nathan, please," Leighburg said. "I'm as paranoid as anyone you know, but don't go around making accusations without evidence. And I've got to tell you, although what you've told me provides some basis for negotiation, or failing that, possibly litigation, that's not going to be enough to get your license to practice architecture."

"I've got more," Nathan said.

"Well, what is it?"

"Section 4703.08," Nathan said. "I've got it right here."

"Go ahead," Leighburg said again.

> *"Sec. 4703.08. The state board of examiners of architects may, **in lieu of all examinations**, accept satisfactory evidence of anyone of the qualifications set forth under the divisions of this section:*
>
> *"(A) A diploma of graduation from an accredited architectural school or college showing that the applicant has completed a technical and professional course of not less than five years' duration, which course is approved by the board, and, in addition thereto, has had at least three years of satisfactory experience, two years of which shall have been in the office of a reputable architect meeting all the qualifications for practice under sections 4703.01 to 4703.19 of the Revised Code; provided the board may require applicants under this division to furnish satisfactory evidence of knowledge of professional practice and supervision of construction."*

Leighburg was silent again. Then he said, "Nathan, I'm going to transfer you to my secretary. Please make arrangements with her to come into my office this week, if you possibly can–early next week at the latest."

Chapter XVI
Rubin, May, 2005

Rubin had never kept a diary, and, thinking about it, had to admit, without feeling at all superior–certainly not to Harry Rosenberg--that he did not understand why anyone would. He did not remember whether either Samuel Pepys or John Evelyn had ever made their motivations clear. A diary seemed to be a form of anticipatory narcissism, imagining that in future years one would want to resuscitate the self one had been, presumably to cherish the memories, to wave fondly at the Ghost of Person Past leaving its ethereal traces in the yellowing pages, the faded ink. It wasn't like keeping letters one had received from friends or relatives or colleagues, archival collections for future biographers or garbage men; or old photographs maintained in albums painstakingly organized to lend some semblance of progression to the contents, miniature museums of quaint costumes in awkward poses. No, a diary was composition, usually improvised, for the sake of turning fleeting thoughts, emotions, and what were regarded as important events into something permanent, into an artifact, a product to affirm one's presence in some particular space at some particular time. But at the moment of composition, improvised or studied, did the diarist envision his future self squinting and fumbling at the pages, warmed by ancient firings of synapses then long atrophied? What, if not some such silliness, did the diarist expect? Why had Harry written all these pages?

Some twenty or so years earlier, Rubin had served on a jury and had tried, in the evenings back in his apartment–he had not yet purchased his condominium–to record that experience, mostly because it raised unsettling questions far beyond the actual case. He remembered trying to reconstruct the drama of the courtroom, the presiding judge's repeated assertions of dominance over both the defense counsel, a Mr. Bauer, and the prosecuting attorney, a Mr. Holgren; the interplay between the two lawyers and the witnesses and each other; and the strange dynamics between the jurors outside the jury box–at lunch, under the supervision of an officer of the court, like school children, or outside the courtroom in the morning, waiting for it to open--forbidden to discuss the case. He remembered how attractive he thought the judge was, a lady in a flowing black robe that somehow managed to hint at a full figure, well maintained. Much to his surprise, he had found himself wanting to be elected foreman, and had tried to ingratiate himself with his fellows for that purpose. There were eight ladies, mostly middle-aged and working class, and four men: Rubin, an older man with a neatly trimmed white beard and mustache, a young Chinese American, and an ex-Navy man who, Rubin thought, would be his chief rival. Rubin wanted to guide the discussions in the jury room when at last they were led there by the bailiff, to analyze the relevant facts, to propose possibilities of interpretation, to demonstrate what he liked to think of as his critical intelligence, and then to persuade his fellow jurors that he was right and the defendant was guilty. Or innocent. He couldn't remember what verdict he had first intended to promote.

The case came back to him with astonishing clarity. Felonious assault and using a firearm while committing a felony. Three black soldiers who had had too much to drink had parked their car on their way into some sort of carnival on the grounds of a high school in the area. The soldier who owned the car kept a small automatic pistol in the glove compartment. One of his companions, Staff Specialist Beard, a big man built like a heavyweight boxer, had noticed it and slipped it into his pocket on his way out of the car. They had parked, apparently rather carelessly, near another car from which a large family of Chicanos, complete with small children, was emerging just at that moment. It turned out that the relationships were not entirely familial; the group was essentially a small tribe with a chief, a very short, powerfully built man, Juan Aguirre, who, it was claimed, had called a younger man to help with a small child. The younger man's nickname was alleged to be "Boy." That was the spark: the drunken soldier who owned the car, hearing Aguirre call "Boy!," assumed that he was the victim of a racial insult, and set out to rectify the matter immediately. Whatever was about to take place at that moment was at once defused by Staff Specialist Beard, who calmed the drunk, shook Aguirre's hand, wished them all a nice day, and turned to go to the carnival with the other two soldiers. But Aguirre called "Boy!" again, the drunken soldier whirled around and rushed him, and in no time found himself pinned against the car by the much stronger Chicano–who, it turned out at the trial, was himself a veteran and had been trained in karate. Whatever he was going to do to the drunken soldier, however, was aborted by a blow to his jaw delivered by Staff Specialist Beard, who was then threatened with physical harm

by Aguirre's consort. Beard took the gun from his pocket, pointed it at
the lady, yelled "Do you want to die, bitch?"–Rubin remembered the line
distinctly because the rhetorical question seemed inconsistent with the
appellation–and then got on one knee and proceeded to try to eject the
clip from the pistol. A round fell out of the clip and rolled away, later to
be found by one of the policemen dispatched to the scene--an Evidence
Specialist, Rubin recalled–but Beard was not otherwise successful. "It all
happened so fast!" That was the chief point of agreement among all the
witnesses. But there was no doubt, either, that Beard had broken
Aguirre's jaw and that he had pointed the gun, operational or not, at the
lady.

To his surprise and chagrin, Rubin was not elected foreman of the
jury. The Navy veteran with whom, Rubin had thought, he'd had a
pleasant breakfast a couple of days earlier, had obviously recognized
Rubin's ambition and set out to block it almost as soon as all the jurors
were seated around the table. The older man with the neatly trimmed
beard and mustache was already sitting at the head of the table, and the
ex-Navy man argued forcefully that in the interests of time and with due
respect for experience, the older man should be declared foreman
without further discussion and they should get on with it in the hopes of
coming to a verdict well before dinner time. The eight ladies nodded in
agreement, the older man said that he was willing, the Chinese American
concurred, and Rubin, feeling exposed and foolish, had no choice but to
go along. He had had no idea that he had been so transparent.

The ensuing discussion had taken quite a while. The facts were not
in dispute. Beard had done what he had done, and Aguirre had had
months of discomfort even after the necessary surgery. But who had
provoked what? Why had the instigator of the entire episode not been
called to the stand? Everyone had seen him during the first three days of
the trial, sitting on a bench outside the courtroom, waiting to be called to
testify; then he had disappeared. Where, exactly, had the cars been
parked? Why, instead of all the confusing descriptions of who had rushed
whom and wrestled one another against this car or that, had the jury not
been shown a diagram of vehicles, paths, and action? Rubin remembered
that he had been willing to agree to dismiss the charge of felonious
assault inasmuch as Beard had first tried to act as peacemaker and had
not struck Aguirre until the man was apparently about to maim his
friend. But he *had* taken the pistol, he *had* pointed it at the lady, he *had*
cried "Do you want to die, bitch?" As for his claim that he had tried to
eject the clip from the pistol, was that credible? Why hadn't he
succeeded?

It was the young Chinese American who brought Rubin around. First he asked for the pistol–it had been submitted to the jury among the items of physical evidence they were allowed to examine–inserted the empty clip, and then demonstrated that he could not eject it, just as Beard had said. Rubin was surprised. Then he asked Rubin a question: "If you agree to dismiss the charge of felonious assault, that is, that no felony was committed, how can you argue that Beard used a firearm in the commission of a felony?" Rubin had to grant the point. He had been the last holdout, he remembered now, for a guilty verdict, and his retreat was greeted with an audible sigh of relief by all the ladies: it was still early in the afternoon. After the foreman had announced the verdict of not guilty, the jury was polled, the defendant (probably at Mr. Bauer's suggestion, Rubin thought) shouted "Thank you!" to the jury, the judge met briefly with the jury and mistook Rubin for the foreman, which Rubin regarded as partial compensation, and then they were dismissed.

The defeated prosecutor, Mr. Holgren, had been waiting for them in the hall. He wanted to know what he had done wrong, whether he had offended the jury in some way. Rubin explained the demonstration and the reasoning that had led to their verdict, and then asked his own questions. The prosecutor said that the system was designed so that "we'd rather free the guilty than jail the innocent," that the instigator of the affair had faced charges of his own, had decided to plead guilty in the middle of Beard's trial, and had therefore not been called to the stand by either the prosecution or defense, and that there *had* been a diagram, drawn by the Evidence Specialist, but that it had been ruled inadmissible because it had been drawn after the cars had been moved. Rubin pondered this perspective while the few remaining jurors who had listened to the explanation melted away. "Now I've got two problems," Holgren told Rubin. "What are those?" Rubin asked. "One is that I've got to explain to Juan Aguirre why you didn't convict the man who broke his jaw," he said. "The other is living with Scott Bauer. He's all set to crow like a rooster."

What Rubin found particularly unsettling about the experience was his role in it. He still had doubts about the verdict: after all, Beard hadn't merely intervened, he had broken Aguirre's jaw. He still didn't understand why he had wanted to be the jury's foreman, and was still strangely disappointed by his failure. But the main source of his discomfiture was the responsibility of the power entrusted to him by the system that, Holgren had said, was weighted in presumption of innocence. "We'd rather free the guilty than jail the innocent." Had Beard been found guilty on both counts, he could have been sentenced to twenty years in jail. He probably wouldn't have received nearly so severe a sentence, but he certainly would have been sentenced to jail, and one-twelfth of the reason would have been Rubin's vote. On the other hand, as matters stood, Aguirre no doubt felt that Rubin's vote was one-twelfth of the reason he had been denied justice and compensation. "Look," Rubin wanted to say to Aguirre, "I didn't have a choice. I was called for jury duty, selected at random, approved by both lawyers and the judge, and had to base my decision not on the answers to questions I didn't get to ask but on the evidence we heard. You shouldn't have been such a smartass with those drunks, showing off for your lady. Sorry about your jaw, but don't go looking for more trouble than you can handle."

But Aguirre hadn't come to him for an explanation. Mr. Holgren had had to provide that, however unconvincingly. What Rubin had to explain to himself was why he had been so uncomfortable about having to make any kind of decision about guilt or innocence. It wasn't, he told himself, as if he'd never had to make decisions that affected people's lives very directly. He had voted, more than once, to put people out of the doctoral program at Michigan. One of the candidates thus ejected from his chosen career had wound up in Vietnam. Rubin did not know whether he had survived, any more than he knew what had happened to other people he had voted against in other contexts: not to interview, not to hire, not to promote to a tenured professorship. His role in those instances had not been pleasant, but he had always rationalized his decisions: he was upholding standards, was the short and long of it, standards as he saw them, and that was part of his job as an academician. Of course lives were affected, profoundly so, even if not as dramatically as what would have been in store for Staff Specialist Beard had the verdict gone against him. Surely it was the same throughout the professions. There were examinations, requirements, rituals of all kinds for entrance, and then, once a toehold had been gained, continued tests of ability, suitability, compatibility with the way things were, the council of elders, the royal court, the *Sanhedrin*. The establishment, as it was known in the seventies. He had been subjected to all of that himself, and once he had been accepted and become part of that establishment–tenure, doctoral committee chairmanships, author of reports and recommendations having to do with policies and procedures, membership on grant award committees, occasionally a recipient of a grant himself for one purpose or another, with quite a bit of leeway about how to spend the money–he had seen himself as a respected and respectable citizen of his world, upholding the best of the traditions he had inherited but always open to changes, to new ideas, to different perspectives. If he participated in and affirmed his agreement with decisions that the affected party found painful, there was always a compelling reason. He remembered an exchange with a graduate student deeply unhappy with a low grade he had given him for a very sloppy, disappointing paper, who had requested a better grade not in defense of his paper but in anxiety about his status in the program. "You ask me to change the rules of the game after the game has been played," Rubin had written in answer to the student's emotional plea, "but you do not consider how unfair that would be to those of your classmates who listened to and followed the instructions, did the work, found the time to correct their papers before they handed them in, and received grades reflecting the quality of their work–as did you." He heard nothing further from the student. He was sure he had done the right thing. What was so different about the trial, the discussion in the jury room, the verdict? And why did he remember the case so clearly twenty years later when–he realized with a start–he wasn't sure that he had taken his pills that morning?

Suddenly, staring at Harry's diaries, he knew. It was all very well for Holgren to say that the system was weighted in favor of the presumption of innocence; for the judge to insist that potential jurors affirm their belief in the defendant's innocence until proven guilty, to insist that the lawyers submit to her interpretation of the propriety and relevance of their questions and objections and the witnesses' testimony, and to instruct the jurors what to ignore and what not to discuss and how to proceed; for the ex-Navy man to block Rubin's desire to be foreman and to engineer the selection of his preferred alternative; for the discussion to be implicitly but tangibly foreshortened by the majority's desire to go home to supper. All that was a dance, carefully choreographed, no doubt, over many generations, and admittedly superior in many respects to almost every other such ritual of which Rubin had ever heard. But it did not disguise the ugliness of what had happened, the raw violence, the racial antipathy between the two little groups. A carelessly parked car and a shout of "Boy!" and suddenly their lives were as precarious as– well, as Harry's back in Greece in the nineteen forties, blowing up German troop trains. And the jury was the threat to Beard.

So it was the lack of cover that had troubled Rubin, he realized, the nakedness of the confrontation with the violence he and his fellow jurors were asked to inflict upon--or to spare--Staff Specialist Beard. Up to twenty years of jail. Say he'd been found guilty and he'd gotten only five years, with the possibility of parole after three, as well as having to reimburse Aguirre for medical expenses, time lost from work, and so on. All for a flash of misdirected temper, a sudden tug of misplaced loyalty.

A life ruined forever, surely. And yet, how did he know that those decisions he had made as a regular part of his academic responsibilities, not to grant tenure, not to hire, not to interview, not to pass, had not, in some instances, had similarly ruinous effects? Under the patina of civility, of tacit understanding, of gentlemen's agreements, under the banner of standards that somehow always defied precise definition, how many lives had he and his fellow committee members derailed, obstructed, forced into frustration, perhaps even despair? Rubin had a vision of unpaid bills, ruined marriages, abandoned children, grieving grandparents, former instructors once regarded as promising, now gaunt clerks at Walmart's with useless Ph.D.'s, experts on medieval heraldry or nineteenth century nature poetry growing old and grey in the kitchen utensils department, all because of some devastating witticism he had permitted himself at a too lengthy meeting of the Promotions Committee.

Too melodramatic, he told himself, still with Harry's diaries in his hands. No theme music from "Jaws," please, no piano thundering in the orchestra pit as the mustachioed villain ties the heroine to the railroad tracks. Enough to recognize the ubiquity of violence in its many different forms, and the possibilities of its commission afforded by its many disguises. What, after all, was the alternative? Not to participate, that's all. To be so afraid of being wrong that one refused to act. Refused to get involved. Refused, ever, to help. He remembered an argument he'd once had with a man, a Jew, who, because he was a conscientious objector, had served as some kind of medic in World War II. He had maintained that there was never any justification for killing anyone, under any circumstances. It wasn't a question of religion, the man had said, but of moral absolutes. On edge, Rubin described how his father had died in Berlin in 1938. "And if you had come by that alley," he had asked, "you wouldn't have lifted a finger to help him, is that right?" "No," the man had said, "I would have tried to stop them. At least I hope so." "How?" Rubin had pressed him. "With pleas? With money? With Talmudic arguments?" "I don't know," the man had said. "But not with violence." "Then they would have killed you both," Rubin had said, "and you know it. But you would have kept your moral superiority, your self-righteousness, and what you think of as your integrity. You remind me of all the *goyim* and some crazy Jews, too, who want the Israelis to throw flowers at the suicide bombers, the Peace and Justice crowd always willing to lecture Jews about the futility, even the immorality, of any measures of self-defense except talk. 'Negotiations,' they call it. What if there's no one to negotiate with? How do you negotiate with murderers? Don't you understand that your version of holiness absolutely stinks, positively *reeks*, of sanctimony? To hell with you." And he had gotten up and walked off.

It's always a trade-off, he thought: giving a poor or lazy student a low grade to protect the value of the high grades he gave to insightful and hard-working students; refusing to hire a questionable candidate or to keep a weak instructor to protect both present and future students and, not coincidentally, the reputation of the department; demonstrating, in a review, that a colleague's book or research proposal or stance vis-à-vis the canon–the traditional materials of the traditional curriculum--had little to recommend it, despite the colleague's standing in the profession, risking his lifelong enmity. Surely all professions exhibited analogous dilemmas. Ultimately all such standards were arbitrary, all decisions were personal, and all discussions of them had to remain as private as possible if the institution, the organization, the establishment were not to dissolve into permanent internecine warfare.

He had seen the consequences of revelations of who had said what about whom, and how it had been said. The poison lasted unto death. Academicians might not write books about the toxicity that occasionally bubbled to the surface in their universities, as did journalists and former government officials about the venom more and more apparent in the Bush administration, but that was probably only because of the limitations of the market. There was no escaping responsibility for the judgments one made or refused to make, but you didn't have to trumpet your opinion of someone else's shortcomings to the entire world. So, imperfect though the system was, with its preference for freeing the guilty over jailing the innocent, even some of its disguises of its own violence could be justified as relatively humane. Process *was* important, sometimes critically so.

Had Harry written anything about any of this? Talk about having to participate in raw violence, what could be more violent than blowing up troop trains? He started to flip the pages of the first diary, "***Personal Diary:*** 1941-50." He lighted on a passage written some time in 1944.

> *"But just how many men will go?" I asked. "I think six will be enough," he said. "And how many of them in this mule pack train?" "It's a bit smaller than we'd hoped," he said. "Only about thirty or forty men and about the same number of mules." My face must have shown how crazy this seemed to me. "Don't worry," he said, grinning. "It won't be nearly as bad as it sounds." I didn't tell him what I thought. But I couldn't fall asleep in my sleeping bag for hours. And when I finally did, it*

seemed to be only for a few minutes before an andarte woke me up, muttering "fyge amesos." It was still dark. The Major said that we'd eat on the way, and we started down the trail, six men, five of them crazy and one full of misgivings, and two mules, who gave no indication of their opinions.

We had walked for perhaps four hours when the Major signaled us to halt. We had reached a very narrow and steep valley. The main trail, a path not more than two or three feet wide, skirting the edge of a soft shale cliff, was directly across from us. There was a sheer precipitous drop of some forty feet from the path down to the little mountain stream racing through the rocky chasm below. Above, the jagged irregular face of the cliff rose almost perpendicularly to the sky. There were no trees, no bushes, no boulders for protection. Anyone who had started to come around the cliff would have to continue to the other end of the path. Turning around would have been impossible.

The Major deployed two of the men to the right and two to the left. He and I remained in the center, behind a large rock. He pulled out a big piece of kalomboki from his pocket and began to gnaw at it. I wasn't hungry and sat staring at the path across from us, trying to visualize what was going to happen.

We waited for about a century before the men on the right gave the bird call signaling that they saw the Germans coming. A moment later we saw them too, coming up the mountain ever so slowly, beating their mules and swearing as they zigzagged back and forth along the twisting, narrow path. The day had turned hot, but all days are hot when you are climbing mountains. They had shed some of their clothing. More importantly, they were not carrying their weapons—we saw them dangling from the backs of their mules. But the two Germans in front, the advance guard, had their guns on their shoulders and I saw the andartes noting the fact. Some of the Germans were singing, and one was sarcastically describing the scenic splendors of the Greek mountains as if he were reading a railway travel poster. Suddenly I saw Spiro, on my right, rise and hurl a grenade across the narrow valley, blowing out the path behind the last mule. Only a split second later there was another explosion on the left and the track disappeared in front *of the column. The mule train stretched out in front of us, unable to advance or to retreat and without any cover. Our three Bren guns went into action immediately. All that could be heard interspersed with the chattering of the guns were the screams of the Germans, the braying of the mules, and the thuds of the bodies hitting the river bed below us. Our attention was primarily on the mules since all their weapons were on their backs, and with the animals out of the way, we would face nothing but forty defenseless men. The Germans tried to get to their guns, but the mules fell to their death. One German was climbing the sheer face of the cliff, trying to escape, but a burst of fire caught him in his back and he tumbled haphazardly down the slope into the stream. Some mules and men were groaning and thrashing around below us. We continued to fire and after a minute or so, all was quiet. The trail was stained with blood everywhere. The scarred rock looked as if some giant animal had tried to claw his way along the face of the cliff. We had executed them all, men and beasts. They hadn't gotten off a single shot.*

We loaded some of the salvageable weapons and supplies on our mules and left a man to guard the remainder until it could be hauled away. The Major looked at the scene one last time before we moved out. "Stupid fools," he said. "They never learn." He turned to me. "Do you see? There will always be a part of Greece that is free. We will always hold these mountains." I nodded. I understood..

Jesus Leaping Christ, Rubin thought. No wonder Harry had never said much about his time in Greece. The joke about the mules was unexpected–Harry had not been given much to joking--but the detail that fascinated Rubin was the German sarcastically describing the gorgeous scenery like a railway travel poster. Complaining in a way to amuse his fellows on what had had to be a very difficult climb. Harry must have understood enough German–perhaps he knew Yiddish from home–to pick up not only what the man had been saying but his intent. Rubin could imagine it: "*Ja, meine Herren, hier sind die herrlichen Berge Griechenlands, das Heim des ersten Herrenvolk in ganz Europa--*" and then the grenades and the terrible machine gun fire.

This didn't sound all that heroic. An ambush that, as Harry had correctly said, had been an execution. Necessary, of course, and no doubt arduous, and surely not without its effects on Harry's psyche, but it hadn't been combat as Rubin had always imagined it. He turned more pages. And there *was* a passage of the kind he had expected.

Dusk fell slowly, almost painfully. We were divided into five groups, to attack from different directions. My group was to approach down a shallow ditch running perpendicular to the railroad track, meeting it just south of the café. While the fighting for the station was going on, we were to sneak down the track laying demolition charges behind us. The signal was given. We went single file down the mountain, silently, quietly, expectantly. To our great disappointment, we saw the villagers leave: they had learned of the attack. Then the Germans must have as well, and we had lost the element of surprise. We came to a flat field lying in front of us in the darkness. Then, as we passed by a small clump of trees, we saw a light in the distance as if through a hole in the wall: our target, the station. We found the small ditch angling to the right in the direction of the railroad track. Half crouched, we sloshed through the mud, shielded by a waist-high stand of wheat on either side. We approached the buildings of the station. There was no sign of any life. At last we reached our position between the station and a pillbox on the track south of the station. Our watches reached 2320, the deadline, and ticked on. Nothing happened. We waited. Then, just before 2345, a white Verey light came up from the station, illuminating the entire sky as it arced its way over the buildings. All hell broke loose behind us at the pillbox, and, as if in answer, the other pillbox, far to the north, began firing. We lay in the mud, listening to the rattle of the machine guns, the heavy mortar fire, the barking of the rifles, waiting for the signal to send us storming down the tracks. Then an armored train pulled into the station, fire coming from a gun mounted on its last car. Not only had they known that we were coming, they had had time to call for reinforcements. The mortar fire grew heavier, and although many of the projectiles were duds, many were not. Parachute flares flew over us and every mortar in the German Army seemed directed against us. Costas, Yannis, and I had just gone out to blow up a small bridge crossing our little ditch when the train backed out of the station until its last car was just over the bridge. We were already under it laying the explosives. Several Germans jumped off the train to investigate.

The men back in the ditch opened fire. Costas and Yannis ran out the other side of the bridge and down the ditch in the opposite direction. I pressed myself into the mud. Then, when the gun on the last car started shooting in the direction Costas and Yannis had run, I ran the other way, toward the andartes back in the ditch. They were starting to retreat. Soon Captain Mortimer, Peter, and I were alone in the ditch. The Germans were attempting to clear the path on either side of the track. We saw several Germans jump off the train, spread out, and head toward us. They moved only when the sky was lit up by flares fired from the train behind them; we moved the moment the flares subsided. I had my Marlin submachine gun on full automatic with my finger on the trigger. I knew that one shot would draw all the guns on the train down on us, and I wasn't at all anxious to do that, but I wasn't going to go down by myself either. The Germans seemed to run out of flares, and back we went through the flat field, heading for a mountain pass beyond the village. The battle continued below, but our part was over. Not only didn't we succeed, we had taken a severe beating.

Rubin paused. Harry had known far more about violence than he had ever let on. One tough man. Never lost that military bearing. Always very direct. And he had become a professor, of all things, a professor of architecture. Well, why not? As Gerald liked to point out, teasing him, he himself had come to this country at the age of eight, "unable to speak a mumblin' word," as Gerald put it, and had become a professor of English and American literature. So why shouldn't Harry Rosenberg, New York-born son of Russian Jewish refugees from some horrible pogrom, find himself shooting Germans in Greece and teaching budding architects in Columbus? Life was one unpredictable mess of surprises of all kinds.

In fact, he thought, this was normality for uncountable millions: upheavals, unspeakable violence, tragedy, brutal death. What had happened to Rubin's father, what had almost happened to Harry's parents, what Harry had done to that sarcastic German, what the Germans had done to the Greeks–it was all the usual stuff of human history. White Americans had built their great democracy, their altars to personal freedom, their hallowed way of life not just by exterminating most of the natives of the continent   and confining the wretched remnants to waste lands the "settlers" did not want, not just by importing Africans like so many beasts of burden condemned as expendable property for unborn generations, but also by constructing glorious myths attesting to their own valor, their values, their intrinsic superiority. And of the ways in which those myths had taken root, none had been more effective than Hollywood's. Small-town America, Mickey Rooney and Judy Garland, Lassie, Jimmy Stewart, not a cotton field or a mining camp or a sweat shop in sight. Rubin remembered how Ronald Reagan, talking to reporters about World War II, described what a heroic American pilot's last thoughts had been just before he entered eternity. The old President had been describing a scene from a World War II movie that had become part of the furniture of his mind. The stories of the Bible, the Homeric legends, the tales of the Vikings, of pirates, pioneers, cowboys and Indians, cops and robbers, Al Capone and Elliott Ness, the saga of the Corleones, the Kennedys, band leaders, ball players, and boxers–it was all served up in living color with theme music and pop corn, forever indistinguishable in popular culture from televised church services, wrestling matches, and other carnival acts led by sweating impresarios.

The bell rang. Rubin put Harry's diaries on his desk and went downstairs to open the door. It was Wayne, the condominium association's manager and resident philosopher, expert on all things in need of repair, present or potential, and, Rubin had found, an inexhaustible teller of stories, many of which defied belief but to whose veracity Wayne swore on his mother's Bible. Rubin was not at all sure that the lady had ever *had* a Bible. Or that, as Wayne claimed, she had been a burlesque dancer, a career she had had to give up when she had become pregnant with him.

"Yes, Wayne, how are you? Good to see you! What can I do for you?"

"It's what I can do for you, Doc," Wayne said. He always called Rubin "Doc," never "Mr. Rubin" or "Professor," and the notion that he might have called him "Walter" did not seem to have occurred to him. Nor had Rubin suggested it. "Can I come in? It'll just be a few minutes."

"Of course, of course!" Rubin said. "How about a cup of coffee? It's still fresh, and I've got some pastry rolls--"

"No, just the coffee will be fine, Doc," Wayne said. "I'm always up for another cup of coffee, ever since I was ten. Coffee was a way of life in my family." They went into the kitchen, Rubin motioned Wayne to a chair and poured a cup of coffee for him, and then, since there was still plenty in the pot, he poured a cup for himself. Wayne, a tall, rather gangly man of about sixty who always wore a baseball cap–Rubin knew he was completely bald under it–positioned himself in the chair so that his feet wouldn't interfere with Rubin's, pushed his cap back slightly, and nodded appreciatively.

"Figured I'd take a chance on you being in, Doc," Wayne said, waving away Rubin's offer of cream and sugar. "Thanks, I take it black–what it is, Doc, is your roof. One of the boys thought he saw a couple of loose shingles on your roof, on the back side, so I came over to take a look and yep, we need to get up there and fix it before you start telling us your attic is floating away and your ceiling is coming down. Have you noticed any leaks anywhere, upstairs, I mean?"

"No," Rubin said, surprised. "Why would shingles come loose? We haven't had any really strong storms this year that I remember. Just the nails working themselves loose over time?"

"Could be," Wayne said. "Could be Old Man Time. Often is. Things never stay the same, you know. Just like a marriage, certainly my marriages. Never stayed the same, none of 'em. Or could be some critter–squirrels, most likely–gnawing here, gnawing there, loosening a corner, say, and the next thing you know, some raccoon gets curious, they do, you know, always poking around, thinking that everything's their business and maybe they can eat it. And then the water starts to work at whatever they've begun, and the mischief gets serious. You can't argue with water, you know. Water wins. What you have to do is to persuade it to go elsewhere, that's your only defense."

"Ummmm," Rubin said. "I'm sure you're right. So you came to tell me that you're going to fix my roof?"

"Oh, we'll fix it, all right," Wayne said, taking a big gulp of his coffee. "The question is, when would be a good time for you? There's going to be some stomping around and pounding and yelling, you know, and we'd probably like to do it when we wouldn't disturb you too much, although we'd like to do it in the morning if that's all right."

"How long would it take, do you think?"

"Don't know for sure until I get up there myself," Wayne said. "But I wouldn't think it would take more than an hour, two at the very most. When would be a good day?"

"Tomorrow?"

"Uh, no, not tomorrow, although we could go up there and see just how many shingles we need to replace and if there's any other damage we need to take care of–then we'd have to go order the shingles or see if the lumber yard has the right kind in stock, they probably don't. We don't keep a supply of shingles up at the shed, you know, wouldn't be practical, don't have that much spare space as it is."

"Yes, I see," Rubin said. His mind was still full of Harry's exploits in 1944. "Lots of logistics involved, I see that. Planning and scheduling, like a military campaign. Deploying the troops to maximum advantage."

"Well, maybe, in a way," Wayne said, a little uneasily. "That wasn't anything they asked me about when I was in the Coast Guard. I didn't know you were in the service, Doc."

Rubin laughed. "No, I wasn't, Wayne," he said. "But I've been reading a diary–did you know that Professor Rosenberg was in World War II and saw a lot of action?"

"No!" Wayne said. "Professor Rosenberg? I knew he was a feisty little old guy, but I had no idea he'd been in the war! In combat, you say?"

"In Greece, with the Greek underground," Rubin said. He saw that Wayne was very interested. "Another cup of coffee? I think there's enough here. And what about a cinnamon roll?"

"Well, sure, if I'm not taking too much of your time, Doc," Wayne said. Rubin could tell that he wanted to hear more about Harry. He poured the coffee and got the roll.

"Harry left me some of his papers," Rubin said, "and among them were some diaries, including one he had kept of his time in the war. He had parachuted behind the German lines, along with others–Americans, British, some Canadians–to join one of the major Greek underground groups who were fighting the Germans. You may remember that the Germans invaded Greece to help out the Italians, who had gotten pretty badly beaten by the Greeks."

"No, Doc, I don't know a whole lot about World War II," Wayne said, munching a cinnamon roll. "I mean, I've seen a lot of the movies, you know, about us fighting the Krauts and the Japs too, you know, and of course I know how it came out, but you know, I wasn't born until 1946, so by the time I got to school they didn't have much left to say about it."

"Yes, of course," Rubin said. "Well, the Greek resistance movement was fierce, first against the Italians, and then against the Germans, and the Allies helped them not just with supplies and equipment but also with volunteers like Harry. The trouble was that the Greeks were divided against each other, with a large communist group and an anti-communist group fighting each other as well as the Germans."

"Fighting each other?" Wayne asked with wonder. "You mean, like these Iraqis today? What you call them, Sunnis and Shites or whatever they are?"

"Well, yes, in a way, except of course that those are branches of Islam with a long history of conflict--" Rubin saw that he was losing Wayne in his reversion to his former profession. "It was about control, really, under the convenient labels of the time, communism and anti-communism. The question really was who was to be in charge once the Germans had been driven out."

"Ah," Wayne said. "It's always about control, you know. What side was the professor on?"

"Oh, with the anti-communists," Rubin said. "Harry's parents had been refugees from Russia, before he was born, of course, but he grew up, he told me, in a household that was anti-communist because it was so anti-Russian. He had no use for the communists, Russian, Greek, any kind. But that wasn't nearly as important to him as was doing his duty as an American. He was very patriotic."

"Really!" Wayne said. "And I thought I knew him pretty well! That never came up!"

"What did you talk to him about?" Rubin wanted to know.

"Birds," Wayne said immediately. "He knew a lot about birds, and that kinda surprised me, because I like birds too, although I'm more interested in seabirds, you know, osprey, gulls, shrikes, and I like hawks and falcons and eagles, too, but he liked song birds, mostly. But we talked about other things too, you know, buildings–of course he knew a lot about that, although maybe not so much about carpentry and plumbing, which kinda surprised me–but other things too. Life, quite a bit about life."

Rubin knew that meant Wayne's various marriages. He could never remember how many times Wayne had been married. He wasn't sure that Wayne could either. "What do you remember Harry saying about life?" he asked. "I mean, anything in particular?"

"Well, I'll tell you, although I wouldn't if the professor were still alive," Wayne said. "He didn't care much for his children, either one of them. And that kinda surprised me, you know. He'd told me that his first marriage hadn't been a happy one, like mine wasn't neither, nor the next couple, but I never had any children, and I used to think that maybe if I had it might have been different with whoever the mother would have been. So he said, no, not necessarily, his children hadn't helped his marriage, his first one, you know, not a bit, maybe made it worse, and then they had grown up and he'd found he didn't like either one of them. I never met the daughter, but I met the son, and to tell you the truth, Doc, I didn't care much for him myself." He drained his coffee. Rubin gave him what was left in the pot.

"Why not?" he asked, remembering his last encounter with Marvin and curious whether Wayne had found him unpleasant for the same reasons.

"I thought he was rude, not just to me, which he was, but to his Dad too, and he seemed so full of himself, didn't have any interest in anything that didn't have a direct bearing on him or his schedule or his whatyoucallit, position, I guess, and he was so impatient with his Dad, you know, the professor was over eighty and you'd think the son would indulge him a bit, but no, he sure didn't. No, I didn't care for him at all."

"In fact," Rubin said calmly, "a self-centered, egotistical, unfeeling bastard."

Wayne grinned. "Yes, you might put it that way," he said. "So you met him too."

"Unfortunately, yes," Rubin said. "And I agree with you. I was surprised too, because Harry wasn't at all like that. Harry cared about a lot of things, and was loyal to a lot of things. As I say, patriotic, for one thing."

"So he fought in the war," Wayne said.

"Yes," Rubin said, "fought and made a bad marriage and somehow got out of that and changed his profession—he had been in practice on his own, before he became a professor--" Wayne nodded, apparently familiar with that part of Harry's history—"and then something happened, I'm not sure what, that made him decide to leave Columbus after his second wife died and come up here. Quite a change at his age. He must have been almost sixty then." Had Harry confided in Wayne, perhaps in their conversations about birds or his disappointment in his children? One thing always led to another, especially with Wayne.

"Well, Doc, I know there was something that happened in Columbus with the professor," Wayne said, "because he sort of hinted at something, pretty mysterious, but I could never quite get him to tell me what it was all about. I didn't want to ask directly, you know, couldn't do that. I had the feeling that it was definitely something on the other side of the law, not that he was himself involved in it, but that he knew about it or at least was pretty sure he did. Have you read all of his diary?"

"No," Rubin said, "just the first part having to do with his time in Greece."

"Well," Wayne said, "you might find something if you keep reading. Let me know—I liked the old gent a lot, you know, and I've got to tell you, I'm curious. Although that's not always a good thing, as one of my wives told me one time. Marlene. No, it wasn't Marlene. She just got so pissed at me she always clammed up. It was the one who never stopped telling me about all my faults, Benita. Benita never stopped. I was too damn curious for my own good, she said. Maybe the professor was, too. Doc, I've got to run along—we'll let you know when we get the shingles and then we'll pick a morning when we can get that done, won't take more than an hour or two." He got up. "Thanks very much for the coffee and roll, Doc–always nice talking to you."

Rubin got up and opened the door for him. "Always a pleasure, Wayne," he said. "If I'm not home when you want to schedule the repair, just leave a message on the machine."

"Sure, Doc," Wayne said. "Thanks again." He left. Rubin watched him go, wondering what Harry might have said that had made Wayne curious about whatever had happened in Columbus. Or what Harry had been curious about. And maybe looked into. Whatever it had been, it had involved Nathan Goldstein.

Chapter XVII
Nathan, 1978-1979

Years later, when Nathan looked back on this period of his life, he recalled the time as a blur of frustration: consultations, preparation of testimony, hearings, appeals, legalities, struggles, humiliation, a great deal of effort but too little, too late. After getting fired by Chuck Schneider– something blowzy Olga had achieved after Nathan had met her advances with evasions--he had survived on pickup jobs that came to him largely as the result of his friendship with Sid Greenstein. His torrid affair with Cheryl Weinglass had eventually ended badly. People moved in and out of his circle of acquaintances, sometimes to help him and encourage him, but sometimes to exploit him. But in the center of all the turmoil was his determination not to quit. He had set out to be a licensed architect, and had acquired a business education as well, and his goal was to combine the disciplines and show what could be done, partly for the sake of his profession, partly for the clients he would have, but mostly because it was his commitment to what he felt was his identity. He remembered a conversation with a German Jew, visiting relatives in Cleveland. After the conclusion of World War II, he had moved back to Germany and resumed his German citizenship. "But why, for God's sake?" Nathan had wanted to know. "Why would you want to live in that country again, after everything that happened?" "Because I have a right to do so," said the man, eyes blazing. "Because I want them to see me, walking around, free, a man, just as I had been. Because I want them to wait on me in the stores, to sit next to me on the bus, to stand next to me in line, waiting, whether to vote or to go to a movie. Because I can. Because it is my right." Nathan felt a sudden surge of kinship. It wasn't a question of intruding where they were not wanted. It was a question of having the courage and the steadfastness to claim what was rightfully theirs.

*****

Frank Leighburg's involvement produced agreement on the part of the State Board of Examiners of Architects to grant Nathan a hearing on his petition. Leighburg, reviewing the Ohio Revised Code in some detail, had found passages highly relevant to Nathan's status.

> *Section 4703.08A ... The state board of examiners of architects may, in lieu of all examinations, accept satisfactory evidence of any one of the qualification set forth under the divisions of this section....*
>
> *A diploma of graduation from an accredited architectural school or college showing that the applicant has completed a technical and professional course of not less than five years' duration which course is approved by the board... and, in addition thereto, has had at least three years of satisfactory experience, two years of which shall have been in the office of a reputable architect meeting all the qualifications for practice under sections 47603.01 to 4703.19 of the Revised Code....*

Nathan met those requirements and had the documentation, and Leighburg agreed that his service as Prescott's substitute instructor in the professional practice course at Ohio State, when Prescott had been in the hospital, would meet the requirement of the last part of the statute: *" ... provided the board may require applicants under this division to furnish satisfactory evidence of knowledge of professional practice and supervision of construction."* The evidence would include Wilson's letter thanking Nathan for his work in teaching Prescott's "Professional Practice" course, Nathan's MBA, and letters from his previous employers. Particularly telling would be Prescott's letter of recommendation, describing Nathan as "regarded as one of the top students to graduate from Ohio State University and highly qualified to be brilliant in the architectural profession."

As for Wheeler's destruction of Nathan's Ohio graphics examinations, he had claimed, on the phone with Leighburg, that he had not been aware of the part of Section 4743.02 of the Ohio Revised Code that stated that *"... examination papers of each applicant shall be open for inspection by the applicant or his attorney for at least ninety days subsequent to the announcement of the applicant's grade...."* Leighburg agreed with Nathan that Wheeler was probably lying, but, he said, there would be no way to prove it. And if Wheeler had been ordered to destroy the exams, as was likely, he certainly wouldn't admit it at the hearing.

When they arrived at the hearing, they found Charnesky seated at the head of a long conference table with four other members of the State Board on his left. Wheeler and a tall young black man were seated on his right. Nathan thought that Wheeler seemed pale and nervous, fiddling with his pen and papers, but he did manage to give Nathan a slight nod. Nathan, Leighburg, and Leighburg's assistant, Sara Mandel, were motioned to three chairs, isolated by empty chairs on their right and left, at the foot of the table. The tall young black man turned out be Jonah Richards, Assistant Attorney General of the State of Ohio. Nathan wondered how many Assistant Attorney Generals the State of Ohio employed. Richards, who seemed only a little older than Nathan, no doubt would have something to prove on the way up his career ladder. A stenographer sat in the corner of the room ready with her machine to record every word of the hearing. Leighburg had requested her presence. The Board had agreed, but at Nathan's expense.

After the opening formalities, Leighburg began by saying that he would present satisfactory evidence showing that Mr. Goldstein had complied with Section 4703.08 Part A of the Ohio Revised Code and was fully qualified to be a licensed architect in the State of Ohio. Richards offered neither an opening statement of his own nor a challenge to Leighburg's. Leighburg asked the members of the Board to identify themselves "for the record," a phrase that would be repeated with what Nathan found maddening frequency throughout the hearing. The members did so. Then Leighburg stated that Mr. Goldstein's position was that the hearing was being held "pursuant to Section 4703.08 Part A of the Ohio Revised Code," and Richards immediately objected on the grounds of irrelevance, inasmuch as Mr. Goldstein had not passed the NCARB professional examination.

Nathan was so astounded that he started to speak, although Leighburg had instructed him to remain silent unless he was asked a direct question. Leighburg squeezed his arm just in time. Talk about Catch-22, Nathan thought. My argument is that the statute provides an alternative to the examination, and this man seems to be saying that I have to pass the examination to claim the right to that alternative! But Leighburg was making the same point in more legalistic language. The language was an arena in which the attorneys jousted back and forth, thrusting and parrying, as conscious, Nathan thought, of the stenographer and her machine as any combatants in the Coliseum might have been of the Emperor and his court. Their duel seemed to be mostly "for the record," perhaps for eventual exegesis by law professors and the admiration of their students.

"For the record," Nathan heard Leighburg saying, "I want this Board to understand that my office has called Mr. Wheeler on two occasions regarding the kind of evidence this Board might require to demonstrate Mr. Goldstein's knowledge of professional practice and supervision of construction, and that Mr. Wheeler, on both occasions, stated that he had no information regarding this matter, so for the record, we ask again, this time of the entire Board, if the Board would specify the criteria by which it would judge Mr. Goldstein's knowledge of professional practice and supervision of construction."

"Objection," Richards said. Nathan was still wincing at Leighburg's use of the phrase "supervision of construction." He had told Leighburg several times that architects don't supervise construction, they observe it on behalf of their clients, even though the word "supervision" was in the statute. The difference was important, Nathan had insisted, contractually as well as substantively.

"On what basis?" Leighburg asked.

"For the record," Richards said. "My objection will become clearer when I call Mr. Wheeler as a witness."

"At this point," Leighburg said sharply, "your intention to call Mr. Wheeler as a witness is irrelevant. I have asked this Board a direct question concerning any criteria they might have that would lead us–Mr. Goldstein and his attorneys–to understand that they will objectively evaluate his knowledge of the professional practice of architecture and the supervision of construction."

"I am not sure," Richards replied, "that they have any such criteria. Again, this will become clearer after I call Mr. Wheeler as a witness."

Round and round, Nathan thought. It was getting increasingly hard to follow what the lawyers were disagreeing about. Leighburg attempted to introduce Frank Wilson's letter to Nathan, thanking him for teaching Prescott's "Professional Practice" course, and dated exactly two and a half years earlier, as evidence of Nathan's knowledge of professional practice.

"I object," Richards said.

"For what reason?" Leighburg asked.

"For the record," Richards said. "How does that letter have anything to do with his failure to pass the examination, or with his qualifications for a license without passing the examination? I object to all evidence you're submitting today except for what I've already stipulated to concerning Mr. Goldstein's degrees and experience, insofar, and only insofar, as they apply to Section 4703.07 of the Ohio Revised Code."

Nathan sighed. He wanted to light a cigarette, but saw that no one else was smoking, and pushed his pack of Marlboros back into his shirt pocket.

Leighburg was speaking with considerable firmness, enunciating his words clearly and modulating his tone as he directed himself not only to Richards but to all the Board members. But they sat there impassively, giving no sign of following the argument.

Leighburg was enumerating Nathan's qualifications in great detail when Charnesky suddenly interrupted, startling both Richards and Leighburg. "Obviously," Charnesky said, "Mr. Goldstein's academic and other qualifications have already been approved by this Board. That's why he was allowed to sit for the NCARB exam. We use the examination process to see if the candidate is fit, because our first responsibility is to the public, to protect the public's health, safety, and welfare. Now the law you keep referring to, Mr. Legbeg, Section 4703.08--"

"Leighburg," Leighburg corrected him.

"Yes, sorry, *Leigh-burg*, that law hasn't been used since 1931, isn't that right, Jim?" Charnesky continued, turning to Wheeler, who seemed to nod. "That's what I believe is called a grandfather clause," Charnesky continued, now looking at Richards, who also nodded on cue. "So at the time the law was written," Charnesky said to Leighburg, "in 1931, when registration of architects in Ohio went into effect, there were a number of people already practicing architecture in this state, of course, and these were the people admitted under 4703.08, to get the law on the books, you see." Charnesky's manner and tone suggested that he had now clarified everything. Nathan glanced at Leighburg. Had he been outflanked? Was there an answer to this? Was his whole case disappearing into the era of the Hoover administration? Who had been in charge of things in Ohio at that time, or did that matter?

"I certainly don't want to interpret your remarks, or any Board member's remarks," Leighburg said, "but I would ask at this time whether the Board is now seeking to introduce evidence into this hearing."

"No, I'm not," Charnesky said.

"For the record," Richards said quickly, "at this point in time, whatever the president of the Board says can be evidence or it doesn't have to be evidence. The president is expressing his knowledge and expertise. There is case law on top of case law that supports that proposition. The president, who is conducting this hearing, can act as though he were a judicial officer."

"Please proceed with your presentation, Mr. *Leigh-burg*," Charnesky said, again pronouncing Leighburg's name with exaggerated care. Nathan thought he seemed very pleased with himself.

Leighburg went into some detail about what Nathan had done as the instructor of Prescott's course on professional practice, and what text he had used. It had been approved and printed by the American Institute of Architects, he said. To his surprise, Nathan saw a frown flit over Charnesky's face at the reference. Leighburg continued, describing the examinations Nathan had given, and how he had determined the grades the students received. "I understand," Leighburg said, "that every member of this Board is also a member of the AIA, and I assume, therefore, that you are all familiar with the AIA book and its relevance to the professional practice of architecture, and to the architect's observations of construction." Nathan was pleased that this time Leighburg had gotten it right. Leighburg amplified the point by citing various passages from the AIA's "Owner-Contractor Agreement," dated, he emphasized, April, 1978, "just last month." Nathan relaxed a little; his case seemed to be getting stronger. But Leighburg continued along this line for almost fifteen minutes, and Nathan began to worry again that the fixed expressions across the table indicated mental absence, not attention. When Leighburg finally finished, Richards swung into action immediately.

"I would like to call my first witness under direct examination, Mr. James P. Wheeler," Richards said. His tone suggested that now, at last, they would all get to the heart of the matter. Charnesky and the other members of the Board shifted in their chairs and sat up straighter.

Richards quickly established who Wheeler was, what his position was, what his duties were, what qualifications he possessed, and that he did indeed know "an individual named Nathan Goldstein."

Wheeler is nervous, Nathan thought: these are boilerplate questions, and he's not snapping the answers back as briskly as they're being asked. He's anticipating something he doesn't want to discuss.

It took a while to get there, however. Richards asked that the record show that Mr. Goldstein's request for a hearing had been received and that the request had been granted. He then proceeded to question Wheeler about the limitations on the rights of individuals to inspect the Board's records, including examination questions and their answers, and established, at some length, that Mr. Goldstein had failed the NCARB examination twice, in December of both 1976 and 1977. Damn it, Nathan thought, he's going over things that everybody here knows and are irrelevant anyway. What a waste of time. He glanced at Leighburg, inclining his head to suggest that he ought to object, but his lawyer remained silent and expressionless.

"Is Mr. Goldstein nevertheless eligible to take the NCARB

examination yet again?" Richards asked.

"Yes, in December, this coming December," Wheeler said.

"Now, to your knowledge," Richards said, looking first at Charnesky and then at Wheeler, "does Mr. Goldstein or his case come under any of the grandfather provisions of the laws governing licensing of architects, I believe that would be Section 4703.08 of the Ohio Revised Code?" Wheeler hesitated, glancing at Charnesky, who suddenly looked concerned. "Strike that," Richards said quickly, correcting himself with a shake of his head. "Withdraw my last question. To the best of your knowledge, Mr. Wheeler, without reference to Mr. Goldstein, what are the requirements for a license to practice architecture in the State of Ohio?"

"Under Section 4703.07 of the Ohio Revised Code, the applicant must sit for the NCARB examination," Wheeler said.

"Everyone, without exception?"

"All candidates who apply under 4703.07, yes," Wheeler said.

"Does this Board allow individuals to obtain licenses to practice architecture without taking the NCARB examination?"

"Not under 4703.07, no," Wheeler said.

"Now this next question is very important," Richards said portentously. "Does this Board allow individuals who have *not* passed the NCARB examination, does it grant them licenses to practice architecture in Ohio? Do you want me to rephrase that question?"

"No, you don't need to rephrase it," Wheeler said. "The answer is yes it does, but only under Parts B and C of Section 4703.08."

"What about Part A?"

"To my knowledge," Wheeler said, "not since 1931. As far as I know and am aware, this Board has not granted anyone a license to practice architecture under Section 4703.08 Part A since 1931, almost half a century ago."

This sounds too rehearsed, Nathan thought. He glanced at Leighburg again, but again saw no expression.

"What do Parts B and C deal with?" Richards asked.

"I have 4703.08 in front of me," Wheeler said. "One second—okay, here is Part B: that allows the Board to grant a license to a person from another state or country, a person whose qualifications, in the considered judgment of the Board, justify such an action, or is an architect who holds a certificate of good standing in the profession, issued by the NCARB. Part C more specifically concerns any foreign architect, that is to say a citizen of another country, who has lawfully practiced architecture for ten years or more."

"I see," Richards said. "Now, since 1931, Mr. Wheeler, to the best of your knowledge, has anyone in the State of Ohio been admitted to the practice of architecture under 4703.08 Part A?"

Over and over, Nathan thought, expelling his breath impatiently and shifting around in his chair, he keeps going over the same ground! He caught Leighburg's warning look.

"No, to the best of my knowledge, no person since 1931. As Mr. Charnesky stated earlier, Part A is what is called a grandfather clause."

"Okay," Richards said. "Now, I have a copy also, and I call your attention, Mr. Wheeler, to the last sentence after the colon in Part A of Section 4703.08: *'provided the board may require applicants under this division to furnish satisfactory evidence of knowledge or professional practice and supervision of construction.'* The question that I want to ask you is this: what does the Board consider such satisfactory evidence to be furnished by applicants under this Part?"

"I don't think I can answer that," Wheeler said. "I don't know of any situation like that, at least that has occurred since I have been in this position, and no such ruling has been made by the Board that I am aware of. As I just explained, and as Mr. Charnesky explained earlier, Part A is a grandfather clause and has not been used since 1931."

"Okay," Richards said. "Now let's talk specifically about Mr. Goldstein's application for a license, against this background, based on our analysis of the relevant parts of the statute. Has Mr. Goldstein applied under 4703.08 Part A?"

"Well, only as indicated in Mr. Leighburg's letter of April 11, 1978," Wheeler said.

"The Board's Exhibit Number 1?"

"Yes," Wheeler said.

"Have either Mr. Leighburg or Mr. Goldstein asked you for any type of application for a license to practice architecture without examination?"

"No, neither one," Wheeler said.

"So you have no application from them to present to this Board?"

"Just Mr. Leighburg's letter, the Board's Exhibit Number 1," Wheeler said.

"So at this point in time," Richards asked, "what would Mr. Goldstein have to do to become licensed to practice architecture in the State of Ohio?"

"At this point in time," Wheeler said smoothly, "Mr. Goldstein's application, the one we have on file, is asking for registration under Section 4703.07, so he would have to pass the NCARB examination first."

"And so far he has failed it twice, is that correct?"

"Yes, twice," Wheeler said. Round and round, Nathan thought again. If this was the legal system the Founding Fathers had envisioned, everyone in the room ought to be wearing powdered wigs and buckled shoes.

"I have nothing further," Richards said.

"Thank you," Leighburg said at once. "I would like to cross-examine Mr. Wheeler at this time." The Board members looked at Wheeler, Wheeler looked nervously at Leighburg, and Charnesky, glancing at Richards, mumbled that Leighburg could proceed.

"Mr. Wheeler," Leighburg asked, "is there an application form requesting consideration for licensure under Section 4703.07?"

"Is there a form?" Wheeler repeated, his voice quavering a little, Nathan thought.

"Yes, Mr. Wheeler," Leighburg said, "we have been discussing Mr. Goldstein's request to be considered for licensure under Section 4703.07, and Mr. Richards has made a point of stressing that no application form to that effect is on file, only my letter of April 11, 1978, and so I ask you again, is there, in fact, an application form, something an applicant under 4703.07 can in fact file?"

Nathan noticed that Wheeler was becoming pale. "Yes, under .07, there's a form," he said, his voice dropping.

"Would you repeat that, Mr. Wheeler?" Leighburg asked. "I couldn't quite make out what you said."

"Yes, there's a form," Wheeler said more distinctly.

"Who provides that form?"

"The Board of Examiners, this Board," Wheeler said.

"Does this form, under .07, have a number?"

"Yes, it's Form A-6," Wheeler said.

"And what is the number of the form under 4703.08?" Leighburg asked, stressing the "eight."

Wheeler hesitated.

"Mr. Wheeler?"

"There is no form under .08," Wheeler said softly.

Richards intervened with another objection and the two attorneys fenced for what seemed to Nathan to be a very long several minutes. Finally Leighburg was allowed to proceed. "You testified earlier," Leighburg said to Wheeler, "let me read from our notes to make sure that I'm quoting you correctly, that applicants' examination papers which are not graded by members of examining boards or their employees, and which are not available for inspection as a result of contractual arrangements with the testing company, don't need to be made available for inspection, is that correct?"

"I–I think so," Wheeler said, his voice cracking. This is so obviously a coverup, Nathan thought, he's going to wet his pants.

"This is under Section 4743.02 of the Ohio Revised Code and more specifically, your contract with the testing company, is that correct?"

"Yes," Wheeler said uneasily.

"And 4743.02 is one of the main statutes in the Code that governs the way you keep records, is that correct?"

"I--I think--" Wheeler started to say when Richards intervened: "I object," he said loudly. "You are leading the witness!"

"All right, I'll be more specific," Leighburg said. "When Mr. Goldstein came to your office on–let's see–it was on February 18 of this year, to review his records, you showed him only his answer sheets. And when he asked to see his Ohio Graphic Exam, which he had passed, you told him that those files had been destroyed. Is that correct?"

"Yes, that's correct, but I wasn't--"

"I just want your answer, Mr. Wheeler, not an explanation," Leighburg said swiftly. "So Mr. Goldstein's whole Graphic Examination file, including two previous graphic exams, was destroyed. Now I'm going to read the concluding part of the last sentence of this Section of the Code into the record, as follows: '... but it shall be the applicant's right to have any such paper regraded manually, upon written request of either himself or his attorney made to the board within ninety days after announcement of the grade.' And Mr. Goldstein met with you on February 18, exactly three months ago today, is that correct?"

"Yes," Wheeler said, looking down.

"And your letter to Mr. Goldstein informing him that he again failed the NCARB examination, an official letter on this Board's stationery, was dated January 24, 1978?" Leighburg got up to give copies of the letter to Wheeler and Richards and then returned to his chair. Wheeler and Richards examined the letter and Richards nodded.

"Yes," Wheeler said.

"So less than ninety days–to be precise, only twenty-five days–had elapsed from the date of your letter to Mr. Goldstein when he arrived in your office asking to review his entire file, is that correct?"

"I guess so," Wheeler mumbled.

"Excuse me?"

"Yes, that's correct," Wheeler said more clearly. Nathan wondered if the worm was getting ready to turn. Or the cornered rat would bare his teeth. For a moment he saw everyone in costumes: Wheeler as a giant rat, Leighburg as animal tamer, whip in one hand, three-legged stool in the other, Charnesky as the top-hatted circus master. Was he the clown? Was this all just some sort of charade?

"But the statute we have just cited," Leighburg continued, "4743.02, mandates that you hold all examination papers for a minimum of ninety days, and here only twenty-five days had elapsed when you told Mr. Goldstein that you had destroyed his examination papers. How do you explain that, Mr. Wheeler?"

"I–I was not aware," Wheeler stuttered, "of that part of the statute, about the minimum of ninety days--" he stopped speaking and looked pleadingly first at Richards and then at Charnesky. Leighburg let the pause linger on, fixing Wheeler with an unremitting stare. Damn it, Nathan thought, Frank is enjoying this too much. It's a show for him, but it's my career we're talking about.

"Did you destroy Mr. Goldstein's examination papers on your own volition or were you instructed to do so by someone else?" Leighburg asked, glaring at Wheeler.

"Objection!" Richards almost shouted. "I strenuously object! I instruct Mr. Wheeler not to answer that question! I move that that question be stricken from the record!"

"I don't understand your objection," Leighburg said, raising his voice as well. "On what grounds--"

"Objection sustained," Charnesky yelled. "The reporter will strike Mr. Leighburg's question from the record. I don't know where you intend to go with this, Mr. Leighburg, but you're beginning to try my patience. If this continues, I'll stop this hearing immediately. Move to other issues, Mr. Leighburg."

Leighburg was quiet for a long moment, staring at Charnesky. "All right," he said. "Mr. Wheeler, please describe the difference between the NCARB examination and the Ohio graphic design examination."

"The difference?"

"Yes," Leighburg said. "Let me put it this way. Is the NCARB exam multiple choice?"

"Yes, it is," Wheeler said.

"And the Ohio graphic design exam asks the applicant to present his own design solution to some sort of design problem?"

"Yes, that's right," Wheeler said.

"Are the two examinations prepared by the same testing bureau or organization?"

"No, they're not," Wheeler said. "The NCARB is a national exam, multiple choice, as you said, given in all fifty states and five of the territories. It's prepared, as the name says, by the National Council of Architectural Registration Boards in Washington. But the Ohio graphic design exam is written and graded here in Ohio." Wheeler seemed more at ease, Nathan thought, discussing the examinations in general terms.

"Would you go into some detail about the Ohio exam?" Leighburg asked.

"Well," Wheeler said, "each applicant is sent a preliminary building program a couple of months before the examination is given. During the exam itself applicants are given a more detailed building program, from which they have to design a site, a building, and provide a site plan, a building plan, building sections, details and notes to describe his solution to the problem so that it can be judged for its adequacy in all these respects."

"But the NCARB exam, you said, unlike what you've just described, is one hundred percent multiple choice. That means, of course, that it's machine-graded. Who grades that exam?"

"The Educational Testing Service, in Princeton," Wheeler said.

"And the four parts of that exam are given over a two-day period, I'm told—what are those four parts, Mr. Wheeler?"

"Environmental analysis, building programming, design and technology, and construction," Wheeler said.

"And Mr. Goldstein has passed three of those? Which part hasn't he passed?"

"Design," Wheeler said.

"What is the passing grade for that part?"

Wheeler consulted his notes. "Seventy-five," he said.

"And what was Mr. Goldstein's score?"

"Seventy-three," Wheeler said.

"So, Mr. Goldstein's performance on the design portion of the NCARB exam, presumably intended to test his design skills as did the Ohio exam that he passed satisfactorily—but different in format insofar as it was cast as a multiple choice exam rather than as a design problem—was short by two points?"

"Yes," Wheeler said.

"So the lack of the availability of Mr. Goldstein's graphic design examination, is this right, Mr. Wheeler, prevents this Board from being able to evaluate Mr. Goldstein's talents in this area of architectural expertise?"

Wheeler looked confused.

"I'll rephrase," Leighburg said. "Had the Board had access to Mr.

Goldstein's recent Ohio graphics exam, which he passed satisfactorily, and to the 1976 and 1977 exams, they would have been able to objectively evaluate Mr. Goldstein's approach to a design problem and how he provided solutions. But they could not do that because that file, clearly in violation of Section 4743.02 of the Ohio Revised Code, had been destroyed, is that correct?"

"Objection!" Richards shouted. "All right, Mr. Leighburg, I warned you--" Charnesky interrupted. "I withdraw the question," Leighburg interjected quickly. "Let's return to the NCARB examination--Mr. Wheeler, does anyone on this Board review the NCARB multiple choice questions or answers?"

Wheeler seemed uncomfortable again, Nathan thought. "Yes, I suppose from time to time all Board members have an opportunity to look at the questions and answers, if they choose to do so," Wheeler said.

"To your knowledge, Mr. Wheeler, did any member of this Board review the NCARB exam taken by Mr. Goldstein?"

Wheeler looked even more uncomfortable.

"Mr. Wheeler?"

"I think Mr. Charnesky may have looked at it at a recent meeting in Washington," Wheeler said, "you know, in preparation for this hearing."

"In Washington, D.C.?" Leighburg asked.

"At NCARB headquarters," Wheeler explained.

"In the AIA building in Washington?"

"What the hell does that have to do with anything?" Charnesky shouted angrily. "I'm warning you for the last time, Leighburg! Richards?"

"I object!" Richards yelled on cue.

"Objection sustained!" Charnesky, still shouting, was visibly angry. "I move that the question be stricken from the record. Will the court reporter, stenographer, whatever your title is, please acknowledge that the question has been stricken from the record?"

The stenographer nodded. "I have stricken the question, 'In the AIA building in Washington?" she said.

"Now go back and strike the references to NCARB headquarters and Washington," Charnesky instructed her.

"May I ask why these questions and references are to be stricken?" Leighburg asked.

"Because," Charnesky sputtered, "because--because they're irrelevant and immaterial, that's why, and now do you have anything else that's germane to this hearing or don't you? We can't sit here indefinitely and argue about the Board's use of the NCARB examination and the testing procedure and all of that, we're in the fourth hour of this hearing and you're taking our time for no clear purpose!"

Leighburg slowly arranged his papers into a neat pile. He seemed to take an extra moment to collect himself. "We are not here to challenge the validity of the NCARB examination," he said carefully, looking directly at Charnesky, "but to present Mr. Goldstein's qualifications for licensure under 4703.08 Part A. I have now been interrupted several times during my cross-examination of Mr. Wheeler. I would like to remind the Board that I did not call Mr. Wheeler as a witness."

"I think Mr. Leighburg has a right to proceed," Richards said.

Charnesky was still angry. "As far as I'm concerned," he growled, "this is just some legal maneuvering going back and forth that's not getting us anywhere." That's because you're not *letting* it get anywhere, Nathan thought. "He's within his rights, however," Richards said mildly. Charnesky scowled at Richards, as if Richards had switched sides. "And I think I have the right to terminate this hearing if and when I choose," he said. "And if you don't like that," he said, addressing himself to Leighburg now, "you can bring a suit against this Board, that's *your* right."

"I think I can say on behalf of Mr. Goldstein that the last thing he would want to do is to bring a lawsuit against this Board," Leighburg said. "Mr. Goldstein has worked long and hard to enter the profession this Board guards. We hope this Board will permit due process to unfold so that a decision can be reached without any trace of malfeasance or nonfeasance."

Charnesky still wasn't mollified. "It may be the last thing he wants to do," he said, still growling, "but if you keep going with this legal obstructionism, he can try that. Let me tell you, Mr. Leighburg, you are not impressing this Board with your going on and on about totally irrelevant things. The issue is whether we will allow him to obtain a license without having passed the NCARB exam, and that's the *only* issue before us."

"All right," Leighburg said. His manner was neither apologetic nor aggressive. Charnesky's outburst slowly drifted away like an unexpected thunderstorm, still surprising but apparently leaving no permanent damage. "Let me return to the matter of the letters of recommendation submitted on behalf of Mr. Goldstein, letters that were included in Mr. Goldstein's file maintained by Mr. Wheeler," Leighburg said. "I referred to Dean Wilson's letter previously, and Mr. Goldstein reviewed those letters in Mr. Wheeler's office. Mr. Wheeler, are those letters in the file here today?"

"Yes, they are," Wheeler replied.

"I ask you to furnish these letters at this time so that they may be marked and introduced as evidence," Leighburg said.

"Objection!" Richards shouted, startling everyone. "I oppose that strenuously! You're asking this Board to open their files to allow you to use their information to help your presentation! That's not fair to the Board!"

"Under the Ohio Rules of Civil Procedure," Leighburg said calmly, "if one party in litigation desires to use a document in possession of a second party, that second party is required to give the first party that particular document. If this Board upholds Mr. Richards' objection, I will ask to be permitted to proffer them into evidence and if I am not permitted to do that, a reviewing court will not be able to determine whether the Board's decision not to admit these letters into evidence was technically correct." Nathan remembered an old jigsaw puzzle he had tried to put together when he was about eight. The picture on the box was of a great clipper ship, plowing through the waves. It seemed straightforward enough, and he had tried to put the pieces together according to the picture. But either the pieces no longer fit into each other or some were missing or some other pieces from another puzzle had gotten mixed in, and he had given up in disgust.

"You can exercise your right under 119.09 to make a proffer," Richards was saying, not to be outdone in legal scholarship, "and I will continue to object at some future point in time, but I ask for a ruling from this Board at this time." Nathan sat up. Will continue to object at some future point--did Richards already know what the Board would decide?

"Objection sustained," Charnesky said. "We've already discussed introducing those letters, Mr. Leighburg, and again I advise you to move on."

"All right," Leighburg said, "Following Mr. Richards' mention of Section 119.09, we ask that those letters be proffered."

"Do you want them marked?" Richards asked.

"Yes, I do," Leighburg answered. The letters of recommendation, written by Arnold Prescott, Sidney Greenstein, and Frank Wilson were marked as the Applicant's Exhibit 22 but Leighburg, despite another effort on his part, was not allowed to read anything from them into the record. Nathan, hungry, thirsty, and tired, was beginning to agree with Charnesky that Leighburg was dragging things out pointlessly, just as Leighburg conceded that he had no more questions for Mr. Wheeler.

"I do have a few more questions," Richards said, "but they're for Mr. Goldstein. I ask that Mr. Goldstein be sworn in at this time." The surprise was general. "Why--" Charnesky and two other Board members started to ask, and Leighburg looked concerned. But Nathan was very pleased. At last I'm going to get a chance, he thought.

"I'm doing this under 119.09," Richards said, "allowing an agency to call any party under oath as if on cross-examination. Mr. Goldstein, please state your full name for the record."

The next several minutes were devoted to establishing Nathan's address, employment, education, and years of experience. "Now, Mr. Goldstein," Richards said, "think about my next question. It is this. Do you feel that you've made an application under 4703.08 Part A for a license to practice architecture without examination?"

"Yes, I do," Nathan said.

"Do you want to expound on that?"

Nathan took a deep breath. "Yes, I do," he said again. "Although what I want to say will summarize what you've already heard. I want to emphasize that I have not accused anyone of intentionally destroying my Ohio graphic design exams, but surely you can all acknowledge that, had they been available to the Board, the members could have come to their own conclusions about my abilities in design, the only portion of the NCARB that I failed, and that only by two points." Wheeler was looking down at the table, but Richards was looking at Nathan sympathetically and Charnesky and the other Board members seemed resigned to hearing him out. Leighburg, he saw, was listening very intently, on the alert, probably, for any slip. Nathan did not know what he should be careful about. Tell it like it is, he said to himself. Richards seemed to be giving him a chance.

Nathan told his story–not what had happened at Ohio State, but his story of the development of his convictions about the profession of architecture, buttressed by his discovery of the "Dober Report," issued in 1974. It did not take him long. He wanted the Board to understand his convictions, his sincerity, and his eagerness to join the profession. They listened, he thought, with more affability than he had expected. But the result was the same. "I agree with much of what Mr. Goldstein said about business and architecture," Charnesky said, "but it's irrelevant to this hearing."

"It is," Richards said. "I request that Mr. Goldstein's statement be stricken from the record. I have no further questions." So why did you give me this chance, Nathan thought–just some sympathy for a Jewish boy, a gesture for the sake of the civil rights movement? Schwerner, Chaney, and Goodman?

Leighburg had no more questions either. Everyone seemed to be anxious to finish. The attorneys fenced one more duel, about the use of the term "capricious," and Richards concluded his remarks with what Nathan took to be an attempt to be gracious.

"Much of what Mr. Goldstein said in his presentation may be true," Richards said, as if he hadn't moved to have it stricken from the record. "And sometimes the law's operation does indeed appear to treat certain individuals harshly. This may very well be one of those instances. Nevertheless, I maintain that this Board should not make an exception to what has been a uniform procedure since 1931, should not license Mr. Goldstein under 4703.08 Part A, because, as Mr. Wheeler has testified, not one architect has been granted a license under that grandfather clause since 1931. An exception now, in 1978, after almost half a century, would not only be highly irregular, it might very well have serious unforeseen consequences, legally and for the profession of architecture as well."

"Thank you," Charnesky said. "We have heard the evidence. I think the Board understands and appreciates the issue very fully, Mr. Richards. This concludes the formal hearing."

On their way back to Cleveland, Leighburg said that the key element of the Board's position was the fact that no architect had been licensed in Ohio since 1931 under 4703.08 Part A, demonstrating that Part A had been intended only to grandfather the practitioners of that time. "Our appeal to the Court of Common Pleas, assuming that the Board's decision goes the way I think it will," Leighburg said, "will have to be based on the Board's abuse of discretion. And that's not going to be easy to show."

Nobody said much else for the remainder of the trip.

*****

Leighburg's prediction proved accurate. He called Nathan the following month to tell him that the Board had denied Nathan's application. Leighburg went on to say that he was preparing a brief to the Cuyahoga County Court of Common Pleas to appeal that decision, using abuse of discretion as the basis. But a few weeks later he called Nathan again to tell him that the Board's decision had been upheld.

"What's our next step?" Nathan asked

"We can file an appeal," Leighburg said. "Again, the basis would be the Board's abuse of discretion, and see what the Court of Appeals says. What do you want me to do?"

"I don't think we have much to lose," Nathan said.

"Okay," Leighburg said. "I'll be in touch."

Nathan remembered the explanation of the grandfather clause. It had excused the Ohio practitioners of 1931, when the statute had become law, from taking the examination which now once again stood between him and professional practice. He would have to take it again in December. It would be his third time. He had no reason to think that he would have any better chance of passing it this time. Grandfather Claus hadn't slid down his chimney with presents for him the past two Christmases, and wasn't likely to prove any kinder this year. Don't get Jewishly paranoid, he told himself: go to the library and see what you can find out about the old bastard. He realized that, in a way, he was checking on the work Frank Leighburg presumably had already done, and he felt disloyal, but he got up, took his attaché case with paper and pens, and went to Case Western University's Law Library once again. He was becoming quite familiar with it.

It was mid-summer and not many people were in the library. The reference librarian, an attractive young lady who turned out to be a second-year law student, was glad to help him. He explained what he wanted to look up and told her that he had previously acquainted himself with the relevant sections of the Ohio Revised Code, but had found nothing about or sounding like a grandfather clause. "I see," she said. "That's very interesting. Let me see what I can find for you. Would you mind waiting for a little while? It'll take me maybe twenty minutes?"

"Certainly," he said. "I really appreciate your help." She flashed a smile, disappeared, and he found a seat near the reference desk. The journals on the adjoining table looked too formidable for casual examination. Or soporific. He waited.

When she returned, she motioned that he was to accompany her through the stacks. Nathan saw that she had taken notes on a legal pad. They came to a long row of shelves holding volume after volume of the Ohio General Code. She consulted an index, muttered a number to herself, and found Volume 114. She turned the pages until she found what she wanted. "This is the initial act defining the qualifications for the practice of architecture in Ohio," she told Nathan. "The General Code Section Number was 1334. It became 4703 under the Ohio Revised Code, and the section of interest to you, 4703.08 Part A, was revised by the legislature several times–let's see–in 1965, 1969, and 1973."

"*What?*" Nathan yelped. "How can that be? I was told by an Assistant Attorney General of this state, and by the president of a state board, that 4703.08 *included* the grandfather clause of 1931! But if that section was revised as recently as five years ago, it's current law, isn't it?

So it *doesn't* include the clause?"

"No, it doesn't, you're right," the girl said. "You probably looked at only the 1973 revisions. Now you can follow the development of this law–here," she said, giving Nathan a piece of paper on which she had written volume and page numbers, "you should check these after you finish with Volume 114. I'm sure I can trust you to put them back in the proper sequence?" She smiled.

"Of course, thank you so much," Nathan said.

"And if you need any more help, I'll be at the reference desk until eight this evening," she said.

"I'll be sure to ask," Nathan said. "You've been most helpful already." She left and he took Volume 114 to a long wooden table, sat down, and began to read House Bill 282 of the Eighty-Ninth General Assembly of Ohio, January 5, 1931, to July 1, 1931: *"To define the qualifications for the practice of architecture in the state of Ohio, providing for the examination and registration of architects by a state board of examiners; defining the powers and duties of said board of examiners; and providing penalties for the violation of this act."* He came to Section 1334-07, *"License issued without examination, when."* The language that followed was familiar to Nathan: it was in all essential respects identical with the language Leighburg had cited at the Board's hearing in May. He got the other volumes the reference librarian had noted on the paper she'd given him. Section 4703.08 Part A, according to what he had just read, had indeed been based on the 1931 law, but had been reasserted by the Legislature in 1965, 1969, and 1973. Nothing grandfatherly about it: it was *current* Ohio law. Then where was the grandfather clause? He went back to Volume 114, found House Bill 282, and this time read Part C of Section 1334.7, *"License issued without examination, when."*

Section 1334-7 Part C. The board of examiners shall grant a certificate of qualification to practice and shall register without examination any one who has been engaged in the practice of architecture in this state for at least one year immediately previous to the date of approval of this act as a member of a reputable firm of architects under his or her own name; provided that applicants under this subdivision shall present proof of competency and qualifications to the board; and provided further, that the application for such certificate and registration shall be made within one year after the date of approval of this act.

So that was the grandfather clause. That's what had not been used to grant licenses to architects since 1931, not Section 4703.08, as they had told him. Section 4703.08 *was* applicable. They had *lied*–Wheeler, Charnesky, Richards, the whole bunch of them. Well, maybe not Richards: he might just not have bothered to do his homework. Any more, it occurred to Nathan, than Leighburg had bothered to do his. Nathan got up and looked for a copy machine. He made copies of all the relevant sections of the General Code and the Revised Code, shelved the volumes in the right places, went to the reference desk to thank the librarian once more, and left. That evening he called Leighburg at his home to announce his discovery.

He was in for another shock.

"I'm sorry to have to tell you this," Leighburg said. "Obviously you've found some highly relevant information, but Nathan, it's too late."

"What are you talking about, too late?" Nathan yelled. "They lied to us!"

"We're not allowed to bring in new evidence during the appeals process," Leighburg said. "I'm sorry, but that's the way it is."

"But this is our entire case!" Nathan shouted.

"I'm sorry, Nathan," Leighburg said again.

*****

Nathan's efforts to interest the media and Jewish organizations–the Cleveland *Plain Dealer*, *Newsweek*, *U.S. News*, the Jewish Community Federation, the Anti-Defamation League–were all unsuccessful. But early in October, he received a call from the Executive Director of the National Center for the Study of Professions, a Mr. Jeffrey Wullinger. Nathan had called the Center a few days earlier and had left a message on the recorder. The Center published a quarterly newsletter, called *ProForum*, and Mr. Wullinger wanted to hear what Nathan had to say. They talked for almost two hours.

"This is extremely interesting," Wullinger said toward the end of their conversation. "You should know that both Wisconsin and California are moving toward replacing the NCARB exam because of the many doubts raised about its validity. They're developing their own licensing exams, especially since NCARB has been stonewalling them. So your story is very timely indeed. All right, send me a draft as soon as you can, just the essentials, and we'll try to use it in our first issue next year. In the meantime I'll send you a few copies of past issues so that you'll have a feel for style, maximum length, and so on."

"Thanks so much for your interest," Nathan said. "This is very encouraging!"

"That's what we're here for," Wullinger said. "Oh, and go ahead and make those appointments you mentioned with the Federal Trade Commission and the Justice people, I think that those are definitely things you should do."

"Great, thanks again," Nathan said. He felt better. The copies of *ProForum* arrived within the week. He wrote to the FTC and the Department of Justice to request appointments, preferably for the same day, with appropriate officials, and continued his work on projects for Sid Greenstein. And with a heavy heart and clenching his jaw, he once again began his preparations for the NCARB examination.

Wullinger called Nathan about a week after the examination to alert him to a development in the Ohio Senate. A bill had been introduced to remove Section 4703.08 Part A from the Ohio Revised Code. Wullinger, unfamiliar with the intricacies of Ohio politics, did not know who had lobbied for it or what influences were at work, but thought that Nathan might want to inform himself about what was going on behind the scenes. "I certainly do," Nathan said. "I might know some people who know some people. Thanks very much. I'll stay in touch." He put Senate Bill 15 on his list. It was getting longer.

A few days later Nathan called the Wisconsin Examining Board of Architects, Landscape Architects, and Professional Engineers. Wullinger had given him the name of that board's administrator, a Peter Candor, and had said that he had already told Candor about Nathan's situation. When Nathan reached Candor, he found him fully informed.

"The only suggestion I have for you," Candor said, "is that you might try discussing your problem with the Governor's office. In Wisconsin, the governor appoints the public and professional board members. Is that how it's done in Ohio?"

"Yes," Nathan said, "but here there are no members representing the public, just practicing Ohio architects. I've already spoken to one of Governor Rhodes' staff people, after I had written to the Governor, and I was told that he didn't want to get involved since the case was already before Ohio courts."

"Ummm," Candor said. "I guess that's to be expected, that he wouldn't want to get involved, courts or no courts. That's politics. What about your legislature, know anyone there? They wrote the legislation empowering the Ohio Board."

"I hadn't thought of that," Nathan admitted.

"Regulatory law is relatively new," Candor said. "Criminal and civil law has evolved for centuries, but this is something different. Let's see, Wullinger told me about Senate Bill 15 –hang on while I check my notes--"

Nathan waited.

"Good Lord, they really don't want to let you into the profession," Candor said. "The Ohio Board is behind this, obviously. This would remove that Section 4703.08 Part A, under which you applied, from the law."

"What do you suggest?" Nathan asked.

"I don't have any contacts or leverage in Ohio," Candor said. "If you're planning to oppose the bill at a hearing, however, perhaps I could fly into Columbus and testify in support of your position, depending on the schedule, of course, theirs, yours, and mine. Do you happen to know the dates?"

"I've talked to a clerk in Senator Casey's office–Casey is one of the bill's sponsors–the first hearing in the Senate is scheduled for January 30 and then, if necessary, in the first or second week of February. Very soon, in other words," Nathan said. "The clerk thought that the bill would very likely pass in the Senate. But the hearings in the House probably wouldn't begin until the middle of March, he thought."

"Ah, good," Candor said. "That's much better for me. Okay, keep me posted and I'll plan on coming to Columbus in mid-March."

"What would your testimony be, if I may ask?"

"I'd tell the House Committee about the problems we've found in the NCARB exam, here in Wisconsin and also in California," Candor said. "If the exam is going to be the only way to get an architectural license in Ohio, then the Legislature ought to know that they are endorsing a very questionable standard of measurement. If this thing were a drug, a pill of some kind, it wouldn't get by the Food and Drug Administration, that's what I'll tell them. Oh, and Nathan, you might want to consider contacting some local architects and others who would also testify in opposition to this bill."

"Yes, thanks, I think I can do that," Nathan said. "I'm really delighted by your offer to testify. I'm sure that'll be invaluable."

"Well, Wullinger's description of your history on this really upset me," Candor said. "And my opposite number in Columbus–what's his name?"

"Jim Wheeler," Nathan said.

"Yes, Wheeler, he's got to be a liar or an idiot, but probably a liar.

He destroyed your exam and then claimed he didn't know about the statute prohibiting that, is that right?"

"His exact words were that he wasn't *aware* of the statute," Nathan said.

"Ridiculous," Candor said.

"Yes," Nathan said. "Mr. Candor, I should let you know, too, that I've got meetings scheduled in Washington both at the Federal Trade Commission and the Justice Department. I'm going to see them both on February 19. So I want you to know that I'm doing whatever I can on my end."

"I think I understand the Justice Department," Candor said, "but the FTC?"

"I think the Ohio Board is guilty of restraint of trade, and I want to see what the FTC thinks of that."

"Back to the NCARB exam for a moment," Candor said. "Have you got paper and pen handy?"

"Yes, I do," Nathan said.

"Take this name down," Candor said. "David Whitaker. He's a public member of the California Board. I'll give you his address in a moment, it's in my book here. He's written some letters highly critical of the NCARB exam–I'll send you copies–here--" Candor dictated Whitaker's address in Santa Monica. "And I'll also send you a copy of the Wisconsin Tagatz report, also critical of the exam, and some guidelines printed in the *Federal Register* last summer, I'll send those. Those were EEOC guidelines, Equal Employment Opportunity Commission."

"Yes, I'm learning how to swim in the federal alphabet soup," Nathan said, writing as fast as he could.

"One more name," Candor said. "This is a professor of architecture at the University of Illinois: Ian McCleary." Candor spelled the name. "He's made some noise about the exam's content, but he's also criticized the way it's graded and the pass-fail cut-offs. You might want to contact him directly and ask for copies of what he's published about it. Letters, mostly, to journals. Very sensible stuff." Candor was done.

"I really don't know how to thank you for all this help," Nathan said. "You've been more than kind."

"Pleasure," Candor said. "Call me after you get back from Washington–I'll want to hear how your meetings went. And let me know about House hearings on that bill as soon as you can. Good luck, Nathan."

Candor's wish was left unfulfilled in the next morning's mail, when

Nathan once again received a letter from Wheeler beginning "We are sorry to inform you that you have failed...." Nathan stopped reading, crumbled the letter into a ball, and threw it across the room. "They really don't want to let you into the profession," Candor had said. Not all conspiracy theories are crazy, Nathan thought.

*****

Nathan took the shuttle bus from the Baltimore/Washington International Airport to the offices of the Federal Trade Commission on Pennsylvania Avenue. He was much too early for his 10:30 meeting, and walked up to Seventh Street and then down to the National Mall. He could see the Washington Monument to the west and the Capitol to the east. Lefant, he remembered from his architectural history class, had conceived the mall in 1791, but it had not been developed until the early years of the twentieth century. No doubt politicians hadn't seen much reason to spend perfectly good federal dollars that they could use for their constituents back home for an area whose residents couldn't vote for or against them. Now *there* was an injustice in the system, Nathan thought, still being perpetuated, that made what he was fighting seem like very small potatoes. On the other hand, here was the National Mall, and there, as he was walking around it, he could see the National Gallery of Art, the Ulysses S. Grant Memorial, the United States Botanical Garden, and the National Air and Space Museum. Maybe the city's residents benefited from the dollars the tourists spent. As for the selection of the architects, the negotiation of their fees, the budgets for the construction, the inevitable overruns, all the money spent on what he was admiring, who knew how that was all arranged? It was time to go to his meeting.

The FTC Bureau of Consumer Protection was itself protected by a formidable black lady behind a formidable desk, and behind her, on the wall, was a large portrait of President Jimmy Carter whose fixed smile also looked quite steely. But once Nathan had identified himself and given the lady the name of the man he had come to see–a Mr. Marc Robbins–the lady apologized very pleasantly and said that Mr. Robbins would be available in about ten minutes. She offered him a cup of coffee and did not seem perturbed by Nathan's polite refusal. He noticed, however, that President Carter looked no friendlier.

When Nathan was eventually directed to Robbins' office, a rather small room devoid of amenities, he found a man about his own age sitting at a worn desk. The familiarity of his appearance was at once reinforced by his greeting: he stood up, extended his hand, and said "Good to see you again, Nathan."

Nathan was startled. Robbins grinned. "You don't remember me, obviously," he said. "No particular reason why you should. I was a couple of years ahead of you at Beachwood High School."

"Yes, of course!" Nathan said, his memory suddenly sparked. "You were active in a lot of extra-curricular things, but you were also near the top of your class! Marc Robbins, of course! I don't know why I didn't connect your name to Beachwood High!"

"Well, it's been almost fourteen years since I graduated," Robbins said. "But I remember seeing you wrestle for the varsity one time when I was back in Cleveland visiting my family, watching you pin some fellow a lot bigger than you were. I think the other school was Byzantine?"

"You were there? Yes, he was much heavier than I was," Nathan said, "but he wasn't in very good shape. I remember that match not just because I beat him but because my Dad was in the stands, and that made it feel especially good to pin that guy in the third period. Well! What a small world!"

"Yes," Robbins said, motioning Nathan to an armchair and sitting down in another, to the side of his desk. "Nathan, I gave your complaint some attention not only because of our Beachwood High connection, but also because your friend Sid Greenstein is also a good friend of my father's, and Sid has told my father something about the problems you're having trying to get your license. This was before I received your materials so critical of the NCARB examination. And those materials have led to interest, on the part of the FTC, in taking a closer look at the procedures that you think are being used to limit the number of architects entering the profession. So in a way, you've already had some success here."

"But?" Nathan asked. "Sounds like there's a 'but' coming?"

"Yes," Robbins said. "Even though our connection, going to the same school and having Sid Greenstein as a mutual friend, isn't very substantial, it *is* a connection, and that means that another FTC attorney will conduct the investigation. I have to stay away from it. But let me give you some background."

"Please do," Nathan said. "This is all foreign territory to me. I just raised a question."

"Monopolistic behavior, or practices that appear to amount to restraint of competition, whether or not they are the result of overt conspiracies, are against the law. Our antitrust authority, which is what it's called, comes primarily from the Federal Trade Commission Act and the Clayton Act, and those represent the outcome of a very long history of struggle, all the way up to and including the Supreme Court, about how business is to be conducted in this country. Well, I won't go into the details, don't worry, but if we determine that your complaint has validity, we might recommend that the Commission take formal action, or alternatively we could work toward a consent decree. Formal action, that is, enforcement, requires litigation in the federal court or before an administrative law judge."

Lawyers, Nathan thought. They live in their own world. So do we all, no doubt.

"Our antitrust division," Robbins was saying, "also works with the antitrust division of the Department of Justice, and we don't want to--"

Nathan couldn't help interrupting. "I have a meeting over there this afternoon," he said.

"Very good!" Robbins exclaimed. "Did you send them all the materials you sent me?"

"Yes, I did," Nathan said.

"Our investigation--I can tell you this much, there will be at least a preliminary investigation--will look at both the validity and fairness of the NCARB exam and at the registration process more generally," Robbins said. "We'll ask whether the examination is job-validated, whether there is any verifiable correlation between level of architectural education and success on the exam, and whether there's any evidence of racial discrimination in the registration process. What time is your meeting at Justice?"

"Two o'clock," Nathan said.

"You know where you're going?"

"Down Pennsylvania Avenue, about five minutes from here."

"Right," Robbins said, glancing at his watch. "You've got time to grab a bite on Constitution Avenue, opposite the National Mall. You know that area?"

"Yes," Nathan said. "I took a walk there before our meeting."

"Okay," Robbins said. "We'll call you later this week to get more details, including whom to contact at Justice. It's been good to see you again, Nathan."

"Thanks so much for your interest, Marc," Nathan said. They shook hands and Nathan left. He walked down Constitution Avenue to the Capital Gang restaurant. He made his way through several men in top coats and suits, leaving the restaurant, and heard one of them say rather angrily to another, "I paid you for that already, damn it, now get it done." Nathan glanced at him and they locked eyes for a moment. The man looked nothing like Charnesky, but somehow reminded Nathan of Charnesky signaling Richards to object on cue. He went into the restaurant.

He was just in time for his appointment at the Department of Justice with a Mr. Herbert Barber, but once again that proved too early. No receptionist was at the desk, and a wispy man whom he stopped from hurrying past to ask if Mr. Barber was in didn't know, and indicated a seat where Nathan was to wait for developments. He thought of his journeys to architectural firms around the country, searching for a suitable job, only to take the job with Becker back in his home town. Here the only familiar sight was the same portrait of President Carter that he had seen at the FTC. Carter, not surprisingly, looked just as unfriendly here. It was his blue eyes, Nathan decided. Steely. Cold. All those bare teeth underneath didn't help either. He looked at the sports section of the Washington *Post,* saw nothing of interest to him, and found the crime stories much more absorbing. A government official had been charged with soliciting bribes. His lawyer was quoted as saying that he looked forward to proving his client's innocence. A man who had been arrested for assault and battery and domestic abuse had claimed that "she'd had it coming, and so did he." Suddenly the receptionist, another black woman, appeared, took off her coat, hung it up in a closet Nathan hadn't noticed, turned to him, and asked if he was Mr. Goldstein. Nathan confirmed his identity and saw a smile he wanted to recommend to President Carter.

"I'm sorry to have kept you waiting," she said. "I was visiting someone at the hospital, the time got away from me, and it's not always easy to get a cab in this city. Mr. Barber is expecting you. I'll tell him you're here."

Mr. Barber, a man about fifty, was also black. Maybe the cab drivers hadn't gotten the message yet, Nathan thought, but the government was beginning to. Mr. Barber's office was considerably larger than Marc Robbins' and had a window with a view. Unfortunately, the sky was overcast. Barber got down to business almost immediately.

"I've reviewed your materials," he said, "and I've also looked into our files on your profession. And I was surprised by what I found. A few years ago, in 1971, we were alarmed about a ban on competitive bidding by the American Society of Civil Engineers. Alarmed enough to begin a civil investigation. That led to a look at the American Institute of Architects because they had a similar ban. After it became clear to both ASCE and the AIA that we were ready to take legal action, they both dropped those bans. The AIA had required all their members to use standard fee schedules depending on building type, project scope, construction costs, and some other factors."

"Yes, I heard about that," Nathan said.

"And now," Barber continued, "the AIA and their local affiliates are promoting something called qualifications-based selection."

"Yes, I'm familiar with that too," Nathan said.

"What do you think of it?"

"Frankly," Nathan said, "it seems that small and even medium-sized firms lacking the right connections don't have much of a chance under this system. It's the old story: not what you know, but who you know. I'm talking about major government contracts, of course, whether federal, state, or local. The right lobbyists are very expensive. The big firms can afford them, partly because the size of the jobs they get more than covers that cost of doing business. And under the qualifications-based selection procedures, I've heard, the firm negotiates their fee after the contract has been awarded."

"I see," Barber said. "What about the smaller jobs?"

"Oh, once in a while some of those go to smaller firms, I think," Nathan said.

"So there's *some* equity in the system?"

"Not in my opinion," Nathan said. He wondered when they would get to the reason he was in Barber's office, but continued. "There are a few small and medium-sized firms that are one-hit wonders, you might say. They get one, maybe two jobs every few years. But I'd guess that less than ten percent of the firms in this country get more than ninety percent of the billings. And the qualifications-based selection system operates in a way so that the same firms win the major contracts time and again. So I don't see any equity."

"Maybe that's something we'll need to look into in the future," Barber said. He glanced at his watch. "Look, I know you're here to tell me about the NCARB exam this afternoon, but before we get to that, I'd like you to take a few minutes to glance at this paper written by one of our Deputy Assistant Attorney Generals here in the Antitrust Division." He handed Nathan a report. "While you do that, I have to run down the hall to check on a meeting scheduled for later this afternoon," Barber said, rising and moving toward the door. "Please excuse me–I won't be long."

Nathan, surprised and feeling a little awkward alone in Barber's office, glanced at the report's first page. His attention was captured almost at once.

... The objective of any self-respecting cartel is to achieve power over price. But economic theory and empirical observation teach us that a successful cartel harbors the seeds of its own destruction. Cartel members will want to cheat on an agreed-upon rate by offering a lower price in hope of increased market shares and revenues. Similarly, the more effective the cartel in raising cost, the more interesting that particular market will be to outsiders. Firms will be attracted to an industry whose profits seem exorbitant or prices significantly above the costs of production....

That seems to work quite well for the architectural firms I've just been describing to Barber, Nathan thought. They control most markets through politics. Their so-called qualifications-based selection system allows them to negotiate their fees after the fact. And the continuous supply of cheap intern architects means that their labor costs are minimal. He turned to the last page to read the conclusion.

... The competitive problems of occupational licensing are in my judgment a symptom of a much deeper problem. Market economies depend on unrestricted entry. Efforts to restrict entry can be expected to grow in intensity as the economy moves further from an industrial to service-oriented structure, and a strategy that is focused on local government is one that, because of relative invisibility, stands the greatest chance of success. Public attention must be focused on the costs of such restrictive regulation so that state and local lawmakers will be alert to this trend. The Antitrust Division will continue to do all in its power as an enforcement agency and as an advocate for competitive policy to insure that markets for services remain open and competitive.

Well, amen! Nathan thought. So I'm not alone in the wilderness! If a federal whatever junior Attorney General—why don't the lower ranks get called colonel or major, as long as the top guy is a general, Nathan wondered parenthetically—can sound off like this, the Ohio Legislature had better pay attention and drop that S.B. 15! He grinned, stretched, and saw Barber come back into the room.

"Find it interesting?" Barber asked.

"Very much so," Nathan said. "I certainly see some relevance here to taking the NCARB exam."

"I thought that you would," Barber said. He sat down behind his desk, pulled a note pad toward his right, and took a pen from his shirt pocket. "Okay, start at the beginning." Nathan told his story, including the latest development, his meeting with Robbins earlier that afternoon. Barber made another note. "Okay," he said, "have we covered all the bases?" Nathan hesitated. "There's something else?" Barber asked. "You seem to have a question?"

"I'm not sure that it's a question," Nathan said, "but if you have another few minutes, I'd like to tell you what happened to me when I was finishing my master's in architecture at Ohio State, and see whether you think it has any bearing on what we've been talking about."

"Your master's?" Barber said. "When was that?"

"Almost four years ago," Nathan said.

Barber was visibly dubious. He glanced at his watch. "All right," he said, "but I'm going to have to leave fairly soon."

"I'll be quick," Nathan said, "but first let me ask you about the Supreme Court decision, some time ago, having to do with professional associations stopping their members from advertising their services to the public–have I got that right?"

"Yes," Barber said. "A couple of years ago the Court held that it was unconstitutional for a bar association–it was the Arizona State Bar–to prohibit attorneys from advertising their prices and services. The Court held–as a lawyer, this was of considerable interest to me, so I remember it well– *Bates v. Arizona*, 1977–that the Arizona Bar's concerns about adverse impacts on the stature of the profession could be addressed by rules less restrictive than a complete prohibition of the practice. Oh, I think I see why you brought that up: I remember we noted in our AIA file that, soon after that decision, the American Institute of Architects amended its own rules prohibiting their members from advertising. Do you have some additional information related to that?"

A sudden ray of sunshine from the window found its way across Barber's desk and onto the wall next to Nathan's chair. "Maybe so," Nathan said. "I was doing a marketing study as part of my master's degree program at Ohio State, intended to examine the familiarity of small and medium-sized architectural firms in the Columbus area with modern marketing practices. My notion was that they weren't, and that might be part of the reason why they weren't really competitive with the big firms who kept getting the big contracts. I was working under two professors of architecture and one of management, got the questionnaire approved, and even ran a small pilot. My plan was to follow the survey with a series of selective interviews as part of the dissemination of results–in fact, I hoped that would be the motivation for respondents to participate, to learn something they could use in their businesses. Just before I was to send the questionnaire out to the firms whose participation I wanted to solicit, I set up some meetings with state officials of the AIA to get letters of support, and I also asked the Executive Vice President of the national, here in Washington, for a similar letter. My committee thought that such letters would be very helpful in increasing the participation rate, and of course I thought so too."

"Who was the Executive Vice President?" Barber asked.

"A man named Roger Fleming," Nathan said. "As far as I know, he's still in that job."

"So what happened?" Barber asked.

"The Assistant Dean and my three faculty advisors had been very supportive and encouraging, and in fact had just prepared an application for an internal grant in support of the work–the anticipated expenses included printing, mailing, coding the responses, that sort of thing–and were looking forward to the letters of support we all expected. What happened instead was that the day after the application had been signed and submitted, the Assistant Dean called me in, told me the application was being withdrawn, and said that I was to stop the study immediately."

"Really!" Barber was genuinely surprised, Nathan saw. "When was this?"

"I started in 1974, and the study was stopped in 1975," Nathan said.

"So two years *before* the *Bates v. Arizona* decision," Barber said. "Did the Assistant Dean give you an explanation, why your study was being stopped?"

"No, not really," Nathan said. "Some gobbledygook about my research not fitting into what the School's Executive Committee considered the proper direction of the graduate program, or something like that."

"And you didn't believe that," Barber said.

"Would you?"

"No, I wouldn't, for more than one reason," Barber said. "But I can't see how this could be relevant to your current problem with the NCARB exam."

"I have to admit that I hope it isn't," Nathan said. "But I have an uneasy feeling that it might be."

"I don't know how to respond to that," Barber said, "but frankly, you've given us plenty to look at with the documents you've brought to our attention, especially in the overall context of restraint of trade, controlling competition, and in effect restricting the labor force of architect interns. I'm pretty sure that we'll concentrate on the NCARB exam, its validity, and its effect on our national economy, but we'll see." He got up.

"Thanks so much for your interest," Nathan said, getting up himself.

Barber extended his hand. "Give me a call next week," he said. "I plan to review your case myself, and I might have some additional questions. Have a good trip back, Mr. Goldstein."

"Yes, I look forward to hearing from you, Mr. Barber," Nathan said.

When he got home late that evening, Nathan found an oversized envelope on the table in front of the mail boxes in his building, addressed to him. It was from Wullinger at the National Center for the Study of Professions. He tore it open. It was a copy of the Center's monthly newsletter, *ProForum*. The lead article was entitled "One Architect in Search of a License." It's my story, in print at last, Nathan thought. I'm no longer telling it just to one person at a time. I'm not alone any more. The next step would be to line up his ducks for the hearing in the Ohio House on its version of Senate Bill 15.

*****

The ducks—reports, articles, letters from officials and their organizations, professors, practitioners, supporters of all kinds-- comprised an impressive array. They now included a group called the Society of American Registered Architects, SARA, founded in 1956 to include "all architects, regardless of their roles in the architectural community." Nathan took Candor's advice and went to see the President *pro tem* of the Ohio Senate, Senator Theodore M. Madison, who also happened to be the senator from his district. At a meeting with Madison in his office in a worn, weary neighborhood on East Seventieth Street, Nathan explained how the section of the law that S.B. 15—which had passed the Ohio Senate unanimously—was to repeal was not the grandfather clause originally used in 1931, despite what the Senate had been told by the bill's sponsors, but legislation revised as recently as 1973. The senator, who reminded Nathan of a black preacher he had seen on television, read the materials and exclaimed that he, and indeed the Senate as a whole, had been "hoodwinked." Nathan agreed, thinking that other terms for the deception might be even more appropriate. The senator promised to fire off a letter to Wheeler, demanding to know the history of all applicants since 1931 for a license to practice architecture in Ohio without taking an examination. "Sometimes," Madison told

Nathan, "politics is more powerful than justice." Nathan was reminded of Jackie Presser–"make your own connections"--and decided to pursue Madison's implicit advice. The House committee's hearing was scheduled only two weeks later, and he could hear the clock ticking. On his way home, he went to see Elliott Ross at his office.

"I need a favor, Elliott," Nathan said, after the initial pleasantries. "You're still close to Bill Lewin, aren't you?"

"Sure," Ross said. "That's one big *macher* I cultivate every chance I get. He's about the most influential Jew in Cleveland. Maybe in Ohio. And certainly one of the biggest developers. What's up?"

"I've heard that Lewin contributes to both parties, quite substantially, too, is that right?"

"Right," Ross said, "and not only that, he raises a lot of money for them from his friends. A *lot*. Regularly. Money talks, and big money gets heard, believe me."

Nathan told Ross about the hearing scheduled for the end of March and, without going into too much detail, his interest in it. "Ummm," Ross said. "And you want to testify."

"I do," Nathan said, "and so does a man who's coming from Wisconsin for that purpose, and I want to submit a truckload of material to document my case. To get all that admitted and to have it make an impact, I need some strings pulled, I think. All I've really got on my side at this point is justice. Now I need politics."

"Never hurts," Ross said. "Who's the chairman of the House committee?"

"Gene Spagnelli," Nathan said.

"From one of those towns near the airport?"

"I'm not sure," Nathan said. "Is that important?"

"No, I guess not," Ross said. "I'm sure Bill knows him well. He knows everybody well. Tell you what–give me a day and I'll call you. And then we'll go out for a drink, and I'll tell you about Lewin and you tell me what's been going on in your life."

"Deal," Nathan said.

Ross didn't call the next day, or the next, but Nathan began to see some fruits of his labors when he received copies of an exchange of correspondence between Madison and Wheeler. Without once referring to Nathan, Madison had repeated the essence of the information Nathan had provided about the actual grandfather clause of 1931 and the fact that the applicable statutes had been renewed, with new standards, by the Ohio Legislature in 1965, 1969, and 1973. He asked Wheeler for the history of all applications for licensure without examination from 1931 to the present date, as well as for the Board's records of their approvals and denials. "As I am sure that you are aware," Madison had written, "the State Board of Examiners of Architects has been entrusted by this legislature to fulfill their obligations to meet the intent of the regulatory laws of Ohio." Wheeler's response claimed that "reviewing the minutes of more than 500 board meetings is time consuming," but that Madison would receive the requested information "as quickly as possible." He can't ignore the President *pro tem* of the State Senate, Nathan thought, but he'll delay as long as he can. I need another shoulder at this door. He looked in his rolodex and found the number for Prescott and Associates in Columbus. It had been quite a while.

A man's voice that Nathan didn't recognize answered. "Prescott and Associates."

"Arnold Prescott, please," Nathan said.

"Just a minute," the man said. Not the usual "May I tell him who's calling?," Nathan thought. Business must not be so good for Arnold. Then he heard Prescott's voice: "Hello? This is Arnold Prescott?"

"Arnold!" Nathan said. "It's Nathan Goldstein–how are you, first of all?"

There was a pause. "Nathan Goldstein," Prescott repeated. He sounded thoughtful rather than surprised.

For an instant Nathan wondered whether Prescott was having trouble remembering him. "Nathan, how good to hear from you," Prescott said. "To answer your question, I never got back to a full one hundred percent after the surgery, and I seem to take an awful lot of pills–just a minute, Nathan--" Nathan heard the receiver being laid down and Prescott calling, in a rather high-pitched tone Nathan didn't recognize, "Brian, don't forget to stop at the pharmacy on your way back!" Then Prescott picked up the phone again. "Nathan?"

"Yes, I'm here, Arnold," Nathan said.

"Sorry, Brian was just leaving, and I wanted to remind him–you remember Brian from the program, Brian Keating?"

"Brian Keating?" Nathan *was* surprised, not thoughtful. "The fellow who sent his drawings along with mine for the Brussels Prize competition, and got an honorable mention? Or whatever it was?"

Another pause. "Yes," Prescott said. "He works for me now. At least for the time being. Anyway, Nathan, I'm no longer as active as I was in the profession, for health reasons, but I do try to keep up and heard about you not too long ago–let's see, when was it? I saw Paul Charnesky at the Kon Tiki some weeks ago, and heard that you had failed the NCARB again, but there was something last year that Paul told me about too–yes, Nathan, didn't you have some sort of hearing with lawyers and testimony, trying to get the State Board of Examiners to grant you a license without having passed the exam even then?"

"Yes, that's right, last April, almost a year ago," Nathan said. He didn't like the way Prescott had phrased it. "And among the documents I tried to get into the record were your letter of recommendation and Dean Wilson's letter about how well I had done teaching the course I took over when you went into the hospital, but the Board denied my application. Maybe Mr. Charnesky mentioned that to you as well."

Another pause. "I believe he did, yes," Prescott said. "Nathan, I'm feeling a little tired–is there something you wanted to discuss or ask me?"

"Yes, there is," Nathan said. "Sorry that you're not feeling well, Arnold, I'll be quick. Are you familiar with Senate Bill 15 and the version the Ohio House is about to hold hearings on?"

"Yes," Prescott said. "I attended a couple of the hearings in the Senate just a few weeks ago–oh, I think I see–Nathan, you do know that the bill passed the Senate unanimously?"

"Yes, I know that," Nathan said, "and I also know how that happened. The point is, I'm planning to come to Columbus next Thursday to testify at the House hearing, and--"

"Are you sure that's a good idea?" Prescott interrupted.

"Yes, I think it's a very good idea," Nathan said. "I'm not giving up after everything I've done, everything I've worked for. You know my situation. The Board denied my application under that statute, falsely, I happen to know, and now they're pulling political strings to get rid of the statute altogether. Well, they're not the only ones with strings to pull. I–"

"Nathan," Prescott interrupted again, "While I was President of the Architects Society of Ohio, I made some friends on the State Board of Examiners, and I know some things too. It's not as simple as you seem to think. There's a lot of background--"

"What do you mean, you know some things too? What things?" Nathan was fighting to keep his voice under control, but he was getting very angry. This wasn't going at all well.

"That's all I can say about it," Prescott said. "All I want to say about it."

"Arnold, I'll be in Columbus by eleven next Thursday–can we meet for lunch?"

"Lunch? No, I won't have time for that next Thursday," Prescott said.

"Well, I could stop by your office to say hello," Nathan said, recovering a friendly tone.

"Ummm–all right," Prescott said, "but I'll have only a couple of minutes, I'm afraid."

"Okay, at least I'll see you," Nathan said. "It's been well over a year, since I was your guest at the Christian Men's camp."

"Yes," Prescott said. "Nathan, let me change the subject, I want to ask you something myself. About Brian. Did you ever hear anything about–well–about his dating habits?"

"His *dating* habits?" Nathan was astounded by the question. "No, certainly not, Arnold, I had no contact with him except for that time about the Brussels Prize competition. He was going to share the shipping costs with me, but somehow he never did. That's all I remember. Why do you ask?"

"Well, I have some suspicions," Prescott said. "And lately, he's made me uncomfortable several times, if you know what I mean."

"You mean you haven't lost your sex appeal?" Nathan couldn't help himself. But his tone made it clear, he hoped, that he was joking. He was relieved when Prescott chuckled. "I'm glad you haven't lost your sense of humor," Prescott said.

"Right," Nathan said. "So we're on for next Thursday?"

""Yes, at my office, promptly at noon. Goodbye, Nathan." He hung up. Of course, promptly, Nathan thought. He remembered Prescott's annoyance with even a moment's tardiness.

As long as I'm making calls, Nathan thought, replacing Prescott's card in the rolodex and extracting Elliott Ross's. He dialed the number. He got Mary, the secretary. She told him that Ross was out of the office for the day, but that he had managed to get an appointment for Nathan with Lewin for the next morning, at seven, in fact. She had tried to call Nathan several times but his answering machine was full.

Nathan apologized, started to explain, thought better of it, thanked Mary, asked her to thank Elliott, made sure he had Lewin's address, said good-bye, and heaved a sigh of relief. What a break! Especially after his quite unsatisfactory conversation with Prescott!

Bill Lewin, the founder, president, and chairman of Emerald City Enterprises, was a very wealthy man. His office building, however, indicated nothing of the sort. It was a modest two-story brick building behind a lumber yard in an area not far from Cleveland Hopkins Airport. The only sign that Nathan saw was on the simple glass door that seemed to be the main entrance. Maybe he's so influential because he doesn't flaunt his money, Nathan thought. He had met Lewin once–Ross had introduced him at a Turkish bath Lewin frequented–and he remembered a powerfully built, hairy-chested, balding man of average height with an intense black stare. It was his bushy eyebrows, Nathan thought. No, it was the eyes underneath. They sized you up and found you wanting.

He was directed to Lewin's office at once, even though he was almost fifteen minutes early, and when he knocked on the door, a voice answered immediately. "Is that you, Goldstein?"

"Yes," Nathan said, feeling as if he were outside the principal's office.

"Come in," the voice said. "Leave the door open." This should take about a minute, Nathan thought.

Lewin's office was no more lavish than the building. "Good morning, Mr. Lewin," Nathan said, walking up to Lewin's desk, covered with several file folders, and extending his right hand. "Thank you for taking the time--"

"Yes, have a seat," Lewin interrupted, shaking Nathan's hand without rising and indicating a chair, almost in the same motion. "Ross explained the problems you're having getting your architect's license. There's a bill, already passed by the Senate, and something similar is before a House committee now, is that right? You're against the bill? And the committee is chaired by Gene Spagnelli?"

"Yes, right on all counts," Nathan said, taken aback by Lewin's brusque manner. I bet he isn't like this when *he* wants a favor, Nathan thought.

"Okay. I've known Gene for years. I'll make a call. Get to the hearing early. Introduce yourself to Gene before the hearing starts." Lewin seemed to be done.

"How will I know who Mr. Spagnelli is?" Nathan managed to ask.

Lewin's eyes looked very black. "He'll be the one sitting behind the name plate that reads Eugene Spagnelli," he said. Nathan blushed. "Sorry," he said.

Lewin nodded toward the door. "Keep me posted on how he treats you," he said. "Okay."

"Thanks very much, Mr. Lewin," Nathan said, rising.

"Hope this helps you, Goldstein," Lewin said. He reached for a file folder and Nathan left, glancing at his watch in the hall. Just about two minutes. Time is money. The question was what he'd have to pay for it when the time came. There wasn't much doubt that godfathers, whatever their ethnicity, never forgot to exact a price for whatever favors they bestowed. Unless, of course, they weren't favors.

*****

At precisely twelve o'clock on the following Thursday, Nathan opened the door to Prescott's office and found Prescott and his wife Betty standing together in front of what appeared to be the receptionist's desk. Their stance seemed to be planned, and didn't look at all welcoming. Nathan, quickly overcoming his initial shock, extended his hand and said, "Arnold, good to see you again, and you too, of course, Betty, how are you both?"

Prescott opened his mouth but his wife was too quick for him. "Arnold has his good days and his bad days," she said. "I'm here to help with some of the typing. And you, Nathan? I've heard you've been making quite a name for yourself?"

"Now Betty, give the man a chance," Prescott said, finally taking Nathan's hand but only very briefly. Betty leaned back against the desk, her arms crossed over her chest. Why the hostility, Nathan wondered–what problems have I ever made for them? "I just came by to say hello," he said.

"Are you planning to testify at the House hearing tonight?" Prescott asked.

"Yes, I am," Nathan said, "as I told you on the phone. You didn't think it was a good idea."

"Arnold, we have to finish typing the specifications," Betty said.

"I know," Prescott said to her, but with his eyes on Nathan. "Nathan, I'm going to be blunt. No, I don't think it's a good idea. I don't want to go into details, but I do want you to consider other options. You have two degrees in business. There are sure to be attractive opportunities in that area for you. You need to consider leaving the architectural profession, Nathan."

Nathan was too astounded to respond. Prescott continued.

"Sometimes," he said, "when life does not turn out as you thought it would, it's wise to make changes. I had to do that in my first marriage. I had to do that with my son. I had to do that when I got sick and had to stop teaching, as you may know. I may have to do it again, I don't know. My point is that you should consider the facts–that your independent study here was stopped by the Dean–that you haven't been able to pass the NCARB exam–and that you've aroused the serious opposition of the architectural establishment in this state. It's time to consider alternatives, Nathan."

Nathan was still in shock, but he had recovered his speech. "No, it's time for you to realize that I'm not a quitter, Arnold," he said, trying his best to keep his voice level. "It's time you remembered our conversation about Frank Lloyd Wright at your house. It's past time for you to tell me whatever it is you're keeping from me instead of telling me you don't want to go into details. You're the one who wrote, in your letter of recommendation, that I had the potential to be brilliant in the profession. After all your encouragement, after all our work together, you are the very last person I would have expected to tell me to leave the profession. I'll be damned first, Arnold."

Prescott had visibly winced at the mention of the conversation about Wright, at Nathan's accusation that he was keeping something from him, and at Nathan's reminder of his own assessment of Nathan's potential. He began to speak, but his wife cut him off.

"No, Arnold, you don't need to answer that," she said. "I think you better go, Nathan. Now."

Nathan looked at Prescott, waiting one more long moment. Prescott wouldn't meet his stare but turned his palms up helplessly. Nathan turned, shaking his head in disbelief, and left. The door closed behind him automatically.

*****

Nathan found Peter Candor at the Columbus airport without any difficulty, and they immediately confirmed the liking they had taken to each other over the telephone. They agreed to have an early dinner so that they could get to the hearing of the Ohio House's Small and General Business Subcommittee in plenty of time to introduce themselves to the chairman, Gene Spagnelli, as Lewin had told Nathan to do. They went over the outlines of their testimony while they ate dinner. Nathan had put the ugliness with the Prescotts on a shelf in the back of his mind, and once again felt determined and optimistic. Here was the Executive Secretary of the State of Wisconsin's architects' licensing board, in Columbus at his own expense to help him make his case. Things were going to turn his way.

They arrived some fifteen minutes before the hearing was to begin, and, to Nathan's surprise, found some people already seated. But the chairs directly in front of the raised platform were still empty. Nathan found two in the very center, immediately facing the nameplate he was looking for on the long table on the platform: "Mr. Eugene A. Spagnelli." He did not tell Candor about his question to Lewin or Lewin's sardonic answer. This time he would not ask if the man sitting in Mr. Spagnelli's chair was indeed Mr. Spagnelli. The room filled up and, a few minutes before seven, so did the chairs on the platform. As soon as a man sat down in Spagnelli's chair, Nathan rose, motioning to Candor to accompany him, and walked up. "Hello," he said to the man, "my name is Nathan Goldstein." Spagnelli got up at once and shook Nathan's hand. "Yes, I was told to expect you," he said, smiling broadly. "Let's go over there for just a moment--" he pointed to the side of the room. Nathan and Candor followed him, aware that people were looking at them. "I've heard good things about you, and I've also heard something about how architects' board has been treating you," Spagnelli murmured. "Yes, that's why we're here," Nathan said, noting that Lewin's name hadn't been mentioned. "I want you to meet Peter Candor, the Executive Secretary of Wisconsin's board, who flew here today just to testify this evening. He's on the list of witnesses." Spagnelli shook Candor's hand, smiled, indicated that they had better get started, and they returned to their seats.

The first three witnesses to testify were architects, all members of the AIA, from Cleveland, Columbus, and Cincinnati. All spoke in favor of the proposed legislation. Candor was the first to testify against it. After presenting his credentials, he came right to the point. "In my opinion," he said, "the proposed legislation would have the effect of granting Ohio's State Board of Examiners of Architects wide open discretionary powers. This could easily prove to be an unconscionable burden on new applicants, making them subject to additional licensing examinations and additional undefined work experience that the Board itself has admitted is difficult to evaluate objectively. But not only are the arguments in favor of the proposed legislation remarkably weak, especially noteworthy is the fact that the Ohio Board and the American Institute of Architects are *collaborating* to make them, strongly suggesting a perception on both their parts that both are threatened by a system that permits alternatives to licensing by means other than the NCARB examination. This is especially peculiar in the light of studies conducted by both the States of California and Wisconsin of the validity of that examination, studies that have resulted in agreement by both states that the examination is seriously defective. It is not credible that the Ohio Board is not aware of these studies and their findings. Certainly the AIA knows all about them. The proposed legislation, however, instead of making wider use of existing provisions to license applicants based on their education and experience, is a giant step in exactly the opposite direction. It will make a bad situation very much worse."

There was a stir throughout the room, and, for a moment, an audible mutter. He isn't treading on just a *few* toes, Nathan thought. But Candor wasn't finished.

"I also want to express my outrage," Candor said, in a matter-of-fact tone that made his description of his emotion all the more effective, "about the Ohio Board's treatment of an applicant architect sitting in this room this evening, Mr. Nathan Goldstein. Not only did the Ohio Board, in my opinion, act with malfeasance and nonfeasance in rejecting Mr. Goldstein's application under the section of the existing law that the proposed legislation would repeal, the Board or its agent destroyed a portion of Mr. Goldstein's examination file in violation of Ohio law! And now they come, with the full support of the AIA, to have that law removed! In my opinion, their behavior merits investigation, not legislation. Thank you very much." Candor's abrupt close, rehearsed at dinner, was also dramatic, Nathan thought. And he was the next witness. He went to the platform carrying copies of all his many documents, already bound in separate folders, and passed them out to all the committee members. He had several left over and offered them to Spagnelli, who took them. Then Nathan went to the lectern.

He described his handouts very briefly, identifying the people who could not attend the hearing but had requested that their testimony be included in the record. He described two reports by federal officials, also included in the documents he had distributed, raising serious concerns about professional licensing boards across the country. These were boards, created by their state legislatures, he emphasized, that were using their authority to restrict entry to the professions they were to license and monitor, not in the public's interest but rather in the interests of powerful members of their respective professions. Then he told the committee about the grandfather clause and its difference from the legislation, thrice renewed in recent years, that the bill before them would remove. He concluded with what he hoped would be taken at face value: a sincere declaration of his good faith.

"I want to acknowledge that getting to this point has been a long and arduous road for me," he said. "There were times that people I had trusted advised me to quit, told me to abandon my quest as naive, told me that politics, not justice, is what wins. But I have also found people like Mr. Candor, and their support is now a matter of record, who encouraged me to persevere. Those are the people I want to believe, the people who think that justice prevails in the long run. If, as Mr. Candor has demonstrated, it is possible for Wisconsin to ensure that the gatekeepers of the architectural profession in that state are more concerned about the public interest than their own, then surely we can do the same in Ohio. Thank you very much."

"And thank you for your testimony and for these documents, Mr.

Goldstein," Spagnelli said. "Does any member of the Subcommittee have any questions for Mr. Goldstein?" He looked to his right and left. There were no questions. "Our next witness," Spagnelli announced, "is Mr. James Wheeler, Executive Secretary of the Ohio State Board of Examiners of Architects." Nathan turned to see Wheeler get up in the back of the room and begin to make his way to the lectern. But the man sitting next to Spagnelli whispered something to him, and Spagnelli held up his hand, palm outward, stopping Wheeler in the aisle. "Mr. Wheeler," Spagnelli said, "we are looking forward to your testimony, but it is getting late, and I wonder if you could defer your presentation until our next meeting on–ummm–April 5?"

"Yes, certainly," Wheeler said, starting to turn back.

"Oh, and Mr. Wheeler," Spagnelli continued, spinning Wheeler around again, "this Subcommittee is very concerned about the testimony we have heard this evening from both Mr. Candor and Mr. Goldstein. Consequently, I want the entire State Board of Examiners present at the next hearing, certainly its president, Mr.–ummm–Charnesky."

Nathan watched the color drain from Wheeler's face. "For what–what reason?" Wheeler managed to ask.

"Because I want to hear testimony from your Board that would explain its apparently very poor treatment of Mr. Goldstein," Spagnelli said. "In conclusion, I want to express our appreciation to all the witnesses who testified, whether they came from near or far. Our next hearing is scheduled for seven p.m. in these chambers for April 5. Thank you very much. This hearing is adjourned."

Wheeler returned to his seat, whispering to the man in the next chair. They both looked grim. Nathan, feeling a hand on his shoulder, turned to see Candor grinning broadly. He grinned back. But their smiles were premature.

Chapter XVIII
Rosenberg's Diaries, 1979

Thursday, March 1, 1979. Everything is set. I am surprised how sure I am that I am doing the right thing. I had thought that change, especially such a profound one, would entail much pain and regret. But the pain seems to have come to an end with Susan's death last year. She had suffered terribly. The whole experience was far worse than anything I've known, including Greece. I was completely helpless. There was almost nothing I could do for her. She complained very little, but it was clear that she was in more and more pain. And her protracted suffering was all so meaningless. Of course she didn't want a priest. She had no use for the Church. And Rabbi Liebermann was no more comfort to me than the doctors. The fact that Susan had never converted didn't sit well with him, I know. Now I am just anxious to wind things up here, to get out of this house–no longer our house–to get out of this school, to get out of Columbus.

I don't understand how I could have been so blind about so many things. Perhaps I was so happy with Susan that I thought that people generally were well intentioned, well disposed, sincere, honest. I have never made friends easily, but I did feel comfortable with almost all my colleagues, not including Webber. Of course I did not consider him a colleague. He was an academic politician, an administrator, not a teacher. I don't even know if he was any good as an architect. Budgets, accreditation, knowing the big names, the big firms, the politics, the alumni if they were rich and influential, those were his concerns. I did get along with Wilson, though, until the business with Goldstein. I don't know what to make of this man they brought in last year to replace Webber, Ken'ichi Toya, and I no longer care.

Mrs. Pearsall's suspicions were never fully confirmed, and I am not even certain that I understood her hints as fully as I should have, about what she overheard of Webber's conversation with Fleming. Still, both Jack Montague and Habib Farzin were quite certain that Webber was under pressure to stop Goldstein. If they are right, then it would make sense to think that the pressure came from Fleming. And he must have been thinking of his Board of Directors. The AIA is critically involved with the periodic accreditation process. What Prescott and I saw as a very promising approach to stimulate creativity and competition in the profession, those people would very likely have seen as a serious threat. We should have realized what Goldstein was getting himself into.

It's a shame that Goldstein has not passed his NCARB examination. I would never have predicted that he would have such trouble with it. Prescott told me that Goldstein has also failed the Ohio design exam, also surprising. His work in design here was excellent. I think he has taken the NCARB exam several times. Now he is trying to get his license without taking the examination. I am told that not only is he on solid legal ground, there are also any number of precedents for such action. But this business with hearings and appeals and now, I hear, legislation–I don't know if he isn't going to make even more trouble for himself. I can imagine what they're saying about him, just what they said about me. Pushy Jew.

Anyway, the place in Ann Arbor is going to work out very well, I think. It will certainly be big enough, and it won't be hard to give up mowing the lawn and all that outdoor maintenance. Good Lord, I'm going to be 57 this year. And the change in colleagues, students, campus will be just what I need, I'm sure.

I miss Susan terribly.

Monday, March 5. I called Prescott at his house this morning after a very restless night, dreaming about Goldstein. To my surprise, his assistant answered the phone–that Keating fellow. I am trying very hard not to be prejudiced but I don't like him, not just because I suspect that he is what is now called "gay." If he is gay, he is gay in a very different way from Murray. Keating is somehow rough and aggressive, demanding this, asking for that. In the two courses he took from me, he always had either some excuse for not having his work done on time or according to specs, or some reason why what he had done should be accepted as an improvement over the assignment. Murray was gentle, easy to get along with, often curious about things, never one to insist on having his way. He was such a sweet kid. Another dagger permanently in my heart, altogether too many, but there is no point in complaining. Not about Murray, not about Susan, not about anything I can't do anything about. Too late. Like that time in Greece, with Mortimer, when we lost the element of surprise, and got caught in the ditch. Too late to call it off. We took a terrible beating that night.

Anyway, Keating asked me to hold on, and then Prescott's wife came on the phone, surprising me again. Betty. I've met her at School functions, of course. She and Susan didn't particularly take to each other, I don't know why not. Anyway, she said that Prescott–"Arnold"– wasn't feeling all that well and what message did I want to leave. I said I didn't have a message for him, but a question, about a former student with whom we had both worked a few years ago. What question, she asked. That irritated me, and I said that I would appreciate it if she'd ask her husband to call me when he was feeling better. I was about to give her my number when she said "Just a minute," and after a pause, Prescott got on the phone.

He did sound weak. He never got over his heart attack and isn't the man he was. But he certainly remembered the business with Goldstein well enough. I told him what I had heard about Goldstein's efforts with the Legislature, and he said that he had heard the same things. I asked him if he thought this was wise on Goldstein's part and he said no, he didn't think so, although he admired Goldstein for fighting. I asked him if Goldstein had been in touch with him and he said no. Then I got to the touchy part. When Webber had called the two of us into his office, to tell us that he had ordered Wilson to stop Goldstein's study, I had gotten very angry and walked out. But Prescott had stayed, I don't know for how long. "Arnold," I said, "I know you don't have to tell me if you don't want to, but somehow Goldstein is on my conscience as unfinished business on our part. Can you tell me if Webber said anything to you after I left, anything, I mean, that we could pass on to Goldstein that he might be able to use now?"

He didn't answer right away, so I knew there was something. Then he said, "No, not really," so I knew there was something, and since I had not disguised my anger in Webber's office, it might well have been about me and Goldstein together. So I can guess what that would have been, and why Prescott hesitated. But that wouldn't be anything that Goldstein could use or should even know about.

Thursday, March 8. I'm going up to Ann Arbor early tomorrow morning–assuming that the weather will cooperate, I hate driving in snow, especially on the highway–to make some measurements in the condo and try to plan what furniture to bring and what to get rid of here. I'll be back in time for *shul.* Susan's things will go to some organization here. It's quite surprising how much stuff people accumulate over the years. I suppose I should bring some of the old family things just in case Marvin and Minna want them eventually, although God knows they've shown precious little interest in me, let alone their grandparents' things. Maybe when they're old themselves, these things will mean something to them. The *menorah*. The *Seder* plate. The few pictures. Maybe not.

For some time I thought that they were bitter against me because of the divorce, and then, later, because I married Susan. But although I still think that they were angry that I got married again, reducing whatever they were hoping to inherit, now I don't think that they ever held the divorce against me. On the contrary, they were probably glad to see me go. I don't really know how close they were to their mother, but they never liked me and I don't think I ever liked them. Not even when they were little. They weren't "cute," they were whiny. Their mother was overly protective, overly indulgent, and although she fell all over herself to spoil them, I don't think that they ever appreciated her. Where do people get the idea that all Jewish families are close and loving? God knows there were problems in my family, not just Murray, but between my parents, something deep that they never told me about but that they couldn't hide either. I never had the courage to try to find out. My father wasn't a man his son could question, and my mother had a way of avoiding things she didn't want to or couldn't talk about. I could never confront her about anything.

I wonder if that's somehow related to my concern about Goldstein, as he were somehow a surrogate for Murray or Marvin, the bright, forthcoming, talented younger brother or son I wanted. That's not fair: Murray was bright and forthcoming, although if he had any talents I don't know what they were. But Marvin, no. And I don't like that woman he married, either, Sarah. When they have children, God forbid, I won't like them either.

Wednesday, March 14. The good news is that the Claptons have made an offer on the house, and although it's several thousand less than I would have liked, I think I'll take it. I want to be done with it, and think about other things. The not so good news is that they won't be able to take possession until about the middle of August, when they arrive in Columbus. They have their own place to sell in Lawrence. They don't want me to leave the house empty for almost three months, and I can't say I blame them. They've offered to pay me to stay until August, although of course they know I'll be up in Ann Arbor more and more frequently, and I think we could work out something so the amount will offset what I'll have to pay in association fees, taxes, and insurance in Ann Arbor during that time. I'm not going to get a mortgage. I don't need to do that, and I am not going to get so smart about the market that I could turn the difference into a substantial profit. Maxwell Goodman suggested that I go to a broker and see what they could do, but I like the idea of owning the condo outright and being done with monthly payments and interest. There are sure to be investment opportunities in Ann Arbor, maybe in real estate, and I won't have any trouble finding something to do with the money I won't spend on the mortgage.

But what the Claptons want me to do means is that I'll have to delay the move. I can't live here without some furniture, and I don't want to rent any. I like my own familiar things. What would Susan tell me to do? I keep thinking that she'd agree with this plan, but there's something else she'd tell me to do as well.

Sunday, March 18. I know what it is. She would tell me to take this opportunity to visit old friends, depending on their schedules. I haven't had a real break in a long time, what with her illness and then, after she died, coping with that fact. I haven't coped with it at all, of course. I could visit the Cohens in Long Island, if they're not going to Israel this year. Maybe the Millers in Charleston. And Mortimer in Washington. He should have some time, now that he's retired at last from that company he joined after he finally left the Army. The last time I saw him was at his wedding four years ago to that much younger woman–she could have been his daughter! Beautiful girl, as I remember. Her name was Joyce something. He was so proud of her.

Susan was ten years younger than I am, but she's gone and I'm still here. I need to get out of Columbus. I can't just housesit for the Claptons, and it won't take me very long to find a routine in Ann Arbor, once the term starts.

I'll make some calls.

Tuesday, March 20. I understand the House committee has scheduled a hearing for next week on that bill removing the alternative to the NCARB exam for licensing requirements for architects in Ohio. I'd like to attend that hearing, partly because I expect that Goldstein will show up and I'd like to see him again. But I'm not sure I'll be able to go. I've gotten some inquiries about what I've listed for sale, and I told them that I'd be here every evening next week. Of course I'm not really obligated to stick to that, any more than they're obligated to show up when they said they would, but having said I'd be here I think I should keep my word.

I'm contradicting myself. What's really at work is that I don't want anyone to help me sell things that Susan and I bought together, or anything of which she was especially fond. I think it would be painful to come back and find that some anonymous dealer has bought, say, her lovely old vitrine and carried it off, just leaving the money. I want it admired. I want to sell it to someone who will let me tell him–her, more likely–how much it meant to Susan. I know this is all foolishness. I don't care. So I'll probably stay here, waiting for buyers. Unless, of course, everything has been sold before that hearing.

Thursday, March 22. I made my calls. The Millers are leaving next month for California to visit their children there, and aren't sure when they'll be back. But the Cohens would like me to visit any time before August–they aren't planning to go to Israel this year. I'd like to combine that visit with one to Mortimer in Washington–actually, he lives in Chevy Chase now, very fancy--and Mortimer said he'd love to have me visit but he wasn't sure yet when the best time would be.

Mortimer didn't sound quite right. I didn't ask, of course, but something seemed to be the matter. He said he'd get back to me soon.

Monday, March 26. The hearing on that bill is scheduled for Thursday evening, and so far no one has made an appointment to look at the things I still have for sale. I've sold a few things, including the garden tools and equipment–won't need those in a condominium!–but I don't think I'll go. Goldstein was a very good student and I liked him better and better as I got to know him, but he was Prescott's student much more than mine, even after his study was stopped and he took that extra course with me. Prescott took him to lunch quite regularly at that restaurant he liked. I never liked luncheon meetings of any kind, and I don't think I ever took a student to lunch. In fact, I've never been able to develop a really close relationship with a student. I wonder why that is. I suppose I've never gotten used to all this informality, people calling each other by their first names as if they were relatives, nonchalance about status, pretenses of equality, everything phrased very carefully, not just criticism but instructions of any kind. God forbid you should offend anyone, minority, woman, physically handicapped, fat, thin, "gay," anybody. Not my style. Sex now is something you do or "have," not something you are. What you are now is a "gender." My important characteristics are apparently that I am a middle-class, middle-aged-to-elderly white male assumed (incorrectly) to be in a position of some authority in a minor professional college at a large mid-western university. Therefore, I'm part of the "establishment" the current generation despises. In their eyes, I belong to the cohort responsible for the Vietnam war, racial injustice, economic oppression, widespread hypocrisy, subjugation of women, pollution of our natural resources, and Watergate. That I am a first-generation American from a working-class family, a veteran of World War II, a pretty good architect, a dedicated teacher, a practicing Jew, a grieving widower, and a bitterly disappointed father–none of that gets into the profile.

Good Lord, what brought that on? I was thinking about Goldstein. I don't really know how he sees me. But I won't go to the hearing. Maybe Prescott will go. I'll call him Friday morning.

Friday, March 30. My God, what a story! Prescott was practically incoherent. He hadn't gone to the hearing either, but he'd called Paul Charnesky, the president of the Board of Examiners of Architects, and found out that Goldstein was indeed at the hearing last night. Wheeler, the Board's staff man, attended. Goldstein and someone he had brought in from Wisconsin, Wheeler's opposite number there, testified in opposition to the bill. They said that the NCARB examination is highly suspect. Wisconsin and California are abandoning it as invalid, unreliable, and unrelated to what architects actually have to do. But that's not all. Goldstein apparently claimed a history of abuse by Wheeler and the Board of Examiners, which Charnesky of course told Prescott was absurd, but which impressed the Committee's Chairman, Gene Spagnelli. I've heard of him. He's said to be in Bill Lewin's pocket, up in Cleveland. Spagnelli told Wheeler to have the entire Board present at the Committee's meeting next week, certainly Charnesky! Well, that was an unexpected turn of events, not just for Charnesky but for Prescott too. Although now that I think about it, maybe Prescott was influenced by my phone call earlier this month, when I told him that I was having conscience pangs about Goldstein. In any case, Prescott told Charnesky that he knew why Goldstein had in effect been blackballed all these years, who was behind it, and that he wasn't going to be part of it any more! I was astounded. But apparently not as much as Charnesky. First, Prescott said, he denied everything, which was to be expected. Then he started to tell Prescott that there would be consequences for him too, that Charnesky would see to it that there would be enough unpleasantness to go around. That did it for Prescott, he said. I wanted to interrupt and ask Prescott just exactly what he knew, what he meant about Goldstein's having been blackballed all these years and so on, but Prescott was still so worked up that I didn't get the chance. He said that Charnesky was no better than a hired thug, and that he told him so. And he told him that he was through with the whole thing, and that he would call Spagnelli to see if he could present testimony next week. "That did it," Prescott said, sounding pretty satisfied with himself. "He really changed then. He said he wasn't going to be the fall guy for anyone. He said he'd call Washington and tell Fleming that, in just that way. He asked me to hold off calling Spagnelli, begged me, really, and said he'd call me back as soon as he'd made it clear to Fleming that he wasn't going to be part of all this himself any longer either. He said he'd talk to Fleming, and of course to Wheeler, and then he'd call me back. So I'm waiting. I'm not sure how much time to give him, but I had better hear from him by Monday, or else."

I wasn't sure that I had followed all that, but I didn't know what to ask, exactly. So I said, "Arnold, are you sure about all of this? Aren't you taking an awful chance? What did Charnesky do, do you know, that he's now so frightened by? And what did he mean by consequences?"

"Harry," he said, and I noticed that suddenly he had found his old voice, strong and clear, "believe me, I know what I'm doing. I've lived with this ever since that disgraceful meeting with Webber, when you walked out as I should have, and I've had enough. Convictions aren't worth anything if you don't have the courage to act on them. I am ashamed to admit that I've learned that very late in life, and I learned it from Nathan perhaps more than from anyone else. Betty has told me time and again to keep my mouth shut, not to get worked up over this, to be careful about my health. You can't undo the past, she keeps saying. Well, I can't live like that any more. I don't know what Paul meant by consequences, and I don't care." Suddenly he stopped and I asked, "Arnold?"

"Maybe Betty does have a point," Prescott said, and his voice quavered again. "I have to be careful. Harry, I have to take a pill now—let's talk later. If Paul calls me today, I'll call you right away. I have to go now."

"Of course, Arnold," I started to say, but he had hung up.

So things have somehow come to a head. I'm certainly going to go to the meeting next week—I'll have to find out where and when. I wonder what Charnesky meant about talking to Wheeler. "Of course to Wheeler." I thought Wheeler was just the staff man, proctoring exams, keeping records, taking the minutes, that sort of thing. How could Wheeler have been part of anything? Unless he had done something on Charnesky's orders? Prescott probably knows. I'll ask him when he calls me back.

But what a story. I can't imagine how all this started to leak out. But there's no stopping it now.

And Betty Prescott tried to stop her husband from doing the right thing. I suppose most wives don't want their husbands to make trouble for themselves, especially if they've had heart trouble. Still, I think I see why Susan didn't care for her. Much too calculating. If Susan had thought that I was keeping quiet about a mess like this just to keep my own ass covered, she would have made her contempt very clear. "Horns of what dilemma?" she would have said. "I see the bull, but no dilemma!"

God, I miss her.

Tuesday, April 3. <u>Charnesky is dead!!</u> It was on the radio this morning–he was killed by a hit-and-run driver early this morning, walking his dog as usual a couple of miles up from me on Olentangy River Road! There was a witness, a newspaper delivery boy, but too far away to say more than it was an old pickup truck that came out of nowhere, smashed into Charnesky and the dog, and then hightailed it out of there. The police are investigating, but the boy didn't even get a glimpse of the driver or the license plate, couldn't even say what kind of a pickup truck it was, so they seem to be lacking clues of any kind. I have no idea how something like that could be investigated. The driver is probably somewhere in West Virginia by now, making sure that the truck's new dents are indistinguishable from previous damage. Or it was a stolen truck, and has been abandoned hours ago. The dog was apparently killed instantly and although Charnesky wasn't pronounced dead until they got him to the hospital, nothing in the report indicated that he was conscious before he died.

I have to admit that I never liked Charnesky–not that I knew him at all well, we didn't live really near one another–but this is terrible. The man had a family, kids in college somewhere, I think, and of course he was important in the profession in this state. And influential in the national, too, I remember hearing, close to Fleming and some of the national Board directors. This is very strange. More than strange. The weather wasn't at all bad this morning, presumably this happened well after dawn, and he was going on his usual route at his regular time, the report said. And that area isn't one where you see a lot of pickup trucks, except for maybe lawn maintenance crews or repair people, but not at that hour of the morning.

And he just had that showdown with Prescott about Goldstein a few days ago! I'll call Prescott.

Wednesday, April 4. <u>And now Prescott is dead!!</u> I tried calling him several times yesterday to talk about Charnesky and find out if he knew anything more than had been reported. But all I ever got was a busy signal. The news this morning reported that he'd died of a heart attack yesterday afternoon. He was found by his assistant Keating in his house with the phone off the hook–so apparently he was on the phone when his heart stopped. With whom? Charnesky was already dead himself! "Strange coincidence," the reporter said, two prominent local architects holding important positions in the profession dead within twenty-four hours of each other, accident and heart attack! Strange, yes, coincidence– I'm not so sure! Of course Prescott's heart had been weak for some years now, and he was on various drugs. I can't just call Betty now, I'm sure she's got her hands full–Prescott had a son by his first wife, as I remember. I wonder if he's any help to her now. And she had children from a previous marriage as well. But I don't think I should just sit here either. I'll go over there and offer to help in any way I can. It's the right thing to do. Susan would agree. I knew Prescott for years. We weren't close, but we were friendly. I thought he was a little strange in some ways, the way he'd jump from one topic to another, but I'm sure that he thought I was odd myself.

Wednesday, continued. <u>Unbelievable</u>. I thought that Betty Prescott would be surrounded by relatives, and that it was likely that someone would tell me to call back within a few days, she was in no condition, etc., etc. Nothing of the sort. Her children don't live in Columbus, and she didn't say a word about Prescott's son (I didn't dare ask), but she seemed genuinely glad that I had come, apparently at a very awkward moment with that Keating fellow. He was there, trying to tell Betty that he *had* gotten Prescott's prescription refilled, that he *had* replaced it in the bathroom cabinet on the lower shelf on the left as always, and he could not explain why Prescott apparently hadn't found it, had taken something else according to the EMS crew that he said he had called immediately, as soon as he'd come in and found Prescott on the floor. Of course Betty looked terrible but to my surprise she wasn't distraught, she was furious. She wasn't screaming at him, but she wasn't letting him leave either, as he obviously wanted to. She seemed to be convinced that Keating was lying, that either he hadn't gotten the prescription refilled or had misplaced it or hadn't called the Emergency people until he had watched Prescott die–why would he do that? What made her imply such things? Nothing made any sense to me, and I said that perhaps I should go, but she kept saying, "No, please stay, I'm just trying to get to the bottom of this"–the bottom of *what*, I wanted to ask.

Finally Keating managed to leave, and Betty asked me to stay a little while and of course I sat down. I don't remember that I had ever been in Prescott's house before. Well, they were never in ours either–we just met at School functions and that sort of thing. Anyway, Betty just sat still for rather a long while, and then she started to talk, how she had never liked Keating, never trusted him, had her suspicions of him. I didn't let on that I might know what she was talking about. "Arnold had liked him as a student," she said, "and he hired him as his assistant because he thought he was talented and creative, but over time, Arnold told me, Brian made him uncomfortable in certain ways, and then he began to doubt that Brian had ever done everything he'd claimed to do, won some prize or other. In fact, Arnold was planning to let Brian go, after they'd finished their current project, and he had told him so." I didn't ask in what ways Keating had made Prescott uncomfortable. Then Betty really surprised me.

"Harry," she said, "this may shock you so soon after Arnold's death–yesterday, my God–but I have to plan his funeral services. Arnold was not on speaking terms with his son, and to tell you the truth, I don't know where he is. I've notified Arnold's brother and sisters and said that I'd let them know about the funeral, but I can tell you now, of course I expect them to come but I don't want them to speak. They never approved of me. They liked Arnold's first wife, who, I know very well, made him miserable." I suddenly found myself liking Prescott better than I ever had before. "Harry," she continued, "I'd like you to say a few words. As a colleague. About Arnold as a teacher. He was very proud to be an adjunct professor at the university, just as proud as of his role in his professional society. Would you do that? For Arnold's memory?"

"I'd be honored," I said at once. "When are you thinking of holding the--"

"I'll have to let you know," she said. "There are some other people I'm going to ask to speak too, you understand, and I have to make arrangements with our pastor, naturally–oh–you won't be troubled about coming to our church? I mean--"

"Not at all," I said immediately, thinking how much Susan would have enjoyed this. "As I said, I'm honored to be asked, and I'm sure that I'll have something to say about him as a teacher." Then suddenly there were people at the door, friends of Betty's and Arnold's, embraces and hugs and tears, and I was able to slip away.

Keating. It's possible that Betty's suspicions are well founded. There's something cold and vicious in that man. Certainly not the kind of man I'd want to be out on patrol with.

I wonder what made me think of that.

The hearing is tomorrow night. I don't know, now, whether I'll go or not. Goldstein will probably drive down again–I'd think he'd have heard what's happened here–and if he sees me, and he would, he'd want to know what I knew. I don't know enough to tell him anything, and just to report my last conversation with Prescott would be sure to upset him. He might just be at the center of things without having the faintest idea about his role. Hell, I don't know either. No, I won't go, and it's not that I don't want to see him, it's that I don't want to tell him what I am beginning to think without having any proof. I don't even know what kind of proof I'm talking about.

I'll call Wheeler on Friday to learn how the hearing went, whether that bill is being withdrawn, whether there's anything new about Charnesky's death. What a mess. I'm sure there'll be a lot of questions about what's going on in Columbus when I get to Ann Arbor.

Friday, April 6. I reached Wheeler this morning. At first he was amazingly cheerful, considering the events of this past week. And his good mood became all the more astonishing when he told me that *he* had been on the phone with Prescott when Prescott had had his fatal heart attack, and he had been telling Prescott about Charnesky's death! I couldn't believe his tone–not just calm and factual, but positively upbeat! It was too much for me and I interrupted him: "Wheeler," I shouted, "you're telling me about these things as if they were normal! Don't you realize what you're saying? These men died this week, your boss, my colleague, and you sound as if you were almost glad! As if these were problems solved, obstacles overcome! What the hell is going on?"

There was a long pause and then he said, in a very different tone, "Professor Rosenberg, I'm truly sorry if I gave you the impression that I'm not shocked and grieved by what has happened–I really am. I think I'm a bit giddy, a little overwhelmed. I was the one, last night, who had to inform Representative Spagnelli that Mr. Charnesky's death made his request for testimony from the members of the Board quite impossible to comply with, and of course he agreed immediately, under the circumstances. So now the Board, once the funeral has been held, will have to elect a new President, and considering the calendar, that won't be scheduled, I'd think, until early fall. So I really do have a lot on my mind, an awful lot to do. I'm answering a complicated inquiry from Senator Madison now, and that's going to take quite a bit of time yet. And as I said, I'm terribly sorry if I gave you the impression that somehow I was indifferent to what has happened here this week. Not at all. I didn't know Mr. Prescott very well, but of course the Board and I will extend our sympathy to his family as well."

That calmed me down somewhat, but at the same time I felt he wasn't telling me everything, not by any means. "Do you know," I asked, "whether Mr. Charnesky called the AIA office in Washington shortly before the accident? Say last Friday? Specifically, do you know if he talked to Roger Fleming at the AIA?"

Again a pause before he answered. "No, I don't, Professor," he said. I thought his tone now was guarded. "Why do you ask?"

Too late to stop now. Press the detonator. "Because I know that he told Prescott that he intended to do just that, just a day or two earlier, and that it had to do with a scandal about how a former student of ours had been treated, the one who testified to Spagnelli's committee," I said. "And you know him too, Mr. Wheeler," I continued, "and you certainly know more about his treatment than I do. I'm talking about Nathan Goldstein."

"Yes, of course I know Goldstein," Wheeler said, sounding neutral. "And I know that he's claimed to have been treated unfairly for some time now, not just last week but for a long time-- about his exams, which he's failed several times, and then at a hearing he insisted on, which the Board held last year, complete with lawyers and so on, and in correspondence with everyone around the country. He's made quite a spectacle of himself. If he ever does pass the examination, he's going to find himself without any friends in this state. I happen to know that the Board, including Mr. Charnesky, regarded him as an embarrassment to the profession. And so do a number of eminent practitioners, not just architects but influential people in related spheres of business."

"What are you talking about? Who? What influential people?" I demanded.

He was wound up now, and, like me, had grown incautious. "Bill Lewin in Cleveland, for one," he said. "Word gets around, Professor. I happen to know that it was Lewin who put Spagnelli up to that business of ordering the Board to appear at last night's meeting, and I also happen to know that Lewin changed his mind and called Spagnelli off. So Paul's terrible accident didn't change anything in that regard: Goldstein was already isolated, abandoned, really. Goldstein has dug his own grave. I don't mean to sound morbid, considering what's happened, so let me rephrase that and just say that he's made his own bed and now let him lie in it."

I ignored the vitriol. "Why did Lewin change his mind?" I asked, still harshly.

"Well, maybe somebody told him what a troublemaker Goldstein really is," Wheeler said. "How he's done nothing but make accusations and write articles and get as much publicity for himself as he possibly can, running everywhere and crying how unfairly he's been treated, when the truth is that he's been treated just like everyone else. Why would someone like Bill Lewin want to support someone like that? So my guess is that somebody told him that there's no percentage in that, and he changed his mind. Spagnelli certainly didn't want to talk to him last night, and I saw Goldstein try."

"No percentage," I repeated.

"That's right, Professor," Wheeler said. "Look, I know Goldstein was your student as well as Prescott's and you probably have a very different opinion of him, but let me tell you, the way I described him is the way he's seen generally, by the Board of Examiners and by other people too. Is there anything else? I really have to get back to work here."

"No," I said, "nothing else. Yes, I do have a very different opinion of Goldstein, but then, I'm not involved with percentages. Goodbye." And I hung up before he could.

It's going to take me a while to digest all this. Something is terribly wrong. It's as if I'd lifted the roof off an old evil, something that's been rotting and stinking underneath an old building always regarded as beautiful. But the foundations were never up to code.

Susan would see whatever it is. She trusted her instincts. I haven't trusted mine since that night in Greece with Mortimer. But I always trusted Susan's.

So the bill wasn't withdrawn. If the House approves it, it'll go to committee and then it's sure to pass. I wonder what Wheeler is doing for Madison. Whatever it is, it looks very much like Goldstein's about to lose his long battle.

Monday, April 9.   The services for poor Prescott were held yesterday. Betty Prescott had prepared me for both Webber's and Keating's remarks, that is, that they would make some. I wasn't surprised that Webber had wanted to say something–he probably didn't but had been asked to by the OSU administration as the dean who had originally hired Prescott–but that Betty had agreed to have Keating speak, after that scene at her house, did take me aback. She told me that she had thought about it and had decided that she   had no basis for the accusations she had implied in my presence, that she could have taken him at his word, even though she didn't like him and didn't trust him. And he had wanted to speak. He knew that all kinds of people in the profession would be there and he's looking for a job, is my guess.

But there was something else, related to those accusations of hers. She said that she'd gotten the death certificate, and that the cause of death was listed as a cardiovascular infarction, nothing suspicious at all in view of Prescott's history of heart trouble. Since I had been present at the scene she'd had with Keating, she wanted me to have a copy of the death certificate. I didn't dare ask whether this was her idea or Keating's, as if Keating were somehow clearing himself–but how could he get her to agree to make a copy for me? Threaten her with legal action of some kind? Now all concerned are aware that the official verdict is that there was nothing suspicious about Prescott's death, and Keating's slate is clean. I decided immediately that I didn't give a damn about Keating and thanked her for the copy she wanted to give me, since that seemed to be what she wanted. And I also decided that my remarks would have to do with Prescott's relationship with Goldstein, how he'd tried to help him after Webber had stopped his study out of the blue. And I did. I looked directly at Webber while I was reading my remarks. He knew what I was saying, and so did Montague and some of the others who were there.

Susan would have wanted me to be even more direct, probably. I didn't mention Goldstein by name. She might have thought that I should have. But I'm not sure.

So that's that. Charnesky's services were also held yesterday. Nothing further about his accident, if that's what it was. The police are keeping the case open, and are asking anyone who might know anything to come forward.

For some reason I don't believe that this is the end of it.

Thursday, May 24. I'm ready to leave tomorrow morning for my visit first with the Cohens in Long Island–I look forward to going to their synagogue with them tomorrow night, that will be an interesting and welcome change from Rabbi Liebermann–and then, next Tuesday, to Washington to see Mortimer. Something *is* wrong in the Mortimer household: he fumbled around on the phone and finally got himself to ask me if I could stay in a hotel in the city. Of course I immediately said that in fact I'd prefer to. And that's true enough, in some ways, especially with a private bathroom and no fuss for anyone with the housekeeping. I didn't expect an explanation. But Mortimer tried to provide one, something about remodeling part of the kitchen, how much longer it was taking than they'd expected, and how it was too much of a mess to impose on an old friend like me. It didn't sound very plausible. "You and I have been in far worse messes than whatever shape your kitchen is in," I said. I meant the reference to that awful night in the ditch as a light touch, a ridiculous comparison, but he didn't chuckle or respond in kind, just made some noise I didn't know how to interpret. So I continued, saying that I'd love it if he and his wife would do me the honor to be my guests at dinner in a fancy downtown restaurant of their choosing. Wrong again. "I'm not sure that Joyce will be able to join us, Harry," he said. "She's been pretty busy lately with various things, and is traveling quite a bit for a couple of her organizations–we'll see." So I said that I was sorry to hear that, for his sake as well as my own–maybe I shouldn't have said that, it occurs to me–but that I looked forward to seeing him again and that we had a lot of catching up to do. He kind of grunted and asked if he could make a reservation for me, did I have a favorite hotel in the district. I asked him to see if he could get me into

the Hay-Adams near the AIA headquarters in the 1700 block on New
York Avenue, and he said he'd see what he could do. I thought that I
might go over to the AIA and see who's around and what's going on.
They usually have some uptodate materials to give out, and I might be
able to use some of them in Ann Arbor.

But first, the Cohens–Myron and Edna. My oldest friends, all the
way back to Brooklyn in the 1920's. They never said anything directly,
but they knew how miserable I was with Barbara, and how happy with
Susan. They were always polite to Barbara but I know they *loved* Susan.

As I did, God knows.

Sunday, June 3. Well. I hardly know what to say to myself. I had a
wonderful time with the Cohens–it's funny how elderly people, reunited
with boyhood friends, so easily revert to the warmth, familiarity,
references, and especially jokes they knew when they saw each other
every day, decades ago. Myron is a very funny man, just like his
namesake. And Edna has always been delightful. They agreed to visit
me in Ann Arbor, once I'm settled in, and that will be marvelous, I'm
sure. They are well, their children are well, their grandchildren are
beautiful, and I confess–and they know–that my happiness for them is
accompanied by some quite painful regrets for myself. It's not envy of
them, it's a sharp awareness of what I don't have.

But that's not what's on my mind. It's what I did in Washington. It's
what I said to Mortimer. I am not and never have been an impulsive man.
Nobody can handle explosives without very steady nerves and an acute
sense of timing. Nor do I consider myself loose-tongued. I can keep
secrets. I was discreet in discussing my suspicions of Webber in the
Goldstein case with Farzin and Montague, and I never discussed them at
all with Prescott. He was probably aware of them, however. So why did
I blurt out what I'd seen to Mortimer? Was it some sense of debt for that
awful night in Greece? How did I repay him with my news? Or was it
my anger at what I saw, a decent man betrayed by what I am now
convinced is a villain and a scoundrel–what an old-fashioned term–first
whatever he arranged to happen to Goldstein and then Charnesky and
for all I know Prescott, and now this? Or both? Most of all, what would
Susan say about what I did?

The room in the Hay-Adams was very nice (and not any less
expensive than I remembered), although it wasn't one with the advertised
view of the White House. I didn't mind; I had voted for Ford. After I
checked in, early Wednesday afternoon, I called Mortimer to let him
know that I'd arrived, but I got his answering machine, so I said that he
could call me after 5:30 so I'd get a chance to stretch my legs. Then I

went out, over to New York Avenue and the AIA headquarters. It was a warm, slightly muggy afternoon, but pleasant enough for a walk, and I hadn't been in Washington in about four years, and enjoyed it as always. Less than a block from the AIA, a few yards ahead of me, I noticed a man who looked familiar, his hand on the elbow of a woman whose profile also looked familiar, guiding her to a waiting cab at the curb. I stopped—I don't know why—and saw him kiss her on the mouth just before she got into the cab. She turned to do so, and I saw her face and recognized her. She was Joyce Mortimer. Although I hadn't seen her since her wedding, when of course she had been dressed very differently and had had a different hair style, she was too beautiful to forget. I am certain that it was Joyce. And as her cab pulled away, the man turned, gave me a glance, and although he obviously didn't know me, I recognized him too. Tall, very well dressed, graying, slightly long hair with fashionable side burns, a handsome man in his late forties or early fifties. It was Roger Fleming. I've seen him at various national meetings, and of course his picture is often in the periodic AIA publications.

He went into the building and I stood there, dazed by what I had seen, and for a long moment unsure about what I should do. Then I found myself following him inside. He was at the far end of the lobby, talking to a woman, some pleasantries, smiling and nodding, unaware of me. Then he went off, either down the hall or to the elevators, I couldn't tell. I saw a table near the receptionist's desk, covered with brochures and pamphlets of the kind I had come to inspect and possibly take, so I did so, exchanging a word or two with the young woman behind the desk. Then I thanked her and looked down the lobby again, where Fleming had gone. No one was there. I left with my brochures and walked back to the hotel. Now, I thought, I can guess what's been troubling Mortimer. At the least he must have some pretty strong suspicions, especially given the age difference between them.

Mortimer is some ten years older than I am, I think, in his late sixties. He retired as a Brigadier General from the Army—when I knew him in Greece, he had been a Captain—and went to work for one of those companies that exist largely on defense contracts of one kind or another, not munitions or supplies, but consultative work, strategic planning, coordination. I don't really know what the hell that's all about. But I knew Mortimer to be a tough man, analytical, logical, unafraid to come to unpleasant conclusions. He had been an excellent commanding officer, and the disaster in Greece that night was in no way his fault. Whoever had been careless about letting our plans become known, it certainly wasn't Mortimer.

He had been married then too, and had had small children, two boys. I don't know what happened to his marriage–he never told me and of course I never inquired. I know that he was very proud of both of his sons, who also became career military men, so that part of his past was happy. But between his divorce and the time he found Joyce, although I didn't see him often, I knew that he was lonely and drank too much. Joyce, although she was almost twenty-five years younger than he was–in fact, I think she's barely over forty now–changed his life. He was what is called "crazy about her." He was deliriously happy. And she seemed to be in love with him–a much older man, of course, but very successful, probably quite wealthy, well regarded, influential, good-looking, vigorous. Why not?

Well, here we are, four years later. Why not indeed.

The fact is that I think Mortimer saved my life that night in the ditch, staying while I was making my way back, and, with Peter, ready to provide cover if the Germans' lights had reached me. He and Peter could have gotten the hell out of there well before I started to crawl back. But they didn't, and that had to be Mortimer's deliberate decision. Peter might or might not have stayed on his own, but he would never have disobeyed the Captain, nobody would have. And the Captain had me covered.

Peter got himself killed within two weeks after that night, but Mortimer and I survived the rest of it all without a scratch. And somehow there's often a strange bond between the man who saved another man's life and the man whose life he saved. We never discussed it, not once, although we weren't afraid to refer to it, obliquely, anyway. But we were both conscious of it, an invisible but powerful bond.

So I sat in the room, waiting for his call, deliberating about whether or not I should say anything and, if so, what. I decided that I wouldn't. If he brought up his marital problems, even in a roundabout way, I would listen sympathetically and try to think of something encouraging to say. All I could think of, in the room, was "I wouldn't leap to any conclusions without definitive proof" or something similarly inane.

But when it came up, as of course it did, over a drink after dessert, and I idiotically said something like that, Mortimer gave me a long look and said, "I don't expect to catch Joyce in bed with whoever it is, Harry. What kind of proof are you talking about? Should I hire one of those sleazy private investigators so popular in pulp fiction and bad movies?"

And out it came. "I know who it is, John," I said. I couldn't believe what I'd said. I was almost as shocked as he was. He just stared at me open-mouthed. We both froze. Once again I was transported back to that ditch in Greece. The Germans had turned the lights on and we didn't dare move.

"What?" he finally said. "What? Who? What? First you tell me I should have definite proof and then you say you know who it is? Harry? Goddamnit?"

I held up my hand to stop him, took a big swallow of whatever I'd ordered, and found my voice. I told him, as briefly as I could, what I'd seen. He stared at me as if every sentence were a knife. All the time I was talking–hesitating and stumbling–I heard two voices in my head, my own, saying that I had *promised* myself *not* to say anything, and Susan's, asking me what I was doing. I couldn't answer her. But once again, it was too late to stop. Finally I was done. It had taken perhaps a minute, no more than two. It had seemed like half an hour. I saw tears in his eyes when I looked at him.

"All right," he finally said. "I'll look into it. I knew, of course, that there had to be another man, but since I didn't have that definite proof you just provided, I had been hoping, despite everything, that there wasn't. Well, this is one of those times that hope doesn't triumph over experience. All right."

"You aren't going to do anything foolish?" I asked. I could have kicked myself around the block. First I confirm his worst fears and then I ask an idiotic question like that.

Another long look. "Foolish, no," he said, quite deliberately. "But I'm certainly going to do something. Now I want to ask you a question."

"Of course," I said.

"You weren't really planning to tell me what you told me, were you?"

"No, I wasn't," I admitted.

"So why did you?"

"John," I said, "I'm not really sure. Maybe, without knowing it, I felt I owed you what truth I have. Maybe there's something else at work too."

"What something else?"

"It has nothing to do with you or Joyce but everything with Fleming," I said.

"What do you mean?"

"It's a long, complicated story," I said, "and it's mostly about my suspicions. I have no definite proof, if you don't mind my using that phrase again. It involves a former student of mine, a former colleague, and an official of the Ohio State Board of Examiners of Architects. The last two are recently dead. Very recently. And mysteriously."

Mortimer waited.

"No women involved," I continued, "at least not as far as I know, but money, power, influence, and those are usually about money too. The student challenged the system. The system, by which I think I mean the nexus or if you prefer the interplay of the profession with its educational establishment and credentialing or licensing processes, ate him up. Various people in high positions seem to have yielded to pressures of various kinds, political, financial, emotional, certainly involving career considerations and future benefits. And behind all this, as far as I've been able to figure out, was the man I saw kissing your wife this afternoon."

"And you think that's why you told me that you saw them?" Mortimer asked. His tone was almost clinical.

"John, I don't know," I said. "It may have been part of the reason. Maybe I've been wanting to accuse Fleming of all that without proof because I think he is behind it. Maybe what I actually saw functioned as a kind of corroboration of what I just told you I suspect he engineered in Columbus. I'm not good at self-analysis, John. I don't have Susan any more to tell me what's behind what I'm thinking, and what I'm conscious of right now is how sorry I am that you're in such pain and how much I miss Susan to help us through this, both of us."

"Yes," he said. "I didn't know Susan well, of course, but she was a wonderful woman, I could see that, and I also saw how much you two loved each other. And yes, I'm in pain. But that's not your fault, not at all. You already know that for some time now I've suspected something was deeply wrong at home. All you did was to confirm that."

"And to give you a name," I added.

"Yes," he said. "Harry, let's call it a night. I'll call you at Hay-Adams about nine o'clock, is that all right?"

"I'm an early riser," I said. I was very glad that the evening was about to end. Somewhere inside me, I was still shocked by what I had done.

"Good," he said. "You know your way back? It's just a couple of blocks--"

"Sure," I said, and motioned the waiter.

"Let me get this," he said.

"Not a chance," I said. "Next time."

But there was no next time, not during this visit. Mortimer called the next morning and (to my embarrassment) thanked me for my friendship, on which, he said, he'd now have to impose: he had to go out of town for a few days, something had come up, and he was very sorry, etc. He assured me that it had nothing to do with our conversation of the previous evening. I didn't let on, this time, that I didn't believe him. He said that he'd be sure to get in touch with me in Columbus, well before my move to Ann Arbor. "I certainly hope so!" I said. Then we said goodbye, I called the airline and changed my reservation, and was back in Columbus before dinner time.

I can't believe what I did. I can't imagine what Susan would have said.

Suddenly I'm anxious to start a new life. Too many memories. I don't know if I'll continue this diary either. Recently it's become almost a confessional, as if I had converted to a kind of non-institutional Catholicism, and I don't need to do that. But I went to services on Friday evening, and I know I can't confide in Rabbi Liebermann. Too pompous, too predictable, and not really insightful. The people at the synagogue I attended that one time in Ann Arbor–I thought of it as a trial run–seemed friendly enough, but I had no particular impression of the rabbi. I don't even recall his name.

Chapter XIX

Nathan and Rubin – 2005

Nathan Goldstein was in an excellent mood. He had exercised, weighed himself, noted that he had dropped a couple of pounds, and felt caught up with most of the details that had been silently calling for his attention around his house. And his mood was enhanced by a flattering letter he had just received from George Hsu, with whom he had become friendly at an international conference held in Hong Kong in December, 2004. Nathan had been one of only two Americans invited to give a paper. George, an architect affiliated both with a large firm and one of the universities in Hong Kong, had been highly complimentary about Nathan's paper, "The Organization Behavior Component of Facilities Management," and in the ensuing conversation had invited him first to a private tour of his native city, and then to his home, to meet his wife and two children and to have a "real" Chinese dinner. Nathan had been delighted by both, and they had stayed in touch. The letter's main purpose was to convey an enclosure, an article George had published in a Chinese journal but whose acknowledgments, in English, included "Mr. Nathan Goldstein, FARA, CFM, MBA, of Cleveland, Ohio, a pioneer in the application of the principles of organizational behavior to the planning, design, and management of complex built space." The article, in Chinese, would remain forever incomprehensible to Nathan, but the acknowledgment, although somewhat inaccurate, was very pleasant and George's letter contained more of the same.

Nathan's paper had been well received at the symposium, sponsored by the International Council for Research and Innovation in Building and Construction, still known by the acronym for its former name, *Conseil International du Bâtiment*, the CIB. George's compliments were among many he had gotten. He regarded the experience not so much as a triumph as a validation, long delayed but finally achieved, of his synthesis of business principles with the practice of architecture. That it had occurred on an international rather than a merely local or regional stage pleased him all the more. The CIB, established in 1953 with the support of the United Nations, was regarded as the world's most prestigious group concerned with international cooperation and exchange of information having to do with research and innovation in building and construction. George's letter stimulated reflection.

A quarter of a century had gone by since he had passed the NCARB examination in December, 1979, some months after Charnesky's mysterious accident and Prescott's fatal heart attack the very next day. Those months had included several setbacks. Ohio Senate Bill 15 had passed, making it impossible for Ohio architects to obtain a license without success on the NCARB exam. The evidence that Nathan and Peter Candor had produced about its imprecision, unreliability, and arbitrariness had been ignored. Consensus that its many serious flaws should lead to its abandonment by the profession was growing, but so far was beginning to show results only in California and Wisconsin. In Ohio, after the bill had been signed into law by the Governor, Wheeler had sent Senator Madison a list of some four hundred names of Ohio architects who had been granted licenses under Section 4703.08 Part A of the Ohio Revised Code, well after 1931, the critical point that Charnesky and his Board had tried to keep hidden. But it was too late for the Senator to undo his colleagues' action: the vote had been twenty-nine to one. As for Nathan's testimony to Congress in favor of both the Truth in Testing Act and the Educational Testing Act of 1979, both bills had died in committee. And Nathan's setbacks had certainly included his difficulties after he had opened his practice in Cleveland. In too many instances to be dismissed as coincidence, in his efforts to do business with developers and other businessmen, to win contracts from local and state governmental agencies, and especially to volunteer for work in his local chapter of the AIA, he had felt resistance, sometimes quite overt, sometimes more subtle. He had survived mostly by working for corporations and businesses, and for governmental agencies. It had been stressful, so much so that it had been a major factor in the breakup of his marriage.

He had turned to marketing as an alternative career. It had been very successful almost from the start. His degrees and experience in architecture gave him a cachet few of his new colleagues could rival. He found that he was good at business, that he enjoyed making money, and most of all that, whoever his enemies had been, they had no influence in his new world. He became a vice president of the company he had joined, active in various professional organizations, and a frequent contributor to their newsletters and other publications. He traveled to all parts of the country, made new friends, enjoyed an occasional affair, and came to terms with his regrets. But he forgot nothing, and occasionally, after he had hired a new secretary or had recommended that someone should be promoted at his firm–or not–was aware of the irony of his status as an insider.

George's letter reminded him of the conversation he'd had so many years ago with Arnold Prescott about Frank Lloyd Wright, the first time he'd been invited to Prescott's house, after Prescott's operation. Should Prescott, as president of the Architects Society of Ohio, have attempted to persuade his organization's members to accept Wright as an innovator, a creative thinker whose ideas merited careful appraisal, further development, perhaps even adoption in various respects? So Nathan thought then and so Nathan thought now. Or was Prescott right, regardless of his own opinion, in simply reflecting his members' general consensus that Wright had little to offer and could be safely rejected as a deviant from conventional wisdom? In retrospect, their brief disagreement, entirely hypothetical, seemed prophetic to Nathan, remembering the last time he had talked to–yelled at–Prescott, ending up with Betty Prescott ordering Nathan to leave the office. Prescott had told him that he should consider leaving the profession. Nathan had gotten angry. A few days later Prescott had had another heart attack and died. Nathan, still feeling betrayed, had not gone to the funeral. It was all a long time ago, he told himself, but it had led, step by step, to everything that had followed, even to George's letter.

Thinking about Prescott brought Rosenberg to mind. He had gotten along well with him, he reflected. He had sent him a copy of the testimony he had presented to the Congressional subcommittee holding hearings on The Truth in Testing Act of 1979, and, in the early eighties, had twice sent him cards for *Rosh Ha-shana* at Michigan's College of Architecture. But he had gotten no response. Rosenberg, Nathan realized, must have retired years ago. He found himself suddenly curious about his old professor, whether he was still alive, still active, still living in Ann Arbor. Rosenberg might be pleased to hear from him now, he thought, especially if Nathan told him that his influence had been most helpful to him, as indicated by the reception his Hong Kong paper had gotten. Nathan reached for the phone. "I'd like the area code and number for the University of Michigan's College of Architecture in Ann Arbor, please," he told the operator.

*****

The telephone interrupted Rubin's examination of the remaining materials in Harry Rosenberg's two-drawer metal file cabinet. He had gone through almost everything now but a few folders and the packet of letters, still held together by the old string. Now that he had finished reading Harry's diaries, he did not expect to find any new revelations that would illuminate what he had come to think of as "the Nathan Goldstein saga." The letters, he was quite sure, would be letters Harry had gotten from Susan over the years, had treasured forever, and whose privacy he should respect. Perhaps something in one of the file folders would tell him the end of the story. But first, the phone. "Hello?" he answered.

He was in for a shock. "Professor Rubin? Professor Walter Rubin?" It was a man's voice he could not identify.

"Yes, this is Walter Rubin," he said.

"Professor Rubin, my name is Nathan Goldstein," the voice said. "I'm calling from Cleveland, Ohio, where I--"

"*Nathan Goldstein*?" Rubin interrupted. "The architect? Harry Rosenberg's former student?"

There was an audible intake of breath on the other end. "You've heard of me?" Nathan asked.

"I certainly have," Rubin said. "I've heard of you and now I'm reading about you, and you might be surprised by how much I know about you."

"I don't understand," Nathan said. "What do you mean?"

"Mr. Goldstein, your professor, Harry Rosenberg, was a good friend of mine," Rubin said. "And not only did he tell me something about you and your experience when your study was stopped at Ohio State, when he died not long ago he left me some files and a diary in which he goes into some details from his perspective. I suspect I now know some things about your case that you don't."

"My case?" Nathan asked. "I'm a case?"

Rubin caught himself. He was surprised by his own excitement. "I'm very sorry, Mr. Goldstein," he said. "I've begun to think of the whole story as a case, as I'll be happy to explain. But first let me apologize for cutting you off–I haven't even given you a chance to tell me why you called me!"

This is bizarre, Nathan thought. What am I getting myself into? How could Rosenberg have–let's find out. "Well, all right," he said. "I got your name from a secretary at the University of Michigan's College of Architecture. I had called them to get Professor Rosenberg's address, if they had it, because I wanted to send him a copy of a paper I gave some months ago in Hong Kong, a paper which has attracted some quite favorable attention. It was to be a way of saying thanks for everything he did and tried to do for me so many years ago. But I learned that he had died recently."

"Yes?" Rubin asked.

"Whoever the secretary was that I talked to–she told me her name, something Indian, I think–I mean she was from India–was apparently quite fond of Professor Rosenberg. So she was pleased to hear how highly I had thought of him, and she thought that he would have greatly appreciated my sending the paper. He always enjoyed hearing from former students, she said. I was surprised, because I'd tried to stay in touch with him, oh, twenty-five years ago or so, and he hadn't ever answered. But I didn't tell her that. Anyway, she remembered your letter to your local newspaper about him, after he'd died. She doesn't know you, she said, but she liked your letter so much that she clipped it and posted it on her office's bulletin board. In fact, she went to get it to make sure that she gave me your right name."

"Yes?" Rubin asked again.

"Well, I was sorry to hear that he had died, of course, and I was hoping that you could tell me a little more about it and perhaps something about your friendship with him as well, and now you tell me that you know a good deal about me and about my experience at Ohio State."

"Yes, I think so," Rubin said. "I think I know who stopped your study and why. I think I know why you had such trouble passing your national licensing examination. I think I know why you were unable to stop that legislation barring alternative ways to obtain architectural licenses in Ohio. There's a lot I *don't* know, of course, and I don't know that Harry's suspicions, which are now mine, would be found convincing in a court of law, but I'm really pretty sure that I have the general picture."

"Why do you think my study was stopped?" Nathan asked.

"Because of its implications for the big money in your profession," Rubin said. "Your study, had it been completed and then publicized, might well have opened the gates to serious competition among architectural firms throughout the country doing the business of what they call the free market. That business is often done well out of the light of day. So you get collusion. Price fixing. Rigged bids or sole bids, in some cases. Under the table agreements. You surely know much more about that than I do. Not just about the many pork barrel politicians who vote in the nation's interests as explained to them by the corporate and other lobbyists, but the puppet masters behind the curtains. I think your case–sorry–your experience was unusual inasmuch as you became the victim of a conscious, orchestrated conspiracy, and that probably doesn't happen very often. Usually, I'd guess that what I just described is simply understood as the normal way of doing business, and has been so understood for generations. Harry and your other advisor, Arnold Prescott, seem to have lost sight of that until your dean explained it to them."

"Dean Webber," Nathan said.

"Yes," Rubin said. "But he was under pressure himself, and acted in what I suppose he thought were the best interests of the school. That rationalization is always the same, whether it's called the greater good, or national security, or patriotism, or some god or other. Think of Abraham's readiness to sacrifice his own son in the name of obedience to the God who had commanded him to do so. Like Adolf Eichmann, 'I was only following orders.' Nothing has changed. Webber no doubt saw himself protecting his school, his alumni, his students, his faculty, doing his job, in other words, and since he authorized arrangements so that you did get your degree, no harm was done."

"No harm?" Nathan repeated incredulously. "That episode determined my whole career!"

"No, I'm talking about what must have been Webber's point of view," Rubin explained.

"Well, you do seem to know a lot about what happened," Nathan said. "But I don't understand why. If you don't mind my saying so, Professor Rubin, so far you haven't told me much that I haven't thought myself. I knew I had been screwed over, to be blunt, knew it for years. And I have some idea of the importance of money in our society, and I do know something about its power to motivate people in my profession and so on. My question is why you and Professor Rosenberg seem to have discussed my experience so extensively. Were those conversations just between the two of you or were others participating as well?"

Rubin felt himself blushing. "I'm afraid both of us found your–umm--experience, first at Ohio State and then later in your efforts to pass the licensing examination, too unusual and yet too emblematic to keep to ourselves," he said, aware that, in his embarrassment, he was spewing academic jargon. "But," he hurried on, "we each told only a couple of other people about it. Harry told me something, and he seems to have mentioned it, in another context, in Washington to his former commanding officer from World War II days. That was years ago. I told my closest friend and his wife something about it at a restaurant in New

York, just this last April. No architects, any of them. And most of what I think I know, as I said, comes from Harry's diaries and files. I haven't shown those to anyone, and don't intend to. I don't have anything really conclusive anyway."

There was a pause. Then Nathan cleared his throat and said, "Professor Rubin, I have to say that I'm amazed by what you're telling me and getting more amazed every minute. What's this about Professor Rosenberg's commanding officer in World War II? How could he possibly have been involved with anything that happened to me thirty years later? And why would your friend and his wife be interested in any of this? How did this come up at your dinner in New York, just by-the-way conversation about an interesting case involving a man none of you had ever heard of?"

Actually, a damned good question, Rubin thought. "The connection to Harry's commanding officer had to do with–well--I know what it was, but it's not so easy to explain," Rubin said carefully. Goldstein had a right to ask the question if not to get an answer, but the telephone did not permit all the usual nonverbal signals required to convey, simultaneously, both a paucity of facts and an overabundance of interpretation. Nevertheless, Rubin found himself gesturing to his invisible listener. "Look," he said, "let's leave that one for the moment. Harry was genuinely troubled by what happened to you, and as he got older and quite naturally spent more time looking back than forward, he was bothered more and more. At first, as I listened to him, I thought he suspected you of somehow being implicated in what happened, whether to that official of the Ohio architectural examination board--"

"Charnesky?" Nathan interrupted.

"Yes, or to Prescott, or both--"

"How do you mean, implicated?" Nathan asked.

"Responsible, in ways he couldn't really specify and tell me about," Rubin said. "But the point is that I was wrong and he didn't suspect you at all. No, what troubled him, more and more, as I said–I'm really quite certain of this–was that he hadn't done anything effective on your behalf. I'm not sure that he knew what he might have done–he probably didn't– but he felt that he should have tried. He saw it as a matter of justice, and he thought that he should have spoken up on your behalf for that reason. He was that kind of man."

"Justice," Nathan repeated. "That never came up in our conversations, as I remember."

"Not so different, really, from what's also called fairness," Rubin said. "What happened to you was manifestly unfair, or in Harry's terms, unjust. He was part of what happened to you, by lack of action. The silent majority may not have approved of what the Nazis did, may not have actively participated, but neither did they try to stop it. Or if some did, they were ineffective. In either case, they were not blameless. And that's the sort of conscience pang that gnawed at Harry, if not at the Germans."

"Quite a comparison," Nathan said. Rubin heard the doubt in his voice. "I'm perfectly aware of the differences in scale and scope, Mr. Goldstein," he said, annoyed, even while he said it, by the professorial manner he couldn't seem to suppress. "I'm trying to suggest what I think was the source of Harry's discomfort. He had a conscience. He felt he had let you down, rather badly, he must have thought. He was appalled by what he took to be the later ramifications and consequences, which he thought probably included all kinds of chicanery and fraud, and eventually even Charnesky's accident and Prescott's heart attack. If that's what they were. He had no proof of anything, so of course neither do I."

"I'm certain that he was on the right track," Nathan said. "There was a lot that he didn't know about, a lot that happened that fits right in with what he thought as you describe it, a lot I could tell you. And it occurs to me that what you're telling me about his conscience might also explain, in a weird kind of way, why he never answered the New Year's cards I sent him a couple of times. He was embarrassed. But what about that commanding officer? And why did you discuss all this with your friends in New York?"

Rubin hesitated. Was it appropriate to tell Goldstein what Harry had seen on New York Avenue in Washington that spring day in 1979, and what he had said to John Mortimer? He didn't know what, if anything, had happened as a result, and Harry's confusion about his motives hadn't been resolved. He ignored Goldstein's first question. "My friend in New York is a very knowledgeable man who spent some years in Washington at the Department of Education," he said. "I told him something about your experience and Harry's suspicions because I thought he could enlighten me about how the accreditation process works for professional schools. Harry's notion, and I think he was right, was that what worried your Dean Webber was exactly that, accreditation. I didn't know much about how it all works–I was a professor of English and we have no national licensing standards or anything like that–and so my friend explained something about it to me. At that point it was partly a matter of my curiosity and partly wanting to tell Harry whether or not he had grounds for his suspicions. But when I got back from New York the next day, I learned that Harry had suffered a stroke and was in the hospital. He died there the night I came back, in fact."

"I see," Nathan said. "And the commanding officer? Why did Professor Rosenberg discuss my case, as you called it, with him? In what context?"

That was the question Harry had asked himself and couldn't answer satisfactorily, Rubin thought. "I'm not sure that I know why he did that, Mr. Goldstein," Rubin said. "But from his diary, it seems that Harry didn't either. His diary concludes with that question, in fact, and as far as I know, he never returned to it. And perhaps that's why he talked to me about it, and left me these papers and files in his will, so that I would look into it. I think he hoped that I'd agree that he'd done the right thing, eventually. He wasn't at all sure himself."

Nathan thought that this was beginning to sound like double talk. Rubin was holding something back. "So he described the conversation with the commanding officer in his diary?"

"Yes," Rubin said. "But there was more to it than what happened to you in Columbus. In fact, that was not the more important part. And the more important part really had nothing to do with you."

"Then why did my name come up at all?" Nathan asked.

"It didn't," Rubin said. "Not your name. Just your, well, case."

Nathan felt a rush of impatience. "Professor Rubin," he said, "I'd like to get a straight answer, if I can. We're going around in circles here, and I don't understand why. You're talking about things that determined the course my life took, but they happened a very long time ago, and I don't see why you should be, well, so coy."

He's right, of course, Rubin thought. But I don't owe him an explanation. And I don't have one anyway, as I've tried to tell him. "I've about exhausted what I know, Mr. Goldstein," he said. "I really don't have anything else to tell you."

"You've finished going through Professor Rosenberg's diaries, is that right?" Nathan asked, as if Rubin hadn't just tried to end the conversation

"The diaries, yes, I've looked at those," Rubin said. "There are still a couple of files and some old letters, but I don't expect to find anything in them having to do with you. I think the letters are mostly from Harry's second wife, Susan."

"I see," Nathan said. "I never met her. I know that she was ill when I was Professor Rosenberg's student, and I think she died about a year or so before Charnesky's accident and Arnold's heart attack and all that business. I suppose you're right–there wouldn't be anything about me in those letters."

"No, I don't think so," Rubin said. "Well, if that's all then, Mr. Goldstein–"

"Just in case, though," Nathan interrupted, "in *my* case, as you said, Professor Rubin, pun intended, if you do find something else, let me give you my telephone number. Would that be all right? Would you mind calling me if you do find something you think I'd be interested in?"

"I wouldn't mind at all, I just don't think it's likely," Rubin said. "But let me get a pencil, just a minute, please."

"Of course," Nathan said. Rubin got the pencil, took Nathan's number, and they said good-bye, both thinking what a strange conversation it had been. I'll never hear another word, Nathan thought. Too bad. He knows something he doesn't want to tell me, and there's nothing I can do about it. I certainly would like to see Rosenberg's diaries. At least I didn't make Harry's mistake, Rubin thought, telling Goldstein more than he needs to know. Too bad, though: I would have liked to meet him, to put a face to the Nathan Goldstein saga. I have to remember to tell Gerald about this.

The thought made Rubin uneasy because he realized that he had forgotten something else he should have remembered. He couldn't think of what it was. The doorbell rang just as Rubin returned to Harry's old letters. He went downstairs to answer it. It was Wayne and two of the maintenance crew. "Hi, Doc," Wayne said, his baseball cap resting rather far back on his bald head. "We've got the shingles and would like to do the job this morning, if that's OK with you–it won't take more than an hour or so."

"Good," Rubin said. "That's fine. Why don't you tell them to go ahead and join me for a cup of coffee? Can you do that?"

"Well, let me get 'em started first," Wayne said. "Sure, I'm always up for a cup of coffee."

"Good," Rubin said again. "I was just finishing up going through Harry Rosenberg's last files–about ten minutes?"

"Right," Wayne said. "I'll take a look up there and make sure we've got enough new shingles–I'm pretty sure we do." He turned and motioned to his two helpers to bring their ladder around the back. Rubin went back upstairs. Most of the letters were indeed from Susan, and he didn't want to read them. There were some letters from friends, and he put those back in the stack as well. But the last envelope, without a return address, caught his attention. It was addressed to Harry in a handwriting, clearly a man's, he hadn't seen before. The envelope contained only an undated newspaper clipping, with no indication of the paper's name.

REGIONAL BRIEFING
CHEVY CHASE

Body of Architectural Society Official Found Near His Car

The body of a man identified as Roger Fleming, Executive Vice President of the American Institute of Architects, was found just off Worthington Place in Chevy Chase early this morning by a resident of the area. Police determined that Mr. Fleming had been shot three times in the chest with a .45 caliber weapon, apparently at fairly close range. No one had reported the sound of gunfire, however, and police speculated that some sort of silencer may have been used. The time of death was tentatively established as only a few hours earlier, approximately at 4 a.m. Robbery was ruled out as a motive inasmuch as Mr. Fleming's keys to his Mercedes, parked nearby, were in his hand, and he was identified from the contents of the wallet in his pocket.

It is not known why or when Mr. Fleming, a resident of Arlington, was in Chevy Chase yesterday. Ms. Louise Hart, Mr. Fleming's secretary at the AIA office on New York Avenue, said that she knew of no reason. Police have requested that anyone with knowledge that may be related to the incident come forward.

–Norma Joseph

BANGBANGBANG! Rubin almost jumped out of his skin. His heart pounded. Then he realized that the sound had come from above, from the roof, and that Wayne was showing his crew how to use the nail gun. "Jesus Leaping Christ!" Rubin said to the newspaper clipping still in his hand. "What timing! I may need something stronger than coffee!" He put the clipping back in the envelope and looked at the postmark. It was blurred, but he could make out "1980."

No wonder Harry hadn't been able to forget the episode, or to continue his diary. He must have sensed what his revelation to his friend might trigger. As, apparently, it had. His wish to see justice done had made Mortimer an instrument of Harry's revenge. Shakespearean! And yet, Harry had not consciously planned to avenge Goldstein, Charnesky, and perhaps even poor Prescott by having Mortimer lurk in thick underbrush in the dead of night, revolver in hand, waiting for Fleming to leave his wife's bed and make his way back to his car. No, Harry had shocked himself by blurting out, quite unintentionally, that he knew the identity of Joyce's lover, and, as a possible explanation, had attributed his lapse to his sense of debt to Mortimer for that night in the Greek ditch. Still, this was undoubtedly the result of Harry's indiscretion. And, it occurred to Rubin, perhaps related as well to Harry's disgust when Rubin had unashamedly mentioned his affair with Alice Horowitz.

The bell rang again and Rubin remembered that he had invited Wayne for coffee. He was no longer in the mood for friendly chitchat, he thought, but he couldn't ask Wayne, now, to come for his coffee at another time. But neither did he intend to tell him about his discovery. Having the coffee wouldn't take that long, and besides, Harry's name probably wouldn't even come up in the conversation. He went downstairs to let Wayne in.

"Gonna be fine, Doc," Wayne said. "Forty-five minutes at the most." "Good, good," Rubin said, motioning Wayne to the kitchen table and getting the coffee. "Cinnamon roll?"

"Well, yes, thanks, Doc," Wayne said. "That'd go nicely with the coffee. So, you were saying you were taking another look at the professor's papers?"

That explains the cinnamon roll, Rubin thought: he wants to hear all about it. "Yes," he said, "some old letters, mostly from his second wife, with whom he had a very happy marriage--" Wayne nodded to show he knew about it-"but I haven't found anything that would explain whatever happened in Columbus. If something did." He had said far too much to Goldstein, Rubin thought, and he certainly wasn't going to tell the whole story to Wayne. Wayne didn't have the proper security clearance, or "need to know," or whatever the Patriot Act specified.

Wayne sipped his black coffee, looking disappointed. "Nothing about what happened in Columbus," he said, more as a conclusion than a question.

Rubin was embarrassed once again. Now either he was going to have to lie or he'd have to be more forthcoming. What the hell: Harry was dead and Goldstein lived in Cleveland. "No, that's not right," he said. "There was quite a bit about what happened in Columbus, but not a satisfactory or convincing explanation for it. That's not exactly the same thing."

Wayne bit into the cinnamon roll and waited.

"It had to do with one of Harry's former students, mostly," Rubin continued, urged on by Wayne's unwavering eyes. "Somehow the student was badly treated by the administration of the school, and Harry seems to have figured out why–the student was doing research that the professional organization, the national organization of architects, didn't want done. They'd heard about it, decided that it would threaten their interests, and pressured the administration to stop it. Well, Harry figured it out, as I say, and he didn't protect the student, and as time passed, and some other things happened, he got to feeling guilty about it. Thought he should have done something to help the student, or at least tried to."

Wayne looked at him unblinkingly. "Other things happened," he repeated.

"Yes," Rubin said. "The student finished his degree, but then he failed the licensing examination. More than once, in fact. Then the student tried to get his license another way, which the law permitted, and somehow that law was going to be changed so that this other way would no longer be open to him, and apparently there was a lot going on behind the scenes–you know, politics, pressure, probably financial considerations. Then the official who was going to have to testify to the committee considering changes in the law was killed in a mysterious accident–got hit by a truck that kept on going. And another professor, Harry's partner working with the student, died the very next day of a heart attack. That professor seems to have known much more about what was going on than Harry did, and his death meant that Harry would never really find out what the truth was."

Wayne had finished the cinnamon roll and now finished his coffee. Rubin refilled his cup. "Thanks, Doc," Wayne said. "So that was it? That's the whole story?"

"It really ate at Harry," Rubin said by way of not quite answering Wayne's question. "I think it bothered him more and more as time passed. His conscience, I mean. He seems to have become convinced that he should have tried to help the student, that he was guilty of being a bystander to an injustice that he should have tried to stop or at least expose."

"Yes, that sounds like him," Wayne said. "He was unusual that way. But what you told me last time about his having fought with the Greeks against the Germans–have I got that right?"

"Yes, with the Greek underground fighters," Rubin said.

"Well, that fits with what you're telling me now," Wayne said. "He saw that as his duty, I guess. And then with this student, he must have felt he didn't do his duty. I wonder where that came from, though."

"You mean his sense of duty?"

"That's right," Wayne said. "Most people I know, and I was married to some of 'em, have a keen sense of *other* people's duty, like mine, for instance. Irene, for instance, she knew what my duty was to her every minute of the day, and she could go into great detail about it. Could and did. So one time, while she was explaining to me in what ways and by how much I was coming up short, I asked her what she thought her duty to me was, as my wife at that time. Well, it turned out that she hadn't really spent much time thinking about that. Hadn't seen the need to consider that. Wasn't inclined to speculate about it. So I said that I didn't think that duty was a credit card, you know, where she could charge and charge and I'd have to pay and pay. Turned out that's pretty much how she saw it, though. I had to cancel that card just as soon as I could."

"I don't think you've told me about her before," Rubin said.

"Well, luckily I found out about this difference in how we saw duty not all that long after I made the mistake of marrying her," Wayne said. "So there wasn't all that much to tell you, as I could have done about two or three of the others. But now the professor, he seems to have thought that he had a kinda duty, or duties, you might say, to do the right thing, whether to help them Greeks or to help this student."

"Yes," Rubin said. "And he felt he hadn't helped the student as he should have."

"What did he think he should have done?" Wayne asked.

"I'm not sure that he knew," Rubin said. "But he didn't think he should have remained silent. Silence doesn't ever help. Speaking out may or may not do any good–that depends on how it's done, and also, of course, what the circumstances are–but that's a chance you take, when you speak out. But silence, well, that's a guarantee that nothing will happen."

"You're right, Doc," Wayne said. "But sometimes that's best, that nothing happens. If people told everything they knew, or thought they knew, could the rest of us bear it?"

Rubin was startled. He hadn't expected the conversation to take such a turn. Whatever was in the back of Wayne's mind that had prompted his question, it was probably closely associated with something very painful. He remembered that Harry's diary entry, recording his conversation with his friend Mortimer in the Washington restaurant, mentioned the tears in Mortimer's eyes. Perhaps Wayne, now apparently so detached from what had to be all those personal upheavals with marriages and divorces following each other in what seemed like unending succession, actually had managed to grow only very thin scar tissue.

"No, I don't suppose so," Rubin said. "You're right. There's such a thing as discretion, tact, empathy—a feeling for what other people feel. So the question is not only how to speak up effectively, but when. And that depends, doesn't it, on the circumstances."

"Always does," Wayne agreed. "Suppose the professor *had* spoken up on behalf of this student—not that I know much about being a student, certainly not about being a college student—what might have happened? Just don't seem likely that people would have said, you know, Professor Rosenberg, you are right, this boy has been treated very poorly, we'll fix that right away, and thanks for calling this to our attention?"

Rubin had to grin. "Right again, Wayne," he said. "That's not the way universities work. Not unless something hits the fan so hard that it splatters all over the newspapers. And even then there are people assigned to what's called 'damage control.' In the Reagan administration, it was called 'plausible deniability,' I think. The idea was that you could get away with a lot of things, including flouting whatever law you liked, provided you could come up with something that would explain it away. You may remember the Iran-Contra affair in the eighties, when the president was caught redhanded trading arms to Iran for hostages in Lebanon, and lying about it because he'd said he'd never do that. And then later, it turned out that Oliver North had been funneling a lot of the money from the sale of the weapons to Iran straight to the rebels in Nicaragua, also in direct violation of the law. A lot of people were involved, but as I remember, nobody went to jail. Not so different from this administration. Or Clinton's, if you recall."

"Oh, Clinton," Wayne said. "But that was a little different from selling weapons to Iran or supporting the rebels in Nicaragua. He just got caught, as so many husbands do, lying about what he shouldn't have been doing, and it didn't help him that all those other husbands had to admit that they had been doing the same thing, because they didn't happen to be president when they were doing it. Church-going hypocrites, some of 'em. Hell, some of 'em were ministers or deacons, wasn't they? What's worse? Being president or a preacher, when you get caught? Well, Doc, we aren't going out to interview them to get the answer to that one, not today, anyway, so I better get back up on your roof and see how the boys are coming along. Thanks for the coffee and the roll. Good to talk to you."

"You're very welcome, Wayne," Rubin said. "Enjoyed the chat. Come back soon, and thanks for fixing my roof." Wayne waved, smiling, and was gone. Rubin went back upstairs. He saw Nathan's telephone number on the piece of paper where he had left it on his desk. He wondered what Wayne would have said about his reluctance to tell Nathan what he knew. He wondered what Harry would have said. He wondered what Gerald would say. Then he remembered that he hadn't taken his pills that morning. He picked up the phone.

It was Nathan's turn to be astonished. "Mr. Goldstein," he heard Rubin's voice say, "this is Walter Rubin. I'm grateful to you for giving me your telephone number–I did find something of interest after all. Do you have a moment?"

"Actually," Nathan said truthfully, "I was on my way out to visit my mother–she's expecting me, and gets nervous when I'm late–you say you did find something?"

"Yes," Rubin said, "but I don't want to delay you, and perhaps the phone just isn't the best way to describe what I've got–and it occurs to me that I'd like to show you Harry's diary–to tell you the truth, I'd like to meet you. I've spent a fair amount of time thinking about you, and your call, earlier, has made me very curious."

"And I'd like to meet you, Professor Rubin," Nathan said, "and I'd certainly like to see Professor Rosenberg's diary. Did you want to come to Cleveland or would you prefer to have me come to Ann Arbor?"

"Is there a place in between, do you think?" Rubin asked. "I think Sandusky is about halfway?"

"Yes, but there's nothing very interesting in Sandusky as far as I know," Nathan said. "What about Toledo? That's much closer to Ann Arbor than to Cleveland, but it has an excellent art museum–do you know it?"

"Yes, that's a very good idea," Rubin said. "That would be an easy drive for me, certainly, and perhaps not too far for you, and we could meet in the museum–let's see–do you know the Cloister, on the upper level?"

"I'm sure I can find it," Nathan said. "I haven't been to the Toledo Museum in a while–I went to see Frank Gehry's Center for the Visual Arts next to the concert hall, the Peristyle, a couple of years ago, I like Gehry's work very much–but as I remember, it's quite easy to find your way around, especially with one of those maps they give you. The parking lot is in the back, isn't it?"

"Yes," Rubin said, "you have to circle around the Museum to get to the parking lot, but there's an entrance right across the street, you don't have to walk all the way around to Monroe Street."

"I remember now," Nathan said. "When should we meet there? And how will I know you?"

"Saturday would be good for me–you know, they have a nice little cafeteria there, would you like to meet around lunch time?"

"Saturday would be very good," Nathan said, "but let's meet where you suggested, in the Cloister, that's sure to be more private, and then we can see whether the cafeteria is too crowded or not. How will I know you?"

"I'm seventy-five years old, Mr. Goldstein," Rubin said, "and I can't say that I don't look it. And speaking of what I look like, I look Jewish, because I'm that too. So if you see an old Jewish man by himself, in the Cloister around noon this Saturday, probably sitting on a bench, that's quite likely to be me. What do you look like?"

Nathan laughed. "I suspect you know, Professor," he said. "Would you like me to wear a *kippah*? I have a very short beard, I'm about six feet tall, and I don't look Irish!"

"I think we'll recognize each other," Rubin said. "Very good! I look forward to meeting you, Mr. Goldstein!"

"Likewise, Professor!" Nathan said. They hung up, pleased with themselves and each other.

*****

The rain was surprisingly heavy that Friday night. Although it had stopped well before Rubin got into his Chrysler on Saturday morning to drive to the Toledo Museum of Art, Ann Arbor's streets were still wet and puddles glistened along U.S. 23. The sky was still heavy with rain clouds. Rubin was anxious about the slick pavement. But he was also delighted to have arranged the meeting with Nathan. Trying to imagine Nathan's reaction to what he was going to learn from Harry's diary and the newspaper clipping in Rubin's attaché case on the passenger seat next to him, he was almost to Dundee before he realized that once again he had neglected to take his pills with his breakfast. He had to change the drill, he thought. What he always remembered was to make his morning coffee. If he put the pill containers next to the coffee pot, on the counter, he couldn't help but remember to take them. Keeping them on the kitchen table in the bowl with the paper napkin holder, the sugar, and the dry creamer obviously wasn't working, at least not often enough.

The news on the radio was, as usual, depressing, having to do with car bombs in Iraq, rockets and retaliation in Israel and the Palestinian territories, an ambush in Afghanistan, fires in California, drought, famine, and slaughter in Africa, and investigations of corruption in Washington. A whirlwind five-minute tour of disasters around the globe. "Intelligent design!" Rubin snorted, twisting the dial to find music he liked. "What a misnomer! Unadulterated sadism, that's what this is!" He couldn't find anything he could tolerate and turned the radio off. Popular music, in his day, had been Frank Sinatra and Nat King Cole, people who could sing and, in Cole's case, play the piano with the best of them. Then there had been "rock and roll," white ripoffs of what had been known as rhythm and blues, Elvis Presley and whoever, and then the British invasion, and do-wop and soul and Jimi Hendrix and white groups with names like the Flush Toilets making sounds to match. And black groups like Fats Domino and Ray Charles, the alleged genius, who had found that there was a lot more money in blending gospel sounds with suggestive lyrics than in imitating Nat King Cole. And now rap and hiphop, self-degradation accompanied by noise and calisthenics. Rubin liked what Wynton Marsalis had called hiphop: a minstrel show. He wondered what Gerald would say.

Traffic was light and he got to the Sylvania exit with plenty of time to spare. Rubin turned east on Monroe Street. He remembered this stretch from years ago, shortly after he had come to Ann Arbor in the late fifties and occasionally had driven to Toledo to hear jazz or to visit the Museum or the Zoo. It had been relatively rural then, quite pleasant, a two-lane road connecting the village of Sylvania to other suburbs. As you drove into town, eventually it became a major city artery, going all the way down to the Maumee River. But now this stretch featured used car lots, one after another, fast food places, suspicious specialty stores, gas stations, and dreary shopping malls for ecumenical consumers with small children and large automobiles. And pot holes, damn it, he thought, as he skirted a big one.

He entered Toledo without noting the city limits–the shabbiness was seamless–but soon saw the sign to turn right to the Museum's parking lot and was pleased, as always, by the glimpse of the huge, classic building. At long last he was to meet Nathan Goldstein, he thought, smiling. He found a space almost at once, pulled in, turned the engine off, and glanced at his wrist watch. It was ten of twelve. Perhaps Goldstein had arrived a little early as well. He opened the Chrysler's door, undid his seat belt, reached for the attaché case, and started to get out.

The pain in Rubin's chest was as sharp and sudden as if he had been stabbed. Somehow, he thought, he had fallen on the corner of a suitcase, whether one of the several he had been carrying in his rush through the train terminal or someone else's, he wasn't sure. People seemed to be gathering around him as he tried to struggle to his feet and stuff his clothes back into his carry-on, but the zipper had gotten stuck on his shirts and underwear, and he couldn't seem to pull it, and he couldn't get up. He looked around to see if he could ask someone to help him and saw two figures in the distance, toward the train track, where it was growing lighter, motioning him to hurry and catch up with them: the train was leaving. They looked familiar, a man and a woman, in their thirties, he thought, how could that be, they were his parents and he was seventy-five. Yes, it was his father, waving him on, *Komm, Walter, mach schnell*, his beloved father and mother, but the damned zipper wouldn't budge and here was another suitcase he had dropped. Someone was bending over him, a Jewish face, thank God, because the huge men were coming, he heard them shouting, *Was ist denn da los?* The suitcase was open, spilling its contents, toothpaste, a razor, shaving cream, Harry Rosenberg's diary, and another suitcase was pressing into his side, he didn't *have* that many suitcases.

"Too much baggage," Rubin muttered, tried to chuckle, coughed, and died. Nathan, bending over him, saw that the old man was gone. He glanced at the attaché case on the passenger seat. Whatever Rubin had wanted to show him was undoubtedly in it. It was too late. He adjusted Rubin's body behind the steering wheel so that he could close the door and ran to the Museum to call the guard. Too late, he thought, too late. Like so much else.

www.ingramcontent.com/pod-product-compliance
Lightning Source LLC
Chambersburg PA
CBHW030749030726
47497CB00001B/202